sisters of the triple moon

Book one

Kiss A Demon Goodbye

ᛈᚢᛋᛋ ᛉ ᛇᚷᛗᚦᚾᛁᚾ ᚢᛈᛁᛈᛇᛗᛇᚾᛉ

by

Elaine Tenborg

Rauna by Sanna Ketutar Jensen

"Bright Blessings!"
Elaine Tenborg

In memory of *Mia* – August 2004 to March 2006
You were our own wee Pip, and we miss you so very much.

Acknowledgments

Research is an inevitable part of writing. Had I any idea of how much time would be spent gathering data, possibly I would never have started this book.

The World Wide Web is a marvelous invention, and without it, much of what went into the book, wouldn't have been easily accessible. The hundreds of hours spent searching for information, verifying its correctness, and sorting through what was useful and what wasn't, was an overwhelming task. The websites I visited are too numerous to mention, so I can only say thank you to all those who took the time to make the information available to anyone with internet access.

Magi Frost, Wiccan High Priestess, mentor and friend, who introduced me to the Wiccan faith, and the joy and healing power of firewalking. My visits to Raimar Retreat will always be remembered as special times.

Shewolf Silver Shadows, solitary practitioner and instructor of traditional witchcraft, author and friend, who graciously permitted me to join her writing group, and who is solely responsible for getting me to actually sit down and write.

Jodyna Krain, numerologist, who gave me a wonderful insight into numbers and how they relate to one's life path.

My husband, *Allen Tenborg*, who was my rock, my editor, my inspiration. Without his support, there would be no book. He put up with unwashed dishes, late meals and an empty bed through so much of my writing.

My Mother, *Pauline Thun*, who always told me I could do anything I put my mind to. Those words have seen me through many rough times, and gave me the courage to attempt writing. She also threatened to never read another word written by me, unless I changed the outcome of one chapter, so just for you, Mom, the chapter has been rewritten.

My sister, *Mikki Lawrence* and my brother, *Cam Thun*, whose encouragement and unflagging belief in me helped to make it seem more real during the times of self-doubt, and there were many.

My daughter, *Shawndra-Lyn Pollock* and my son, *Rob Schellenberg*, who gave me the thumbs up on the love scene. A romance writer I am definitely not!

A special thanks to my son, *Michael Schellenberg*, who gave the love scene his blessing only after a spirited discussion on the fine line between that which is sensual and that which is pornographic.

Doris Hope, dear friend and sounding board, who listened, encouraged and who actually understood where I was coming from.

A very special thank you to my dear friend *Ket Jensen*, for granting me permission to use Rauna and her story in my book, and for trusting me to do right by her.

Author's Note

References to historical events and places, all cities and towns, sanctuaries, zoos, parks, highways and historical monuments, do exist and are used in a fictitious manner. The author is solely responsible for any errors in the description of such places.

The foreign languages used in this work have been meticulously researched. The author is solely responsible for any errors in spelling, use of, or order of the words.

When one picks up a novel of the fantasy genre, some expect to find strange new worlds and wonderful creatures never before seen. *Sisters of the Triple Moon: Kiss a Demon Goodbye* is a tale of our world as we know it, mixed with witchcraft, demons and a dash of history.
The author hopes the reader is not disappointed.

Prologue

The candles flickered and danced on the breeze, giving an eerie appearance to the clearing deep in the woods. The silhouettes of the occupants in the circle cast indistinct shadows as they walked counter clockwise, their chanting harsh on the otherwise quiet night air. The fire in the center of the circle had burned down and only red embers remained.

The identical, dark hooded robes gave anonymity to those gathered, except for the leader, whose robe was maroon, not black. The hoods were pulled as far forward as possible, and only the one in command knew the identity of the others.

He stepped forward, the blade of the sword in his right hand reflecting the glow from the coals. He reached out his arms and gripped the hilt with both hands, holding the blade over the embers. He felt the power fill and consume him. He was omnipotent and before long, the entire world would bow down to him; before long, the entire world would tremble in fear at the very sound of his name.

He remembered seeing his first world globe. He remembered feeling the power for the first time as he stood there, watching it spinning it on its axis. He had known then his destiny, and since that day on his fifth birthday, he had been preparing.

It was almost time. Soon, he would summon up three of the most powerful inhabitants of the underworlds, and under his command they would give him supremacy over the veil known as earth.

The sword began to glow, taking on a life of its own. He could feel the vibration coming from the blade and for a fraction of a second, a seed of doubt hesitated on the periphery of his mind and then it was gone. He waited until he could no longer control the sword, its vibration shaking his entire body. He released it and took a step back.

It dropped to the center of the coals and as its point entered the earth, the embers of the fire flared. Blue flames shot skyward, dwarfing the cloaked figures. The acrid smell of sulfur lay heavy in the air. The flames vanished as quickly as they had come, leaving in their wake an entity more abominable, more hideous than anyone's imagination could ever hope to conjure.

All in the circle were familiar with this particular fiend. It had been summoned before. With the promise of freedom held like a flower in front of a honeybee, the demon came when called and did as it was commanded.

In the beginning, the conjurer had asked it to turn into a more pleasing aspect, but now he found he liked the demons menacing appearance. He slid his hood back slightly and eyed the apparition. It was over ten feet tall and as he watched, it grew smaller until it was shorter than he was. That was the only firm order it had been given; when it was summoned, it must take on a form shorter than that of the sorcerer.

When it was done, the magician's eyes glittered and he smiled. However, there was no warmth in either the smile or his eyes, only derision and greed. He gave his orders to the demon and bid it carry them out. It had one week in the veil of earth's time.

The demon grew in size again and with a noxious blast of putrid air it vanished, leaving those in the circle gasping for breath, their stomachs roiling. The sorcerer stepped forward and gripped the handle of the sword. With a mighty heave, he pulled it from the earth and raised it to the skies.

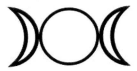

1. Shattered Peace

"She what?" Salem's eyes looked as if they might pop right out of his face. "Tell me you're joking, Neffy; please tell me you're joking."

Nefertiti shook her head. "*Puleeze!* Do *not* keep calling me Neffy. I *am* a *purebred* Persian and as such, I *deserve* to be called by my proper name. Just because *you* don't have any breeding doesn't mean you have to drag me down to your level. And no, I am *not* joking. The Mistress wants to go surfing in Hawaii. I overheard her telling Pip."

Just then, Pip came running through the door. Pip never walked if it could be helped. The youngest of the three, she was full of energy and always look-ing for adventure.

"Guess what, guess what?" Pip ran around the room, jumped on the bed and off again. She pounced on a forgotten sock that lay half hidden under the chair.

"We've heard." Salem licked his paw, as much as to say the news was old.

Nefertiti turned and regally strolled to the window to assure herself every-thing was as it should be outside. She saw the look on Pip's face and knew she was disappointed. She loved to be the one bringing news and she would think this was the greatest. Pip hated the long winters. *Don't we all?* They all wished at times the Mistress wasn't so fond of living in the far north, but it bothered Pip more than Salem or herself.

The Yukon Territory is a vast, sparsely inhabited land with a total popula-tion of thirty one thousand and twenty two thousand of those people live in the capitol of Whitehorse. This suited Joly James just fine. She'd staked a gold mining claim on a creek fifty miles from the nearest community. She built a twelve by twelve foot cabin and furnished it with the basics, a wood stove, a single bed, a small table, one chair, a dresser, a bookcase and her pride and joy, an old rocking chair that had been passed down through sev-eral generations. She had moved rocks and boulders and spent days turning the soil to make a vegetable garden, and afterward she planted flowers and herbs around the cabin and the garden.

In order to maintain her lease on the property she needed to have an active mining operation, so in the summer months she shoveled rocks and sand from the creek into a sluice box she'd gotten from an old-timer who'd given up ever striking it rich and had moved back to civilization. Between the shoveling and tending the garden, she didn't have time to think during the endless summer days. In the evenings, she would go for walks with her three furry friends, picking berries and searching for wild plants she could use.

The winters were long and cold. She spent her days sewing or reading while trying not to think about her past. It was also at this time she sometimes took short trips away from the Territory to visit new places or try something different.

Like now. She had gotten it into her head she wanted to try surfing, so that was where they were off to. Joly knew Pip would be the only one happy with her decision. Pip was game to try anything new especially if it meant leaving the north country. Nefertiti's glorious long gray and black coat kept her warm and although Salem's fur was short, his extra weight saw him through, but Pip was tiny and so full of energy she never gained weight and her coat like Salem's, was short. When she wasn't bouncing off the walls, Pip was happiest snuggled into an old afghan that once belonged to Joly's Grandmother.

Joly came through the door with an armful of wood. She smiled at her friends. "I take it Pip has told you the news. I'll go to town on Friday and make the arrangements."

She put the wood by the stove and turned to shut the door. It was the first week of October and snow had fallen on several occasions, but the day had been sunny and relatively warm, though the smell of winter lay heavy in the crisp air.

She didn't like the autumn season. *Too many memories!* Joly tried not to remember; how she wished she could forget, but she would *never* forget. The pain shot through her slender body once again. *Keep busy!* But it was too late. The waves of anger and sorrow rose to the front and with a wail; she threw herself on the bed. The tears fell and her loud wracking sobs drowned out the sound of the wood crackling merrily in the stove.

Nefertiti, Salem and Pip were beside her in an instant, cuddling in close, sending waves of comfort and healing to her. They all wished there was more they could do, but this was something their Mistress had to work through herself.

A long time later she became quiet and although her shoulders still shook, her three friends knew the worst was over for this time. Nefertiti went back to the window to look outside. Salem walked to Joly's face and licked her cheek. Joly lie still a moment and then lifted her tear stained face. "I'm sorry, Salem, I'm not sure what brought that on."

Nefertiti watched as the Mistress reached down to stroke Pip who lie snuggled against her chest. "What would I do without all of you?" Joly rose and went to the sink. Pouring water into a basin, she washed her face and started preparing their evening meal.

Salem and Pip joined Nefertiti at the window. Pip spoke first, "Her heart was pounding like crazy; I was really worried about her. It's been a while since she so totally broke down."

Salem agreed. "Yes. She was a long time coming out of it. Maybe it's a good thing she's planning a trip now. We don't usually travel until after Candlemas, but I have a feeling this October could be a rough one on her."

Nefertiti agreed with her companions. The ninth anniversary was almost upon them. She knew the Mistress kept her memories locked away deep inside so she rarely thought of them. She was aware the Mistress had never mourned, had never grieved the way all living beings needed to, so when the door to her memories cracked open, it was as if the Bad Time had happened recently.

Nefertiti watched the evening approach, her senses tuned to the outdoors. This was her specialty. She sensed long before the others when something was not right outside. And although nothing evil had sought them out in this location, she was ever vigilant because one just never knew. She'd been with their Mistress the longest. Ever since the Bad Time, when the Mistress had been alone and more dead than alive. She'd sensed the urgent need of a special, magical human and found her in a dirty alley in Europe. A more disheveled human Nefertiti didn't think she had ever seen, but she knew this was where she was needed and she had been watching out for the Mistress ever since.

She thought back to her life prior to Mistress Joly. She had been the pampered feline of Mistress Antoinette. Her home was an eighteen room chateau in the French Alps. She remembered the day of the accident and how she'd heard the cries of terror via her mind, but the doors and windows were closed and she was unable to go to her. The Mistress and her daughter were driving down the mountain highway when something went wrong. She'd lost control of the little red car she always drove and slid over the embankment. The Mister, grief stricken beyond words had instructed the maid to get rid of the *cat* and any other reminders of his wife. She overheard the conversation and knew invisibility was the key to her survival. She spent the next three months in the stables making do with scraps fed to her by a sympathetic cook and chauffeur.

She awoke one morning with the urge to head north. She waited until the cook put food out for her and then she left. She lost track of the days as her senses drove her steadily onward. When she arrived at the large expanse of water she was nonplussed as to what she should do. She finally managed to sneak aboard a ship and when she debarked, she knew she was close to her destination. It took her several days to get to the big city, where she'd had to avoid traffic, dogs and dead ends.

She'd had a terrible time convincing the Mistress they belonged together, but in the end, they came to Canada and the Mistress began the long process of healing. Nefertiti watched out for her because she was unable to watch out for herself. Nefertiti knew she had the power but she never used it.

She thought about the plane trip and how she'd had to convince everyone the Mistress came in contact with, that she was nothing more than a plush toy. It was the most intensive bit of chicanery she'd ever pulled off. The Mistress had been so out of it, Nefertiti didn't think she even noticed the illusion.

It was four years later when Salem showed up out of the blue. She and the Mistress had been to town and sensing nothing out of the ordinary Nefertiti left her side for only a minute. Salem never talked about his past so where he came from no one knew, but on that day he saved the Mistress' life. Nefertiti had just disappeared from sight when a truck came careening around the corner as Mistress Joly was crossing the street. Salem made a super leap into the middle of her back. The Mistress had stumbled forward falling to the ground, as the truck roared over the spot where she stood a moment before. The Mistress had scraped her hands and knees but other than that, was none the worse for wear.

She didn't care for Salem but she was aware that the Mistress needed him. Salem could sense immediate danger and on several occasions had saved their Mistress from various mishaps. The latest one being when the Mistress went to move the stepladder, forgetting the hammer was resting on the top of it. As she picked it up, the hammer slid off falling toward her head. Salem had leapt up and bumped it with his shoulder so it fell harmlessly to the ground. His shoulder was sore for several days but their Mistress was fine.

Pip was another story. Her extrasensory perception was so attuned to the Mistress' internal workings, it was at times scary. Pip had walked all the way to their cabin, from where she didn't know. Her paws were raw when she arrived on the doorstep bedraggled and so thin one could almost see through her. Nefertiti knew she was coming, but knew she wasn't a threat. She did want to know why Pip was there, but she waited until the Mistress had cleaned up her paws and fed her before she questioned her.

Pip said she'd been born in a small, dirty house, one of a litter of seven. The Mister yelled a lot and hit the Mistress and their children. When the kittens were barely old enough to eat on their own, he'd tossed them outside to fend for themselves. She watched as a hawk took one of her brothers and an owl grabbed her sister. A dog took two more of her siblings. The youngest girl favored Pip and fed her when she was able, but when school resumed at the end of summer Pip rarely saw her, and knew if she was to survive she needed to move on.

She said she had followed her heart, and sometime into her long journey, she discovered she was being guided by a force larger than she was. It wasn't until she approached the cabin that she realized this was where she needed to be. Pip proved to be invaluable when it came to the Mistress' health. Pip knew long before there were any physical signs, when she was getting a cold, the flu, or even an infection. Although she was a pain in the backside with her exuberance, she and Salem knew Pip was as needed as they were.

A few days later they went to town and Joly prepared for the trip to Hawaii. They would leave on the twenty-sixth.

Returning home quite late, Joly quickly fixed a small meal. They ate in silent comfort, and then Joly washed up the few dishes and prepared for bed. As she turned back the covers, climbed in and curled into a fetal position, Salem and Pip joined her. Pip as always, slept as close to her heart as she could. Salem curled up next to her head.

Nefertiti slept by the window ever alert to the air currents around her. Even the shifting of the wind from one direction to another would have her on her feet searching, sensing, always checking.

The nights were always quiet inside the cabin. The only sounds coming from the wood stove, as the pine and birch logs crackled and popped.

Joly never dreamed. She didn't dare dream, as the nightmares were so real she would never have survived them. Every night before bed, Joly practiced the only magic she did nowadays. She cast her circle, drew in the pentagram, lit her candles, and prepared the herbs and liquid she needed to ensure her sleep would be undisturbed.

While she was doing this, her three friends were making their own preparations; Nefertiti worked a sealing spell around the door and window against intruders, as well as another around the whole of the cabin. Salem made a circle around the bed and put another one there. Pip sat on the bed and worked her own magic to ensure the Mistress would have a comfortable and peaceful sleep. They didn't know if Joly was aware of their cautiousness, but it didn't matter. It was a necessity. They all knew their Mistress had immense power. They could feel it emanating from her very soul. Nefertiti had told the other two that among witches she was a queen, and she must be protected at all cost until she was able to protect herself.

Salem was having the most wonderful dream. He was back down south where he had been born and his Mother, sisters, and brother were with him. The barn where they made their home was warm and dry; the scent of the fresh mown hay was sweet in the air. They were well fed by the Mistress, something the Mister frowned on, but he never stopped her from bringing milk and treats to them. He grumbled about no mousing being done by fat cats, but he admitted that he rarely ever saw any rodents.

The dream shifted.

He'd felt the need to leave his snug home and head north. He traveled for many weeks, sometimes managing to con a sympathetic motorist into taking him some of the distance. He'd had to stop doing that when one well-meaning soul had turned around and headed back the way he had come from. It had taken him a two day journey on foot to return to the point where he'd gotten into the car. He'd been shot at by some idiot in a truck, chased by numerous dogs and some animal he still couldn't identify. He'd gotten to the point where he was sure he would never get to the north. He remembered one of the children saying Santa lived as far north as you could go and he was positive that was where he was going to end up.

He'd been lurking in the small town a couple of days, resting and searching for food when he sensed someone was in mortal danger. He'd sprinted down alleys and streets narrowly avoiding being run over by some jerk in a blue truck. He'd cut through a couple of yards and was running full out when he saw her crossing the road. He knew sure as his name was Salem, she wasn't going to make it. He wasn't sure where the extra speed came from, but he was almost flying as he crossed the street, and launched himself into the middle of her back. He saw the truck out of the corner of his eye. It was the same one that had almost ran him over only minutes before.

The long, low growl startled him, causing disorientation for a second or two. Then he was on his feet in a flash, his head swinging around.

Nefertiti was crouched below the window, every hair of her fur standing on end. Just her eyes were peering over the top of the sill.

"What is it, Neffy?" He opened his senses, but found nothing.

"Something bad is coming, something really bad."

Pip sat by her Mistress, not moving. She was terrified, but said nothing. She knew they had done all they could to protect the Mistress. She didn't know what kind of bad thing was coming, but when she pictured *bad*, she saw a man, loud, mean and usually drunk on something called beer.

She hoped it wasn't the man coming. Even with the sealing spells, he could break the door down. She had seen him do it before.

Salem felt it then. *Evil!* Evil was outside, and soon it was all around them! He stayed where he was. It would do no good to join Nefertiti at the window. The spells had been cast. They would be safe.

Pip cowered in terror. This wasn't the man. This was something much worse, something she had no knowledge of... and yet, she thought she recognized it.

From somewhere deep inside of her, she remembered another life, another evil entity and she finally understood why she was there. This was the reason for protecting the Mistress. This was the reason the Mistress needed to heal. It was this evil and others like it that she was destined to rid the world of.

The Evil swirled around the cabin for hours. It checked every nook and cranny looking for a way to enter. When it touched the cracks, they could hear it hiss as Nefertiti's spell repelled it again and again.

Morning arrived but it was still dark this far north. Their Mistress stirred. She moaned as she stretched. She opened her eyes. As she sat up, they could tell the instant she felt it. The hatred was so all encompassing, she cringed.

The demon heard her and renewed its efforts to enter. It knew she was inside and it wanted her. It had been searching for her for years and it had finally found her. It was *not* about to go away without her. It felt the fear coming from inside and had it been able to laugh it would have. It liked fear; it thrived on fear. Fear was good! It fed on the fear and grew stronger. It swirled back and forth, up and down, but it could not find an opening. It grew angrier! It hadn't thought she would be so well protected.

Joly moved to get out of bed. Salem touched her arm with his paw to stop her. She looked at him and reached over to stroke him. He sat on his haunches and stared into Joly's eyes. She realized he needed to communicate with her. She rolled over onto her stomach bringing her face level with his. She knew she needed to concentrate but the fear was making it hard.

She sat up again. "Wait." She closed her eyes and sent her thoughts to a place she had not been to in many years.

Joly went home.

She saw her home as if it was yesterday. The ivy climbing the walls and all the brightly colored flowers, so lovingly cared for by her Mother. Joly felt a stab of pain but willed it away. She walked up the front steps and opened the door. The smell of freshly baked bread made her mouth water. She moved forward through the entry hall and looked into the living room. Spotless as always but empty. Then she heard singing, soft and cheerful her Mother's voice drifted over Joly, bringing tears to her eyes.

She turned the corner into the kitchen. Her Father sat at the table, the newspaper and a cup of steaming coffee in front of him. Her Mother was standing at the sink watching something through the window. She was still singing softly.

Joly reached her hand forward, unable to speak with the huge lump in her throat.

Her Father looked up and smiled.

"So there you are! We wondered when we would see you." He was conscious of Morgana turning from the sink.

"Ah, my sweet, sweet Joly Anne, it took you far too long to come." With a graceful, unhurried movement, she walked across the kitchen and put her arms around Joly.

They were always aware of what Joly was doing, but in their veil known as Summerland, they knew only tranquility. They no longer had the ability to worry and stress was something for those who had not yet crossed over.

Feeling her fear and knowing what was transpiring in her world, Colin stood and joined them, one arm around the woman he loved as much in death as he had in life, and the other around their precious daughter. He felt her absorb their peace and serenity, felt the fear leave, and he released her back to her world.

She opened her eyes. Her heartbeat had slowed and even though *It* was still outside, the fear was gone. She lie back down on the bed and faced Salem.

They looked into each others eyes and neither blinked. Joly let herself relax and she took a deep breath. As she slowly exhaled, she pictured her thoughts going to Salem's mind and she watched Salem exhale and pictured his thoughts coming to her. She continued to look directly into his eyes and felt herself being absorbed into them. She knew Salem was experiencing the same effect. Soon they became one and she could hear his thoughts.

"Mistress, you are safe within these walls but we would prefer you stay on the bed, at least until It leaves."

"Why?"

"It's very riled and we feel the less movement from you, the better."

"Yes, alright. Thank you, Salem."

Salem turned away.

Joly shook her head and looked around. Nefertiti was crouched at the window. With her long fur standing on end, she looked like a giant black and gray furball. Joly stifled the urge to laugh. She knew Nefertiti would be horribly offended.

Pip! *Where's Pip?* She turned and glanced behind her. Pip was lying there with her eyes so big; they looked like they were about to burst. Joly laughed and it felt good so she laughed again. She reached over, picked Pip up and brought her onto her lap.

"Poor Pip. You've nothing to be afraid of."

The demon heard her laugher and while it fed on fear the reverse was also true. Joly's laughter took its strength and weakened it. Also, daylight was coming. It knew it had lost this round but it would be back. *Oh, yes! It would be back!* The evil being slithered away in the darkness that was blackest just before dawn.

Joly had a lot of preparing ahead of her. Once Nefertiti gave the all clear, she jumped out of bed, washed, dressed, and prepared a light breakfast.

Daylight was slow in coming. Fog had rolled in giving the area an otherworldly appearance. Not a breath of wind stirred; even the birds and squirrels were quiet.

Joly knew what had to be done. She went to the bed and reached underneath. She gripped the handle of the trunk and pulled it out. Squatting down she snapped the two clasps into the open position, and taking the cord from around her neck, she inserted one of the attached keys into its opening. The lock clicked and she removed the key, returning the cord to her neck. Placing both hands on the corners of the lid, she paused. There was no more hiding, no more pretending she was like most people. The time had arrived for her to resume the roll that had been charted for her since her birth. Her destiny would wait no longer.

Joly lifted the lid and looked inside. Lying on top were her robes, just as they were when she had placed them there so many years ago. She carefully removed them and placing them on a hanger, she put them in the closet. Next to come out of the trunk were two large wooden boxes. These she pushed to the side. On the bottom was another wooden box, this one was long and wide, but not very high. She struggled to get a good grip on it and lifted it out. She took it over by the table and set it on the floor. Kneeling, Joly gently opened one clasp and then the other. Lifting the lid, she felt a shiver radiate through her body.

Eying the contents, Joly paused. Memories rushed in overwhelming her, fragments fighting to be recognized first; her wonderful parents, dear Morag, silly Bettina, funny Raoul, serious Broderick, and Duncan, her beloved Duncan. She heard the chanting, smelled the candles, felt the cool night air, and then the vile, putrid odor of something that should have never been.

They were a small coven that pursued that which was not good. They searched out evil spirits and demons and when they found them, the group banished them back to where they came from. Joly's parents were part of the coven and from the time of her birth, they had been training Joly in the craft.

Joly's childhood was for the most part, like any other child's. She went to school, had friends, joined the drama club, went on sleepovers, and was active in sports. However, she had a secret, one she knew she could not tell anyone. She was different from her playmates and their families. She was a witch! She understood most people did not believe in witches or magic, but that was okay. Her parents taught her tolerance and control.

Her best friend from the time they were toddlers, had always been Duncan. He too was a witch, the son of two other coven members. They had loved each other forever and knew they had been together in other lifetimes, other places. When Joly graduated, they made their wedding plans and were married on August first, Lughnassad. The next three months were the happiest she had known.

Then came the summons to Europe. Another demon was wreaking havoc and gaining strength daily. The group knew they had to stop it. Defeat never entered anyone's mind. They had always been successful.

The circle was cast, the pentagram drawn. The altar was ready, as were they. They knew how to get the demon to appear, but they were not prepared for the size or strength of it! They hadn't brought enough holy water, sea salt or herbs. They fought valiantly with every magical potion and spell they knew.

Joly saw the demon seize her Father, saw it slay her Mother, and watched as it killed two others. Duncan took his eyes off it for a moment and told her to run, "Go, Darlin', now! Get out of here!" She refused! She would not leave her beloved. Duncan had grabbed her, picked her up and thrown her with all his might. She had landed well clear of the circle. As she lie there trying to catch her breath, she turned her head and saw Duncan go down, watched as he struggled to rise, saw someone throw more sea salt, watched the demon writhe in agony, shrink, then grow again. She looked on in horror as a small, almost transparent tentacle reached out to Duncan. Suddenly, he was still.

The scream froze the last two in their tracks; it was like nothing she had ever heard before. The hair on her arms and legs stood on end. The banshee wail went on and on and on.

Joly couldn't imagine what kind of animal could make a noise like that. Why, even the demon had quit fighting and seemed to be listening.

Joly shook her head. She didn't have time to think about the past now. Realizing her cheeks were wet, she drew her hands across her face and wiped the tears away.

Feeling warmth on her hip she looked down and found Pip snuggled against her. Joly looked around and saw Salem and Nefertiti both watching her from the table. "I'm okay. Honest." She smiled at them all and sniffled. "I guess I was woolgathering." Her attention returned to the box in front of her.

On the left was a large leather bound book. Joly lay her hand on it. This had been her parents Book of Shadows. All their spells, rituals, recipes and anything to do with the craft were entered here. She left the book alone and moved to the middle. She lifted the rectangular box onto her lap and opened it. Inside was an assortment of feathers in one section, and seashells filled the other side. Joly closed the lid and placed it on the table.

The box on the right was opened but not removed. In it lay her tarot cards, the runes that had been made especially for her and her crystal ball. She smiled as she looked at the crystal. Her Father had given it to her on her tenth birthday. Her Mother had not been pleased, saying she was too young. It was one of the few times Joly ever heard them disagree. They had finally compromised, her parents would keep the crystal ball under lock and key, but Joly was free to use it when one of them was there to supervise. Joly closed the lid.

Her attention returned to the book. She carefully lifted it and stood up to put it on the table beside the box. She then went over to the other two boxes and brought them to the table. Opening the heavier of the two, she looked down at the display of rocks and crystals.

Her attention drifted to the last box. With fingers that were trembling, she raised the lid. Inside were several identical long narrow boxes but Joly knew the contents of each were very different. She started to reach her hand in but drew it back. She wasn't ready.

Joly moved to the cabinet by the sink. Opening the door, she removed several vials of oils and some candles. Closing that door, she opened the one next to it. She reached in, closed her hand around her chalice and removed it.

Unable to delay any longer, she walked back to the table and opened the Book of Shadows. Her Mother's unruly handwriting jumped out at her. She drew in a deep breath and began searching. There were basically two ways to confine a demon, but she didn't have the means to do either. There was a third way, one that wasn't recommended, but she thought she could pull it off.

An hour later, satisfied that she knew what to do, she closed the book and reached for her jacket. Salem jumped off the table and went to the door.

Joly walked to the clearing. The air was damp and the fog, although not as thick as earlier, was still hanging below the treetops. She carefully removed sticks, branches, rocks and other debris; until she was sure the ground was clean. On the way back to the cabin, she stopped at the woodpile and grabbed an armload of wood.

Back inside Joly heated a large kettle of water. At the sink, she mixed oils of lemon, lavender, anise, cinnamon, and jasmine. She set out a clean towel, poured the water into her small tub and added the oil mixture. She undressed and climbed in. The tub was too small for any amount of comfort so she always bathed with speed. Getting out she wrapped the towel around her, and poured another kettle of water into the sink. Washing her long chestnut brown hair with no running water was a chore, but she refused to cut it. Duncan had loved her hair, loved to run his beautiful long fingers through it. *Don't think!*

She went to the tiny closet and took out her robes. She pulled the emerald green silk gown down over her head and tied the soft rope belt, then went to brush her hair. She slipped on the flowing emerald velvet cloak, did up the clasp and slid into her shoes.

Looking out the window Joly could see she was fast running out of time. She carefully gathered up the altar cloth, chalice, bell and candles. Heading outside, she set up the altar on a board placed over a level tree stump in the clearing. Back inside, drawing in a deep breath Joly reached again for the box she hadn't opened before. Lifting the lid, she picked up the third box from the left. As she did, she heard her Father's voice, *"When you decide you need to use this, there is no turning back. Be very careful!"*

Joly opened the box. It still took her breath away, even after all these years! The ebony wand was the most beautiful one she had ever seen. The Gabon ebony had come from Africa and a master artisan had crafted it especially for her. She had decorated it over a period of several weeks with tiny shells, feathers and stones, wanting it to be perfect.

She removed the wand from the box and placed it in one of the deep pockets of her robe. She picked up the vials of oil and herbs from the counter and a large blue bottle from the cupboard, along with a glass container of sea salt. Back outside Joly placed the items on the altar and raced back to the house. She grabbed her athame and looked around making sure she hadn't forgotten anything.

Salem and Pip went and sat under the steps. Nefertiti walked over to the clearing to ensure everything was in its proper place. She checked the area and saw a small pine cone; she went and picked it up in her teeth and removed it. She returned to sit with the other two. At her feet sat a small black bag.

Joly started her ritual. She took her besom and swept the clearing while chanting the cleansing spell. She cast the double circle with her athame, drew in the pentagram and symbols, sprinkled the sea salt and holy water around the edge. She chanted her spells with a surety that belied her age and inexperience. She was in total control.

"Dark is the Night
Just as the Day is Light,
Evil is wrong, just as good is right,
And good will win this fight!"
Joly kept chanting.

Dusk was coming fast. The fog continued to hover with no breeze to sweep it away.

In the trees it was already dark and something moved, disturbing the quiet air. The gray-black shadow hovered at the edge of the forest waiting for the dark. It grew impatient wanting that which had been denied it so many years before. It hadn't expected to find her in an isolated area. It had searched every city the world over expecting her to find safety in numbers. It hadn't even been looking for her here. It had just been passing through when it caught a whiff of something it hadn't smelled in years.

The demon had been there in Europe when Joly lost everyone dear to her. It was a very small, young demon and had remained undetected while the battle raged. It didn't know what the call to the circle meant and it followed its mentor only to discover the horrors of sea salt, holy water, herbs and other terrible hurtful things. It caught her scent and decided it had to have her. When she was thrown beyond the circle it was furious. It had almost given itself away when it stabbed the one who threw her. The potions had burned terribly but no one noticed there were two evil beings in the circle. When the fight was over and the circle removed, it was too late. She was gone and it had been searching for her ever since.

The time had come. It slithered forward to get its reward.

Joly felt the goosebumps rise on her arms and knew it was coming. She could smell the evil radiating from the hateful thing and shivered in anticipation. *Come on you slime ball!* She continued chanting.

It had no thought other than to get the one it had in its senses. As it twisted and undulated toward her it was conscious of her every breath. It was almost there when it realized she wasn't going to be so easy to grab. She was in a protective circle. The demon roared its displeasure! It had searched for so long. Confused, it was unable to think clearly. The demon swirled around the Sacred Circle, its anger and scent palatable on the night air.

Wait! The circle was not complete; the line did not join in one spot. It was a very tiny gap but it was all that the demon needed. It thinned itself and slid through. It ran into another invisible wall. There was another circle. If she was careless once, perhaps she had been careless again. It searched. There! The tiniest hole but small meant nothing to the demon. It oozed through.

It was so intent on reaching the object in front of it; it never noticed a small dark shadow stealthily approach with a bag in its mouth. The corner of the bag had been cut open, and the sea salt that had been blessed with holy water trickled out to complete the sealing of the outer circle.

Joly stood as close to the top point of the pentacle as she could without stepping outside the inner circle. She continued her chanting as though unaware of the anger and hatred being radiated toward her from the other side. She waited as long as she could. When she knew the dark beast was almost through the inner circle and inside the pentacle, she quickly opened the invisible gate and stepped to the outer circle. She waved her athame and said the words to close the gate. She waited until the wraith like appendages approached her.

The demon attacked! It reached out to consume her but she wasn't there! It bumped into the edge of the Sacred Circle and let out a scream of pain.

She ran around to the crack the demon had slid through. She spread more sea salt and holy water, sealing the monster inside the pentacle.

It turned to exit the circle the way it entered and found the hole was sealed. The air vibrated with its scream of rage and the fetid odor it emitted was nauseating!

Joly gagged, swallowed, and picked up the bell on the altar. Walking in a clockwise direction, she circled the pentagram three times ringing the bell and calling upon the good spirits to hear her.

The demon howled. It wanted to feed upon something, anything. It needed to feed its anger. It needed to grow stronger. It reached out to grab Joly, its tentacles stretched to the limit but it connected with empty air.

Joly returned the bell to the altar, removed the stopper and picked up a vial of holy water and a handful of sea salt. She stood at the upper point of the circle. Chanting the words she hadn't said in nine years, she threw the salt and holy water at the demon. It screamed in pain and sent out more vile odors. Still chanting, Joly threw the herb mixture, more salt and holy water. She reached into her pocket and withdrew her wand. She could feel the vibration within the wood as she pointed it at the demon. She swirled the wand in a clockwise direction, and drew on her inner power. She felt it rise from the pit of her stomach and as it ran down her arm, she said the words she had heard her Father say, feeling each one as it left her mouth.

The tip of the wand sparked and the powerful charge sped through the air. It hit the demon dead on, and it screamed as it writhed in pain.

The three cats sat in the shadows, their eyes glued to the circle. The youngest from time to time assuring the other two that all was well. In fact, Mistress Joly's heartbeat had never been stronger and she had never seemed so alive.

Joly threw more salt and holy water, more herbs and she used her wand repeatedly. The demon weakened. It knew it had lost and was about to be banished back to the world it had escaped from nine years before. As her words got louder, it became a duel between the demon's crazed howls and Joly's chant.

When she sensed the battle was ended, her chanting ceased. She tossed a final vial of holy water at the apparition. Her wand quivered, the end twisted and sparked. As the water and electrical charge struck the monster, the howling stopped. The world went still.

Then the demon screamed a scream equal to the one heard so many years before. It writhed in agony, and appeared to be sucked into the earth.

The silence was absolute!

Joly was exhausted, but knew there was more to do before calling it a day. First, she had to take down the circle. Starting on the east point, she snuffed out the candle sending a blessing to the corresponding element. She worked her way around the circle. Then she went to the altar, gave thanks, and instructed the spirits to depart in peace.

Joly gathered everything from the altar and returned to the cabin. It was cool, as the fire had almost burned out. She added wood and made one last trip to the clearing assuring herself it was as clean as when she started.

She fed the cats, took off her robes, washed and climbed into bed.

"Did you see that?" Salem asked Nefertiti.

"Yes." She answered.

The Mistress had gone to bed without casting the spell to keep her from dreaming. "Do you think she forgot?"

Pip answered. "No, she didn't forget. She no longer needs it. Our Mistress has rejoined the land of the living."

She slept long and deep. She dreamed of her parents and her husband and still she slept. Pip and Salem watched over her while Nefertiti kept an eye on the world beyond their doorstep.

"Jacinta... where are you?" Emilia Escobar de Juarez whirled in a circle, her dark eyes flashing and a smile playing on her lips.

Silence.

"Come on now, you've proven your point, *niña*."

"Boo!"

Emilia jumped, laughed and swung around. The young girl stood grinning at her Mother. "See, I told you I could do it."

"Si, you did. Very good, my *hija*." Emilia smiled and shook her head. Jacinta was good, too good for her age. Her magical powers were far beyond

what Emilia's own had been at fourteen. Jacinta was practicing invisibility and she had managed to cloak herself for several minutes. Emilia could have opened her senses and found her, but she'd wanted to see what the child could do.

"What next, *Madre*?"

"I think it's time to go and have a bite to eat."

"Can we play one more… please? Then I promise to go in."

"What do you have in mind?"

"Umm… *levitación*?"

"*Levitación*. All right. Where's your feather?"

"No feather. Something heavier." She smiled impishly as she searched the ground. She picked up a small flat stone and held it up for her Mother's inspection.

Emilia knew she must have been practicing on her own, if she wanted to try with a rock. She walked to the swing and sat down to watch.

Jacinta sat cross-legged on the ground; she closed her eyes and was still for a minute, then she cupped her hands in the air around the small stone. For seconds nothing happened, and then slowly, the stone rose and floated above the earth.

Emilia watched Jacinta's facial expressions. Her powers of concentration were intense, so this was a fairly new trick. The stone hovered for a minute and then began to float toward Emilia. It had only traveled a foot or so when White Wind barked and jumped off the veranda. He grabbed the rock; his tail wagging and dropped it at Jacinta's feet.

"*Viento Blanco!* You wrecked it."

"Very good, *niña*, you've been practicing."

Jacinta pouted. "It was supposed to go to your hand."

Emilia laughed. "*Viento Blanco* had other ideas." She patted the white German Shepherd and put her arm around her daughter.

"Let's go and eat. I'm hungry."

As they walked up the steps, the air currents changed. The dog growled. Emilia looked down the road. Someone had just entered the property. Her wards had been disturbed. There was the sound of a vehicle and soon a red pickup drove into sight. It was her neighbor whose property bordered hers to the south.

A hard lump settled in Emilia's stomach. She gently pushed Jacinta to the door. "Go inside *niña* and take *Viento Blanco* with you. Put the kettle on for tea. I'll be there in a minute." The dog was still growling as he followed Jacinta inside.

Iago Flores Vargas got out of the truck and nodded to Emilia. He looked around the property, before he advanced to where she stood.

"*Buenas tardes, Señora* Escobar de Juarez." He smiled up at the woman, but the smile did not reach his eyes.

"Good afternoon. What can I do for you?" She felt the lump move in her stomach and hoped she wasn't going to be ill in front of Iago.

He nodded to himself and again glanced around the property. He removed his *sombrero*, took a hanky from his pocket and mopped his brow.

She knew courtesy required that she invite him in for a cool drink, but she wanted him off the *rancho* and the sooner the better.

"*Señora*, you have not responded to the letter from my lawyer."

"My apologies, *Señor* Vargas. I am not interested in selling the *rancho*. I should have let *Señor* Ramirez know that."

"You know… it's been a year since Ernesto died. I have watched you struggle with the *rancho,* with the cattle. You are not meant for such back-breaking work. You should be enjoying life, spending time with your *hija*… maybe looking for a new *esposo*.

"*Señor* Vargas, I am not interested in looking for a husband, I do spend time with my daughter and the *rancho* is operating fine. Now I'm sorry, I have things to do. Good day." She turned to go inside.

"*Señora*."

She turned and faced Iago. *"Si?"*

"I would advise you to reconsider my offer. Women alone… sometimes they have trouble, bad trouble. Things happen…" He shook his head and re-placed the *sombrero*. "I would be careful if I were you."

"*Adiós, Señora.*" He walked back to his truck, got in and turned it around, running over the edge of one of her flower beds.

When he was out of sight, she crumpled to the steps, shaking.

She couldn't let Jacinta find her like this; she stood, centered and grounded. They were *Sisters of the Triple Moon*. Everything would be fine. She went inside and greeted Jacinta with a smile on her face.

It was thirty-six hours before Joly stirred.

There were so many things to take care of. Joly needed to cancel the Hawaii trip, but she could do that on her way south. There wasn't much holy water left, so she would have to replenish it, but the full moon was five days away.

Joly repacked everything into the trunk and pulled out the suitcase from under the bed. Living out in the bush alone, she hadn't needed much in the way of clothing. Jeans and sweatshirts were her mainstay, a couple of T-shirts for when it was hot, fleece pants and long underwear for when it was cold, two night gowns, underwear, socks, slippers and shoes. She had her snowsuit, winter jacket and boots, and a summer jacket and jac-shirt.

She packed the things she knew she wouldn't need again. She heated water and did a small load of laundry, hanging it on a line that was strung across the room.

The stars shone brightly in the cool, crisp air. The full moon hung almost directly over the clearing. Joly swept and cleansed it. She set up her altar and walked down to the creek. Breaking the thin ice, she dipped a large wooden bowl in the cold water, filling it. Walking back to the altar she grounded herself. She cast her circle and holding her arms outstretched to the east, she called upon the God and Goddess to bless the water. Continuing the incantation, she added rosewater to the bowl, lifted it high in the air and said the words of consecration. Setting it back on the altar, she added sea salt to the bowl and consecrated it. Calling on the spirits of the light and the Moon Goddess Selene, she asked them to bless the water; assuring them it would be used to heal, protect and guide. She took down her circle, thanking the spirits as she bade them to depart in peace. She poured the holy water into a clean blue decanter and dismantled her altar, leaving the bottle to sit in the moonlight to absorb the pure light from the Moon Goddess.

Everything was packed and loaded in the old pick-up truck. It didn't look like someone was moving out of the Territory. Her trunk and suitcase were in the back of the truck, along with her rocking chair and three boxes of books. Two other boxes contained her herbs, oils, and various other items she used regularly. There was also a large green garbage bag. The pickup bed was covered with a blue tarp to protect the contents from the elements.

Joly took a last look around the cabin peering into the cupboards making sure nothing had been forgotten. She'd filled the wood box with split wood and kindling, and made sure there was coffee and sugar in sealed containers.

It was the unwritten law of the land. In case someone became lost and stumbled upon an empty cabin, everything was ready for them to light a fire and heat a pot of coffee. Doors were never locked. There were also cans of beans and soup left in the cupboard. A frozen, starving prospector or hunter would welcome a hot meal. She also left a couple of comforters in a metal garbage can, so the mice couldn't destroy them.

Outside, she walked around the cabin double-checking everything. Satisfied all was taken care of; she climbed into the truck where her three feline friends sat waiting. Nefertiti was lying on the back of the seat where she had a view of everything around her. Salem was on the passenger's seat and Pip curled up against Joly's thigh. Joly turned the key, the engine catching immediately. She put it into first gear, and touching her foot to the accelerator they slowly moved down the rutted trail toward the highway.

Hours later, they drove down Two Mile Hill into the city of Whitehorse. Joly stopped at the PetroCanada and fueled up, checked the oil and tires and washed the windshield and headlights. She drove down Fourth Avenue watching for a small side street that had an herb and natural foods store. Finding a parking spot, Joly went into the store and picked up some rosewater, lavender oil and sea salt. Satisfied she had everything she might need for her long journey south, she paid for the items and went back to the truck. She drove over a couple of blocks to the grocery store and picked up some fruit, cans of tuna and chicken, and several bottles of water.

Back in the truck, she headed up the South Access road past the dam to the Alaska Highway. There was a motel across from the airport and she headed there to get a room for the night.

They left early the next morning long before daylight. It was early after-noon when they arrived at Watson Lake. She gassed up the truck, used the washroom and headed down the road. They stopped at a pullout just outside of town where they all got out to stretch and get some air. While her famil-iars were checking out the area Joly leaned against the truck and considered what she was doing.

She was headed home, but she didn't know why. She only knew this was the next step she needed to take. She'd been back to the house briefly when Nefertiti and she had gotten back to Canada. She had arranged for a neighbor to look after the lawn and flower gardens, and gave him a key so he could check inside. Her parents had kept the old house in good repair but one just never knew when a water pipe might burst.

Her main reason for going there at all at the time was to get her parents Book of Shadows. This was something that could not be left lying around for some dim-witted burglar to get his light-fingered hands on. It had been a hard thing to do, going in the house and knowing she would never see them again, except for when she dream-walked while meditating.

It was funny. She thought she should be going to see Duncan, when she took the dream-walks but maybe he couldn't ground her like her parents could. It was true he had always made her heart race. She smiled. It would be hard to calm and ground a body whose heart was getting ready to jump right out of the very skin that contained it. She loved him so very much! She was only twenty-eight, but she knew she would never fall in love or marry again.

A brush against her leg jolted her back to the present. Pip was looking at her, head slightly cocked as if to say, hey lady, get with the program! She grinned at the wee cat and opened the door.

They crossed the invisible border into British Columbia. They were physically in the middle of nowhere, but Joly felt a surge of delight. She had been born and raised in British Columbia and it didn't matter what part of the province she was in, she thought of the whole of it as home.

It was a long, lonely highway between Watson Lake and Fort Nelson and she wasn't sure she would be able to drive that far without stopping. She found herself wishing she'd bought a couple of cassettes, so she would have some music. It had been nine years since she wanted to listen to music, and the cassette player in the truck had never been used.

She had bought the truck brand new, but there was still very little mileage on it. She had driven it up to the Territory and while she looked around for a place to call her own. When she bought the claim the truck hauled lumber, insulation, shingles and all the necessities for building her cabin. It had brought the sluice box and mining equipment, the wood burning stove, the little bit of furniture she required, and groceries. Since that time, she usually went to town once a month for supplies. The rest of the time the truck sat.

Something was wrong! Pip leapt to her feet yowling. Salem and Nefertiti startled out of sound sleeps began growling, their fur on end.

Joly jerked awake. She had dozed off, and if not for Pip sensing the slowing of her heartbeat, she didn't know what might have happened. Shaking, she pulled off to the side of the road and got out of the truck. It was dark and the road wasn't wide enough to park for any length of time. She would have to look for a pullout. She walked around the truck several times, breathing deeply in the cold night air. Satisfied she was awake; she jumped back in the truck. Thanking Pip for her vigilance, she pulled back on the road.

They hadn't gone far when Joly spotted a large pullout. She turned off the highway and drove to the far side away from the traffic. Getting out, she realized they were beside a lake. The moon reflected on the water and ice had formed around the edge. Joly stretched and loosened a corner of the tarp. She pulled out the garbage bag. Inside was a pillow, her Grandmother's afghan and a blanket.

Back inside the truck, she laid the afghan out for Pip and Salem. She wedged the pillow against the window and covered herself with the blanket. Reaching up, she stroked Nefertiti, knowing that while she was getting the bedding, a protective circle had been drawn around the truck. Snuggling into her pillow, she relaxed and closed her eyes.

As much as Pip loved the afghan, she wasn't happy. She couldn't curl up against her Mistress the way she always did, so she stuck her nose under the edge of the blanket and wriggled her way onto Joly's lap.

Joly's first thought was; why was she in a sitting position? Her next immediate thought was how cold she was. Opening her eyes, the events of the past two days came flooding back. She sat up to start the engine and felt a weight on her lap. Lifting the blanket, she saw two large amber eyes looking back at her. Joly smiled and carefully stretched her foot out to the gas pedal, turning the key at the same time. The truck roared to life.

It had been a long time since she had driven any distance, and Joly felt a little sheepish knowing she had put all their lives in danger. She would not try to make so many kilometers this time.

After getting out for a stretch, opening a can of chicken for the four-legged passengers and grabbing a banana and an apple for herself, they were on the road again. It was still early and very dark. Joly drove carefully, alert for any wild animals that might attempt to cross the road in front of her.

They pulled into Fort Nelson at nine-thirty. Joly gassed up and found a grocery store where she purchased a few things. Then she went looking for a place that sold music and finding one, she picked up a couple of country cassettes. Then they hit the road again. They made it to Dawson Creek, the urge to get home stronger now, and she was confused by the feelings. There was nothing there and no one was waiting for her.

The next night they stopped at Williams Lake. She slept fitfully, her first night of uneasy sleep in many years. The urge to get home was stronger now. They were on the road early. She would be home by noon. As she got closer she found herself speeding and she had to keep easing off the accelerator.

Pip was worried, and told the others so. Nefertiti could not sense anything out of the ordinary, nor could Salem. They weren't sure what to make it.

Joly turned off Highway 97 and onto Number 7 highway, just before Hope. It wasn't the freeway, but the road wasn't as busy and she knew she could make good time.

Nefertiti's senses were on high alert as she sat on the back of the seat, her head swinging slowly back and forth, searching, ever searching.

Salem moved to the wide dashboard, watching the road in front of them, and then turning his head slightly to look at his Mistress. He didn't like what he saw. Her eyes had a glazed look and she was breathing fast, almost panting. She needed to ground herself, but she didn't seem aware anything was amiss.

Pip was huddled against Joly, feeling the strong vibrations of unreasonable fear coming from inside her loving Mistress.

Close! She was so close! Past the island where she and everyone dear to her had had so many good times, over the bridge where Duncan and she had loved to watch the swans, across the railway tracks, closer! Ever closer!

When she came around the corner and saw the traffic light ahead was red, she hit the brakes. Salem was forced against the windshield, Pip flew onto the floor and Nefertiti flew through the air to bounce off the front of the dash.

Joly was horrified! She sat, shaking and crying. A car horn blared behind her making her jump. Through her tears, she managed to drive ahead until she was across the intersection, where she pulled into the little grocery store parking lot. Laying her head on the steering wheel, she cried.

Pip and Salem sat as close to her as they could, sending their waves of healing comfort. Nefertiti regained her position on the back of the seat, watching, searching, but found nothing.

Some time later, Joly lifted her head slowly, ran her arm across her teary face and forced herself to look at her companions. "I'm sorry, I'm so sorry, I don't know what I was I doing, I don't know…" Her voice trailed off and she shuddered, another sob escaping. She took them one at a time and gave them a gentle hug and kiss.

She pulled out, turning right on the one-way street, going down several blocks and turning right again. She hesitated, wondering if she should go down the alley and park in the back, or should she park on the street. She opted for the street and drove up to the corner, turning right again.

Home! She was finally home! Joly pulled off the road and parked in front of her parents home, her home, the only place she ever lived until she married.

She got out of the truck and stretched, walked around the front of it and opened the gate. Returning to the pickup, she opened the passenger door and scooped up all three cats. Joly walked down the sidewalk and up the wide steps to the front door. "Stay put you three." She put them down to dig out her key.

Inserting it in the lock, the key turned easily and gripping the doorknob Joly drew in a deep breath, and pushed open the door.

Joan Ardell heard a vehicle stop and doors opening and closing. She might be getting old, but her hearing was fine. Reaching for her cane, she stood up and shuffled over to the dining room window. Peering around the edge of the lace curtain, she saw an unfamiliar truck parked next door. *Now who's that? No one's lived in that house in what, eight or ten years? Harold McNabb from down the street has a key and checks the place regular as clockwork. He had also taken care of the lawn and gardens until he had gotten too crippled to do it anymore. Now he had that boy, what was his name, Casper, Jasper, something like that, who came over and did the work. Harold still supervised and made sure it was done to his standards. I guess he must be being paid for it, but he's pretty close-mouthed, and I've never been able to find out what the deal was.*

It was a sad, sad thing what happened to those people. The James' had always seemed nice enough, and it wasn't that they weren't friendly, there was just something... I never could put my finger on it. What was her name... oh yes, Morgana. What kind of name is that, anyhow? She had been quite striking with her dark hair and brilliant green eyes. Piercing, they were. Sometimes it felt like she was looking right inside of you. And... Colin, yes, that was his name. He was nice as pie and always fixing up their place. He had a smile that would just knock your socks off! Yes, he'd been a looker all right. They had a girl, wonder what happened to her. She survived whatever accident it was they were in, but she never came back here. She had an odd name, what was it? She had been a pretty young thing, always seemed to be very popular, but there was something about her... remember watching her lie on the grass for hours, staring into her cat's eyes. It was creepy, like they were communicating or something. Didn't she lose her husband too? Yes, that young Duncan McEwan, from across the street. Damn, my memory isn't what it was! His parents are gone too, as far as I know, and their house hadn't been lived in since, either. It isn't right, leaving perfectly good houses like that empty. It's downright spooky, when you think about it.

I wonder if I should phone Harold and tell him someone's in the house. Maybe it's finally being put up for sale. Real estate agents don't drive trucks, do they?

The first thing that struck Joly was the smell, or rather, the lack of it. It did smell slightly musty, but it smelled... unlived in. She laughed. It had been nine years since it was occupied, so the smell was natural. That was about to change.

"Well my friends, check it out and make yourselves at home, I'm going to bring in the stuff, then run down to the store for groceries." She turned and went back outside. Walking down the sidewalk, she saw movement out of the corner of her eye, and turned her head. The curtain next door was moving and she could vaguely see the outline of someone's head. Joly wondered if Mrs. Ardell still lived there. Maybe she should go over and say hello, and let whoever it was know she had returned. A small chill went through her body, and she remembered the urgency that she had felt earlier. Thinking about it, she realized she was still tense. No, she needed to get organized first, and then she would call on the neighbor.

It didn't take her long to unload the truck, but the feeling of the eyes drilling through the curtain next door, began to unnerve her. She was glad when she carried the last load up the steps and could go inside and shut the door.

Nothing had been touched in nine years, other than the fridge being cleaned out and the garbage's emptied. The appliances and anything electrical had been unplugged. Mr. McNabb had the furnace serviced every fall and she knew he ran the water through the pipes regularly. The hot water tank had quit working four years prior and a new one had been installed. Layers of dust covered all the surfaces and a mixture of cobwebs and spider webs crisscrossed their way throughout the house. Joly peered under the kitchen sink and found the cleaning supplies still sitting there. She grabbed a clean cloth, filled a bucket with soapy water, and started cleaning. By four, she had the downstairs looking and smelling clean.

In the short time Nefertiti had been in the house nine years earlier, she had checked the place out from top to bottom. She liked what she had seen, but she felt it was too big. It would be harder to protect than the little cabin in the woods. She knew which room was Joly's; it was a smaller room facing west. The big bedroom had a bay window that faced north and two smaller windows that faced east. Nefertiti chose the master bedroom, getting comfortable on the wide windowsill. From there she had a view of Mount Baker, Washington in the distance, the Fraser Valley and the river below.

Salem had never seen anything like it. He felt like a king. *Wow!* It was surely a mansion. He couldn't get enough. He went through the rooms several times. He truly hoped he would never have to move again. He couldn't figure out which room he liked the most. The living room had such a homey feeling, but so did the kitchen. He sensed that people had spent a lot of time in the kitchen. It was large, with a table and four chairs directly ahead when you walked in. To the right was another door, leading outside to an enclosed porch and to the left of it, a counter ran to the corner and around the adjacent wall. He jumped up on the counter and looked out the window. The house was on the side of a hill, so the back yard sloped downwards. There was a driveway, lawn and trees. He couldn't wait to explore the outside.

Pip was amazed at the stairs! Now here was room to wind up and run to her hearts content. *Yes!* This was going to be just too much fun. And the windows, so many windows to look out, and so much to see! She was going to like living here. She ran from room to room, and every few minutes, she would either run up the stairs or back down. She found her Mistress' bed and knew where she would sleep, but until then, she had so much exploring to do.

Her stomach was growling and Joly realized she hadn't eaten since morning. Grabbing her purse, she yelled to the cats that she would be right back, as she went out the door. As she stepped outside it hit her! *Something wasn't right*. She glanced around, but nothing seemed amiss. She shrugged her shoulders; she just wasn't use to being in a city again with all the noise and smells that went with it. She walked quickly to the truck, jumped in and drove the short distance to the mall.

Nefertiti sensed something in the air. It wasn't a threat, but whatever it was, it wasn't good. She needed to protect this place and she needed help. Where was everyone? She let out a loud yowl and waited. Nothing. That was the trouble with a big place; she leapt off the sill and headed into the hallway. There were four bedrooms and a bathroom on this floor. She meowed again. Still nothing. The others must be downstairs.

She was halfway down when a furry black cannonball raced up the stairs, almost knocking her over. "Pip," she yelled, "we have trouble."

Pip put on the brakes at the top of the stairs, but she was unused to hardwood floors and she skidded into the wall. Shaking her head, she ran back to the stairs and down, catching up with Nefertiti at the bottom. "What's wrong?" she asked, and without pausing to get an answer, continued, "Salem's in the kitchen."

"That figures," muttered Nefertiti. "He always needs to be near the food." They walked down the hall to the kitchen. Salem was in the window, his head swinging back and forth.

Pip as always, wanted to be the first with the news. "Salem, Salem... Nefertiti says there's trouble!"

Salem turned and looked down at them. "I know. I can feel it, but I can't figure out what it is." He jumped down and walked across the room. "Neffy, what do you think it is and what should we do?"

"Something bad is happening somewhere. We need to protect the house and hope the Mistress returns soon. I've never seen you do a sealing spell. Can you? *And by the Gods!* Quit calling me Neffy!"

"Sorry Nefertiti, and yes, of course I can! I never bothered before, because you always did it. I did seal the Mistress' bed, always. You know that. Pip, what about you, have you ever done any magic?" They both looked at the little one.

Pip hung her head and quietly said, "I've only removed the negativity from the space where the Mistress sleeps." Then she looked at Nefertiti and boldly asked how could she help?

Nefertiti shook her head in disgust, not only was Pip a pain, but next to useless too. It was almost too much for her. "Stay out of our way," she growled, and turning to Salem, she told him to start upstairs.

Joly paid for her groceries and pushed the shopping cart toward the exit. The closer she got to the door, the slower she walked, until she stopped about three feet away from it. Others were leaving and every time the automatic door opened, Joly felt the urge to run in the other direction. *Gods!* What was wrong with her? She forced herself to approach the door and as it swung open, she shuddered. She gripped the bar of the cart, and pushed it forward.

She ran to her truck and throwing the bags in the box, she jumped in and fumbled with the key. She was shaking so badly, she couldn't fit it in the hole at first and when it finally slid home, Joly started the truck and narrowly missing a car, she backed out. Throwing it into first gear, she hit the gas and raced out of the parking lot. The Gods were with her at the light and she sped through the intersection and up the hill, turning into the alley. She had the door open almost before the truck had stopped, and running to the back door, she again fumbled with the keys. Only when she was inside, with the door closed and locked, did she stop and take a deep breath.

Pip was at her feet and rubbing up against her legs. Joly was shaking so badly she had trouble reaching down to pick the little kitty up. Once she had a hold of Pip, she leaned back against the door trying to control her ragged breathing. It was a few minutes before she realized Pip was looking at her with unblinking eyes. "What Pip, do you need to talk to me?"

Pip nodded. She had never tried to do a meeting of the minds before and she was unsure of herself, but she was determined to do something. The look she had gotten from Nefertiti had hurt, really hurt.

Joly lay down on the floor, resting the top half of her body on her arms. She looked into Pip's eyes and concentrated on her breathing. It was a long time before the two minds became one.

"Mistress, you have the *power*. You need to start using it again. You need to ground yourself and take control. Mistress, the time has come for you to be all that you used to be. Mistress? Do you hear me?"

"Yes, Pip, I hear you. I'm afraid, Pip, so afraid. I was young. I had guidance. I don't know if I can do this. Pip, what should I do?"

"Firstly Mistress, you need to ground yourself. Then I think you need to go back outside and fetch in the groceries. The danger is not here. It's in the air, but it's not close, at least not now. When you have done that, then you need to remember how to protect, not just yourself, but also the house and the property. And while you are remembering, I think you need to have a cup of tea, preferably peppermint and mullein. Can you do this Mistress?"

"I'll try Pip, I'll try." Joly blinked.

The shaking had stopped and she felt calmer, but quite tired. The mind meld demanded great concentration and this had been a long session. She got to her feet and stretched. Grounding. This she could do, and taking a deep breath, she slowly released it, willing herself to relax.

Pip was exhausted; she didn't think she had felt this tired when she had traveled all those miles to reach the Mistress. She was too tired to stand.

Looking up at her Mistress, she saw that she was grounding herself. Good! Forcing herself up, she wobbled to her feet and headed toward the stairs.

Joly took a deep breath, and opened the door. Standing in the doorway, she forced herself to stay calm and lifting her head, she sniffed the air. Yes, something bad was happening somewhere, but it wasn't close by. She went out to the truck and several trips later, had everything inside the house.

Entering the property from the back lane, Joly was in the basement of the old house. Her Dad had fixed it up, dividing it into four rooms. She was in the rec room; this had been where she and her friends had gathered to watch television, have sleepovers and just generally hang out together. Going through the door, she entered a small hallway. The door on the left was the laundry room. Straight ahead, was her Dad's workshop and to the right of it, was her Mother's room. It was a mixture of sewing, crafts, and storage. There was a small bathroom, closet and the stairs to her right.

Joly headed up the stairs with the first load of bags. Once she had them all in the kitchen, she put the kettle on the stove and put the groceries away.

Sitting at the table sipping her tea, Joly knew she needed a plan. She had spent too many years alone and safe. Now it was time to get organized. What should she do first? Her stomach rumbled and she laughed.

Okay, first thing was to eat. She got to her feet and started preparing their meal. She didn't have a lot of energy left, so she hard-boiled three eggs, then separating the yolks from the whites; she cut up the whites and made a simple tuna salad for herself. She opened another can of tuna, divided it into three portions and added a cut up yolk to each one, for her companions.

For the first time since arriving home, she was alone with her thoughts while she sat eating. Memories flooded her mind as she thought about what Pip had said. ... *the time has come for you to be all that you used to be.*

She *did* need guidance! She'd only been eighteen, and while she had known what was expected of her in her future, she had not had the intensive training that had only just begun. Her stomach muscles knotted as the fear again took hold. Joly knew she was going to fall apart, but she didn't care. She was home and she was all alone in the world. She put her fork down and pushed her plate away.

Pip knew instantly when Joly started to lose it. She had been grooming herself when she felt the first waves of fear and self-pity wash over her Mistress. Pip didn't normally get angry; in fact, she wasn't sure she had ever been angry before. But she got *very* angry now, and by the Gods! She was not going to sit there and let this happen.

Salem and Nefertiti had also been washing when they sensed their Mistress was in need of their healing energies. Before they could move, Pip jumped up on the table, hissing, growling and spitting.

Joly laid her head on her arms and let the tears flow. It took several seconds for her to become aware of the angry little kitty spitting in her face. It took another few seconds to gulp down the sobs and look at Pip. In that time, Pip reached out and scratched her on the arm. Joly jumped and withdrawing her arms off the table, she was suddenly very much back in the present.

"Pip! Settle down, what are you doing?" She hiccupped a sob back, staring incredulously at the angry creature in front of her. Pip quit her growling almost as fast as she had started. She sat there and stared her beloved Mistress in the eye, willing her to be strong and to remember.

Joly looked into Pip's eyes and remembered what had transpired on the basement floor. *"Mistress, the time has come for you to be all that you used to be."*

Joly took Pip in her arms and hugged her. "You are so right little girl, I'm being foolish and I hope you will accept my apologies." She hugged Pip again and set her down on the floor. "I have things to do, don't I, so I had best get started, don't you think?"

Joly went to the closed door at the top of the second staircase. When the house had been built many years before, the top floor had been three small bedrooms. Her parents had turned it into their craft room. They tore out all the interior walls and made one large room with windows on three sides. It was there that the altar was set up and spells were cast. Anything to do with the craft was kept there. The door was kept locked against any who might decide to do a little exploring. In the past, it was Joly's friends who were always coming and going that it was meant to deter. Joly took the cord from her neck. The cord held three items, two were keys, one for the trunk, one for this room and the third was the silver pentagram her Mother had given her so many years before.

She opened the door and entered. Going quickly to the trunk she had put in there earlier, she knelt down, unlocked it and returned the cord to her neck. She removed her robes and the two large boxes and put them by the cupboard her Dad had built along the back wall. Returning to the trunk, she removed the Book of Shadows and returned it to the table she had taken it from on her last trip home. She pulled out the chair her Mother had always used to make her entries into the Book, and she sat down to read.

Nefertiti and Salem were astounded! They had never seen Pip angry before. She had always been very timid and very much afraid of her own shadow. Pip followed her Mistress to the craft room without looking in their direction. They had followed her and now sat in the doorway watching.

"Pip, come here," Nefertiti demanded. Pip looked at her without moving.

"My place is with the Mistress." Her attention returned to Joly.

Salem chuckled and Nefertiti glared at him. "Don't start," she warned.

Salem figured he had best leave, so he headed back to the kitchen, thinking, *"Way to go, Pip."*

Nefertiti was baffled. She wasn't sure what she should do, and that was unheard of. She *always* knew what had to be done. She sat there undecided.

Joly closed the book and stood. There was so much information she was having trouble absorbing it all. Wards... she had never placed any and she was sure she would do it all wrong. She had watched her Father place them, but it was so long ago. She walked over to the cupboard and began searching through it. She needed quartz crystals for the house, steel railroad spikes for the yard and white candles.

Two hours later, she was done. She had protected her home as best as she was able. Joly only hoped the wards would work. She had been nervous while she was outside placing them in the four corners of the property. The air was filled with a permeable darkness that was not natural. While she had been placing the two on the south side of the property, she felt the malevolent force coming from somewhere in the eastern United States. It was far away, but for her to be feeling it so strongly here, she knew it foretold of something very bad happening.

Nefertiti, still feeling put out by Pip's behavior, had followed the Mistress and Pip at a distance, making sure all was done properly. Pip never left Joly's side throughout the evening, and never showed any sign that she knew Nefertiti was even there.

Back inside, Joly heated water with a bay leaf in it and made a cup of agrimony tea.

She felt like a child again, as she prepared to sleep in her childhood bed. She half expected to hear her Mother ascending the stairs to say goodnight to her. She pulled the covers back, climbed in and curled up into a ball. Pip snuggled up against her. Salem joined them and found his spot by his Mistress' head.

Nefertiti looked in from the doorway and softly padded down the hall to the master bedroom. She jumped up on the window ledge and curled up, ears ever alert to the changing air currents outside.

As she drifted off to sleep, Joly's last thoughts were of Morag, and why was Morag calling her?

2. The Gift

The old woman shifted her weight in the chair. She was sitting on some-thing lumpy. Either the cushion was folded up underneath her or the baggy sweatpants they made her wear were creased under her butt.

This had been one of her better days. There weren't too many of them. She had sat out in the garden for almost two hours completely undisturbed, been visited by several birds, thoroughly enjoyed the warmth of the sun and she had communed with nature. Of course she had gotten hell when discov-ered. Too much sun wasn't good for you, you know. *Balls!* The Sun God had been her friend for more years than she cared to count.

It was Tuesday. Stephen should be along anytime. She didn't pretend to understand him, but he was her son and she did love him dearly. Sometimes she wished he would visit more than once a week, but then what would they talk about? They were like two strangers. He lived for his computers and she understood nothing about them. "But Mother, I'm in touch with the world." *Ha!* So was she, or at least she had been, and she didn't need some damn machine that plugged into a wall. She knew they made computers that didn't need to plug in, but that was a moot point. They still couldn't take one to what was happening this very moment in some remote part of the world.

"Ah, there you are dear, come along now and let's have a snack." The nursing assistant wheeled her into the day room and up to a vacant space at one of the tables. A half a banana, two cookies and a glass of milk were wait-ing for her.

Oh yippee! It's a wonder I haven't starved to death. She ate without tast-ing the food, her mind wandering along the pathways of her past.

Stephen McEwan was in a hurry. The tall, slender, red headed man pushed through the doors and turned left, careening into an older woman who was leaving. He muttered an apology without slowing down, continuing on to the day room. Pausing briefly at the door, he quickly scanned the room. Spotting his Mother by the window, he strode over to her. He leaned down, giving her a peck on her cheek and a quick squeeze of her shoulder.

"How are you, Mother?" He turned and looked out the window without waiting for an answer.

She was slow in answering, preferring to admire the athletic build of her son. He had always had a restless energy and she had never been able to figure out where he got it from. He looked so much like his Dad. "I'm fine, Stephen, and you?"

He turned and looked at her for the first time since his arrival. She looked better than usual, not quite so old and haggard. There was a sparkle in her eyes and for a second it threw him. "You look good today, did something happen?"

"Yes, I managed to sneak away to the garden and spent two glorious hours alone. Of course I got hell when they discovered me, but it was worth it. You didn't answer me Stephen, how are you doing? You look tired."

"I've been rather busy. Computer technology is advancing so fast that it's difficult to keep on top of it at times. Every minute away from the office, I feel like I'm missing something vital. Speaking of which, I must be getting back. I'm expecting a couple of important calls and I can't afford to miss them. Do you need anything, Mother?"

He looked impatient to be off, but she was going to hold him up a couple of extra minutes. "Stephen, I know I've asked this before, but I'm going to ask again. I'd like my crystal ball, please."

"Mother, the answer is still no. You know it would either be stolen or you would be labeled..." his voice trailed off.

"What would I be labeled?" she asked, peering intently at him, "Maybe I'd be labeled a witch? Damn, that would never do now, would it?" Her voice had a risen a bit and it angered Stephen.

"We have been through this several times before, and I don't have time to stand here and argue with you. I will not have you ostracized by the very people you have to live with." His voice had grown quite loud and he saw several people in the room were avidly watching and listening.

He squatted down to his Mother's level, "I'm sorry. I shouldn't have raised my voice, but I can't understand why you keep asking. What makes you think I would change my mind? We've been through this several times, and you should know by now what my answer is going to be."

She put her wrinkled hand on his arm. "Stephen, for how many years was the craft my life? Why can't you understand that it's not something you just up and one day quit? Think about this, Son. Could you get up tomorrow and not have anything to do with computers, ever again?"

He stood. "I have to go, Mother. I'll see you next week. I'm glad you had a good day, but please, try not to upset the staff too much." He leaned over to give her another peck on her cheek, whirled and was gone.

She watched him go and whispered, "Goodbye, Son."

Stephen was upset. He was late and had probably missed at least one of his calls. He turned his cell phone back on. He hated the facilities rule on no cell phones, but was always careful to comply. This was the third place he had put his Mother in and he didn't want to jeopardize her stay there. Lord knows, in time she would do that on her own.

As he slid behind the wheel of his Porsche, he allowed his thoughts to wander, something he rarely did these days.

The craft. God, how he had come to detest the word. He had grown up in a house of witches. His whole family had practiced the craft. As a youngster, they had tried to get him interested, but it just wasn't there for him. His idea of a good time had been ripping apart anything involving electronics and computers topped his list.

He had gotten used to his family disappearing for days at a time doing whatever it was they were doing. He never asked because he didn't care. When he was very young, they would leave him at friends, and then when he was old enough, he was left on his own. This suited him fine as long as he had something to tinker with.

For a time he had tried to get their attention to focus on things he had either built or fixed, but he finally gave up. Then one day it clicked; their having no interest in what he was doing, was the same as his having no interest in what they were doing. It was a revelation of sorts, and after that, he found it easier to live with them.

When he graduated at the top of his class, they had all been there smiling and obviously happy and proud. It had been one of the best days of his life, and one of the few times where *he* had been the center of their attention.

He had gone to university, built his career, married and enjoyed a very successful and busy life. Occasionally, he would think about his family and he would call every couple of months or so, but he rarely ever saw them. He had no time and they had nothing in common.

His thoughts drifted to the only time he had ever been really sick. He had caught pneumonia, and as usual he was too busy to slow down. He had ended up in the hospital.

He was lying in his bed feeling sorry for himself when he heard a commotion in the hallway. Seconds later his Mother had stormed through the door looking madder than hell.

"The nerve of that twit, telling them she was your only relative! I should put a damn spell on her... one where her nails keep breaking or her hair turns frizzy. What do you think?" She paused in her tirade to look at her son. "Damn... you look like hell, Stephen."

He had never thought of his Mother as being funny, but he started chuckling. This led to a coughing fit, which had his Mother hammering on his back, then he laughed again and the whole thing repeated itself.

He'd hoped his wife wouldn't arrive while his Mother was there. They despised one another, with his Mother referring to Elise as That Twit, and Elise calling his Mother, That Woman!

When he could finally talk without choking, he asked, "Mother, how did you know I was here?"

She had looked at him in amazement. "Why Stephen, with my crystal ball of course! How do you think I kept track of you through the years? I always knew where you were and how you were doing. Do you think I would have left you all those times if I couldn't keep my eye on you? I even knew when you took up with that twit. I remember saying to your Father how I hoped you wouldn't end up marrying her, but of course you did."

He remembered being absolutely stupefied. His Mother had actually sounded like she cared. He never thought she had.

The horn blaring jolted him back to the present. He went through the green light and turned into the parking lot. Locking his car and alarming it, he headed to his office building, still deep in thought.

Elise had arrived at the hospital a short while later, impeccably groomed as always. Stephen found himself trying to picture her long perfectly mani- cured nails broken and her tightly coiled French knot in a mass of frizzes. He'd had to choke back a laugh that got him coughing again. Elise had wrinkled her nose in distaste, more worried about him giving her the 'bug' than being concerned about his health.

Things had changed slightly after that. He tried to remember to call his Mother more often. Not that they had any more to say to each other, but there was something. He could never define it, but then he had never been in touch with his feelings, so his brother once told him.

It was during one of these calls that she told him they were leaving the country for a few days, but they should be back inside a week. This wasn't unusual, they were always traveling, doing whatever it was witches did. What was unusual was that he knew before hand. Usually he found out about the trips after they returned

He had called again two weeks later expecting to hear how the weather was overseas, but all he got was the unending ringing of the phone. He tried again a couple of days later and still there was no answer. He wasn't unduly concerned, but there was an uneasy feeling; something he couldn't really put his finger on, but it was there nonetheless.

When his receptionist paged him the next day saying there some woman on the line who claimed to be his Mother, he felt a terrible sense of forebod- ing. His Mother never phoned him. He had hastily picked up the phone and heard her crying. Never in his entire life had he seen her cry! What could possibly have happened?

There was an accident; a horrible, horrible accident. Everyone was dead, including his Father and brother. She had lost the use of her legs; they said she would never walk again. Could he come and get her?

He'd booked a reservation on the first flight he could get, and he and Elise had their first big fight. "You're not going to Britain without me!"

"Yes, I am!"

"That woman..." She didn't have a chance to finish her sentence. It was

the only time he had ever yelled at her.

"That woman is my Mother! She is hurt and I am going to get her and bring her back here."

"Here!' she had shrieked. " Not to my house you won't. I won't have it!" He had stormed out.

On the flight over, he had time to think. He knew Elise was right. The two women could never live in the same house. He would have to find somewhere else for her. Somewhere that she would be looked after. Money was no object. She would have the best.

He'd hardly recognized her. Her dark auburn hair had turned white and she had aged twenty years. She was a big woman, not fat, but well proportioned for someone who was five foot eleven inches tall, but she looked small sitting in the wheelchair. He wasn't sure what he was supposed to do with her. She had always seemed so independent, and if she ever needed anything, his Father had been there to see to it.

The doctors told him they had never seen anything like it. It was as if the skin and flesh on the upper part of her legs had melted, ran down and then solidified. When she was asked, she said she didn't remember what happened. There were no open wounds, just masses of skin and flesh where they didn't belong. Her thighs were thin sticks and her knees looked chubby, but it was the lower part of her legs that was unbelievable. From just below the knees all the way to her feet there were uneven knobs of skin covered flesh. Her ankles were the worst; where they had once been shapely, they were now huge and distended. She couldn't wear shoes and the slippers they got for her, had to be cut across the top, so they would slide on. Her pants also had to have the seams cut in the legs, so they fit over the massive misshapen ankles. They said surgery was not an option.

She had been adamant that he take her out in the country; down some Godforsaken back road and into the bush, so that she could complete whatever it was that witches needed to complete. He had refused at first, but she had raised such a commotion the nurses had come running, so he quickly said he would. The trip had been a nightmare. He wasn't used to driving on the wrong side of the road with the steering wheel on the wrong side of the car, and she wasn't sure where they were going. Twice they had ended up in farmers' fields.

When they finally found the place, it was too uneven for the wheelchair, but she refused to let him carry her. He ended up having to remove brush and rocks by hand. She made the trip to the clearing alone. He waited by the car for an hour, watching as she moved here and there, murmuring to herself. He watched as she raised her arms to the sky and knew she was talking to her Gods and Goddesses. She had a lapful of stuff with her when she got back to the car. She had put her hand on his arm as they were driving back to civilization and thanked him. He actually felt glad he had done it. She looked more peaceful.

The trip back to Canada was uneventful. His Mother refused to talk about the accident and there were no bodies to bring back to bury. She wept a lot and when she wasn't crying, she would get a far away look on her face, which said don't bother me. He didn't.

He had made several calls from England and had found a nursing home that would look after her until he could find something permanent. She didn't seem to care one way or the other. She did ask him to take her home so she could get a few things, which he did.

He found an excellent extended care facility that was a fifteen minute drive from his office. She lasted there less than two years. She had to wear adult diapers and when she was ignored by the staff and had to go, she would scream and yell until someone came and cleaned her up. It was the same story at the second place he found. She had done better there, or perhaps the staff were more attentive. Eventually though, they too got tired of her hollering and he was asked to find her another place.

He had lost track of time and wasn't really too sure how long she had been at the current one. He had already received several phone calls in regards to her tantrums and had been asked to talk to her. This, he had a problem with. How did one tell his own Mother that there were times she would have to put up with some discomfort until someone found the time to take care of her needs? Staffing shortages were a problem, not just in the extended care units, but also at hospitals across the country. He had finally tried talking to her, but she wouldn't listen. "Would you sit quietly in your crap? Well, neither will I! If I couldn't sit on a toilet, it would be different, but I can and I will. It doesn't take that long for someone to assist me onto it."

He didn't know what he would do if they asked her to leave this place. There were no other good ones in the area, and his time was so short, he couldn't be driving miles to visit her.

He thought about what she had said just before he left. He knew he would go stark raving mad if he didn't have a computer within reach. Could it be the same for her? He hadn't thought about it in that context before. Maybe he should let her have it. God knows what the staff would think. Maybe he could bargain with her, tell her she could have it, but only on the condition she didn't complain so vocally when she needed to use the washroom. Yes, that might work, and maybe he could tell the staff the crystal ball was a toy that might help to keep her quiet.

She looked at the reflection in the mirror. She looked *old*. She wasn't really. She had just turned fifty-seven, but the freckled face staring back at her looked to be well over seventy. She felt seventy most of the time, but she knew this didn't have to be the way of it. All she needed was a healer, a topnotch healer and she knew of only one that could help.

Damn! She needed her crystal ball. She could search and find the one she needed, if she was still alive. At least she would know one way or the other. She had tried reaching the dear child with her mind, but there had never been any response, never any sense that she was anywhere close.

Elaine Tenborg

She had tried only once to explain to Stephen that she could be healed. He had scoffed and informed her that if the best surgeons couldn't repair her, that certainly a laying on of hands wouldn't help. She wondered again how this child could be hers. If he hadn't looked so much like his Father, she would have thought two babies had been switched at birth. She knew many witches gave birth to non-witch children, but still, Stephen seemed to be an enigma.

She shuddered. Thoughts came creeping in of another child, a magical reddish-blonde haired little boy with a big smile and a bubbling laugh.

She had caught him scrying with her crystal ball when he was three. His kitty was missing and he had found it in the crystal, locked in a shed two doors down. It was an accident of course; the kitten had wandered in unseen.

He hadn't looked like her or Brody, but he had learned the craft as easily as he learned to talk. He could watch a spell being cast just once and then usually, he was able to cast it on his own. They had had to watch him closely, worried that he would do something outrageous, but he seemed to know that being a witch and the magic that went with being one, was serious business. He never tried to use magic when he was playing, although he had giggled and threatened to turn Stephen into a frog on more than one occasion. He loved his big brother and couldn't understand why Stephen never had any time for him. Stephen would ignore the threats, just as he ignored most of what happened in their home.

He had grown up a happy and carefree spirit, seemingly just as content, whether he was reading a book or out playing ball. His best friend had lived across the street and they were inseparable. Where one was, they always knew the other was nearby. The parents, Morgana and Colin had been her and Brody's best friends, and they too had practiced the craft. Their daughter also had been born with the knowledge, and they all knew she had the gift of healing, but they never forced her, allowing her to discover her own strengths and weaknesses as she grew up.

Gone, they were all gone. She had watched in horror as the monster had devoured Colin, reached out and slashed Morgana, content to let her fall to the ground. Then it had lashed out at the other two that were part of their circle, taking them down as well. The four that remained had given everything they had, trying to send the beast back to where it belonged.

She had seen out of the corner of her eye, her son pick up his bride of three months and throw her out of the circle and out of the demons reach. By doing that, he had compromised the sacred circle, releasing the demon from its confines. Weak from everything they had thrown at it, it had slashed at his leg, sending him to the ground. The beast seemed to be everywhere. She and Brody had renewed their efforts trying to get its attention, chanting and throwing the sea salt and holy water. It was roaring and as it seemed to grow smaller in size; their strength seemed to be drawn into it. It swelled again and an almost transparent arm like piece of it seemed to reach right inside her boy's robe, and her son had suddenly lay still.

The scream! She would hear that scream for the rest of her life. Never had she heard anything like it and she hoped the hell she never would again. The look of absolute terror and anguish on her dear daughter-in-law's face would also remain with her forever.

She had turned and saw that the demon was frozen in place, almost as if hypnotized by the sound. She saw Brody gathering up the last of the sea salt and holy water. He pointed his wand at the beast, murmured the words of banishment and let go with everything he had left to give. The super-natural charge hit the demon with such a force that for seconds it was still, and then with a screech of rage it started disappearing back into the hell from which it had been summoned. With a last burst of strength, it reached out a tentacle like arm, and cut a swath around the circle catching her across the front of her legs. The pain was like a million flaming knives searing into them. She had screamed and fallen to the ground. She expected to breathe her last then, but glancing around; she realized Brody was its target. As it writhed in agony, shrinking, screaming and releasing a palatable mist of hatred and anger, it had grabbed her Brody and taken him with it.

Morag shook her head to clear it of the unbidden visions and wheeled herself to the doorway. She needed to use the bathroom, but as usual, there was no staff to be seen. She had tried before to do it by herself and the episode had ended in disaster. She wheeled down to the staff room. Empty. She spotted one of the aides going into the day room and wheeled after her.

Stephen drove out to the old house wondering just what he was doing. He had taken the afternoon off work, which was insane with the talks for the merger just around the corner, but he'd remembered this was the anniversary of his Father's and brother's deaths. He felt something was about to happen, but for the life of him, he couldn't figure out what.

He knew his Mother would be having a rough day and it had seemed like a good time to give her the crystal. He hadn't been to the house in years. His Mother had asked him to hire someone to look after the property after the accident and he had. He had tried to talk her into selling it, but she wouldn't hear of it. She had told him she would need her home to return to, when she could walk again. He had gotten so angry he had stormed out of the nursing home, returned to work and seemingly had made life pure hell for his secretary the rest of the afternoon. She had informed him at quitting time that she wouldn't be back.

He stopped for the light and when it changed to green, he drove up the hill, turning right onto the side street. Pulling up in front of the place, he sat for a moment looking out through the windows. Not much had changed over the years. The whole block consisted of older homes and for the most part, they looked to be well cared for. Looking across the street he noticed an older pickup parked in front of the James' old place, and next door to it he saw a curtain flutter. "Don't tell me that nosey old biddy still lives there? What was her name anyhow?" *Christ!* Now he was talking to himself.

He jumped out of the car and strode up the sidewalk, letting himself in through the front door. His intention was to grab the crystal ball and get back to the city, but once inside, he found himself wandering through the rooms, remembering different bits of his past.

He paused thoughtfully when he reached his little brother's room. Duncan had been a pain in the ass, but he never deserved to die. A small voice came unbidden to his mind.

"I could turn you into frog you know, Stephen. Stephen, what would you do then, huh? Stephen? Stephen? How come you never talk to me Stephen?"

He shook his head to clear the memory. He would give anything to see Duncan again. He would talk to him, about what he had no idea, but damn it, he'd talk to him!

He continued through the house until he got to the locked door, and reaching into his pocket, he pulled out the key, inserted it and turned the lock. As he opened the door, he was hit with the dry, musty scent of a room that has been closed up for a long time. He had a house sitting company taking care of the house and grounds, but no one had been in this room since before the accident. Turning on the light, he suddenly felt like he was in one of the horror movies he'd seen on television. The dust and webs covered the room from top to bottom. *"My God,* Mother would be horrified!"

Stephen dumped the last bucket of filthy water down the sink. He wiped his hands and rolled down his shirtsleeves, buttoning the cuffs. Striding back to the room, he gazed around satisfied that it at least looked clean, even if it wasn't. He wasn't used to cleaning, but he'd done his best to make it look habitable, although God knows when someone would enter through this door again.

He walked over to the cabinet and opened the door. His Mother's crystal ball was sitting in its stand. *Damn!* Where was the case for it? He wasn't about to walk anywhere in public, carrying it out in the open. After a quick search, he found it on the bottom shelf tucked away at the back. Bringing it out, he lifted the lid and reached for the ball. As he was about to pick it up, he thought he saw a glint of light come from it. Startled, he pulled his hand back. Nonplussed, he stood for a moment staring at it. Then with a nervous laugh, he reached in and picked it up. He felt the vibration immediately and almost dropped it. He placed the crystal ball in the satiny interior of the box, grabbed the stand and tucked it in beside it. He closed the lid and quickly walked to the door, shutting off the light as he left the room. After carefully locking the door, Stephen walked to the front entrance and back outside.

The darkness surprised him. Glancing at his watch, he was shocked. He had been at the house almost four hours! Suddenly it struck him... something wasn't right. He looked up and down the street, but all he saw was a couple of teenagers horsing around. Where on earth had that thought come from? Everything was fine. He was just tired. He got into his car, did a U-turn and headed back to the city.

Ninety minutes later, he pulled into the extended care facility's parking lot.

Morag had not had a good day. She never did on this anniversary date, but today had been worse than most. She had awoken in the morning not feeling well and for some reason her legs were tingling. After a thorough checking over, the nurse could find nothing wrong, so insisted she dress and be wheeled out to the day room. Her normally healthy appetite had deserted her and she picked at her breakfast. Then she had tried to sneak out to the garden and been caught. This had brought on a scolding from the nurse and she had been wheeled back to the day room. Not wanting to be there, she had wheeled herself back to her room, where she had spent the rest of the morning holding on to the five by seven framed picture of her and Brody.

At lunch, the nurse had wheeled her back out to eat. She wasn't hungry, so after trying to choke down some of the baked macaroni, she gave up and wheeled herself to the window. Her legs were still tingling and she wondered what it meant. They had never done that before. She had been there for sometime when she realized no one else was around, so she headed for the door once again. This time she managed to get all the way to the enclosed garden space. There was something in the air. Whatever it was it was very faint, but there *was* something and it didn't feel right. She was trying to figure out just what it was when the nurse found her. The nurse was mad and this in turn made her mad, so she told the nurse where to go.

The nurse had none too gently wheeled her back to the day room. By this time Morag realized she needed to use the washroom, so she asked the nurse to assist her. The nurse, still upset, had told her she could darn well go in her pants and had walked away. Morag proceeded to turn the air blue with her cussing which had brought the head nurse running. Morag had been wheeled to her room and thoroughly chastised. Then had come the threat of being evicted from the facility, and wouldn't her son be pleased to hear that. Morag, usually more than up to the task of giving as good as she got, but not feeling well, coupled with the anniversary of the death of her husband and son, not to mention the others, was too much for her and she broke down in tears. She had not cried since Stephen had brought her home. She refused to cry knowing it wouldn't bring her loved ones back.

The nurse was astonished to see the vulgar, loud-mouthed woman crying. Since Morag McEwan's arrival just over three years before, the staff had come to expect the temper tantrums, the screaming, the foul mouth, anything, but not this. Terry Delaney rubbed Morag's shoulder, wondering what she should say to the woman who obviously needed a friend, but just as obviously didn't want one. Opting for companionable silence Terry kept up a gentle touch, letting Morag know that she wasn't alone.

Morag cried for a long time; letting the pain and frustration of the past nine years come bubbling to the surface. They weren't gentle sobs but loud, keening cries of release.

When the great wracking sobs eased and the violent shaking became small tremors, Terry spoke gently to Morag, "Come on, let's get you to the washroom, and then maybe you'd like to lie down for a bit."

"No!" Morag was adamant. "What I would like, is to go out to the garden. *Please!*"

Terry knelt down so she was eye level to Morag, "You know we can't let you out there alone. What if you fell out of the chair? Morag, please try to be reasonable and look at it from our viewpoint."

"What if you wheeled me out there and put me in the exact spot I want to be? What if I promise not to move? Please nurse, I really need some fresh air and I need the solitude right now. Nine years ago today I lost my husband and son. I need some quiet time to just be alone with my memories."

Terry was amazed. That was the most Morag had spoken at any given time except for when she was throwing a tantrum. "I didn't realize this was the anniversary. I'm so sorry Morag. Tell you what, I'll do it today because of what day it is, but don't expect this to become a habit, okay?"

"Thank you."

Terry had expected to take Morag outside and simply guide her to a certain spot. She wasn't prepared for what actually did happen. They got to the garden area, which was surrounded by a hedge of caragana to muffle the sounds of the traffic on the nearby street. Several paved pathways meandered around various flowerbeds of different shapes and sizes. Morag pointed to the far side and Terry pushed her over there.

She set the brake and was turning to go, when Morag spoke. "No, not here, maybe over there," and she pointed to another spot.

Terry noticed that as they were moving along, Morag had her face up, almost as if she were smelling the air, and she also had her hands resting out in front of her with her palms up and her fingers splayed.

As they were approaching the new spot, Morag shook her head, "No, not here. Can you stop for a minute?"

This scenario repeated itself several times and Terry was fast losing her patience. As she was pushing Morag to yet another location, Morag suddenly shouted, "Here. Stop here!"

Terry stopped. *Now what?*

Morag did the nose thing again and asked Terry to turn her so she would be facing southeast. Terry stood waiting.

Morag looked around at her, "You can go now, I'll be fine right here."

Terry looked at her watch. The afternoon was almost gone, "You've got thirty minutes Morag, then its supper time." Morag murmured something that Terry assumed was an agreement.

Once she was alone, Morag grounded herself and cleared all conscious thought from her mind. Closing her eyes, she felt herself relaxing, her mind empty but open. There was a floating sensation and her inner conscience took over. Yes, there it was. Preparations were in the works for something bad. She had sensed this before on several occasions, but it appeared stronger this time. It always came from the same direction... the eastern part of the States. *Damn, I wish I had my crystal ball!* She tried to get a clearer sense of it, but to no avail. Before she knew it, the nurse was back to take her in for supper.

Morag still had no appetite, so after picking at her food, she wheeled herself back to her room. She was sitting by the window, feeling the power of whatever was happening, growing stronger. She didn't like it. *Gods!* It had been a rotten day, and what was with her legs? They were still tingling. She was glad the day was almost over.

Stephen charged through the doors as if he owned the place, looking this way and that for his Mother. Not seeing her, he headed to her room. He never walked quietly, always being in too much of a hurry. Everyone either saw or heard him heading down the hall, but when he got to the doorway of Morag's room she appeared to be deep in thought, and unaware he was there.

Suddenly feeling like an idiot for what he was about to do, he paused and watched his Mother for a moment. She seemed to be focused on something outside, but from where he was standing, he couldn't see what it was. Stephen surprised himself when he found himself asking, "A penny for your thoughts?"

Morag jumped. "Gods, Stephen, you scared me half to death. What are you doing here? This isn't Tuesday and you never come in the evening. Is everything alright?" She turned her chair to face him.

"Everything is fine Mother. I just want to talk to you."

"Stephen, you never *just* want to talk to me, so quit lying and get to the point. They called you, didn't they? Told you to find me another place. Well, I'm sorry. I told her to rot in hell, and I'm not sorry I did. I don't have to take the crap some of these nurses dole out. Just because I can't walk or take care of my needs doesn't make me less a person than they are."

Stephen looked confused. He hadn't been prepared for the tirade that she had just hit him with. He had been too focused on how he was going to give her the crystal ball and elicit a promise of good behavior from her. "Uh, no. No one called me, but I am here about your temper. I'd like to try and make a deal with you."

"A *deal*? Stephen, you don't make deals. You bulldoze your way through obstacles, trampling over anyone who dares to get in your way. I used to watch you sitting in your fancy boardroom not caring who you hurt, just as long as you got whatever it was you wanted." Morag paused to draw a breath and then continued, "I've seen that big house you and that twit live in. Does it make you any happier than when you lived at home? Do you think we couldn't have bought some fancy schmancy house? You have power of attorney; you know we could have, but you know why we didn't? Because a home is what you make it and we were happy where we were. Do you go home at night Stephen and feel welcome? Does that monster house wrap itself around you and give you a warm, fuzzy feeling? I doubt it, but my house did. Every time I walked through the door I felt my home embrace me, and welcome my return. This has *not* been a good day and I'm tired, so what do you want, Stephen?"

He was angry. He had come in good faith with something his Mother dearly wanted, and she had the gall to sit there and lecture him. He was half-tempted to turn around and leave without giving her the box.

Morag could see his teeth were clenched and that he was shaking from the effort to withhold his anger. She wheeled over to him and took his hand. "Stephen, I don't want to fight with you, but I think you needed to hear that, and Gods knows, no one else will ever stand up to you. You wield too much power, Son. You need to take a step back and have a good look at what you've become. As your Mother, I will always love you, but as a person, I don't even like you." She turned and rolled back to the window.

He didn't remember her ever telling him that she loved him. His anger dissipated. He was embarrassed by the things she had said. It was all untrue of course, but the picture she painted certainly was grim. He would have to set her straight on a few things, but not tonight. She did look tired and he needed to get home. Elise had been upset with him when he phoned and told her he was stopping in to see his Mother. He had stopped at some florist's shop and had two dozen red roses delivered to her. He hoped that would placate her, as he really didn't need another confrontation tonight.

Stephen walked over and knelt down beside the chair. He opened the bag he'd had tucked under his arm and drew out the box.

All color left Morag's face when she saw what was in his hands. She held her breath, suddenly hearing the words screaming in her mind, "*I'd like to try and make a deal with you.*"

"What..." her voice cracked. She swallowed and tried again, "What kind of deal?" The question came out in a whisper.

Stephen watched the terror mixed with hope in her eyes, and knew without a doubt that even if she refused to agree, he would leave the box with her. He could almost taste her fear. "Mother, I'd like you to quit telling the nurses to rot in hell and to stop the tantrums you throw when you don't get immediate attention. Can you do that, for me?" He paused, and then continued with an unrehearsed speech. "Can you do that for your son, the one that you love, not the one that you don't like?"

Morag knew he was sweating, she couldn't see it but she could smell it. That was all he wanted? That was the deal she had to agree to? She smiled a shaky smile and reached out and tousled his hair. "Yes Stephen, I think I can do that, at least I can try."

He handed her the green brocaded box. She gripped it tightly and hugged it to her chest. The tears trickled down her cheeks. "Thank you, Son."

"You're welcome, Mother. I have to go now. Enjoy!" He got to his feet and bending over, he hugged his Mother for the first time in many years. He held her head in his big hands and kissed her on the forehead.

She grabbed his face, pulling it to her and gave him a soft kiss on the lips.

He smiled at her, a real smile, not the fake, absentminded one that most people got. "Goodnight, Mother." He whirled and disappeared out the door.

He stopped at the nursing station and told them he had given his Mother a gift. It was something that might help take her mind off her problems. It had been a long time since he had given her anything and she had seemed inordinately pleased by his gesture. It was a smallish box, so if she insisted on taking it everywhere with her, please allow her to do so. She had also promised to try to behave.

They thanked him for his continued efforts, not believing a word he said, and agreed that as long as it didn't become a nuisance, she would be able to carry her gift with her.

Stephen walked out into the dark and again had the feeling that something wasn't right. He paused at the door of the Porsche, and without realizing what he was doing, he sniffed the air.

"Mommy, Mommy, I had a bad dream."

"Shh, hush now honey, it's just those grimlies. Go back to sleep and Mommy will take care of them."

Christ! Where had that thought come from? He'd forgotten all about the nightmares he'd had as a small child. His Mother had tucked him back in and he had always slept soundly the rest of the night. She had indeed taken care of them.

Morag sat for a long time gripping the beautiful green box. She didn't understand her son at all. So many times he had said absolutely not and now, here it was. He would have had to drive out to the house. She wondered if it was being taken care of. Gods! It would be so nice to go home again, even if just for a visit.

Finally, she wheeled over to the small writing desk and sat the box down. Slowly she lifted the padded lid and looked inside. Gods, it was beautiful! She had never lost her amazement over the beauty of it.

She had been in the city shopping, and seeing a small pagan shop, she had gone inside. She hadn't expected to see anything unusual, but as she browsed, she could feel a humming sensation. It wasn't unpleasant, but it was unusual. Curiosity got the best of her and she asked the old East Indian behind the counter what was causing it.

"What humming," he asked, and she had been surprised. She described the feeling to him, but he didn't seem to know what she was talking about. She had continued browsing, noticing that sometimes the humming was more

intense and other times barely perceptible. She then moved purposefully around the shop until she came to the place that the humming seemed to be the strongest. Looking around, she saw nothing out of the ordinary. The cabinet she was in front of had a storage section under the display shelves.

She called the proprietor over and asked what was kept in the storage area. He told her it was empty. She told him it was not.

He was adamant, "Yes Miss, it is very empty. All our stock is on display."

Morag knew differently. "Sir, I will give you one hundred dollars for whatever is behind that door."

He had laughed. "Only one hundred dollars, Miss?" Then she understood. It had been some kind of test.

He bent down and slid open the door; reached in and pulled out a cardboard box. Setting it on the counter, he opened it. Inside, she could see a beautiful green brocade box, decorated with pagan symbols. The humming was vibrant now, coursing through her.

"May I?" She asked.

He had given her a little bow and waved his hand in agreement.

She found her hands were shaking slightly as she lifted it out and set it down. Lifting the lid, she had gasped. The pale green crystal appeared to twinkle as she gazed upon it. She touched it lightly with her fingertips and felt the power emanating from it. She knew she had to have it, at any cost. "How much, sir?"

He smiled and told her the oddest story.

Thirty-five years before, an old woman had walked into the shop. She had put the green box on the counter and told him he must tuck it away out of sight. That some day, someone would come through the door and sense it was hidden away. That he must deny anything was hidden, until he was offered a sum of money for it. Only then could he admit to its existence, and then he should charge the amount that had been offered.

"So Miss, it is yours for one hundred dollars."

Morag had been intrigued. "I am the first person in thirty-five years to know it was here?"

"Oh no, Miss, there have been others, maybe three, maybe four, they knew it was here, but you see, they did not want it badly enough to offer money for it. So I told them the same as you, there is nothing here, and the others, they left. But you, you were meant to have it. So, one hundred dollars please."

Morag had paid him and then walked out of the little shop carrying her treasure, and feeling as if she had won the lottery.

Picking up the crystal, she could feel the power pulsating through it and into her. She had scryed with many different crystals. She was good and she never had any problems seeing whatever it was she needed to see. But this one, it truly was special. It always seemed to know just where she wanted to go, and the clarity; everything was crystal clear, never any foggy patches, like with so many. She had tried to get Brody to scry with it, but he refused to touch it; preferring on the few occasions he used one, to using the clear one he had had forever. He never told her why.

Morag cleared her mind of all the thoughts that seemed to be jumbling together and looked into the clear crystal. It had been a long time and she was willing to let the ball take her wherever. Mists swirled into the center of the ball, and then cleared. There was a sense of traveling high over the trees. Morag looked away. *Gods, I'm dizzy!* Best to take it slow. She removed the stand from the case and set the crystal ball on it. She wheeled herself away and turned to look at it from a distance.

Stephen drove along the winding highway without conscious thought. They had bought the house right after they were married. He had wanted a Cape Cod style home, but as Elise was the one who had to decorate it, he had left the final decision up to her. He had been surprised with her choice, as they had agreed that neither of them wanted children. The five bedroom house was extremely large for the two of them, but Elise had assured him that when they had company, he would appreciate the spaciousness.

He couldn't remember when they'd last had company, but it had been quite some time ago. The third bay in the three car garage had never been used. Elise had some idea of buying a boat to put in it, but as they never went boating, he saw no point. The music room had never been used to his knowledge and the baby grand sat gathering dust. They had watched an occasional movie in the theater, but again, the room was mostly unused.

He swung into the long curving driveway and as he approached the house, he stopped. Getting out of the car, he stood and gave the house and grounds a thorough scan. Even though it was dark, the grounds were well lit with numerous spot and landscape lights. *Fancy schmancy* his Mother had called it. She was right. He climbed back into the car and hitting the remote, he drove into the garage. Entering through the side door, he paused.

Do you go home at night Stephen and feel welcome; does that monster house wrap its self around you and give you a warm, fuzzy feeling? No, it didn't. Thinking about it, he decided it felt more like walking into some sort of mausoleum.

There were a couple of points that had been brought up that morning concerning the merger which he needed to go and brush up on, so he headed for his office.

Polina Petrova was having one of those moments when all seemed to be right with the world. She was in her secret place and as she leaned against the big old oak tree, she felt as one with the universe. She hugged herself, happy to be alive.

She could feel the energy building inside, she felt light as air, and she wondered if she might just float away. She laughed at the thought and stood up. She shook her hands to rid herself of the excess energy.

Hey... I wonder... She dug in her backpack and pulled out her wand. She allowed the energy to build and pointed the wand at a small bush ten feet away. She released the energy; the tip of the wand sparked and a branch of the bush caught fire.

Oh shit! She ran over and clapped her hands over the burning leaves until the flames were out. She knelt in front of the plant. "I'm so sorry. Forgive me for harming you. I didn't know."

She looked at the wand on the ground as if she had never seen it before.

My power. I've just received my power. "Thank you, Goddess."

She removed a candle from the backpack, lit it and knelt. Full of right-eousness, she solemnly intoned, "I am a Sister of the Triple Moon. I will devote my life to the good of Mother Earth. If I ever abuse my power..." She wondered what the worst thing could be. "... may I die a slow death."

The nurse came in and stared at the sparkling crystal ball. "So Morag, I see you have a new toy." She smiled. "Do you think you can tell me what my future holds?"

Toy? Toy! Morag was ready to set her straight, when she remembered *the deal*. Then the thought crossed her mind that if they knew or even suspected she could scry, then they would take her crystal away, or maybe even have her kicked out. She bit back the retort that had been about to leave her lips and smiled sweetly, "I think first, I need to figure out how it works, but isn't it beautiful?"

The nurse agreed and suggested it was time to get ready for bed. She was prepared for Morag's nightly refusal. Morag always wanted to be last. It was because she was a night person, so she said. Morag wheeled over to the bed, retrieving her nightie from under the pillow and wheeled herself to the wash-room. "Just give me a couple of minutes."

The nurse's mouth dropped open. *What, no fight?*

Morag removed her shirt and quickly washed, then slid the flannel nightie over her head. Wheeling back out, she went to the writing table, picked up her treasure and put it back in the box, then took it over to the nightstand, carefully setting it down.

"Ready" she said, as she wheeled back to the bathroom. The nurse went in and with the help of a hoist lifted Morag off the chair, removed her pants and put her on the toilet. Then she left, giving Morag some privacy.

She returned a few minutes later and hoisting Morag back into the chair, she wheeled her to the bed. Another hoist was set up there, and again Morag was strapped in and raised up over her bed. Then she was lowered onto the bed, the straps removed and the nurse straightened the bottom of her gown. The covers were pulled up and the nurse said goodnight. Morag responded in kind and closed her eyes. Her door was left slightly open, so that night checks could be done, without disturbing her.

Morag lay there listening. When all was quiet and she knew the staff were having a much-needed break, she reached over and turned her bed light on; then reaching for the box, she removed the crystal ball. She needed to know what was happening somewhere southeast. The air had been sour all evening. She held the crystal toward the light and letting her mind clear, she gazed through the ball.

The crystal's response was immediate. It took her to a clearing in a forest and in the darkness, the remains of a fire glowed. She saw the robed figures, counted thirteen and knew dark magic was taking place. She saw the sword drop into the center of the embers, saw the huge dark beast appear. Whoever was in charge had strong powers.

Damn! The time was flying by; they'd be coming to do night checks soon and she still had one more thing she wanted to do before going to sleep. Her legs were still tingling and it was driving her crazy.

Was her daughter-in-law still alive, and if she was... where was she? Morag's gaze went back to the crystal. "Joly McEwan, where are you? I need you Joly. Show yourself to me." She looked deep into the crystal ball.

As the crystal receded from the woods, Morag glimpsed the dark beast leaving the circle. It had been sent on a mission. She knew without a doubt there would be grave repercussions from this night's visitation.

"Morag, what are you doing? It's past lights out time. You know the rules. If that *gift* is going to interfere with your well being, which includes a good night's sleep, we will have no choice but to give it back to your son." The night nurse braced herself for Morag's tirade.

Morag dropped the crystal ball. "*Shit!* You scared the hell out of me. You don't need to be sneaking up on people like that." She paused, again remembering Stephen's words. She clamped her mouth shut, willing herself not to say more. She picked up the crystal from the bed where she had dropped it and placed it back in its box. Joly would have to wait until tomorrow.

"I'm sorry; it's just that Stephen doesn't often give me gifts, so I just wanted to look at it again." She pulled the covers up around her neck. "Good night Nurse."

The nurse stood there with her mouth open. What was this? No name calling, no being told where to go and how to get there. What was she up to? Surely this turn around would be short lived, but what the heck. She might as well enjoy it while it lasted. "Good night Morag."

Morag listened to the creaking of the nurse's rubber soled shoes as she walked down the hall. *Damn!* This was going to be harder than she had thought. She was tired. It had been a long day and she wished her legs would quit tingling.

Morag drifted off to sleep, thinking about being able to walk again.

3. Escape

Slowly coming out of a sleep that had been plagued by dreams, Joly opened her eyes to see Salem looking at her. "Good morning, Salem, how did you sleep? I've had better for sure, but suppose I'll survive." She reached down and stroked Pip. "Time to rise and shine little one."

She threw the covers back and sat up. "I sure did have some weird dreams last night, but the strangest thing happened as I was going to sleep. Let's go down and get our day started and I'll tell you about it." She grabbed her robe, slid into it and headed for the door.

As she reached it, Nefertiti walked into sight. "Good morning Nefertiti. How was your night? Where did you sleep?" Nefertiti turned her head and looked toward the room that had been her parents. "Ah, I see." They all headed to the kitchen, where Joly put the kettle on to make tea.

Preparing everyone's breakfast, she told them, "I had a really strange thing happen last night. As I was going to sleep, I thought I heard Morag calling me. I don't think I've told you about her. I guess I haven't really told you much about my past at all, but anyways, back to Morag."

"She lived right across the street with her husband Broderick and their two sons, Stephen and..." she paused, swallowed and continued with a huskiness to her voice. "...and Duncan. She was a wonderful lady, always very much into nature. Her back yard was an amazing place; it was like walking into another world. She designed it with hedges, trees and shrubs to block out the sounds of the city and the traffic. It's a small yard, like the one here, but it was laid out with meandering pathways so that when you walked around a corner, there was a completely new view to see. Morag always talked to the birds; Gods, she loved her birds. She had feeders everywhere. Different kinds for the different birds. There were finch feeders, chickadee feeders, feeders for the wrens and sparrows. The Stellar's Jays had their platforms for nuts and fruit. It was an incredible place."

"My parents were best friends with Morag and Broderick, so we spent a lot of time over there, and they came over here lots too. Duncan and I, well, we were always together. I loved him so much!" Joly wiped at a solitary tear that had rolled down her cheek.

"They were part of our group and they were in England with us nine years ago. That *thing* took everyone I loved. I still don't know why I was left alive. I guess there must be a reason, but for the life of me, I don't know what it is."

"Stephen wasn't with us, but he was an odd sort. He wasn't a witch and never did anything with us. I wonder where he is now. He sure did look like Broderick though. Broderick was very quiet, where Morag was a talker. It was funny to see them together. They seemed so mismatched, but when they looked at each other, you could see the love in their eyes."

Joly set the three dishes of rice and chicken down for the cats and she sat down to her fruit cup and whole grain toast. In between mouthfuls, she continued, "Morag called him Brody. That always struck me funny. He did *not* look like a Brody. He was far too serious. Broderick suited him."

"I don't know what happened that night. After seeing Duncan go down, I kind of lost it. I don't remember anything. Something was screaming, I do remember that. It was an awful sound. The rest is blank until Nefertiti insisted I go with her. I didn't want to go anywhere. I don't know how I got to that place where you found me, but you were so insistent, weren't you, dear?" She smiled at Nefertiti and shook her head.

"I don't know why after all this time I would hear Morag calling to me. That is just so weird."

"Anyhow, I'm going to shower and get dressed. Then I'll go next door and see who was watching me yesterday. I am *so* looking forward to a real shower!"

After Joly headed up the stairs, Nefertiti stalked over to Pip and smacked her across the face. "And just what was that all about yesterday?" she demanded. "You actually hurt our Mistress."

Pip had expected repercussions, but she had not expected a physical attack. She let out a yip and backed away from Nefertiti. "The Mistress needed guidance and it was the only way I could get her attention. Don't you hit me again Nefertiti. You're not my boss." Pip turned and walked out of the kitchen. When she reached the bottom of the stairs, she started running and didn't stop until she was on her Mistress' bed. She was shaking, and feeling quite dumb because of it. Nefertiti scared her, but she didn't want her to know that, or Nefertiti might make life unbearable for her.

Salem had been sitting in the kitchen window and when Pip was slapped, he jumped down. He listened to the altercation and after Pip left the room, he looked at Nefertiti. "Neffy, I don't think you had any reason to slap Pip. What she did yesterday worked better than anything you or I have done. I think you need to get a grip on yourself. Sometimes, you get to thinking that everything has to be done your way. That's not the way of it, and you know it." He turned and jumped back on the counter and lay down in his spot in front of the window.

Nefertiti glared at Salem's retreating figure. As he lay down, she walked over to the counter and jumped up. Salem looked at her as she reached out and smacked him across the nose. *"Quit calling me Neffy!"* She turned and jumped down. Salem got to his feet and looking over the edge of the counter; he gauged the distance and jumped, landing on top of Nefertiti.

Joly heard the fight from upstairs and wrapping her towel around her, she ran down to the kitchen. *"Hey!"* she yelled. "Hey, Nefertiti, Salem! Stop it right now!" She grabbed a cup and filling it with water; she threw the contents on the two cats. The fight stopped as the cats sprung apart, both looking wildly around for the source of their discomfort. When they saw Joly standing there with the empty cup still in her hands, they hung their heads and slunk off in different directions. Nefertiti headed up to the master bedroom and Salem disappeared into the living room.

Morag had just finished her oatmeal and toast when the nurse came to take her for her bath. Morag hated bathing. She had always been a shower person, never understanding how someone could climb out of their dirty bathwater and consider themselves clean. She was wheeled down to the tub room and after undressing; she was strapped into the harness and lifted into the over-sized tub. It was filled half-full with warm water. Morag would have liked her water warmer, but had gotten used to the tepid water, which all these places seemed to prefer.

They left her alone for a few minutes and she sat there looking at her legs. They always reminded her of her first attempts at making buns. Instead of twelve nice even shapes in the pan, Morag could never seem to get the sizes the same, and the pan would be filled with all these misshapen roundish lumps of dough that were different sizes. Her Mother had always laughed.

She took the washcloth and bar of soap and started washing herself. The soap smelled horrible and she wondered where they bought it. Gods, what she'd give for a hot shower and her homemade shea and cocoa butter soap scented with almond and orange oils. As she scrubbed, she thought of Joly. Last night, she thought she had sensed something just as the nurse startled her. She was anxious to try again and see what it was.

Joly headed up the sidewalk to the house next door. Knocking, she waited. When it didn't seem as if anyone was about to answer, she turned to leave. As she skipped down the steps, the door opened. Turning around, Joly had trouble concealing her surprise. "Mrs. Ardell?" she managed to squeak. The old woman nodded.

Joly couldn't believe anyone could change that much in so few years. Her neighbor had always scared her, when she was young. Mrs. Ardell had been an imposing figure, tall and sinewy, and always, she would be frowning or glaring, except when she was talking to Daddy. Then she would be nice as pie, smiling and giggling.

This wizened woman leaning heavily on her cane bore little resemblance to the one that Joly had grown up next to. The face had aged considerably, and the body seemed to have shrunk to half the size of before.

"Mrs. Ardell, I don't know if you remember me. My name is Joly James. I used to live next door." She paused, the old woman said nothing, so she continued, "I just wanted to let you know I've moved back, so in case you noticed the lights on or anything like that, I didn't want you to think there were burglars in the house." She paused and again the old lady said nothing. Joly turned to go, "Nice to see you again." *Damn, you lie, girl!*

"Wait!" The voice cracked like a whip and startled Joly so she stumbled on the steps, almost falling. She managed to catch herself, and turned around, suddenly feeling like she was six years old again. She was terrified.

"You said James. I remember you got married. I'm not senile, you know."

Joly finally breathed. *Wow, is that all?* She tried to smile, "Yes, I was married to Duncan McEwan, but we were only married for three months. It didn't seem right to call myself a McEwan after that, so I just went back to using James."

Joan Ardell nodded. She should invite the girl in for tea, but she couldn't shake the picture of her being eyeball to eyeball with that cat.

"Mrs. Ardell, would you mind, uh, if I used your phone. I need to get mine reconnected."

She nodded, and stepped back from the door. "Come in. You might as well have a cup of tea, while you're here." Joan pointed to where the phone was, then went and plugged the kettle in.

Morag was back in her room, dressed and ready for the day. She thought she should have at least an hour without interruption, so wheeling to the table at the side of her bed; she opened the box and removed her crystal ball. She wheeled over to the window and clearing her mind, she willed the crystal to lead her to Joly.

"Hi Mrs. McEwan," a bubbly voice piped from the doorway. Morag was getting irate. For nine years, she spent hours alone, with no one talking to her. Since she had her crystal back, she couldn't seem to get a moment's peace. It was one of the young volunteers. She had to put in so many hours of volunteering as part of the requirements for entry into some part of the nursing profession. Morag couldn't remember what she was training for. "I thought you would like to go outside today. It's another gorgeous day for this time of year, and I'm sure there won't be too many more of them."

Outside. Yesterday, she would have given up her teeth to get outside, and now all she wanted was to be left alone. Gods! It was enough to make a body weep.

Morag smiled at the girl. She really was a sweetheart, and she had done nothing wrong, so no point in getting mad at her. "Sure dear, just give me a minute." Morag put the crystal on the bed and rolled over to the chair in the corner to get her sweater. Wheeling back, she picked up the crystal and went to the door. The young girl wheeled Morag out to the garden, set the brakes and sat down on a bench.

Morag spent the next hour, answering questions about the crystal ball, making up stories as she went, knowing she didn't dare tell this innocent the truth. Lunchtime arrived and Morag was wheeled back inside.

Joly spent an uncomfortable half hour having tea with her neighbor and breathed a sigh of relief when she finally was able to leave. She had called the telephone company and arranged to have the phone hooked up the next day. She could tell Mrs. Ardell wanted to question her, but for some reason, she didn't. She just sat there looking nervous. *What on earth did she have to be nervous about?* Joly shook her head as she walked the few steps home. It was very strange.

Back inside, she went to the fridge and took out a package of chicken breasts to thaw for supper. She made a salad for her lunch and as she sat eating, she again wondered why she had felt the need to come home.

Morag had eaten her lunch without complaining and then gone to her room. Afternoon lie-downs were optional and she rarely agreed to them, but she was wondering if that were the only way she'd get some peace and quiet to do some serious scrying. When the nurse walked by without stopping, she decided the heck with it and rolled over to the window with her crystal ball.

She scryed to the forest first, and took a careful look at the clearing. She could tell it had been in use for some time as the scent of evil permeated the area. She wondered where the demon had disappeared to and once again regretted not having the use of her legs. She wasn't sure she had the ability to banish it on her own, but she would still have done her best to track it down and send it back to where it had been summoned from.

Clearing her mind, she asked her Gods and Goddesses to help her find the one she was looking for. She looked through the crystal and watched as the center misted, then cleared. *I know that place!* It was the James' house. Why on earth had the crystal brought her here?

She never entered homes anymore. When she was young, she went wherever she had a mind to go, but she eventually learned not to do that after running into couples in compromising positions, people walking around sky clad in the privacy of their homes, others in showers or sitting on the throne.

Joly was lost in thought when a vision of Morag came to her, again calling out her name. Joly jumped! *What is going on?* She quickly walked down the hall to the front door and opening it, she walked out onto the steps. Joly gasped! The sense of Morag was all around her.

Morag sucked in her breath! *It's Joly on the steps.* She looked older, but there was no mistaking that it was she. Morag willed Joly to turn toward her and was rewarded with a look in her direction.

Joly could feel Morag, could hear her calling to her. She was somewhere west, not too far away. Unconsciously, she mouthed the name, Morag. *My Gods! Morag's alive!*

Morag saw and was ecstatic! Yes! She had found her; she still didn't understand why Joly was at home, but that no longer mattered. What mattered was getting Joly to come to her.

Joly realized Morag was scrying, that was how she had found her. She laughed as the tears came. She was no longer alone.

Morag saw the tears through her own. This was why her legs had been tingling. Joly must have just returned to the area. From where, she didn't know, but it didn't matter. She knew Joly had no idea how strong her healing powers were. Her parents had known, as had she and Brody. They knew all she had to do was stand in a room and the power would reach out to all in it. But her power was stronger than that, so strong it could reach across miles and begin healing.

Morag wondered if she could guide Joly to her. The staff wouldn't let the patients' use the phone and she couldn't ask them to try to get a phone number for her, as she didn't want them to know how to contact Joly. She was planning to finally escape from this hole, but she had to be careful. Stephen had many resources and he would use them all to find her.

Morag willed Joly to come. *Come to me!*

Joly heard and was confused. How was she going to find Morag? She didn't know, but she knew she had to try. She ran back in the house and grabbed her purse and keys. Locking the door, she ran down the sidewalk and jumped in the truck. Turning the key, she did a U-turn and headed down to the highway. She turned right and sped toward Vancouver.

The three felines all rushed to the living room window, arriving in time to see the truck disappear around the corner. They sat there wondering what had gotten into their Mistress. She never went anywhere without them. They settled down to wait for her return.

Morag watched her as she drove closer. She wasn't sure how to get her to this place. She couldn't visualize the streets, as she was unfamiliar with them. She could scry the city, but she'd lose connection with Joly if she concentrated on trying to read all the street names. She would have to do it the hard way.

Joly drove fast, too fast, but her heart was pounding and she was driving to the beat of it. She could feel Morag, could feel her coming closer. It was a long time since she had been in the city and she took a wrong turn, ending up on a one-way street going the wrong way. With vehicles honking at her, she pulled off on a side street. Finding a parking spot, she pulled into it and stopped. She put her hands to her head and tried to clear her thoughts, to give Morag a better chance at guiding her.

She was headed in the wrong direction now, so she needed to get turned around. Where was she going? North Vancouver maybe or West Vancouver. *Okay, I'm coming Morag.*

She eased out into the traffic and going around the block, she finally got herself headed in the right direction again. She headed toward the Burrard Street Bridge. Crossing the span, she sensed Morag's closeness. The urge to speed up was overwhelming, but Joly forced herself to drive slower in order to keep Morag strong in her mind. *Now where?* Morag seemed to be fading. *No! Morag come back!*

Park, Joly, park, now!

What? Okay. Joly pulled into a small strip mall. She found a parking spot and pulled in to wait. What she was waiting for, she wasn't sure. Oh Gods! She had left the cats behind. She was in trouble now. They would be a long time in forgiving her; she was sure.

"Morag, are you alright? I've been talking to you and you didn't seem to hear me at all."

The nurse did sound worried, but Morag was upset over the interruption. "You control everything I can do in this place. Now you want to control my mind too. I don't think so. If I want to sit and dream, I damned well will and no one is going to stop me. Now go away and leave me to my thoughts. They seem to be all I can call my own these days."

"Sorry, I didn't mean to upset you." She left and Morag looked into the crystal again. She thought Joly was probably close enough she could just think her here, but the crystal was more reliable, plus she could see as Joly got closer.

Joly, can you hear me? Morag could see her sitting in the parking lot. *Come to me.*

Joly heard and pulled back on the road. She realized she had passed the street where she needed to turn. She turned around and drove slowly; trying to pick up which street the voice inside her was coming from. There! She made a left hand turn. Several blocks later, she knew she was close, but how close? She took another turn into what appeared to be a semi residential area.

Suddenly Morag's voice seemed to be shouting. *Stop! Stop! Get out of your truck and walk.*

Joly parked and started walking. There was a tall hedge beside her, blocking the view of whatever lay behind. Someone valued their privacy, she thought to herself. She got to the end of the block and turned the corner. Still following the path of the hedge, she could see an entryway up ahead. Was this where Morag was?

Morag put the crystal on its stand and wheeled out of her room, heading to the front doors. *Gods, let me get outside without being stopped.* She was through the doors and wheeling down the sidewalk.

Joly reached the end of the hedge and looked down the sidewalk. Some white haired woman in a wheelchair was rolling quickly toward her. She tried to hear Morag, but there was nothing.

"Joly! Gods girl, you're a sight for sore eyes!"

Joly stared. "Morag? Is that you?" She started to cry. Morag reached her and leaned forward and wrapping her arms around Joly, she held her tightly.

Joly felt the familiar sense of belonging that always happened when the two of them were close. She welcomed it and clung on to her old friend and neighbor as if she would never let her go.

Joly was gripping Morag so hard, it hurt, but she stayed silent. Gods knows what this child had been through the past few years.

"Child, listen to me. I don't have much time. They won't let me out here alone and I need to tell you some things before they find me."

Joly looked at her quizzically, "But you're not alone, I'm here."

"Listen to me Joly. I need you to get me away from here. Stephen will try to find me, but I need you to help me heal, to help me to walk again. I can't do that here. I haven't had a visitor in years. If they see you, they will want to know who you are, and then they will tell Stephen. Stephen can't know who I'm with. He would just bring me back here. Joly, is any of this sinking in? Oh, my sweet child, how I want to just sit and hold you, but there will be time for that later."

"You're not allowed to leave here? How terrible. Yes, come with me. Let's go now." She ran around to the back of the chair and started pushing Morag toward the end of the sidewalk.

"Now?" Morag wasn't ready. Things were moving too fast. "My crystal ball, I can't leave without it."

"Yes you can. You have to. We're doing this now, before either you or I change our minds, and I'm not about to lose you again. I thought I was losing my mind last night. It *was* you?" They turned the corner and were out of sight of the building.

"Yes child, but I got caught with the crystal and had to put it away."

They reached the corner and Joly raced around it. She thought her heart was going to leap out of her throat.

At the truck, Joly opened the passenger door. "How are you possibly going to lift me up there? Oh Joly, this isn't going to work, girl." Joly heard the disappointment. She smiled.

"No problem. I've spent the past several years mining." She reached down and easily lifted Morag onto the seat. Only then did she become aware of the massive amount of flesh around Morag's ankles. "Oh my Gods!

Morag, what happened?"

"Let's get out of here child. There will be time enough for telling."

Joly struggled with the wheelchair for a minute before figuring out how to collapse it, and throwing it in the box; she jumped in and fired up the truck. She did another U-turn and sped down the street watching the rear view mirror, but she saw nothing.

Morag's heart was pounding as she thought about Stephen and his reaction. He would come out to the house. That would be the first place he would look. She was too obvious in her chair. She couldn't stay at Joly's. Gods! They needed a plan.

Joly wondered what she was going to do with Morag. Mrs. Ardell didn't miss anything and the wheelchair was a dead give away. If Stephen came out knocking on doors, she would know exactly where his Mother was. Could she be charged with kidnapping? Gods, this was a mess. *Wait! I've got it! Let me think. Yes, that would work. I wonder what time Mrs. Nosy goes to bed. Once it's dark, I should be okay.*

Stephen was stupefied! "What do you mean, you've lost my Mother? How can you lose someone in a wheelchair for God's sake? You damn well better have found her by the time I get there or you will not have a job come morning, I promise you!" He slammed the phone down and left his office running.

Morag spoke first. "Joly dear, I think we have a problem."

"No Morag, we don't. I have it figured out, I think. Are you on medications or anything?"

"No, why?"

"I just wondered if you had need of anything."

"Nothing except my crystal ball."

"We'll have to let Stephen know you're okay. We'll ask him to fetch it and at least you'll know it's safe. If you need to use one, you can use mine. I can't take you home until its dark. Do you remember Mrs. Ardell? She still watches everything that happens on the street. Is there somewhere you want to go until we can sneak you into the house?"

"There's only one place I would like to go and that's home, but that's out of the question of course, so wherever you want to go is fine."

"You need clothes, so lets go shopping."

Joly stopped at a mall and they spent two hours getting Morag outfitted with a new wardrobe. Morag was excited to be able to buy what she wanted, not what was required. Joly bought some jeans and a couple of shirts and some undergarments.

From there, they went out for supper. Morag was in seventh heaven. She had the biggest steak the restaurant sold, a baked potato with sour cream, veggies and a roll. Joly laughed at her friend's appetite, but she also ordered a small steak with a salad and roll.

It was dark when they left the restaurant. Joly wheeled her over to a phone booth. "You need to call Stephen. He'll be worried, I'm sure."

Morag didn't know his number, so Joly got it from information. He answered the phone before the first ring had ended.

"Stephen…"

"Mother, where the hell are you? You've had me worried sick. The police are out looking for you with the dogs. What possessed you to disappear like that?"

"Stephen, *shut up!*" Morag didn't want to fight, but she wasn't going to listen to him rant and rave either. He was quiet. "Thank you. Now you listen to me. I am not going back to that prison. I am fine. In fact, I have never been finer. I want you to pay up whatever is owed and sign me out of there. All I want is my crystal ball and the picture of your Dad and me. The rest of my stuff can be donated to whoever can use it. Call off the search. You won't find me. I still have my resources too. Have I made myself clear?"

"Mother, I don't know what you are up to, but I promise you, I will find you. You can't exactly hide in that chair. I honestly don't understand what you are trying to do here. Have you completely lost your senses? It's that damn crystal ball, isn't it? Something you saw, someone you contacted somehow. I will *not* just let you wander off on your own." He paused, "What do you mean you want your crystal ball? You don't have it with you?"

"No, I left it behind, I didn't mean to, but things happened so fast. Please get it, before it disappears. No, you won't find me, so go back to your empire and let me be. I will be in touch. You are my son; I'm not disappearing out of your life forever, just until I can get back on my feet. I have to go now. Good bye Stephen."

"Mother? Mother?" She was gone. *What the hell?* He should have had a tracer put on his phone, but he hadn't been expecting her to call. He'd been waiting to hear from the police, kidnappers or the hospital.

Joly lifted Morag into the truck, collapsed the wheelchair and put it in the box. Climbing into the cab she turned the key, eased out into the heavy traffic on the Lougheed Highway and headed toward home.

Turning up the street and hitting a green light, she sped across the intersection and up the hill. Instead of turning at the corner, she slowed and looked down the street to see if any lights were on at her neighbors. She didn't see any, but it was better to be cautious. Joly turned at the next street, drove down a block and turned again. At the corner she turned once more, coming toward her place from the opposite direction. She wished she could enter from the alley, but she didn't think she could pack Morag up all the stairs to the main floor, so she had to park out front. As she drove by Mrs.

Ardell's, she saw no sign of lights.

She eased to the curb and quietly slid to a stop. "Wait here for a sec." She opened her door and gently closing it; she went to the back and lifted out the chair. She unlocked the door, set the chair up, and went back to the truck. She was watching for curtain movement next door, but she saw none. Opening the passenger door, she reached in and lifted Morag into her arms. She quickly carried Morag into the house and set her in the chair. Then she ran back to the truck, grabbed the shopping bags and shut the door, locking it with her key fob. Back in the house, she shut and locked the door and only then did she turn on a light.

Three little faces were looking intently at the two of them. "Oh great heavens, I forgot about you three. I'm so sorry, but I had an emergency. Morag, I'd like you to meet my companions. This is Salem," Joly reached down to stroke the nearest cat. "This is Nefertiti and this little one is Pip." She stroked each one in turn. "I'd like you all to meet Morag. She's going to be living with us for awhile."

Morag looked each one over carefully. "You don't catch birds, do you?" she asked them. They all shook their heads. "Good! Then we may get along."

Joly laughed. "Have you ever known any of my feline friends to be birders?"

"No" replied Morag, "but I thought I should check. Joly, I hate to be a nuisance, but I do have to use the facilities."

"No problem, you know where it is. Wheel yourself down there and I'll be right with you."

Joly turned her attention to the three sitting in front of her. "Okay, we have a change of plans here. We have to get Morag away and the sooner the better. I'll pack tonight and tomorrow we head back up north. That's one place no one will be looking for her. Her son had her put away in an institution. We're going to help her to walk again, and then she can come back here. I'll feed you in a few minutes."

Joly went to assist Morag, leaving behind three concerned kitties. Nefertiti spoke first. "Someone is looking for her? There will be no peace, that being the case. We'll have to be vigilant."

"Yes," replied Salem, "And not only that, but it's going to be very crowded in that small cabin. We'll have to watch our tails with those wheels."

Pip looked glum. "I hate the cold; I don't want to go back there."

Salem looked at Pip, "Don't start whining. Do you think any of us want to go back up there?"

Joly made sure all the curtains and drapes were closed on the main floor, and then left Morag while she went and fed the cats. Morag went into the living room. No light had been turned on and Morag sat in the dark and closed her eyes. Gods, it had been a long day. She wasn't used to so much excitement and she was exhausted.

Joly brought down bedding from upstairs and made up the chesterfield for Morag to sleep on. She told her about the cabin and that they would head up there in the morning. Joly helped Morag into a nightie and then lifted her onto the sofa and tucked her in. "Sleep well my friend." She leaned down and kissed Morag goodnight.

She headed to the magic room first and repacked her trunk. Then, running downstairs she packed her suitcase. She hadn't unpacked the books, so she put the three boxes with the trunk. She grabbed the two empty boxes from the basement and refilled them. Then she found two more and packed them with the groceries she had purchased. She got the rocker from her bedroom and lugged it back downstairs. She dug out another suitcase from the basement for Morag to use and brought it upstairs.

She hadn't notified Mr. McNabb that she had returned, so she wrote a note letting him know she had been home and she left it on the table. She would have to take her garbage with her and throw it in a dumpster somewhere. What else was there to do? Taking a garbage bag upstairs, she packed two pillows, the afghan, and two blankets.

She was tired, but she couldn't sleep yet. She quietly went outside and began loading the truck. When she had everything loaded, she tarped it. As she was standing there, she happened to look down at her license plate.

Yukon, it screamed at her. How many people would have seen it? Not Mrs. Ardell, because she had always parked the truck in the other direction and the Yukon Territory only required one plate on the rear of the vehicle, not two like British Columbia did. She needed to turn the truck around, but if the police were looking for Morag, would they be interested in an out of province vehicle parked across the street from her house?

She decided she needed to park in the back, so unlocking the door she got in and tried to start the truck quietly. She eased up the clutch and coasted onto the street, turning left and driving down into the alley. She tried to coast into her driveway, but as it was uphill she had to give it some gas. Then stepping on the brake, she shut it off. She sat for a moment watching the windows next door. All appeared quiet. She got out and closed the door by pushing her shoulder against it. It made a quiet click as it shut. The back door was locked and she fumbled with the keys in the dark. Finally, she was inside. She went upstairs and put the kettle on. She needed a cup of elderberry tea, and then it would be time to get some sleep.

Joan Ardell was not having a good night. Every time she would doze off to sleep, something would wake her. There seemed to be all sorts of noises happening outside, yet every time she went to the windows and checked; she could see nothing and all was quiet. She was sure the sounds were coming from next door, but the only thing she had noticed was that the James' girl had moved her truck from the front to the back. That was a little strange for this hour of the night, but then, not everyone went to bed early, as she did. She finally decided to stay up for awhile and keep watch. She didn't like not knowing what was going on in her neighborhood. So many people didn't care nowadays, but she was always watchful. One could never be too careful. She moved her chair by the window and placed a coverlet over her to ward off the chill. She watched alertly for some time, the only movement being the vehicles going up and down the street that ran parallel to hers. Some time in the wee hours of the morning, Joan finally succumbed to sleep.

Joly drank her tea and checked on Morag. She was sleeping peacefully, so Joly headed to her own bed. They would have to leave very early so as not to be seen. Joly hadn't used an alarm clock in years, but thought she should tonight. Her own internal alarm worked excellently, but she didn't want to take a chance. She walked into her parent's room, said goodnight to Nefertiti, and then crawled into her own bed. She patted Pip and stroked Salem, curled up and went to sleep.

She awoke with a start and lying there for a second wondered why; then the memories of the day before flooded her mind. As she sat up the alarm rang and she reached over to shut it off. Quickly dressing, she trotted down the stairs and put the kettle on. She went to the living room and found Morag sitting up waiting for her. She lit a candle, not wanting to turn on any lights and helped Morag to dress. They went into the kitchen and had a quick breakfast of toast and tea, while they discussed their plans.

Joly fed the cats and washed up the dishes. She packed Morag's things and took the suitcases down to the basement. Running back upstairs, she grabbed the bag of garbage and took that down. Quietly opening the door, she lifted the tarp and quickly loaded the rest of the things.

She wasn't sure how she was going to get Morag down the stairs, but she didn't dare chance starting the truck and driving around the front.

They were ready to leave. Joly lifted Morag into a chair, lugged the wheelchair downstairs and set it up, remembering at the last second to set the brakes. Back upstairs, she asked Morag if she was ready.

"Oh yes, my dear, I have faith, I know you won't drop me."

Joly lifted her up and made her way to the stairwell. Morag wasn't overly heavy, but the stairs were narrow and steep. One step at a time, they made their way down. Reaching the bottom, Joly placed Morag back in her chair and breathed a huge sigh of relief. It hadn't been as bad as she thought it might be. While Morag wheeled herself to the door, Joly ran back upstairs and snuffed out the candle. Back in the basement, she opened the door and took the three cats out to the truck. Then she picked Morag up again and carried her out.

Making sure the door was locked, she collapsed the wheelchair and loaded it as quietly as she could, ensuring the tarp was snug before she jumped into the cab. Releasing the emergency brake, she pushed the clutch in and let the truck roll down the incline and into the back lane. "Here we go."

Joly started the truck and in one fluid movement, had it easing ahead and down the lane. Reaching the corner, she turned on the lights and drove out into the early morning traffic.

Joan Ardell was feeling extremely crotchety. She had awoken with a crick in her neck and a sore back from sleeping upright all night. She had slept longer than usual, which didn't improve her mood. Looking out her window, she saw the truck was gone from next door. She thought it was strange she hadn't heard it start up. She rarely if ever, missed anything like that. And why would that girl be out this early anyhow?

Later that morning after having her breakfast and tea, Joan was ensconced in her armchair channel surfing when her doorbell rang. She was still in a foul mood and decided that whoever it was, they could just go away.

She didn't know it was the police who were doing a door-to-door canvass, trying to find out if anyone had seen anything suspicious in the neighborhood since yesterday, when an older woman in a wheelchair went missing.

The trip north was uneventful. They took their time, enjoying the scenery and talking about everything except the last time they had been together. They stayed in motels along the way, with Joly signing them in as mother and daughter. Morag's picture had been in the paper and on television, so she stayed in the truck while Joly registered them and Joly would buy take out or easily prepared meals they could eat in their room.

In Whitehorse, Joly bought a good supply of groceries, easily reverting to the way she had shopped for so many years. She also bought some heavy winter clothing for Morag. She had stopped in Prince George and found an herbal shop where she had purchased several different oils and herbs for working on Morag's legs. She also purchased a good roll away cot.

It was late afternoon when she turned into the yard at her cabin. Being so far north it was already dark, and the fresh snow sparkled like diamonds as the headlights bounced over the landscape. Joly left Morag in the truck, while she lit an oil lamp and got a fire burning. While the cabin was warming up Joly unloaded the truck. By the time she was finished, the chill was off the cabin and she carried Morag into her new home.

Joly unpacked the groceries and took the meat and frozen goods outside to her meat safe. She prepared a quick supper of pasta with a vegetable sauce for her and Morag and fed the cats chicken with cooked egg yolks.

Once the dishes were washed and put away, Joly set up the roll away and made up the two beds. She helped Morag prepare for the night and lifted her into the bed in the corner. She readied herself and after banking the fire, she went to bed on the new roll away.

Nefertiti had already taken her place by the window. Salem jumped onto the bed and curled up beside Morag's head. She smiled at him and gave him a pat. Pip waited for Joly to get comfortable and then curled up beside her.

Morning came slowly in the far north. It was still dark when Joly and Morag started their day. Joly stoked the fire and added wood. She dressed and taking stock of her oils, she removed the bay, lemon, lavender, calendula and pennyroyal. Opening her trunk, she removed the box that held her stones and she took out a selenite, a lapis lazuli, and two black onyxes. Joly lit two red and two white candles and placed one at each corner of the bed that Morag was lying in.

Taking the bay and lavender oils, she carefully mixed one teaspoon of each together and then added one-half a teaspoon of lemon oil. To this mixture, she added a teaspoon of calendula oil. Joly mixed the oils well making sure that they were blended.

Morag watched with interest, finally commenting, "You know... you are a healer. You don't need all the oils and stuff. You would do just fine with only your hands."

Joly smiled, "Yes, that well may be, but please bear with me and let me do it my way. I have not done a healing in many years and I had only found out how powerful my capabilities were, when..." Joly's voice trailed off.

Morag was surprised. "You knew you were a Sister of the Triple Moon? I didn't know you had been told."

"Yes, Daddy told me. Um, I don't think Mom knew he had, though. It was after my eighteenth birthday. Daddy said it was time I knew, as I needed to be prepared in case I was called. He said Mom insisted there was lots of time, that I was young yet and she didn't want me to be forced."

"I see. Yet you chose to ignore what you had been told, to isolate yourself up here for all this time."

"No, I didn't ignore it. I haven't unpacked the books yet, but when I do, you will see what I have spent all these years reading about. I may not have the experience, but I do know the theory inside out and backwards."

"I see." Morag wondered if she should tell Joly that she too was a Sister of the Triple Moon. No, not yet, she decided. Joly had enough to concentrate on right now. There would be time enough for that later.

Joly went outside in her bare feet and grounded herself. She knew the healing would drain all her strength if she weren't prepared. Back inside, she picked up the stones and the oil mixture. Walking over to Morag she pulled the covers down and lifted Morag's nightie to her hips. She placed the selenite and quartz stones on the bed between Morag's knees. The two black onyxes were placed on the lumps of flesh where two slender ankles should have been. Taking the oil, Joly poured a small amount on Morag's thigh and as she massaged it into the emaciated skin, she envisioned the healing light of the Goddess descending from above, entering through her crown chakra, down through her arms and out through her finger tips. She repeated the procedure on the other thigh, then moving the onyxes to the thighs; Joly massaged the oil into the massive ankles and shins. Ninety minutes later, she was done. She took the pennyroyal and massaged it over the legs. Removing the stones, she washed her hands. "Alrighty then. Ready to get up?"

Morag laughed. "If you don't want a wet bed, it might be a plan. Thank you dear. They feel good right now. The tingling drives me crazy, though."

Joly blew out the candles and removed them. "I know. Be happy about it. It means you're healing."

As she helped Morag dress and get ready for the day, she asked, "So tell me, how did you know I was a Sister of the Triple Moon?"

Morag smiled. *So much for telling her later.* "Because I too, am one."

"I wondered if you were. When Daddy said I would know others like me by a sense of unity, I thought about you. That's why I always feel so... I don't know... complete, whole... something like that, when you're near. It was so weird when I was growing up. My Mom was just the best you know, yet I never had that feeling with her, and sometimes it bothered me. Kind of like I was being unfaithful to her, you know what I mean?"

"Yes, I think so. I've always thought of it as a feeling of oneness."

"Yes, that describes it perfectly. Do you know how many of us there are?"

"Do you?"

Joly looked puzzled. "No."

"Neither do I child. I am only a witch like you. I can do many things, but there are still some things beyond my control."

"I'm sorry. I guess I wasn't thinking."

"No need to be sorry. I do have my thoughts on the matter, but they are only thoughts. I think there are probably either seven or nine of us."

"Nine because it's the square of three, right, and three is the number of the universe."

Morag smiled. "Correct... and why might it be seven?"

"Umm..." Joly shrugged her shoulders. "I don't know. Seven is the number of magic, but what else is there?"

Morag chuckled. "Why would you need something else? Seven is the number of magic, and isn't that what we are all about?"

"Oh." Joly blushed. *How embarrassing.* "I guess it's a little obvious I've been away from the craft for awhile."

"Just a little." Morag leaned forward and gave her a hug. "But we will soon change that. Now what's for breakfast?"

4. The Summoning

10 P.M. – Russia – The snow had been cleared away and the circle drawn in where he sensed the worst of the tortures had occurred. They were at an old concentration camp and the suffering had been horrendous. He smiled as the preparations were made, the sacrifice offered, and the dark one invoked.

He was so close to having his life's dream and there was nothing to stop him now. *Oh yes there is*, the small voice in his head niggled at him.

No… no, there wasn't. There was only one person in the entire world that might have been able to stop him, and he'd taken care of that, years before. He was home free and the world was his.

2 A.M. – Yukon Territory, Canada – Nefertiti leapt to her feet growling, her fur on end. Salem and Pip also awoke and they joined Nefertiti at the window. "Something very evil is happening somewhere to the west."

"Yes, the smell is bad."

Morag moaned and thrashed about in her bed. Then Joly began tossing and turning, and soon a sharp cry escaped her.

Pip jumped off the table to go and lie beside her, sending calming energies to her Mistress. Salem joined her, while Nefertiti kept vigil at the window.

For the next hour a great darkness hovered and there was no peace for the two women. The cats did their best to calm them, but the terror in their subconscious minds was too great.

5 A.M. – Florida, U.S.A. – *"Babushka?* Grandmamma, are you awake?"

"Da, Polina, Come in bed with me."

"I'm scared, Grandmamma."

"Shh, I know. It is bad, but it will go away soon, I think." The old woman lifted the covers and sixteen year old Polina crawled in and curled against her Grandmother.

They huddled together as the darkness closed in around them.

Veronika Ivanova's thoughts were fragmented and she tried to piece them together in between the bouts of horror that kept slamming into her. Her grandchildren, Polina and Sergei had made many trips to the Otherworld. They laughed about them and thought it to be great fun. She wondered if this terror was the result of one of these trips. As she let her mind relax and clear, she sensed the evil was being invoked at that moment in time.

Het, no… the grandchildren were innocent.

Polina was terrified of the dark images, but she was more afraid of the trouble she would be in, after they were gone. She was sure *Babushka* would blame her and Sergei for bringing them. They had played too much in the Otherworld. She decided this must be their punishment, and she wondered how Sergei was making out.

7 A.M. – Argentina, South America – *"Madre, Madre…* help me. Make it go away."

Emilia Escobar de Juarez rushed into the room. Her daughter lay on the floor with her arms around her head. White Wind whined as he pushed his nose against her arm. "Hush *niña.* I'm here." She sat on the floor and held Jacinta tightly in her arms.

The darkness surrounded them and pushed itself in on them. Emilia forced herself to calm. She centered and envisioned the light entering her. She allowed it to fill her and it overflowed and surrounded her and her daughter. The dog curled against Emilia, as she rocked back and forth in the cocoon of protection, her precious child safe in her arms.

As she rocked, she thought of the evil and what it might mean. If she was to be called away, it could be a disaster. The neighboring landowners didn't think it was right that the widow should have control of so much land. Since Ernesto died, they had been trying to wear her down and talk her into selling at a price that would have laughable, had it not been so pathetic. Then there was the veiled threat from Iago Vargas two weeks prior.

She would have to make some arrangements in case she was called.

10 A.M. – Great Britain – The tiny cottage she called home was closing in on her. She never had problems with small spaces, but now she had to get out. Rhiannon Robinson opened the door, and as the evil swirled around her she fell to her knees. Visions of horror and terror slammed into her and she hung on to the floor and cried. She managed to close the door, but it didn't help. The darkness overpowered her and unseen voices cried out for help, but she couldn't help herself, never mind the invisible ones who called to her.

12 Noon – Finland – Rauna Rantanen was watching the snow fall, when the sense of evil appeared from nowhere and surrounded her. She opened her senses, but found she was unfamiliar with whatever it was. As the force grew stronger, Rauna knew she needed to take herself away from the present. She went and sat in her chair in front of the fire and withdrew into her mind, allowing it to take her where it would. It took her to her past.

After the obligatory nine years at school, Rauna had had enough. Her father was proud of her line of 10's on the certificate and they celebrated her success by a fire. Rauna had been happy, and when she went to bed, her dad had continued drinking moonshine and dancing.

Next morning she had found him lying by the ashes in the rain, with a happy smile on his old face. He had had a heart attack and died. Rauna sat in the rain by her Dad's body, wept a little, and thought a lot.

4:30 P.M. – India – Rupinder Rati stared at the ledger in front of her with unseeing eyes. They were in deep trouble. The crops needed to be harvested and there were no workers to do the job.

The darkness slammed into her and when she realized what it was, she smiled for the first time that day. Someone somewhere, was doing some sorcery and it gave her an idea.

For the next hour her thoughts were fragmented, and in between the bouts of terror, she tried to come up with a plan. When the darkness passed, she went looking for her brother.

8:30 P.M. – Australia – Shelley Sawyer had known fear only once in her life. Right now, she was mad as a cut snake. This wasn't the first time she had killed, but it was the first time she'd killed someone in her own home. She would need her brother's help to remove her boyfriend's body.

The darkness closed in on her. It took her a few seconds to figure out what was happening and then she really got mad. Somewhere, some bozo was summoning up some massive evil. Her hit list was already long enough and she really didn't need to add some dickhead sorcerer to it.

She wondered if she could drag Darren to the entry. She leaned over to grab his legs when the visions slammed into her. She fell to the floor and struggled back to her feet. The visions of horrors so terrible as to be indescribable hit her again and again.

She didn't know what the feeling was that overtook her, but as she sat down, the trembling so violent she could no longer stand, she recognized what it was. She was scared!

Sometime after three the darkness lifted, but it did not disappear. The women calmed and slept quietly for the rest of the night.

Joly awoke with a sense of foreboding. She lay there as she tried to figure out why. Something didn't feel right, but she couldn't put her finger on it, so she shrugged it off and got up. She lit the lamp, stoked the fire and put the kettle on.

Morag awoke and listened to the sounds of the other woman. She knew

Joly felt it; she sensed the other's unrest. How could anyone not? She wondered if Joly would say anything. She opened her eyes and said, "Good morning."

"Good morning, Morag." She smiled, but Morag noticed the dark circles under her eyes. She had not slept well. Ah well, she would feel more herself after she did the healing.

Joly was quiet throughout the morning and each time she went outside, she looked skyward, but she wasn't sure why.

10 P.M. – Africa – The wind swirled the sand as if it knew what was about to happen. The twelve men in black robes had covered the lower half of their faces to keep the sand out. The thirteenth left his face bare, but the sand did not bother him. He had protected himself and was safe from outside forces.

Below them was a mass grave, where dozens of innocents had been tossed, like so much trash. The sorcerer could feel the confused souls and knew they would continue to be restless for a long time to come. There would be no help for these ones.

Again, the circle was drawn, the sacrifice offered and the dark forces invoked.

Those who circled around the great one were afraid, but they were more afraid of not obeying.

11 A.M. – Whitehorse – Nefertiti hissed and her fur stood on end. Salem snarled and Pip yowled.

The air grew heavy and dark.

"Gods, what is it?" Joly frowned as she looked toward the window.

Morag did not like what she was seeing and feeling. Something somewhere was not right. "I don't know dear, but you might want to shield yourself." She didn't want to frighten Joly, but she knew evil forces were out and about. She wondered what day it was and then she knew. It was Samhain, All Hallow's Eve, the night the veils were the thinnest between the worlds. *Gods!* Something was being released into the veil of earth. Something monstrous! And then she remembered the feeling of the early morning. Two? Could that be? *Oh Gods, no! No, no, no!* She turned away so Joly couldn't see her face. The whole idea was too appalling to even contemplate. She forced herself into a semblance of composure and turned to face the room.

Joly was grounding herself. Good! Morag did the same and then visualized the shield to protect herself from the outside forces. She built the glass box around her head; saw the security alarm and the protective gate that would keep the evil and whatever visions it might send from entering her mind.

Joly was sitting in her rocking chair, her feet up under her chin with her arms wrapped around her legs. The chair slowly rocked back and forth.

"Are you alright dear?" She wheeled over to Joly and put her hand on the other woman's arm.

Joly nodded. "Yes. It felt like a terrible weight was coming down from the skies and was slowly squishing us."

Morag smiled. "Yes, it was a nasty feeling. You shielded?"

"Yes, but it's been many years since I have. It's holding though."

"Good."

Pip was on Joly's lap and Salem on Morag's.

Nefertiti sat at the window, with only her eyes peering over the sill. Time seemed to stop. She had sealed the little building as soon as she felt it, but the air still hung heavy and she knew this did not bode well.

2 P.M. – Florida, U.S.A. – Veronika felt the evil building. She didn't understand it and she was afraid. She headed down the stairs to Sergei's room. He called it his lab, but it was just a bedroom, cluttered with books, computer components and clothing. She looked around, not sure what she was looking for.

Both the grandchildren had a bedroom here. They spent as much time with their old *Babushka*, as they did with their Mother.

Veronika turned to go back upstairs. She was half way up when the visions slammed into her. Her hand went to her heart and she lost her balance. She grabbed for the banister and missed. She stepped back and her foot came down on air. She lost her balance and fell, her shoulder scraping the wall as she tried again to grab onto the railing.

At the bottom of the stairs, she winced in pain. From the angle of her leg, she knew it was broken. She opened her mind and called to Polina and Sergei, but the call was fragmented with bouts of terror and fear.

Several blacks away, Polina wrapped her hands around her head and yelled," I'm sorry. We won't bother you any more. Now go awa-a-y-y-y..." She thought she heard *Babushka* calling to her, but she wasn't sure. The pain and the images wouldn't let her think.

She stumbled to her room and threw herself on the bed. The visions grew worse and she screamed almost continually for the next forty-five minutes.

4 P.M. – Argentina, South America – Emilia had put in another hard day. The strange episode of the morning had left her with scattered thoughts, so she had to do everything twice. She was tired and as she drove into the yard, she was looking forward to a hot cup of tea. The darkness closed in on her and as she wondered where her daughter was, the door flew open and Jacinta and White Wind came running down the steps.

Emilia got out of the jeep and the girl flew into her arms.

"What is it, *Madre*?"

"I don't know *niña*." She held her daughter against her as they hurried into the house. She welcomed the coolness and led the child to the living room. They curled up on the sofa and she encircled them with the protective white light.

Whatever the evil was, it was building and getting stronger.

White Wind whined and jumped on the sofa beside the two women.

Emilia thought about the *Sisters of the Triple Moon*. She knew there was a reason for them to be there, but when she had been told that her child would also be one, she'd assumed that they wouldn't be called until Jacinta was older. She wondered now, if she had assumed wrong.

7 P.M. – Great Britain – The rain poured out of the black skies and Rhiannon sat curled up in an old blanket, thinking about the things she needed to do the next day.

When the evil forces descended on her, she whimpered and sunk deeper into the ancient armchair. Her nails dug into the arms of the chair and she wished for the first time that she had a friend. *What the bleedin' 'ell is 'appenin'?*

As the clock advanced toward the eight, the sense of darkness grew stronger. Images flashed through her mind… images of monsters and terror so hideous it left her trembling with tears running down her cheeks.

10 P.M. – Finland – Rauna was almost asleep when the horrors of the day returned. She remained in bed and again drifted into herself. Her thoughts continued from where they had left off earlier.

She was only fifteen, society would see her as a child and take her away to be *taken care of*, and with her certificate they would expect her to continue studying – to throw away three more years. However, as a fifteen year old, she could always act like a stupid wimp and say that she didn't know. So she dragged her father into the woods and left him there, dancing a little farewell ceremony in his honor, asking Mother to accept him back and thanking Her for the time she had with him. The animals and birds would take care of the body.

1:30 A.M. – India – The darkness hung heavy in the air and the sleeping woman tossed in her bed. The covers fell to the floor as she thrashed around. Her dreams of terror drifted deep into her subconscious, beyond the part of her mind that ever knew consciousness and there it buried itself in the part of her that knew true fear. The guttural cries sounded more animalistic than human.

5:30 A.M. – Australia – Shelley dreamed of Darren and his wonderful love making. He was a considerate lover and had always pleasured her first, before taking his own satisfaction. She moaned as his tongue did wondrous things to her nether region. He slid up her belly and sucked on her nipples before continuing up to her neck.

The darkness closed in and as he raised his head to kiss her, his face distorted into an oozing, pustule ridden demon.

She screamed and tried to wake, but the dream refused to release her and she spent the next hour fighting for her life.

By twelve-thirty the darkness began to lift. Joly rose to put the kettle on. She splashed cool water on her face and took the basin to Morag who did the same.

Morag handed the basin back to Joly. "Do you have this place warded?"

Joly shook her head. "No. I'm not sure I know how. I did the house and yard when I was home, but I don't know if I did them right."

"You did fine dear. I felt them when I was there. Do you have clear crystals, preferably with points and a white candle?"

"Yes, I have those." She pulled the trunk out from under the bed, unlocked it and dug through it until she found the crystals.

"You'll need to clean and charge them."

"Yes, I know that much." Joly poured hot water into the basin, added soap and washed and dried them. Then she grounded herself and envisioned the white light entering her body, flowing through her hands and into the crystals.

Morag instructed her to run each one through the flame of the candle, and then place them with the points up in the four corners of the room, while chanting the protection spell.

"Goddess of light, God of the day,
Protect this home and keep evil away,
Goddess of dark, God of the night,
Selene will protect us with her light."

While Joly was busy doing that, Morag thought about the two occurrences. If it was as she thought and two demons had been summoned to earth, then she needed to get on her feet in a hurry. It didn't matter that they had vanished for the time being. They would have to return to where they had been summoned from, at least once in every twelve month period. She would be watching for them. In the meantime, she knew the earth was in for a rough time of it. Evil things never seen before would be taking place everywhere.

She thought about the *Sisters of the Triple Moon* and she knew why they were there at this time.

They passed the afternoon quietly and Joly was putting the last of the supper dishes away when it hit again.

10 P.M. – U.S.A. – The rain had not let up, so they were forced to meet indoors. The old manor house appeared to welcome them. They had used it before, when they were unable to gather in the outdoors.

The final circle was drawn, the last sacrifice made and the ultimate evil invoked.

Those in the circle knew they were doomed the moment they saw it, but when the sorcerer waved his hand in their direction and said, "Feast," the twelve men experienced overwhelming terror. They ran, but the dark beast grabbed them as if they were small children and one by one, they were no more.

The youngest of the coven thought he was home free. He made it to the doorway, and was almost through when he felt the dagger enter his back. As he twisted and fell, he saw their leader wipe his blood off the knife with his finger and then he licked the finger clean. The three-headed monster fastened its eyes upon him, and he wondered briefly which head would consume him.

As the light faded from his eyes, he saw a dog and felt it lick his face. He smiled, and the last sound he heard was the crunch of bones as the dog bit his face off.

6 P.M. – Yukon Territory, Canada – It hit so hard and fast, Joly dropped the plate she was holding. It shattered into dozens of fragments and Joly ignored it as she quickly called upon her mind's security alarm. She felt the protective shield slide into place. "Gods Morag, what the hell is it?"

"Is your crystal handy dear?"

She went and dragged the trunk out, unlocked it, retrieved the ball and handed it to Morag.

She held the crystal for a few seconds, absorbing and becoming one with the vibrations that were unique to each crystal ball.

She watched as the mists appeared and receded. The crystal took her to the darkness of the eastern U.S. The huge house was a dark shadow in the night. The rain made it even harder to make out any detail. A multi win-dowed room on the left flickered with candle light. She bade the crystal to go closer. She could make out the blurred figures circling, could hear the chant-ing, while a lone figure stood apart from the rest with a chalice raised high. On the altar something small flopped in its death throws.

Morag knew the chalice held the warm blood from the unfortunate sacri-fice. She watched as all those present drank from the cup, and then saw the remains thrown in the center of their circle. The chanting grew louder.

"Do you see anything?"

Morag looked at Joly who had finished sweeping up the broken plate. "Yes, there's a circle and its not a sacred one." She looked back into the crys-tal just in time to see an evil more horrendous than she could fathom, rising up from the floor. The crystal dropped to her lap, the vision remaining with her.

The dark beast stood some ten feet tall with three heads, each with horns. She had seen four arms and a tail that whipped around in aimless fashion. The body appeared to undulate like a pit of angry snakes. The eyes of two heads flashed bright orange, but the third, the eyes of the serpent glowed black, and it had struck at the window, looking directly at her.

It had sensed her intrusion.

Gods! If the other two were this terrible, Mother Earth was in serious trouble.

9 P.M. – Florida, U.S.A. – Veronika lay in the hospital bed, her leg in a cast. They were keeping her in overnight for observation. Sergei had been across the city when he'd sensed her cry for help and had arrived thirty minutes later.

The darkness descended around her and over her and in her. She cried out and clung to the bedding as wave after wave of terror bounced off of her.

A nurse heard the cry and entered the room to see Veronika thrashing about. She rushed over and put the sides of the bed up; afraid the woman was going to throw herself on the floor. She tried to talk to Veronika, but got no response. She saw the fear on the woman's face, but could see no reason for it. She left to call the doctor. The woman obviously needed a sedative.

When the doctor arrived, the visions were gone and Veronika lay quietly in her bed. The doctor questioned her and she said she'd had a bad dream. He cocked an eyebrow at the nurse, shook his head and left.

The visions returned and Veronika's tongue bled from biting on it, with trying not to scream. When her thoughts melded and became whole, she wondered how Polina was making out. She hoped Sergei was with her; he was the only one who would understand.

The scream was in her throat and she kept swallowing. Polina did not want to alert her Mother that something was wrong. She stumbled to Sergei's room, but he wasn't home. She slid to the floor in the hall and stuffed the hem of her sweatshirt in her mouth. She allowed the scream to release into the worn cotton and repeatedly banged her head against the wall.

Time had no meaning, and it wasn't until much later that she realized she was being held and rocked by her Mother.

12 Midnight – Argentina, South America – Emilia sensed the darkness, and rushed out of her office toward her daughter's room. As she hurried through the rooms she envisioned the light entering her, and by the time she reached the bedroom, she was surrounded in protection.

Jacinta lie asleep, tossing and turning, moans and sharp cries breaking the silence of the night. White Wind lay at her feet, a low growl on his breath.

Emilia sat beside the girl and gently picked her up, cradling her on her lap. The child stilled and Emilia relaxed.

The first two had been nine hours apart. This one only seven hours later. If there was another one before morning, she would stay home tomorrow.

This evil was the beginning of something *muy* bad. *Madre Tierra* was going to go through some bad times. She was a *Hermana*, a Sister and she had a responsibility. Mother Earth came before her small piece of paradise.

She smiled down at her daughter. She knew her *niña* would not be happy if she was called away. They had never spent even one day apart, but Jacinta was too young to go. She would have to stay with Emilia's brother, Marco.

3 A.M. – Great Britain – The heavy rain had lightened to a drizzle. Rhiannon slept fitfully in her chair. She had been afraid to move from it when the earlier attack ended and she fell asleep with the visions still fresh in her mind.

When the third attack began, Rhiannon huddled deeper in the chair, and a high pitched hum drew itself up from her very soul. She slept through the darkness but the visions ingrained themselves deep in her subconscious and would stay with her.

5 A.M. – Finland – The darkness slunk into the cabin and to the small bed in the corner, Rauna unconsciously withdrew into her self. Her thoughts returned to the day her Father died.

That evening she sat late and planned how to manage the year ahead. Her father owned the cottage and a couple of square miles around it, and there was money to get from the forest in the form of berries and mushrooms. She was a skilled picker and well known in the store nearby, so that would not be a problem – she would get enough money to pay taxes and to buy the necessary things for the winter and next summer. She had a hard summer in front of her, but she knew she would manage. Her father had been so old that she had done a lot of the work already, and now she wouldn't need to work for two – and she wouldn't need to go to school next August, so that gave her more time.

She worked like a small squirrel all summer and autumn, and when the winter came, she had her cottage well prepared. The cellar was filled with food from forest, garden and lake, wood piled high in the shed and everything was well taken care of, waiting for the next spring.

8:30 A.M. – India – Rupinder told her brother she was taking a trip to the city. He wanted to go with her, but she told him he must keep trying to find workers. They were going to lose their crops if they weren't harvested soon.

The darkness surrounded them, but Jagdish barely felt it. He watched in amazement at the transformation of his sister. She ruled their small empire with total control, but now she fell onto the cushions that surrounded the low table. She tried to smile but it turned into a grimace as the visions overwhelmed her. Jagdish went and held her, but he finally gave up and let her go, when she almost broke his arm from the force of holding and twisting it.

12:30 P.M. – Australia – Shelley was feeling narky. She'd had a horrible night filled with dreams of terror. Whoever the sorcerer was, he or she had strong power. She would have to get rid of him, but she would not stray from her agenda.

Darren was buried out back of beyond. She called his parents asking for him, but they didn't know where he was. She smiled as she hung up the phone and the darkness descended once again. *"Bloody hell! Nick off!"*

She had never been afraid of anything, but the visions were terrifying. She threw herself on the sofa and pulled a cushion over her head. It didn't help, and by the time the darkness passed, Shelley had cried her first tears in memory.

The next morning Rauna walked through the forest. She had a habit of taking a morning walk in the forest surrounding her little cottage, keeping in touch with nature and the year. This morning there was a nasty feeling lying behind the peaceful existence around her. There were some mouse prints in the thin white layer of snow, and there an owl had got herself a nice nibble for the night. The short anguish had already melted into the normality of the forest, so that wasn't the cause for the disruption. Rauna couldn't see what was wrong, so she decided to go home and look around a little better, in the Other Realm.

Back home she made herself a bowl of mugwort tea, with some cinnamon and mint to make it taste better. She put a couple of logs into the fire, petted her crow, and sat comfortably by the fire drinking the tea. She looked deep into her bowl of tea while drinking, and when the cup was empty she put it in front of her, and started to look into the fire. Flames were playing on the logs forming abstract figures, and after a while Rauna closed her eyes.

She climbed up the World Tree and was above the clouds. Animals were uneasy and Rauna began to walk to see what was wrong. She walked into the White Forest that looked similar to the birch forest with new fallen snow she had been walking in just a while ago. There too, were the small paw prints of the mouse, and there too, were the wing marks of the owl in the snow... "Oh my..." What was normal in the Real World was a bad omen in this world.

She walked out of the woods and saw a thick pillar of black smoke on the horizon in the south. "I see..." She spread her wings and flew to the smoke.

The arid desert was empty but the remains of evil hovered in the vicinity. She could sense that many bones lie under the cover of sand. Sometime long past a mass burial had taken place here and many restless spirits still searched for peace.

She saw the remains of the circle and something dark on the sand. On closer inspection she saw the stain was blood.

As she looked about, she noticed another pillar of black smoke to the northeast. She flew toward it.

It was snowy and the tracks were visible from the air. She sensed the evilness of the area before arriving. Again there was evidence of a circle and the blood was red in the snow. Some distance away, she saw the head of a rooster. The snow was melted in places and where there was soil showing through, she sensed terrible evil and despair.

As she looked around she spotted another pillar of smoke, this one to the southeast. She flew toward it.

There was a grand house, abandoned but not empty. She could feel the stench from afar and got very cautious. That kind of foul smell could only mean something bad, and she didn't want to meet anything bad without knowing more. The house was big and beautiful. There were traces of someone leaving the building and some lives had been taken. The unknown presence of evil was still the strongest sensation in the place. It didn't have a form; it was more a promise of turbulence and destruction.

Rauna went closer to see through the windows. They were all black. She was afraid, but also curious. This was something she didn't have any experience of at all. She entered the house carefully, with every nerve tingling and every sense alert, ready to flee at the first sight or trouble.

The thing was lying on the floor. It was just a black, formless mass. Rauna took one look at it, and backed out as quickly as she could.

The thing didn't seem to have noticed her, but one never knew. It reminded her of dragons, and dragons always noticed everything. Rauna stayed at the vicinity of the house for a while, just to be sure that the thing didn't follow. She looked around so she would recognize the place when she saw it in the Real World. When she was certain that the thing wouldn't follow, she hurried back home.

It was a relief to see the fireplace and the cup. Fire had almost died - it was mostly grey ashes and just some red lines sparkling on the coals. Rauna crawled to the fireplace and started a new fire. She had been gone longer than expected, and her body was stiff. The crow was looking at her all-knowingly, amused but slightly worried. The water was still hot, so she staggered up on her feet and made herself another cup of tea. This time, chamomile with plenty of honey to calm her upset mind, and to fill up the energy used on the journey.

"You know what, Crow," she said while drinking the tea. "We have to go to America. That's one place I have never been in... I wonder what the custom regulations are concerning birds." Then she laughed.

After a quiet night with no visitations or dreams, both Joly and Morag felt better. Joly did her healing magic on Morag's legs and while she prepared breakfast, Morag scryed to the southeast.

The day was overcast in Pennsylvania but with daylight, Morag could see everything. The crystal took her to the old manor house. It was a huge place, a symbol of wealth from days long past. The area was deserted as she thought it would be. She checked the outside first; there were several out buildings at the back. The property was large, with many trees, over grown shrubs and lawns. It was very private. No wonder the evil one felt safe there. She entered the building.

She could tell the place had been deserted for quite some time, but overall, appeared to be in good shape. She could feel the evil and wondered at its strength. She wandered through several of the rooms before entering what appeared to be a sunroom, the scene of the previous night's dirty deeds. The altar was there, but it had been cleaned. The only items on it were two candles. The flooring was hardwood and appeared worn where the circle had been. It would seem they had used this room before. She thought about the circle in the woods and wondered if the two groups were the same. She thought it was probable. There was a black stain on the floor in the center of the worn area. It was large, larger than what she had seen the night before, so more than one sacrifice had taken place here.

Well, they had the location for one of the demons. She allowed the crystal to take her where it would.

"Morag?"

She looked up.

"You didn't hear me. Breakfast is ready."

"Sorry dear." She put the crystal down and turned to face the table.

The days passed in comfortable companionship. Morag spent time reading Joly's books, occasionally quizzing her on the contents. The books on physics covered everything from thermodynamics, electromagnetism, astrophysics, aerodynamics and wave motion. Other books on biology, chemistry, astronomy and more showed the wear and tear of continual usage.

Joly chopped wood, hauled water and went for short walks when the weather was nice. The cats spent most of their time sleeping, with Nefertiti always being alert to the air currents around them. Salem was still as vigilant as ever with his Mistress, but he liked to curl up with Morag. Pip spent most of her time snuggled in the old afghan dreaming about a large house with stairs and lots of running room.

Rauna emptied the cauldron and water bucket, and prepared to travel. The water would freeze when the warmth vanished, and she didn't want her cauldron to break. She marked the well in case someone came by and needed it. She put a ward on the house which was more effective than any locks, because if people wanted to get into the house, they would break a window. That would let the snow and rain in, which would damage it more than some stolen items. The ward would make people unwilling to disturb anything. It just might be so, that someone got lost and needed a place safe from nature. Then she took her bag and the crow and left.

Rauna was a small woman, only five foot five inches, and rather thin. One wouldn't have thought it of her, but she was a very good walker. She could travel quickly and lightly over long distances, almost flying. The USA was surrounded by oceans, so one couldn't walk there. Rauna didn't want to use an aeroplane because of the crow, but she had some friends who had a boat.

Valentin Konovsky worked on one of the icebreakers in Petropavlovsk. He hadn't heard from Rauna for a very long time, so he was surprised to see her coming, walking in the blizzard in late November. Rauna's fur lined cloak was heavy from snow, and the crow huddled in the cover of the hood.

"Rauna, my friend! What are you doing here at this time of the year?"

"Hello, Valentin," said Rauna and smiled. "I need a lift."

"Oh?" Valentin was very surprised. "You need a lift back home to Finland and come to see me in Kamchatka..."

Rauna laughed. "Yes, dear. I need a lift to Alaska, you see..."

"I see," said Valentin and laughed. "And knowing you, no is not an answer... so we need to visit Anchorage for some reason soon."

"Yes, preferably so. The ice over the Bering Strait cannot be trusted; I'd take that route otherwise."

"I know," snorted Valentin. "Do you have a place to stay until I can arrange your trip?"

"Always," smiled Rauna.

As they talked a dog sleigh came by and a young native woman greeted the friends.

"Grandpa told me that you were here, so I came to pick you up," said she.

Rauna stayed a couple of weeks with the woman's grandfather, an old Itelmen shaman. They talked about the evil that had arrived in the world, and the best way to deal with it.

"We don't have any experience with spirits materializing to our world that way. There are evil people who work for them, and people possessed by evil spirits, but this is a whole new entity..."

"I have read of demonology and summoning spirits to do the wizard's bidding, and I have heard of djinns – they can sometimes escape their masters and run amok in the world."

"Yes, could be. If it is a runaway slave, it doesn't need to take a human form to fit the world. But I would think it wants to."

"Yes," agreed Rauna and thought about it. With all the movies and books about supernatural beings and aliens, people would not be as afraid of a monster. "An evil man or something that looks like a man, can achieve more..." She sighed. "Do you think we have more of them coming through?"

"It's like with fish – if you have a hole in the net, one fish will see it, and the others will follow the first one... we need to find the hole and mend it, wherever the spirits are."

They drank their tea in silence.

The next day Rauna left the house. Valentin was a bit surprised to see her, as he was just about to send a message to her, but he was pleased because now no time needed to be wasted for fetching her. They sailed within an hour. The sea journey was pleasant, two peaceful days through ice-covered water; evenings spend with singing and storytelling. On December fifteenth, she arrived at Anchorage.

Rauna was not a person you would remember, or even look at twice. She was an older woman with ash brown hair in dark, worn out clothes. She looked very much like the crow on her shoulder. That one thing might have stopped you, if you were a little more awake than people usually are. Rauna and the crow fitted together so well, that people didn't even notice the crow.

Some people saw her at another time and were met by her eyes, they were golden amber with stars and an amused glint playing in them. No, people didn't usually notice her, but she noticed them. So when she arrived in Anchorage, she disappeared in the city without anyone even noticing that she had arrived in the USA.

The pencil thin muscles of Morag's thighs became more prominent and the great lumps around the ankles appeared to be shrinking. Joly still used the oils, feeling the massage was as beneficial as sending the power through her hands.

Yule was right around the corner. Joly needed to go to town and get a few supplies. She also wanted to pick up some things for the holiday. Morag also wanted to do some shopping. She felt badly that she had to borrow the money from her daughter-in-law, but Joly knew she would be paid back when Morag could resume her normal life.

They discussed whether it would be safe for Morag to go out in public and decided that this far north, they had little to fear. Joly said they would drive down to Whitehorse, rather than go to the small town that was nearest. One thing she wanted to pick up was a walker. Although Morag wasn't ready for it yet, Joly wanted to be prepared.

The weather had been nice for several days, so Joly decided they would leave the following morning, before it turned nasty again. Morag wanted to forgo the treatment in the morning so they could leave earlier, but Joly refused to hear about it. The treatment came first and that was that.

It was early afternoon when Morag suddenly looked up from the book she was reading and cocked her head as if she was listening to something. Joly caught the movement and looked at her quizzically.

Morag shook her head. "I don't know. There was something, but it seems to be gone now."

Joly looked at Nefertiti, but she had both eyes closed, although one ear was twitching back and forth like a radar antenna. She herself, could sense nothing amiss.

A few minutes later, Morag's head snapped up again. After several seconds, she wheeled to the table and picked up the crystal ball. "There is something, but I can't seem to put my finger on it."

Morag turned toward the light and held the crystal in the air. She gazed into it and watched as the familiar mists emerged and retreated.

Morag's voice thundered through the small room.

Kiss A Demon Goodbye

"By all the Gods! What in Sam hell does that boy think he's doing?"

Stephen had done everything he could. He had filed a missing persons report with the police. He had contacted both major newspapers and taken out full-page ads. He had appeared on television, begging the public to please be on the lookout for his missing Mother. He had hired a company to do up flyers and distribute them. He had employed a detective agency and had both his home and work phones tapped.

He had also started a lawsuit against the company that ran the facility his Mother had gone missing from. He had given a horrific dressing down to the officials that ran the place and with no satisfaction received from that end, he gathered up his Mother's things and let them know in no uncertain terms that when he found his Mother, she certainly would not be returning to this particular establishment.

Six weeks had passed and no one seemed to have seen anything. It was as if Morag McEwan had vanished off the face of the earth. There had been sightings, the usual, "I think I saw her on a bus, on the train, at the airport. I'm sure it was her shopping, having dinner, etc." They were checked and all proved to be false. The only report that seemed halfway hopeful had ended up a dead end. A woman that answered to his Mother's description had been seen having supper in a restaurant with another woman, the night she went missing. However, the woman had paid cash for the meal, so there was nothing to trace. Who the other woman was, Stephen couldn't even begin to guess at. The only people she had ever been close to, that might have been willing to help her disappear, were all dead.

Stephen was beside himself. The past few days had brought no new leads at all. Everyone's phones seemed to have quit ringing. He didn't know where to turn. He found himself going through his Mother's belongings again. He kept hoping he would find some clue amongst her meager possessions. When he moved the box containing her crystal ball to look at some papers underneath, he felt the urge to look at the crystal. He scoffed, thinking how pointless it was. If it actually worked, it certainly wouldn't work for him. Opening the box, he was struck by the beauty of the crystal. He could see why his Mother set so much in store by it. She had always loved beautiful things.

He reached in and gently grasped hold of the crystal. Once again, there was the shock of a vibration running through his fingers and up his arm. He persevered and lifted it out. He held it in both his hands and walked over by the window. How would one go about calling up a vision in this clear, circular ball? He didn't have a clue, and for the first time he felt some regret that he hadn't at least tried to learn some of his parent's ways. He stood there forlornly, wondering for the millionth time where his Mother was.

Not realizing it, he had been staring into the crystal as his thoughts wandered. He noticed the crystal had turned cloudy, no, not really cloudy, it was more like a mist he decided, but the shock of what he was seeing had him scrambling back to the box and none too gently dropping the crystal back in its home.

He stood there hyperventilating. Forcefully calming himself, he decided he had been seeing things. Something must have gotten in his eye. He picked up the crystal again, and still a bit shaky, walked back to the window.

Looking outside, he decided his vision was clear and he again looked down at the crystal. This time, he purposefully thought about his Mother while concentrating on the glinting orb in his hands. The mists appeared again and Stephen decided he was losing his mind. He was not a witch, had never been a witch, and had no desire to be a witch. *What is with my eyes?* Maybe he needed to see an optometrist. That was probably the answer. He did a lot of close up work and his eyesight was suffering.

The mists swirled around and started to recede. Yes, it was his eyes he decided. He couldn't do this anymore. It was pointless. He walked back to the box, put the crystal ball inside and closed the lid. *Christ, Mother, where the hell are you?* Stephen went to the bed and lay down, the tears welling up and spilling over to run down his cheeks.

Morag watched as Stephen lie down, saw his tears fall and felt her own tears falling too. This strange man-child of hers actually had a heart after all. It also appeared he was extremely distraught over her disappearance. Distraught enough to try scrying. By the Gods, he had succeeded too, although he didn't seem to be aware of it. Maybe, just maybe, there was some hope for him after all.

Morag looked across the small room to Joly. "My son," she hiccupped, "He seems to be trying to reach me through my crystal. I think I better phone him when we go to town." Joly walked over, put her arms around her friend, and held her tightly, while Morag cried quietly into her breast. Salem jumped on Morag's lap and curled up, sending his healing energies to her.

5. A Yuletide Visitor

They left right after Morag's treatment. They were both quiet, Morag trying to figure out what to say to her son and Joly concentrating on the icy
road. The ice didn't make her nervous, but the knowledge that there would be
patches of black ice did. The trip took longer than usual, and as they descended Two Mile Hill into Whitehorse, she was reminded of something else
that happened in the winter. Cold clear weather brought ice fog in the city
and it was thick as pea soup. One minute the sky was clear, the next, they
couldn't see six feet in front of them. Joly braked, felt the truck slide, eased
off and the truck righted itself. Once again she touched the brakes and again
the truck slewed sideways. They hit a patch of sand and came to a stop.

Morag gave a nervous chuckle, "I'm not sure this was such a good idea."

Joly gave her a sheepish smile, "I'm sorry, I forgot about the ice fog. It
happens here every winter. We should be okay now." She eased the truck
forward and they made it down the hill and into town.

They decided the best place for Morag to make her call would be from a
pay phone in one of the bigger hotels. There would be some semblance of
quiet, and hopefully it would be busy enough that they would not be too obvious. Morag wanted to make the call first and get it out of the way. She was
sure Stephen would have the phone lines tapped and knew she would have to
keep the call short, but that didn't mean she would be successful.

Joly turned down the side street to the hotel and parked. She went in to
check for a pay phone and to see how busy it was. The phones were handy,
almost right inside the doors. The restaurant was on the left and there were a
few customers inside. The front desk was to the right and the clerk never
even looked up as Joly stood there looking around. It would do, she decided.
She called information and got Stephen's work number from the operator, all
the while watching the people around her. She also asked for the cost to call
North Vancouver.

She wheeled Morag in the doors and over to the phones. She put a handful of change in Morag's lap and stood back.

Morag's hand shook as she punched in the number and deposited the required amount of coins. The phone at the other end began ringing.

An efficient voice answered, "McEwan Microsystems, how may I help you?"

Morag hesitated, "I'd like to speak to Stephen McEwan please."

"May I tell him who's calling, please?"

Another hesitation, "Tell him it's his Mother."

The receptionist audibly drew in her breath, "One moment please," she quickly replied.

Seconds later she heard the heard the click of the phone and felt her stomach muscles tighten.

"*Mother.*" He was shouting.

"Stephen, how are you?"

"Jesus Christ, Mother, where the hell are you? I have been worried sick about you. Do you realize the police are looking for you? What the hell do you think you are doing? You can't just disappear and expect people to sit back and not give a damn. *Christ...*"

"*Stephen, quit swearing!*" It was an order.

"Mother, I'm sorry."

"I am fine. I told you the last time I spoke with you that I was fine. Why you feel it necessary to have the police looking for me, I'll never know, so call off the search and just trust me. I haven't lost the use of my brain Stephen, just my legs." She drew in a deep breath.

"Mother, where are you? At least tell me that."

"No Stephen, I won't, because I don't need you on my doorstep tomorrow, or the next day, or the next. I told you before, I will walk again and I am working to that end now. Just leave me be, Son, I am fine. I have to run. I will call you again in a few weeks. I love you. Have a nice Yule, Son."

Morag hung up the phone and looked at Joly, shaking her head. Joly wheeled the chair back outside and to the truck.

They were quiet as Joly slowly drove through the ice fog to the city's main department store. Morag sat with her head bowed, wondering if she had done the right thing after all.

Emilia stood on the rise with her hands on her hips. She looked over the *rancho* with a practiced eye. All appeared calm.

She thought again of the evil from two months prior. She shivered though the day was warm with the beginnings of summer. She turned and raised her foot to the stirrup and mounted the grey gelding.

She would do her best to make this holiday season special for her *niña*. The tree had been put up on the eighth as was the custom and Jacinta had decorated it. The gifts were under it and more were hidden to be added from *Papa Noel* on *Navidad* morning.

Navidad eve was a time for families to gather to celebrate. Their family was not close by, so they would be alone as usual. Even though they weren't Christian, she still enjoyed the festivities and being with family.

She'd thought about going to her brother's, but she was afraid to leave the *rancho*. The men that worked for her would be celebrating with their families, and probably wouldn't notice if anything went amiss.

There had been an incident in *Noviembre*. Her wards had been set off late in the evening and she had grabbed the rifle and headed out. White Wind had received the command, *"silencio"* and quietly went with her to an eastern pasture. The men were not quiet. It appeared they were about to rustle some of her cattle. She had quickly fired two shots over their heads, frightening the cattle and scaring the *bastardos* enough that they jumped in their trucks and left. There had been no sign of them since, but she was sure they would be back.

She rode slowly toward the *casa*, idly wondering where Jacinta was. She usually rode out early on her horse, but there had been no sign of her. Estrella would be pacing in the barn wondering where her young mistress was. Just then, she heard White Wind barking in the distance. Soon the dog and Jacinta came into view. She saw her Mother and waved, turning her horse toward Emilia.

"*Madre*, I was riding to the west. The fence is down."

Oh no! "Let's go and see, *niña*."

They loped to where Jacinta had seen the break.

Emilia dismounted and checked the wires. Yes, they had been cut. She had been here two days earlier and all was well. This had just happened. Whoever was responsible had not entered the property, so possibly had been frightened away. Or else they were preparing for something. She wandered onto the neighbor's side of the fence. There were faint tire marks.

"*Madre*, was it done on purpose?"

"Yes, it was. I will return tonight and keep watch. Now, let's go home."

"*Madre*, do you think *Papa Noel* will bring me my bridle?" she grinned mischievously.

Emilia chuckled. "Maybe *Papa Noel* has no *dinero* this year to bring a gift. Did you think of that?"

"*Madre…*" Jacinta laughed. "You know *Papa Noel* doesn't need *dinero*. Luisa said he has elves and they make everything."

Emilia smiled. "Elves? I see." Life was simple for the young ones, but *Papa Noel* would not let her down. The fancy black bridle with the silver conchos was tucked in the back of her closet. It was the only thing Jacinta had asked for and she had put her order in early, first mentioning it back in August.

Although she had to watch her spending, they were far from destitute. She had opened another account and put money away in case she needed to travel. She had spoken with her *hermano* and told him Jacinta might need to stay with him, should she need to leave.

Marco had understood. He knew of her destiny and that of his niece.

Joly left the truck running and locked it with her second set of keys, so the cats would stay warm. Then she wheeled Morag into the gaily decorated store. The store was crowded with shoppers and she felt they were safe amongst them all. Morag placed a carry basket on her lap and Joly gave her some money to pay for her purchases. "I'll meet you back here in an hour, okay?"

Morag nodded.

Joly quickly headed to the seasonal section and filled her cart with different decorations. Then she went to the health aisle and was disappointed to find they didn't sell walkers. She would have to go elsewhere. The clerk gave her directions to a pharmacy that carried the requested item. Moving quickly, she headed for the clothing department. She had decided her gift to Morag would be a festive outfit, as all they had purchased in Vancouver were basic everyday clothing. Morag had been a sharp dresser in the years prior to the accident and grumbled regularly how much she hated the damned clothes she had to wear now.

She spotted a gorgeous black velvet, ankle-length skirt with gathering around the waist and crossed her fingers hoping they would have Morag's size. *Yes!* She grabbed it before anyone else might decide to take it. Now for a blouse. She moved over a couple of aisles searching, but saw nothing that would suit. She was ready to give up when she saw it; a ruby red sweater with a cowled neckline and three quarter length sleeves. *Oh please, please, let them have Morag's size.* She searched in vain. Every one was too small.

"May I help you?" The sales clerk materialized out of nowhere.

"Yes please. I'd like this sweater in a large, if you have it."

"I'm sorry; all our stock is on the floor. We did have it in large, but I guess they're all gone. Is there something else I can help you find?"

"No, no thank you. This would have been perfect for a very dear friend of mine. I wanted it to go with this skirt."

"Oh yes, they would have looked great together, wouldn't they? I'm so sorry."

"That's all right. I'll just have another look around, thank you." Joly moved away, disappointed. Morag would have loved it, but she would never fit a medium. Joly wandered for a bit longer, then realizing the time, she headed toward the checkouts. She would have to go elsewhere for a top.

The lineups were long and as she searched for the shortest one, she spotted Morag by the door. She was sitting and smiling at something Joly couldn't see, with her arms wrapped around several bulky packages. Joly smiled unconsciously. Good, Morag looked to be feeling better.

The line moved slowly forward. Morag spotted her and waved.

"Miss, oh Miss. Miss, hello." Joly became conscious of the voice and turned to see who was being so insistent. It was the girl from the women's fashion department. She was looking at Joly and waving something in her hand. She fought her way through the crowd and stopped before Joly, beaming from ear to ear.

"I'm so glad I caught you. Look, I was doing the returns and this was in the basket. It's a large. That was the size you wanted, right?" She held out the ruby red sweater to Joly.

Impulsively, Joly hugged her. "Thank you so much! You have just made my day."

"I'm glad I was able to help you, Miss, Merry Christmas."

"And a Happy Yule to you,' Joly responded. She clutched the sweater and grinned foolishly.

With her purchases paid for, she and Morag headed to the truck. Joly drove down Fourth Avenue, looking for the turn off to the pharmacy. Finally spotting it she turned and parked. Leaving Morag in the truck, she dashed in and asked about walkers. Yes, they had them. They showed Joly several models and she chose one of the cheaper ones. There was no point in spending a lot of money on something that Morag would only use for a short time. She paid for it and carried it out to the truck and put it in the back with the rest of the purchases.

Their next stop was the grocery store where they did the shopping together. Morag was an excellent cook, but she wasn't too sure about cooking on a wood stove. Joly teased her until they were both laughing so hard the tears were running down their cheeks. Still giggling, they stood in the line up quite unaware of the attention they were garnering.

After paying for and loading the groceries, it was time to eat. They went to a nearby fast food place, opting to eat in the truck. Sitting in companionable silence, the five of them ate their supper.

They were still sitting in the parking lot when Joly noticed there seemed to be an unusual amount of police cars driving around.

Morag saw Joly's frown and followed her gaze. "Oh dear, do you think they're looking for me?"

"I don't know, but maybe we had better think about heading back home."

She put the truck in gear and headed for the street. When she went to turn onto it, she saw that farther down a roadblock had been set up. Morag saw too, and pinched her lips together.

Joly wanted to reassure Morag, so suggested the roadblock was a stop check for drunk drivers. Just to be on the safe side, Joly turned in the other direction and headed toward the south access road. She didn't see any roadblocks this way. She got to the end of Fourth Avenue and went around the loop.

Emilia sat just out of sight of the fence line. She had her rifle and a jar of cold tea. She waited in the dark, looking at the stars and listening to the sounds of the night. The dog lay quietly beside her. She thought about her husband, Ernesto, and the good times they'd had.

By one in the morning, she was wondering if anything was going to happen. When White Wind growled, she listened. At first she heard nothing, but soon there was the distant sound of vehicles.

She took the safety off the rifle and ran forward until she could see the headlights. As the vehicles neared, the lights were turned off. They didn't slow down when they reached the fence line, but drove through it.

Emilia looked down the gun sight. "*Diosa*, be with me and help my aim to be true." She fired and heard the satisfying pop of a tire. The lead truck stopped. The driver jumped out, checked the tire and went to talk to the driver of the vehicle behind him.

She lined up the sight and again asked for the Goddess' guiding hand. She fired and heard the shell hit metal. There were the sounds of cursing, and a hurried conversation. The shadowy form ran back to his truck and turned it around. The other three vehicles followed, as they drove back across the fence line.

Emilia waited another hour. When there were no more sounds of intruders, she called the dog and went to her jeep. She drove home, lit a candle to thank the Goddess and went to bed.

Morag spotted a large boat and asked Joly about it. Joly told her it was an old stern-wheeler called the S.S. Klondike, which was built in nineteen thirty-seven. It was now a tourist attraction during the summer, having been completely restored in nineteen eighty-one.

Morag, trying to relax looked at the scenery around her. "How did Whitehorse get its name, Joly, Do you know?"

"Yes, back in the eighteen hundreds when the gold rush was on, there was some very dangerous rapids right where the dam is. They looked like white horses manes and hence the name Whitehorse."

A large group of buildings painted blue caught her eye and she asked about them. Joly told her that it was the Yukon hydro electrical generating station, which provided a great deal of the electricity to the Territory. It built its power from the dam in behind which fed the turbines, generating the electricity.

Morag needed to see it. She wasn't sure why, but she knew from experience to follow her intuition. "Can we stop to see it?"

Joly wondered if it was safe, but took the exit and drove toward the dam. The ice fog had finally dissipated, but the light was fast fading. This far north there was only about six hours of daylight at this time of year. They would be just able to see the workings of the dam before it got too dark.

Driving up on the top of it, Joly noticed someone was standing alone, looking out over Schwatka Lake. There was no car in sight. "My Gods, whoever that is, they must be freezing! Why would someone be out here in this weather? You don't think it could be someone contemplating suicide, do you?"

"Oh, I wouldn't think so. Let's go over and speak with them. Maybe we can drive whoever it is to a warmer place."

Rauna looked at the water plant, disappointed that there were no rapids anymore, no white horses that had given the city its name. She wondered why the shaman had told her to come here. The water made the city misty and in the middle of the winter, that was a killer. Even in her thick fur cloak, she huddled. Then she heard a car coming up behind her.

She laughed. Okay, *this* is why she was supposed to be here.

They pulled up beside the figure who was wearing a heavy dark cloak. Morag rolled down her window and leaned out. She heard a sound come from the figure, but was unable to tell whether it was laughter or sobbing. "Hello, are you all right?"

The person turned around. "Hello. Yes, I'm all right, thank you." The voice belonged to a woman, who walked to the cab and rested her hand on the open window, her fingers touching Morag's coat.

"Oh… interesting…"

Morag was shocked. The feeling of recognition was overpowering. She had only felt it twice before. The *Sisters of the Triple Moon* did not just *accidentally* meet. This was obviously why her intuition had told her to come up here.

Oh yes, there were occasions when two came together, like when she first realized that Joly was one. And many years ago when she and Brody had been in Europe, they had taken instruction from an old shaman who had a young daughter. She too, was a Sister.

The cloak covered the face so well, it was impossible to tell if she was young or old. "You must be chilled, even dressed as warm as you are. Would you like to come with us, to warm up and perhaps to talk?" Morag turned to Joly, "You don't mind, I hope."

Joly peered around Morag and smiled at the hooded face. "Of course not. I just hope you don't mind three well behaved felines."

"I think I am supposed to come with you, thank you. I don't mind felines." Rauna smiled back at the driver, and added, "I hope none of you mind corvines." She moved her hood backwards revealing the hooded crow sitting in it. "He doesn't mind felines either and is fully capable of taking care of himself if need be, but I don't think there will be any need of that here."

She peeked inside the cab and was met by three pairs of cat's eyes.

Nefertiti was less than pleased. "Just what we need," she muttered, "a crow. Where's the justice?"

Salem said nothing, but wondered where he was going sit now. The truck was going to be very crowded. Oh well, surely Miss Morag wouldn't mind him curling up on her lap.

Pip's eyes grew large! *Holy!* The bird was as big as she was, and his beak looked to be very sharp. She decided to stick very, very close to the Mistress.

There was no point in taking any chances.

Morag looked at the face in the hood. It was older now, but yes, she had seen it before. This was indeed, the old shaman's daughter. "Your name is Rauna, I believe. Get in my dear, before you freeze to death, and by all means, your crow is more than welcome. I doubt you will remember me, but I met you many years ago when you were a child. My name is Morag and this is my daughter-in-law, Joly."

Morag awkwardly slid closer to Joly, dragging her legs over. She picked Salem up and placed him on her lap. Pip was squished in between Joly and Morag and let out a sharp yelp. She managed to extract herself and she jumped up on the back of the seat beside Nefertiti. She pushed her way past the Persian and lay down on the far side, by Joly's neck.

"Thank you for picking me up. Yes, I'm Rauna, and no, I don't remember you. I'm sorry." She opened the door and lifting the front of her cloak out of the way, she pulled herself up into the cab and onto the seat. As she sat beside Morag their arms touched, and even through the heavy clothing, she felt the sense of being one with the woman beside her. She pulled the door shut, enjoying the feel of the warmth inside.

"Why do I feel as if I know you? It's a little disturbing."

Morag smiled. "You'll get used to it if you are around us for long. It will happen any time you are near me or Joly. I have known Joly all her life and we don't even notice the sensation now. Are you aware that it is a sign of the *Sisters of the Triple Moon*?"

"The *Sisters of the Triple Moon*? What's that?" asked Rauna.

"Oh my! I can see we need to do some serious talking."

"Are you hungry, should we stop and get you something to eat?" Joly asked. She was concerned about the time. She turned around and headed back to the road.

"Jolene, was it? No, I'm not hungry, but it was kind of you to ask."

Joly smiled. People were always getting her name wrong. "Actually, it's Joly, j-o-l-y."

Rauna decided to make her acquaintance with the large tom first, because the black and grey Persian queen looked at her as if she was, well, something a cat wouldn't ever in a million years drag in, and the little one had fled behind the young witch driving the truck.

Salem recognized a good person when he saw one and benevolently marked the fingertips given to him. Then he acknowledged the crow.

"I am interested in information. At Samhain, something bad was let into this world, and it needs to be stopped. I don't know anything of that kind of evil. A friend of mine, Kutkh, told me to come here to find help, and then you came. So, I suppose you are to help me with this. What do you know?"

Morag nodded. "Yes, there appears to be three of them. We felt it too. I went and had a look at the last one."

"I was there the next morning. Three black pillars of smoke rose to the heavens and at the house, something very evil was inside. I have never seen anything like that. It looked like it was sleeping, but as I don't know it, I can't say. There was death in the air."

"Oh my dear, you shouldn't have ventured inside. That could have been the end of you. You must never approach these *things* when you are alone and unprotected."

Rauna laughed. "Well, I need to know what I'm up against. I was very careful, and some experience I do have. It's not useful to anyone if people never dare to explore. I had my wards on, and the Otherworld was there. If something had happened, just about every shaman in the world would know exactly what by now, and that was worth the risk."

"Dear, shamans deal with spirits. This is not a spirit; it's a demon. These are two very different things. And remember this; it is *never* worth the risk, if a life is going to be needlessly thrown away. And what this means is there will be a lot of evil happening everywhere, and by everywhere, I mean *all over the planet.*"

Mumbling to herself, she shook her head. "Sorry child, I was crippled by a demon some years ago, and without the use of my legs, I've been out of touch with the world."

Rauna leaned over to see her legs. Morag lifted the blanket so she could see the swollen misshapen ankles. "They are actually starting to look much better now."

"A demon did that? It looks like I really need to learn about demons..."

"Joly came to my rescue before Samhain and has been healing the damn useless things. It won't be long and I'll be out and about, but for now I have to make do with a crystal."

"There are things one can see better without eyes. I haven't used the crystal myself, but I'm sure you can see things in it that wouldn't be quite as obvious otherwise... I wonder; could you show me how to use one of those? I might see something you haven't seen. Different eyes see different things."

"But of course dear. It would be my pleasure. I too, use senses that don't involve the use of eyes. I have been lax in my duties the past few years. I must pull myself together and resume using the gifts the Gods so graciously endowed me with."

Joly turned off the highway, and driving slowly down the rutted trail, she pulled into the yard.

"Wait here, while I get some heat into the place." She left the truck running and jumped out, with Salem hot on her heels. Entering the cold building, she lit a lamp and quickly got a fire going in the stove. Then she went out to the back of the truck and unloaded the wheelchair taking it inside so it could warm up.

"Is she always that independent?" Rauna asked, a bit irritated by the forced idleness. Then she shrugged it off. If the young witch wanted it this way, she was free to choose, after all, Rauna was a guest.

"You will have to have some patience with Joly; she lost both her parents and her husband of three months; my son, all to the same demon that did this to my legs. She has lived here, isolated from the world for over nine years. She is used to doing things on her own. I have been here six weeks now, and she is still adjusting to not being alone."

"I see..." Rauna said looking after Joly.

"Morag, tell me more about demons. They feel like fairytale characters to me, like something out of 'Arabian Nights'. I know the evil spirits, but this didn't feel like that. Even evil spirits are understandable and follow rules. Do these things have rules?"

"The only rules demons follow are their own. I can see we have lots of work ahead of us, if we are to make you knowledgeable about these things."

Joly made several trips back and forth, unloading all their purchases and putting the groceries away, all the while thinking about the new guest. She was anxious to hear all about this newcomer, especially since she too, seemed to be one of the Sisters.

She and Morag could sleep together, that was no problem. Rauna could have the roll away cot. They could make do with the one chair and the rocking chair. Morag had the wheelchair. She did have enough plates and cutlery, but just. It would be crowded, but over all, it would work just fine.

By the time she had everything put away; the little cabin was feeling warm and cozy. She ran back out and opened the passenger door. "You can come in now, Rauna, it's finally warm."

"Thank you. I appreciate your kindness," said Rauna while she slipped down, out of the truck. She waited to see if Joly needed help with Morag, but understood that necessity had caused the two women's co-operation. She watched how Morag dragged herself toward the door and how Joly reached in and lifted her out.

She opened the door for them and while Joly put her precious cargo gently down in her chair, Rauna took off her cape. The crow chose the rocking chair of the two remaining seats and sat comfortably on its back.

Salem waited while Morag removed her coat, and then jumped up on her lap.

Pip and Nefertiti followed them inside. Nefertiti headed for her usual spot by the window. She lay down and glared at Crow, letting him know that this was *her* domain, and that he had better not try anything while he was here.

The crow stared back, telling her the only reason he wouldn't do anything was that he wasn't interested, not because he was afraid of a *cat*.

Pip wanted to know more about the Lady, but was terrified of the bird. She sat by the stove, basking in its heat, delicately sniffing in Rauna's direction.

Joly went to the small closet and hung up her and Morag's coats.

"I wonder where I can hang my cape… it's rather snowy and cold, and I'm afraid it is going to spread the moisture all over the cabin. I have a cabin like this, but there's only me and the Crow. I can spread it on the floor by the fireplace and turn it over every now and then so it dries up, but here's not enough room."

"Here Rauna, why don't we hang it over the clothesline?" Joly reached out to give her a hand. The feeling of being one startled them both.

"I don't think I will ever get used to that," Rauna said.

They managed to drape the cloak over the line, although its great weight made the line sag drastically.

Rauna joined Crow on the rocking chair, enjoying the heat from the fire, while Joly heated water to make tea.

Morag looked at Rauna, "I would like to know what has happened to you since I saw you last. And what of your father? He was quite old then. You were a child of about twelve, maybe thirteen."

"Ah," said Rauna.

"Joly, my father was a shaman, one of the last ones in Finland. He wasn't much appreciated back there; paganism was, and still is considered as something ridiculous and people don't take these things seriously. But he was well known outside Finland, and he used to visit different gatherings in the summer, when he could take me with him. My mother died while I was very little, I don't remember her much."

"Morag, I'm sorry to tell you that my father died twenty-five years ago, when I was fifteen."

"Oh, I'm so sorry to hear that. He was a great man. My husband and I learned a lot from him."

"Yes, he was. I didn't realize how lucky I was to have him as my father. I took him and his knowledge for granted and only later started to understand what heritage he left to me." Rauna smiled gently. "I haven't been able to go to the summer meetings so often. I have to take care of the farm, but I do go to at least one meeting, and then I walk around Europe and Asia in the winter when there's nothing to do back home. Everyone has wonderful stories to tell of my father, and I feel very blessed." She paused.

"The life has moved on as it does, slowly but steadily, and there has been a little problem every now and then, as there always is. And then, on All Hallow's Eve, there were three comings of darkness and I could feel the evil. Come morning, I felt that something was wrong. I couldn't see what it was, and I thought it was just something small, something happening in Finland, but I went up to see around anyway and ask if I could do something."

"I saw these huge black pillars in the distance and realized that it was something seriously wrong. I flew there... and here... well, one's in the USA. I looked around and there were no people there... I was a bit disturbed... you know... they're on both sides of the ocean, and it really isn't any of my business, but I was there. I have to do something, I was called..."

Joly poured chamomile and honey tea for the three of them and placed a plate of banana cookies on the table. She put treats down for the cats and looked at the crow. "Excuse me for interrupting, but would your friend like something? I bought apples. Maybe I could cut one up for him?"

"I'm sure he would like that. Thank you."

Morag took a sip of tea and cleared her throat. "But it is your business, my dear. Please, do continue."

"I decided to come to America and see if anyone here could help me. I wouldn't hunt a raccoon without knowing a little more of them, so I won't hunt demons either without knowing more of them. I look at your legs Morag, and understand that it might not be enough. You are a professional, and if that can happen to you, what ever might happen to a novice?"

Rauna continued. "Maybe it is that Sister thing you speak of, Morag," she laughed. "I just find it hard to think of myself as a "Sister of the Triple Moon." It sounds like something too grand for me, but I heard the call and I came, so I suppose that makes me some kind of a sister. And then there's the sense of..."

"Yes, you were called; you have the oneness that we all share. You need the knowledge that goes with it. You were right to come, although I'm not sure why you were sent to me. I can teach you many things it's true, but with these useless legs, I will be doing no fighting of demons or anything else in the near future."

Joly looked at Morag with something akin to fear in her eyes, "Does this mean I should be going?"

"No child, your place is here with me, at least for the time being. Once I am walking again, we will see what's happening out there." Morag yawned.

"It's getting late and I think we all need some sleep. I know I do. Joly dear, what are we doing for sleeping arrangements?"

"I thought you and I could sleep in the corner bed and I'll give the roll away to Rauna. I'm sorry Morag, in all the excitement; I forgot how late it was."

Joly unfolded the rollaway and handed Rauna clean sheets, "Do you mind? I'd like to get Morag ready."

Rauna shook her head and taking the sheets, she prepared her bed. After doing that, she disappeared outside for ten minutes then came back in wearing nothing but her shirt. She got into bed.

Joly poured water into a basin and took it and a bar of soap over to Morag, who washed up, then brushed her teeth. She used a bedpan and Joly got her into her nightie and carried her to the bed, tucking her in. She leaned over and gave her friend a kiss, wishing her sweet dreams.

Morag smiled, and then looked over at Rauna. "Sleep well Rauna, my dear. We will start your education in the morning."

Rauna smiled back and said, "Good night, all."

Salem jumped up on the bed and curled up by Morag's head. Nefertiti looked at him and commented, "You'll have to move, you know. The Mistress needs a place for her head."

"Oh, I forgot!" Salem jumped to his feet and padded down to the foot of the bed, where he once again curled up. "Thanks Neffy," he murmured as he was already dozing off to sleep.

Pip edged around the room until she got to the bed. Jumping up on it, she went and nudged Salem and asked, "How did you do that?"

"Do what?" he responded sleepily.

"Well, you know?"

Salem lifted his head and looked at the annoyance standing in front of him, "No Pip, I don't know. What *is* your problem?"

"The *bird*, Salem!" Pip looked around to see if *it* was listening, but it didn't appear to be.

"Oh for the love of... Pip, you're being stupid. It's a crow. We see crows every day, outside. Now go to bed." Salem tucked his face under a paw, hoping Pip would leave, but just knowing he would never get that lucky.

"But Salem, that's just it, they're *outside*, not in our house," Pip was frantic Why couldn't Salem see that this just wasn't right?

Salem had had enough. He opened his eyes again, just in time to see Pip being scooped up off the bed.

Pip let out a scream. *The monster bird has me! This is it! I'm a goner!*

Gentle hands turned her around and she saw her Mistress' face. *Oh... how embarrassing!* Pip felt like a fool, but was ever so thankful to be held close and cuddled.

Joly wanted to laugh, but knew she didn't dare. Her eyes twinkling, she looked at Rauna. "I think this little one needs an introduction. She has always been a bit skittish, and I know your crow is making her very nervous. Pip, this is Rauna, now why don't you say hello, in that sweet little voice of yours?"

Pip felt quite brave in her Mistress' arms, so ventured a look in Rauna's direction, and let out a sound that was closer to a squeak, than a meow. Joly placed Pip on Rauna's bed and stepped back.

Pip crouched down, but extended her head toward Rauna, sniffing. Rauna reached over and let Pip smell her fingers, then reached back and stroked her fur.

"Hello, Little One..." The hand was very gentle and felt very nice, and Pip leaned to it, but then she remembered the bird and stiffened. "You are worried about the bird, aren't you, Little One,' Rauna said with low, soft voice.

Pip nodded.

"He is very scary, I know. He has sharp claws but not as sharp as yours, you know. And he eats meat, just like you do. But he has no teeth, and you have two nice, white and very sharp rows in your mouth, don't you."

"He doesn't have any teeth?" said Pip very amazed.

Crow chuckled.

"No, not one tooth."

Pip looked at the crow.

"And, Little One, you see that he actually isn't that much bigger than you are."

"No..., no he isn't. Uh, hello Crow."

"Hello Cat." He turned his head and looked at Pip with one eye to see him better. Pip thought it was weird.

"It's okay, Little One," said Rauna with her low, almost hypnotic voice. "You have more time tomorrow to get to know each other. He won't eat you or harm any of you, so you can sleep calmly this night."

Pip went back to her Mistress' bed, thinking she had done very well. And it really hadn't been too terribly scary after all.

After washing her face and brushing her teeth, Joly stoked the fire, adding a few logs, and then she blew out the lamp. She climbed into bed beside Morag, who silently welcomed the healing body.

The warmth of Morag's body startled her and she realized that she had slept with no one since Duncan. Damn, but she missed him. She curled up as best she could, and with Pip tightly against her, she fell asleep and dreamed of a laughing young man with the bluest of eyes.

Rauna felt the people in the other bed, the two women; the three cats. She remembered the lonely winters in her cottage that had driven her to seek company all through the world and was grateful for the sounds of life. The crow chuckled in his dream and Rauna knew he was happy with the company as well. She had never married, but she had had her crushes and history with men. She thought of the younger woman who had lost her husband, and the older woman, who had lost her son. These people had paid more than was reasonable, and they were still doing this. The older woman was annoyed of the fact that her legs stopped her from going after the demons... and not to revenge her son, but because it was the right thing to do. The younger had opened up her life and home to a complete stranger, simply because it was the right thing to do. What extraordinary courage.

She wondered what she was supposed to give to these two, who would never ask for anything. Knowing that the dreams would tell her, she fell asleep.

Nefertiti looked out the window, thinking about all that she had heard this night. She had better have a talk with those other two in the morning. This was not good news. Their Mistress wasn't ready. She had just started healing; she needed more time. Her senses told her that all was well for the time being, so she curled up, and with her ears ever twitching, she slept.

At five in the morning, Rauna was awake. She listened to the breathing in the room, got up silently, rekindled the fire, took her clothes and went out. The morning was still dark and the stars shone brightly. It was very cold, but Rauna enjoyed the feeling of the snow on her bare feet. It was too bad there was no lake around. She rubbed herself with the clean snow and dressed. Then she took a walk to familiarize herself with the surroundings.

A short distance away from the cottage was a small clearing with a stump near the middle of it. Someone had done some magic there; there were traces of a circle and other magical markings on the ground. Rauna went around the place careful not to disturb anything. The spruce forest was peaceful and quiet as it should be early in a midwinter morning.

Crow found the leftovers of a fox's dinner and served himself an early breakfast.

Joly awakened slowly. Her first thought was that there was someone in bed with her, and then she remembered she had slept with Morag. She gently eased the covers back, not wanting to disturb her, and sat up. Expecting the chill of the morning, she was pleasantly surprised to feel warmth. That was strange… what time was it anyhow? She thought it was morning, but maybe it was still early night. She looked down at her watch, peering at the illuminated face. She was right, it was morning and it was almost eight. She had slept later than normal. She got up and tiptoed to the stove. It was very warm.

Rauna? Maybe she had gotten up and put more wood on the fire. Joly clicked her lighter and held it up, looking around. The bed was empty. It was strange she had heard nothing, but at least she now knew why the cabin was toasty warm. *What a treat.*

"Dear, when you're finished sneaking around, I have to use the bedpan."

Joly jumped and laughed. "Sorry, I'm feeling a little discombobbled here. Let me get some light happening." She reached for the lamp and lit the wick.

Soon, Joly was working on Morag's legs, massaging her healing magic into the withered thighs and fleshy ankles.

"I wonder where Rauna disappeared to. It's funny I never heard her get up or stoke the fire."

"No, I heard nothing either, but I was tired from the events of yesterday. Rauna seems to be very self-sufficient, so I'm sure she's fine."

Just then, the door opened and stamping the snow off her boots, Rauna entered, closing the door behind her.

"Good morning, Rauna," Joly and Morag said in unison.

"Good morning," Rauna responded, removing her cloak and laying it over the back of the rocking chair. "I took a walk around the cottage, I hope you don't mind." She thought of something and smiled. "I know it's a bit late to ask."

"No, that's fine. Just make yourself at home."

"There's this clearing with a tree stump. Someone has been doing some magic there, so I didn't go there, if you wonder. It's going to be a cold day, but all is well."

"Yes, there are so few large clearings around, I draw my circle there. The cold is expected at this time of year, but the cabin is warm. Thank you for adding wood to the stove this morning. It was a nice change to get up to a warm room."

Curious to see the full extent of Morag's leg injuries, Rauna walked over to the bed. She was surprised to see Morag's legs. The thighs, which would normally have been about twenty-five inches around, were only about ten inches in circumference and her ankles, which should have been ten inches around, were about twenty-five inches.

"You say a demon did that... How is it possible?"

Joly replied, "The demon changed the actual chemistry in the legs. I am having to rebuild the cells in the upper legs, one by one, by taking the altered cell in the lower leg, altering it back and moving it up. I guess it's a lot more complicated than that, but that's basically what I see happening, as I do this."

Morag interrupted, "She is a strong healer, she doesn't need to do a laying on of the hands, but the massage sure does feel good."

"That's what healing is. I can feel she's good," Rauna laughed.

When Joly was finished, she helped Morag to dress and put her in the wheelchair, and then she went to prepare breakfast. She opened a small trap door in the floor and dug out some vegetables for an omelet. While it was cooking, she sliced some twelve-grain bread and toasted it over the open flame. The kettle steamed and peppermint tea was made.

While Joly was doing this, Morag rolled over and picked up the box that contained Joly's crystal ball. "Right after breakfast we'll start you off with a scrying lesson and see how you do."

"Wonderful!"

While they were waiting, Morag explained how scrying with a crystal worked and what to expect. "Once you can scry in one way, many options are open to you. You need not carry a crystal with you when you travel, although I prefer to, but one can scry in the flames of a fire, by looking into a pool or container of water. Once you are proficient at scrying in the normal ways, you can also scry by looking at clouds, tealeaves, mirrors, even by looking in the eyes of another person or animal. Almost anything will work."

She smiled at Rauna, wondering once again, what it would have been like to have a daughter. Brody and she had tried to have more children, but it had never happened. Joly was close as she would ever get, but she could feel the old motherly instinct kicking in with this lovely woman from across the ocean.

Rauna smiled back. She had never had a mother, and had never needed one, but the sense of oneness with this woman caused her to think of herself as a daughter. She had always felt older than the other children, and never had any real friends, and these two women felt like a family – the sense of belonging and unionship was something she had never felt before.

Joly fed the cats dishes of chicken with bits of egg yolk and she offered the crow some cooked egg, raisins and a cut up apple, commenting, "I'm not sure what Rauna feeds you, but I think you'll enjoy this."

Joly announced breakfast was ready and they gathered around the small table. The conversation was varied and lively, the three of them getting along like old friends.

When they were done, Joly said she would clean up, if the other two wanted to get started. The water hot, she poured it into the sink and as she washed, dried and put the dishes away, she listened to the teacher and the pupil, thinking how blessed she was, to have such wonderful people in her life.

It was three days until Yule, and Joly decided she would start decorating. The cabin was small and wouldn't need much, but she had bought several foil ornaments that would hang from the ceiling and lots of garland. It had been many years since she celebrated this festive season and she was looking forward to it. She must remember to ask Morag what they could give Rauna for a gift.

Morag picked up the crystal and handed it to Rauna. "Have a look at it my dear. This one is Joly's. Mine unfortunately is locked up back home. Once you're attuned to them, most will work for you. All crystal balls are made from clear quartz, some will have a tint of color, others will have rainbows in them. Mine is green and is very old. Older crystals have more messages as they have experienced more energies and stored more information. As you will know with your Father being a shaman, crystals are life forms and they can have a lot to say. They send and receive signals, like any communication device. They will also balance your energies while you are working with them. Do you feel or sense anything, dear?"

"Yes… I think so... a vibration of sorts."

"Yes, you are receiving. Good. Most crystals have a flat area or if you like, a window, through which you can see, once you're attuned to it, although you will find that you will be continually turning it, as the different angles will show you different things. You should have good light to see, although even candle light will work, once you know what to expect. I prefer to stand either at a window or outside, but I have been found peering intently into mine with only a lighter." Morag chuckled. "You make do when you have to."

Rauna was quiet, her hands turning the crystal. Occasionally she would stop and peer into it.

"If you ever want to buy a crystal, be sure to get one that calls to you. Crystals have different frequencies as you know. You simply need to be able to tune in to the one you are holding, to adjust your energies to that of the crystal. Listen to your thoughts. You will know when the connection is right."

Joly put the two bags of decorations on the table and sorted through them. She pulled out the green garland and went to get the scissors. She hung the garland around the door and cut another one to fit around the window.

Pip looked around to see what there was to do. Salem was curled up on Miss Morag's lap and Nefertiti had gone outside. She didn't want to sleep. She wanted to do *something,* but what? The bird, *yes!* Pip walked over to the rocking chair and looked up. She jumped up on Rauna's lap, startling her. Rauna set the crystal down in its stand and she lightly ran her hand down Pip's back.

Pip continued her journey up Rauna's arm to her shoulder.

"Hello Crow."

"Hello Cat." The crow peered around the back of Rauna's head.

"I think you're nicer looking than the crows we have here. I like your black and white colors."

"Thank you, Cat."

"Uhh... my name is Pip."

"You're a cat, not a pip."

"Yes, I'm a cat, but my name is Pip. There's a difference."

"Well, that's silly. Why would I want someone to call me Woodpecker when I am Crow?"

"But what if there were two of you? How would you know when someone is talking to you and not the other one?"

"You look at their eyes, Cat. If they're looking at you, then you know they're talking to you."

"I see. Uh... nice talking to you, Crow." She climbed down from Rauna's shoulder. She didn't see at all, and thought Crow's reasoning was dumb.

Joly was balancing on the bed, trying to stick a pin in the ceiling that had a foil bell attached to it. Salem was watching closely, ready to jump to her rescue, if he was needed.

The next day Rauna again asked Morag about the demons.

"As you are one of the Sisters, you do indeed need to know about them. But before we get into them, I would like to know what you are able to do. You obviously must have discovered your powers by now, at least some of them. Enlighten me, please."

"Well, I'm a shaman... World is multidimensional, build like an onion of several layers, and these layers lay around each other, between each other, within each other, blended to each other. People are not used to seeing the different layers, dimensions or realities, so they don't see them. To me world is... a little bit like looking at these weird three-dimensional pictures. Everything looks as if it was a picture made of several slightly opaque pictures… and the images don't quite match. I am able to choose any of these layers and work with it, and move from one dimension to another and back again. I can also see the… currents or strings of whatever you might call them. That's a bit like looking at a photo taken very slowly in the middle of the night on a heavy trafficked road - a lot of white and red lines all over the place. That's a bit how it looks… leylines and all that. It actually doesn't look, like seeing with eyes, it's more like a feeling, or… I just know. But that is how I know when there's a magic circle or some kind of energy field, or where animals are going to go or what kind of weather is coming. And I can… er… how to put this… pull the strings, so that I get the weather I want, or get the animals to come or go, or get the people to not see me. It's also how I see what's wrong with people. Your legs look as if they were upside down and inside out and everything is just wrong. I have never seen anything like that. It's hard to explain what I can do… it's who I have always been and the way world has always been."

Morag chuckled. "You are definitely your Father's daughter. I can remember him telling Brody and me almost exactly the same thing. Your Father taught us a bit of a shaman's ways. Our powers were always more traditional I suppose, but I am able to do some of the things you mentioned. I don't actually see the onion, although I understand the concept. I too, can sense circles and energy fields. I can also manipulate the weather, but I rarely see any reason to. The Gods have been taking care of our planet since the beginning. I think they know what they're doing. I also talk to the birds. I suppose I can talk to all the animals, but the birds have always been my passion. I can summon them and give them instructions if the need arises."

"Morag, what are these demons?"

"The first type began their existence as Gods, or perhaps you're familiar with the term Titans. Before mankind came along, when all that existed were Gods, some of these Gods began preying on other gods, needing I suppose, to feel more powerful than they already were. Eventually the evil Gods were destroyed, some banished to Tartarus, and some were cunning enough to escape the realm they were in. It is of course this group where the Christians get their strange beliefs."

"The second type is extra dimensional, but their origins are unknown and therefore they can't be classified as true demons. What I mean by extra dimensional is that they came into existence as a demon or an evil entity. These would include such beings as nightmares, fears, headaches or one's own personal demons. You weren't born with them, so their arrival and inhabitation of your body, mind or spirit is no different than that of a true demon who tries to inhabit a person's body in what we know as possession. Also included in this group are the mental illnesses and brain disorders, such as epilepsy, autism and such. "

"Demons of the third type are also extra dimensional in origin. Some of these demons have found their way to Earth at some point in their life; others have remained in their own plane, awaiting discovery by dimension-travelers and sorcerers. These can be weak beings that wreak havoc in small ways that most people would think of as having some bad luck or having a dumb accident. These weak ones are sometimes servants or messengers of the stronger ones. There is also a fourth type of demon that I will briefly mention here. It is a combination of an escapee god and a demon. Not much is known about them, other than in another plane; the two evils got together and spawned a new type of extra dimensional demon. As this new type is virtually impossible to tell from the original, we class the two as one. The worst of the evil entities are the ones that would take over mankind. These have no thought other than to gain more strength by overpowering and defeating those weaker than itself. It's these ones that we traveled the world over, banishing back to the abyss they spewed from."

"How do you beat them? What do I need to consider while fighting? I mean, is there any rules in banishing demons? Are there tools or something else I could use to fight demons? You don't use your bodies; you use your mind. Do I need to learn to separate my mind from my body to use the mind alone? Have I understood correctly?"

"I wish we could fight them with our minds. We generally fight them with sea salt, holy water and herb mixtures. By holy water, I don't mean the Christian church version, although I'm sure theirs would work just as well. We make our own from rose water, spring water and sea salt. There is a ritual and it is consecrated by Selene, the Moon Goddess. Wands too, are good against them."

"I have seen your legs, so I know I am dealing with very serious matters… do you know how and why that happened?"

"Demons," said Morag, "are always unpredictable. No two are ever the same. They get their start in various ways and that is what makes it hard to fight them. If we were able to tell where they came from, we would be better able to have a plan of attack, but as that's not possible, we have to try and be prepared for every eventuality. As you can see, we are not always successful. That one was a bitter fight; it was a very nasty, determined creature. We lost six of our group that night."

"Six!"

"Yes. Along with Joly's parents and husband, I also lost my Brody. As well, we lost two dear friends, Bettina and Raoul."

"I'm so sorry to hear that," Rauna said, her low voice filled with compassion.

"We badly underestimated its power. I have relived that fight a million times. We should have had a double circle; we hadn't brought enough sea salt and holy water. At times, it was almost as if there were two of them. It seemed to be everywhere." Morag paused for a moment, once again momentarily reliving the worst day of her life. "That's the why of it. How did it happen? The buggar lashed out at me. I was too close. I suppose I'm lucky it had something else on its mind because it could have stopped and taken me with it. It chose to take my husband instead."

"How can I shield myself from that happening to me? I am a shaman, and I have always done my fighting in a very physical way, even in the astral world, the fights are physical. I am in a body there, even when my body wouldn't be defined physical in the same sense we use the word here. I have arms and feet, and I wrestle with the evil spirit… is it similar when fighting with demons?"

"Rauna… you cannot fight a demon physically, like in hand to hand combat. You can never allow a demon entity to touch you. You will most likely die if that happens. If they actually grab you, you will be absorbed into their being and they will grow stronger, or if they just take a swipe at you, you can end up like I did."

She wondered how to continue with Joly standing there. "They can also reach inside of you and either give you a heart attack… or… they have been known to remove a person's heart, right through the skin."

She watched Joly, who was biting her lip, as she continued to string garland across the ceiling. As Joly turned her head, Morag saw the glint of a tear. She saw that Pip had sat up and was watching her mistress closely.

"Can you see them? I mean, can you be sure that there only was one? If it felt as if there were two of them, maybe there was?"

"Yes, they can make themselves visible when they choose to, the same as any spirit can. They are usually an undefined blobbish shape, although in their realm, they do have a definite shape. They grow and shrink at will, shaping themselves into whatever they think is needed. They can thin themselves to fit through a hole the size of a pin and smaller or they can stretch themselves into a tall or wide entity to scare or attack. They need to consume a living, breathing body, be it animal or human in order to grow. This is why it's so very important that we or someone always be on guard, on the lookout for them. They could conceivably take over the world, if there was no one around to keep them in check. The chances of that ever happening are pretty slim, but just the same, we do need to be vigilant."

She paused. "I'm sorry… I kind of went off on a tangent there. What was it you asked… was there only one? Yes, there was only one. Oh, I suppose another one could have been present, but it's unlikely. They do need to make themselves visible in order to consume someone and there was only the one that showed itself. They also seem to need to be visible to fight, thank the Gods! If you remember only one thing of this conversation, Rauna, remember never to underestimate what is out there. You cannot always tell before hand what power it will have, although for those who are experienced in fighting them, there are things to look for, clues if you like, that can give you an idea of its strength. You must be prepared, always!"

Rauna was having trouble talking about the demons. The talk made her feel uncomfortable, a feeling she wasn't used to. She excused herself to go for a walk.

Morag wheeled over to the counter and began preparing cookie dough. "If we're going to celebrate Yule, let's do it right. It's been a long time since I've made shortbread. I wonder if I remember how. It will be a new experience for me baking in a wood stove."

"Gingersnaps too?" Joly grinned at her.

Morag laughed, remembering when Joly was younger. Every Yule season, when she was over to see Duncan, she made a special trip into the kitchen looking for gingersnaps. Morag had made dozens of them, but they never lasted. And when Duncan went across the street, he had his fingers in Morgana's cookie jar. She made chocolate chewies and he had loved them.

Morag made gingersnaps and when Rauna came back in she discovered she had a sweet tooth. She and Joly made short work of the cookies.

They laughed a lot and the cats were pleased to see their Mistress on the road to being healed.

Yule Eve day, Emilia stayed home to cook and bake. It was early afternoon when White Wind's ears perked up. Seconds later, Emilia felt the disturbance of her wards. *Now what?*

The dog's tail was wagging as he stood with his nose against the door. Emilia opened it and he ran outside, joyfully barking.

When an older green car came into sight, Emilia felt the tears. She ran lightly down the steps and as the driver got out, she threw herself in his arms.

"Marco, is it really you? Welcome, my brother."

"Happy Yule, Emilia." As he held her, he could feel the distant fear. He was glad he had decided to come.

Yule Eve arrived. In the small cabin the morning was like any other, but the afternoon brought a flurry of activity. Morag made cabbage rolls and Joly made raspberry jello and custard sauce.

Rauna did a lot of thinking. She still didn't understand the demon thing, but was reluctant to pursue the topic. It was Yule, a time for celebration, not sober talks about things that should never be.

That evening with their appetite's sated, they were relaxing when Joly went and got two packages from under the bed. She handed one to Morag and the other to Rauna.

"Happy Yule my friend. Happy Yule, my new friend."

Morag's eyes were glistening as she took the brightly wrapped package from Joly.

"You shouldn't have, my dear. You've done enough without this."

Rauna was speechless. She had not expected this. She sat quietly, as she watched as Morag opened her gift, her own clutched tightly in her lap.

Morag removed the paper and opened the box. Her eyes opened wide when she saw the red sweater.

"It's so beautiful!" She lifted out and held it up. "My Gods, it's been many years since I had something this lovely to wear."

She folded it carefully and went to put it back in the box when she realized there was something else in it. With a quizzical look, she reached down and withdrew the skirt. When she saw what it was, she burst into tears.

Joly went over to her and gave her a hug.

"Do you like it?"

In between her sniffles, she nodded. "Yes." She held the skirt to her breast. "You have no idea what this means to me. No idea at all."

"Well, I know you always liked wearing skirts, so it seemed like the right thing to get for you."

"Come here child and let me hug you."

They hugged and then Morag rolled over to the corner and withdrew two packages from a bag.

"Happy Yule to you, Joly and Happy Yule to you, Rauna."

Joly was surprised. She hadn't been expecting anything.

Rauna held her two packages, looking at the colorful wrapping. She felt tears in her eyes. She was overwhelmed by the kindness shown to her.

Joly excitedly opened the paper to find a jewelers box inside. She wasn't much into jewelry and with living in the bush; the only thing she wore was the cord around her neck. She never even wore her watch unless she was going to town. She removed the lid and stared momentarily at the cotton batting. She lifted it up and gasped.

Nestled on the under layer of cotton was an antique ring. Joly recognized it immediately. With her mouth open and a puzzled expression, she looked at Morag. "I don't understand."

"Well dear, as you know, it belonged to my Mother. I have no one else to pass it along to other than Elise, and I wasn't about to give it to her. You're like a daughter to me. I understand that you may not want to wear it, and that's all right. I just wanted you to have it."

Joly took it out of the box. Although the wide gold band was worn around the edges, the intricate design of Celtic knots that covered the entire surface was still prominent. She closed her fingers around it, and with tears in her eyes, she went and knelt by Morag. She laid her head on Morag's lap, and with her shoulders heaving from the silent tears; Morag rubbed her back.

Morag had wondered about giving the ring to her at this time. She knew Joly would be thinking of her Mother's rings and the fact she would never see them again. She decided to give it to her anyway, hoping it might help her to move on with her life.

After the tears stopped and Joly wiped her eyes, she slid the ring on her finger. "It's so beautiful. I won't promise to wear it, but you know I'll cherish it forever."

Rauna went over to have a look and exclaimed at the exquisite workmanship. She still had not opened her gifts.

"Come on Rauna. It's your turn."

She was feeling self conscious as she looked at the two packages... another feeling foreign to her. She was going to have to leave. She could easily become too dependent on these two amazing women.

She slowly put the one package on her lap and opened the other. It was the one Joly had handed to her. Inside the long thin box was an almost white wood wand. Rauna had never owned a wand, had never needed one and she thought of Morag telling her how they fought the demons. She managed a smile and looked at Joly. "It's beautiful. Thank you."

Joly smiled back. "It's made from English Holly and has very strong protective qualities. I thought you might have use of it in your travels."

Rauna nodded thoughtfully. She sat it back in the satin lining, closed the lid and put it in her pocket. She opened the gift from Morag. Inside were two boxes of Canadian maple sugar candies in the shape of maple leaves. She grinned.

Morag chuckled. "For that sweet tooth of yours dear."

Rauna reached in her pocket and slowly withdrew two small items. "Happy Yule to you Morag, Happy Yule to you Joly." She handed them each a stone. She hadn't known what to give them, but she had dreamed and the dream told her what she had, that they could use and would appreciate. And she always carried a pocketful of different stones and crystals.

Joly looked at hers quizzically, "I seem to be familiar with this, but I'm not sure."

Rauna smiled. "It's soapstone, it's mined in Finland."

"Soapstone... I have a wonderful collection of stones, but I don't have this one. Thank you." She looked at it again. "It's a healing stone as I recall."

Rauna nodded. "Among other things, yes." She wasn't sure she should tell the young witch its other properties of peace, stability and release. Things she had come to realize Joly needed.

Morag looked at Rauna. "I don't recognize this stone at all. Tell me about it." She looked back at the stone of varying shades of blues and golds. She wasn't sure, but she thought there were some deep reds in it also. She could feel the energy emanating from it. It had strong power.

"It is found only in Finland and was discovered in 1940. It is called the Stone of Light, more commonly known as spectrolite. It's from the feldspar family. It has wonderful healing properties and is also very good for meditation. If you have trouble sleeping, put it under your pillow, but only the ones with blue in them. There are red ones, but they are quite rare."

"How very wonderful. Thank you so much Rauna. I will cherish this." She shook her head. "I thought I knew all the stones. You've reminded me that there is always more to learn." She rolled over to Rauna and hugged her.

The next day was spent quietly, the women lost in thoughts of previous Yule's spent with loved ones who were no longer with them. They prepared their Yule meal together, with Joly peeling potatoes and Rauna doing the carrots. Morag, proudly wearing her new skirt and sweater stuffed the roasting chicken Joly had bought. The smells of it cooking made everyone's mouths water, especially the three cats. Joly mashed the potatoes and heated a can of corn to go with the carrots, dressing and gravy. Dessert was the last of the gingersnaps and shortbread.

Rauna knew she must leave the next day. There were things she needed to find out and she was growing too attached to these women.

As they prepared for bed, Morag rolled over to Rauna and gave her a hug. "Keep well my dear."
Rauna returned the hug. "You too."
Joly hugged her next. "Stay safe my friend. I'll miss you."
Rauna had said nothing about leaving. She felt the tears start. These women were incredible. She tucked herself into bed.

The next morning when Joly and Morag awoke, Rauna was gone, as they knew she would be. The little cabin seemed empty without her. She had blended in so well they hardly noticed she was there, but now there seemed to be a hole, a piece missing.

Nefertiti was more relaxed. She didn't like crowds to begin with and there had been too many for the small space.
Salem didn't seem to care one way or the other. He still watched out for his Mistress and spent a lot of time with Morag.
Pip missed both Rauna and Crow. There was something special about Rauna's touch. As for Crow, well... how many felines could say they actually talked to a bird?

When Joly took the decorations down two days later, she commented on how much change the year had brought. Morag agreed whole-heartedly with her, looking at her legs as she did so.

6. The Invisible Box

The New Year arrived. It was bitterly cold and Joly only went outside to empty the bedpan and bring in wood.

Morag's thighs were filling out and Joly knew it wouldn't be long before she could try to walk again. The lumpy ankles were slimming down nicely and Morag was able to wear large men's socks without sewing two together.

Morag was reading another book when she looked up. "Joly dear, I've been thinking about something and I do hate to stir up bad memories, but we need to go back to England. There are still some unanswered questions. What do you think?"

"What questions?" She didn't want to think of the past.

"What happened to the bodies, my dear? They weren't all taken by that demon we were fighting. Someone had to have found them? None of them were there when Stephen took me back, and I know animals didn't carry them away. There were no signs of blood or drag marks and I did check very carefully while I was there."

"Oh my Gods, Morag! I never thought about that. Yes, you're right; there should have been some sign of them." Her voice broke as she sat down on the bed and continued, "Mom and Duncan..." The tears started flowing. Morag wheeled over to her and wrapped Joly in her arms.

"There, there my child, cry now and get it out. You need to be able to re-member them with happiness, think of the good times; they wouldn't want you to be forever grieving. Possibly this has been part of the problem. You have had no closure. Perhaps we can find their graves, and then maybe you can begin your healing, child."

Morag held her for a long time.

The three felines also huddled in close, muttering amongst themselves.

"Is that a good idea, do you think, Neffy, going back over there?"

"I don't know, I wouldn't think so, but I'm not human, and they do tend to have some rather strange ideas."

"Nefertiti, will we be able to go with them?" Pip looked at her with big eyes, wondering what would happen to them if they were left behind.

"Pip, I don't have all the answers, you know." But she thought to herself that it was likely. Their Mistress had always taken them everywhere, except for the time when she rushed out to rescue Miss Morag.

Joly lifted her head and sniffing noisily; she got up to blow her nose. "Yes, maybe you're right, maybe we do need to do that, although Gods knows, I don't relish the thought."

Morag smiled. "Well then, that gives us something to work toward. We will have to get our passports updated and the cats will need their shots and whatever else is required."

"*Shots!*" Pip let out a loud yowl. "*No!* No shots, I hate getting shots!"

"Would you rather be left behind to fend for yourself?" Salem licked his paw, quivering at the very thought himself, but he wasn't about to let that scaredy-cat know it.

"Passports? How will you get your passport?"

"I'll be walking by then, dear. We'll have to make a trip south, if you don't mind?"

"No, of course not. I wasn't thinking. I'm sort of rattled over the idea."

They spent the rest of the day making plans and talking more about the past than they had before.

"Joly, can you satisfy my curiosity about something? What happened to you after I left you? I sent the police to get you after I answered what seemed to be a million questions. They came back and said no one was there."

"I don't know. I don't know where I was when Nefertiti insisted I go with her. I was in the city I guess, but I don't know how I got there. I hoped you could tell me."

"I got you to the city dear. I dragged you and myself as far as the road. It took me three days to get us there. Some kind soul stopped, but when he saw the state the two of us were in, he was horrified. Our robes were filthy and torn. We were covered in dirt and there were twigs and grass in our hair. I think he was going to leave us there, but I begged him to take us to a hospital. He had a truck and he finally agreed, but only if we rode in the back. He had to lift both of us in, but he must have had second thoughts as he was driving. As soon as he got to the outskirts of London, he stopped and said he wouldn't take us any farther.

I refused to be left on the side of the road and I'm afraid I went a little crazy. I told him I was a witch and I threatened to turn him into a tree so all the dogs could piss on him. He turned white at that and got back into the truck. They're a superstitious lot over there. He drove us to an alley where he very unceremoniously dumped us, telling me the hospital was around the corner. He left and I started crawling. It wasn't around the corner. It was a couple of blocks away. Someone saw me and called the police. They were the ones who took me to the hospital.

I know my directions weren't very good, but I'm sure you must have still been there. I don't understand why they never found you. I thought something bad must have happened; that you had been carted away, maybe picked up by some rapists or druggies. When there had been no word by the time Stephen arrived, I thought you were probably at the bottom of the river or dumped somewhere that no one would ever find you. I'm so sorry my dear that I wasn't able to try harder to find you."

"Don't be silly; you did more than you should have with the condition of your legs. I don't know how you managed to drag yourself anywhere, never mind taking me with you.

Nefertiti found me and kept at me to get up. She would growl and bite me. I kept pushing her away for the longest time. It finally seemed like it would be easier to go with her than to keep fighting her. I think I had been there a couple of days, but I don't really know. I was so weak I could barely walk, but Nefertiti kept nipping at me. Whenever she thought I had done well, she would rub against me. But it was the growling and biting that kept me going. She was very determined.

We got to the hotel and I smuggled her in under my cape. The desk clerk didn't want me in there, I was such a mess, but I told him I would only be there long enough to clean up and pack. He hadn't been paid, so he had no choice but to let me in. I packed up the stuff in our room and had a shower, and then I went and got a key for Mom and Dad's room. I packed up their stuff as well. I ended up falling asleep on their bed. I guess it was the next day when I woke up again. I called the airlines and got us on the next flight out. I don't know why Nefertiti was allowed on the plane with no papers, but the Gods must have been watching out for me that day.

I went home and dropped everything off, made some arrangements for the house, packed a few things, called Dad's lawyer, bought the truck and headed out. I had no idea where we were going; I just kept driving. We would stop to eat and sleep, but that was it, until we got up here. Even then, I wandered around aimlessly for a while, before deciding I'd had enough traveling. I was talking to some people and they suggested that I might want to stake a claim, which is what I did. The building of the cabin kept me busy and it was a healing thing for me, to a point. Then in the summer months, I had the claim to work, wood to cut, my garden, it all helped, I guess."

"Ah Joly, you come from a strong family. You will always do well, even if you don't think so."

Morag's legs continued their struggle to return to normal and whenever Joly was outside, she had been trying to stand on her own. She had almost succeeded a time or two, but her legs were very weak.

The day arrived when Joly thought she was ready for the walker. It had been hidden outside in her little shed and was cold as ice. She walked over to the stove with it, not looking in Morag's direction. She set it down and turned around. "Happy Candlemas, Morag."

Morag's face was a mix of emotions. Joly watched as each one tried for supremacy. Shock, surprise, fear, hope, Morag's mouth opened and closed.

Joly laughed to ease the tension-filled room. "Morag, you look like a fish out of water. Say something."

Morag started crying. Joly rushed to her and hugged her. "Hey, hey, it's not that bad, is it?"

"My Gods child, you *are* full of surprises, aren't you? Where did that come from? Do you think I'm ready?" Morag was sniffling, the tears glistening on her cheeks.

"I bought it when we were in the city and yes, I do think you are ready for it. I don't expect you to grab hold of it and do the hundred yard dash or anything, but I think you're ready to take a step or two. Let it warm up a bit and then we'll give it a try, okay?" Morag nodded and went to blow her nose.

The three cats checked out the new contraption, unsure as to whether it would be an improvement over the wheels of the chair. The wheels on this thing were much smaller, but they would hurt just as much.

Some time later, Joly took the walker over to Morag. "Ready?"

She helped Morag into a standing position with Morag clutched onto the handles. The walker rolled forward and Joly grabbed it to steady it. "You have brakes here," she showed Morag. They were on the handles similar to bicycles brakes. Morag tried them; they held the walker as she tried to steady herself on her feet. She was standing, although she was hunched well over the handles trying to hold her weight up.

Joly clapped her hands in delight. "Yes, it won't be long and you *will* be ready for that hundred yard dash, I see that now."

Morag slowly released the brakes and the walker rolled ahead a couple of inches. Morag clamped down on the brakes again and determinedly shuffled one foot ahead, then the other. She did this several times, until she was by the table and then she unceremoniously dropped into the chair, breathing heavily.

Joly rushed over and hugged her. "Wow, you did just fantastic! I knew you were ready. How do you feel? Talk to me."

"Gods child, let me catch my breath," she panted. A few minutes later, Morag smiled. "Joly, I am so overwhelmed; I don't know what to say. I knew you could fix these ugly legs, but I never knew just how good it was going to feel to move somewhere without that damned chair. Thank you my dear, thank you so very much." She held her arms out to Joly and they hugged.

The snow had not yet started to melt, but the days were getting longer and there was a definite scent of spring in the air. The cats were venturing outside more during the day and Morag had bundled up and sat out in the fresh air for a short while.

She had mastered the walker with no problems and the wheelchair sat empty by the bed. Morag rarely sat in it now, hating the very sight of it. She decided to donate it to someone who needed one, when they went south.

Unbeknownst to Joly, Morag was walking without the walker, taking short steps whenever Joly was outside. She still shuffled, but her legs grew stronger everyday.

Joly had to make a trip to the nearby village to pick up supplies. Morag opted to stay home, ostensibly to have a nice supper ready, when Joly got back. In reality, she wanted to try walking for a longer period, without Joly around.

Salem and Nefertiti opted to make the trip with their Mistress and Pip decided to stay at the cabin.

The truck had barely driven down the rutted track, when Morag was up and toddling across the floor. "Pip dear, I'm not sure why you chose to stay with me. Just what would you do if I fell?" Pip said nothing, looking at her with knowing eyes. She laughed. "You are quite a creature little one, but I am glad to have the company."

For the next three hours Morag practiced picking up her feet as she walked, trying to rid herself of the shuffling gait. It was hard. Her muscles were still trying to mend and she knew she was pushing their limits, but she kept on. She was anxious to go across the ocean. She knew Joly felt some trepidation about the trip, but she did not. She wanted to know where her son's body was, as well as those of Morgana, Bettina and Raoul. She needed closure, as did Joly.

When Joly walked through the door, Morag was sitting reading. The smells of baking and cooking permeated the air. "Mmmm, it smells good in here. I have some news for you," she smiled.

"What kind of news?"

"There's a boy in the village, he had cancer and they had to remove his leg. His family makes too much money to qualify for a free wheelchair, but they can't afford to buy one. I thought you might like to give him yours."

"Oh how terrible! How old is he?"

"I'm not sure. I got the impression he was in his early teens."

"When can we go, dear?"

Joly chuckled, "Boy, you can't wait to get it out of here, can you?"

"No, I can't," Morag laughed. "I'm sorry for the boy, but I'm so glad the chair will have a new home."

They left the following morning. When they got to the village, Joly stopped at the store to get directions to the boy's home. A short drive later, they pulled up at a yellow house. Morag insisted she was going to the door, so Joly got the walker from the back and helped her out of the truck. She then lifted the wheelchair out and wheeled it to the door. They knocked and waited.

The door opened to reveal a small dark woman in jeans and a plaid shirt. "Yes?" she inquired, and then she saw the chair. Her face played through the emotions of hope and disappointment.

Morag spoke, "I understand you're in need of a wheelchair. I'd like to give you this one, as I have no need for it anymore."

The woman's face lit up. "Really? You're not kidding? Oh my God! I don't believe this. I don't know what to say."

She remembered her manners. "I'm sorry, please, won't you come in?" She stood back, while Joly lifted the chair in and Morag made her way in with the walker.

They were shown into a small, but tidy living room. They were offered coffee, but declined. The woman said her son was in the bedroom and asked if they would like to give him the chair personally? They agreed and made their way down a short hallway and into a bedroom.

The boy was lying on the bed staring at the ceiling. It was apparent he had been crying. Morag guessed his age to be around fourteen.

He looked at them as they entered, then turned his head away.

"Look Dustin, these ladies have brought you something."

Dustin never moved. Morag looked around the room and spotted several shelves filled with rocks and crystals. "Oh my, you have quite a collection here, don't you Dustin?"

Morag turned to his Mother and asked if she could have a few minutes alone with Dustin. The woman looked doubtful, but did not want to offend the giver of the wondrous gift. She and Joly returned to the living room.

For the next twenty minutes or so, all they could hear was the murmur of Morag's voice, when finally, they heard Dustin talking too. For another few minutes the two voices continued, and then there were the sounds of Morag saying goodbye. Dustin responded and Morag came down the hall and into the living room. She was smiling. "You have a lovely boy. I'm honored to have been able to spend some time with him. Thank you."

The woman shook her head. "No, 'tis I who should be thanking you. I still can't believe you're giving the wheelchair away with no strings attached."

"Ah, but you're wrong. There are strings attached."

The woman looked crestfallen. "What…?"

"Nothing too serious and definitely something you are able to do. I've already talked to Dustin about it and he's agreed. He said he is a candidate for a prosthesis and I asked that when he no longer has any use for the chair, that he pass it along to someone else who is in need."

"Oh yes" the woman smiled, "We certainly will do that." They moved to the door and said their goodbyes. As Morag eased her walker outside, a voice from the bedroom shouted, "Thank you."

Morag shouted back, "You're welcome."

They made their way to the truck and headed back home.

Joly was curious. "So what did you do in there? I couldn't believe it when I heard Dustin talking to you."

"Simple my dear. Dustin's Mother is trying to act as if nothing has changed. Dustin resents this, and has been bottling all of his emotions up inside. I just needed to draw him out, which I did by talking about something he was obviously interested in, his stone collection. He is going to make himself a medicine pouch to help overcome his negative feelings. I also suggested he do a smudging with cedar. He agreed. He is also going to make a dream pillow."

"The medicine pouch, it will contain snowflake obsidian?"

"Yes, as well as a piece of malachite, some St. John's Wort and whatever else he feels will help. He realizes he needs to talk to Mama also, and get her past the denial stage. They will do fine now."

"Morag, you are so awesome, you know that?"

"Common sense, my dear, nothing awesome about it at all."

Veronika was recharging her wards when Sergei arrived. He stood and watched her for a few minutes.

"*Babushka*, you're one of the special witches. What magic do you do?"

She looked at him. "Why?"

"Just curious. I never see you do anything special."

"Magic is serious business, not game. When I need to use, I use. Otherwise, leave it alone."

"But how do you learn if you don't practice different things?"

She thought about Russia. "I know what I can do. I don't need practice."

"Do the wards really work?"

"Have you ever surprised me when you come?"

He thought about it. "No, you always know. How do they work exactly?"

"They make invisible box; anyone comes inside it, I know."

"Even from the sky?"

"*Da*, even from the sky."

He nodded. "I'll be in my lab if you need me." He headed to the basement.

Veronika went out and placed her wards. She thought about their conversation and smiled. Practice? She looked around and spotted a piece of paper that had blown into her yard. *You want practice... I give you practice.* She pointed her finger and felt the power fill her. When it felt like she might explode, she released the energy. The electrical charge shot across the lawn and the paper burst in flame. She chuckled.

Morag was mobile enough that she wanted to spend some time in her own home. It had been many years since she had been alone and while she knew it would seem lonely at first, she knew she was ready. Joly would be just across the street and she would see her daily for the healing.

When they first discussed leaving, Pip was ecstatic. "Yes," she cried, "Yes, we're going back to the big house." She darted around the small room, bouncing off the furniture.

Salem too, was pleased they were leaving. He pictured the kitchen window and the sunshine beating through the glass. He lay on the bed contentedly purring.

Nefertiti, ever the worrier, sighed, thinking of the large house they would again need to protect. It might not be so bad this time, she finally decided, as the Mistress was now able to provide her own protection spells. Provided she remembered, that is. They might have to remind her, but that was no problem. And Miss Morag could certainly take care of herself. She knew that was one human that didn't need mollycoddling. She wondered if Salem might go and live with her, but decided it was unlikely. As much as he seemed to like her, he was always on the watch for the Mistress. Oh well, one could dream.

They packed with little fanfare and were ready to leave two days later. The trip south went well and their arrival in Mission coincided with Ostara, or the spring equinox, which pleased them both. It meant not only the beginning of summer and new growth, but it was also a new beginning for the two of them.

Hesitant to bother Mrs. Ardell again, Joly found a pay phone and made the call to have her phone hooked up. She also called Mr. McNabb and let him know she was back. With Morag's blessing, she made a third call. She reached Stephen at his office. When the receptionist balked at putting Joly through, she mentioned his Mother, which brought a flurry of activity and momentarily, his voice boomed in her ear.

"Yes? Who is this? What do you know about my Mother?"

"And a good afternoon to you too, Stephen. This is your sister-in-law, Joly. Your Mother is at my house." She got no further.

"*Joly?* Joly is dead! What the hell is going on? Who *is* this? What have you done with my Mother?" You're in serious trouble, you know. You can't just kidnap someone and think to get away with it."

"Stephen, shut up!" Joly had been prepared for a blast, but this was ridiculous. "I did not kidnap your Mother. She wants to see you by the way, if you would quit yelling long enough for me to tell you."

"*What?* Where is she? She had better be in good shape, or I'll have you..."

"Stephen, she's walking, do you hear me? She's walking, so quit threatening me. All I did was help her to walk again. That's all she ever wanted and you know it."

Stephen knew a trick was being played on him. There was no way on God's green earth that his Mother could ever walk again and that was a fact, but he decided to back off a bit. He didn't know what this girl was up to, but he sure as hell didn't want her disappearing with his Mother again.

"Sorry," he said gruffly, "This has been a very difficult time for me. Where is my Mother, please?"

"She's at my house. You know… across the street from hers in Mission."

This female was playing her part to the hilt. What the hell did she want? He decided to play along.

"Yes, and what would you like me to do?"

"Your Mother would like you to come out and let her into her house, Stephen. I think she would also like to see you. When can you come?"

It was an obvious setup. Well, he wasn't buying. "Fine, I'll be there in ninety minutes."

"Great, I'll let her know. Bye."

Stephen immediately called the police and let told them some kind of shake down was in the works. He asked them to meet him at his Mother's house and not do anything until he got there. He rushed out of his office telling the receptionist he would be back later. He drove like a maniac to his old hometown, dreading what he might find when he got there. He made the left hand turn and hit a red light. *Gods teeth, is there no justice?* He tapped impatiently on the steering wheel while he waited for the green light, and then burned rubber going through it.

Joly replaced the receiver, feeling drained. Gods, how did Morag handle the pompous ass? She walked back to the truck and drove home.

The coastal weather was a real change for them all and the five of them contentedly sat outside. Spring had arrived in all its glory in this part of the world. The sun was brilliant and warm. Flowers were in bloom. It was heaven compared to what they had left behind.

Salem was finally able to check out the back yard, as was Pip. Nefertiti chose to stay near the Mistress.

They noticed a couple of police cars drive by, but neither thought anything about it. They heard the tires squeal as the car turned at the corner. The Porsche screeched to a stop across the street and directly behind it were two police vehicles.

Morag shook her head as she leaned on the walker to stand.

"Damn fool boy," she muttered as she walked toward the road.

Stephen was out of his car and looking around when he saw her coming toward him. She looked good, younger. She wasn't walking unaided, but by God, she really was walking. He ran to her and without any thought, he grabbed her and gave her a bear hug. "Mother, oh God, Mother, you have no idea how glad I am to see you."

"I'm glad to see you too, Stephen, but perhaps you'd like to tell these nice policemen they're really not needed here."

As Stephen glanced around, he spotted her. *By God, it is Joly.* She was older, and she was gorgeous. *What the hell?*

"Mother, I would like to know what's going on."

"And I'll tell you Son, but not out here in the middle of the street. Perhaps you would be kind enough to let me in my house. I've been away far too long and I would dearly love to see it again."

Stephen went and talked to the police, told them it was a mistake and that he would be by the station later to explain.

Morag told Joly she would see her later. They agreed to have supper together, and then they would go shopping for groceries. They hugged and Joly watched through teary eyes as her friend finally walked through the door of the home she had missed for so many years.

The knock on the door startled her. Joly wasn't expecting Morag for another hour. She smiled as she opened the door. Stephen was standing there.

Gods! It was like looking at Broderick. She could see why Morag had been so in love with him. He stood easily at six feet, if not taller and he was extremely good looking. She idly wondered if he had a good marriage.

"Hi Stephen."

"Joly." He paused, wondering what to say. "You look good."

She smiled. "Not too bad for a dead person, eh?"

Stephen turned red and she laughed. "Come in, I'm sorry, I shouldn't tease you. You've had an awful shock." She stepped back.

"Uh... to say the least. What you did with Mother, I don't know what to say. She looks great. She said she could be healed. I didn't believe her. Stupid, I know."

"We witches can do marvelous things sometimes. I'm just glad I was able to help her."

"Yes, well... I just wanted to thank you, and to apologize. I wasn't very nice on the phone. I'm sorry."

"No you weren't. I'm glad I'm not an opponent of yours. You'd gobble me up and spit me out without giving it a second thought, wouldn't you?"

"Uh... yes, well... Mother said I need to come down off my high horse. I think after today, I may need to do some reflecting, make some changes. Uh... I guess I can see now that everything isn't always black and white."

"Good. Your Mother would be pleased to hear you say that. And yes, I will accept your apology, but please, the next time someone wants to tell you something, hear them out before you start spitting nails at them."

"No guarantees, but I'll try. I'll go now. I just wanted to say thank you. I know I don't show it, but I do love her, you know."

"I know, Stephen, she loves you too."

He turned and opened the door. "Uh... guess I'll see you sometime. You take care. Goodbye."

"Bye now." She shut the door and turned thoughtfully to the box she had been unpacking.

Stephen climbed in the car and started it. God, he felt like a fool. Stuttering? What was wrong with him? Christ, he couldn't remember ever stumbling over his words. Joly must think him to be some kind of idiot, and he didn't blame her.

The following two weeks brought about changes in everyone's lives. Joly learned to be alone with her thoughts again. She still saw Morag every morning and every couple of days they would eat together. She had cleaned her home from top to bottom and decided to paint some of the rooms. They didn't really need it, but she had far too much time on her hands.

Morag was on her own for the first time in over nine years. As much as she loved it, she found she missed hearing the movements of another person, the conversation and camaraderie. She even missed the cats. The coast was having one of their renowned springs and the weather had been beautiful. Morag spent most of her days out in the back yard. She never used the walker in the house anymore, but she took it outside, just in case.

Stephen came out to the valley every three or four days to visit her. He bought her two canes, thinking she might find them easier to use around the house. He discovered his business was still running fine, even though he wasn't there quite as often. He found his Mother was actually an interesting person to talk with. He didn't often see Joly, but whenever he did, he'd find himself stuttering again.

Morag watched the interplay between her two favorite people and wondered about the future of both.

Joly took Morag shopping and she bought so many clothes, Joly threatened to go and rent a moving van. Morag delighted in being able to try clothing on, and she bought so many skirts that Joly swore she would never be able to wear them all. She finally could fit into sandals and bought them in every color available. She vowed that no matter how cold it got, she would never wear another pair of sweat pants.

The birds discovered Morag was home and her yard was filled with the sounds of singing and chirping. Morag spent hours outside, feeding and talking to them. She would sit with a glass of iced tea and think how wonderful it all would be, if it didn't have to end.

But of course it did have to, and sooner than she had thought. She was only half listening to the news one evening, when something caught her ear about the land dying. Her attention turned to what was being said. There was an area of forest in which everything was dying or dead. The horticulturists and land management people were baffled. No one had been able to figure out what was causing it. There were no beetle infestations, the soil had been tested and was fine. The location was east, about three hours away. Morag thought it sounded suspiciously like something unnatural was causing it.

She got out her crystal ball and had a look. The area was quite large, it looked to be about ten acres, and it definitely was not caused by man. She phoned Joly and told her they had to go.

They took the next day to prepare and left the following morning. They reached the road nearest the area around lunchtime. Joly parked the truck and they donned backpacks filled with all the things they might need. Morag was using her canes, and with Joly walking in front, they slowly progressed through the thickly treed area. The three cats fanned out and walked with them, one on each side, with Nefertiti leading the way. What they were looking for was about a kilometer in, but it took them over an hour to reach it. They knew they were near when they heard Nefertiti let out a loud growl.

It was a very eerie thing to be walking along, seeing and hearing the birds, the evergreens looking healthy, the deciduous trees with their new spring coats, and patches of low growing greenery, when suddenly it was as if they were transported to another world.

They came through a thick stand of trees and there was absolute stillness and silence. The aspens and willows were leafless, their trunks turning black. The evergreens were brown. There was no sign of anything growing; there were no birds, there was nothing.

Joly took two steps backwards into the trees and she could again hear the birds. Walking forward, it was as if an invisible wall separated one world from the other. Nefertiti had stopped on the green side of the invisible line, and she walked back and forth sniffing the ground and the air. Soon Salem and Pip were doing the same thing.

Morag knew why this piece of news hadn't been broadcast. No one would have believed it for starters, and there would have been pandemonium eventually, with the sightseers flocking to see the anomaly, the religious nuts forecasting the end of the world and the rest of the population running scared. It was caused by magic; of that there was no doubt. But what kind of magic, caused by whom and why? This was what they needed to find out.

Joly told Morag to rest. She would walk the perimeter to see if she could find anything. She called Salem and set off. Morag removed her backpack and slid down against a dead tree.

"Be careful, my dear."

Morag cleared her mind, breathed deeply and tried to sense if anything was in the vicinity. She sensed nothing. Opening the backpack, she removed her crystal ball and tried scrying. She waited for the mists to appear, but nothing happened. "What the…?"

She struggled to her feet and moved out of the dead zone. Again she held her crystal and waited. The mists appeared, receded and she searched, but all she saw was Joly, who was making her way around the edge. Salem was walking on the outside of the bewitched area, and every so often he would walk up to the invisible line sniffing and searching, then he'd resume walking, keeping pace with his Mistress.

Morag sat down again and leaned her head against the tree. She closed her eyes and sent her mind back through the years, searching for anything she might have knowledge on, that would help her with this.

Nefertiti was upset. Her coat was a mess, her Mistress had called Salem to go with her, they were in the middle of nowhere, she was hungry and Pip was whining. And to top it off, an invisible wall that humans could walk through, but felines could not.

Pip didn't understand the barrier. There was nothing there; why couldn't she get through it? Her Mistress was gone who knows where, Nefertiti had her hackles up over something as usual, and Miss Morag was resting. She decided to follow her Mistress and Salem.

Joly walked slowly, not wanting to miss anything, but when she arrived back at Morag's location an hour later, she was none the wiser. She had seen nothing, felt nothing.

Morag listened to her, and said, "I know it's a spell, a powerful one at that, but with nothing else to go on, I'm not really sure what our next move should be. It's hard to undo, when we don't know what's been done."

Salem rubbed up against her leg, and Joly absentmindedly reached down and patted him. This was not what he wanted; he needed to talk to her. He meowed and waited.

Joly looked around and spotted Nefertiti, who appeared to be glaring at Salem, but where was Pip? "Pip! Pip, come here." There was quiet while they all listened, but there was no answering meow. *"Pip!"*

Morag looked in the crystal, but couldn't see her. She suggested that the little cat would return. They had only to wait.

"Yes, I'm sure you're right. I don't understand her taking off like that. It's not like her. If she's going to start disappearing, I'll have to leave her at home. I'm going to go back in. We have another hour or so, before we need to leave. I'm going to head for the middle this time. Are you all right?"

"I'm fine dear. Take Nefertiti with you."

"Okay, come Nefertiti, let's go for a walk." Joly headed into the dead trees.

Nefertiti yowled!

Joly turned to see what the problem was. "Come on, silly. I know it's spooky, but there's nothing to hurt you."

Nefertiti tried again and let out another yowl. Joly walked back and squatted down in front of her. "Nefertiti, come." Again, she tried. Joly saw her nose flatten against the concealed barrier.

"Okay sweetie, I see the problem." She looked up. "Morag, it's not that the cats don't want to come through, they can't."

Morag struggled to her feet. When she saw what was happening, she looked up and around, "Alright, so we have a barrier that allows humans through, but not animals. Well, that's a step in the right direction. At least we've learned something. If we can't hear any sounds of birds on the other side, then I would think that this wall extends up and possibly has a roof over it." She paused, and looked around.

She bent down and picked up a small rock. She tossed it across to the dead side. "Okay, it only keeps animals out, not inert items. But why is the plant life dying?" Morag stepped across the hidden line. She walked around, checking the dead weeds and shrubs. She put her hand on an aspen and stood in deep thought, then she walked over and did the same with a fir tree.

She walked back to the green side and disappeared into the thick growth. Joly stepped over the line and could hear Morag talking in low tones. A few minutes later, she returned.

"Joly dear, go for your walk now. Please check for any dead animals or birds. I'll stay here with Nefertiti and Salem and watch for Pip."

"Alright." Joly turned and headed for the middle of the dead area. The growth was thick and the dried branches snapped and scratched as she made her way toward the center. She saw no sign that any wildlife had died although she could see deserted nests in the trees, and she found a spot under some fallen dead wood where some animal had lain. Farther along, she spotted a burrow and then she came to a clearing. She checked her watch. She had been walking for close to thirty minutes, so she was probably near the center.

She spent twenty minutes searching a meadow, but other than a flattened area in the middle of it, she found nothing. She called out, "Hello." Her voice did not echo, but died as it left her mouth. She continued on, heading into the brush on the far side. Some time later, as she was fighting her way through a particularly dense growth area, she thought she heard something. She paused, and wiped at the perspiration that was snaking its way down her brow. Standing still, she listened, but heard nothing.

Continuing on, her feet crunching dry twigs, she was trying to get around several fallen trees. She decided it would be easier to go over them, so pulled herself up on a large tree trunk. She was easing her way across them when again, she thought she heard something. She stopped and listened. There was nothing, just the sound of her heavy breathing. It was so quiet she could hear her heart beating. Looking around, she spotted an area that appeared to be thinner in density, so she headed that way. She was thankful she had worn her heavy hiking boots and thick jeans. Even so, she knew her legs were covered in scratches.

She made her way down to some lower deadfall, and could finally see the ground ahead. A few more steps and she was at the edge of the mess of fallen trees. She grabbed a handhold on either side and stepped down. Feeling with her foot for solid ground, she felt something squishy. She pulled her foot back and peered down.

Pip lay on her side and appeared lifeless. "*Pip! Oh no! Pip!* Hold on,

Sweetie, I'm coming." Joly stretched her leg and hit solid ground on the far side of the still animal. She clambered down and bent over the cat.

"Pip! Please Pip!" She was crying and couldn't see through her tears. She picked Pip up and sat heavily. She rested her head on Pip's body, letting her tears fall freely.

She felt the slightest movement and Pip let out a tiny sound. It was more a gasp, than a cry. Joly jumped to her feet and protecting the wee cat as best as she could, she started running toward the edge of the dead area. Having already walked it, she knew it was easier going, and she needed to get to an area where she had some room, so she could try to heal her little friend.

Joly crashed through the brush, the branches tearing at her hair and ripping across her face. She felt nothing but her fear.

She had been running blindly and she crossed the invisible line without realizing it. The sounds of birds singing finally penetrated her whirlwind of thoughts. Gasping, she crashed to the ground, holding Pip tightly against her. She knew she needed to control her breathing in order to concentrate. Joly placed Pip on her legs and stroked the soft fur, while she tried to pull herself together.

Pip gasped, and then she gasped again, drawing the badly needed fresh air into her small lungs. She turned her head, looked at her Mistress and gave a small squeak of thanks.

Joly wiped the tears from her eyes, and watched the transformation of the small animal going from almost dead, to very much alive. Ten minutes later, although still weak, Pip appeared to be back to normal.

Joly got to her feet and headed back to the perimeter of the dead territory, so she would have a guide to get back to Morag.

Morag was concerned. She had dozed off and awoke to find that Pip hadn't returned and neither had Joly. She picked up her crystal to see what was happening. She found the two of them together, sitting on the ground. Pip looked injured. Gods! What had happened out there? She cursed the being that had damaged her legs and kept her from being able to scramble through the brush.

She watched as the two of them made their way back toward her.

Nefertiti sensed their return before Salem and ran to meet them. "Pip!" "What happened?"

Salem caught up to her and not far behind, Morag stumbled through the bush. She had forgotten her canes and was grasping at branches to keep her balance.

"Gods, child! What happened?"

"I don't know, I don't know." She was glad to be back with everyone.

They returned to where the backpacks were and Joly and Morag sat down. Pip left Joly's arms and went to talk to the other two.

Joly and Morag watched the interaction between the three and Joly spoke. "I'll need to talk to Salem, but it will have to wait. It's getting late and we need to get out of here."

Morag agreed. They each had an apple and took a short rest.

Joly fed the cats and put water out for them. Pip appeared recovered from her ordeal, and Joly was anxious to find out what had happened.

They made their way to the truck. They were exhausted, so Joly drove to the nearby town of Kamloops, and got a motel room for the night. After settling in, and cleaning up her scratched face, Joly and Salem found a grocery store where she picked up a few things for their supper.

By the time she returned, Morag had showered and was sitting on the bed with Pip, who was curled up sleeping. Nefertiti was still grooming herself, trying unsuccessfully to get all the burrs and twigs out of her coat.

Joly showered while Morag dished up the barbecued chicken and salads. By the time she was finished, the cats had eaten their portion of chicken and were washing their faces.

Joly and Morag ate quietly, thinking about the days events. When they were finished, Morag cleaned up the mess while Joly went outside and grounded herself, in preparation to talk to Salem.

Back inside, she lay down on the floor, setting her chin in the palms of her hands. Salem joined her and they began the process of melding.

"Pip couldn't breathe, Mistress. There is no air in the box. She was looking for you and me. She found a way in, and then she couldn't breathe and she got mixed up. She knew she needed to get out, but she couldn't think clearly and couldn't figure out where the opening was. She said she heard you and tried to call, but she was weak and didn't know if you heard her."

"I heard Pip, Salem, but I didn't know it was her. I stopped a couple of times to listen, but it was quiet each time. You called it a box. What do you mean?"

"A box, Mistress, it's a box. It is closed in on all sides and has a top on it. I don't know where Pip entered it. I didn't see an opening when you and I walked around the edge. Pip said that's why everything is dying. There's no air at all in there. I tried to get your attention earlier, to tell you there was a solid wall that we couldn't get through, but you weren't paying attention. I know Nefertiti showed you, but I did try to tell you."

"I'm sorry, Salem; sometimes I don't pay attention when I should. Do you think Pip can find the opening again?"

"Pip doesn't want to go back, Mistress. She said if I walk against the barrier, I can find it for you."

"Alright. I don't know what we'll do with her, but I guess we'll figure something out. Thank you, Salem. Go in peace."

"You're welcome, Mistress."

Joly was drained. She had been tired before, now she was exhausted. She climbed to her feet and fell on the bed. She managed to give Morag a quick run down, before sleep claimed her.

Shelley Sawyer was mad. The trap hadn't worked like it was supposed to. All the bloody work had been for nothing. She needed to get rid of these two witches. She sensed they were staying near by and knew they'd go back the next day. She wracked her brain, wondering what she'd done wrong. She had tested the box on her brother and damn near killed him. She was glad she'd thought to leave a small exit hole. It should have worked the same for these two.

A witch is a witch, right? They're Sisters... does that make a difference?

Morning arrived before anyone was ready for it. They were still tired from the events of the day before and by the time they got mobile, it was close to eleven.

Morag and Joly now knew what the problem with the land was, but they still didn't know why. A spell had been cast that allowed humans through the area, but there was no air for the wildlife or vegetation. They needed to find the opening Pip had discovered. They needed to know if it might be a weak point in the spell. If it was, they would start there with trying to undo it. If it wasn't, then they would have to try something else.

The weather remained sunny and warm, with a few clouds lazily drifting across the sky.

By one, they were at the bewitched location. Morag would wait until they found the opening to conserve her strength. She sat down by her tree again and looked down, smiling.

Pip had made the trip in Joly's backpack, and now she lay beside Morag. She did not intend to do any more wandering, nor did she plan on going anywhere near the opening to the void.

Joly set off with Nefertiti and Salem. Joly could not find the opening as she couldn't see the wall, so it was up to the two cats to find it. It was slow going as the felines took turns pressing against the wall. At times it was almost impossible, with tree trunks resting against it.

Joly was lost in thought when she saw Nefertiti lose her balance and fall in toward the dead area.

"Nefertiti, are you alright?"

Nefertiti took several steps inward, then turned around and headed back. Salem took a turn also, checking to see that he too, could enter.

Joly took a piece of rope from her pocket and tied it around the nearest tree for a reference point. Then kneeling at the invisible entrance, she picked up Salem and gently slid him along the wall, edging him closer to where she thought the opening was. Soon, the front part of his body edged inwards.

Then she slid him upwards, needing to know the height of the opening. She had only raised him about two feet off the ground when she felt the resistance. She slid him across the top about one foot, when he was stopped again.

Joly carefully marked both sides of the entrance with two more pieces of rope. Whoever had cast this spell wasn't very big, if they themselves used the opening. Her work done for the time being, the three of them headed back to Morag and Pip.

Morag watched the marking of the small hole through her crystal, so when Joly and the cats returned, there was no need for explanations.

They ate while discussing the reasons for the hole. Joly and Morag were crunching on raw vegetables and fruit, while the cats shared some tuna and dry food.

"There should be no need for a hole. Humans can walk through the wall."

"Could it have been made by something not human?" Joly asked.

"Not too likely. Animals aren't so stupid that they would block off their own land and if it were a demon or such, they wouldn't have made it so humans could walk through it. They would probably enjoy watching people crashing into an invisible wall. No, what we have here is this. Someone does not want to harm wildlife, and so however they manifested it, they did make sure the animals and birds got out. This same someone did not want people to discover the wall, and built it so people could walk through not sensing anything. I cannot guess why this has been done. Why would anyone want to kill off the vegetation? The wildlife that they obviously value needs the vegetation to survive. Possibly it's someone playing with their abilities, trying them out. It's all very strange, my dear."

"Getting back to the hole, do you think it could be a weak point?"

"I don't know. I'm hoping so, because if not, we are going to have a difficult time with so large an area. Alright dear, I think I'm ready to make the trip."

They packaged up the remains of their lunch and Joly helped Morag to her feet. Using her canes, Morag followed Joly into the trees, with the cats following closely behind.

When they got to the place, Morag quickly started her preparations. Being out in the middle of nowhere, it was tricky to have a purifying bath, but Morag had been in difficult situations before. She stripped down, while Joly opened two bottles of water. Joly dug in her backpack and brought out a small vial of mixed oils. She poured half into each of the bottles of water, and capped them, then gently shook them to mix the solution. Joly walked over to Morag, who stood back from their working area, and held the bottles up over Morag's shoulders. Joly slowly poured the water. Morag washed herself as it trickled down her body, while she centered and thought of the task ahead. When the bottles were empty, Joly stood back letting Morag begin the ritual.

Morag cast her circle half in and half out of the bewitched area. Leaning on a cane, she drew in the pentacle with her athame, along with various symbols. Then she took a black and red candle, which had been rubbed in rue and olive oil from Joly, along with a small container of incense and with the help of Salem, she centered them in the opening. She took four candles, green, red, blue and yellow and placed them in the four quarters. Then she took four white candles and placed them in between the colored ones.

While Morag was doing this, Joly opened a new bottle of spring water and poured it into a small wooden bowl. Then she opened a bag of sea salt and sprinkled it around the edge of the circle. Morag put the bag of salt and the bowl of water with the incense and two-colored candle in the center.

When Morag was satisfied that all was ready, she stepped into the circle and facing north, she raised her hands and spoke:

"I call upon you Gods and Goddesses of old,
I call upon you Gods and Goddesses of new.
I call upon the Four Quarters
For justice to be done.
I pledged to honor you in all ways,
I vowed to work for the good of all.
The universe maintains a balance.
The balance has been disrupted.
Sorcery and deviltry has caused a shift.
Help me to reverse the spell and heal this earth."

As Morag walked to the yellow candle of the east, Joly bent down, lit it and handed it to Morag. There was only a slight breeze, and she hoped the Gods would be with them. Joly continued around the circle lighting the white candles.

Holding it with both hands, Morag raised the candle to the east.

"I call upon the element of air
To bring your winds and blow these walls away."

She handed the candle to Joly who placed it back on the ground. They walked to the red candle of the south. Joly lit it and handed it to Morag.

"I call upon the element of fire
To light these walls and burn them to the ground."

She then walked to the blue candle of the west.

"I call upon the element of water
To bring the rain and wash these walls away."

Walking to the north Morag took the green candle and raised it, said:

"I call upon the element of earth
To shake these walls and bring them down."

Joly watched, spellbound. She thought she had never seen Morag look so magnificent. At one with the nature surrounding her, Morag seemed unaware of her nudity. She spoke beseechingly to the higher powers, as she padded barefoot around the circle.

She opened the invisible gate and Joly stepped outside the circle. She closed it again and continued.

Involved with the ritual, Joly didn't notice the three cats move under a large canopied tree. Nor did she notice the sky was no longer clear, that clouds were rushing in on a high wind.

Morag walked to the center and lit the bi-colored candle. Using the candle, she lit the charcoal that was mixed in with the incense. A thin trickle of smoke arose from the container.

Morag lifted the incense and walked to the edge of the circle where nothing was growing. She gently blew on the incense, walking from the left side of the circle to the right. Returning to the center, she held the container up high, and cried out,

"What was sent forth, I send back for them to see
By Air and the Law of Three."

Morag set the container down and lifted the candle, again walking the half circle on the barren side, and returning to the center.

"What was sent forth, I send back for them to see
By Fire and the Law of Three."

She set the candle down and picked up the bowl of water. Walking again from the left to the right, Morag dipped her fingers in the water and sprinkled it upon the ground. Back at the center, she called out,

"What was sent forth, I send back for them to see
By Water and the Law of Three."

Setting the bowl down, Morag lifted the salt and again walked the half circle, sprinkling the salt, then she went to the center, and cried out again,

"What was sent forth, I send back for them to see
By Earth and the Law of Three."

The wind was blowing harder and the flames on the candles were dancing in the breeze. Joly was holding her hair off her face when she finally realized the weather had changed. She sent a quick prayer to the Gods to hold off on any storms until they were done. She was amazed none of the candles had blown out.

The cats knew they were in for a soaking and weren't pleased. Pip was hoping she would get to ride inside the backpack again for the trip back to the truck.

Thunder crashed, and the three cats jumped.

Morag appeared unaware of the change in the weather. She moved with a steadiness and surety, as she continued trying to undo the evil that had been done to the land.

"With incense smoke and candle flame
Away from here, I send all bane.
With water pure and earthly salt
Let any harm come to naught.
What was sent must go back.
Three times light and three times black.
What they reap, they must sow

As above and so below."

Thunderclouds heaved their way across the sky and lightning flashed. The first drops of rain splattered to the ground. Joly watched, completely mesmerized by Morag's ritual.

"Earth and Air, Water and Fire,
Hear me! Reverse, by my desire!
I invoke the Law of Three
This is right, and it shall be."

Morag fell to her knees. She put her head down, picked up the bowl of salt, and poured it onto the earth, then took the bowl of water and poured it over the salt. She shook the smoldering incense over top and picked up the candle, blew it out and set it on top of the incense. She lifted her head and shouted,

"Energy spent for evil and bane
Go back now from whence you came!"

Morag stumbled to her feet, weaved a bit, and then regained her balance. She closed her circle, snuffed the colored candles and staggered over to Joly, who grabbed her and eased her to the ground. Joly got her clothing and in the relative dryness under the tree, helped to get Morag dressed.

She wished they had some hot tea. She knew Morag was chilled and it was a long walk back to the truck. She looked over at her friend, who was resting her eyes. Joly had questions but knew they would have to wait.

The sky opened up and the rain came down in sheets. Thunder reared its head and roared as lightning stabbed at the earth. The wind swirled and cried, unable to decide what it wanted to do. A distant rumbling sounded, different from the thunder.

The cats huddled in close to stay dry, to provide warmth for Morag and to receive warmth in return. They heard the rumble and knew what it was. The earth started to tremble.

Joly sat up thinking she was imaging things. It couldn't be an earthquake, could it? The lightning was crackling overhead and they heard the whistling before it struck. One of the dead trees in the bewitched area burst into flame.

Morag abruptly sat up, watching with the rest. The rain came down in bucketfuls, the wind howled and the earth shook. The tree burned fast and the flames were immense. The spectacular show lasted less than five minutes and as fast as it had started, it ended.

The fire burned itself out, the wind quit blowing, the earth ceased quivering and the rain stopped. The clouds disappeared almost magically, and the sun reappeared.

Joly was stunned! She had seen many things when she was with her parents, but this was the most spectacular piece of magic she had ever been privileged to view. From the moment Morag had cast her circle to this instant, Joly knew she would never forget one thing about this day.

"Salem and Nefertiti, would you be so kind?" Morag smiled at them as she waved her hand toward the place where they could not go.

The two of them walked to where the invisible line was and gingerly, they both put a paw through the space where a wall had stood only minutes ago.

Walking forward, they sniffed the air and carefully checked everything.

"There Pip, see, it's alright now. No other animals will be in danger of having what happened to you, happening to them."

Pip responded with a purr.

When Morag had rested, they gathered everything together and began their retreat back to the truck. Joly decided they would stay one more night at the motel to give Morag time to recover. She had expended a lot of energy and the walk through the woods took a long time.

Even with the help of her canes, Morag had to stop every few feet and rest. Her legs felt like jelly and she couldn't wait to sit down. Morag knew she was holding the others up, but she couldn't help it. Her legs felt the same as the first day she had leaned over the walker and shuffled across the room of the small cabin. Eventually, they reached the truck and Joly had to lift Morag up onto the seat.

By the time they got to the highway, Morag was fast asleep. Back at the motel, Joly lifted Morag out and carried her to the bed. She never stirred. Joly covered her up and leaving Pip with Morag, she went to buy a few groceries for their evening meal and some fruit for the morning's breakfast. Morag continued to sleep through the evening. Joly and the cats ate and retired early.

They made it look so easy. What had taken her two days to build, they had undone in an hour. *I got the rough end of the pineapple on this one.* Shelley threw her shoe at the wall. She was up a gum tree and knew it. She decided to cut her losses and go home. She needed time to think and decide what to do next.

Morag awoke and wondered where she was. The events of the previous day came flooding back. They had been successful and when she got back home, she would thank the Gods and Goddesses properly. They would probably never know who had cast the spell in the woods, but it didn't matter. The evil had been undone and the animals and vegetation were safe.

She stretched and gingerly sat up, half expecting to be sore, but she felt no aches or pain. She headed to the washroom, had a shower and dressed. By the time she was finished, Joly was up.

"Hey, how are you feeling? You look great!"

Morag smiled. "Actually, I feel great. Sometimes, it feels just plain good to be alive and today is one of those days. I am starving though. Do we have something to eat?"

After a breakfast of fruit and cheese, they packed up their belongings and drove home. Morag was in a chatty mood and they shared lots of laughter.

Joly had painted all four bedrooms. She found it to be a cathartic experience painting her parents room. At first she had felt guilty moving anything on the dressers. Then, once things had been put away and the furniture was slid away from the walls, she began to feel more relaxed. Her Mother had painted the walls a strange shade of pinkish brown and the trim in sunshine yellow. The scatter rugs were a deeper shade of the pinkish brown. The bedspread, curtains, doilies and runners were all a soft lemony yellow. It was a cheerful room and Joly had always enjoyed going in there and talking to her Mother.

She had been undecided on the new colors and had taken dozens of paint chips home. She browsed the linen departments of several stores trying to get a feel of what she was after. She even thought about asking Morag for help, but decided this was something she had to do on her own. When it finally came to her what she wanted, it became an obsession to get the job done. The walls were painted a light cyan hue and everything else was done in darker tones of the same color. Joly had always loved greens of any shade and when the room was finished, she decided she was ready to make it hers.

She packed up all her parents' things and carted all the boxes to the basement. Then she sorted through what remained of her old possessions and packed up many of the things she had outgrown. Most of her things had been at the apartment where she and Duncan had lived. The few remaining items were moved into her new bedroom.

Morag was pleased to see Joly moving on with her life and decided Joly had the right idea. She didn't know if she was ready to tackle painting a room, but thought that with Stephen's assistance, she might be able to. The phone call did not go well.

"*What?* Are you insane Mother? Why do you think we have money? It's to hire people to do these things. Now I'll not hear another word on this. I'll find someone reliable and send him out to talk to you."

She decided not to argue with him, but when the painter arrived, she informed him she had changed her mind. Then she phoned Joly. "Hi dear, are you busy? I've decided you had a great idea with the painting and I thought I might do the same thing. Do you still have the color chips? Would you mind bringing them over? I'll put the kettle on for tea."

Morag's bedroom had been a combination of both her and Broderick. The walls were a dusty rose; the carpet and trim were grey. The bedspread was shades of dusty rose, grey and burgundy. There were splashes of burgundy in the doilies and runners.

Joly said the room was far too pale and told Morag she should be more adventurous with her color selection. Morag laughed, "Maybe purple with pink polka-dots?"

"Well, maybe not that adventurous," Joly replied, looking over the room in question. "Do you want a total make over, or are you going to keep some things the same?"

Morag thought of the many years of bliss that she had had with her soul mate. They had been like two peas in a pod and she remembered the fun they had when they decorated the room. If she listened carefully, she could still hear her Brody.

"Darlin', the room must be soft and romantic, like you. When I walk in here, I want to feel like I've arrived in Utopia. It must be colored with passion, but not be garish. You are not a prostitute. You are my lover."

She wiped a tear away. "I don't know. I suppose if I am redoing it, it should be totally redone, right?"

"Do you think you're ready for this kind of change? Maybe you should wait, or maybe start with a different room."

"Yes, maybe you're right. I think I'll paint Stephen's room instead. What do you say to pale pink and powder blue?" She laughed, picturing the look of horror on her son's face. "Well, I always did want a daughter, maybe I could pretend." She chuckled again.

Stephen had never liked color, and even as a child, his clothes were conservative. Over the years, his room was always painted varying shades of beige. The carpet was a medium brown. The curtains and bedspread were shades of beige and dark greens.

"Morag, you can have a blast painting this room. I don't think you have to paint it pink, I think anything other than brown will knock his socks off."

"Yes, you're right. Okay, this will be a guest room. I do have so much company." She laughed again, quite enjoying the thought of Stephen finding his old room redone. "Let me see…" She was sifting through the paint chips, dividing them into two piles. Then taking the one pile, she went through it again. "What do you think?" she asked as she held up two samples.

"Wow! I think it'll look great." The walls would be a pale yellow and the trim would be sky blue.

"Unfortunately, I'll need some help. I thought Stephen might, but…" she trailed off, knowing Joly would understand.

"No problem. When do you want to start?"

"Tomorrow too soon for you? Maybe we could pick up the paint today, and then I can spend the rest of the day clearing everything out."

"No, that's fine. Let me run home and grab my purse and keys."

The days passed quickly. Morag found a blue carpet she liked and Joly pulled up the old one. After the room was painted, the contractor came and laid it. They shopped for bedding and discovered a blue and yellow bed set at a big mall in Surrey.

Morag had managed to do a lot of the painting, and she knew she was almost ready to travel. Her ankles continued to slim down and she found some wide loafers she could slip her feet into. She was so excited; she had bought them in white, brown and black.

Joly's birthday arrived on May fifth, and Morag invited her and the three cats over for supper. Joly was surprised to see Stephen's car as they walked across the street. She was more surprised to find he was staying to eat with them.

It was a relaxed meal with lots of lively conversation. Joly discovered Stephen wasn't as stuffy as she had always pictured him, and that he was actually a good conversationalist.

After the meal, Morag brought out a cake topped with candles. Joly was overwhelmed, and more so when she discovered it was an ice cream cake; her all time favorite. Morag had ordered it and Stephen picked it up on his way out.

The biggest surprise was still to come when Morag and Stephen both presented Joly with gifts. She was curious to see what Stephen had gotten her, but she made herself wait and opened Morag's gift first. She hated ripping beautiful paper, so she slowly and carefully removed the tape and neatly folded the paper. It was a large box, but light. She knew it was clothing, but she wasn't prepared for what she saw when she removed the lid.

Morag had known Joly wouldn't have replaced the ritual robes from the disaster in England. She knew Joly had another set, but their group had always had two sets. She also knew Joly liked green, but she decided another color was called for; something that wouldn't remind her of that time.

Joly carefully lifted the gown out of the box. It was a rich rose color with a deep V neckline, which was decorated with embroidery. It had leg o' mutton sleeves, with inserts of embroidered arcane symbols and beading. The lower part of the sleeves ended in points over the back of the hand. The fitted bodice flared at the waist with a loosely gathered skirt. The silk lined cape was a deeper rose. Both were made of the softest jersey. Joly couldn't resist putting the dress against her face. Putting them back in the box, Joly went and gave Morag a hug. Her eyes were glistening and she was having trouble controlling her emotions. It had been ten years since she'd had a birthday celebration, and it was overwhelming.

She picked up the gift from Stephen and saw it had been professionally wrapped. She smiled. Again, she carefully unwrapped the paper she wanted so badly to shred. She was very curious!

Stephen was on tenterhooks waiting for Joly to open his gift. He had never been in a pagan shop before, but once inside, he found himself mesmerized with the array of items available. He had spotted the ideal gift almost immediately, but spent an hour browsing. Now, he held his breath.

When she opened the small box, she had trouble concealing her shock and dismay! Inside was a six-inch tall statue of the Goddess Bastet, in her cat form. Joly swallowed hard and forcing a smile of delight, went over to Stephen and gave him a hug.

Morag knew the second she saw what was in the box, that tears would be shed before the day was over. She had known Stephen was picking up a small gift, but she certainly hadn't expected it to be what it was. *Damn!* She should have asked him what he had gotten her, before Joly had come over.

The small party broke up shortly afterwards, with Joly promising to model the robes in the near future.

Stephen had seen something in her look, but was unsure what it was. After Joly was gone, Stephen asked his Mother if something was wrong.

"I think Joly was just overwhelmed with it all. It's been years since she had a birthday celebration."

At home, she burst into tears and threw herself on her bed. The cats had no idea what was wrong, so they cuddled in with her and hoped to be enlightened when this bout of tears was over.

The tears finally stopped falling and other than the occasional sob, the slender body on the bed lay still. The mind inside the body was anything but. It was filled with images of a birthday ten years before.

Her Mom and Dad had gone all out for her eighteenth birthday. The entire back yard had been decorated with streamers, balloons, candles protected by clear glass covers, ornamental balls and bells. The afternoon had been her friends' time. They had laughed and giggled and acted very silly; eaten chips and drank sodas until they were feeling ill.

With the arrival of the evening, their group had arrived with their own gifts and their own special celebration. Duncan kept his arms around her, never leaving her side. Every few minutes he would whisper in her ear, "Hey, Darlin', bet you can't guess what I got you?" Then he would chuckle. Joly elbowed him in the ribs after about the tenth time and Duncan just laughed louder.

The time arrived to open the gifts and Joly was determined to leave Duncan's until last. This didn't sit well with him and he kept up a running chatter of, "Mine next, mine next. Aww... come on, Darlin', open mine next." The others in the group laughed and teased the two of them, but they both took it in good fun.

She finally did get to Duncan's gift and she made sure to open it as slowly as possible, prolonging the agony for both of them. Duncan was almost sitting on her lap by this time, and was trying to hurry her along. She kept procrastinating until the entire group was urging her to hurry it up.

With the paper removed she opened the end of the long box. It was heavy and she was curious. Peering in the opening, all she could see was tissue.

"That's it then. There's just paper in here." And with that, she sat the box on the ground.

Duncan was beside himself. He grabbed the box and dumped it upside down in Joly's lap. Something very heavy, still wrapped in tissue, fell with a solidness onto her legs.

Duncan sat beaming, as she finally unwound the tissue. There were many gasps when the gift was finally revealed. It was an eighteen-inch tall statue of the Goddess Bastet in her cat form, complete with a solid gold collar, medallion, necklace and earring. The hieroglyphics had been meticulously painted around the base in gold paint. The eyes were so lifelike that they seemed to follow one as they moved from place to place.

She had thrown her arms around Duncan and almost knocked him out, when the statue connected with the back of his head. There was much good natured ribbing about what the statue would be used for once they were married.

The statue sat on her dresser and kept watch over her. It was the one unnecessary possession that made the trip to the far north and back again.

Joly finally moved on the bed. She turned over and looked at Bastet. With a final shudder, she arose and taking the small gift from Stephen, she sat it beside the large cat. She choked up a chuckle and said to no one in particular, "For two brothers who are nothing alike, they sure do have similar tastes."

A few days later, Morag broached the subject of travel with Joly, unsure of what reaction she would get. She had watched her while they were painting Stephen's room. Every so often, Joly disappeared down the hall, and Morag knew she was in Duncan's room. Neither had said anything and nothing had been said about Stephen's gift.

"Yes, I've been wondering when you would feel you were ready. I've renewed my passport and the cats have all had their shots. We're ready whenever you are." She spoke bravely, and if Morag hadn't known her so well, she would have thought Joly was prepared. But there was a quaver in her voice, and as slight as it was, Morag knew she was fighting her fear.

They bought their plane tickets and made reservations at a pet friendly hotel in London. Morag let Stephen know she was leaving and he offered to drive them to the airport. They packed and Joly contacted Mr. McNabb, letting him know she was leaving the country for two weeks. Would he please keep an eye on the house?

At the airport, Stephen surprised Joly with a hug. "I know you'll take care of Mother, but you need to take care of yourself too." He gave her a quick kiss on the forehead. After saying good-bye to his Mother, they passed through the scanner and waited to board the plane.

The flight was uneventful, with the exception of a comment made by Morag. Joly had laid her head back to rest her eyes. Morag had a magazine on her lap, but hadn't shown much interest in it, when she asked, "Joly, do you ever wish you'd been pregnant when we lost Duncan?"

Her head shot up. "*My Gods, Morag!* Where did that come from?"

"I don't know, I'd like to have had a Grandbaby, and it won't happen with Stephen. I was just curious."

"This may seem harsh, but no, I have never wished it. I was in no shape to look after myself, let alone a child."

"But don't you think you would have healed more quickly, if you'd had a distraction?"

"Morag, my love for Duncan was and is, all encompassing. I'm sure that given the chance, we would someday have had children, but we were young. We just wanted to be alone with each other. I'm not sorry I don't have his child. I don't think I could stand looking at a miniature of Duncan, knowing I could never again have the real thing. Now, if you don't mind, can we just drop it?"

"Of course Dear. I'm sorry. I was just curious."

With tears in her eyes, Joly patted Morag's hand. "Now you know."

In the baggage compartment, there were sounds of discontent.

"Why do we have to travel in here? It's scary." This came from a little black cat with several patches of fur missing as well as a piece of her left ear.

"Pip, you know why. Now quit being such a nitwit and go to sleep." Salem wondered at times, where he dredged up the patience to deal with everyone. Neffy was at the other end of the carrier, ignoring both of them. The Mistress had given her the option of having her own carrier, but Neffy knew that it would be more awkward for the Mistress, with two carriers, so she opted to travel in the big one. She had made it abundantly clear though, that he and Pip should remain at the other end.

Salem chuckled to himself, remembering the scene in the vet's office. Pip sure had given the doctor a run for his money. Salem didn't think there was one area of the office that Pip hadn't covered in her race to get away from the needle. The Mistress had been horrified, but even that hadn't slowed Pip down. Pip had destroyed the room, knocking everything over. Anything that was on the small counter had been sent flying including two bottles of liquid, which had broken on the floor.

He chuckled again, as he pictured the look on Neffy's face. She was as horrified as their Mistress. She had sat in the corner pretending she didn't even know Pip. When Pip had finally taken cover half under and half in behind her, she'd come to life. Neffy wasn't much of a scrapper, but boy oh boy, she had sure laid a licking on Pip. Pip ended up cowering under the Mistress' legs, which was the wrong place to go. The Mistress had scooped her up and unceremoniously placed her on the table. The doctor grabbed her by the scruff of the neck and slammed the needle home.

7. Demon Dogs and Odd Occurrences

Alexander Alexander was in his garden when he noticed someone watching him. He looked up and there was this dark pair looking at him. Alexander smiled widely recognizing the two and left his work to go to greet them.

"Rauna, my darling! What brings you to San Francisco?"

"Lexy dear," Rauna smiled.

Alexander bent over the fence to kiss Rauna.

"I need your help. You know I haven't cared much for demonology and all this Crowley thing, and I know you are an expert in the issue."

"Oh… you are in deep shit." Alexander laughed.

"Yes, I am… and it really isn't that funny, you know."

"Yes, I do know, but you have to let a girl laugh every now and then. It keeps me young."

"You Erisian, you." Rauna laughed at Alexander's mischievous grin.

"Besides, it's a sign of freedom to laugh when you are afraid instead of being afraid when you laugh…"

Alexander opened the gate to let Rauna in.

"That too," said Rauna.

Alexander Alexander was over 6' tall and had the most delightful Latin looks, dark velvet eyes, bronze skin and black curls. The usual pinks and blues he wore became him very nicely, but it was unusual even in San Francisco, to see a handsome man walk around in long skirts and a skimpy little top with silver coins. Every step he took was accompanied by the chime of silver bells of his anklets, bracelets and belly chains. Even his earrings had silver bells and coins to add to the music. Rauna looked very out of place in Alexander's garden. Alexander himself fitted perfectly in the tropical paradise, being like a huge bird of paradise

"No, I really am happy because you need my help. I have been waiting for that since we first met in the U.K."

"Oh… have you? Why?"

"Because… a girl needs to be needed…" His smile was a little sarcastic. "And I like to be needed by you."

"I see." Rauna's smile mirrored the sarcasms. "Good. I need you, Alexander."

"Good. Now, come in, dear, and have a cup of tea with me."

"Cup of tea, huh? I hope it's proper British tea and not some weird Californian blend."

Alexander burst into enormous laughter. "I have only weird Californian blends, darling! We *are* in California now, not in some cold, misty island."

"Oh, dear me now," said Rauna.

Alexander prepared a pot of red herbal tea, a blend of cinnamon, licorice root and hibiscus.

"I am happy to see you, dear. Now, tell Uncle Alexander it all."

"Uncle? Oh, too bad... I was planning to do things with you I don't do with my uncles... such a pity. But, sure, Uncle Alexander, if that's what you want." Rauna winked.

Alexander blushed and said, "Well... it's just a way to talk... don't take it too seriously, darling."

Rauna smiled and looked at Alexander for a while in silence, and then she continued.

"About eight months ago I noticed three huge black smoke pillars in the Other Dimension, and went to see what they were. I couldn't recognize anything, so I decided to come and see it in person. I met a couple of people on my way, and found out that we have a demon problem. Now, I don't know much of demons, Morag told me something, but it's still very blurry... I find it hard to believe in demons..."

"Well... they don't have any problems in believing in you, dear, and that makes it quite hard on you."

"Yes, I have noticed... I was attacked in Minnesota by a small angry one, and it was close. I didn't lose the fight... I was saved by a local witch. She just happened to be there and just happened to know what to do, which was my fortune. I am not used to being rescued by others, and I don't want to get used to it either, so I need to learn, and learn fast."

Alexander sipped his tea in silence for a moment.

"You say that we have a demon problem... I assume that by "we" you mean the world."

"Yes... I think I do."

"And you usually like to diminish any problems you have, so I assume this is serious."

"Yes, I believe it is so."

"So what is it exactly you want from me?"

"Your knowledge, dear Alexander. All you know about demons and demonic dimensions, how to fight them, how to drive them back, how to close the portals between worlds, how to recognize those things."

"And why don't you leave this to those who can do something about such things? Like this Maura you mentioned... I assume she knows more of demons than you do."

"Ah... you know me. If there's something you can do, why leave it to others?"

"Why indeed... maybe because it seems to be an American problem, as you are here – and you are not American?"

"It is not an American problem, but an international problem. All the people I have been discussing this with during my journey agree with me on this. I feel obligated. I started to solve this problem, so I have to finish this, otherwise I can't live with myself."

"That of course is an important point of view," Alexander said. "Are you hungry?"

"Uh... not particularly... but I think Crow might appreciate something to eat. Do you have meat?"

"Darling, this is California! And that is a crow. They are all-eaters, you know. It has to be satisfied with what I have."

"Oh, something weird vegan food – with avocado."

"Yes, of course."

Alexander started cooking. One could see he was very comfortable in the large kitchen and he made a show of impressing Rauna with his skills with the knife. Rauna had never been much interested in food or cooking, and wasn't paying much attention. Crow flew over to see what Alexander was doing, and was rewarded with a tasty little piece of this or that, as Alexander worked. When he was finished, he set a beautifully arranged plate in front of Rauna, and Rauna ate, not noticing what was on her plate.

Alexander was somewhat amused, as this part of Rauna never stopped amazing him – to him food was important, how could anyone ignore *food* – and part of him was a bit offended, as this usually affected all his female friends to no extent. But – the food was good, well made with superb ingredients, so he concentrated on enjoying his own portion and decided to be happy that Rauna was there instead.

After leaving the plane, clearing customs and retrieving their bags and the carrier, they took a taxi to their hotel. They checked in and settled in their suite. There was a large sitting room with sofas and chairs, a fireplace, a decorative dining table and chairs, an enclosed hutch that housed the television set and several small tables and sideboards with lamps or statuettes on them. There were also two bedrooms, as well as the bathroom.

The three cats were happy to be loose once again. Nefertiti found a spot on the wide windowsill and she lie down to watch the action on the street below. Salem stretched his legs and then went and curled up on a chair. Pip, as was customary, felt the need to check out every square inch of the rooms, which kept her occupied for some time.

Joly placed an order at the desk for a rental car. She had her international drivers' license, but was unsure how she would make out driving on the left side of the road from the right side of the car. She had requested a truck, but the rental place was unable to accommodate her, so she was also going to have to adapt to driving something low to the ground.

They were tired and needed time to adjust to the time difference of eight hours. They called room service for tea and a bite to eat, and then retired for the night.

Morag awoke early and climbed out of bed, padding into the sitting room, leaving Salem curled up on the bed. There was no sign of Joly yet, so she decided to check out the area. She retrieved her crystal ball from her suitcase and sat beside a window. Relaxed, she looked into the crystal, and watched the mists form and retreat.

They had brought no tools of the trade with them except for the crystal. They were here to search for the graves and then they would be flying home again.

Now that Morag had the use of her legs, she knew they needed to think about the evil that had been unleashed the previous year. She knew the *Sisters of the Triple Moon* were being called together. She didn't know when it had last happened. It was only for very strong, serious evil that the calling came.

Looking in the crystal, she toured the city and parts of the countryside. It was a beautiful day and she was looking forward to getting outside. She hoped they could clear up the mystery of the bodies quickly, and then maybe do a little sightseeing.

Just then Joly appeared, with Pip following on her heels. "Good morning! It looks marvelous outside."

"Yes, it does. Did you want to eat here, or go out?"

Joly looked at the cats and decided they should eat in the room. They ordered breakfast and Joly had a shower and dressed, and then Morag did the same. By that time their breakfast had arrived and they sat down to eat.

Afterward, they went down and Joly retrieved the keys for their car. They found it in the parking lot and Joly jumped in on the left side. Realizing her mistake, she got back out again and the two of them had a good laugh.

The cats weren't sure if they liked the extra room or not. Nefertiti liked the fact that she had more room to stretch out in the back window, but found it was harder to keep an eye on everything around them. Salem decided the back seat looked comfortable, but lonely. He preferred to stay in the front beside Morag. Pip explored all parts of the car and then returned to Joly's side.

"Where do you want to go first?" Joly asked, unfolding a city map she had picked up at the front desk.

"We need to find Colindale; I think he said it was off Edgware Road. He also mentioned the M1 highway. I should have gotten him to write it down."

"It's okay, I've found Edgware. I'll wait until we're closer, to refine the search." Joly pulled out and slowly headed into the traffic. "This could be tricky." She automatically wanted to head over to the right hand lane, but forced herself to think differently than normal. Before long, they were on the M1 and making good time.

When they got closer to where they were going, Joly pulled off the highway and parked to look at the map again. With a few wrong turns, she finally got them to Colindale and the library. She found a parking space and pulled in. Looking at the cats, she told them they were going to have to stay put.

Entering the library, they requested the papers they wanted and sat down to wait. "Are you sure that's all we need?" Joly wondered.

"Yes, I was still there on the first, so I'm sure there was no one else around. Stephen brought me back to the place on the seventh and there was no sign of anyone, so they had to have been moved somewhere in that time. That's still six days with many papers to go through. We'll be here awhile."

"Yes, I suppose you're right."

Eventually the papers arrived. They sat down at a long table and began sifting through them, looking for anything on unidentified bodies being found in the area where they had been.

Two hours later, Morag got up and stretched. "I'm going to go out for a bit of air. Do you want me to let the cats out?"

"No, I don't think so. They should be fine for awhile yet, but they might like to see a familiar face." Joly smiled and handed Morag the keys. "When you come back, I'll take a breather."

Joly finished the paper she had been going through and put it in the pile of read papers. Picking up the next one, she laid it in front of her and scanned the front page. Nothing. She opened it to the next page. Scanning both pages, she found nothing. She flipped to the next one. Nothing. Joly felt her eyes blurring and looked up and around the room. It was time for a break. She stood and stretched, looking to see if Morag was on her way back. There was no sign of her, so Joly sat down again and turned to the next page.

Morag returned and looked questionably at Joly. Joly shook her head. "My turn." She got up and went outside.

Morag reached for another paper and unfolded it in front of her. There it was, half way down the page. *Unidentified bodies found by two locals.* Morag read the article.

What the hell? There was a serious problem with it. One that she could not let Joly see while here. She checked the date and quickly checked the other papers for that day. There was one other mention of it. She grabbed the two papers and went to find the photocopy machine.

She was paying for the copies as Joly walked back in the door. Morag quickly threw them in her purse and went to meet her.

Joly looked at Morag's face and knew she had found it. There was something else though, but what it was, she couldn't tell. She turned and fell in step with Morag. As they walked through the doors, she asked, "It was there?"

"Yes, in two papers. Let's go back to the hotel, dear. I am in desperate need of a cup of tea, and a soft cushion for my backside."

The drive back to the hotel was filled with tension. Joly kept waiting for Morag to say something, but she remained quiet throughout the drive. Joly decided it was because of the finality of it all. She couldn't let herself think about that. She would never be able to see to drive.

Once they were back in their room and tea was ordered, Morag went to her room, softly closing the door. Joly started pacing, wondering what was wrong.

In her room, Morag sat on the edge of the bed and reread the two articles. *My Gods!* What was this going to do to Joly? She dreaded the thought, but knew she couldn't put it off any longer.

Entering the sitting room, she found Joly receiving the trolley with their tea and biscuits. Once the waiter was gone, Morag handed the articles to Joly, who had enough sense to sit down before reading.

A gruesome discovery was made yesterday, by two local men. Three bodies were found in a clearing two kilometers east of town. Two were female Caucasians and one was a male of Hispanic descent.

There was no identification found on any of them. They all appeared to be dressed in Halloween costumes.

One female is approximately thirty-five to forty years old, with long dark brown hair and green eyes. The other female is approximately thirty-five years old, with long light brown hair and blue eyes. The male is approximately forty years old, with medium length black hair and brown eyes.

No identification has been made and the investigation continues.

The article went on to describe the location where they were found, who found them, and said there were no visible signs for the cause of death. The other article said pretty much the same thing.

Joly read the article three times, before it finally sunk in; Duncan had not been found with the others.

"Morag, where's Duncan?" The question needed no answer, as Joly knew Morag was as in the dark as she was. "*Where is Duncan?*" Her voice rose.

Morag went over to Joly and sat beside her, putting her arms around her. "I don't know, dear, I just don't know."

Joly leapt to her feet. "What the hell, Morag, what's going on here?" She started pacing.

The three cats were all watching their Mistress closely, as was Morag.

"I want to go and see my Mother's grave. Can we do that?"

"Yes, of course dear. Would you like to take some flowers?"

"Yes… yes, that would be nice. Do you think they will be marked? I mean, how do we find them?"

"Well dear, I'm not sure, because we don't want to draw attention to ourselves, do we?"

They decided to wait until the following day. Joly went to her room, and a short time later Morag looked in to see Joly asleep with tears on her cheeks.

Morag got out her crystal ball and began scrying. She asked to be taken to the graveyard where the three were buried. The crystal did not fail her. As it zoomed in on the graveyard, Morag caught the name on the gates and filed it away in her memory.

It was a neat and tidy cemetery and not too big. They would be able to wander around freely. There was no house or records office in the vicinity that she could see. She backed away, and the crystal took her to the town. She had a quick look, deciding that it was a very quiet place, as she didn't even see anyone on the main street.

When Joly came out of the bedroom, she found Morag looking out the window.

"See anything interesting?"

"No, not really. It's just that the city is so busy, so vibrant. It's so different from Vancouver. Shall we go out for a walk?"

"Yes, I'd like that. Just let me wash the sleepy dust out of my eyes." Joly walked to the bathroom.

They spent two hours window shopping and sightseeing in the neighborhood of the hotel. It was a somber time, but the different scenery kept their minds somewhat occupied. When they got back to their room, they again ordered room service for their evening meal.

Neither of them was into watching television, so they said goodnight early, and were in bed by nine.

A short while later, Morag could hear the sounds of crying next door. She thought about going to Joly, but realized there was nothing she could do. She noticed Salem had gone with his mistress, and knew the three cats were doing as much as anyone could.

Joly cried herself to sleep, but it was not a peaceful sleep. She dreamed of Duncan, of his laughter and his kisses, of how beautifully he made love to her, of the last time she saw him as he tumbled to the ground, of how still he was. She tried to go to him, but she was bound to the place she was in and she could not move. She called his name over and over, but there was no reply.

When morning came and Joly awoke, she felt like she'd had no sleep at all. Salem was by her head and Pip was curled up by her stomach. She looked at the window where Nefertiti lay watching her. She had to smile. Who else had three guardians, such as she had?

"Good morning," she croaked. She cleared her throat and tried again. "Good morning." That was a little better. She crawled out of bed and digging some clean clothes out of the suitcase, she headed for the shower.

Morag heard Joly go to the bathroom and got up. She headed into Joly's room and spoke to the cats. "How is she?"

Morag watched the cocked heads and the nods and took it to mean she was as good as could be expected. "Good. Just so you know; we're going to her Mother's grave today. Don't expect it to be a good day."

Salem was the first to speak. "Why do humans punish themselves this way?" He was quite baffled.

Nefertiti responded, "Why do humans do so many strange things? It's the way they're made. We aren't here to question. We're here to support."

"I wasn't questioning, Neffy. I was simply wondering out loud. Sorry…"

Pip decided she wasn't going to get involved. She still looked awful from the last altercation. The Mistress had healed the wounds, but the fur would be awhile growing back. She got up and joined Morag in the sitting room.

Joly and Morag switched places and while Morag was showering, Joly ordered breakfast. She was desperate for a cup of tea and she knew the three little ones were probably starving.

After eating, they got ready to leave. On the way to the lobby, Joly asked Morag if she thought they could have some simple markers made for the graves. "Just something with their first names. I think they deserve that much."

"You're right of course, dear, but let's wait until we've been there first. We'll take some flowers for now and hope that we can find them."

They stopped along the way and purchased three bouquets of mixed flowers.

The day was overcast, but the rain was holding off. It didn't look promising, but Morag was hoping the Gods would be with them. Cemeteries weren't her favorite place to begin with, never mind having to search in a downpour. It wasn't that she was afraid of the dead, far from it. She just preferred to walk among the living.

Joly turned off the main highway and drove down a narrow paved road toward the town. It was early afternoon and the sky was still grey. Joly hoped it wouldn't rain. She needed closure on at least one part of her life. She didn't often admit it, but she did know it, and going to see where her Mother was buried seemed like a good time to be truthful, at least to herself.

They reached the town and Joly stopped. "How pretty!" she exclaimed. The town was picturesque with a square in the center. The grounds needed some attention, but it was still attractive. Morag was looking around. There was something not right here. There was still no sign of any people. It was quite eerie in a way. She pulled back on the road and slowly drove down the little town's main street.

Morag saw some faces peering out of windows. Well, at least it wasn't a ghost town. She noticed someone waving and waved back. Her senses weren't usually wrong, but maybe the feeling had to do with the graveyard.

They found the cemetery with no trouble. Joly parked and got out, holding the door open for the cats.

The three jumped out and Nefertiti immediately came to a halt. Her nose in the air, she sniffed frantically about. Hissing, she jumped up on the hood of the car and took another sniff.

Salem too, was checking out the air. There was definitely trouble nearby. "Do you smell it, Pip?"

"Yes!" Pip was poised to jump back in the car, when Joly shut the door.

Joly also sniffed. "I smell something, but I don't think it's a threat. What do you think it is Morag?"

"I don't know dear, but let's hurry." She headed toward the gate. Joly and the cats followed. Morag looked around, but felt nothing nearby. Whatever it was, was back in the town.

"Do you want to split up, you take one side, and I'll take the other?" Joly sensed Morag wanted to leave as quickly as possible. She knew she should too, but her Mother's remains were here. She understood that her Mother was not, that her earthly spirit was long gone to Summerland, but still, it was the closest she would ever be to her again, other than in her meditative state.

"Yes, good idea dear. I'll go this way; you take the left. Does anyone want to come with me?" She looked at the three cats.

Before anyone could speak or move, a voice came from beyond the trees, "What are yer doing 'ere? Don't yer know the dogs are loose? Are yer both crazy?" A figure showed itself in the shadows. "You 'ad better lock them cats away, if yer don't want them eaten fer an afternoon snack! What's the matter? Don't yer speak the English language?" The woman came out of the shadows.

Morag recognized her for what she was and stepped forward. "Merry Meet!" she spoke to the woman whose age was undetermined, due to the distance between them.

Joly took the hint, and stepped forward. "Merry Meet!"

The woman stopped and looked at them. "What would be the next festival?"

Morag and Joly answered in unison, "Beltane."

The woman stepped forward. "Merry Meet! Me name is Rhiannon."

"I'm Morag; this is my daughter-in-law, Joly. These are her three protectors, Nefertiti, Salem and Pip."

"And yer 'ave no need of a protector, Morag?" The woman approached them. She appeared to be in her mid twenties. She had long auburn hair that fell in soft waves over her shoulders. When she got close, her eyes were the feature that caught and held Morag. They were so pale; there was no color to speak of. The irises might have been light grey, but Morag couldn't tell.

"I haven't needed one for a long time, but sometimes things change."

"Dat is true. Now, I ask again, why are yer 'ere?"

Joly answered. "We've come a long way. Somewhere here, is my Mother and two of her friends. Perhaps you know the whereabouts of her grave. They would have been buried here almost ten years ago."

The woman looked startled. "Yer from America, or Canada?"

Joly answered, "We're Canadian, from British Columbia."

"Ahh… dat explains it then. Follow me." Rhiannon swung around and briskly walked between the rows, until she came to some invisible marker. Pointing, she explained, "The younger slag lays there, the older one there and the Spaniard is over there."

Joly walked to where her Mother's bones were buried. She looked down at the earth and then up to the sky. "I'm sorry Mom; I didn't mean to take so long to come." The tears came and the sobbing, at first quietly, and then loudly and unashamedly. "Momma, where's Duncan?" This ended in a wail.

Morag stepped back and Rhiannon followed. "There were four of them; the missing one was her husband and my son, Duncan."

"There were only three found. Could 'e 'ave been dragged away by animals?"

"I don't think so. I was there; I cleaned up the area. There were no drag marks, no blood. I was in a wheelchair. I couldn't stay. My other son took me there. He is not one of us. It was a difficult time."

"Ahh… dat explains the small wheel marks I clocked. I knew what I was seein'; knew what 'ad 'appened, but there was no fourth body. Now I know; I will clock what I can find aht fer yer. It was a long time ago. There may be nothin'…" she trailed off, looking back at Joly. "They must 'ave been young."

Morag looked over at Joly, "yes, she was eighteen, Duncan was twenty-one. They had been married three months."

Joly walked over to them. Tears streaked her face, but she seemed unaware of them. "Rhiannon, do you think we can put markers up, with their first names?"

"If yer give me their names, I will do dat fer yer. I 'ave come often, wonderin' what I was visitin'. It will be a relief fer me to know. Now, we really must leave. The dogs are loose. We don't want them to find us."

"The flowers! Wait!" Joly ran back to the car and reached in the back seat for the three bouquets. She grabbed them and ran back to her Mother's grave. Carefully she placed one on the sunken area, and then she walked over to Raoul's grave and did the same.

Morag had walked back, so Joly handed her the last bouquet. Morag took it and placed it on Bettina's grave. "We won the battle, Bettina. Wish you and Raoul had been there for the end."

Rhiannon led the way back toward the gate. They were talking about the markers, when suddenly Morag's head whipped around and at the same time Nefertiti let out a terrible scream. Salem and Pip's scream followed a second later. Rhiannon whirled around. "Run!" she yelled.

Out of the trees came a pack of about twenty dogs. They looked normal at first glance, but then the abnormalities showed themselves. The dogs ran quiet, but they seemed to be of a single thought. Their path was a straight one, directly to the three women.

The three women started running, but by the time they reached the gate, they knew they would never make it to the car. The dogs were almost upon them. Their chests were wet from the saliva that was dripping from their mouths and their eyes were glazed.

Rhiannon cried out, "Protect yer 'ead!" She threw herself on the ground, covering her head with her arms. Morag knew she could communicate with humans, but she had never been good with animals. Her passion had always been the birds. *The birds!* She could mentally call to any within hearing distance, but she knew there wasn't time for them to arrive. She too, lay down and covered her head, waiting for the first stab of pain and the tearing of her flesh. "Joly, get down and protect your head!"

Joly was stunned! *What's wrong with the dogs?* They looked like normal family pets. She saw a couple of huskies, a collie, two or three spaniels, a rottie, three or four terriers, half a dozen shepherds, several labs, both black and golden and even a poodle. *This is crazy!*

She knew this was the end... and then, the fear made itself known. The adrenalin started pumping its way through her body and she could feel the perspiration forming in little beads on her forehead. She knew she should follow the other two and throw herself to the ground, but she was frozen in place.

The sound came from inside her. A high-pitched squeal that was so intense, she wanted to scream, but she could not; she wanted to cover her ears to get away from it, but she could not, she wanted to run, but she could not.

The air around them grew cool, and then it became cold. The temperature dropped fast and she could see the frost forming on the dogs' wet coats. The saliva dripping from their mouths turned to ice. The dogs slowed, feeling the effects of a temperature that now hovered around minus forty Celsius.

Stop!

Where had that come from?

Stop! What are you doing? I said stop!

What the...?

The lead dog, a husky, hesitated and seemed unsure what to do.

I said stop! Why are you doing this?

The husky whined and came to a stop. The others followed suit. Most of them were now shivering.

Why are you doing this? Answer me! Now!

They were hurting us.

Who?

The humans. We didn't want to, but the whistling and screeching in the ears was too much. It drives us crazy. The humans would talk and it was like they were screaming. It hurt to listen to them. Our skin crawls like it's full of fleas. Our humans would pet us and it was like they were sticking us with pointed things. We can't stand it, so we have to get away from it. We bite and snap to try to tell them to back off, but it's not always enough. You can only take so much before you go crazy and attack.

How many people have you hurt?

I don't know.

Are there more of you?

Yes.

Go and round them up. Bring them to the town square. This has gone far enough.

Yes, Miss. They turned and ran back the way they had come.

Both Morag and Rhiannon were watching from the ground in amazement. As well, six large eyes were watching from the top of the car.

There was a coating of heavy frost covering everything and as Joly relaxed, as her heart slowed, the air again warmed, the frost melted, leaving a dew like dampness on the ground, the grass, and all that it had touched.

Joly was drained and she stumbled. She went down on one knee, drew a shaky breath, gathered her strength and pushed herself back upright. She managed to walk the remaining distance to the car, where she slid to the ground and leaned against a tire.

Rhiannon and Morag got to their feet, and shivering they followed Joly, both looking warily around.

"Wha… 'ow did she do dat?" Rhiannon asked incredulously.

"I'm not sure. She seems to have powers we never knew she had. I find that very interesting."

They reached the car and Joly.

"Dat was a pretty impressive piece of work, Joly. Thank yer."

"Uh… no problem. You're welcome. Morag, just what the hell was that?"

Morag laughed and it felt damn good. "Well dear, I would say that you just discovered another power."

"I'm not sure I want it."

"I can see where it might take some getting used to."

"Well, I have a meeting with these dogs, so I guess we best get going." Joly struggled to her feet.

"What?" Rhiannon couldn't take much more of this. She might be a witch, but she sure couldn't do that kind of magic. "A meetin'? Where?"

"Back at the town square, with the rest of the dogs. These fellows are rounding up the others." She said it so nonchalantly, that Morag chuckled.

"The town square, in front of all the people? Are yer *crazy*?"

"I don't live here. When I leave, these people will never see me again. It matters not what they think, as long as they get their pets back, right?"

"I can't go wiv yer. They already butchers at me funny. Give me the names and I will do the markers. If yer give me yer address, I will try to send yer a picture."

"That won't be necessary dear. We'll look in the crystal and see. Thank you so much." Morag took a notepad out of her purse and wrote the three names down, tore the page out and handed it to Rhiannon. "If you ever come to British Columbia, look us up. Just call my name and I'll hear you."

Rhiannon looked at her in disbelief.

Morag got into the car. Joly and the cats were already in and waiting. They waved at Rhiannon and drove back down the road toward the town.

Rhiannon stood there with her mouth hanging slightly open. "What the bloody 'ell *are* them crumpet?"

When they got back to the town, Joly parked the car telling the cats to wait. She looked at Morag, "Do you want to wait here too?"

"No, I'd like a cup of tea. Do you think there's a coffee shop open here?"

"I'll go and ask." Joly jumped out of the car and walked to the nearest store. She saw a hardware sign on it and walked inside. Seeing a woman at the till, she asked about a coffee shop.

The woman looked at her strangely and shook her head no. Joly thought about forcing an answer, but decided against it. These people were terrified of the dogs and now a stranger had come to town. It was probably a little much for these country folk. She turned and walked back outside.

Looking down the street, she saw a large pack of dogs at the square. Most of them seemed to be sitting in the rotunda. She walked back over to the car and told Morag there didn't seem to be anywhere she could get a cup of tea. They would stop at the first place they saw, when they were done here.

Morag nodded. "I'll wait here dear, unless you want me to come with you."

"No, I'll be fine. This will take a while."

Joly walked down the center of the street. She didn't want the dogs to think she was sneaking up on them. Out of the corner of her eye, she saw movement at a couple of windows. That was all right. Let the people watch. She wanted them to see that their dogs were going to be okay.

As she approached the square, a husky came to meet her. She thought it was the one she had talked with earlier. She looked around. There were a lot of dogs here. She thought maybe forty or fifty. She wondered about talking to them. She had never talked to any animals other than cats and she had always done a meld with the felines. She didn't understand how she had talked to the dogs. She decided it was the fear that made it possible. She wondered if she would be able to talk to them now.

She stopped to ground herself, to prepare, so she wouldn't be drained at the end of the session. She had a long drive back to the city. She opened her mind and allowed her thoughts to flow.

Greetings canines! Thank you for coming. I talked to some of you earlier. I would like to know when all this started. Do any of you know? She paused, wondering if they heard her. There was some whining, but none spoke. She took that as a positive sign and continued.

I want you to listen to me. You have masters, right? Masters who were good to you. Some of you had children to play with. This looks like a nice town. Most of you are probably very lucky to live here. You should be proud and happy, not hurting the ones you love and care for.

There were murmurs of assent.

This is what we will do. When you are done here, you will go back to your owners, docile and submissive. I don't know what all of you have done. Maybe some of you won't be welcome back. She paused, seeing movement over to her left.

It was Rhiannon, standing at the edge of the wood. *Those of you who are not accepted back into your homes; you will go to that woman over there.* They all turned to look. *She will accept you and take care of you.*

Now, I want you to come to me, one by one. I will heal you from this madness that takes over. Are you all here?

Yes.

Who will be first? This will not hurt. I would never do anything to cause you pain. You have all suffered enough.

I will. The husky approached Joly, afraid, but hopeful, his skin quivering in anticipation and his tail nervously tucked between his legs.

Joly knew her healing powers were strong, but she was so used to working with aids that for a moment, doubt crept into her mind. She had no tools, no candles, no stones. Shaking it off, she held her hands out in front of her and concentrated on receiving the power from the spirits. She could feel it enter through her crown chakra, flow down through her third eye, her throat and descend down to her heart. The power flowed into her hands, and throughout the rest of her body. She felt light as air, intangible, and she became one with the universe.

She leaned forward and put her hands on each side of the dog's head. Slowly, she ran her hands down his body, down each of his legs, under his belly and down his tail. She returned to his head and stroked all around it, paying special attention to the ears and she finished by moving her hands down his chest, pausing over his heart. She could feel the power flowing into the animal at her feet, and she could feel his heartbeat and she knew when he was healed. Joly stood and shook her hands, ridding them of the excess power that had accumulated.

You are healed. In the name of the Goddess Diana, protector of all animals, go in peace. She looked at the others. *Next.*

Another dog stepped forward. The healing continued until finally, the last dog was at her feet. When Joly had finished its healing, she stood and for the first time in over four hours, she turned and faced the street. She shook her hands one last time and sent a quiet thank you to her Goddess of healing.

The street was filled with the townspeople. There were some quiet murmurings, but mostly the people were silent. A few of the dogs were with their people, but most hung back.

"Listen to me. The dogs are okay now. They were filled with some sort of evil sickness. I have healed them. I have communicated with them. They are sorry for the grief they caused. They were in a lot of pain. When you touched them, it was like sticking a knife in them. You increased their pain. This is why they did what they did. They want to go back home, but they know not all of you will be forgiving. They understand this."

"I see some of you have already taken the first step in receiving your beloved dog back into your lives. Who else will do the same?'

No one moved. There were whispers amongst the people, but that was all.

"Oh come on! Surely there are more among you, who want their pets back?"

There was a flurry of movement in the crowd and a young voice cried, "Chip, I want my Chip."

Another voice filled with fright shouted, 'No, Melody, no!"

A young girl of about eight came running out of the group, toward the dogs. A collie ran to the girl and she wrapped her arms around the dog. The dog was licking her face. Right behind the girl was a woman, hurrying to catch up.

When the woman approached the girl and dog, the dog got on his belly and crawled to the woman. "Oh Chip, 'ow do I know I can trust yer?"

Joly spoke, "You can trust him. The evil that possessed them is no more. They *are* your pets again. Trust them."

Slowly, others came forward. Names were called and dogs everywhere were crawling on their bellies, or had their heads down and their tails tucked between their legs.

Joly's work was done here. She walked back to the car and got in. She laid her head on the steering wheel.

"You all right, dear?" Morag put her hand on Joly's shoulder. She could feel the power still radiating from beneath Joly's clothing and she was awed. This was power as she had never seen before.

"Yes, yes I'm fine. Let's go find that cup of tea." She raised her head, started the car and pulled out, driving slowly past all the people milling about in the street.

Some waved; others looked at her suspiciously. The dogs all wagged their tails. At the edge of the trees, Rhiannon stood with three dogs sitting beside her. She too, waved.

They left the town and headed back to the highway.

"Morag, can you tell me what happened back there... when it got cold?"

"I don't know too much about it dear. It's called cryokinesis. I have seen it in minor forms, where the temperature drops a few degrees, but I have never seen it drop like you made it drop today. It's my understanding that those with the power of cryokinesis, usually also have the reverse power of pyrokinesis. This can be either a strong or weak force."

"Pyro… as in fire?"

"That's right dear."

"My Gods! This is all too much to absorb right now. I need to eat and then I think I need to sleep on this. Maybe it won't look so scary tomorrow."

Morag smiled, and thought to herself that the scariness probably would not go away anytime soon. There was evil in the world, and she had a feeling this new discovery was going to be one of many.

By the time they reached the hotel it was getting late. They went up to their room and once again ordered room service. When their supper arrived, they ate quietly, both thinking about all that had transpired.

After they finished eating, Morag asked Joly what she would like to do the following day. They still had six days left, before their flight.

"Well, I suppose seeing as we're here, we should take in some sightseeing. There's a lot of history here. It would be nice to see some of it."

"Good! We'll do that then, and now I'm off to bed. It's been a rather taxing day. Goodnight dear." Morag headed to the bedroom.

"Goodnight Morag, sleep well."

Morning arrived with the sun shining brightly and the British people thankful for a beautiful day.

Morag and Joly were up early and after having breakfast, they headed down to the car with the three cats. Joly headed out of the city, deciding they would explore some of the countryside, while taking advantage of the sun.

They spent the next few days exploring castles and museums; they took a ferry over to the Isle of Wight, toured the Roman Baths and Shakespeare's birthplace. They checked out Piccadilly Circus, toured the Tower of London, looked at the Crown Jewels, and saw Anne Hathaway's Cottage.

On one of the days, they drove to Stropshire. They visited the Stiperstones, saw the Devil's Chair and Old Tom, and toured the ancient mines. They were told about some megaliths that were just southwest of where they were, so they headed in that direction.

They pulled into the parking lot and set out on foot. There were several places to visit. Their first stop was the Whetstones Cairn and the remains of a destroyed circle. Then they began walking over to Mitchell's Fold circle, also known as Medgel's Fold. Some said this was where King Arthur had pulled the sword out of the stone.

Joly was feeling strange and mentioned it to Morag.

"What do you mean, dear?"

"I'm not sure; I just feel odd, kind of lightheaded or something." They got to Mitchell's Fold and began examining the ancient circle.

Morag was looking at the view toward Wales, when she heard a strange sound behind her. She turned around to see Joly crumpled on the ground by the tall stone known as the petrified witch. Morag rushed over to her and propped her up against her lap. After a minute of moaning and tossing her head back and forth, Joly opened her eyes.

"My Gods, you gave me a fright child. Are you alright?"

Joly sat up, wrapping her hands around her ears. "I think so. I have this roaring in my ears, though. It sounds like a waterfall running through them."

Morag helped her to her feet and they headed toward the parking lot. As soon as they were away from Mitchell's Fold, Joly's ears cleared and she said she was fine.

"That was really weird. I want to try something." Joly turned around and headed back toward the petrified witch stone. As she neared it, the roaring started again in her ears. Joly backed off until it quit and she stood looking at the stone. She felt lightheaded, but stayed. She let herself be drawn into the feeling; she lost all sense of the world around her. Her mind whirled with color. It was like being on a merry go round. The colors whirled faster and faster. Joly's knees gave out, and she sank to the ground. She held her hands out toward the stone, willing it to talk to her.

There was no sense of time, no sense of place, no sense of being. There were just colors, whirling around at warp speed. Finally, the colors slowed and began to fade. They were replaced by a heavy mist and in the middle of it, was the Witch Stone. At the base of the rock, a figure sat. The distance was too great to see who it might be or what they were doing. The person was there for a long time, when finally they arose and walked toward Joly. The figure's features became clear and Joly saw it was a woman. Her clothing was dark and she wore a dark cloak. Her head was down, but when she approached the area where Joly stood, the woman raised her face and looked directly at her. Joly was stunned! It was like looking in a mirror. The woman was the spitting image of her.

Although the woman was looking at Joly, she showed no sign of actually seeing her. Joly gave the woman a full scan as she passed by. She noticed the crystal in the woman's hands, almost hidden under the cloak.

Everything went black; the silence was complete. Slowly, Joly returned to the present. Shaking her head gently she focused and saw Morag closely watching her.

Morag spoke first, "Well, I hope the trip was a good one."

"Uhh… yes, I suppose it was. It was actually quite strange." Joly struggled to her feet and taking Morag's arm, they walked back to the car.

They had one day left for touring and then it was back to Canada. It was another beautiful day, so they headed north to see Hadrian's Wall and some more of the diverse countryside.

There was much to see and they were in no real hurry. They had passed the turn off to York, when Morag stiffened.

"Joly, *stop, now!*" she ordered, her voice not sounding like her at all.

Joly looked at her, but couldn't see anything wrong. She pulled off to the side of the highway.

Morag got out and ran back several yards, stopping every few feet, looking around and appearing to listen. She wandered back and forth for several minutes with a strange look on her face.

Joly finally got out and walked back to where she was standing, looking around. "What is it, what's wrong?"

Morag looked at her daughter-in-law as if she had never seen her before. Her eyes were wild and her mouth was moving, but nothing was being said.

Joly was worried. "Morag?" She took Morag's arm, but Morag pulled away. Morag turned and walked away, heading down the road away from the car.

"Morag! Please, you're scaring me. What is it?" Joly followed her. She knew Morag had sensed something, but what, and why wouldn't she answer?

Morag kept searching. *He's here! I felt him! Why can't I find him now? Maybe I haven't gone far enough back.* She kept on walking, her senses wide open and her heart pounding. She felt a tugging on her arm.

"Morag... *please!* Talk to me."

Morag turned around, startled. She blinked a couple of times.

"Joly! What...?" she trailed off, with her memory finally finding its way back to the present. "Oh Gods, child, I am *so* sorry. I think I'm losing my mind." She looked around one more time and then grabbing Joly's hand, she started back to the car. "Let's go and see this wall, okay?"

The relaxed mood that had been with them previously had disappeared. Morag appeared to be deep in thought the rest of the day, and although she said the right things, Joly could tell her heart wasn't into sightseeing.

Driving back to London, as they approached the York area, Joly could sense Morag tensing up. She slowed down in case she had to stop again, but apparently whatever Morag had sensed the first time was no longer there.

They ate at a small restaurant just off the highway. Morag was still quiet and Joly left her to her thoughts.

It was late when they got to the hotel and when they got to their suite, Morag said goodnight and disappeared into her room, closing the door behind her.

Joly was concerned, as well as puzzled. She hoped Morag would be her old self, come morning.

"Well, we might as well tuck in, too." She headed for her room with the three cats following.

The next morning was a wet and dreary one. The rain that had held off all week had finally arrived.

Joly was up early after a restless night. She was worried about Morag. She went and showered, and then packed in preparation for the flight home.

Morag was up, but was still in her room. She had her crystal ball at the window and had searched the entire area around York, but found nothing.

She placed the crystal back on its stand and leaned back in the chair. Was she losing her mind? Did she want her son found that badly, that she was now imagining sensing him? Her senses had never failed her. Duncan had been there, she was sure of it. And if he was there, then he was alive. But that didn't make any sense either. If he had somehow survived the attack, he would have gone back home.

He had hated England, complaining from the time they had gotten off the plane. It had been cold and wet and Joly had teased him with an old nursery rhyme, changing the words and singing it with a phony British accent.

"Its ryning, it's pouring,
Duncan's going to be snoring.
'E'll bump his 'ead on the end of 'is bed
So 'e cawn't get up in the morning."

Morag smiled at the memory and stood. She needed to get ready. She was getting old, damn it. She had to have been imagining it. If he were there, she certainly would have found him, either by scrying or with her senses. So, what *had* she felt? That was the million dollar question.

She wouldn't be telling Joly about this. Joly would never leave England if she thought for a moment there was a chance Duncan was still alive.

Time to put on a happy face. She opened the door.

"Good morning, dear," Morag said cheerfully, as she went to the washroom.

Joly tried to read her face, but saw nothing. "Good morning," she replied. *Weird.* She shrugged. Morag was almost sixty. She was entitled to act odd on occasion, she supposed.

The rest of the morning passed quickly and before they knew it, it was time to head for the airport.

The cats weren't impressed with having to get back in the carrier, but they went without complaining. Salem and Pip were keeping the image of the large house they were returning to, foremost in their thoughts. Nefertiti was just glad that they were going home. She didn't like traveling and she certainly hadn't wanted to return here. She'd been right in her thinking too, with all the strange things that had happened. Thank the Gods; it was over!

8. Alyce and the Riddle

Stephen met them at the airport. He was quieter than usual and Morag asked him what was wrong.

"Nothing, Mother," he replied with a shortness that said to leave it alone.

But Morag wouldn't. "Well, something's wrong. You're not yourself."

"I have a lot on my mind. Work is pretty hectic now."

"Bull tweet!" Morag replied, "You forget who you're talking to."

Stephen glanced in the rear view mirror at Joly and then looked across at his Mother, wondering exactly what to say. It was a personal matter as far as he was concerned, but he knew his Mother. She wouldn't be happy until she had dragged it out of him. It wasn't that he didn't want to tell her, he just wasn't sure he wanted Joly to hear. At least not yet.

"Yes Mother, you're right of course, but it's nothing serious. Elise and I had words, but I'm sure we can work out the problem."

"Ahh… I see. Trouble on the home front. I wondered how long before it happened."

"You're making it sound worse than it is, Mother. It's nothing major."

"Of course it is, Stephen, or you wouldn't be worrying so. It was bound to happen sooner or later. I'm amazed you two lasted this long, but it's probably because you're never home."

The rest of the trip was completed in silence.

Jimmy Smith was looking for something. He wasn't sure what it was he had lost. He just knew he was missing something and needed to find it. He no longer asked people to help him search, because most just gave him a funny look.

He knew what they called him and he didn't like any of the names. Slow, dimwitted, idiot, retarded, mentally challenged, mentally handicapped, stupid, dumb. He didn't think he was any of those, but he guessed it was because he spoke really slow and sometimes, when he was excited, he would stutter. He also walked with a limp, slightly dragging one leg.

The doctor said he had been born that way, but he didn't remember being born. He thought the universe had opened its arms one day and gently deposited him on the earth. He didn't remember having a Mother or Father, which was another reason he was sure the universe had placed him there. He had tried to tell people this, but they laughed at him. He knew they lived on the planet earth, but he found it much easier to think in terms of the universe. He felt as one with the universe and he loved sitting out in the back yard at night, looking through his telescope. He knew all the stars and planets names and where in the sky to find them. The telescope had been a wonderful gift from the couple he lived with.

Hans and Gisela Werner had taken him in many years before, when he was very young. They had given him a small room in the back of their house. Hans ran a fix it shop, repairing anything from refrigerators to radios. Jimmy helped him whenever Hans got too busy or when tiny transistors needed soldering or chips needed to be replaced. Jimmy had long narrow fingers that would go into small places that Hans' pudgy fingers wouldn't fit. Jimmy was good with electronics and very careful with the work he did. Hans would pay him a little bit for the work, but he didn't need much money. He liked to go to the coffee shop every day and he would sit and have a soda or a hot chocolate, depending on the weather. Sometimes he would buy a new shirt or pants, but Gisela bought most of his clothes.

When Hans didn't need help, Jimmy would wander up and down the streets with an old shopping cart, picking up bottles for recycling. He always walked by the Hallett's house, hoping for a glimpse of Jenny Hallett. Jenny was married, but that was okay with Jimmy. He just liked to look at her. He thought she was the most beautiful woman in the universe, with her long dark hair and sparkling brown eyes. Jimmy thought that maybe he was in love with her, but he wasn't sure. Whenever Jimmy saw Jenny, he would speak to her and she was one of the ones who treated him like anyone else. She always smiled and spoke with him.

Jenny had three boys and one of them was named James. Jimmy liked it that the boy was called James and not Jimmy. He wished people would call him James, but no one ever did. When someone asked him his name, he would tell them it was James, but they would just call him Jimmy anyhow. He really liked the name James.

Gisela Werner was a big woman. Jimmy thought she must weigh eighty or ninety kilograms. She was all bosom and she loved to give hugs. Jimmy thought he was going to be smothered one day from one of her hugs.

Hans and Gisela had seven children, but Jimmy had never met any of them. They all lived far away in different parts of the world. Every year, the two of them would go away to visit one of their offspring, leaving Jimmy behind to look after the little house and the shop. Jimmy was very proud of the trust they placed in him. Jimmy was very good with numbers and Hans trusted him implicitly.

This particular day had been a special one for Jimmy. He had been at the edge of town, when he thought he had found what he was missing. He stepped forward to get it and it was gone. He couldn't even remember what it was that he thought he had seen. He had gone home and told Gisela. She had embraced him until he thought the end of his universe was about to happen.

Then Gisela told him of her news. Their daughter Traute was coming home for a visit. They would pick her up at the airport and they were going to take Jimmy with them. He had never been to the airport and thought this was great news.

Jimmy went to his room and sat on the edge of his small cot. He thought it was really strange that whatever he was missing had almost been found today. He had always known that it was missing, but this was the first time he had almost found it. He just didn't know how to go about finding it again. He wished he could remember what it was.

Jimmy's room was stark and bare. Gisela had told him he could decorate it anyway he wanted to, but he had never shown any interest in adding anything to it. He had purchased a small portable radio and it sat beside the bed. Jimmy never turned it off. At first, Gisela had gone in when Jimmy wasn't home and turned it off, but she finally decided that if he wanted it left on, who was she to question it. He asked for nothing from her or Hans, and it was turned so low that outside of the bedroom no one could hear it.

There was only one other purchase that was evident in his room. Jimmy had seen a picture frame in a store one day and he knew he had to have it. The frame sat on his dresser, empty. Jimmy would often stand in front of it, staring at it. Gisela found this to be such a sad thing and whenever she caught him looking at it, her heart would break for this man-child that she loved so dearly.

Jimmy was a towhead with blonde hair so pale; it looked white. He was a good-looking man, close to six feet tall, with a slender build. He had blue eyes and a smile that lit up his whole face. Jimmy never laughed, but he almost always, had a smile on his face. Jimmy didn't really know how to be unhappy. He could be hurt by the nasty things that were said about him, or he would be sad if he heard about someone hurting an animal but these bouts never lasted. Jimmy would be back to whistling in no time at all, very content with his small piece of the universe.

Gisela understood Jimmy and she knew what he was looking for. She just didn't know how to help him find it. She knew that others made fun of him and she hated the small mindedness of some people. There were others that knew what he had lost, but most people were so involved with their own lives, that they never thought much about Jimmy's problem.

Hans too, knew Jimmy had lost something, but he figured it was best if it was never found. Hans was glad they had him. Jimmy filled a void in Gisela's life. She wasn't happy unless she had someone to fuss over. She had been lost when the last of their children left home. When they had heard about Jimmy needing a permanent home, Hans had been doubtful about taking on the responsibility of a stranger, but Jimmy had proven his worth many times since then and Hans couldn't imagine life without Jimmy being a part of it.

Morag unpacked, started a load of laundry and headed out to her back yard to feed her birds. That done, she went and made a jug of iced tea with lemon, and then she picked up her crystal ball and went back outside.

With the birds singing and chirping, she began scrying. She wasn't sure what she was looking for, but her intuition said something needed to be looked into. With all the unrest in the world and the problem down south, she knew there would be many things showing up in the crystal, but she was after one thing. She would know it when she found it.

Morag was so in tune with her crystal that it never took much on her part to make it work. She browsed through different parts of the world without really even thinking about it. She saw so much unrest and devastation; she became disheartened. Resting the crystal in her lap, she leaned her head back on the lawn chair and closed her eyes. She would rest a minute and then go in to check the laundry.

Joly and the cats were happy to be home again. Joly went up to her bedroom and unpacked, taking an armful of dirty clothes to the basement.

Pip was racing through the house, happy to have the room to run again. Salem walked around checking that nothing had changed while they were away and then he went and sat in the kitchen window. Nefertiti also checked out the house and asked to be let outside so she could check out there also.

Joly had decided on the flight back that she needed to find something to occupy her time. She was only twenty-eight. She couldn't spend the rest of her life lying about the house waiting for a call to go and save the world, or at least a part of it. The only problem with this decision was that she had no idea what it was she wanted to do.

As a teenager, she had never thought past getting married to Duncan and having his babies. The nine years she had spent up north, she had never thought past the next day.

Her parents and Duncan had been her whole world. She was at a loss how to proceed. She knew she could go and talk to Morag, but she was another one whose life had revolved around her husband. She probably wouldn't know what to suggest, anyhow.

Joly felt the need to connect to her past. She went to the magic room and unlocking the door, she headed for her parents Book of Shadows. Sitting down, she opened the book.

The Charge of the Goddess graced the first page. Someone had done it up in a beautiful calligraphy script, and although Joly knew it by heart, she read it again. It had always moved her with its beauty.

Turning the page brought her Mother's handwriting into view. She could never understand why a woman who was so particular about her dress, her home and everything else, would have such atrocious handwriting. When she asked her about it, she had just laughed and said no one was perfect.

The first section was on the planets, the sun and moon, the lunar phases, planetary hours and colors, cardinal points, esbats, planetary trees, planetary herbs and planetary numbers. Joly moved on to the next section, skimming most of the first one as she had the majority of it memorized. Section two was on the elements, their correspondences and meanings.

Suddenly she had a thought. She quickly flipped through the book until she found the section she wanted. What had Morag called it? Cryo something. She scanned the pages looking for the word. She found something else instead.

The handwriting was not familiar at all. She had never seen it before in all the times she had looked through the book. It was a very large book, so that wasn't too surprising, but just the same it was odd.

The paper was protected by a clear plastic sleeve, but Joly could tell it was very old. There were crease marks throughout the page, which she could picture her Mother ironing with care. It was a small piece of paper, only about six inches by four inches. The edges were ragged and it was hard to read as the spelling was very strange.

My cystale dyd shewe me that a wytch bye the name of Morgana shal haue a gyrle childe. This childe shal bee borne in a countrey far from heere. The stars saye shee will bee borne at the fyfth houre and the fyfty seventh minute of the sixeth daye of the fyfth monthe of the Cymreig Nos Galon Mai. This childe will haue mightie power and shee will fight much eville. Shee shal bee known as a Syster of the Tryple Moone. So say I and so it shal bee.

Alyce Gryffyd   1632

What? Gryffyd? Wasn't that the spelling of Griffith years ago? Joly was having trouble grasping it. Griffith was her Mother's family name. Re-reading the article, she shook her head. *She shall be known as a Sister of the Triple Moon.* Was it talking about her? That wasn't quite her birth date, she had been born on the fifth of May, not the sixth. What on earth was Cymreig Nos Galon Mai? *I need Morag!*

Joly ran across the street and rang the bell. She waited a minute, then skipped down the steps and headed around to the back of the house. Opening the gate and closing it behind her, she walked along the stepping stones to the back yard. She had to smile when she came around the corner and saw Morag sleeping in her chair. Joly spotted the crystal ball in her lap, and knew she had better not startle her.

Morag opened her eyes and looked at Joly. "Thought you could sneak up on me, didn't you? You should know better than that. How many times did you and Duncan try that trick? It never worked then and it surely won't work now." She smiled and groaned as she got to her feet. "Stiffened up, sitting here. Guess I need to get mobile."

"Can you come over to my place? There's something in Mom's book I need you to see."

Joly looked odd, something seemed to have shaken her up. "Let's go," she replied.

Joly led Morag to the book. "Did you ever see this; did Mom ever show it to you?"

Morag read the ancient script carefully and then read it again. "No dear, I've never seen this before. It's incredible! My Gods, child, do you realize that your birth was foretold over three hundred years ago?" Morag was overwhelmed. To actually see something like this was a moment to savor. She had heard there were documents like this kicking around, but she had *never* expected to see one. She feasted her eyes on the handwriting again.

"Morag, what's Cymreig Nos Galon Mai?"

"Cymreig Nos Galon Mai? Let's see. Mai is the month of May. Cymreig Nos Galon…? I know that, I think. Just give me a second." She searched her memory, pictures and script running through her mind like a movie. Cymreig? Cymreig? A language… a country… Cym… wait! Cymru was Wales, so Cymreig would be… Welsh. Nos Galon? A Welsh something… yes! Beltane, that's what it meant. She had learned that when she was young, learning the Sabbats and the different words people used for them.

"Cymreig Nos Galon Mai is Welsh dear, for Beltane. Well, not literally. The Welsh don't actually celebrate Beltane. The Scots and the Irish do. Beltane is celebrated on the eve of May first. Nos Galon Mai is usually celebrated on May fifth, or whichever day the sun and… I believe it's Taurus, meet at something like fifteen degrees. Occasionally that happens on the fourth or the sixth, but not usually. It's one of the main Welsh festivals, celebrating the love and marriage between the Sun God and the Moon Goddess. This is when they mate and conceive the spring for the following year. If I recall my history right, there are a couple of other things also happening on that day. One I think is a yearly battle between a God and a mortal over a woman."

"Anyways, what this is saying is that at the exact moment of the beginning of spring, which must have occurred at five fifty-seven, a girl child would be born who would be known as a Sister of the Triple Moon. Do you know what time you were born?"

"Umm… Mom did tell me, I thought it was around eight, though, not five or six. It's written down somewhere. I know it was in the morning, but I was born on the fifth, not the sixth."

"Hmm… look at what it says, Joly. It says that *the stars say* she will be born at five fifty-seven. This is obviously in astral time. If we were to compare this time, with that of your actual time of birth, they probably are one and the same. If you can find me your birth time, I will do up the charts for comparison."

Morag shook her head, still looking at the writing, "This Alyce was obviously a powerful scryer. When you think back to how things were three hundred years ago, most people were illiterate, and also extremely superstitious. Alyce must have wondered at first, what she was seeing. The message must have been very strong for her to write it down. Remember that back then witches were not popular, and to be found with this piece of paper, it would surely have meant death for her."

"It's really interesting that the writing is in English but she refers to the day in Welsh. I wonder why. Wasn't Morgana's ancestry Welsh?"

"Yes, both sides of her family were."

"I wonder how your Mother came by this."

"I don't know. I've never seen it before. I was about to look up that cryo thing, when I came across it."

Morag laughed. "Cryokinesis my dear and I'm not sure that Morgana would have anything about it in her Book. It's not something that a lot of people are too interested in. It would probably be classed as more of a parlor game than anything. Sort of like... oh, is your drink getting warm, here, let me cool it off for you, as the person holds the glass and drops the temperature of the contents a degree or two."

"And the pyro... is it kinesis also?"

"Yes, it is pyrokinesis. The ability to cause something to either melt or burst into flame, depending what you're focusing on. I do know that it's very rare for a strong cryokinetic to also be a strong pyrokinetic. There is another name for one who is equally strong with both forces. I believe they're called thermokinetics."

"Come into the kitchen and I'll make some tea." Joly led the way down the stairs. As she was filling the kettle, she spoke, "So tell me Morag, what do you know about the Sisters and if my power is so unusual, what's yours?"

Morag looked at Salem, who was in the middle of a giant stretch. "Well, I can't say I know a whole lot about the Sisters. I do know there are several; I'm not even sure how many, but it will be a power number. That problem that arose on All Hallow's Eve was probably the catalyst for why we are here. It's all leading up to some sort of major event. I also feel that something else is taking place. We will be going on another trip and soon, I think. I get the feeling we will need to have all our vaccinations for this next one."

"Vaccinations? Such as?"

"The works, I think. Polio, rabies, typhoid, hepatitis, diphtheria, and we probably should take some malaria medication with us."

"Wow! Where on earth are we going?"

"I'm not sure. I was having a look earlier, but ended up dozing. The time difference is playing hell with this old body. I think it'll be an early night tonight."

"Yes, for me too."

Salem let out a loud meow, getting the attention of the two women. He looked back and forth from Joly to Morag, clearly wanting something.

Joly walked over and stroked his back, thinking over their conversation. "You're wondering if you'll be going on this next journey, aren't you?"

Salem arched his back and made a small sound.

Morag shook her head. "No Salem, I can't see you making this next trip, I'm sorry. If we're going where we need rabies shots, it's a place you really don't want to be. I'm thinking somewhere in Asia."

"Why would my birth have been forecast over three hundred years ago?"

"I'm not sure child, but obviously you are here for a reason. There's no getting away from it. You, my dear, are destined for important deeds."

"Umm... I was thinking about maybe getting a job or some..."

"*No!*" Morag was emphatic. "No job, no work, no anything that might interfere with our duties. We are here to help the earth and that is our *soul reason* for being here. There will be no outside duties that might take away our concentration, our will to leave on a moments notice. *Do I make myself clear?*"

"Yes Morag." Joly was mortified; she hadn't expected Morag to tear into her like that. She had always been a relatively good child and rarely had she been spoken to in a raised voice. She remembered the last time she had been yelled at.

Go, Darlin', now! Get out of here!" Duncan was shouting at her.

She was trying to remove the top from another bottle of holy water. "No!" she had shouted back. "Not without you."

"I said now! I don't want you hurt." He had picked her up and thrown her. He threw her so hard she had literally flown through the air.

The tears welled up in her eyes. Morag saw and went to her, enclosing the lithe body in a warm and welcoming hug. "I'm sorry child, I didn't mean to yell."

"It's okay; I was thinking about the last time I was yelled at. It was when Duncan wanted me out of the circle."

"Oh Gods child, forgive me. I didn't mean to stir up memories."

"It's okay. No forgiveness needed. You did nothing wrong." Joly went to the forgotten kettle, and prepared some chamomile tea with honey.

"I guess I didn't realize the scope of being a Sister." Joly laughed, but it was a rather sad laugh. She poured the tea and sat down.

Morag smiled at her beloved daughter-in-law. "We are changing that my dear, with every spell that has been cast, with every evil banished and with every healing. You are doing fine. I know the in betweens can seem long, but with what happened last All Hallow's Eve, be prepared for an escalation. Don't expect to see much of your home for the next while."

"I guess that means I should be calling the doctor as soon as possible, to get my shots."

"Yes, me too." Morag thoughtfully took a sip of tea, thinking about their next trip.

Morag had faithfully looked into her crystal ball every day, but had seen nothing that called to her. In fact, the crystal had taken her to another Canadian city on several occasions.

She and Joly had both gotten all their vaccinations and they had gone shopping for a summer wardrobe. Joly had bought several pairs of shorts and tank tops, while Morag had opted for knee length skirts and sleeveless cotton blouses.

Knee length… she still couldn't believe it. Her ankles were almost their normal shapely selves again and Morag thanked the Gods daily for sending Joly to her.

Joly decided that if she needed to be ready to leave on a moments notice, she might as well continue painting. It was something that kept her busy, but could be left without worrying about it.

She had installed a cat door on the back door in the basement. Then she had called Mr. McNabb and asked if he would be willing to come over and feed the cats when she was away. He had agreed and also insisted that he should still be taking care of the lawns and flowerbeds. Joly had laughed and although she didn't think it was necessary, she told him to go ahead.

Morag was dozing in her lawn chair, the voices of the birds chittering in the background, when she heard a loud cry for help. Sitting bolt upright, she looked around trying to determine which direction it had come from. It wasn't Joly's voice, and for that, she was thankful.

She listened, but heard nothing. Getting out of the chair, Morag walked to the back of the yard and looked down the alley. It was empty. She opened the gate and walked down to the cross road then down to the next corner. There was nothing. Walking down the front sidewalk to her home, she realized why she was seeing nothing.

The cry for help had come via her mind.

Morag had learned at an early age to block out all the voices she heard. She had almost been driven crazy as a young child, by the voices. They were everywhere. She had been lucky. Her Mother had known about the voices and understood where they were coming from. Morag's Grandmother too, had heard them and learned how to block them out. It was her Grannie who had sat patiently with Morag, as she writhed in pain, listening to the shouts, the cries, the screams. Grannie had taught her how to center and ground herself, then once she had mastered that, Grannie taught her how to shield herself against the outside interference. Morag had learned how to protect herself and how to seal away the voices.

The only time she let them out, was when she needed to reach someone, and she had learned how to put the many in a grouping by themselves, so that she might hear the one she needed to reach. She had also learned how to receive unexpected messages via the mind, without unlocking the horrors that lived there.

This cry for help had been meant for her. It was a female's voice, maybe slightly accented; she wasn't sure.

Morag went into the house and grabbed her crystal ball. She watched the mists fill the crystal and recede. *Take me to the voice,* she silently urged. The crystal did not fail her.

She laughed when she saw where the crystal had taken her. Another Canadian city. No wonder she had kept ending up there. She was in Edmonton, Alberta, actually just west of Edmonton, in a fairly large suburb.

The woman was there and sensed when Morag had focused on her. She whipped around in shock, obviously not expecting this kind of response to her cry.

Morag spoke to her via her mind, *"I heard your cry for help. Do you need me to come to you?"*

The woman was perhaps thirty-five and was obviously Indo-Canadian, even though she was dressed in western attire.

Rekha Dhaliwal was shocked! She had communicated this way many a time with her sister and her Nani, her Grandmother, but never had she expected to get a reply from a total stranger. She had just been venting, letting off steam, when she had let out the cry for help.

Rekha finally decided that she should answer this woman's voice, before the woman disappeared. Tentatively, she called out, *"Hello?"*

Morag sat smiling to herself. The woman probably had no idea that she was being watched. Most people couldn't sense it. Joly and Duncan both had been able to. How many times had she tried to sneak into wherever they were, to see what they were up to? They had always been sitting or standing, facing her, beaming their cherubic smiles, as much as to say, ha-ha, can't fool us.

"Hello, my name is Morag. I'm talking to you from B.C. You have need of me, I believe."

"B.C.? You have strong power Morag. My name is Rekha. My family in India have major problems and need help. Not the kind of help a person can give, but the magical kind of help."

"I understand Rekha; I have the magical power, as does my daughter-in-law. Do you need us to come to you for direction, or should we go directly to India?"

"Can you go directly to India? I can give you instruction on where to go and who to see. You will be talking with my cousin, Pinga. She speaks English good. Time is critical. My village and the one next to it are starving. They don't know why. They are eating and dying. It isn't a normal thing."

"Give me the directions. We will be on the first available flight over."

Rekha gave Morag the directions. Morag had to put the crystal down to write everything out, but the voice communication remained strong.

Joly was sorting through some things of her Mother's, when she came across her original birth certificate. There was her time of birth, eight sixteen in the morning. She would have to tell Morag. She was curious about this time difference and wondered what the translated version would say. Was she in fact, the one in the prophesy?

She thought it was time for a break anyways, and decided to run over to see Morag with the news. She headed for the door, yelling as she went, "I'm headed across the street."

Joly reached to ring the doorbell, when the door opened. Morag smiled at her.

"My Gods child, talk about timing. I was just coming to tell you to pack. We're heading to India. I've already made the reservations. We leave the day after tomorrow." Morag paused to take a breath, and then continued, "Come in, come in. Sorry, I'm quite excited about this trip." She turned and led the way to the kitchen, talking non stop.

Joly sat at the table awestruck. Morag was incredible when she had a mission. She was so animated; she was constantly on the move, seemingly unable to stop for even a moment. Her hands were waving about as she paced back and forth, describing the problem, where they were going; what they could take with them and what they couldn't. There were several things they would have to purchase once they were in India.

Suddenly she came to a halt. "My Gods child, here I am going on and you haven't been able to get a word in edgewise. You came over for a reason."

Joly grinned and chuckled, "You were on a roll. I didn't want to interrupt you. I brought over my birth certificate for you to look at. I just found it."

"Oh wonderful! I'll bring my stuff on the plane and I can work on it, on the flight over. It won't take long to figure it out."

They had some iced tea and talked about the trip. Joly went home and sorted through her clothes. She knew she couldn't wear shorts and she idly wondered how the woman of India could stand all the clothes they wore in the heat. She decided to only take a few things and thought she would buy some things there.

She went to the small safe her Dad had installed in the basement floor and removed her passport. She'd had it updated before they went to England, so it was fine. She needed to run to the store and get some cat food. Other than that, and cleaning out her fridge, she was ready to go.

Stephen drove them to the airport. He seemed more his usual self, which both Joly and Morag were thankful for. He again kissed them both goodbye, this time aiming for Joly's cheek.

She smiled, thinking how lucky Elise really was, and she hoped the woman knew it. Stephen was a good provider, a hard worker and she was sure that there must be times when he was fun. She had never seen him really enjoying life, but he had been relaxed and interesting on the night of her birthday. No one could go through life, being all business and serious. Way too serious. Her thoughts turned to his brother, and she wondered again, how two boys could be so different.

Duncan with the twinkling deep blue eyes, Duncan the jokester, Duncan whose laugh was larger than life, Duncan the consummate lover. *Gods!* How was she going to get through the next fifty years without him?

Once on the plane, Morag got busy with the process of figuring out Joly's time of birth according to the stars, her sidereal time of birth. It was a piece of cake figuring out the time in Mission, and she had that done before their meal arrived. Eight sixteen A.M. on May the fifth of her birth year was twenty-two hundred hours, by star time. Moreover, she had also figured out where Joly's sun was. At the exact moment of her birth, the sun had gone into fifteen degrees of Taurus. *Cymreig Nos Galon!*

Morag was anxious now to see what a seer from the seventeenth century had seen in her crystal ball.

The tasteless meal over with, Morag went back to her drawings and numbers. This was something she used to do a lot of and it was something she enjoyed doing. She had tried doing charts when she first went into the extended care hospital, but the reception from the staff had not been pleasant, so she had mainly given it up. She had done the occasional one, when she found someone who liked to grab the daily paper to read their horoscope.

Joly looked at the paper on the table in front of Morag and smiled. It made no sense to her whatsoever. It actually resembled someone's piece of scrap paper that was doing equations and didn't want to mark up their finished report. There were scribbles and numbers going in every direction, and Joly wondered how Morag could possibly know what was where.

Joly put her head back and closed her eyes. The image of a woman came into her mind. It was the woman from the witch stone. Joly was still amazed that the woman looked so much like herself. She wondered if it was her. She knew she had lived before, several times, but as much as the woman looked like her, it just didn't *feel* like her. She wished she had been able to communicate with her.

Joly was dozing when a muffled oath aroused her. She blinked open her eyes and looked at Morag, who was triumphantly holding up two pieces of paper.

"It *is* you, my dear. Look!" Morag put the pages down in front of Joly.

Joly choked back a fit of the giggles. It must be the altitude, she thought to herself. The two pages of scribbles were in her lap. She was supposed to understand this? "Sorry Morag," she chuckled, "You'll have to explain what I'm looking at."

Morag looked quite put out. "Explain? Why it's as plain as the nose on your face." She took the papers back and held one up.

"This is you in Mission, born at eight sixteen on the fifth of May. The eight sixteen converts to fifteen sixteen in universal time, which converts to twenty-two hundred in sidereal or star time. Do you see that?"

Joly held back the smile. She did see the three figures that Morag had just mentioned. "Yes," she replied.

"And here," Morag pointed at an actual graph that was filled with squiggles and numbers, "See... do you see?" she was insistent.

Joly thought she had better try to see, so she took the paper and stared at it, wondering what on earth she was supposed to be seeing. She did know something about astrological graphs, but this wasn't the normal well laid out drawn to scale type. Suddenly though, she did see! The sun was in fifteen degrees Taurus. She turned and grinned at Morag. "So, you were right. I was born at the first moment of spring."

"Yes, you were. Now look at this other one. I had to do this one backwards, because we had no place of origin, right?"

Joly nodded and Morag continued, "There's eight hours difference between B.C. time and London, England time, so when you were born it was already four sixteen in the afternoon over there. But now, there's the Daylight Savings time that we have to deal with. Universal time has no changes, so we have to take away the hour, which makes it only three sixteen in the afternoon, in London. You still with me?"

Joly snapped to attention. She had been almost hypnotized by Morag's beating on the paper with her pen. "Yes, of course. Can you wait a minute?" Joly got up and headed down the aisle. She needed a break and she didn't want to be rude. She had only needed the answer, not all the technical jargon that had gotten the result.

She splashed some cool water on her face and had a drink, then headed back to her seat. "Sorry," she spoke as she sat down.

"No problem, but you do pick the weirdest time to get up and leave. Now, where was I? Oh, yes. Then I had to figure out the longitude and where it was at three sixteen. And where Taurus and the sun were. It was no picnic, you know. Anyhow, I then had to figure out the Sidereal or star time in England," Morag stabbed at the paper again, "Which was five fifty-seven on the morning of the sixth. *Exactly* the time that Alyce Gryffyd forecast!" Morag triumphantly threw the papers in Joly's lap.

"Wow!" Joly was suitably impressed. It hadn't taken Morag long at all to figure it out. She was very good with numbers. She had helped with the math homework lots when she and Duncan were in school.

"Dumb question, Morag."

"There's no such thing as a dumb question, you know that."

"Where was this forecast made from? Do you know?"

"Of course I know. It's right here." Morag grabbed the papers back, gave them a quick scan and handed the one back to Joly. "It's right there," she pointed.

Three degrees, one minute west. Fifty-two degrees, thirty-four minutes north. Well, that was definitely in the boundaries of England. "I don't suppose you brought an atlas," commented Joly.

Morag guffawed and got the attention of several people seated nearby.

"My Gods child, you do make me laugh. Thank you."

Joly sat there puzzled, wondering what was so hilarious in Morag's eyes, when suddenly it clicked. They had no need of an atlas, they were witches and they could scry themselves to anywhere in the world. She started to chuckle, and soon the tears were running down her face. She glanced at Morag and saw she was crying, too. Joly grabbed Morag's arm and gave it a squeeze. She was so glad she wasn't alone in the world anymore.

The trip to India had to be completed in two legs. First, they would be going back to England, where they had a layover of a day, and then they would head out to Lucknow in India.

Morag had booked them into the same hotel they had stayed at before.

Morag dug her crystal ball out of the luggage to see if she could find where the prophecy of Joly's birth had been made. The crystal showed the treetops and castles, towns and rivers, as it took her to her intended destination. When it slowed down, Morag was surprised. She recognized the countryside as one of the places they had visited the last time they were here.

The crystal homed in on its intended target. Morag bade it stop, before it got too close. *Where was this?* There! The circle, she could see it plain as day. It was much more noticeable from overhead than it was from when they toured it on the ground. She willed the crystal to take her closer. Then she was there.

My Gods! That was the rock where Joly had passed out. What was it called? Something about a witch. Witches Stone, something like that. Joly's birth had been forecast from this very spot. No wonder she was sensitive to the area. Morag couldn't wait to tell her.

She did wonder though, what Joly had seen the last time, when she had returned to the circle. Morag had watched her sink to her knees, holding her hands out in front of her. That she had been receiving, there was no doubt. When she had asked Joly, all she'd gotten for a reply was that it was very foggy and she couldn't see much. Maybe not much, but she saw something. It was unlike Joly not to share, so it did make her very curious.

When Joly came in from her walk, Morag delivered the news, watching closely to see her reaction. It wasn't what she expected.

"Alyce... my Gods, it was Alyce I saw. She had the crystal with her."

"You actually saw her?"

"Yes! I should have told you, but it was kind of freaky. Alyce could be my twin. She looked right at me and I thought I was looking in a mirror. She was at the stone for quite awhile, and then she got to her feet and walked toward me. She had the crystal under her cloak."

"You don't think this was you in a past life?"

"I thought about it, but it didn't seem right. No, I don't think it was me."

"I hope not child. You really don't want to be running into yourself now, you know that?"

"Yes, I know. I don't think she and I are one. That we're related, yes, but

I think it ends there. Morag, I know we weren't going to go anywhere, but I think I'd like to see if I could find out more about her. Maybe church records, something. What do you think?"

"Well, we're here. You might as well. It's much easier to search from the location, than it is to search from afar. You'd better go and rent a car then."

The sky was overcast as Morag and Joly left London heading in a north-westerly direction on the M1 highway. She switched highways several times until she got to Shrewsbury and then she turned south.

Joly was tense. She wasn't sure she was going to find anything out about Alyce, but she was hoping. She had never gotten into the genealogy thing, being content with knowing her family ties back into the late eighteen hundreds, early nineteen hundreds. Her Mother had been able to go back farther and delighted in rattling off the names of forebears long gone. It was funny though, she didn't recall her Mother ever mentioning an Alyce.

Joly drove across the border into Wales, heading for Montgomery. As it was the largest town in the area, she hoped they could instruct her as to the best way to conduct this search. They only had today, so she needed to make the most of it.

Upon arriving in Montgomery, Joly was distressed to see how small the town was. She had expected something larger. She quickly located the town hall, which sat at the end of the main street. Running inside, she enquired about old records, and was told that what she was looking for was probably located back at Shrewsbury.

Back in the car, she told Morag. It was less than a half hour back to Shrewsbury, so it wasn't a great error.

Driving back, Joly slowed the car when she reached the turnoff for Priestweston. She didn't have the luxury of time, but she felt an urge, and she knew from past experience, to follow her senses.

She pulled into the parking lot and was out of the car almost before she had shut the motor off. She almost ran toward the stone circle, her breath coming in small gasps. As before, the closer she approached to the stone witch, the louder the roaring in her head. She was determined to be closer this time and she advanced until it was almost overpowering.

Joly centered on the roaring, letting it consume her. She sank to her knees, without knowing she had done so. The light show began, the colors swirling, dancing, whirling about. Once again, the colors slowly faded, leaving a thick mist in front of her. There she was. Alyce was seated on the ground, but this time Joly was close enough to see the crystal ball in her hands. Alyce was talking quietly to herself. Joly strained to hear what she was saying, but could only make out the occasional word.

Morag had gotten out of the car and followed Joly. She was concerned. She wasn't one hundred percent sure this Alyce wasn't Joly in a previous life and she knew there would be problems if this turned out to be the case.

She watched as Joly sank to the ground; saw her leaning forward. Then she watched as Joly began crawling toward the tall stone. "No!" she whispered, "Don't go there, Joly. *Stop!*" Morag had not spoken aloud, but Joly did stop and she breathed a sigh of relief. She knew what happened when two bodies merged. It certainly wasn't the pretty effect that was portrayed in the movie, 'Ghost'.

Joly was only about five feet from the stone. Morag thought she remembered Joly saying that Alyce had been right against it. She hoped she remembered correctly.

Alyce lowered the crystal to her lap and sat there a moment. She turned her head in Joly's direction and looked directly into her eyes. "I've seen you before. You're the Sister of the Triple Moon. I spoke with your Mother. Now please, quit bothering me."

Joly was stunned. Alyce *did* see her. "Hello Alyce, my name is..."

"I don't *want* to know your name! Isn't it *enough* that I know about you? Isn't it enough that I see *things*? Do you want me *hanged* for talking to myself, because no one else can see you? Now please, go back where you came from and leave me alone."

Joly dropped her head. She felt badly for Alyce, but she wanted some answers.

"May I ask you one question, Alyce, and then I'll go."

Alyce stood up and walked over to where Joly sat. Looking down at her, she shook her head. "You really do look like me, you know. Strange, I didn't see that in the crystal."

Alyce squatted down in front of Joly, their faces inches apart. "What do you want to know?'

Gods! There were so many things she wanted to ask. How could she pick just one?

"Hard to decide what question you want answered the most?" Alyce asked.

"Yes."

"You know, I told your Mother every thing I could. Why don't you ask her?"

"My Mother was killed by a demon almost ten years ago."

"*No!* You're not that old. Tell me you're not eight and twenty years." It was a demand.

"Uhh... yes, I am. I turned twenty-eight a month ago."

"By the Gods! If you are eight and twenty, then you have already fought a demon by yourself. And you've talked to the dogs?"

"Yes."

"You are going to another country now, are you not?"

"Yes, we leave tomorrow for India."

"You have help. Your friend is very powerful, but not as powerful as you are. She has the wisdom. You *must* listen to her. You will win this battle, with *her* help."

"There are more of you, these Sisters. You will gather together, to fight evils that should never have been let loose. You will not all survive these fights."

"I don't want to know…"

"And I am not about to tell you. But I will tell you one thing." Alyce paused and looked around, and then she lowered her head. "Remember these words, I will *not* repeat them."

"The gift to summon is abandoned in Polaris.
The mirth is secure in the psyche.
Widdershins and fire releases the void.
Gemini becomes the nucleus."

"I will tell you one more thing. Your quest here is for naught. You will find out nothing. I am your Nain, your Grandmother, many times removed. Leave it at that. You need not know more. Go now. *Ymgryfhau, hir yw pob ymaros.*"

Alyce turned and walked away. Joly sat and watched, until she had almost disappeared in the swirling fog. *"Wait!* Alyce, what was that you said, at the end?"

She thought Alyce hadn't heard, but as she shimmered in the outlying mist, she turned and faced Joly once more. "Be strong, Joly. All waiting is long." She turned and was gone.

Joly wasn't aware of the tears falling until she went to stand up.

Morag watched as Joly swiped her arm across her face. *What just happened?* She moved forward to help Joly. When Morag reached her and put her arm around her, Joly cuddled into her and with their arms wrapped around each other, they walked to the car.

Joly dropped into the driver's seat and laid her head on the steering wheel.

Morag sensed she had a headache and said to her, "Come and sit on the ground, Joly. I'll do what I can."

Joly climbed back out and sat down. Morag massaged her neck and head, in behind her ears and her temples. Within minutes, the throbbing eased off and Joly could think again. Thanking Morag, she stood and took the Goddess position, grounding herself to receive the healing energies from above. It wasn't long before her head was clear.

Soon, they were back in the car heading toward Shrewsbury and then London. Joly relayed her conversation with Alyce to Morag. "And you know? She did know my name. She said she didn't want to know it, but then she said it after she walked away."

Morag took a pen and paper and wrote down the riddle, and while they were driving, she tried to figure out what it meant. Parts of it were simple; Widdershins meant counter clockwise, mirth was enjoyment, Gemini was the twins, psyche was the soul. Her piece of paper looked very much like the ones on the plane, by the time they reached their hotel.

Joly chuckled and asked her how she was making out.

"Well, the translation of what you were given seems to be another riddle. We'll be on the plane fifteen hours tomorrow. I'll work on it then."

Joly was tired from her trip into the past, so she went and lay down.

Morag took her crystal ball from its case and scryed to the Leeds area. She still couldn't understand why she had had that momentary sensing of Duncan. She found nothing; she could sense nothing. She called him with her mind, but there was no answer. She put the crystal away, angry with herself for holding onto hope.

She picked up the paper with the riddle and read it again, changing a word here and there. It still made no sense.

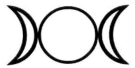

9. Wicked Witches

They boarded the plane to India just before lunchtime and would arrive in Lucknow around seven-thirty the next morning.

Morag and Joly read the information they had gotten from Rekha and what they had found at the library. They quietly planned their strategy from what they had knowledge of. There were always the unknowns that would have to be factored in once they got to the area.

They had things to purchase in the city, before catching a train to the city of Hardoi, where Rekha's cousin was to meet them.

The area where they were going had sodic soil, and only about one third of it was usable for crops. The Indian Government had begun a successful program of reclamation, using a system of water filtering, leaching, drainage and inclusion of gypsum. These reclaimed areas were being carefully monitored and were successfully growing crops.

Poor villages, whose men had had to leave the area to find work, were now able to stay home and work their own fields.

They arrived at Lucknow and took a taxi to the city. It was already twenty-five degrees Celsius and was supposed to reach thirty-five in the afternoon. Morag was glad she was wearing a cotton skirt and blouse. Joly also had chosen cotton, wearing casual pants and a T-shirt.

Morag had booked them into a hotel, even though they were leaving that night. She didn't want to be bothered with their bags while they were shopping. The desk clerk at the small but beautifully appointed hotel on Shahnajaf Road spoke perfect English and was happy to assist them. He arranged for a car and driver to stay with them for the day. They agreed to meet the driver at ten-thirty.

After freshening up in their room, they went to the restaurant for tea and a bite to eat. The restaurant featured a large buffet with many mouth-watering delights. Both Morag and Joly overfilled their plates, wanting to try as many different types of Indian cuisine as possible. The square tables were well spaced apart with wrought iron chairs and padded seats. They ate at a leisurely pace, enjoying what would be their last day of relaxation, before embarking on their mission.

After breakfast they went back to their room, where Joly borrowed Morag's crystal and scryed herself home. Nefertiti knew immediately when Joly honed in on her. Joly had promised to go home every day this way, so the cats would know that all was well on the other side of the world.

Their driver arrived shortly after ten-thirty and they asked him to take them to the *Hazratganj* market. The driver told them his name was Amar and he suggested they might want to try a different market, one that wasn't so expensive. Morag assured him that the prices didn't matter, but that the quality of the goods was of utmost importance.

The market area was large, fanning out in all directions from a central circle. There were several narrow winding lanes arranged like the spokes of a wheel, connected to a wide road that comprised the outer ring of the circle. The central circle had a large concrete base and on this was a tall pole, which was surrounded by a four foot high concrete enclosure. This in turn, was surrounded by four curved wooden detached fences. In between the concrete enclosure and the fencing were several cows. Amar told them that the cows were allowed to wander at will and that they would be seeing them most everywhere they went. The wide road was filled with buses, auto rickshaws, bicycles, bicycle rickshaws and people. All of the vehicles seemed to be honking their horns. Joly wondered how they managed to make their way around the circle with no accidents.

It took them close to an hour to find everything they were looking for, but once Morag was satisfied with her purchases, they asked Amar to take them sightseeing. He took them to see the Residency ruins, the two hundred and twenty foot Clock Tower, Ali Khan's tomb, which was actually a double tomb, as Ali Khan's favorite wife was also buried there. They saw the *Bara Imambara* with its sixty foot high entry door and the largest vaulted hall in the country, with a fifty foot high ceiling. They saw the *Rumi Darwaa*, an ornamental gateway, the *Hussainabad Imambara*, an ornate structure with a gilded dome and a cluster of small turrets and minarets and the *Jami Masjid* with its triple onion shaped domes. There was a large bird sanctuary in Lucknow, but Morag knew she didn't have time to go through it on this trip. As much as she wanted to see it, she knew it would have to wait.

"May I now take you for a refreshment?" Amar wasn't a young man, but he looked quite boyish standing there with a hopeful look on his face.

Morag smiled at him, "Yes that would be lovely."

He took them to a small coffee shop and ordered for them. They were served *Badam Halwa*, which was like almond fudge and a drink that was called *Mango Lassi*, which was made with a yoghurt base.

Amar insisted on taking them to the Chowk district, which was famous for its *Chikan* embroidery. He knew exactly which shop he wanted them to see, and once inside, Morag and Joly could see why.

Neither of them quite knew what to look at first, everything was so beautiful. Morag was drawn to a white *kurtis* with mauve and deep blue embroidered flowers on a six inch hem along the bottom and around the sleeves. There were individual flowers sporadically embroidered all over the blouse. Then she spotted the linens. The bed sheets were pale blue and embroidered in an intricate pattern with white thread.

Joly wanted one of everything, but decided she would have to settle for a couple of tops. She saw an aqua green *lehnga choli* that she had to have and as she was walking toward it, she spotted the dearest little shirt in an almost sheer white material with a white diamond shaped floral pattern covering it.

Morag joined Joly and smiling, asked if she had decided on anything.

"Gads! I love it all," she exclaimed.

Morag laughed, "I spoke with the clerk. They will ship our purchases to Canada, if you want to buy more than your suitcase will hold."

"Really? Wonderful, but we could be here a while."

Morag laughed again and went back to her own shopping. They both bought sheet sets and several tops. Joly bought the *lehnga choli,* which was a strapless halter top with a floor length skirt that rested on her hips and Morag bought several *saris*, thinking she would make curtains out of them. They both bought a salwar kameez, to wear when they got to the village. The people there weren't used to seeing outsiders, especially Caucasian ones, so they thought that they should at least try to fit in, clothing wise.

When they were done, Amar asked if they were pleased.

"Oh yes, Amar, very pleased!" Joly exclaimed.

By this time, they were both tired, so they asked to be taken back to the hotel, so they could have a short rest, before catching their train at six twenty-five. Once in their room, Morag ordered room service for a light supper with tea. While waiting, they repacked their suitcases and after eating, they laid down for a rest.

Before they knew it, Amar was knocking on their door, ready to take them to the train station. They spotted the *Charbagh* station before they arrived. The bright yellow and red of the massive building was impossible to miss. There were several platforms inside, with trains going in various directions. There were sleeping rooms, eating areas and four gardens. The architecture was outstanding, and while waiting for their train, Amar gave them the grand tour.

Morag had already paid Amar, but he seemed reluctant to leave them alone. She did see beggars and what looked to be some drug buying or selling, but she didn't feel she needed protection. Amar felt otherwise.

When their train arrived, Joly impulsively hugged Amar, and he beamed his approval. He gave them his phone number and made them promise to call him when they got back to Lucknow. Morag assured him, they would. They boarded the train and waved to Amar as it left the station.

They were riding on the *Doon Express*, which would stop three times before arriving at Hardoi. All three stops were in the first hour they were on the train, and with the rocking motion, they soon fell asleep.

The change in speed woke Morag, and she reached over to gently shake

Joly. They watched as the city came into sight and soon the train came to a screeching stop. Gathering up their belongings, they headed for the door.

They stepped onto the concrete platform and stood for a moment looking around. There were vendors selling their wares, porters were running back and forth and there was a general air of everyone being in a hurry. Not seeing anyone who looked like they were waiting for the two of them, they headed to the gate following the other passengers. They showed their tickets to the ticket collector and passed through.

Again, they stopped and looked around. Joly wondered what they would do if no one met them. "What now?" she quizzed Morag.

"I guess we wait. We don't have an address, so hopefully someone will show up soon."

They sat outside the station, enjoying the cooler air of the evening. Both were tired from all the traveling, shopping and the time difference.

It was sometime later when a voice shouted, *"Namaskar!* Hello!"

They turned to see a small woman hurrying toward them. She wore rectangular glasses and had her hair pulled back into a ponytail. She was wearing a salwar kameez in shades of gold and red.

"I am Pinga Singh. Very, very sorry to make you wait." She held out her hand to shake Morag's and Joly's.

"I'm Morag McEwan and this is Joly Mc..." She caught herself, "James."

"Very good. Come now. We go to house. You would like tea?"

"I would love to have a cup of tea. Thank you." Morag could hardly wait.

Pinga had a rickshaw waiting and after loading their luggage they got in. They looked around as they headed to their destination. There were no traffic lights and the street was quiet. They saw a bust of Mahatma Gandhi in a triangular garden and several dogs roaming loose. There were neem trees, temples, several children playing cards, and the occasional adult heading home from a day at work.

Soon, they arrived at their destination. The house was small, but clean. They sat at a low table on cushions and had their tea. Pinga told them more about the problem, but seemed to be unwilling to accompany them to the area. She said she would go part way, but then they would be on their own.

"How will we know when we have reached it?" Joly enquired.

"You will know." Pinga responded.

Pinga showed them to their room and said goodnight. There was a double bed and a dresser in the room, along with some religious pictures on the walls. They got ready for bed and Joly scryed herself home to let the cats know all was well.

The knock on the door startled them both.

"Yes," Morag called.

"It's time to go. We leave in one hour." Pinga's voice came to them.

"Damn..." Morag rolled out of the bed. "I feel like I could use another four hours sleep."

"Me too." Joly stretched and slowly sat up. "What's the rush, I wonder. It's barely daylight."

"I don't know, but we'd best get moving. I for one am starved."

"Me too." Joly got to her feet and dug out her new *salwar kameez*. It was a deep forest green, with white embroidery on the sleeves and hem of the blouse. The pants were plain, except for a four inch embroidered hem around the ankles.

She slid the pants up and tied the string at the waist. "One thing about it. They sure don't have to worry about it if they gain a pound or two."

Morag chuckled, as she slid the blouse over her head. Morag's *salwar kameez* was a cornflower blue, with the whole of the blouse embroidered, as well as the ankles of the pants. They checked each other over once they were dressed, and decided that they looked all right. Joly quickly twisted her long hair up behind her head and pinned it. Morag had kept her hair short after leaving the extended care facility.

Barefoot, they padded to the kitchen where tea, fresh fruit and *Roti* bread awaited them. They ate heartily, thankful that they would be leaving on a full stomach.

They could hear voices in another room, but no one came in to meet them.

As soon as they were finished, Pinga rushed them and their belongings out the door and into the waiting rickshaw. The first part of their journey was completed on smooth roads, but soon they came to a rougher road that was quite bumpy. They reached a turnoff that resembled little more than a trail. Pinga told them they would have to go on foot from this point. She would return for them in the evening.

Joly and Morag grabbed the bags, and stood watching as Pinga and the rickshaw disappeared from sight.

"This is really weird, and I don't like it. Where on earth are we going anyhow?" Joly looked around and could see nothing but fields in all directions.

Morag dug out her crystal ball and had a look around. "Well child, it looks like we have quite a walk ahead of us. I think we should put all the clothes in one bag and leave it here. Then we can take turns carrying the other one."

They emptied their cases and switched everything around, and then Morag took the suitcase of clothing and walked into the field and hid it out of sight of the road and pathway.

They started walking. Toward what, they still weren't sure. Morag thought they had about five kilometers to go, but they had only gone about two when they both had the breath knocked out of them.

The air was filled with hatred. It was as if someone had thrown a blanket over them. They both stumbled and the urge to retreat was overpowering. It was difficult to breathe and they both were gasping, trying to inhale lungs full of air.

"What the...?" Morag whipped her head around trying to see what the cause of this was, but she could sense nothing. She reached for her crystal, but saw nothing. The village was still a ways ahead of them.

They pressed forward, feeling the hatred swirling around them, crashing into them in waves. Each step was a struggle to take. They weren't wanted here and someone was trying their best to deter them. They had only gone about twenty feet, when Morag stopped. The air pressure had changed and they were being slowly smothered. Somebody was trying to kill them.

"It's too much Joly. We have to get rid of this." Morag was panting, her breath coming in small puffs.

Morag opened the case and removed two candles, one black and the other, purple. She removed a bowl and sat the black candle in it, and then she opened a bottle of spring water and poured it into the bowl. She cast her circle and lit the candles, placing the bowl in the center of the circle. She held the purple candle as she called upon the Gods and Goddesses and the elements to help her rid the area of the evil within.

Joly stood outside the circle and was battered back and forth by the feelings of hatred. She had trouble standing in one spot. There was no sign of anything, no wind, not even a breeze, but her body was buffeted on all sides from an invisible force that seemed determined to send her to the ground.

Morag spoke her spell, aware of the fight happening a few feet away from her. There was a shift in the air currents. Morag continued with the banishing spell.

Joly felt the shift. The hatred was as intense, but she knew Morag was slowly winning. Still, the will to breathe seemed to be leaving her, and she had to concentrate on every breath. Joly lost track of what Morag was doing; she forgot where she was. She finally decided it was just too much effort and giving up the fight for air, she crumpled to the ground.

Morag knew she was winning, but it was happening too slowly. She saw Joly fall, but was powerless to do anything.

The force that surrounded them was a strong one. There was much power coming from someone, and it *was* a someone that she was fighting. This was no demon, but a human being whose power was as strong as hers.

She heard a hiss and glanced down at the candle in the bowl. The water and the wick were at the same height. Morag placed the purple candle on the ground and knelt in front of the bowl.

"*Spell, be gone; magic be gone.*
Go now, back to whence you came."

The candle spluttered and went out.

Instantly, the pressure vanished and the air became pure. Morag had won this round. She dug a hole and buried the candle, and then poured the water from the dish over it. She stood and lifted the purple candle once more, and finished her ritual. She thanked her Gods and Goddesses. She closed her circle and went to Joly.

Taking a bottle of water, Morag poured some over Joly's forehead and holding her closely, she willed her to take a deep breath.

As if she had heard, Joly did breathe deeply and with a small shudder, she opened her eyes. Seeing Morag looking down at her with concern, she tried to smile, but failed.

"It's alright child, we're okay now. Rest for a minute." Morag held the bottle to Joly's lips and she drank.

The heat was beating down on them, but neither seemed to be aware of it. It was such a relief to be able to breathe normally that nothing else mattered.

Soon Joly sat up and with Morag's help, she got to her feet.

"Gads! I feel like somebody beat the crap out of me."

"Somebody did." Morag got angry. "And whoever it is, we are not done with them yet, mark my words! Now ground yourself, and we'll be on our way."

Thirty minutes later they saw the village in the distance. They could hear a dog barking and they saw people moving around. As they closed the distance they saw people gathering, watching their approach.

A figure removed itself from the group and walked toward them. The woman was very emaciated and tall, but she carried herself proudly. She smiled as she approached them.

"*Namaste! Mubarak ho!*"

Morag put her hands together in front of her chest and bowed slightly, "*Namaste!* I am Morag, this is Joly. We have come to help you."

"*Han,* ahh, sorry. No speak good. I am Gurdev. Rekha send you. *Dhanyawaadh.* Thank you for come. There is much *harsha*... ahh... happy. *Anil*... is good." Gurdev waved her hands about. "We feel light... sorry. Not good tell."

Morag beamed, "You're doing just fine dear. The air is good now. You feel happy because you can breathe."

"*Han*... yes. Breathe is good. Thank you. You did... yes?"

"Yes, we did it."

"Ahh, thank you, *dil kee gaharaeon se.*"

They reached the rest of the villagers and although they looked happy, most of them eyed the two of them suspiciously.

Morag searched through the people, but found no one there that could have tried to kill them. She sensed the suspicion, some fear, but most of all, she felt their pain. These people were very malnourished and many were sick.

A small boy approached Joly, and with big eyes, he tugged on her pant leg. "*Mein bukha hun.*"

Gurdev said something to the boy and with a gentle swat to his behind, she sent him away.

"Excuse me," Joly hesitated, wondering if she was overstepping her bounds. "What did he say?"

"He say he hungry. Is okay." Gurdev led them to a small hut made out of mud, with a thatched roof.

"Come," she invited.

They entered the hut and were both immediately overwhelmed by the poverty that was evident everywhere they looked. It had an earthen floor and poorly made open cupboards, showing the few contents. The dishes were chipped and the bedding thin. A few pieces of clothing were on one of the shelves.

Gurdev poured them some colored water, which they took to be tea, and they gratefully accepted. The heat was extreme and being out in the sun for so long, both were feeling the effects of it. They drank thirstily and when their cups were empty, Gurdev refilled them. She sat smiling at them, obviously happy to have them there.

When the tea was gone, Morag asked Gurdev, "When did this start, all these bad things?"

"Maybe three month. First was *anil*..." she breathed in deeply signifying air. "Next was food, all bad, next was *bimari*, ahh... sick."

"That's fine Gurdev. We have fixed the air. Next, we'll work on fixing the food and sickness. Joly will help with the sickness, while I work on your food."

"Thank you. Very, very good."

"Do you have any idea who might be causing all this to happen?"

"Sorry?"

"Who might be doing this? What person?"

"Ahh... bad *jadu karana*... like you only bad."

"Like us, yes, but do you know who? Name of person?"

Ahh... no *naam*. Not know."

"Okay, thank you. We will find out who it is." Morag smiled and arose from the scrap of material she had been sitting on.

"May we walk around now? Go outside?"

"Yes, *avashya*." Gurdev led them back out into the heat.

The three of them walked through the small village, but Morag could not sense anyone there that could have done the spell casting. Whoever it was wasn't there at present.

The small boy who had tugged on Joly's leg came to walk with them. He reached up and grabbed Joly's hand, seemingly content to walk beside her.

She asked Gurdev what his name was?

Gurdev spoke to the boy. "*Aapka kya naam hai?*"

He shyly looked at Joly and said "*Mera naam Ranjit hai.*"

Joly smiled at him and said "*Namaskar, Ranjit.*"

He grinned at her, "*Aapka kya naam hai?*"

Gurdev spoke, "He want know your name."

"My *naam* is Joly."

"Cho - ly." He laughed and clutched her hand tighter.

Gurdev and Morag smiled.

Joly laughed, and Ranjit laughed with her.

They walked out to the fields and both Morag and Joly could sense the evil surrounding them. Their crops were growing as normal, but when the people went to eat the food it was bad. This was why the village and the one next to it were starving. Everything that came into the area, in the way of food, immediately became inedible.

Morag knew what she had to do. She hadn't done this spell for a long time, but it was easy enough to do. The village needed a strong protection spell, and this was the strongest one she knew. She had thought this might be the case, so she had bought the ingredients in Lucknow.

Joly could feel Ranjit's hunger and it bothered her. There was nothing she could do, other than what she was already doing. She couldn't feed him, but her healing energies were going from her hand into his, and the pain of the hunger had left him.

Once the tour was over, they got to work. They only had the one day to get the major obstacles out of the road. The next day they were scheduled to go to the other village. Then they would return each day, until they found who was responsible for the evildoing.

Morag thought back to everything they had been told. Rekha was from this village. She had somehow managed to get out, get an education and move to Canada, but most of her family was here. Pinga too, was related and although not as educated as Rekha, the two of them had maintained contact. When Rekha had heard that the village was sick, she had flown home to try to help. She had almost died for her efforts. Pinga had managed to get her out and well enough to send back to Canada. There she healed and searched in vain for someone with powers stronger than hers. Her search had been unfruitful, until the day Morag had heard her cry of rage and frustration.

No one seemed to have any idea who was behind the sorcery, but Morag knew it had to be someone who was very angry with not just one or two people, but with the villages themselves. What had the villages done that was so bad, she wondered?

They had been self-sufficient up until this all had taken place. Prior to the reclamation, the men had worked in other more prosperous villages, to feed their families. Although by her standards, Morag deemed the village as totally poverty stricken, she had been told that this was the way they were used to living, and knowing no other way, when they had food on the table, they felt blessed with their lot in life. There was always some dissension on varying topics, but for the most part, they were content.

Morag asked Gurdev if there were others that would be willing to help. She knew most were suspicious, but she hoped that the thought of ridding the area of the evil that had pervaded it, would help them to overcome their doubts.

Gurdev said there were several who had approached her, prior to their arrival, to offer assistance. She turned to go and get them. Morag asked her to bring back nine sturdy metal containers and Gurdev nodded yes.

Morag opened the suitcase and carefully removed several of the contents. She would need to place the containers around the village and she was grateful it was a small one. Both the affected villages had a population of approximately two hundred people.

Joly told Morag she was going to do some healings, and she followed in the direction Gurdev had taken with Ranjit still holding her hand. She saw the villagers looking at her suspiciously, but it didn't bother her. She knew she was here for a good purpose and that was all that mattered.

She could feel the sickness surrounding her and she headed in the direction that it was strongest. She approached the door of the hut and knocked softly. The door was opened by a young girl of about ten.

"*Namaskar,*" Joly greeted her.

"*Namaskar,*" she responded. She opened the door wider to allow Joly admittance. Ranjit hung back, but refused to let go of Joly's hand. She knelt down and hugged him, telling him to wait. She realized he couldn't understand her, so she led him to the side of the door and gently pushed him into a sitting position. She repeated, "Wait," and smiling at him, she entered the hut.

The smell almost gagged her. The odor of sickness permeated the room and had Joly not known better, she would have thought whoever was in here was already long dead.

The girl hung back and watched wide-eyed as Joly approached the place where the woman lay. Joly tried to breathe through her mouth, but it didn't seem to help.

She knelt down and placed her hand on the woman's head. It was hot and very dry. She moved down to the chest area, sensing the shallow breathing. That the woman breathed at all was a miracle. Joly didn't know if she could help this one. She may have been too far gone for a healing, but Joly had to try.

The people were starving to death. How much rotten food, for how long, could people eat? Joly couldn't imagine having to eat anything bad, and the thought of having to do just that, day after day, sickened her.

All she could do for the time being was take away the pain. This woman was too far gone to feel pain, but Joly wanted to instill the will to live for one more day. She couldn't fill their bellies, but if Morag was successful today, they would be bringing food tomorrow.

Joly knew the instant the woman regained consciousness. Soon, her eyelids fluttered and she opened her eyes. She didn't appear surprised to see a Caucasian stranger leaning over her, with her hands moving rhythmically over her wasted body.

Joly smiled and spoke softly, "*Namaste.*"

She needed water. What was the word again? She had memorized it, but now that she needed it, it had deserted her. Salad? No, of course not. Sal... something. Ahh... right, two women's names, Sal and Lil.

She turned to the girl and said, "*Salila* please."

The girl nodded, and went and got a chipped cup and filled it from a bucket. She brought it to Joly who took it and put it to the woman's parched lips. She had no strength to drink, but Joly let the water trickle through the lips, knowing that the throat would automatically swallow. The woman's eyes closed again.

Joly had done all she could here. She rose and pointed to the cup. She looked for a clock, but there didn't appear to be one. She held out her hands counting her fingers, hoping the girl could count. She wanted the girl to give the woman a drink every hour. She would have to get Gurdev to come and speak with her.

She smiled and opened the door, expecting to find Ranjit gone, but he sat exactly as she had placed him. He jumped to his feet when he saw Joly and grabbed onto her hand again. She laughed, and Ranjit laughed too. He had such a cute laugh that Joly laughed again, and so did Ranjit. They walked down the street both laughing, with many people looking on.

Ranjit spoke, *"Hansane wali baat."*

Joly had no idea what he had said, but she took it to be something good, so she nodded. She was becoming attached to this little guy. She must ask Gurdev, where he lived.

She wondered what it would be like to have a child of her own. She would never know of course, but she thought she would have been a good mother.

She headed to the next hut that she felt needed her. She would be busy the rest of the day, this much she knew. Again, she told Ranjit to wait.

He sat down and said, "Wait," and then he laughed.

Morag watched as Joly left, and knew she would do what she could for the ones most ill. Morag took a drink of water and wondered how anyone could live in this heat. At least she and Joly had the power to keep their body temperatures more or less in sync with the atmospheric temperature, but just the same, it was damn hot!

She watched as Gurdev returned with nine others. There were five women and four men. Morag hoped they could follow instructions.

Morag told them what needed to be done and Gurdev translated. Morag was concerned that Gurdev might not understand everything she was saying, so she repeated the instructions several times, until she was satisfied they knew exactly what to do. She also repeatedly warned them that what they were about to do could be dangerous. They didn't seem concerned.

They had each arrived with a container, and one at a time, Morag carefully measured the Epsom salts and herb mixture into each one. Then she measured the hydrogen peroxide and poured it over the salt. She made sure each person had a long match and sent them on their way. Eight of them would fan out around the village; four of them to the cardinal points, north, south, east and west. The other four went to the points in between.

Morag, Gurdev and the remaining woman headed into the center of the village. Gurdev assured Morag, that she knew where the exact center was, although in this case that wasn't really an issue. Once there, Morag placed the container on the ground.

She drew her circle and called upon the Powers to help her. Facing the four quarters, she called upon their help also. She placed the container in the middle of the circle and removed a match.

Gurdev held up a gong-like apparatus and when Morag nodded, she hit the metal with a beater. The sound echoed through the village. Morag nodded again, and again the gong rang. It had been a long time since Morag had performed this particular bit of magic and she had never tried doing it with so many others, but the area was large and she would rather go for overkill, than have it not be enough. She nodded once more and again the gong rang out. Morag struck her match and held it just over the top of the contents.

The salt bomb shot blue flames into the air, some as high as six feet. The other two women were silent as they watched the fire burn. Ten minutes later when the fire burned itself out, Morag realized a crowd had gathered to watch.

Morag raised her head and smelled the air. It smelled fresh, but there was something else. Morag knew what it was. It was the scent of clean. She had rid the area of the spells that had been cast. Now, she and Joly needed to rid the area of the evildoer.

The eight helpers arrived in the center to see what was happening next. Morag told Gurdev to tell the people that all was well once again. Now any food brought in, would be wholesome and fresh.

The rest of the villagers that had gathered heard the news with mixed feelings. Some were happy and cheering, others were still doubtful that anything had been done at all.

Joly heard the ringing of something similar to a bell, and sensed when the evil had been lifted from the village. She was grateful, but wished they had been able to bring some food. It wouldn't have done any good, as it would have turned bad the moment they arrived. Pinga was bringing some things in the evening, to tide the villagers over until the next day, when Morag and Joly would bring a five-ton truck full of food to help them out.

Joly spent the afternoon comforting and removing the pain of hunger. Once she had taken care of the worst cases, she concentrated on the children, small ones first. They didn't understand why there was no food or why their tummy's hurt. The removal of the pain was a short-term thing, but that was all she needed. Just to get them through until the food arrived. The adults would have to be told to not over eat or over feed the small ones. Otherwise, they would just throw it back up.

Morag spent the afternoon walking. She wandered far out into the fields and down beaten pathways, searching for anything amiss. She found nothing.

Ranjit stayed with Joly, content to wait at each hut for her. She shared her water with him after each healing, and he liked to point out different things as they walked, although she was usually unsure what he was pointing at.

Joly looked at the sun and realized the day was almost gone. They would have to leave soon to meet Pinga.

She took Ranjit's hand and went looking for Morag. They met up at the edge of the village.

"Did you find anything?"

"Nothing. Whoever it is nowhere around today. He or she could be at the next village. After we drop the food tomorrow, we will head over and do a repeat of today."

Morag looked at Joly's small companion, "What are you going to do with the little one? He doesn't look like he is going to let you leave." She smiled at Ranjit, who grinned back at her.

"*Aapka kya naam hai?*"

"My name? It's Morag."

"Morg." He laughed. "Morg, Cho-ly." He laughed again and squeezed Joly's hand.

"I don't know. I thought I would ask Gurdev where he lives and take him home. It's funny no one has come to get him and he hasn't shown any attachment to anyone we've met in our travels today. He sure is cute though, isn't he?"

"Yes, he is."

They went in search of Gurdev, who was gathering up some of the villagers to walk back to the road with them. They would bring back the food that Pinga was bringing out.

Joly asked Gurdev where Ranjit lived.

"Ranjit live here." She waved her hand around, taking in the whole village.

"Which house?"

"No house. He is all…" She paused trying to find the right words. "No *mata*, no *baba*; he village boy."

Joly wasn't sure she had understood this correctly. "He has no parents? Where does he sleep?"

Gurdev shrugged her shoulders. "He sleep…" Again, she encompassed the village with a wave of her hand.

Joly was not happy. "You're telling me, he sleeps wherever he happens to be? That he has *no home* to go to at night?"

"Village watch. All feed. He good, okay."

Oh my Gods, she thought to herself. I can't leave him here. No wonder he hasn't left my side today. He has no one. Everyone is busy with their own families, dealing with the starvation and their sick.

"I will take him with me when we leave. He *will* have a home with me." Joly left no room for argument.

Morag wasn't surprised. She had been watching the interaction and saw the bonding that was taking place. So… she going to get the chance to be a grandmother after all. She snorted, and Gurdev and Joly both looked at her.

"Sorry," she chuckled. "Are we going to get him on the plane?"

"Of course we are."

Gurdev looked from one to the other. "You take Ranjit?"

"Yes. Is that a problem? He has no home. I will give him a home, an education, love."

"He say." She spoke to the boy rapidly in Hindi. He replied, never letting go of Joly's hand.

"He say go. You are good. *Dhanya-waadh.*"

No argument? Wow! Joly was surprised. She had expected to have to fight to take Ranjit out of there. She looked down at him and found he was looking at her.

"*Hum Ho Gaye Aap Ke.*"

Joly looked at Gurdev.

"He say he yours."

Joly knelt down and hugged him. "Yes, you are mine now."

"How old is he?" she asked.

Gurdev shrugged, "Maybe…" She held up the fingers of one hand.

Do you know his birthday? The day he was born?"

She shook her head. She spoke to the other villagers. There was an animated conversation and then Gurdev turned back to Joly.

"I talk Pinga. She talk you."

"Okay."

The group headed toward the road to meet Pinga. The villagers were excited about finally having decent food to eat. Joly and Morag were both looking forward to a good nights sleep.

It was nice to have company on the walk back to the road, even if they couldn't understand what was being said. The trip didn't seem to take near as long as it had in the morning.

Pinga was already waiting with the rickshaw. She and the villagers spent the next ten minutes conversing.

Morag went out into the field and retrieved the suitcase.

Ranjit didn't really seem to be paying attention, but suddenly his head perked up. He turned and looked at Joly. "Cho-ly, *apa jadu-garni. Asla.*" He shook his head no.

Pinga looked over at Ranjit for the first time and seemed to realize that he was holding tightly to Joly's hand. Pinga said something to Gurdev and another animated conversation ensued.

The villagers unloaded the rickshaw and each in turn stopped in front of Joly and Morag, saying thank you, "*Dhanya-waadh.*"

They headed back toward the village and Morag, Joly and Ranjit climbed into the rickshaw, along with Pinga.

Everyone was quiet for the first few minutes, when Pinga suddenly spoke sharply to Ranjit. He answered her quietly and she was again silent.

A few minutes later, Pinga turned to Joly and asked, "Why you take Ranjit?"

Joly smiled and said, "I can give him a good home, an education, lots of attention and love. Besides, I don't think he would let me leave him behind."

Pinga nodded. "You will have much trouble at customs. Is not right to make him happy, then have to leave behind. You should not do this, I think."

"I won't have trouble at customs and he won't be left behind."

"We see. Morag, truck is ready for tomorrow. You need to pay, then can take."

"Good! We'll do that first thing and take it to the village. How far is it to the next village?"

"Maybe ten kilometer."

"Across the fields?"

"You not go across the fields?"

"Yes, I think so. We need to check out the land. That is the best way."

"Maybe five, six kilometer across field."

"Good, we'll leave the truck and walk from there."

"*Hawass-bakta,*" Pinga muttered under her breath.

It seemed to take a long time to get back to the city. Both Morag and Joly dozed on and off. Ranjit was too excited to sleep and kept watch on the passing scenery.

They finally arrived at Pinga's and she fed them something she called *Rajma Chawal*, which was rice and kidney beans, and hot tea.

Joly had to monitor Ranjit's eating, as she didn't want him up all night with a sick tummy. It didn't take much for him to be full, his little stomach had shrunk so much over the past three months.

With the full tummy came tiredness, and having never seen a proper bed before, he happily snuggled under the cover and was soon fast asleep.

Joly and Morag weren't far behind him. As soon as Joly had scryed home to Nefertiti, they too, tucked in. They slept on either side of him, giving him a security he had never known existed before.

Morag dreamed of a demon so terrible, it left her trembling in her sleep.

Joly dreamed of running through a field with Duncan and a little dark haired boy in between them, holding tightly onto both of their hands.

Ranjit didn't dream, but he didn't have any nightmares either, for the first time in over two years.

Again, the morning arrived before they were ready for it. They dressed, ate, and then Pinga took them to where the truck was. Morag checked the back of it, to make sure it was fully loaded and she asked for a copy of the manifest. She didn't plan on checking each item off. She couldn't even read it, but maybe one of the villagers would like to.

Pinga said she would lead them to the road to the village and then she would see them that night.

Joly climbed into the driver's seat with Ranjit, bright eyed over the adventure he was on, sitting close to her.

Morag sat on the other side, feeling every day of her age. She didn't want to say anything to Joly, so she tried to appear relaxed. She had not slept well and the vision of the demon was still with her.

Joly eased into the traffic and followed the rickshaw. The traffic was a nightmare with vehicles changing lanes without signaling, pedestrians walking out in front of the traffic and everyone was honking. She had never heard so much honking.

They made it to the turn off and Joly felt better once they were on the side road. The trip to the village was uneventful and the villagers quickly gathered around the truck, once Joly eased to a stop.

Morag handed the manifest to Gurdev and after a quick cup of tea, they began walking to the next village. With her crystal, Morag knew they would never get lost, but Ranjit seemed to know the way.

He was a curious little boy, and he kept up a running chatter. Joly would say words in English and he would repeat them, sometimes insisting that she say the words in Hindi.

Joly noticed Morag was quieter than usual and worried about her. She needed to do a healing on her. She looked tired too.

It wasn't long before they reached the village. Again, they were greeted with some suspicion, but word traveled fast and they knew of the previous day's success. Their contact there was another woman whose name was Sudhara.

Their day went the same as the one before. When they were done, they began to make their way back toward the first village. They were half way there when they had the breath knocked out of them. Ranjit cried out as he stumbled.

The hatred again slammed against them as the invisible blanket slowly began to smother them, but it felt different this time. Morag grabbed her crystal and sure enough, not too far away was the cause of all the problems.

The man stood hidden out of sight although he could see them. Morag saw he had several things with him that she recognized. She also sensed that he had no plans on letting them get back to the village.

He didn't seem to have a crystal, but then not everyone needed one. However, she felt he did not have the ability to see them close up.

"Joly, he means business. How do you want to handle this?"

She remembered, "*Your friend is very powerful, but not as powerful as you are. She has the wisdom. You must listen to her. You will win this battle, with her help.*"

"Umm, what do you think we should do, Morag? I don't want Ranjit hurt."

Morag was pleased with her answer. She was thinking about someone else, not herself. Her healing was almost complete. She had put the past behind her. Soon, they would have to go to the States. Joly was ready.

"He is powerful. Not as powerful as you are, but you will have to be very careful just the same. I think I will draw a circle and keep Ranjit safe within it. You will need to approach him and have it out. Take your wand; you will need it. Also, remember your powers and don't be afraid to use them. He won't hesitate to use everything he has against you."

"My wand... yes, of course." She knelt down to open the case. They were still being buffeted by the evil that surrounded them. She withdrew the small case and opened it. The Rowan wand lay snuggled within. It was the strongest protection against magic of all the wands, and she knew she would have use of it on this day.

Ranjit was silent through all of this. He could feel bad things in the air, as he struggled to draw each breath, but he didn't understand what it was. He knew that Cho-ly and Morg were talking about something, but he didn't know what.

Morag drew her circle and surrounded it with sea salt. She poured holy water around the edge and drew in the pentagram. She said her invocations. She took Ranjit by the hand and led him into the circle, sitting him near the center. Morag lit a white candle and gave it to Ranjit to hold. She lit another white candle and sat beside the boy.

Joly told him to wait and she grounded herself, absorbing all the energy she could. She began walking toward the bushes where the man was hidden. She had trouble standing straight as the hatred swirled around her, slamming her back and forth. Again, the air pressure changed and she knew she had to act fast.

She saw movement and knew where he hid. She thought of the villagers starving because of this person... and then she thought of Ranjit.

The anger bubbled up from soles of her feet and infused her whole body. Anger replaced the blood pumping through her veins; anger replaced the heart that beat in her chest.

"*Damn you!*" she screamed and the air began to cool.

Morag watched as the air around Joly shimmered. She saw the crystals of ice forming on the grass. She and Ranjit were safe from the cold. Icicles began appearing on the bushes. Still Joly moved forward and Morag prayed that the Gods were watching over this child of her heart.

"*Damn you, you bastard,*" Joly screamed again as she advanced on the figure who had come out in the open. The air was freezing now and the figure raised his arm.

Joly saw the flash of the blade the instant before he sent it flying straight toward her. She raised her wand and directed it toward the knife that was now less than fifteen feet from her. The knife closed fast.

Morag sat with her one arm around Ranjit. The other held the candle. They watched as Joly screamed at the man and they saw the knife leave his hand. Ranjit drew in a deep breath and Morag gave him a squeeze of assurance.

Her wand sparked and the knife suddenly didn't exist. It had vanished as if it had never been. Still Joly advanced and the air got even colder.

Ice replaced the anger pumping through her veins. Ice replaced the anger beating in her chest. And still she moved forward.

The distance between the two of them was now less than twenty feet. And still she advanced, her paces sure and steady.

Suddenly a *khukuri*, a curved knife came out of nowhere. It flashed toward Joly at an unbelievable speed. Her wand sparked immediately and this knife too, disappeared.

The man was obviously feeling the effects of the cold, but his hatred overcame it. He advanced now and screamed at Joly. *"Apa kutiya! Apa mah-der chod!"* He lifted a sword and ran at Joly swinging.

Her wand sparked but she overshot. She tried again, and again she overshot.

The ice melted in Joly's veins and her heart, and it was replaced by a roaring inferno of fire. She was burning up, but she had no sense of self, no sense of being.

He was in front of her. He swore at her again, as he lifted the sword for the final blow and sweet victory.

Ranjit opened his mouth to scream and Morag quickly covered it, muffling the sound of terror coming from the small child. Her eyes never left the sword as it was raised.

As he brought his frozen arm back to swing at her neck, Joly sent him the gift of heat.

The fire spewed from her wand with a heat so intense, he was incinerated. His sword dropped harmlessly to the ground, beside the charred remains.

Joly turned and walked back toward her family.

She suddenly realized the air pressure was still wrong. She was still having trouble breathing. *What the...?*

Morag saw her first. She slid out of the bushes silently, and without a sound she ran toward Joly's unprotected back. She held nothing in her hands and Morag knew without a doubt, that the fight had not yet even started. She had been invisible even to her, which said she was most likely a Sister. Morag didn't dare yell, knowing this was something Joly had to do alone.

Ranjit had struggled to his feet when he saw Joly returning to them. Then he saw the woman running toward her and he went to warn her. Morag dropped her candle and grabbed him, and again covered his mouth, holding him tightly.

Joly saw Ranjit stand, saw Morag grab him, knew something was wrong and then she felt her, and knew she was right behind her.

She kept walking, waiting until she could hear the soft padding of feet coming through the grass. She sensed the intake of the evil one's breath and she dove to the right, falling and rolling.

Where she had stood a split second before, the grass disappeared in a mass of flame and smoke.

Joly jumped to her feet and pointed her wand. The heat had not had time to leave her body and her adrenalin was pumping fast and furious. *She was mad!* There was no thought of fear, of losing. This monster in front of her had caused much grief and she was about to pay the ultimate price.

The wand sparked and shot out a flame directly toward the woman. The evil one raised her hand and a bolt of lightning like electricity shot from her fingers, colliding with the fire. The explosion was deafening, the earth scorched.

Joly shot another burst of flame and again it was repelled. They circled each other alternately shooting and repelling.

Morag knew the air would rob Joly of her strength. She had to get rid of it. She spoke quietly to Ranjit, and with much hand signing and shushing of the lips, he appeared to understand he was not to move or make a sound.

Morag went to the case and removed the candles, bottle of water and the bowl. She prepared everything as she had the day before. The time passed, the candle slowly burned down toward the water. Morag watched the fight out of the corner of her eye as she invoked the spirits.

It was an apparent standoff. Neither seemed to be able to get the best of the other. Morag hoped some decent air would change that.

Ranjit sat quietly, still holding his candle. He prayed to *Durga* to protect his new friend and to destroy the one who would destroy Cho-ly. He had wet himself, but he was so involved in what was happening, he didn't realize it.

Joly was tired, but that fact had not been conveyed to her conscious mind. She wasn't aware of her short breaths, her panting. She was only aware of the enemy that stood facing her and her anger bubbled to the surface once again, and it gave her the strength to continue for another round.

Morag continued her ritual, asking the Spirit of Air to help, as he had the previous day. She heard the first splutter of the candle and knelt in front of it.

"Spell, be gone; magic be gone.
Go now, back to whence you came."

The wick went under the water and a small wisp of smoke arose. Morag sensed that the air was pure again. She dug the hole and buried the candle, pouring the water over the dirt. If she was right, the battle should intensify. She looked up to see death coming at her.

Neither of the two warriors had felt the first shift in the air currents, but the sudden clearing of the heavy pressure got the attention of the one who had laid the spell.

Rupinder Rati whirled around and saw the old woman pouring out the water. She sent a charge of electricity toward her and whirled around again to face her adversary.

Joly saw the lightning heading toward the only two people she had in the world. Her wand extended, the eruption of flame was formidable. It spewed toward her enemy.

Morag saw the electrical charge coming, heard it crackling through the air. Without conscious thought, she grabbed Ranjit and threw the two of them sideways, rolling out of the circle. She stood and holding the boy, she began running.

The charge slammed into her protective circle and the explosion deafened the two them and sent them flying through the air. Not being able to continue in a straight line, the lightning turned and went to ground. The crater it dug went deep and the earth where they had been seconds before, sank out of sight.

Rupinder turned in time to see the deadly flame almost upon her. There was no time to defuse it. She threw herself sideways; felt searing heat and knew incredible pain.

She looked and saw why. Where her left arm had been, there was nothing, not even a shred of bone or flesh. She pushed herself to her feet with her one arm. She looked for the woman, but saw death instead.

The flame hit her with such a force, she was instantly cremated and the flame carried her ashes another thirty feet, before slamming down into the ground, burning the grass in a twenty foot circle.

Joly sank to the ground, unable to stand any longer. Her breath came in ragged gasps and as she sat there, she thanked her Gods for lending a hand in giving her victory.

Ranjit, unable to wait another second, jumped to his feet and ran toward Joly. She heard him coming and turned, opening her arms to embrace him, as he crashed into her chest.

Morag followed with a bottle of water for Joly. They sat there quietly and rested. Joly saw the dampness on Ranjit's pants, but said nothing. If he didn't have nightmares after all he had witnessed, she would be surprised.

The heat was beating down on them and they knew they had to go. Joly went with Morag to pack the suitcase. Ranjit didn't want to let go of her hand, so when she showed him that she needed both of them free, he grabbed onto her pant leg. She found she was tripping over him as she moved about, but she said nothing.

Once they started walking, she held his hand tightly. They hadn't gone far when Joly realized Ranjit wasn't going to make it. She stopped and picked him up, resting him on her hip. She could see Morag was tired and she tried to take the suitcase from her, but she was brushed off.

"You have your hands full already. I'm not so feeble I can't carry this damn case back to the village."

They were both relieved when the village came into sight. All Joly wanted to do was head back to town, but there was still one more thing to do first.

Gurdev met them at the truck. Morag checked and saw that it was half full. Good, she thought. It was ready to go.

Gurdev told them that everything had been removed and sorted into two piles, with the one pile being reloaded.

Morag told her they would have no more problems; that the people involved had been dealt with.

They had a cup of lime juice and then got into the truck and headed back to the other village. They unloaded the food and told Sudhara they would be back the next day. They also let her know that the problem had been dealt with.

They drove back to Hardoi. Joly wanted nothing more than to have a shower and relax in the comfort of a hotel room, but they couldn't insult Pinga, so she headed in what she hoped was the right direction.

She took several wrong turns, but finally found the street she needed. They parked in front of the house and walked to the door with Joly carrying Ranjit, who was fast asleep.

Morag knocked and they waited. Finally, the door opened a crack and a woman spoke brusquely to them in rapid Hindi and shut the door in their faces. They had both understood the word Pinga, but nothing else.

Joly looked at Morag, "I take it Pinga is *not* at home."

Morag chuckled. "I think you're right. Well, let's take the truck back. Do you think you can find the place?"

"Eventually."

They both laughed and climbed back in the truck.

After many wrong turns, Joly did eventually find the place. Morag tried to explain to the man at the desk they wanted the truck filled up again, but either he couldn't figure out what she wanted, or he was being deliberately ignorant. She couldn't decide which it was.

"Now what?" Joly asked, wishing again, they could just go and find a hotel.

"Back to Pinga's I guess. We'll just sit in the truck and wait for her to come home."

"I need a drink. Let's see if we can find a restaurant or something."

"Good idea."

They drove around for a while, but were unsure of what might be a restaurant, without actually walking and looking inside. Joly gave up and decided to drive back to Pinga's.

When they got there they were hesitant to knock on the door again. Joly decided she wasn't getting out of the truck and disturbing Ranjit, just to turn around and climb back in.

Morag said that she would go. She climbed out and went to the door. Knocking softly, she waited. Nothing. She knocked louder. Still nothing. She turned and walked back to the truck. As she was climbing in, the door opened and Pinga stepped out.

"Very sorry, did not hear knock. Come in."

Joly climbed down and eased Ranjit into her arms. They walked into the house. Joly asked if she could take Ranjit to the bedroom and was told yes. Joly gently laid him on the bed, concerned if he should wake up and she wasn't there.

Thirst won out and she headed to the kitchen, where Pinga was pouring tea.

They told her about eliminating the evildoers and delivering the food. Also about not being able to get the truck filled, once they were back in Hardoi.

"We go now. Truck ready in morning."

"Can we not get it filled and get it back tonight?"

Joly looked at Morag, wondering about her reasoning, but Morag said nothing.

"Maybe."

"Alright." Morag stood to show she was ready to leave.

Joly pushed herself to her feet. She was exhausted and all she wanted was to go and curl up beside Ranjit. "I'll get Ranjit." She went to leave the room, but Pinga stopped her.

"Leave here. He be okay."

Something in Pinga's stance, the way she said the words, had Joly on full alert. Something wasn't right and her senses were *never* wrong.

"It's alright. I don't want him to wake up and find me gone." Again, she went to leave.

"No!" Pinga's voice was sharp. "He fine. My people talk to him. Tell him you be back." She looked worried.

Now Joly knew something was wrong. She didn't hesitate; she turned and ran to the bedroom.

An old woman was carefully wrapping the sleeping Ranjit in a sheet. She looked startled when Joly went flying into the room.

Joly was angry. She went to the bed and scooped up the boy and walked back to the door.

The old woman muttered under her breath, "*Jadu Karana.*"

Joly had heard that said before. She wondered what it meant, and knew that it wasn't anything complimentary. She walked into the kitchen.

"By the way... Gurdev said you were supposed to tell me something regarding Ranjit. What was it?"

Pinga was having trouble playing the gracious host. It was obvious that she was mad.

"Gurdev say Ranjit born *Diwali* five year ago. Mother was Nalini Devi.

Father was Matsya Kumar. Matsya kill Nalini for not enough dowry. He want motorbike. Her Father say no *Rupee* for bike. One day they find Matsya dead. Someone kill him. Ranjit saw Mother die. He was maybe two."

She headed out of the room. "We go now."

After getting into the truck, Morag wrote the information down. "I wonder what *Diwali* is and when it is."

"We'll find out. Did you get the same feeling as me? They were going to take him away while we were gone. An old woman was already in the bedroom when I got there."

"Yes, I suspected as much. What do you want to do now? It won't be safe to go back there. These people kill one another over the smallest things. A motorcycle? My Gods!"

"Our train leaves when?"

"Six AM. I had already thought to get this load out to the villages tonight, so we could leave in the morning. Now, I know we have to. Are you up to it?"

Joly smiled at her friend. "Of course. As Daddy always said, 'One does what one has to do.' Yes, I'm tired, but I can make it. Once we're back in Lucknow, we will be able to sleep around the clock."

She looked down at Ranjit. "Well, maybe not quite around the clock."

They both chuckled.

Back at the warehouse, Pinga was having an animated conversation with the clerk. It was the same one that Morag had tried talking to.

Pinga spoke to Morag. "He say not ready tonight. Come back morning."

"Tell him he will have it ready tonight or he will be unloading it all again. I will not be back in the morning for it. And tell him I will pay double if it's ready in an hour."

Pinga and the man had an intense argument about something. Finally, the man threw up his arms and walked away.

Pinga looked at Morag. "He say cannot do. Help go home already."

Something in her stance, told them she was lying.

"Alright. If it can't be done, then I guess we'll have to wait. Tell him we'll bring the truck back in the morning."

"No! Leave truck here. They load before you come. You come with me."

"No, I don't think so. We'll bring the truck. You can go Pinga. We'll be behind you."

Pinga stormed out the door, all pretense of civility gone.

Morag called the man back. "You load now?" She waved her hand in the direction of the truck.

The man smiled broadly and gave a quick bow. He hollered at someone out of sight and soon the truck was being quickly loaded.

He tried to cheat her on the price, but given the speed with which the truck had been loaded, Morag paid without haggling.

They climbed back in and headed back to the village.

It was very late when they got back to Hardoi that night. Gurdev had been pleased that she could offer them a meal and they had enjoyed something called *Kaikari Biriyani*, which had been similar to a meatless stew, with vegetables and rice.

Joly had asked about the information Pinga had given her. Gurdev said it was correct. She explained that *Diwali* was a big festival, celebrated all over India. It was usually held in November.

Joly never mentioned the fight with Pinga or that the family planned on taking Ranjit. These people were all related and she didn't want to cause any more problems.

Joly drove to the railway station and parked. They decided this was the safest place to be. Pinga could get someone to come for the truck. She would eventually guess where it could be found.

They dozed on and off through the night. Ranjit woke up once and had to go to the washroom. Joly stood outside the truck with him while he went on the side of the road. He was asleep almost instantly, once he was back in the truck.

Dawn arrived and they decided to go in the station. Joly spotted policemen walking around and hoped they wouldn't question why a Hindi boy was traveling with a white woman. They seemed to not notice.

The train was late, and when it arrived, they quickly climbed aboard.

Ranjit was excited, but also nervous. When the train started up, he clutched onto Joly for dear life and she held him tightly, talking in a low and reassuring voice.

"Can you imagine the reaction when we get on the plane?" Joly laughed and Morag joined in.

Morag was exhausted and slept all the way to Lucknow.

Once he was over his fright, Ranjit enjoyed watching the scenery fly by, and Joly smiled as she watched him.

At Lucknow, Morag phoned the number Amar had given them. They were in luck. He was at home and would leave immediately to pick them up.

Ranjit was terrified of the city, the sounds, and all the people. Even his curiosity couldn't overcome the fright of how big, how loud, how fast, everything was. Joly carried him until they found a place to sit down.

Amar found them there a short time later. He was amazed they had a child with them, but seemed pleased once they explained what had happened.

He took them to the hotel they had stayed at before. Morag told him they would not be going anywhere else until the next day. Amar seemed disappointed, but assured them he would be ready whenever they called.

They went to their room and Morag went straight to bed.

Joly got Ranjit settled down and went to her friend. "You need a healing." It was a statement, not a question.

"I'm fine dear, just weary."

Joly ran her hands over Morag's body. She felt that something was not right. She sent her healing energies into Morag.

Sometime later, she realized that Ranjit was squirming and thought about the washroom. He had never seen an indoor bathroom before and she wondered how he would react to it.

She led him into the small room and showed him the toilet. He stood there wiggling back and forth. Joly tried to sit him on the toilet, but he would have no part of it.

She finally took him by the hand and went down to the lobby. She explained the problem to the desk clerk, who took Ranjit to the washroom, talking all the while to him in Hindi. They were gone a long time, and Joly was getting worried when the door finally opened and Ranjit went running to her, talking non-stop.

The clerk laughed and told her that once he knew what it was all about, he didn't want to leave. "He must have flushed at least a dozen times."

Joly laughed, relieved that that part was taken care of. They wandered through the hotel, Ranjit's curiosity aroused. He wanted to explore every nook and cranny.

Joly noticed the strange looks she was getting and decided it was because of her young companion. She changed her mind, when they went back to their room and she looked in the mirror. *Holy Gods!* She was a mess.

She realized they had not had clean clothes or showers since they had left here, three days ago. Ranjit was filthy also, and she wondered how he would take to having a bath. She needed to buy him some clothes, too.

"*Mein bukha hun* Cho-ly."

Of course he was hungry. They hadn't eaten since last night. Gods! She wasn't doing well as a mother at all. She wasn't sure about taking him to the fancy dining room, so she called the desk. They assured her that room service was no problem.

Ranjit was intrigued by the phone. Joly knew he couldn't understand why she was talking to a thing, but he had seen some strange things the past two days. She was sure he would get used to it. She chuckled when she thought about the television and what his reaction to it, might be.

Their meal arrived and Joly woke Morag. She looked better, but she was still in need of more sleep.

Ranjit was amazed at the assortment of food on his plate and he pestered Joly for the names of each one, carefully repeating them after her.

"Morag, I need to get Ranjit some clothes. Do you think I should take him with me, or would it be better if I left him with you?"

"Why don't you call Amar? He can translate and you would be sure to get the right sizes."

"Yes, I'll do that. Great idea.

Oh my Gods! With all the excitement last night, I forgot to let Nefertiti know we were okay."

Morag went and retrieved her crystal ball and Joly scryed home.

Nefertiti was almost out of her mind with worry and Pip had been getting under her skin for hours. When she finally felt her Mistress, she was extremely relieved.

Ranjit was fascinated by the crystal and Morag let him hold it.

Amar arrived smiling, pleased he could be of service. He talked to Ranjit in Hindi and translated some words into English. He drove them to the market and took the two of them to various stores.

Ranjit didn't own any shoes, had never worn underwear, pajamas or socks, had never owned more than the clothes on his back. To have an extra set of clothing to change into was more than he could understand.

Amar took them to a park and he sat with Ranjit and explained all the different things he was going to have to get used to. Ranjit still couldn't seem to get some of the important things understood, so finally Amar rose and said, "Come. We go to my home. I will show Ranjit some of this."

Joly wasn't sure she should do this, but Amar seemed nice, so she decided to go ahead. They got in his car and he took them through town and into a residential area. His house was small and the yard neatly kept.

Inside, Amar yelled and a woman came through the door from what Joly assumed was the kitchen. "This my wife, Chandra. This Joly and Ranjit. Joly and her friend are the ones who hire me."

Chandra came forward and shook Joly's hand. Her English wasn't as good as Amar's, but it was understandable.

Amar explained what was happening with Ranjit and that he thought maybe showing him some of the things he needed to know about, would help. Chandra agreed.

They covered the lights, refrigerator, small appliances, washing machine, bathtub, sinks, radio, closets and dressers.

Amar was going to turn the television on, but Joly asked him not to. She wanted to save that for later.

Chandra served them iced tea and made some suggestions to help make the transition easier. She also had Joly write out a list of words that Ranjit might use that she thought Joly should know.

Joly spent an all together enjoyable afternoon with the couple and Ranjit asked endless questions.

Amar informed Joly that he would take them out to the airport the following day. Ranjit needed to get used to the idea of flying.

Supper time was fast approaching and Joly suggested it was time to go.

Amar said he would be waiting for their phone call in the morning. Joly thanked him for being such a kind soul. He looked embarrassed after she said it and she worried that maybe she shouldn't have.

Ranjit was trying out new words and said thank you and goodbye to Amar in English.

They went up to the room, both tired but happy. Morag had the television on when they walked in and Ranjit was terrified. He screamed and clutched on to Joly with every ounce of strength he had. Morag turned it off, but it was still a long while before he calmed down.

Joly told Morag about their day and that she had asked Amar not to show him the TV, but she thought maybe she had been wrong. She had no way of explaining to this little boy about the people in the box.

Morag had showered while they were gone and Joly could hardly wait to do the same thing. Once she was sure Ranjit was settled, she disappeared into the bathroom. The hot water felt wonderful and she really didn't want to turn it off, but she had a little boy she wanted to bath before putting him in between the clean sheets.

Ranjit's first bath was an experience that Joly did not want to repeat. He was fine until it came time to actually get into the tub, then he would have no part of it. He leaned over the edge and ran his hand through the water and thought it was great fun, but when Joly tried to lift him in, he kicked and scratched and screamed. Joly felt like she was trying to hang onto a full-grown man, not a tiny malnourished little boy.

Morag joined them in the bathroom and she tried to talk him into getting in the tub. He still refused. They finally decided they were going to have to force him. If he won this round, Joly didn't have a hope of ever getting him to bathe.

Joly had clean clothes on, but she knew they would be dry by morning. She held onto Ranjit as she climbed into the tub and sat down. He tried to scramble back out, but Morag was there to make sure he didn't. Joly managed to push him down in between her legs and she put a scissor-lock around him. Morag handed her the soap and she began a soothing massage on his back. She sent calming energies to him as she washed his arms and neck. Morag took the soap and washed his legs.

Between the two of them, they got him clean, except for his hair. Joly talked soothingly to him throughout the performance and she finally stood up and squatted over Ranjit. She leaned him back into the water. He did some more flailing about, but in the end, when he got out of the tub, he was squeaky clean from head to toe.

She had bought him pajamas and he excitedly put them on. She knew it was the first new items of clothing he had ever worn.

She tucked him in bed and told him a story from her childhood. She knew he didn't understand, but the sound of her voice was soothing, and he was soon fast asleep.

At nine, she called her lawyer in Surrey. She was lucky; he was in and was able to speak to her. She explained about Ranjit and asked how long before he could have the necessary papers drawn up. He thought he could have everything ready in a week. She gave him the address of the hotel and hung up.

"Everything okay?" Morag inquired.

"Yes, he said no problem. Gods, I am so thankful I'm not a normal person. How would I have pulled this off if I were?"

Morag laughed. "If you were a normal person, you wouldn't be in India. At least not out in the villages where we just were."

"How true." She chuckled. "Well, it's been a long day. I'm ready for bed.

You slept all day. How do you feel?"

"Better, but I'm ready to lie down again."

They both crawled in beside Ranjit and within minutes, all were fast asleep.

Rauna thought about her travels and wondered if she was making any headway. She honestly didn't think so. She had heard so many different stories and learned about so many different types of beings… beings she hadn't known existed or ones she thought she would never have to deal with, so had never taken the time to learn about them.

Alexander had paid her fare to Mexico and she had toured through the country, talking to different shamans and witches.

She had gone to Central America and learned about the Catholic tradition of demonology.

She went to the West Indies and she smiled as she thought about Mama Brigitte. Now there was a woman with a zest for life. Everything she did, she did big. She was knowledgeable about evil spirits and evil witches and had taught Rauna about Voodoo.

There had been lots of dancing, drinking, singing and having fun, but now it was time to get back to this demon thing.

She sighed as she thought of her cabin across the ocean and wondered when she would see it again.

The next few days passed quickly. They did some more sightseeing and shopping. Morag spent two days out at the bird sanctuary. On those days, Amar took Joly and Ranjit back to his home.

Amar and Chandra explained the television to Ranjit and turned it on for him to see. As soon as he started to panic, they would turn it off, assuring him that he could do the same thing. Amar showed him the off and on buttons and told him to try it. Ranjit pushed the on button. The picture and voices came on. He hit the off button and they disappeared. Soon, it became a game and he lost his fear.

They were having breakfast when there was a knock at the door. Morag answered it. It was a courier for Joly. She signed for the package and tipped the man.

As soon as the door closed, she tore into it. Everything was there. The passport just needed his picture and Amar knew where to get that done. The birth certificate read Ranjit Duncan James, date of birth October twenty-ninth, place of birth Mission, B.C. Canada. Amar had checked the dates of *Diwali* five years prior. She had decided that although *Diwali* actually lasted five days, that she would have his birth on the Indian New Years day, as this was a new beginning for him.

Ranjit was legally hers. "*Yes!* We can go home now."

They made the reservations and Ranjit was excited about traveling on the plane. Amar had driven them out to the airport twice and Ranjit had watched in fascination at the people getting on the plane and the plane lifting off into the sky. Amar had explained that this was how they would get to his new forever home.

When Amar heard the passport and papers had arrived, he decided they must celebrate. He invited them to his home for supper. Chandra was just as excited for them. They explained to Ranjit that he now belonged to Joly, she had papers that said so, and no one could take him away from her. The papers said she was his mother. Ranjit thought about this and asked Chandra if he could call Cho-ly, *Mata*. Chandra suggested he might want to call her Mommy.

While they were eating, Chandra suggested they should have a Canadian name for Ranjit. Joly agreed. They tried out different ones and asked Ranjit what he thought of each one. He decided he liked Randy best. It sounded close to his name.

The day of departure arrived. Their flight didn't leave until nine-fifteen in the evening and Randy acted up all day, excited about the upcoming adventure. Amar and Chandra drove them to the airport and stayed with them until it was time to go. There were tears and hugs and promises to keep in touch.

When they finally boarded the plane, it was a different story with Randy. He clutched on to Joly, although he never said anything. This was a short flight, as they had a four hour layover in Delhi, before leaving for London. Randy said nothing on the one hour flight. He sat quietly and after looking out the window once, he refused to look out again.

In Delhi, they sat in the airport, Randy sleeping on Joly's lap. When it came time to go through customs Joly was nervous, but they went through without a hitch.

They were on the plane for nine hours and once Randy was awake, he acted like a seasoned traveler. He insisted on sitting by the window and talked continuously. They arrived in London at seven in the morning. Going through customs was harder this time. Joly was asked many questions, but her documents were in order, so they didn't detain her.

The time difference was going to be hard on them all, but especially Randy. He wanted lunch, but it was only breakfast time.

They stayed in the same hotel as they had before. They would be in London twenty-five hours, before leaving for Vancouver. Randy couldn't believe the size of their suite and the two separate bedrooms. He ran from one to the other several times talking non-stop.

Morag wondered if Joly would mention Alyce, but she was so involved with her new child that if she thought of it, she gave no sign. Morag took out her crystal again, mentally kicking herself in the butt for doing so. She scryed up north and throughout England, but neither saw or felt anything. She decided she had to have been imagining things.

Randy wanted to explore the new city, so they went for a walk after eating. He found it very strange to hear all the talking and not being able to understand any of it, except for the occasion word.

By three in the afternoon, Randy was ready for bed. Joly tried keeping him awake longer, but by five, she knew he had to lie down. They had to be at the airport by six-thirty in the morning and she thought he would sleep through until it was time to get up.

Morag managed to stay up until seven and then she too went to bed. Joly scryed home for the last time and then she stood at the window looking out, but she saw nothing.

The voice came unbidden to her mind.

"Joly, I love you so damned much. When we're apart, I feel like part of me is missin' and I'm never whole again, until I'm back with you. I can never get enough of you; you're like an addiction to me. Tell me you'll never leave me; tell me you'll never go away without me."

She had told him what he needed to hear and they had snuggled together and later, they had made incredibly beautiful love.

Where was his body? Where was his spirit? She knew he would have tried to contact her, but she had never felt anything. *Duncan, my love... where are you?*

She realized she was crying again. She went and washed her face and got ready for bed. She climbed in beside Randy, who turned in his sleep and cuddled next to her.

At the airport the following morning, they lost Randy. One second he was there, the next, he was gone. Joly and Morag both panicked and ran in all directions looking for him.

Neither noticed the man, whose eyes followed them everywhere. Neither noticed the man who stared hard at the little boy who was with them. And neither noticed the man who attempted to follow Joly, but lost her in the crowded airport.

Morag found Randy in a restaurant trying to take a muffin without paying for it. Morag paid for it and led him back to Joly, who gave him a lecture on leaving her side.

Randy seemed to be contrite and said he was sorry in Hindi. Joly made him say it in English.

He had his head bowed and was fiddling with the muffin. "So-we Mummy."

Joly burst into tears and hugged him. She sat him down with his muffin and wiped her eyes. "Gods, Morag. This mothering is hard."

"You haven't seen anything yet child. Trust me. He'll break your heart a million times before all is said and done."

They boarded the plane for the last leg of their journey. It would be a long trip with a four year old. Joly had bought him crayons and coloring books, a pre-school alphabet book and several others to keep him occupied for at least part of the journey. They would be aboard for ten hours, but would get into

Vancouver at ten-thirty the same morning. She patiently taught him to say "Hello Stephen" and she laughed as he insisted on saying, "Hello Sea-ven."

The man at the viewing window frowned. He was not happy he had lost her. He needed to talk to her.

Morag sat looking out the window. The sun was shining and reflecting off the metal. The rays refracted and so did Morag's mind. Suddenly there were bits and pieces of micro memories, words, thoughts, pictures. It was a kaleidoscope whirling around. None of it made sense and when her thoughts cleared; she didn't understand what had just happened. She tried to piece it together, but nothing would fall into place. *Weird!* She reached in her purse and dug out the riddle.

Randy was happy. He had things to look at and do. There was the window he could look out if he wanted to. He had someone to call his own. For a four year old who was used to being on his own, this was all new and very exciting.

Joly's thoughts were of home and the things she needed to do, once there. Randy came first. She needed to find a reliable person to look after him, for whenever she had to leave. She decided the easiest way would be to have someone move in. That way Randy would get used to them. She wondered if she should get someone that spoke Hindi, but she wanted him to learn English and decided maybe it wasn't a good idea. He would need to be registered for kindergarten in September. She needed to take him to the doctor to get all his shots and make sure there was nothing else wrong. She needed to take him to the dentist. The list was endless.

Randy slept for a few hours, later into their flight and Joly was glad. The time difference once they were home was going to take some getting used to.

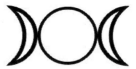

10. Magic and Dreams

Stephen met them at the airport and was shocked speechless when informed that Joly had become a mother to an Indian child. He finally spluttered, "But you can't be serious?"

"Very serious. Would you like to see his birth certificate?"

"No!" Stephen couldn't believe Joly would have done such a dumb thing. *Christ! If she wanted a kid that badly, she could have at least adopted one that looked like her.*

"Hel-lo Sea-ven."

Stephen ignored Randy and went and waited for the luggage in silence.

"Well… he didn't take that bit of news too well, did he?" Joly was upset. She couldn't understand anyone not falling instantly in love with her little guy.

Morag shook her head. "You know, there was no tolerance in our home for discrimination. Well, of course you know that. You damn near lived there. I will never understand that son of mine."

The drive out to Mission was completed in silence, except for Randy's chattering and Joly's soft replies.

The month of July passed in a blur for Joly. She was kept busy with Randy, interviewing prospective nannies, and an outbreak of some type of flu bug had hit the area, mainly attacking children. She went to the hospitals and visited all the children's wards and as she walked through, she sent her healing energies to the children.

Randy quickly adapted to the new life of luxury, thoroughly enjoying the large house and landscaped yard. The regular meals and stress free lifestyle worked wonders on him. He gained weight and filled out so much, that Joly soon needed to buy him more clothing in a larger size. He loved the cats, but Pip was his favorite.

He couldn't understand the idea of having his own room. His toys were there, but he usually took whatever he was playing with downstairs, so he could be near Joly. At bedtime, he headed for Joly's room and the comfort and security of her bed.

Morag too, was busy. There had been several cases of small towns being under different spells and she had been all over the lower mainland and over to Vancouver Island to banish them. Because she had never learned to drive, she took buses to the various places.

Chandra had told Randy that Morag was his Nani, but in English, it was said as Grandmother or Grandma. Randy had chosen to call her Gra-Morg and she delighted in spoiling him with different small things. When he wanted to visit her, she would stand at her gate and Joly would stand at hers, while he crossed the street. He loved Morag's yard with all the birds and was quickly learning to identify them and say their names in English.

There had been a nasty incident with Joan Ardell right after returning from India.

Randy had been out in the back yard, when Joan first spotted him. She didn't much care for the James girl, but she wasn't about to let some little snot-nosed Paki brat destroy anything on her block.

She had shuffled out her back door and waving her cane at him, she had screamed for him to get the hell out of that yard and off her street.

Randy didn't know what she was saying, but he knew she was mad at him and he had gone running inside the house crying. When Joly asked him what was wrong, he had led her to the window and pointed.

Joly went next door with Randy in tow, although he kept pulling back trying to get loose from her grip to go back home. Joly knocked on Joan's door and when she answered, the shock was evident on her face to see Randy with Joly.

"Mrs. Ardell, this is my son, Randy. I'm not sure what you did or said to him, but I would appreciate it if you wouldn't scare him half to death. He's had a rough life and I will *not* have him being afraid in his own back yard." She stopped to draw in a deep breath.

"You can't be serious! Your son? He's a *Paki!* What would you be wanting a Paki kid for, when there's a million *white* children needing a home?"

"Mrs. Ardell... I won't say this again. I do *not* tolerate discrimination of any kind! You will either speak kindly to my son, or you will *not* speak to him at all. *Have I made myself clear?"* Joly was livid.

The image came to her mind once again, of this girl staring into her cat's eyes. Joan didn't scare easily, but this girl made her nervous. "Yes, very clear, but you had better make sure he never sets a foot in *my* yard."

"Or *what*, Mrs. Ardell? What will you do? Hit him with your cane, throw something at him? *What?* Don't you *ever* let me catch you threatening him. He's a little boy with a lot of love to give, and like any child on this earth, he needs love. If you don't want grave repercussions I would suggest you just back off. *I mean it!*"

Joly picked up Randy, swept down the stairs, and at the bottom, she turned around, "And for your information, Randy is *not* a Paki. Paki's come from Pakistan. Randy is from India. Just so you know!" She turned and went home. She was so upset, she was shaking. She wished Morag was home, but she was off doing a banishing somewhere.

Joly had been washing floors, but she was too upset to return to that task. She grabbed her keys, called the cats, got bottles of water and juice from the fridge and said to Randy, "Let's go."

She drove down number 7 highway, headed east. She turned off and headed to the spot that their group had loved to go to. She hadn't been there since returning, but decided it was time. There was no one there, and the five of them spent a relaxing two hours. The Fraser River formed a narrow channel on the one side of the small island they were on and Randy happily played at the edge of the water. He and Joly built roadways and small water channels and played with his little cars. The cats explored the area and relaxed in the warm summer sun.

The other interesting event that took place in July was a sheet of computer paper that Morag received in the mail. She assumed Rekha had sent it, although there was no return address.

The item, printed from the internet, mentioned that two siblings had gone missing from a large village in Hardoi district. Rupinder and Jagdish Rati had not been well liked; in fact, they had been suspected of witchcraft, but nothing had ever been proven. Foul play was suspected.

The article went on to say that they were well known for hiring workers from the poor neighboring villages and either not paying them, or paying them less than had been promised. Since the reclamation work and success of crop growing in the small villages, the brother and sister had been unable to find workers.

Morag and Joly were pleased to know the reason behind the hatred they had felt, and that they had made that small piece of earth, a better and safer place to live.

Jimmy Smith was confused. Things were happening that he didn't understand and in his orderly universe he found this to be unsettling.

The first time he had almost found what he was missing had been exciting. He had been so happy because it confirmed what he had known all along. However, other things had begun to happen and he was no longer happy.

Hans understood what was going on in Jimmy's world and he was worried. When he was at work, he had lots of time to ponder over the boy's problem. He felt no good was going to come from this.

Gisela was busy with her daughter and grandchildren who had arrived for their visit. She realized Jimmy was having problems, but she didn't have time to spend with him and she thought that in the end, it would all work out.

Jimmy was at the park with his shopping cart. It had been a nice day and he had done well with his bottle and can collecting. He was resting on a park bench, thinking about what was happening to him.

Part of me is missing; part of me is missing; part of me is missing. He wished again that whatever it was that he had almost found, had stayed found instead of disappearing again. The scent of magnolia blossoms hit him again and he thought of the denim-clad woman. *I love you. I love you.*

He shook his head and got up from the bench. Pushing his cart, he headed toward Jenny Hallett's house. He always felt better after seeing her. He just hoped she would be outside.

Jenny was outside, and after talking to her for a few minutes, he headed toward the shop. He hoped Hans would have some work for him.

I love you. I love you. I love you. He thought about Jenny. She was married. He didn't think he was supposed to love her. He didn't know if he did love her. He just knew he really liked her.

The phone rang and Joly dashed to answer it. "Hello."

"Joly, it's Kyle Devon. How are you making out with your search for a nanny?"

"Kyle… it's good to hear from you. I haven't found anyone suitable at all. Either I can't understand them and they want to live in, or they don't want to live in and I understand them fine, or else I get bad vibes. Why?"

Her lawyer paused; he felt responsible for Joly even though they had never been close. Colin had been a good client, and later, so had Broderick. He wanted to do right. He too, was a witch, part of a large coven in Surrey, but without the inclination to fight the evil forces of the world. He was content to make sure his clients, mostly witches, were treated to a fair deal in all their legal matters. Moreover, if he had to use a little sorcery to get what he needed for them, so be it. That was obviously the reason the Gods had given him his powers. Randy came to his mind and he smiled, thinking about the child's birth certificate, passport and the other documents he'd had drawn up for Joly. Since then, Kyle had been in touch with the Department of Vital Statistics in Victoria and with a bit of chicanery on his part, Randy's birth certificate had been duly registered.

"There's a girl, the daughter of one of the members of my coven; she wants to move out of the city. She says its getting too crazy for her. Sara Jonathan's an up and coming artist and wants work that gives her time for her drawing and painting. She's twenty-four, very reliable and knows her

Father is a witch."

"Wow! Sounds too good to be true. What's her phone number?"

Kyle gave her the information and asked her about Randy. They talked about him for a few minutes and then discussed Joly's will. Kyle had drawn up a new one for her, naming Randy as sole beneficiary, but until Joly decided who was to be his trustee, Kyle was on hold with it. He told her he at least needed her signature on it, before she headed out of the country again. If necessary, he could always fill in the trustee section, should the necessity arise. She said she would drive in to see him and thanked him.

Joly checked on Randy, who was playing with Pip in the living room and then called Sara who said she said she would drive out that afternoon.

Her doorbell rang and Joly sensed that Morag was back from the Island. She went to answer the door, but Randy had beaten her to it. He and Morag were hugging.

Joly chastised Randy for answering the door without her being there. He knew he wasn't supposed to.

"I know is Gra-Morg. Is okay?" His large brown eyes looked at Joly questioningly.

They both looked at him. "You knew it was Gra-Morg?" Joly was shocked.

"Han. Pip say me."

"Pip told you it was Gra-Morg?"

Randy nodded. "Han."

Joly replied automatically, her thoughts in a swirl of emotion. "Yes Randy, not han, yes."

Then Morag started laughing. Joly looked at her and saw the twinkle in her eyes, and realized something wonderful had just happened. They headed for the kitchen discussing that particular bit of news.

Sara arrived and Joly was pleased with the way the interview went. Randy seemed to like her and Sara instantly fell in love with him. She had her own vehicle and liked the fact she would have a lot of free time when Joly was home. Joly wanted to ensure that she wouldn't change her mind after moving in, so asked her to think about it for a couple of days and then call her with her decision.

Two days later the phone rang. It was Sara. She told Joly she would like to take the job. She had discussed it with her parents and had their full support. If Joly was satisfied, when could she move in?

Joly had already dusted and cleaned the spare room. There hadn't been a lot to do, with her having painted it three months prior. She told Sara to come whenever she was ready.

The following week was a busy one. Sara moved in and Joly had to get used to another person living with her. Randy thought it was great having someone else to play with. Sara turned out to be an easy person to share a home with. Their eating habits were similar, Sara didn't care for TV and preferred to read if she wasn't sketching. The vivacious blonde was an early riser and loved to spend time outdoors.

Morag arrived to meet her and gave Joly her stamp of approval.

Joly needed someone who could speak Hindi, to explain to Randy why Sara was living with them. She went down to the Temple, hoping someone there could help her out. When the man she spoke to found out that an Indo-Canadian child was living with a Caucasian, he got extremely upset. They had many families who would give this child a proper home and religious training and she should turn the child over to the Temple immediately.

Joly almost ran from the Temple to her truck. She needed a spell to make the man forget he had talked to her.

She wondered what she should try next.

As she entered the house, Pip greeted her at the door. "Hi Pip, where's your buddy?"

Pip responded with a soft meow and walked toward the stairs. Suddenly, it hit her. "Pip! Come here. I need to talk to you." She walked into the living room and Pip followed. *Damn!* She needed to do the spell first. "Pip, I have to cast a spell first, and then I'll talk to you." Pip left and Joly ran up to the magic room.

She absentmindedly smiled to herself, as she thought about the day she had shown Sara through the house. When she told Sara the locked door led to the magic room, Sara had raised an eyebrow and Joly realized how silly it must have sounded. She had explained that it was a throwback from her childhood. She knew she should start referring to it as the craft room, but to her, it would always be the magic room. Her Mother had called it that when Joly was very young and it had stuck.

She flipped through the pages of the Book of Shadows and realized this was beyond her. She slammed the door to the magic room behind her and ran across the street to see Morag.

Morag sensed the panic and had the door open before Joly ran up the steps. "Gods, Morag. I need help." She quickly explained what had happened and that she didn't know how to make the man forget she had been there.

Morag began gathering things together while explaining, "Child, it is never a good plan to do a forgetting spell. Too much can go wrong. There are better ways, better things one can do. Tell me what he looked like and when I am ready, you can drive me down there and wait in the truck for me."

Morag went out into her back yard and grounded herself. She envisioned the light from the Gods entering her body and saturating her complete self. The white light overflowed and began to envelop her being.

Joly watched spellbound. Morag's tricks of the trade never ceased to amaze her. She blinked her eyes, as they seemed to blur. Then she realized it was Morag that was blurring, not her.

The white light began to diffuse, taking on the colors and shapes of the surrounding area. Morag vanished into nothingness. "Let's go dear."

The voice beside her startled her and she realized she could see Morag, but just.

They got into the truck and drove down to the Temple. Morag got out and Joly watched as the door to the Temple appeared to open by itself.

She had been waiting fifteen minutes and began to get worried. She pictured the curved knife at the man's waist and relived the moment when such a weapon had been thrown at her. She waited a few more minutes. The truck door opened and Morag climbed in. She wearily smiled at Joly. "It's done," she stated simply as she leaned back into the seat.

"I was getting worried. I had just decided to go and see what was happening."

"These things take time. I couldn't just go in like gangbusters, yelling and hollering. The power of suggestion is just that. A suggestion. And it takes time to convince someone that it is their own mind that is doing the suggesting. Also, as it turned out, he had already called someone regarding you and Randy, so I had to suggest he call them back and explain that it was a false alarm. Keep in mind that this whole operation was tricky because I don't imagine he thinks to himself in English. That made it doubly as hard to do. I do wish you had let me know what you were going to do. I could have told you what the outcome would have been and saved us all this. Anyways... it is done. Now what is your next plan, or do you have one?" They were sitting outside Joly's, but neither made a move to get out.

"I'm sorry Morag. I just thought that they would be willing to help me out. I should have thought about what happened in Hardoi, with Pinga and her family. And yes... I do have a plan of sorts. Randy talks to Pip. I thought I would talk to Pip. See if she communicates fully with him, or do they converse like he and I do."

"Good idea. Let me know how you make out." Morag climbed down and headed for home.

Joly went inside and called to Pip. She came running from upstairs and they went into the living room. Joly lay down on the floor and they began the mind meld.

"What do you need Mistress?"

"Pip, you talk to Randy. I need to know how well he can understand you."

"He understands everything, Mistress."

"Everything? Define everything. Randy speaks Hindi and you speak English. How much can you communicate to him?"

"Mistress, we speak all languages. How else are we to answer the call of where we are needed? Think about it. When Nefertiti found you in England, she didn't know what language you spoke. She said she tried several, before she got a response from you. I speak to Randy in Hindi and I am teaching him English as well."

'Oh for Pete's sake. How stupid of me. Of course I should have realized that."

"It's of no consequence Mistress. Randy is very happy here, by the way.

Was there something you needed me to tell him?"

"I'm glad he's happy. I love him so very much. Yes, I need you to explain to him that sometimes I have to go away and I can't always take him with me. That Sara is here to look after him while I'm gone. I also need you to let him know that I will always come back. That he won't be left alone to fend for himself ever again."

"Mistress, he already knows all this. He wanted to know why Miss Sara was moving in and so I told him. I told Master Randy that you would always *try* to come back, but that maybe some day, you wouldn't be able to. He saw what you did to the two in India. He understands that someday, someone might do that to you. He is very intelligent for a human child. I did assure him that you would probably be around for a long time."

"Thank you Pip. Gods! What would I do without you three?"

"You'd make out just fine Mistress. I am sure of it."

"Thank you Pip. Go in peace."

Joly laid her head on her arms and cried. Pip checked to make sure she was alright before leaving. Her tears were ones of relief and Pip felt she would be fine on her own.

Later, Joly went over to let Morag know what had transpired. Over tea, she explained everything. Morag's reaction was not what she expected.

Morag slapped the table. "Damn! How very stupid of me! I must be getting senile to have not thought about it. I talked to the birds in the sanctuary in Lucknow. I never even thought about the language barrier. Of course, there was none. So it stands to reason that there wouldn't be one with the cats either." She sat there shaking her head and wondering once again, if she was getting too old for all this. She thought of the eastern States and knew she still had things to do, before she could even think about retiring.

That evening after bathing Randy, Joly held him tightly and never wanted to let him go. She guessed the emotions shooting through her body were the so-called maternal feelings that every mother felt. She tucked him into bed and as she did every night, she read him a story.

Later, as she crawled into bed beside Randy, he murmured in his sleep, 'Love you, Mommy." She carefully gathered him to her and fell asleep holding him tightly.

She dreamed.

The blackness was complete, with not a hint of light anywhere. She sensed something in front of her and her eyes dilated, trying to see what it was. Two pinpoints of light appeared a long distance off. As they slowly approached, she became conscious of a sound. She cocked her head, trying to figure out what it was she could hear.

The two points of light soon became identifiable as eyes and as they came closer, she realized that they were huge; each several feet across. Somehow, they looked familiar, but she couldn't place them. They were too large, too overwhelming. The sound grew louder, but no clearer. It almost seemed to be a voice, but it was fuzzy and indistinct. It was a repetition of something. Dum, dum-de, dum. Dum, dum-de, dum. Dum, dum-de, dum. It went on endlessly.

The eyes came closer. She looked for the face that should have surrounded them, but there was none. What was the look in the eyes? They seemed to be trying to tell her something. She watched unwaveringly and soon the eyes came to a stop. They were no more than ten feet away from her. They were brilliant blue and she knew where she had seen them before.

"Duncan? Oh Gods, talk to me honey." But he had no mouth and could say nothing. The intensity of the sound reverberated through her head. The staccato cadence amplified and seemed determined to ensure that she would never hear again. Dum, dum-de, dum. Dum, dum-de, dum. Dum, dum-de, dum.

What was the look in his eyes? Why couldn't she read it? She had always been able to read his face, just as he had been able to read hers. Dum, dum-de, dum. Dum, dum-de, dum.

The eyes began to advance again and she knew it was because she couldn't help him. "Duncan, I love you. I will always love you." Dum, dum-de, dum. Dum, dum-de, dum. Dum, dum-de, dum.

The eyes were about to absorb her into their depths and she knew if that happened; her life would end and she would no longer exist.

Suddenly she knew what it was he was trying to convey, and for the first time, she was afraid.

His eyes were accusing her... Dum, dum-de, dum. Dum, dum-de, dum. Dum...

"Joly, wake up, please... wake up." She stirred and heard the urgency in the voice. *Randy!* She sat up, terror running through her body.

"Thank God! You were having a majorly bad dream. Randy came and got me. Are you all right?"

Joly looked at Sara and then she looked at Randy. She held her arms out and he ran and jumped into them.

"Yes, I'm okay, I think. Thank you, Sara." She moved to get out of bed. Randy refused to let go, so she carried him downstairs and held him, while she made a cup of chamomile and peppermint tea.

She realized Randy was rhythmically rubbing her back and neck, and she knew he was trying to give her the comfort and security that he had never had. She pictured him asleep on the ground and no one answering his cries when he had a nightmare. She squeezed him tightly and smiled at him. "Thank you, Son," she whispered.

After she had her tea and Randy had a small glass of juice, they headed back up to bed. She cuddled Randy close and soon they both drifted off to sleep.

They slept soundly through most of the night, but toward morning, Joly dreamed again. It was a different dream, one with an urgent message. She was needed in Greece, as soon as she could get there. The dream faded away and the rest of the night passed uneventfully.

When Joly awoke, her first thought was of the dream she'd had. She must run over and tell Morag as soon as possible. Randy stirred and his eyes opened. He smiled and her heart melted.

They had a wrestling match and then got ready for the day. While they were eating breakfast, the doorbell rang.

Joly knew it was Morag and wondered why she was there so early. She went and opened the door to let her in. Sara had already poured a cup of tea for her and she joined them at the table, after giving hugs to Randy.

"We have to leave, Joly. We've been called."

"Yes, we're going to Greece."

Morag raised an eyebrow. "You keep surprising me child." She turned to Sara. "Do you have a passport?"

Sara grinned, "Of course, doesn't everyone?"

"Is it up to date?"

"Yes, why?"

"I thought that maybe you'd like to come with us. I hate to separate Joly and Randy this early in their relationship and it'll give you some new sights to sketch."

Sara looked expectantly at Joly.

"If Morag says you can come, who am I to say no. Besides, I don't think I'm ready to leave my son yet." She reached over and laid her hand on Randy's arm.

Salem rubbed up against Morag's leg and she reached down to pet him. He nipped at her finger and she pulled her hand back.

"Salem! Why did you do... oh, I see. Right. Yes, I suppose the three of you can come too. I haven't done any checking, but I'm sure it'll be all right. You may need to have more shots, though"

The earliest flight they could get did not leave for three days. Joly took the cats for an updated rabies shot but this time she left Pip in the carrier. The vet still ended up with scratches, but his examining room wasn't destroyed.

Joly drove into Surrey to see Kyle and signed her new will. She told him if anything happened to her, to name himself as trustee for Randy, as she had no one else. She did suggest Morag, and he said he would give her the option, should the occasion arise. She had taken Randy with her, and Kyle said he could see why she had fallen in love with him.

She took Randy shopping and bought him some shorts outfits and another pair of runners. They went to the Golden Arches for lunch, something Joly did not normally do. Randy didn't want to play with the other children and seemed content to watch them on the slides and playing in the ball pen. He didn't seem to think much of his hamburger either, for which Joly was thankful. She knew it was because he had eaten little meat in his life and she usually cooked chicken or fish, only giving him a small bit of hers.

Veronika was weeding the flower beds when she sensed a change in the air. She sat back on her heels and looked around. There was no one there. She went to check on her wards and found the first three were fine. As she walked to the fourth, she felt energy coming from the ground. She stopped and opened her senses. *Da... there's something there.* She looked to the skies and allowed her mind to go blank.

The air around her was filled with a darkness. It wasn't overpowering, but it was there just the same.

She went in the house and got a black and a purple candle and her other spell casting equipment. She drew her circle near the spot the energy appeared to be coming from. She called upon her Gods and Goddesses and the elements. She poured water into a bowl and set the black candle in it. She lit the purple candle and began to chant.

"With this spell I do weave,
Bad energy is caught, darkness must leave,
You're not of earth, you're not of air.
Good energy will win; our veil to repair.
You don't belong, you must go,
Benevolent winds come and blow."

She continued to chant until she heard the first hiss of water and fire meeting. She waved her hands around the candle flame.

"Spell, be gone; magic be gone.
Go now, back to whence you came."

The candle spluttered and went out.

She closed her circle and wandered through the yard. *Da*, it's gone. She wondered where it had come from.

Morag didn't bother to call Stephen to take them to the airport. Their previous few conversations had not been satisfactory, each one ending with him still in a huff over Randy's adoption. Morag had tried to talk to him about his sudden apparent discrimination when there had never been any prior, but he refused to discuss it.

Morag thought they could take a taxi out to the airport, but Joly suggested that if they could all squeeze in the truck, she would leave it in one of the airport parking lots.

Sara was so pleased with the prospect of new sights to sketch that she was packed and ready to leave the following day.

Their departure day arrived along with overcast skies. They reached the airport by eleven, and after checking in they wandered around until it was time to head for the boarding gate.

Randy was excited to be going on a plane again. He had a new backpack filled with things to keep him occupied on the long flight. He had a great time making the three adults switch seats. He had started out sitting with

Joly. Then he wanted to sit with Morag, so Sara went and sat with his Mother. Then he wanted to sit with Sara, so Joly moved over and joined Morag. It continued until he powered out and fell asleep.

When Randy and Sara were busy with one of his books, Joly spoke to Morag. "Morag, tell me something. Thinking back on my life, if Duncan were to walk down this aisle right now, what have I done that he could accuse me of doing wrong?"

Morag looked into Joly's eyes, sensed she was troubled and replied. "I'm not sure I fully understand the question."

"I had a dream the other night. Duncan came to me and he was accusing me of doing something, but I don't know what. It was just his eyes. The way they looked at me... as if I had done something wrong. There was a voice... it was so loud it was deafening me, but the words weren't clear. It was like someone was talking under water. I think it was three words that kept repeating over and over again. I've been trying to make sense of it, but I just can't."

"Ah, Sweetie... you have never done anything wrong where Duncan was concerned. Perhaps you read the message wrong."

"No, I don't think so."

Nine and a half hours after they left Vancouver, they arrived in London. It was six-thirty in the morning and they had almost two hours until they caught their next flight. They found a restaurant and had breakfast.

Shit! Polina knew she was in trouble. *Babushka* would kill her if she found out. Sergei... well, she knew he wouldn't be happy with her either.

She had sensed the unrest a couple of weeks ago, and decided to banish it on her own. She knew what she was doing. It wasn't her first banishing, but it was the first time she'd done one alone. And she'd succeeded too. But the man... *oh Gods...* the man.

She'd had to go back.

She was in love with a spirit. She laughed.

Tara and Lyn would tease her if they ever found out. They didn't know she was a witch, but sometimes it was so hard not to say anything. Friends were for confiding in and sharing secrets.

She began the long walk home. She wondered if she should go to *Babushka*'s tonight. No, her Mom wasn't so attuned to her. *Babushka* might smell the Otherworld on her and she didn't need that.

Polina walked along lost in thought, dreaming of the young man who had died in the civil war. His name was Griffin and he had the most incredible brown eyes. She smiled and a passerby smiled back at her, but she didn't notice.

Today Griffin had put his arm around her and she thought she'd died and gone to heaven. Well, she had gone to Summerland, but only to see Griffin.

As she turned up her street, her thoughts returned to the present. She hoped Sergei was at *Babushka*'s. He could read her too well and would know she had done something she shouldn't have.

She knew astral traveling could be dangerous. If someone came along and moved your earthly body when you weren't in it, your spirit wouldn't be able to find its way back.

She knew her secret place was safe. She'd been going there for two years and only three times had anyone ever walked by when she was hidden out of sight. No one even knew she was there.

She grinned and she skipped up the steps. She still had another month before school started. She had tons of time to go and see Griffin.

11. Solid Ghosts

The flight from London to Athens took just over three and a half hours and they arrived at two in the afternoon.

There had been a bit of a problem with the cats, as the airlines wouldn't allow pets to fly when the weather was extremely hot and August was the hottest month of the year in Greece, but Joly had gotten lucky. A low-pressure system had moved into Greece and the temperatures were cool enough for the cats to accompany them.

Joly rented a car and they loaded the luggage and cats into it, and made their way to *Alexandras* Avenue where their hotel was located.

Morag had had problems trying to find one that took pets and also had a room large enough for all of them. She had considered getting two rooms, but finally decided that for convenience sake, Sara should share with them and Sara had agreed.

They entered their room and Randy's indrawn breath was heard by all. The room was carpeted in a brilliant royal blue and the headboard above the king size bed was the same color. Randy went over to the giant bed and looked at it from every angle. He turned and looked at Joly.

The bed was actually two double beds pushed together and Joly understood Randy's look of disbelief. She laughed and picked him up, tossed him on the bed and then she jumped on it too. While they had a wrestling match, Sara let the cats out of their carrier.

There was a sofa at the far end of the room for Sara to sleep on, along with the usual armchair, desk and television. The cats explored the new surroundings and once Joly and Randy had finished with their cavorting, Morag went and lay on the bed.

It was five in the morning Vancouver time and although they had all slept on the plane, she was exhausted. To give Morag some quiet time, Joly and Sara took Randy over to the park that was across the street.

The park was a disappointment for them. They were used to the clean, well cared for parks of Canada. There were visible scars of trees that had been cut down, vehicles were parked on the wide walkways and there was garbage strewn about everywhere they looked. They did manage to find a picnic table in a semi clean area and they spent some time there, while Randy burned off his energy running about.

They returned to the hotel two hours later and found Morag standing at the large window looking at the view.

"Did you get some sleep?" Joly was concerned about her friend. She sensed that Morag's heart wasn't into all the traveling and spell casting and she wondered about it. She scanned Morag's body anytime she was close to her and sensed nothing medical wrong.

"A bit," she replied. "I know Greeks customarily eat their evening meal late, but I am starving. Anyone else ready to eat?"

Randy knew the word eat and ran to Morag. "Eat, eat. *Han*... no... no *han*. Yes, eat." He held onto her hand and tried to drag Morag toward the door.

She chuckled and let him lead the way. They went up to the rooftop restaurant and found it didn't open for another hour, and the garden restaurant had closed at two.

"So what does everyone want to do? Do we wait or try the one on the main floor?" Morag asked, looking at the two girls.

"We can eat up here another night. Let's go downstairs. I for one am tired and I'd like to try to get Randy settled down as soon as possible. His internal clock has to be way out whack at the moment."

"I agree." Sara responded, and so they caught the elevator to the main floor.

The restaurant was an elegant one, with white tablecloths and napkins. The chairs were padded in soft gold velvet.

Joly and Morag had the marinated chicken breast and Sara ordered the marinated pork fillet. They asked for an empty plate for Randy and each gave him a portion of theirs. Joly also asked for an extra chicken breast to take up the cats. She wasn't sure how they would take to the marinated flavor of it, but knew if they were hungry enough, they would eat it.

Randy was quite taken with eating in the restaurant and spent most of his time looking around at the other diners, although they were few, with the early hour.

After a leisurely meal they went back to the room. Joly fed the cats and ran a bath for Randy. Once he had gotten used to the daily ritual, he decided he liked bathing and he looked forward to the time in the tub. Joly always stayed in the bathroom with him and they would spend the time practicing new words. He had his little bath toys memorized and would proudly show them off every night.

"Lellow duck, orange boat, geen fish, red fish, blue fish, pur-pil dra-gin," he smiled at Joly, "Wight Mommy?"

"Right honey. You're so smart. I love you."

"Love you," he responded.

She washed and dried him and tucked him into bed. She read him a story and kissed him goodnight. He reached up and wrapped his little arms around Joly's neck. "Love you, Mommy."

"Love you too, Sweetie."

"Not Sweedie, naam is Randy." He giggled at their ongoing joke. He had never had any nicknames and thought it was funny being called all the different endearments.

"Naam is Sweetie, Honey, Punkin Pie, Baby Cakes, Baby and Randy." Joly smiled and gave him one last hug. "Night honey."

Sara had brought her laptop and emailed her parents, telling them about the flight and their first day.

It didn't take long for the room to become quiet, the only sounds being ones of soft breathing.

Nefertiti looked out the window and assuring herself that all was well, she curled up at Sara's feet. Salem was snuggled in beside Morag and Pip was beside Joly.

Veronika stared in amazement at the ground. Whatever it was she had gotten rid of was back and it felt stronger this time. She gathered her things together, cast her circle and redid the spell, changing some of the words.

When she was done, she placed a white candle over the area of ground that the activity appeared to be coming from. She lit the candle and said a protection spell to keep the clean.

Satisfied she had done all she could, she went in and had a cup of tea.

The night passed uneventfully and when daylight showed through the curtains, there were sounds of stirring.

Morag got up first and headed to use the facilities before there was a rush for it. She had slept well and felt better. She knew the culmination of all the bad things that were happening everywhere would soon be upon them. She had decided if she survived the final war, she might take a trip to Hawaii or somewhere similar. She thought somewhere warm and relaxing might be the antidote that she needed.

Sara stretched and sat up, absentmindedly patted Nefertiti, and thought about how her life had changed in the past ten days. She thought about Joly and Randy and wondered how two people could become such an important part of her life so fast. She thought of Morag and decided it was like having another Grandmother, but she knew she would never tell Morag that.

Joly stirred and felt a finger sliding up her arm. Randy was awake and trying to get a rise out of her. She lay very quietly for a few seconds and then growled and pounced gently on top of him. He squealed and the wrestling match was on. Pillows were thrown and the bedding ended up on the floor.

Morag opened the bathroom door and was hit by a pillow that Joly threw at her. Randy thought it was hilarious so he threw one too. Soon, Morag was on the bed tickling him and Joly went to have a shower.

While she brushed her teeth she thought of her family on the other side of the door. She knew she was blessed, but she couldn't help wishing there was one more person in her life. *Why had Duncan been looking at her so accusingly?*

The door burst open and Randy ran toward the toilet. Joly smiled, thinking of all the horsing around that had went on, and thought it was a miracle he hadn't wet himself.

They went and had breakfast and Joly took some food back to the room for the cats. Once they had eaten, Joly put them in the carrier and they all went down to the car.

They were headed northeast to the Plain of *Marathon*. They wanted to get a feel of the place before deciding on the action needed. There had always been the occasional report of hauntings there, but apparently, it had suddenly gotten much worse. People were afraid to go there and as a historical site that was popular to visit, the reason for the fear needed to be stopped.

In 490 BC, the Athenian army of ten thousand soldiers had defeated the Persian army of over one hundred thousand soldiers on the Plain. When the battle was over, more than six thousand Persians lie dead along with one hundred ninety-two Athenians. The reason for the victory was the location. The Plain of *Marathon* lies in a north- south direction along the coast. The Persians arrived by ship, not realizing that each end of the Plain was covered with marshes. Once on land, they could not fan out, and were slaughtered on the shore. The plain was about six miles along the shoreline and a mile and a half deep.

The Athenians had been cremated on an eighty-five foot artificial floor along with animal sacrifices, and then a funeral banquet had followed. The mass grave was covered with a fourteen meter high mound of dirt. The mound had eroded through the years and was currently nine meters high.

They drove out of the city, past the US Embassy and through the industrial area. The road slowly rose in a meandering pattern as they drove past olive groves, fields and country homes. The air was filled with the song of the cicadas. They drove through towns with names like Stavros, Rafina and Nea Makri. Off to their right, the ocean glistened in the sunlight.

They reached the town of Marathon and Joly carefully made her way the two miles to the Plain. She parked the rental car and they got out.

Nefertiti sniffed the air, advanced several paces and sniffed again. She growled and looked at her mistress.

Morag could feel it as soon as she stood up outside the car door. The fear, hatred and anger permeated the air ahead of them. This was a massive uprising of ghosts. They had a monumental task ahead of them.

Sara took Randy by the hand and with her art supplies; they headed toward a rise away from the battlefield.

Joly also felt the ghosts that did not rest. She looked at Nefertiti and the other two cats. "You three can wait here. We're just checking it out. There's nothing to worry about for now."

She and Morag walked toward the plain. There was nothing out of the ordinary to see. There were fields of wild flowers and weeds, trees and shrubbery and surrounding the plain were ancient hills, mostly rock strewn, with drab shrubs growing in the thin soil.

The day was bright and warm, but the chill caused by the ghosts made them wish they had brought jackets. It was easy to see why no one wanted to come to this place. They walked toward the sandy beach and the bay where the Persian ships had sat waiting for the victorious return of their soldiers.

The scene in front of them blurred and suddenly they were in the middle of the battle that had taken place over two centuries earlier. The smell of blood and fear overwhelmed them. The sound of swords clashing and men grunting swirled around them.

A soldier ran through Joly and she was filled with his excitement, his thirst for blood. She smiled and ran several steps, before realizing what she was doing. Stopping abruptly, she stared in horror at the semi-transparent men lying all over the field, many wounded and moaning, some crying out for help, others begging for mercy, and everywhere the blood flowed freely, saturating the parched earth below her feet.

Morag stumbled and fell. She threw out her hands to soften her landing and saw that one hand was about to go through a dead man's chest. She twisted her body and fell heavily onto her side narrowly missing a soldier crawling toward the water. She quickly got to her feet and yelled to Joly, "Let's get out of here."

Back at the car, they both took several deep breaths.

"*By the Gods!* That was just too real." Morag leaned against the car, her eyes never leaving the plain.

Joly felt a moment of fear. The old Joly was trying to make a come back. She shook the feeling off. Whatever was needed to put these ghosts to rest, she could do it. She knew in her heart that she was strong. The past ten months had taught her that.

She too eyed the plain and wondered how Morag would fare through this. She quickly scanned her friend's body but found nothing truly wrong. Morag's heart was beating faster than normal, but so was hers. She saw that Morag was grounding herself and she did the same.

"Mommy, Mommy. Go now. No like here." Randy ran up to Joly and threw his little arms around her. She picked him up and felt his heart beating wildly through the T-shirt he was wearing.

Sara arrived and apologized. She knew Randy needed to be kept away while they scouted the area, but he had suddenly run from her and headed for his Mother.

"No problem, Sara. He is feeling the anger that surrounds this place. Our next trip out, we'll leave you two behind."

"I feel it too," she responded, looking toward the bay. "This is not a good place to be at the moment."

"You're right, but hopefully we can change that."

Morag walked away from the group, wandering seemingly aimlessly about, but Joly knew she did nothing without purpose. She was making plans and when she was ready, she would let Joly know what they were.

Joly wondered what she would do if Morag wasn't there to lend her expertise to all the different things that had been happening. She knew she had the ability to fix what was wrong, but she didn't have the working knowledge. Even reading her parents Book of Shadows didn't tell her all that she needed to know. Maybe when they went back home, she should sit down with the book and really read it. Possibly the knowledge was there and she just hadn't seen it.

Morag returned from her wandering and they climbed back in the car and headed back to Athens.

They had a light lunch and Sara decided to go for a walk, taking Randy with her.

Morag wanted to have a nap and Joly decided to join her.

The blackness was absolute. Again, the two pinpoints of light appeared far off in the distance. Again, the sound became audible. As the eyes grew larger and the sound grew louder, Joly found herself straining, trying to make out what was being said.

"Duncan," she called out. "I don't know what you think I've done. I love you... you know that I love you. I have always loved you. I will always love you. Please tell me why you're so angry."

The eyes closed in and they were just as accusing as the first time she had seen them. The sound reverberated through her mind. Dum, dum-de, dum. Dum, dum-de, dum.

The eyes again stopped several feet away from her and accused her unendingly. Joly knew she should be afraid, but this was her beloved, her Duncan. He would never harm her.

The eyes resumed their approach and this time Joly welcomed it. "Yes my love. Take me with you. I love you, Duncan."

The eyes stopped inches from her. Joly stared into the black pupil of the one eye and willed it to consume her.

She was suddenly aware she understood a word. "You dum-de, dum. You dum-de dum."

"I what, Duncan? For the love of the Gods... what?"

"Joly, wake up dear. Come on now. Come back to me. Joly, wake up." Morag had started out shaking her gently and when she got nowhere with that, she got rougher. Then she slapped Joly across the cheek twice.

Joly moaned and her eyes fluttered. Morag felt instant relief and rocked back on her heels, where she knelt on the bed over her daughter-in-law.

Joly's eyes fluttered again and finally opened. Seeing Morag hovering over her and the look on her face, she realized she had given her a terrible fright.

"Oh Morag, I'm so sorry." Joly sat up and hugged her friend. Morag clung onto the body that was damp from perspiring and stroked the back of Joly's head.

"There's nothing to be sorry for, child. You can't help your dreams. I would like to know what happened in it though."

"Yes… just give me a sec, okay?" Joly got up and walked into the wash-room. She splashed some cool water over her face and relieved herself, all the while trying to make some sense out of the dream.

Returning to the room, Joly sat on the bed, pulling her knees up under her chin and wrapping her arms around them. She told Morag what had happened and how she had wanted to go with Duncan.

"Why, Morag? Why would I do that? It was like Randy didn't exist, like nothing in this life existed. I had no thoughts of anything, except that of wanting to be with him forever."

"Well my dear, there are several things at work here. One, dreams usually have a message. Just what that message might be, I'm not one hundred per-cent sure. It would seem that Duncan is trying to tell you something, but for one reason or another, he is having trouble telling you what it is. I don't think the problem is with you. Wherever he is, something is holding him back; hindering him from what I believe is an honest effort on his part to commu-nicate with you. Two, you have never let Duncan go…"

Joly interrupted, "Morag…"

"Hush child and hear me out. It's true. You spent years alone, supposedly grieving and getting over the bad time."

Joly was furious, "What do you mean… *supposedly?* Duncan was my…"

Morag cut off her tirade. "He was your life, yes, and he was also *my* son. You seem to forget that sometimes. You also seem to forget that Brody is also gone, and he was *my* life! Now, before you interrupt again, listen to me. I said supposedly and I meant it. You did *not* grieve. You hid away and tried to put the past out of your mind. But in reality, all that time alone just helped to feed your anger, your feelings of injustice. I could see it from the moment I laid eyes on you. I see it now, when I look at you. That is why you are so willing to go with him in the dream. You haven't let time heal you. Inside, it's as if you lost Duncan yesterday. And if you only lost him yesterday, then there is no Randy, no helping the planet, there is no me. Do you see what I'm trying to say?"

"No, you're wrong, Morag. I did heal. I did learn to live without the laughter; I did come to grips with knowing I would never see him again. I did." The tears came then and Morag held her as she cried. The three cats joined them on the bed and with Morag; they all sent their healing energies to the lost soul that they loved.

When the sobs became sniffles, Morag sat back and looked at Joly. "Look at me," she commanded.

Joly wiped her eyes with the back of her hand and looked at Morag.

"Can you honestly sit there and tell me that you have come to grips with losing your husband, when almost ten years later, you still can't talk about him without falling apart? You haven't come to grips with anything, my dear. You have been in denial for so long that you don't even realize that you are just now grieving, you are just now healing, you are in fact, just now coming to grips with losing Duncan and that's the truth of the matter. Right?"

"But why the dream? Why now?"

"For one, you would never let yourself dream. You took steps to prevent them. Two, whatever it is Duncan seems to think you did, is probably something that's happened recently. After all, you certainly didn't do anything in the time you spent at the cabin."

Morag looked thoughtfully at Salem who was lying beside her. "There's something else happening now too. I wasn't going to say anything, but it might help you to know. I don't know what it is yet, but it concerns Duncan. I believe he is alive."

"*What?*" The shriek startled Pip, who jumped to her feet growling.

"Joly, I don't know. I'm going with my gut on this and a couple of odd things that I've sensed. I think he's still in England. Why he hasn't contacted anyone, I don't know. But these dreams of yours, added to thoughts and senses of mine…" Her voice faded off.

Joly's heart was beating so rapidly, she thought it might burst right out of her chest. *Her Duncan was alive.* She wanted to sing, to dance; she wanted to cry again. What had happened to him that he hadn't come home to her? Morag's senses were *never* wrong. If she thought he was alive, then he was. She just had to find him and her world would be right again.

"I see the look on your face, dear. Don't go getting your hopes up too high. If he's been lost for this long, he could easily remain lost for just as long again."

"No Morag, no one was looking for him. Now we will when we are done here. We can go back to England and search. It's a small country. We *will* find him."

"You're forgetting something. Our first duty lies with Mother Earth. Only when all this evil is brought to bear, can we pursue other endeavors. I'm not trying to put a damper on your hopes my dear, I'm just reminding you of our duty. The fact that he's trying to communicate with you is a positive thing. I don't understand why I can't find him with the crystal, but I suppose there is a reason."

Morag got off the bed and walked over to the window. Muffled voices could be heard in the hallway and then a key sounded in the lock. The door opened and Randy burst through and ran to his Mother. Sara closed the door and smiling; she dropped some bags on the desk and headed for the washroom.

Randy and Joly snuggled on the bed, and soon the small bundle of energy was fast asleep. Joly eased herself up and joined Morag by the window.

"Have you thought about what we have to do on the plain?" Joly was now anxious to get this operation over with and head home. They had another layover in London and she wondered what she could do to start the search for Duncan.

"Yes dear, we'll go out this afternoon and buy a few things. I was thinking to go back there tonight, but I'm wondering if we shouldn't wait until tomorrow night."

"Why?"

"Well, you've had an unsettling day to this point and I know for myself, I could use another good night's sleep, before getting to the crux of this matter. What do you think?"

"I'd just like to get it over with and go home."

"Ahh Joly, you're speaking with your heart, not your mind. Come on; think about it. Do you truly feel up to the task of banishing thousands of ghosts back to where they belong?"

Joly looked out of the window and wondered why life had become so hard. Perhaps she needed to talk to her parents. She was strong, but right now her whole world seemed to be coming unraveled. She knew her parents would set her straight, but it was so hard going to them. She still missed them so much.

Morag's voice echoed in her mind. *You did not grieve. You hid away and tried to put the past out of your mind.* She supposed that was true of her parents also, and decided she definitely needed to talk to them.

Sara joined them at the window and told them about her and Randy's sightseeing. She sensed something had happened while she was gone and asked about it. Morag glanced at Joly and told Sara about the dream. If Joly was going to keep having them, Sara needed to be aware of it. She also wanted to talk to Sara alone, but would have to wait for the chance, perhaps when Joly was bathing Randy.

She wondered if she had done the right thing by telling Joly she thought Duncan was alive. She hoped Joly was strong enough to not let it interfere in her duty to Gaia.

Morag was hungry and asked the others what they wanted to do. Sara said she and Randy had stopped for a bite to eat when they were sightseeing. She told Joly and Morag to go and she would stay with Randy.

Joly wasn't very hungry, but knew she needed to keep up her strength, so she slipped into her shoes and went down with Morag to the restaurant. They had a light lunch and then went shopping. Morag's main purchase was candles.

When they got back to the room, Randy was up and he did his best to tell them what he and Sara had done on their excursion, and with Sara's help, they heard all about the sights they had seen and places they had gone.

They decided to visit the *Acropolis* and the *Parthenon*. Joly drove carefully through the madcap traffic, but after navigating the roads in England, with traffic driving on the wrong side of the road and driving in India, where there seemed to be no traffic rules at all, she found that the Greek traffic wasn't really so bad.

They toured the *Parthenon*, the museum and the temple of *Athena Nike*. They saw the *Propylaea* and the *Erectheion* with the famous porch of the *Caryatids*.

By this time, it was getting late and they headed back to the hotel, where they had supper and went back to their room.

Joly gave Randy his bath and read him a story. Everyone was tired, and soon they were all in bed.

The next day after breakfast, they did some more sightseeing. If all went as planned that night, they would soon be able to head back to Canada.

They visited the *Kalimarmaro* Stadium, the Temple of *Hephaestus*, the Temple of *Zeus* and the theater of *Dionysus*. They saw the *Agora* and the Tower of Winds. They went to the Shrine of *Asklepios* and made the trip up *Lycabettus* Hill to view all of Athens.

It was mid afternoon when they returned to the hotel. Randy went and lie down on the bed and fell asleep almost immediately. Sara was busy with her sketching. Morag sat on the bed and began a meditation session. Joly quietly left the room and went and had a shower.

When she walked back into the room, Morag was packing the bag they would take with them that night, double-checking that nothing had been forgotten. Once she was satisfied, she lie down for a nap. As they would be up most of the night, Joly joined Randy on their bed and she too dozed off.

Randy woke up and soon had the other two awake. They went down for supper and returned to their room. Randy was full of energy, so Joly took him across the street to the park where they played ball and tag for a couple of hours.

Back in the room Randy had his bath and Joly tucked him in for the night. No one said anything to him about the midnight excursion, and Joly figured they would be back long before he woke in the morning.

At ten-thirty they left. Sara wished them luck as she saw them to the door. Joly hadn't wanted to take the cats, but Salem refused to let her out the door without them, so she lugged the carrier out to the car and Morag carried the bag.

It was just past eleven-thirty when they reached the parking lot. Joly aimed the headlights at the gate and Morag got out to check the lock. It was open. Her power of suggestion sent that afternoon, had worked.

Joly breathed a sigh of relief. She had not looked forward to the two of them having to climb over the fence.

With the cats following closely behind them, they walked toward the battlefield. Morag carried a flashlight, as the ground was uneven and the blackness of the night allowed them little to see by. The moon was hidden and the odd star that peeked through the clouds did not help.

When they sensed they had arrived at the edge of the battlefield, Morag opened the bag and removed the contents. Joly undressed and put on her ritual gown. Once Morag was satisfied everything was there, she too undressed, but rather than wear a robe she chose to proceed sky clad.

Morag sensed something in the air. She thought it felt like the presence of another person, and she shook her head. There were more pressing matters.

The battlefield was quiet, for which they were both thankful. The preceding day's events had startled them and they were wary with what might happen on this night.

"I think we should try working from the center outwards. If you work toward the right, I'll go to the left."

Joly nodded in agreement and then realized that Morag couldn't see her. "Yes, fine."

They gathered up the articles that were lying on the ground, dividing the items equally between them and headed out onto the plain.

Salem walked along beside Joly on her right, inches from her feet. Nefertiti was in the lead and Pip walked on her left.

Salem wished that Miss Morag had someone to walk with her, but the three of them were bound to Mistress Joly and could not leave her side He decided that he would try to keep an eye out for her, as long as it didn't interfere with his watching out for his Mistress.

When they sensed they were near the center of the battlefield, they began their preparations. There was a slight breeze and Joly wondered if it would affect the candles. Morag carefully poured the oil into the two metal bases and replaced the caps. She lit the wicks of the torches and pushed the stakes into the ground. The flames lit up the immediate area making it easier to see.

While she had been doing that, Joly cast their circle and drew in the pentacle, along with various other symbols. She took the holy water and sea salt and chanted as she consecrated the salt. She continued to chant as she poured the salted water around the edge of the circle.

Morag lit a black candle and walking to the eastern point of the circle, she began her invocation of the Four Quarters. At each Quarter, she lit another black candle. Once the invocation was done, Joly stood in the center of the circle and lit some patchouli incense. She held the container to the sky and chanted,

"Where the light shineth, let all darkness flee.
In our world; as above and so below."

As Joly continued her chant, Morag stepped up beside her and lit a second container of incense. She too held it up to the sky and as Joly was beginning the second part of the ritual, Morag began the first part.

The two voices, each saying different words, blended together, creating a harmony of incredible beauty.

As Joly began the chant a second time, she turned counterclockwise in the circle, and as she reached her starting point, she widened her steps until she was making concentric circles going steadily to the right of her starting point. Just before leaving the circle, she reached down and picked up one of the torches.

When Morag began the chant a second time, she did the same thing, only making her circles heading off to the left.

"Spirit ghosts, advance toward the light you see.
You are finished here, now in peace, I bid you go."

Nefertiti sensed it first. Salem became aware of it a split second later. The fur on Pip's back stood on end and she forced herself to concentrate on her beloved Mistress.

Morag and Joly both sensed it at the same time, but continued unerringly with the ritual.

The clearness of the night slowly vanished into a mist. The silence that had only been broken by the words of the two women, slowly dissipated into a low murmur. The mist seemed to bring with it, an unnatural light. The murmuring grew louder and the clash of metal upon metal could be heard. The mists began to take shape and slowly the soldiers could be seen.

Morag and Joly continued chanting, continued making their circles. The cats stayed as close to Joly as they dared, not wanting to trip her.

The soldiers solidified. The sound amplified and the shouts of the men, the striking of iron sword upon iron sword drowned out the words of the two women.

They were no longer part of the modern day. They were transported to another time.

Soldiers with helmets and bronze breastplates throwing javelins, wielding heavy swords and large shields were slowly hacking away at men wearing light armor and bearing short swords. The occasional arrow was seen, but the fighting was too close for the archers to have any effect.

The soldiers continued to solidify, and as they did, the women found themselves in major trouble.

Morag felt it first. She was pushed and nearly fell, only managing at the last second to regain her balance. The men were so solid she could no longer see Joly. She knew they had failed on this attempt. *It was time to get the hell out of there.* She ducked and weaved her way toward the edge of the plain, all the while praying to her Gods to give her protection.

Joly felt the wind from the sword on her arm and knew she was in trouble.

She dropped the incense holder and the torch and turned to get her bearings. She heard a feline yowl and turned again. Nefertiti was calling to her, showing her the way. She clumsily followed, trying to avoid the blades and spears. She managed to get through the first two ranks of men, although she had been pushed and shoved several times. She thought she was home free, as the bulk of the fighting seemed to lay behind her.

Where they came from she wasn't sure, but suddenly there were two men fighting directly in front of her. She tried to go around, but wherever she went they were there, thrusting and parrying. She stepped back and was hit solidly in the middle of her back. The force of the blow propelled her forward directly between the two men.

Time slowed to a crawl and she watched in horror as the double-edged sword was thrust toward her. She watched as it curved in an arc and knew it was destined for her chest. She became aware of the other soldier and saw his sword being brought down toward her arm.

Time seemed to slow even more. Joly wondered if she would get to see her arm amputated or if her heart would be sliced in two first.

The indistinct blur of something flew past her and hit the arm of the soldier with the heavy sword. The swing of the sword was stopped. Joly's heart had only time for one beat when she remembered the other sword. As she swung her head around, a large projectile hit her hard in the chest. She felt the air being pushed out of her lungs and she knew she was falling. She didn't want to see what happened next. She closed her eyes and searched for Duncan. She wanted to see him one last time.

Morag wondered at the insanity of it all. She was sure Brody would have been in his glory, had he been there. He would have grabbed the first available sword and would have joined the Athenians in their victorious fight.

She had been pushed to the ground several times and she finally said, "Screw it!" She crawled on her hands and knees through the blood and gore; she crawled over dead men and around the wounded ones. She had been repeatedly kicked and tripped over; she was sure there wasn't a piece of skin on her body that wasn't black or blue. She knew she would have a black eye come morning. She had no idea if she was still headed in the right direction, but she thought she was.

She wondered if Joly was faring any better than she was. *Gods! They had so underestimated the power of these ghosts.* She briefly wondered what they should do next when she was kicked hard again. She curled up in a ball holding her ribs.

Damn! That one really hurt. She thought at least three ribs had been broken. She just needed to catch her breath and then maybe she would try standing again. Maybe she was close enough to see the edge of the field. She closed her eyes, willing the pain away.

"Mistress, come on now. You can't just lay here. You need to get up.

We've got to go."

Joly opened one eye and found Nefertiti almost glued to her face. She opened the other eye and looked down at her chest, wondering how much blood there would be. She blinked and looked again. She couldn't see any blood. She lifted her hand and ran it down her chest. Looking at it, she saw it came away clean. *What?*

She pushed herself up into a sitting position. The battle still raged all around her. Something small and dark lay just beyond her feet. A soldier was backing up and his foot was dangerously close to whatever it was, when Joly suddenly came alive.

She threw herself forward and over the still form of Salem. The soldier's foot came down hard on her arm. She felt the bone snap. A wave of nausea enveloped her and she shook it off. She looked around and saw Pip beside Nefertiti. She stumbled to her feet using her good arm to push herself up. She reached and lifted Salem up and forced herself forward, following the two cats.

What seemed to be hours later, she saw the edge of the battlefield. She pushed herself forward looking for Morag. As she left the field, the sounds of the battle diminished. The night returned with its blackness and with its silence. She had no idea where she was or where Morag had gotten to.

"Nefertiti?"

She felt a rub against her leg. Soon, she felt a rub on the other leg. The two cats walked slowly, keeping their Mistress tightly between them, so she could feel where to walk. When her foot hit pavement, she began to breathe easier.

The two cats guided her to the car. Once there, she crawled in and turned on the ignition. Then she flipped the headlights on. She crawled back out and walked to the front of the car, Salem still tucked gently in her arm. She squatted down in front of the vehicle and placed Salem on her lap. She ran her hand down his side and felt the weak heartbeat. *He was alive!*

She saw the blood on her hand and wondered where it had come from. Maybe she was wounded after all. Her left arm was useless, so she started Salem's healing with her right arm.

Some minutes later, when she realized nothing was happening, that something was very wrong, she knew she had to do something else. She forced herself back on her feet and laid Salem on the hood of the car. Her dress was wet where she'd had Salem on it. It finally dawned on her that the blood was coming from him and not herself.

She was a mess and she was no good to anyone in the state she was in. She walked to the edge of the pavement and standing on the soil, she grounded herself. She willed away the pain in her arm and welcomed the light into her body. When she felt at peace once more, she turned and walked back to the car.

She tore the skirt from her dress and placed Salem on it. Examining him, she found a wound on his left side. It looked like maybe a sword had cut him open. He was lucky. It really wasn't too deep, but he had lost a lot of blood. Joly held her good hand over the wound and began sending the healing energies to the wound. She sensed when the blood quit flowing out of the opening, but she continued. Only when she saw a small movement, did she stop. She shook her hand to release the energy in it and stroked Salem. "You'll be fine, my friend, you'll be fine."

Joly looked around then and saw that the first hint of daylight was making itself known on the horizon. They needed to leave soon.

Her thoughts turned to Morag and she began to be afraid. Too much time had passed. Something was wrong.

Joly placed Salem in the car and got in herself. She edged the car forward, facing toward the plain. From inside, she could see nothing. She got back out.

"Nefertiti, stay with Salem, please. I won't go back on the field. I just need to see if I can find Morag."

Joly headed toward the field, the illumination from the headlights soon consumed by the darkness. She edged forward as far as she dared. She stood and listened, but all was quiet. She took another couple of steps and heard something beside her.

"Who's there?" she whispered. A tiny cry told her that Pip had followed her. "Hey Pip, glad you're along little girl. Can you sense Morag out here anywhere?"

There was silence. Joly hoped Pip was trying to find Morag, but she couldn't tell. The sky was lighter, but it was still too dark to see. Joly took another few steps forward. She held her breath, expecting at any moment to have swords swinging by her head again. Still nothing.

She thought she heard something, but decided it was wishful thinking or perhaps it had been Pip.

She was feeling fuzzy again. She needed to get her arm set. She sat down and placed her head between her knees, willing the darkness to pass.

She became aware that a lot of time had passed. She lifted her head and saw that dawn had arrived. She knew she must have passed out. She gingerly stood, afraid that the darkness might hit her again, but she stayed on her feet. Not thinking about the possible consequences, she headed out on the field, instinct leading the way. She found the bag and the candles sitting where they had been left. She closed the circle, thanking the Goddesses for being with them. She found her incense holder and torch and placed them in the bag. Now, she just had to find Morag.

She hadn't gone far to her left when she came across Morag's torch. Picking it up she continued on, idly wondering where Pip had gotten to. Another twenty-five feet or so farther on, she found the incense holder. She looked around, but still could see no sign of Morag. She changed her course and headed toward the edge of the field, thinking that was the direction Morag should have taken. She found nothing, so headed back to the middle area.

The sun had risen and there were few clouds in the sky. Joly thought Sara and Randy would enjoy the nice day. All she wanted was to get her arm set and then have at least ten hours of sleep.

She realized she was heading toward the water and as she turned around, she spotted something out of the corner of her eye, something that seemed to be out of place. She turned around again and walked toward whatever it was, still wondering where Pip had gotten to.

As she got closer, she walked faster and faster until she was running. She held her broken arm against her stomach, as she gasped for air.

"Dear Gods, no... *no.*" She reached Morag's battered body and found Pip crouched beside her. Joly knelt down and placed her hand over Morag's heart. A faint beating was felt and Joly became lightheaded once more. She put her head down and rested for a moment.

When the feeling of darkness had passed, she got to her feet and looked around. She felt her heart sinking and wondered what she was going to do. They were only about thirty feet from the waters edge. The gates would be opening soon. They would find the car and the cats, see the gate was open. They would call the police. How was she going to explain all this?

Rauna's quest for knowledge was not going well. The more she tried to understand the problem of demons, the less she seemed to understand. As much as she enjoyed traveling, she was getting tired of it. Nothing was falling into place.

She thought again about the *Sisters of the Triple Moon.* How was it possible she could be one of them? She did not have the powers she had been hearing about in her travels.

Her thoughts went back to her first winter alone. *When winter had come, also had come loneliness and boredom. She had been working all summer and autumn from early morning to late evening, now she had nothing to do. After finishing the fifth pair of stockings, she was so bored with knitting she burned the yarn. She walked through the forest every morning and evening, just to have something to do. She was very sorry for her decision of not going to school for three more years, at least she would have had something to do and company.*

By midwinter she was so tired, sad and bored that she stopped walking in the forest. She stopped eating. She stopped everything. She lie in her bed and didn't even think of anything.

After three days in the ice-cold cottage, she travelled to the Otherworld. She found herself standing in a white landscape with many different animals all looking at her. None of them spoke; they just looked at her wondering what she was doing there. She didn't speak either, wondering the exact same thing. After a while, a Raven flew by and landed in front of her. It talked with the other animals on a low voice; Rauna couldn't hear what they were saying. Then it turned to Rauna and said, "We don't know why you are here."

"I'm dying of loneliness," said Rauna.

"Yes," said the Raven. "But why have you come?"

Rauna looked at the Raven. Her first reaction was "How would I know?" But she wasn't a shaman's daughter for nothing. While she looked into the eyes of the snow white Raven, she remembered what her father had taught her. This was a test; an initiation. Only the best shamans were initiated by the spirit world itself, not by an older shaman. Was she supposed to be a shaman like her father? Was she supposed to be "the best?"

"I have come to receive my power," she said.

"Yes," said the Raven slowly. "Yes, you have. Then receive it."

The Raven started to dance and Rauna danced with it. The Raven led her to the other animals, one after another, and Rauna danced with them all. She danced the dance of a bear, remembering the berry picking tours to the forest, she remembered the passion and compassion, caretaking and strength, and remembered the Bear Medicine, dancing with the bear. She danced with the wolf, remembering the Wolf Medicine – remembering the weakness of loneliness and strength of the pack. She danced with the eagle, she danced with the hare, she danced with the deer and the fox, she danced with the squirrel and she danced with the mouse – she danced with all the animals gathered there, from the majestic moose to the fragile butterfly, and she remembered their Medicine. In the end she danced with the Raven again, and the Raven said, "You will remember."

She awoke on her bed and the cottage was white with frost. She was warm and in her hair were white feathers. She stared at the ceiling for some time, wondering if she dared to think it was just a dream, when she was startled by a knock on the window. She tried to ignore it, but whoever was there, was persistent. Finally Rauna got up from the bed and went to the door. When she opened it a crow flew in. Rauna laughed and decided to live.

Yes, she was a powerful shaman, but what did that have to do with the *Sisters of the Triple Moon*?

12. The Mysterious Benefactor

"You look like you need some help."

Joly almost jumped out of her skin. She whirled around to find a man standing there, smiling at her. He seemed to be about her age, with longish sun-streaked blonde hair and dark eyes. He was good looking and she could see he worked out regularly.

"Where the hell did you come from?"

"Here and there. I take it that's your car in the parking lot?"

"Yes."

He walked forward and taking a blanket from under his arm, he wrapped it around Morag and carefully picked her up.

"I think your cat is injured. Perhaps you should carry her, so we can get out of here faster."

Joly looked in amazement at Pip, wondering what he was talking about. She saw Pip was limping on three feet, the fourth one tucked underneath her.

"Oh my Gods! Pip! I'm so sorry. Come here." Pip limped over and Joly carefully scooped her up with her good arm.

Joly had trouble keeping up to the man. He walked with long strides as though he was used to being out in the open air, striding across uneven ground, carrying a woman that had to weigh one hundred and fifty pounds.

When she reached her bag, she wondered for a moment how she was going to manage both it and the cat. A thought came to her. She put Pip down and opened the bag, then she carefully placed Pip in the bag. Standing, she lifted the bag and lit out after the man, who had kept on walking.

Her arm was throbbing and she wondered if she was going to embarrass herself by keeling over in front of the stranger. The dark feeling did not show itself and Joly hurried along after him.

When he got to the car, he waited for Joly to arrive to open the door. She set the bag down and opened the door. He leaned forward and gently placed Morag on the front seat. When he stood up again, Joly was surprised at how tall he was. He hadn't given the impression of great height, but he towered above her.

"Thank you." She didn't know what else to say.

"You're going to need help getting her out again."

"Yes, but I have a friend that will help."

"Are you sure? I can ride along with you if you like."

"Uhh… no. It's okay, really."

He smiled again and Joly envisioned women swooning at his feet. "You're nervous." He said it as a statement, not as a question.

"Look; you appear out of nowhere, assist me like it's something you do regularly and you seem to think I should just accept it, like it happens to me on a daily basis. Well, I assure you, it doesn't. I do appreciate your help, but I can handle it from here. Again, my thanks." She turned to put the bag in the back seat, still keeping her broken arm close to her body.

"You're hurt!" He reached forward to take the bag from her and he put it on the seat beside Salem.

If he noticed the injured cat, he said nothing, nor did he say anything about Nefertiti sitting in the back window.

He stood and looked at Joly. "You can't drive with that arm. Now I would suggest you get in the back and I will take you where you need to go."

Joly opened her mouth to argue with him, but he spoke first. "You have no need to be afraid of me. Your powers would annihilate me in an instant, if I so much as made a wrong move. Now get in, before the others arrive. They are on their way." He turned and walked back to the gate, locking it.

Joly stood momentarily with her mouth hanging open. *My powers?* What did he know of her powers? She decided she had better find out, so she eased herself into the back seat, placing the bag on the floor. She leaned forward and lifted Pip onto her lap.

The man who seemed to know more about her than she knew about him, got in and closed the door. As he eased the car forward, the first employees arrived, looking at them oddly, as they pulled out of the lot.

The early morning traffic was heavy, but the man seemed to know what he was doing when it came to driving. He asked Joly where she was staying and she gave him the name of the hotel. He raised an eyebrow. She decided he didn't appear to be familiar with staying in first class hotels.

He drove easily through the busy city and pulled into the hotel parking lot, found an empty stall and parked. He stared at the hotel without making an effort to get out, his fingertips tapping on the steering wheel.

"Is there a problem?' Joly leaned forward and looked at him in the rear view mirror.

His eyes looked back at her. "You might say so. The elevators are in the front. I'm wondering how we will get you and your friend past the doorman, the desk clerks and anyone else who might be around."

"Me? What's wrong with me?"

"Have you looked at yourself recently? You are wearing a skirt that is missing most of the front panel and is covered in blood. You have blood smeared over your arms and face. You have what appears to be a broken arm. Your hair looks like it hasn't seen a brush in weeks and you're also barefoot. Does that answer your question?"

She was horrified. With everything that had happened, she hadn't even thought about how she must look. "Umm... I have jeans and a shirt in the bag. Morag's clothes are in there too."

"You want to change here in the parking lot?"

Joly looked around and saw that the lot was actually busy, with people coming and going in all directions. "Uhh... no, I guess not. Is there a service station near by, where we could go?"

"No, but I have an idea."

He started the car again and headed south, soon leaving the heart of the city behind. Joly wondered where he had decided to take them. He drove down the highway with the ease of one who had traveled it many times before.

Tiredness overtook her before she could ask where he was taking them. She knew she hadn't been asleep long when she opened her eyes and found him leaning over her in the back seat. She stifled a scream as he leaned back and stood.

"I'm sorry, I didn't mean to startle you. You didn't want to wake up."

"It's okay. I didn't know what was happening. Where are we?"

"My place. We might run into someone, but I don't think so. If you want to grab your cats, I'll get your friend."

Joly placed Pip back in the bag and looked at Salem. "Nefertiti, I think I'll leave him here. Do you want to stay with him?"

Nefertiti could think of many things she would rather do, but she lie back down in the window. The Mistress had many things she needed to look after. She didn't need a rebellious cat on top of it all.

"Thanks Sweetie." Joly climbed out of the car and picked up the bag. The man was waiting with Morag in his arms. She closed the door and looked around.

She appeared to be in a beachside resort area. She could see the water from where she stood. She turned around and looked at the building. It was modern, not more than a few years old. It looked well cared for. "I'm ready."

He led the way down the sidewalk and using a key card, he opened the door. He held it open until Joly had walked through, and then let it close on its own. She heard the quiet snick of the lock catching. He walked quickly to the elevator and pushed the up button. Seconds later, the door opened. They entered and again, he pushed a button. The elevator whisked them upwards and Joly again felt lightheaded. She grabbed onto the railing and concentrated on willing the blackness away.

"Are you alright?"

"I think so. Just got a little dizzy for a second."

The elevator stopped and the doors opened. He led the way to a door and unlocked it. He walked in and Joly followed. She looked around.

The main feature she could see was the sectional that took up most of the living room. It looked like it was made of crushed velvet and it was white. She tried to picture her cats sitting on it and she could not. There were four deep red cushions placed neatly on it. She wondered if he ever sat on it. In front of the sectional was a square glass coffee table with chrome legs.. She pictured Randy with jammy fingers leaning on it, and smiled. Above the sectional was an incredible piece of artwork, done in charcoal. It was of a man and a woman sitting with their backs to the room. They were nude and appeared to be facing an ocean. Somehow, it seemed familiar, but she was sure she had never seen it before.

"You coming in?" The voice startled her, as he reached behind her to shut the door. She had been off in her own little world.

"Yes. Do you have a phone I can use? I need to let my little boy know that I'm okay."

"Yes, over there." He pointed and she walked over to it. It was on the kitchen counter, which was open to the dining area. She could see a balcony through the French doors and the water's edge was at the other end of the block.

"Do you have a phone book?"

He went and got it, looked up the number and punched it in for her.

"Thank you."

She asked for her room when the front desk clerk answered. Seconds later, she heard Sara's worried voice.

"Sara, it's me. We're okay, more or less."

"Thank God, Joly. I have been worried sick and trying not to show it. Someone here is pretty upset just the same. Where are you? When will you be back?"

""I don't know and I don't know. Let me talk to Randy."

"What do you mean you don't know? You don't know where you are?"

"Not really. Look Sara, it's been a rough night. We do have injuries that need attention. May I speak with Randy, please?"

"Yes, of course."

The soft voice startled Joly. She had been expecting a rambunctious hello, not the timid small voice that had just said, "Mommy?"

"Yes Baby Cakes, it's Mommy. You okay?"

The voice became more normal. "I okay. You okay?"

"I'm fine Sweetie. I'll be home soon. Okay?"

"Mommy? Where Gra-Morg?"

"She's with me Honey. She's okay."

"Where Pip 'n' Nefer-ti 'n' Say-lam?"

"They're with Mommy too. We're all okay, Randy."

"You come?"

"Soon Sweetie, real soon."

"'K Mommy. Love you."

"Love you too Punkin."

She listened to the click of the phone as Randy hung up and slowly put the receiver back in the cradle. *Normalcy. It was so wonderful!*

"Everything alright on the home front?" The voice came from directly behind her and she jumped.

Turning around she gave the man a wan smile. "Yes, thank you."

"Your friend is on the bed." He turned and led the way.

The small bedroom was stark in comparison to the rest of the suite. There were two single beds pushed together with a bedside table on either side. A dresser stood against the far wall. The walls were bare. He obviously didn't have many overnight guests.

He had filled a large bowl with warm water and a bar of soap, a face cloth and a towel lay beside it. He disappeared and came back with the bag. He set it gently down and looked at Joly.

"Do you need help?"

"If I do, I'll call you." She turned her attention to Morag and heard him leave.

She tugged on the blanket that was wrapped around her friend and pulled it off. She laid it on the floor, took the washcloth and began bathing Morag.

As she washed her, she checked for broken bones and anything else that might be damaged. She found the broken ribs and began the healing process. There were numerous cuts and scratches all over her body and she had a dandy black eye. Once Joly was satisfied she hadn't missed anything, she did a body healing, to lessen any pain. The ribs would be sore for a day or two, but the rest she could deal with immediately. Once she was done, she left Morag and turned her attention to the bag. She lifted Pip out and checked her paw. It looked like it had been stepped on. There were no broken bones and she sent her healing powers to the wee cat. A few minutes later, she put Pip down and watched as she gingerly set her leg down and tested her weight on it. She walked normally.

Joly smiled at her and turned her attention back to Morag. She knew Morag's sleep was a magical one. She had obviously thought the end was coming and sent herself somewhere else, so she wouldn't feel anything. Joly just needed to bring her back from wherever she was.

"Morag... come on now. Everything is okay. You can return." Joly massaged Morag's temples and continued talking softly. Morag would have picked a word to facilitate her return. Joly just needed to figure out what it was."

For ten minutes Joly talked about anything she could think of, rambling on about Randy, Duncan and eventually home. Then she had a thought! "Birds, Morag, soon we can go home to your birds."

Morag stirred and then she groaned. Her eyes opened, she started to smile at Joly, and then her eyes opened wide. "You look like hell, my dear!" She paused. "You got us out though. Good! I thought you would." Her voice was rough.

"Well, not exactly, but yes, we are out of there."

Morag looked around the room. "Where are we?"

"Umm… I'm not really sure. It's a long story and I'd rather tell it after we get back to the hotel."

"Gods! I need a drink." She threw her legs over the edge of the bed and sat up. Then she realized she was still nude. Joly handed her clothes to her and went to find the man.

He was standing just outside the doorway with a glass in his hand.

"Oh… thank you."

"No problem. The place is small. I heard her ask for it." He turned and walked away. Suddenly he turned around again. "Come with me."

Joly followed him. He took her to the washroom and told her she could shower if she felt up to it. She thanked him and went back to the bedroom, handing Morag the water.

"Who was that?" she asked after taking a big swallow.

"Umm… our benefactor. He's the one that got us out of there. We're at his home. We were too much of a mess to go to the hotel."

Morag raised an eyebrow. "Were? Have you looked at yourself recently?"

"No, I haven't. If you're okay, I'll go and get cleaned up now."

"I'm fine my dear. Away you go."

Joly picked up the bowl and cloths and headed to the bathroom. Once there, she immediately turned around and walked back to the bedroom.

"Morag, I need some help."

"What's wrong, dear?"

"I have a broken arm. I need it pulled back into place, before I try to heal it."

"Damn! How on earth did you manage that?" Morag got to her feet. She was dressed and other than the black eye, she looked none the worse for wear.

"Someone stood on it. Salem was hurt, he was my first priority."

"And how is he now?" Morag checked to see where the break was and without any warning, she suddenly reefed on it.

Joly had started to reply, when the world went black.

Morag lowered her onto the bed and headed out to find whoever lived there. He was sitting at the dining room table looking out the French doors.

"Excuse me."

This time he jumped. He was startled to see the other woman up and about. He had thought she was more seriously hurt.

"Where's the washroom?"

He got to his feet and showed the crone where it was. "Your friend could have told you."

"She's unconscious. A little difficult under those circumstances, wouldn't you say?" She smiled at him and ran some cold water over a cloth.

He followed her back to the bedroom and saw that the crone was right.

Morag ran the cool cloth over Joly's temples and it wasn't long before her eyelids fluttered and opened.

"*Holy Gods, Morag!* You might have given me some warning." She sat up.

"And have you fight it? No, this worked well. How's it feel?"

Joly moved it slowly around. "Yeah… it's back in place. Thanks."

She got to her feet and went to have a shower. There was no tub in the suite, just a corner shower with a rounded outer wall of acrylic. She looked in the mirror and decided the man deserved a medal for taking her into his home. She truly was a mess.

She stood under the hot water and let it run down her body. She held the broken arm and sent the healing power to it. She could feel it mending. She would have to be careful for a few days, but it was okay for the moment. She would be able to drive back to the hotel. She shampooed her hair and scrubbed her body until she thought the skin was going to peal off.

After drying off and getting dressed, she ran her fingers through her hair. She had no comb or brush and wasn't about to ask for one. She noticed a bottle of purple liquid soap sitting by the edge of the sink and she thought how out of place it looked. She walked to the bedroom and found it empty. She had a sudden vision of the stranger staked to the floor, Morag standing over him demanding answers. She smiled to herself and walked to the living room. No one was there. Maybe Morag had him tied to the edge of the balcony. She chuckled and looked outside. No one.

"Pip?"

A soft rustle and Pip was at her feet.

"Oh good, for a minute, I though I had been transported to a foreign planet."

The outside door opened and Morag and the man came in. He stopped, clearly startled at the transformation in Joly. Morag said she had wanted to go down and see Salem. The gentleman had made sure she hadn't been locked out.

"Yes, well I think we can go now. We're both presentable." Joly turned to the man and went to shake his hand. "Thank you, thank you for everything."

"What do you mean? You're not driving. *I* will take you back to your hotel. Do you have everything?"

"I just need to grab the bag." She turned and went to get it. She didn't want him driving them back, but he had been a gracious host, not overly friendly, but certainly gracious. She could think of no good reason to refuse him.

Morag picked up Pip and the man took the bag from Joly and they went down to the car. Morag sat in the front and Joly climbed in the back and picked Salem up. As they quietly drove, she sent her healing powers to the cat. He was finally conscious, his eyes clear and alert.

When the man parked at the hotel and Joly had the cats back in their carrier, everyone got out of the car. She wondered what she should say to him.

"I'll take the cats up," he informed them not leaving any room for argument. And so the three of them went into the lobby and up the elevator.

As Joly walked to the door, she felt a momentarily shiver and wondered where it had come from. She unlocked the door and a small body cannonballed into her. His arms were wrapped around her tightly and she could feel him vibrating inside. Randy had obviously been very anxious and she felt badly that this had happened so soon in their relationship.

Morag came through the door and Randy went to give her a quick hug, before going back to his Mother.

The man came in and went to set the carrier on the bed.

Joly heard the intake of breath and looked at Sara, who was white as a sheet.

"Jesse?" She whispered.

The man dropped the carrier the last few inches, which brought forth cries of complaint from the occupants.

He whirled around at the sound of the voice. "Sara?"

"What are you doing here?" Sara looked like she was going to faint at any time. Joly slowly eased toward her.

He smiled. "I was helping your friends."

Sara turned away. "Well, they're here, so you can go now."

"Yes, you're right, of course. Nice to see you again Sara."

He turned to Joly and reached out his hand. "A pleasure to make your acquaintance. You are a very incredible woman. I wish we could have met under different circumstances."

Sara let out a snort and embarrassed by it, she ran to the washroom.

He shook Morag's hand. "You my Lady, are one strong woman. I am honored to have met you."

He walked to the door, opened it, walked out and closed it. Morag and Joly stood there staring at the closed door. Finally, Joly shook her head.

"Did he tell you his name?"

"No, and I asked. He pretended he hadn't heard me. I tried to look around his kitchen. There were some papers on the counter, but nothing with his name on it.

The door opened and Sara left the safety of the bathroom. "I'm sorry Joly. I didn't mean to be rude." She walked over to the window.

"Who is he and what's his name? He never did tell us."

"His name is Jesse Alexander. He's an artist, a race car driver... and he's a witch."

Morag let the cats out of the carrier, picked Salem up and placed him on her pillow. She needed to talk to Joly about what had happened, but obviously they couldn't do that with Sara around.

Joly picked up Randy who was still clutched on to her and walked over to Sara. "You were in love with him." It wasn't a question.

"Yes, I was. He walked out one day and never came back. The next thing I heard was that he was racing in Italy or somewhere. He never called… nothing."

"How long ago was that?"

"About a year and a half ago."

"I'm sorry Sara. If I had known, I wouldn't have brought him to the room."

"You had no way of knowing. It's not your fault. If you don't mind, I think I'll go out for a walk."

"Go ahead Sara. We're not going anywhere."

After Sara had left, Morag asked Joly to tell her what had happened. Joly explained how Jesse had appeared out of thin air and knew of her power. That he had been carrying a blanket to cover Morag's nude body. She tried not to leave anything out. When she was finished, Morag sat quietly thinking about what it meant.

Randy, finally convinced that his mother had indeed returned and was okay, relinquished his grip on her. He went over to Morag and touched the bruising around her eye. "Hurt," he stated and leaned up to kiss it. Morag cuddled him and was thankful he hadn't seen her earlier.

Joly was exhausted. She had had no sleep through the night and needed to lie down, but she didn't want to saddle Morag with Randy. She sat on the bed and they colored for a while. It wasn't long before Randy yawned. Joly realized he had probably not had a nap, waiting for her to come home. She put the coloring book aside and lie down, bringing Randy into the security of her arms. Minutes later, they were both fast asleep.

Morag had slept long and well, once she had taken herself off the battlefield. She was wide-awake and needed to get her mind organized. She needed to figure out what their next step was with the ghosts and why had this Jesse Alexander shown up when he did? She decided to go for a walk.

As she walked through the lobby, she heard a familiar voice and looked around. There was Sara with Jesse. They hadn't seen her, so she quickly exited the hotel. He must have been waiting for her when she came down. She hoped there wasn't going to be a problem.

She walked down the street thinking about the past hours and wondered why the ghosts had decided to return to relive their battle. And why had Jesse shown up at the exact moment Joly needed help?

Morag found an open-air coffee shop and sat down for a cup of tea. She did a whole lot of thinking, running different scenarios through her mind. Finally, deciding she had her new plan of attack more or less figured out, she walked back to the hotel, hoping Sara and Jesse were no longer there. She was almost to the hotel when she sensed something and looked around. Jesse was hurrying to catch up with her. She wasn't surprised. She hadn't thought they'd seen the last of him.

"Hello, I'm glad I saw you. I wanted to tell you that you should pay a visit to the Oracle at Delphi. She should solve your little dilemma for you."

"Jesse... why do you show up just when you seem to be needed?"

"I'm sensitive to things like that. I always have been. I suppose you could call it my gift."

"I see." Morag thought for a moment and came to a decision. "Jesse, I would like to talk to you, straight up with no bull shit. Are you capable of doing that?"

He smiled, and a younger woman would have melted. "When needed."

"Well, I think this is needed, but I won't waste my time or yours, if all I'm going to get from you is a run around."

Jesse looked directly into her eyes as he thought. He finally appeared to reach a decision. "We can't talk on the street. Come with me, my Lady." Jesse took her arm and led her to a car that was parked around the corner. He opened the door and helped Morag settle in. Closing the door, he went around to the driver's side and seating himself, he started the car.

Morag heard the purr of the engine, felt the leather seat, realized that the outside noise was nil and knew she was sitting in one horribly expensive vehicle.

"Sara says you race cars. You must do well with it."

"That and other things. I do alright." He paused. "I'm sorry. I have a bad habit of being vague. Yes, amongst other things I do race, and I do very well with it." He glanced over at Morag and smiled.

"Thank you." She smiled and thought they might make out okay.

He drove toward the *Acropolis* and parked below it. He helped Morag out of the car and they walked to the *Agora*. Though there were many tourists wandering around, the place was large enough to be private. They went and sat down.

Morag watched him, saw the conflicting emotions running across his face, and she knew he was not used to opening himself to many, possibly to none.

"Tell me about the craft." She had to start somewhere.

He looked startled, like a bird caught by a predator. "What exactly do you want to know?" he finally responded.

Morag smiled again, it was going to be done the hard way after all. "Joly said you appeared out of nowhere on the battlefield. Is she right?"

He ducked his head, looking with great interest at his shoes.

"Jesse... are we going to do this or not, because if we're not, then you might as well take me back to the hotel?"

"My Lady..."

"Oh for Pete's sake, my name is Morag."

Still showing great interest in his footwear, he nodded his head. "Morag... my Lady, please understand. I have been ridiculed, harassed, put on display... I learned years ago to keep my own counsel. This is hard, very hard for me. It's not that I don't want to do it... well, actually no, I don't want to, but I said I would, and I will. It's just really hard."

"Jesse," Morag put her hand on his arm, "I am a witch. I can do many things, I have done many things, and sometimes I make mistakes, like last night. But I have never ridiculed anyone or harassed anyone. My husband was a witch, one of my sons' is a witch, Joly is my daughter-in-law and she is a witch. Her parents were witches and were our best friends. I am not going to hurt you. I simply need to understand where you are coming from, and the best way to do that is to get some background on you. Now, I can't very well just ask you to tell me about yourself, because you will give me two sentences and expect to be done. So I ask you again, did you just appear on the battlefield this morning?"

"Yes." There was a long pause and Morag wondered if it was going to be worth all the trouble.

"To all intents and purposes, I did. I can make myself invisible. I was actually there all night. Umm… well, I actually hitched a ride out there with you."

"*You lie!*" Morag was mad. "You no more hitched a ride out there with us than I've flown to the moon. Now, either be truthful or take me back to the damn hotel!" She thought about the Plain, and how she'd felt someone else's presence.

Jesse sat up then and turned to face Morag. "You're right of course. No, I was already there, waiting for you. I was up on the hill." He looked at her intently. "I find it interesting that you are more concerned with the truth, than with me saying I was invisible."

"Is that what this is all about? Oh for crying out loud… I can make myself invisible, it's no big deal."

Jesse's mouth dropped. "You can… *really?*"

"Yes, really. Oh Jesse… I can see why you're so hesitant to talk about it. We really do need to talk, not just about that, but about a lot of things."

And they did talk. For hours they sat there oblivious to the surroundings, to the tourists, to everything, except one another. Jesse told Morag about the so-called covens and groups he had belonged to. How they had been amazed at his abilities, sometimes angry, sometimes mean and usually jealous. Morag told him about their group and the things they had done; about the powers that were truly real; about real covens and not so real covens. She also told him about familiars and that the cats would have known if he was in the car with them. She didn't bother to mention that she would also have known. She told him about the evil that had been unleashed and they felt it was due to this, that the long dead soldiers had risen to fight again. Jesse was a good pupil. He listened and asked questions. He learned more that afternoon than he had in his lifetime about the craft.

Morag found out that the reason he had walked out on Sara was because of something that had happened at a coven gathering. He had left the meeting, stopped by his apartment and grabbed a few things, driven out to the freeway, and just kept on driving. He was angry and upset. He realized later he had been wrong to go, to not tell Sara, but by then it had just seemed easier to keep going. Sara didn't know about his ability. He had felt that because she wasn't a witch she wouldn't understand. If other witches couldn't fathom it, how could she?

Jesse also told Morag he had tried to get rid of the soldier ghosts, but he didn't have the knowledge. He also had left the battlefield with bruises. When he realized two other witches had arrived on the scene, he had been hopeful they would have more success than he had had. From the hillside, he had watched the women. He had thought about asking to join them, but was afraid of further ridicule. When the ghosts had departed, he walked out and saw that Morag was unconscious. He knew she needed a blanket. He watched Joly look for her, but hadn't realized she was injured. He apologized, ashamed that he hadn't gone to their aid more quickly.

Morag asked about his car and how was it that it was at the hotel, when he had driven their rental car in from Marathon. He told her he had parked it there in the evening and had rented a car to go out to Marathon. He had a feeling he would need to assist them and had left the rental car in Marathon. He had called the agency and told them where they could pick it up.

"So you knew where we were staying?"

"No... I didn't. I just happened to leave my car at your hotel. I trust the area more than most. It was a fluke." He grinned at Morag again.

Jesse took her to a *taverna* for supper and they continued talking.

Morag called the hotel to let Sara know that all was well and that she might be late getting in. Sara said that Joly was still asleep and that she and Randy had been keeping busy.

Joly stirred, turned over and moaned. She had lain on her broken arm. She lie there for a few minutes focusing on the past twenty-four hours. She wondered what Morag would do next. She thought about Jesse Alexander and wondered what had made him so taciturn. His manners were impeccable and she was sure he could be a great conversationalist if he chose. She listened to the murmuring of Randy and Sara and knew she needed to get up and spend some time with her son before he went to bed. She moaned and when there was no response, she moaned louder. She heard Randy whisper her name to Sara. Joly knew Sara had it figured out when she heard her tell Randy, "Go and see if Mommy's alright."

Joly felt the edge of the bed dip and waited. When she could feel a gentle breath on her face, she growled and pounced. Randy shrieked. Joly tickled him and he tickled her until he had to run for the bathroom. Joly winced as she sat up. She really needed to do another healing on herself. She looked around and asked Sara where Morag was.

""I'm not sure. She called a little while ago and said that she might be late."

Joly figured it was something to do with the ghosts. When Randy came back to the room, she went into the washroom and took her shirt off. The arm was discolored where the two bones had grated against each other. She did a healing, wishing she could do it outside, but it was dark and she didn't want to leave Randy. He hadn't seen much of her lately and she didn't want to scare him by taking him over to the park. He didn't like the dark and Joly tried to ensure that there was always some source of light around, along with the feeling of security.

When she was finished, she went and sat on the bed. Randy snuggled up against her. Joly asked Sara if she was hungry and when she said yes, they went downstairs.

Sara and Joly shared their meal with Randy which was a good thing, as Sara hardly ate any of hers. Going back up on the elevator, Joly asked if she was okay. She smiled too brightly and said yes, which told Joly she was not.

Joly ran a bath for Randy, played with him, read him a story and tucked him in for the night. She walked over and sat beside Sara who was doodling on her sketchpad.

"What's bothering you Sara? Are you still upset over seeing Jesse?"

"No, not upset really. It was just such an unexpected shock."

They had been quiet a minute when Sara asked, "You were in Jesse's house?"

"Yes." Joly expected to be asked what it looked like. She wasn't prepared for the next question.

"Did he have any paintings or anything on his walls?"

Joly remembered that she had said he was an artist. "I was in his kitchen, dining room, living room and the spare bedroom. His walls were bare, with the exception of a gorgeous charcoal drawing over his sectional."

Sara looked startled. "Charcoal? What was it of, do you remember?"

Joly smiled. "Of course I remember. It was so touching; I'd have trouble forgetting it. It was the backs of a nude man and woman..."

Sara's ragged intake of breath stopped Joly in mid sentence. She looked at Sara and saw that she had lost all color and that she looked dangerously close to passing out.

"Sara? Sara! For Gods' sake, talk to me. Sara? Breathe, damn it!" Joly didn't know what else to do, so she grabbed Sara and shook her.

Sara gasped, drew in a deep breath and exhaled. She looked at Joly. "They're facing the ocean, the two of them."

Joly nodded. "That was my impression."

Sara slowly shook her head and spoke so quietly Joly had trouble hearing her.

"I don't believe it. I just don't believe it."

"It obviously means something to you, but why the shock of hearing it's on Jesse's wall?"

Sara smiled a small sad smile. "Jesse and I sketched that together. He did my back, I did his. The ocean view is a spot where we liked to go and watch the sun set."

Joly smiled and hugged Sara. "It's funny. When I looked at it, I thought it looked familiar and I couldn't figure out why. I see the back of you all the time, leaning over, doing things with Randy. No wonder it seemed familiar. But why the shock of Jesse having it?"

"When he never came back, I assumed he had thrown it out. When I asked you about paintings, I was thinking of his own work, not what we had done together. I thought it was long gone."

"Well, it obviously means something to him. As I said, it was the only thing on his walls."

Sara nodded, got to her feet and tidied up and then she got ready for bed. Joly did the same.

Morag asked about the Oracle and Jesse told her. He had made the trip and asked the Oracle to help him to banish the ghosts. Morag wondered aloud why he had told her to go and see this Oracle, if he already had. He explained that she would get a different answer than he did; that the Oracle talked in riddles and that different interpretations were given to different prophesies.

"Speaking of riddles, are you any good at solving them?" Morag reached in her purse and pulled out the worn piece of paper that she had written Alyce's riddle on. She handed it to Jesse.

He read it and smiled. "I see a riddle within a riddle here."

"Yes, I found that too."

"Is this something important? Something you need to have the answer to?"

"It was given to Joly by a Seventeenth Century witch. What do you think?"

"I don't quite understand. Given to Joly, how?"

Morag smiled. Jesse really was very naive in the ways of the craft even after all her explanations. "I just told you."

Jesse shook his head. "You're telling me that Joly actually talked to someone from the Seventeenth Century?"

"Yes."

"In person?"

"Yes."

"My Lady, do you think I'll go home and have nightmares tonight?"

Morag laughed heartily. "I wouldn't think so, but I'm sure you will have trouble getting to sleep. Your mind will be swimming with what you've heard today."

He handed the paper back to Morag. "May I have a copy of this?"

"By all means." She took a small notepad and a pen out of her purse and copied the riddle down, handing it to him when she had finished.

It was after eleven when they left the *taverna* and Jesse drove Morag back to the hotel. When he dropped her at the front entrance, he said, "I have the feeling there's something you haven't told me. It seemed like there was some issue that you kept skirting all evening."

"You are very perceptive Jesse. Yes, there is something, but I don't think you're ready to hear it. You have an awful lot to think about as it is. It's nothing that really concerns you and if I thought your knowing would change anything, I would have told you. Does that satisfy you?"

"Not really, my Lady, but I suppose it'll have to do." He grinned at her and they said goodnight.

The doorman held the door open for Morag to enter, but she stood watching the taillights of Jesse's car until they were out of sight. When she entered the building and walked to the elevator, she was deep in thought. She wondered what Jesse would have had to say, if she had told him about the *Sisters of the Triple Moon*. She was still thinking when she opened the door to their room. A light had been left on for her and everyone was in bed. She quietly washed up and undressed, turned the light out and crawled into bed. She controlled her breathing and soon was fast asleep.

Jesse drove the distance to his apartment without thinking about it. His mind was on the crone and all she had told him. Some of the stuff was pretty unbelievable, but she hadn't questioned his ability. For that he was thankful. That she could make herself invisible didn't really surprise him. He always thought there had to be more of them with the ability. No, the shock had been finally meeting one. He had given up finding anyone. Hell, he didn't even bother looking anymore. He hadn't joined a coven or a group since that night in Coquitlam. What did they call that? A solitary. Yeah, he guessed that's what he was. He was a solitary in more ways than one.

Sara. Damn he missed her, had always missed her. What a shock to see her standing in that room today. His reaction had been even more of a shock. All he had wanted to do was go over and wrap his arms around her and never let her go. Her reaction was probably the normal one, not his. *"... You can go now."* That was his Sara, never one to mince words.

He had known she would go for a walk. It was something she had always done when she was upset. Maybe the outcome of their talk would have been more productive if he had told her the truth. Now he had talked to the crone, he wondered if he shouldn't give it another try.

He pulled into a parking spot and got out, locking the car. He went up to his apartment and let himself in. Turning the light on, he stared at the picture on the wall. In his mind's eye, he could feel his finger tracing Sara's backbone from her neck all the way down. He could hear her soft laughter and feel her swinging around to wrap her arms around him.

Jesse shook away the vision. *Damn!* He was hard as a rock. A cold shower would fix that. He headed to the bathroom. He undressed and looked in the mirror. The splash of purple caught his eye and he looked down at the hand soap. Sara had bought it for him. He used it only occasionally, wondering what he would do when it finally was empty. He didn't know, but he did know that this night he was damn well going to use it.

The cattle were thirsty. The winter had been drier than usual and the spring rains had not yet come.

Emilia knew her neighbors had to haul water in, but she had no need to spend her hard earned *dinero* on a Goddess given commodity.

The cattle were gathered around the dry water hole and looked at her expectantly. She waved her wand through the air and thought of the children's expression, hocus pocus, abracadabra. She smiled.

She felt the power rising through her and as it shot down her arm, she pointed the wand at the dry indentation.

The tip of the wand sparked and shot a charge of energy to the ground.

"There you go my *amigos*, in a moment you shall drink."

She stood with them and waited. Soon she heard the familiar gurgling and as she watched, the soil grew moist and slowly the hole filled with water.

There were many underground springs on the *rancho*. It was simply a matter of directing them to where they would do the most good.

Under the cover of darkness, she would slip over to her neighbors and revive some of their water holes. They did not seem to understand how much water it took to quench an animal's thirst. She didn't do it for the *rancheros*, but for the animals. She could not stand the sounds of distress she heard whenever she opened her senses.

Joly awoke early and decided she would make a quick trip across the street to the park to do a healing on herself. She opened her eyes and saw a light was on. She sat up to see Morag sitting at the desk looking at something. She eased out of bed not wanting to wake Randy and softly walked over to Morag.

"Toss some clothes on and come with me," she whispered. They both dressed and quietly left the room.

Over at the park Joly did another healing on Morag, concentrating mainly on her ribs. She did a healing on her arm and told Morag about the conversation she'd had with Sara. Morag told Joly about the hours she had spent with Jesse. Joly was surprised. She had pictured Morag doing a lot of things, but spending time with Mr. Tightlips was not one of them.

Morag said they would go to Delphi once everyone was up and they had eaten. They walked back to the hotel.

Joly went and checked Salem, who was almost back to normal. His wound was healing nicely and she did another healing on him. She checked Pip's paw and saw that it was fine. She needed to talk to them, so she lowered herself to the carpet. Asking quietly who wanted to tell her about the events on the plain, she waited to see who would respond.

"Mommy!" The happy voice rang from behind her. She turned and sat up to hug her son. They cuddled and talked for a few minutes and then she asked Randy if he could be quiet while she talked to the cats. He grabbed a book and went and sat on the bed, smiling contentedly.

Joly resumed her position and looked at the three cats that were all lined up in front of her. "A group talk? Can we do this? Well, I suppose we can.

We'll give it a try anyhow."

The cats sat closely together and Joly began watching their eyes, concentrating on their breathing. Time passed and finally she began to hear fragments of conversation. The cats appeared to be arguing over who was going to tell the Mistress about the events. When she was sure she had melded completely, she sent a message to them.

"I don't need to hear the bickering. I need to know what happened. I will listen to each of you, one at a time. Nefertiti, you may go first."

"Mistress, Pip wouldn't wait. We were discussing how to disarm the two men, when she just leapt into the air and hit the one with the heavy sword. Things got a little out of hand after that and I saw no choice but to try and get you out of harms way. I threw myself at your chest, hoping to knock you down, which I did. I didn't see how Salem got injured."

"Mistress, they were taking too long. While they were talking, the swords were both being swung at you. I went for the one that seemed like it would do the most damage. I did stop it, Mistress. When I turned around, you were lying on the ground with Nefertiti on top of you and Salem was at your feet, not moving."

"Mistress, I think we came close to failing you and I am sorry. Neffy always wants to talk. It's plan, plan, plan."

"Salem, there is nothing wrong with planning. Thanks to Pip we almost lost our Mistress."

"Neffy, if you would just shut up sometimes and *do* something, things would go much better."

Joly was losing her concentration. *Neffy?* She wanted to laugh, but needed to hear Salem's story. "Salem, continue please."

"Well Mistress, Neffy was insistent on a plan, and I was listening while watching you. Suddenly Pip jumped up and hit the soldier's arm. I saw you turn to look at the other sword and I knew we were out of time. I jumped up to disarm the soldier, but Neffy jumped at the same time and my aim was thrown off. Instead of hitting his arm, I hit the side of his sword. It was at an angle and the edge of it nicked me. I'm sorry Mistress. I don't mean to be a bother."

Joly smiled. She had to get her message across fast. She was going to laugh. "Salem, you did nothing wrong. Injuries happen… to everyone. Pip, you did nothing wrong. You were protecting me and you succeeded. Thank you. Nefertiti… Neffy? Is that what they call you?"

Nefertiti was enraged. "Mistress, my name is *Nefertiti. That* is what I am called. This poor excuse of a feline has no couth. He's a disgrace to my race and I am ashamed to admit I know him."

Joly was losing it, and fast. "Nefertiti, I'm sorry. Talk is good, but not necessarily when there's a lot of action happening. You all succeeded in keeping me from any serious harm. For that, I thank each of you. Please, try to get along. There is no reason to argue amongst yourselves. You are all loved and wanted." Joly choked and managed a quick, "Go in peace."

She put her head down on her arms and snickered. *Neffy*. That was just too funny. Trust Salem. She got to her feet and walked over to the bed. She was still snickering to herself and without realizing, she said it aloud.

Randy heard and quickly picked up on it. "Nef-fy? What Nef-fy?"

Nefertiti was mortified. She was going to get rid of that good for nothing Salem for once and for all. She just wasn't sure yet, how she was going to manage it. It wasn't bad enough that her Mistress knew, but now the chatterbox also knew. She walked to the window, jumped up on the table and looked out, wondering if there was a way she could get Salem to stand in front of a moving vehicle.

Joly knew that Nefertiti was already upset, so she set about getting Randy's mind off the new word. "Nothing honey, Mommy was just talking to herself. Let's get you dressed okay?"

"'Kay."

Joly watched Nefertiti sitting with her back to the room and wondered once again about her history. She had obviously come from somewhere that breeding was extremely important. Joly knew she didn't like Salem, but she had hoped they would somehow at least get along. It didn't seem like it was going to happen, if they were still at odds after all these years. *Neffy*. She would have to watch herself. Gods forbid that she someday slip and call her that. She smiled and turned her attention back to her son.

They went for breakfast and Joly went back to the room to get the cats. They got in the car and headed north. It took a little over two hours to reach the town of Delphi, which sits on the edge of a cliff on the slopes of Mount *Parnassus*, overlooking the Gulf of *Corinth* and a valley filled with olive and cypress trees. The view was incredible and Sara chose to stay where she was to sketch. She asked Randy to stay with her, while Morag and Joly began the walk up to the Sanctuary of *Apollo*. They walked through the *Roman Agora* and took the same path that visitors had taken for thousands of years. The *Sacred Way* wound itself up the side of the hill like a snake. They passed statues that commemorated military victories and other achievements of not only the Greek people, but other peoples as well.

They came upon the reconstructed Treasury of the Athenians, which had been built with the spoils of the victory over the Persians on *Marathon* Plain. Morag and Joly wondered at the meaning of this. How strange that they were there in regards to that very battle and in front of them stood this monument.

They continued up to the *Great Altar* and Morag paused.

It was here... long before Apollo, long before the other Gods that they revered today, that Gaia or Mother Earth, had had her beginnings. Morag had never thought she would be so close to the *One* she revered above all and she was so humbled, so full of awe, that tears trickled down her cheeks. Oblivious to the tourists, the tour guides, the children, even to her daughter-in-law, Morag assumed the Goddess position and gave thanks to the Creator of all.

Joly also knew where it was that they were and she followed Morag's lead, knowing that this was a once in a lifetime experience. One could always make a second or third trip to this place, but there was only ever, one first time. She gave thanks to Gaia and reaffirmed her promise to always do her best to ensure that Mother Earth was looked after. She asked that the Mother look upon them in favor that day and grant their quest to find an answer to lay the *Marathon* soldiers to rest. Morag and Joly poured water from their bottles onto the earth, took a drink, and finished their ritual.

They continued on to the Temple of *Apollo* and walked through what remained of a great building. At the far end was where the Oracle, commonly known as Sybil, had sat, sagely handing out her prophesies and answering the questions of the people.

Morag had felt light-headed for some time, but had attributed it to the altitude. Now, she wasn't so sure that was the reason. She was in an extremely holy place and she could feel the vibrations in the air. Her mouth was dry and she took another drink. Her eyes continued to water.

They approached the area where the Oracle had sat and Joly felt a thrumming coming up from the earth. She wondered at first if there was an earthquake in the making, but then she realized the air was also filled with it.

They each made their request to the empty air in front of them. Although they could see no one, they both felt the presence of an unseen entity.

They stood waiting, wondering what would happen next. The thought that they might fail never entered their minds. The original Oracle had been placed there by Gaia herself. As their lives were dedicated to the preservation of Mother Earth; that she would send them an answer was only natural.

Joly too, began to feel lightheaded and goose bumps appeared on her arms. She took a drink, wondering if she should sit down. She turned to Morag who was turning toward her, and they came together, wrapping their arms around one another. Morag laid her head on Joly's and wept. Joly felt the tears well up in her own eyes and she too, began to cry. The smell of jasmine was overpowering and again the dizziness overtook them.

As they cried, pictures whisked through their minds like a video that had been placed on fast forward. The pictures and thoughts were dizzying, and they clung to one another even tighter. Eventually the video slowed and the pictures became clear. A calendar with the thirteenth circled, the moon low in the sky, a three-headed woman, a pack of black dogs, an altar, a torch, black and white candles.

Time had no meaning. They held on to each other for a second, a minute, an hour, a lifetime.

Sara stood and watched them. Randy wanted to run to his Mother, but Sara held him back, asking him to be quiet. They had gotten worried and made the trip up the *Sacred Way*, Sara stopping here and there to sketch something that caught her eye. She wondered if she should approach them. She moved slowly toward them, holding tightly to Randy's hand and quietly called out their names.

Seconds passed and the two women slowly separated. Their faces were streaked with tears.

Sara wondered what they had experienced and decided she was glad she wasn't a witch. She thought of another witch then, and wondered if her life would have been different if she had been one.

Morag and Joly found their legs and slowly walked toward Sara and Randy. The vision had been so vivid, so terrifyingly real, the dizziness so overpowering, that it was taking some time to come back to the real world. They reached Sara and Randy. Joly took her son's hand and with one on each side of Sara, they walked away from the Temple.

The drive back to Athens was a quiet one, except for Randy's chattering and Joly's replies. Joly looked in the rear view mirror and saw Morag's eyes were closed, but she knew she wasn't sleeping. The task ahead of them was a scary one, leastwise she thought it was and she wasn't looking forward to it. She decided she would rather face another demon, than go back onto the battlefield again.

Back at the hotel Morag asked Sara if she would look up a couple of things on her laptop.

"Sure, what do you need?"

Morag told her and within minutes Sara had the information she needed. It was the eleventh. They had two days to prepare.

Veronika couldn't understand it. She'd never had a spell fail before, but this evil thing in her yard did not seem to want to go away. She noticed the white candle lay on its side and she knew there had been no wind. Whatever it was, it felt stronger than the last time.

She waited until the grandchildren arrived and told them about the strange energy field in the back yard.

They thought that the three of them together might have better luck, so Veronika cast the circle and did the banishment spell. Sergei and Polina helped to reinforce it and when they were done, all appeared to be well.

"See *Babushka*, you should have gotten us here the first time."

"We will see." She glared at the earth where the energy appeared to be coming from.

The next day Morag went shopping for candles and incense. She wandered through the *Plaka*, listened to the street musicians, wandered in and out of small shops and kiosks, toured up and down little side streets. She met a street seller who was selling tablecloths and she found a smaller one she liked. After some heavy bartering, she purchased it for twenty euros. She made several other small purchases and while chatting with one of the clerks, she found out there was a place called The National Gardens, not far from there.

Morag walked over to it and wandered up and down the pathways. She discovered an area of almost forty acres full of flowers, plants, bushes and trees from all over the world. There were over five hundred different varieties of plants under a canopy of trees. It had been built for the Royal Palace of King Otto and Queen Amalia, and had been planted in the mid eighteen hundreds. There were birds and benches, a duck pond and a small zoo. She needed to relax, to plan, and she had found the perfect spot.

He had cloaked himself in invisibility and he sat on the side of the hill watching. He was tired and he knew he needed to get some sleep soon. Why he went back there day after day, night after night, he wasn't sure. He just knew he needed to be there. Nothing had ever happened except with the crone and her sidekick, and they probably would have made out all right without his intervention. How the girl would have explained a naked, unconscious woman, he wasn't sure, but she seemed quite resourceful.

He wiggled his backside on the blanket, trying to get more comfortable. He hadn't been completely honest with the crone, but he figured what he had told her was close enough. He felt like a big enough fool for hanging out at the plain every day, without admitting to someone that's what he was doing. He guessed it was kind of like being a guardian or something. He snorted at the thought and quickly looked around to see if anyone had heard him.

Not many people were going to *Marathon* Plain these days. There were still a few that showed up and went to the museum, and there were the ones that went and took pictures of the mound, so they could go home and show the pictures to Aunt Betty and Uncle Joe, or whoever. But those that ventured out on the plain itself were few and far between.

He wasn't sure what he would do if some tourist did get into trouble on the plain. He had already faced the soldiers and lost. How he could aid some helpless fool, he had no idea. Still, he found himself going back every day, every night.

He wondered if the crone would be back. He wondered if they had gone to Delphi. He had lied about that too. True, he had gone, but he couldn't have told the crone the Sybil's answer if his life had depended on it, but he wasn't about to admit it. That she had answered his question, he had no doubt, but he hadn't been able to figure out what it meant. He didn't consider himself stupid, but the crone had shown him that he was quite ignorant in the ways of the craft. Even after their talk though, he still didn't understand the message he had received. If they had gone like he had told them to, he wondered if they would understand the message that they were given. He decided they would.

He wondered what it was the crone hadn't told him. He shook his head. He was doing far too much wondering. He took a drink of water and concentrated on the field. The ghosts were back, but no people were in the vicinity.

Sara flitted through his thoughts and he tried to push her away. He had enough crap happening, without her entering the picture. She danced around the periphery of his mind, teasing him until he finally gave up and let her in.

Sara. Beautiful, beautiful Sara. He loved her, of that he was sure. He hadn't even looked at another woman since he'd left her. When his thoughts and feelings got too overwhelming, he'd sign up for another race. Pitting his ability against that of a machine seemed to work for a while. Now that he had seen her again, he figured he'd have to hit the track soon, but first, he needed to finish with the ghosts.

Joly and Sara took Randy down to the pool. He was terrified of the large expanse of blue water and only after seeing his Mother and Sara swimming in it, did he consent to sit on the edge and dangle his feet. Joly and Sara played tag, swam and splashed water everywhere until a timid voice called for his Mother. Joly went and picked up Randy who threw his arms and legs tightly around her. She stayed near the edge of the pool until his fear lessened and slowly she introduced him to the joys of swimming. By the time they were ready to go back up to the room, Randy had decided that playing in the *big water* was fun.

When Morag returned she told them about the gardens. Joly told her she had talked to the desk clerk and discovered there was a zoo out by the airport. She thought maybe they could go out there the next day. Morag agreed with her.

Morag got out her crystal and did some scrying, nodding to herself as she looked in it. Randy went over and had a look and after peering intently in it, he looked at Morag and said, "Man."

Morag chuckled, agreed with him, and quickly put the crystal away, in case Sara decided to investigate.

They spent several hours at the zoo the next day where Morag discovered the third largest bird collection in the world. She wandered off on her own, talking to the various birds and forgot for a little while, the reason they were in Greece.

Joly and Randy saw all the wildlife and Sara did some more sketching.

Back at the hotel, they had an early supper and Joly bathed Randy and put him to bed. She was careful this time to tell him that she and Gra-Morg were going out for a little while, but that they should be back before he woke up the next morning. She read him a story and cuddled with him until he was asleep.

Joly gathered the cats together and explained that they had to stay behind. Salem let her know he was not happy with hearing that. She explained that if all went as planned, there could possibly be some dogs involved, and they wouldn't be friendly ones.

Upon hearing that, Pip went and jumped on the bed, curling up beside Randy.

Nefertiti touched her paw to Joly's hand as much as to say, "Be careful."

She was thinking to herself that it really was too bad that the Mistress wouldn't take at least one of them. She looked at Salem and thought he'd look good hanging out of the jaws of a large dog.

Salem brushed against his Mistress and went to see what Sara was drawing. He glanced at Nefertiti and saw the look in her eyes. He'd have to keep an eye on her. She was thinking really evil thoughts and he knew they centered around him.

Morag had packed the bag and they were ready to go. She had one last look in the crystal before they left. Again, she nodded and smiled to herself.

It was dusk when they arrived at the plain. They had just enough time to prepare, before the darkness was complete. Morag found the gate open once again, and was thankful for the birds. Their presence had helped her to meditate and send the suggestion to the keeper of the gate key.

While Joly was busy with the bag, Morag turned toward the hill and waved. Then she got busy. They walked out to the edge of the plain and Joly drew the circle. It was larger than normal, being close to fifteen feet in diameter. At the north end of the circle Morag set up an altar, using her newly purchased tablecloth as an altar cloth. Two black candles and a white candle were placed on the altar, along with a wine goblet that Morag had borrowed from the hotel, a bowl of jasmine incense, a brass bell, a bowl of sea salt, a bowl of water, an athame and a baetylic stone. Morag had had the stone for years and it normally resided at the bottom of her purse. She had cleansed and charged it before leaving the hotel. She filled the goblet with white wine.

While Morag was busy at the altar, Joly took three white candles and placed them at the east, west and south points of the circle. She checked the time. The ritual had to start at moonrise. They had ten minutes to finish their preparations.

Up on the hill, Jesse watched with interest. He had been startled when the crone waved directly to him, but thinking about it, he realized it really wasn't surprising. She was a smart old girl, that one. He wished he could join them, but knew that whatever they were up to, they wouldn't have time to explain what they were doing, or what he might be able to do to help. He picked up the night goggles and put them on.

Morag stripped down and stood facing the hill where the dark shadow kept watch. She did it so that when Joly faced her, her back would be to the hill. They took four bottles of water and two vials of mixed oils and carefully mixed them together, and then took turns pouring the water over one another while they bathed.

They went into the circle and Morag lit the three white candles. She then went to the altar, lit the three candles on it and dipped the athame into the water and blessed it, calling out,

"In the name of the Goddess Hectate, I cast out from thee all impurities and unclean spirits."

She dipped the athame into the sea salt to purify it, and called out,

"Blessed be this salt, in the name of the Goddess Hectate, that which would malign or hinder shall be cast out and all good shall enter herein."

Morag picked up the bowl of salt and poured it into the water. Joly picked up the athame and retraced the circle as she called out,

"I cast this circle three times round,
First for the maiden, with hair unbound
Innocent, carefree and full of play
She is in her spring, loving life each day.
I cast this circle three times round,
Second for the mother, braided, her hair is bound.
Protective and kind, nurturing and strong.
She is in her summer; spring days are gone.
I cast this circle three times round
Third for the crone, with hair again, unbound,
Full of knowledge, shrewd and wise,
She is in her autumn, gone the summer skies."

Joly moved to the center of the circle and beside Morag, they both raised their arms and chanted,

"Circle of power, circle of protection…"

Jesse watched in fascination. He knew he had never seen anything so incredible. After talking to the crone and then watching this, he decided the covens that he had belonged to probably had as much to do with witchcraft as his racing did. No wonder they had all thought him to be some kind of freak. *Damn!* He had been so stupid! Maybe he would move back to Surrey. Maybe he could become part of the crone's group. He thought he might like that. He knew he would certainly learn from her. He wondered what Sara would think and wondered how she would feel if he moved back?

"…in the name of the Goddess Hectate."

Morag moved over to the altar and knelt before it. She picked up the goblet of wine with both hands and she held it in the air as she spoke,

"In your honor great Goddess Hectate do I drink this toast to you and to the Mother."

Morag poured some of the wine onto the ground and drank some. Placing the goblet back on the altar, she picked up the bell and rang it three times. Joly picked up the athame and held it high in the air.

"In this dark hour of night the Goddess Hectate reigns supreme. Hectate, I do honor you and I do praise you."

Joly picked up a container that sat by the altar. She walked clockwise around the circle and poured out the contents as she walked, taking care to swing wide of the altar. When she was finished she moved back to the center.

"Hectate, I call upon you, the Goddess of the moon. Hectate, I call upon you, the Goddess of witches. Hectate, I call upon you, the Goddess of the underworld."

Morag moved to the edge of the circle, lit a match and tossed it to the ground. The circle erupted in flames.

Jesse was on his feet and running down the hill before he realized it was part of the ritual. He stopped, feeling like an idiot and stood still, not wanting to distract the two women. He still couldn't believe they were actually trying to call a Goddess into their circle.

They stood in the middle of the flames, arms upraised, calling out,

"We evoke and conjure thee, Hectate, come into our circle of fire as we do this rite in your honor."

The atmosphere grew heavy and the air currents, crackling with life, swirled around the circle.

Jesse heard the distant baying of dogs and knew he was in trouble. Everyone knew Hectate always traveled with a pack of dogs and they weren't nice dogs. He had to get out of there. He saw their car and said, "To hell with it." He ran for it, opened the door, dove in and slammed the door behind him. His legs were shaking so badly his knees were knocking together.

"Hectate, hear our voices."

The air grew heavier still and the baying of the dogs grew louder.

"Hectate, Goddess of the underworld, we ask that you would banish the ghosts that reside on this plain. This is not their time nor is it their place. Their battle is over. The soldiers need to rest."

The wind howled, as did the dogs. Jesse could hear them all around the vehicle, growling, barking, their nails ripping at the metal and the glass, as they tried to tear their way in. He was terrified and he hunched down in the seat with his eyes tightly shut.

Suddenly, the doors on the car flew open! Jesse wet his pants.

The wind wrapped itself around Morag and turned her around. A void formed in front of her and she saw a vision of Jesse huddled in their rental vehicle.

"Hectate, Goddess of all witches, we ask that you would show mercy on one who follows the path. He has been diligent in his watch."

The car doors slammed shut and the baying of the dogs grew distant. Still Jesse did not move.

The Marathon Plain began to glow, the wind swirled the length and breadth of it. The entire plain appeared to be on fire. Eventually the fire vanished, the glow lessened, the wind condensed and turned conical. It headed to the circle.

Joly and Morag raised their arms and spoke in unison.

"Hail to thee, Hectate!
Hail to thee, Hectate!
Hail to thee, Hectate!"

The funnel came down in front of them and twisted itself into the ground at their feet. The air pressure returned to normal, the wind ceased; there was total and complete silence.

Joly looked around and was surprised to see the candles were still lit. She smiled and wondered at her surprise. Goddesses can do anything; she knew that.

They set about closing their circle and gathering up their things.

The car door slowly opened, Jesse climbed out and slunk away in the darkness to the rental car that sat back in the town, all thoughts of his blanket and water bottle long forgotten.

When they were dressed and had everything packed, they took one last look around. There was no evidence of them having been there, not even so much as a burnt blade of grass. They put the bag in the car and headed back to Athens. Their work was done in Greece. They could go back home.

Morag wondered where Jesse had gotten to. She had felt the wet seat when she got in the car and knew what happened. She saw and felt his fear when Hectate gave her the vision. She felt sorry for him, but now he had witnessed true witchcraft, perhaps it would give him something to go on, something possibly to set a goal for. She knew he loved Sara and she was sure Sara loved him. She wondered if there was any hope for the two of them.

13. Lost and Found

Morag was not happy Joly had talked her into extending their stay in London. True, it was only for one day, but she knew they needed to get back to Canada. The evil was building; she could sense it and she knew there were still other things to do before heading to the states.

They stayed at the same hotel as before. Joly immediately rented a car and after a bite to eat and freshening up, she was ready to go. Morag declined the invitation to accompany her, opting to stay at the hotel to rest. Sara had been to London with her parents and wanted to visit a couple of places she remembered from her trip with them. Randy, when asked if he wanted to accompany Sara or go for a car ride with his mother, surprised them all when he said he wanted to stay with Morag. She agreed to watch him, saying she would enjoy his company.

Salem was not about to let Joly out the door without him, so she agreed to take him along. Nefertiti decided that if Salem was going, so was she. They looked at Pip, expecting her to run to the carrier to join them, but she decided to stay with Randy and Morag. Joly took the two cats down to the car and once inside; she opened the carrier gate to let them loose.

She headed out of the city toward the small village where her Mother had been buried. Rhiannon had agreed to try to find out what had happened to Duncan. Joly hoped she had had some success.

She drove into the village and was amazed at the difference. There were people everywhere, some hurrying down the sidewalk, others standing and talking. The street was spotless, as was the square. There were dogs with their owners and dogs wandering alone. It was a normal scene and Joly felt a burst of pride that she had helped to make it so.

She drove down the street slowly, hoping for a glimpse of Rhiannon, but did not see her. She continued out to the cemetery, thinking she might see her there. She parked at the gates and climbed out. The cats jumped out too, and sniffed the air. It smelled clean and fresh. Joly walked toward the three graves and even from a distance, she could see the markers that had been placed on them.

As she got closer, she smiled. She had expected to see Christian crosses; she should have realized Rhiannon wouldn't have done that. Instead, there were three white five pointed stars attached to sturdy stakes. In the center of each star the occupants name had been painted in sky blue and outlined in dark green.

Joly looked at Bettina's and Raoul's stars first, then she went to her Mother's grave. Looking at the star and seeing Morgana's name written boldly for all to see, Joly realized that indeed, Morag was right as usual. She had been in denial. The tears fell softly down her cheeks as she thought about the last times her Mother had hugged her, had told her she loved her, had laughed with her. Joly swiped at her cheek and whispered, "I love you Mom. I sure do miss you." She turned and walked back to the car.

She laughed, thinking about what she had just done. She surely did make a poor witch, talking to the grave like any good Christian would do. Her parents were in Summerland waiting for her to go and visit, not floating around on some fluffy white cloud, with giant wings sprouting out of their shoulder blades.

She drove back to the village and parked near the square. Leaving the cats in the car, she walked over to the rotunda and thought about the last time she had been there. A dog ran up to her and licked her hand, his tail wagging back and forth. She didn't really recognize him, but knew he was one of the many she had healed that day. She spoke to him, petting him gently. Suddenly she had an idea.

"Hey buddy, can you find Rhiannon for me? I've been looking for her, but I can't seem to find her."

The dog barked and ran across the square and down the street, disappearing around the corner.

Joly went and sat on one of the benches. She was conscious of her pulse racing as she sat, absorbing the rays from the Sun God.

"Joly! Is it truly yer? 'allo! It's 'andsome to clock yer." Rhiannon was smiling. "I didn't Adam and Eve Rocky at first, but 'e was insistent. Come wiv me. I'll make us a pot of Rosy Lea. Where's yer china, 'er name is Morag, right?"

Joly laughed. "Hello Rhiannon. It's good to see you too. I would love a cup of tea, but two of my cats are in the car. May I bring them?"

Joly stood and Rhiannon reached out to grasp her hands.

"Yes, of course. I forgot yer traveled wiv yer cats. Didn't yer 'ave three, ain't it? Where are yer parked? We can drive over to me place."

The sense of oneness shocked them both. Rhiannon stepped back. "What the bleedin' bloody 'ell was dat?"

"My Gods, Rhiannon!" Joly stepped forward and they both felt it again, the sense of having always known each other.

Rhiannon stared at Joly, shaking her head.

"Oh my Gods, Rhiannon. Do you have no idea what it means?"

"It means somefin'? Me Muvver always says I was destined fer 'andy things. How 'andy is dis… stuck aht 'ere, doin' not much of anythin'?"

"We definitely need to talk."

Joly led her to the car and introduced the cats to her. They drove a short way to the edge of town where a small cottage with a thatched roof lay snuggled in the trees. Flower and herb beds were laid out in neat order and looked to be well tended. Two dogs ran to greet them and Joly recognized them as two she had last seen standing by Rhiannon at the edge of the forest.

Rhiannon, Joly and the cats went into the cottage and Rhiannon put the kettle on. Joly asked about the third dog that had been with Rhiannon, when she last seen her.

"Oh, she's around 'ere someplace. Prolly puttin' the scarper on a 'are in the bush. She knows be'er than to catch them, but she does love to put the fear of the Gods into them." She laughed.

Joly looked around the small cottage, feeling totally at home as she did so. Rhiannon lived simply, but everything was put together to convey a feeling of complete comfort. It reminded her somewhat of her cabin although it was larger and there were homey touches everywhere. Dried herbs hung from the ceiling and homemade curtains covered the windows. There was also a curtain-covered doorway leading to what Joly presumed to be the bedroom. There were candles everywhere and Joly could see they were the main source of light in the evenings. There was a small altar set up along one wall.

"So what brings yer back to dis part of the world, Joly? I didn't expect to clock yer again." Rhiannon poured the tea and sat across from Joly. Nefertiti and Salem sat under the table.

"Umm… things have been happening. Strange things. Morag believes Duncan is still alive. You said you would see if you could find anything out for me… us. I was wondering if you had." Joly looked closely into Rhiannon's eyes. It was strange. She really could not tell what color they were.

"I did check around. A bird by the flamin' name of Maddie talked to a stranger around dat time, but I don't fink it was yer Duncan. She says 'e was a simpleton, wi' white barnet and a one-track mind. Says 'e was on an errand or somethin', and apparently 'e got right agitated wiv 'er when she couldn't understand wha' 'e was about."

"Oh. No, it doesn't sound at all like him. So you've heard nothing else?"

"Nothin' at all. Stand on me, guv. I 'ave talked to various people. Dis seems to be the only stranger clocked at dat time."

Joly took a sip of tea and thought. "I wonder… do you think I could maybe talk to this Maddie? I probably won't learn anything, but I just need to be sure I've covered all the bases. I don't want to get back to Canada and decide I missed something. You know what I mean?"

"I understand where yer comin' from. We can scarper over and clock if she's at 'ome. She prolly is. Maddie doesn't wander much. She 'as a bum Mystic Meg."

Joly smiled. She understood most of what Rhiannon was saying, but she did use some colorful language. "Mystic Meg?"

Rhiannon laughed and patted her leg. "Yer doin' brill, Joly. Most people would 'ave asks fer clarification several times by now. Yer know... I can rabbit wi' aht all the color, but dis is me. What I learned when I was a saucepan lid."

Joly nodded. "I enjoy listening to you."

Rhiannon chuckled and then looked curiously at Joly. "So... tell me about dis feelin' and why do I feel like I know yer?"

Joly explained about the *Sisters of the Triple Moon* and what it meant to be one. Rhiannon's eyes grew large as Joly told her about it. Joly watched Rhiannon's eyes with interest. She still couldn't figure out what color they were. She had never seen eyes so pale.

"Yer've got to be kiddin'! Super powers! I don't fink so. I'm a kitchen witch, a garden witch. I can't do anythin' like what I clocked yer do aht at the bleedin' graveyard. Yer wrong. I'm not one of yer kind."

Joly smiled sadly. "I wish I were wrong. It's a great honor, but it's also a burden at times. Like now, when all I want to do is look for Duncan, but I have only today. Tomorrow we fly back to Canada to find out where we go next."

"Why can't yer stay 'ere and wait until yer called, eh darlin'? Wouldn't dat make more sense?"

"We don't know when the next calling will come, or from where. It makes better sense to operate out of our home territory, what with our passports and all. And also, I have my son to think of. He will be going into kindergarten next month. I need to be there if possible."

"Yes, of course. I didn't know yer 'ad a currant bun. How old is 'e?"

"He's four, soon to be five." Joly told her how she had come to be a mother.

"Wow! Dat's somethin'. He's 'ere in Britain wiv yer?"

"Yes, along with his nanny."

They talked some more and Joly thanked Rhiannon for the grave markers. Rhiannon said she had done them herself. She had enjoyed the task and was happy to know that Joly approved. Finally, Joly said she really had to be going.

"Right. Let's go clock if Maddie is around." She put the cups in the sink and they walked outside.

Rhiannon directed Joly to Maddie's house. She left the cats in the car and they walked to the door. Rhiannon knocked and grinned at Joly. "Yer'll get along fine wi' Maddie. She's a up to scratch old bird."

The door opened and a wizened old woman with a stooped back stood before them. Her face resembled a dried prune and her jowls sagged so much they almost hid her neck from view. Thin white hair failed to cover the pale pink scalp.

"Rhiannon..." The voice croaked. Her eyes sparkled and Joly could tell the old woman was pleased to see her.

"Ay Maddie. 'Ow yer doin'? It's been a while. Dis 'ere is Joly. She wants to rabbit to yer about the stranger dat passed through 'ere ten years ago."

Maddie's lips twitched. "Come in." She opened the door wider.

Joly went to enter, but was assaulted by the fetid odor of filth, rotten garbage, unwashed dishes, and the woman in front of her obviously hadn't bathed for quite some time. She stopped; swallowing the bile that had risen to her throat. She swallowed again and breathing shallowly, she stepped into the filthy home. She knew she couldn't stay long; she was already having trouble breathing without choking.

Maddie limped over to a worn sofa that was so dirty the original color had all but disappeared. She sat down heavily. She waved her arm in the direction of a couple of chairs, the loose, wrinkled skin flapping back and forth from her upper arm. The dress she wore was stained with various colors across the front, testament to having been worn through several meals.

Rhiannon quickly led the way, suddenly aware of Joly's discomfort. She went and sat in the ancient armchair, leaving Joly the scarred, rocking chair with a torn cushion of thin material, the stuffing half in and half out.

Joly sat gingerly on the edge of the chair, wanting nothing more than to get out of there. She spoke quickly, "Maddie, Rhiannon tells me you spoke to a stranger ten years ago. That's about the time my husband went missing. I don't think the man you talked to was him, but I need to make sure."

Maddie nodded her head. She looked thoughtful for a moment, and Joly wondered if she was trying to remember the event.

Maddie's mouth opened and the voice croaked again. "He was an odd one, that boy." She paused, took a ragged breath and continued. "He was about twenty with white hair. He walked with a limp, dragging his right leg slightly. He talked in a stilted manner, similar to one who is autistic." She paused again, swallowing loudly.

Joly was shocked at the cultured words coming from the old woman's lips. Her use of proper English, coupled with the state of the home didn't go together.

"Can you tell me how tall he was or the color of his eyes?" Out of the corner of her eye, she saw movement and watched as a large beetle made its way around a giant dust ball that sat in the middle of the floor.

The old woman's mouth twitched again. "His eyes were incredible. They made you think of warm summer skies, they were such a brilliant blue. He wasn't overly tall, perhaps about five foot ten."

Joly thought of Duncan's blue eyes. She had always thought of summer skies too, when she had looked in them.

"Do you have a picture, my dear?" Maddie asked.

"No. I'm sorry. I don't. He said he was on an errand?"

"No, that's not what he said. He said he was on a mission. I tried to get him to tell me what it was. His speech was very fragmented, as if he was having trouble getting the words out. He became very agitated with me. Let me think. I can tell you exactly what it was that he said."

The silence was overpowering in the small room. Joly looked around at the dust and cobwebs that covered everything and wondered what had brought this elegant speaking crone to this. She was beginning to think Maddie had dozed off when finally, her voice crackled to life.

"I go... mission. Those were his exact words."

Joly shot out of the chair. "Are you *sure, absolutely sure?*" The tears welled up and trickled down her cheeks. *Duncan's alive.*

"Yes dear. That obviously means something to you."

"*Yes, yes, yes.*" She laughed as she cried. "That's where we lived. Mission. That's what he was telling you. He was going to Mission. Don't you see? You said he got agitated when you tried to get him to tell you what his mission was. That's why. He wasn't on a mission; he was going to Mission. I have to go. I have to let Morag know. Oh my Gods! This is wonderful. Maddie, thank you so much. You have no idea what this means. All this time we thought he was dead. My Duncan is alive."

Joly headed for the door. Turning back, she went over to Maddie and squatted down in front of the old woman. She grasped Maddie's hands in hers. "Thank you." Her voice came out a whisper. A surprisingly firm squeeze was given back.

"You're more than welcome, Joly. It was nice to meet you. Where will you look now, for your man?"

Joly's head dropped. "I don't know. The surrounding towns and villages, I suppose. I guess you have no idea which way he went from here?"

Again, the lips twitched. Joly decided it was Maddie's way of smiling.

"No, not really. He appeared to be headed toward the M1, but I'm not sure. I'm sorry."

"It's okay Maddie. You have done more than enough, just by remembering what Duncan said to you. I do have to go."

Joly rose to her feet and walked over to Rhiannon. "Thank you my friend. I shall never forget this." They hugged, the sense of belonging together overpowering and then Joly walked to the door, all thoughts of the squalor and stench gone from her mind.

She pulled the door closed and walked to the car. Suddenly she had a thought and she turned and ran back to the cottage. She knocked and walked straight in.

"Maddie, I'm sorry. I forgot to ask... what was he wearing when you saw him? Do you remember?"

The dry, croaking voice sounded put out. "Why wouldn't I remember? Your man was wearing a long cloak of medium brown velvet. He kept it wrapped tightly against himself, so I have no idea what he was wearing underneath it."

"Thank you Maddie. That's what he was wearing the last time I saw him." Joly turned and opened the door again. Pausing, she looked over at Rhiannon.

"Do you have a passport, Rhiannon?"

"Not bleedin' likely. I 'ave no need fer one. I won't be travelin' anywhere."

"Don't count on it. Thanks for everything. Bye now."

Joly closed the door behind her and skipped down the walk.

Once she was in the car, Joly started to shake. Salem walked over to her and put his paw on her arm.

"*Oh my Gods... oh my Gods.* He's alive Salem. Duncan's alive. He's here, somewhere. And tomorrow we leave for home. I don't want to go. I want to stay and find him. Damn it!" She pounded the steering wheel in frustration.

"Do you think the Mistress is okay to drive, Neffy? I mean Nefertiti."

"I'm sure we're about to find out," she responded from her spot by the rear window.

Frustrated beyond anything she had ever known, Joly angrily inserted the key in the slot and started the car. She headed down the street wondering what she could do next. As the street widened and became the road to the highway, she had an idea. She slowed down and began searching both sides of the road.

Joly and Duncan had always thought alike, so she decided it made sense that she should be able to figure out which way he went when he left the village.

She paused briefly in several spots and twice she got out of the car to look over areas that seemed somehow to call to her. When she reached the M1, she pulled off to the side of the road and again got out. She stood staring down the highway, jumbled thoughts running rampant through her mind.

She remembered the trip to Hadrian's Wall, and how Morag had paced up and down the road as if searching for something. Had she in fact, felt Duncan? If so, why hadn't she said anything? *She didn't want to upset me, that's why.*

If that was the case, then Duncan had gone north from this place. North. What was it about that word... north? There was something she was missing, but what?

Joly got back in the car and turned south toward London, her heart heavy, knowing she was so close and yet still so far away from her love.

When Joly walked into the room, Randy was sleeping and Morag had the crystal over by the window. She knew Morag wouldn't enter a home with it, so she decided to tell a white lie and see where it took her.

"Duncan's alive, Morag, just like you thought. I talked to a woman who talked to him ten years ago. There's something wrong with him. He has trouble talking and he was limping. She said he went north."

Morag smiled. "Yes, I thought so. Limping... well, the demon did strike him, so that's not really surprising. Come, sit down and tell me everything."

"There's not much to tell. He was still wearing his robes. He told the woman, her name is Maddie, that he was going to Mission."

Morag raised an eyebrow. "Well… he never quite made it did he? Yet, he went north from there?"

"Yes. Maddie said he had a lot of trouble trying to get words out. She said it was like he was autistic. She asked him what he was doing or something and he told her, 'I go Mission.' Those were his exact words, so she says."

"And then he headed north?"

"Yes."

"Well then, that explains why I felt him when we drove up to Hadrian's Wall that day."

Yes!

"Why didn't you tell me? You had me so worried the way you were acting."

"I'm sorry dear, but there didn't seem to be any reason to upset you. It was a fleeting moment of Duncan being there and then it was gone. It was almost as if I had imagined the whole thing. You have no idea how many times I have looked for him since in that area, but I can find nothing." She held the crystal up and shook her head.

"Morag… I can't go back home tomorrow, not with knowing Duncan is so close. I just can't." She began to cry.

Morag put the ball down and went over to Joly, encasing her in her arms. "I know, dear, I know. We don't have much time, but England is small. With any luck, we won't need long."

"Mommy?" The voice was concerned. Randy had woken and seen his Mother was crying.

"Hey Baby, come here." Joly smiled through her tears and held her arms out. Randy ran to her.

Morag smiled at the two of them and walked back to the window. They would have to cancel their flight. If the search was going to be concentrated up north, they should try and find a hotel that was closer. Maybe she would go down and ask at the desk if there was one they could recommend.

Sara returned and they told her of the change in plans. When she was told why, she was very excited for them.

Joly called the airlines and the car rental agency, and Morag went down and spoke to the desk clerk about accommodations in the York area. By the time she went back to the room, they had reservations at a pet friendly hotel.

The next morning under cloudy skies, they drove to York. They listened to the weather report on the radio and were disheartened to hear that thunder and rain showers were forecast for the next few days.

Joly took the M18 exit just before Doncaster. Rather than stay on the main thoroughfare, she wanted to travel on a quieter road, with the hopes that Morag might be able to sense something. She didn't think Duncan would be living in a city. He had always hated the hustle and bustle, the crowds, the noise of Vancouver, and regardless of what had happened to him, she couldn't see that changing.

Raindrops splattered sporadically on the windshield, as the skies tried to decide whether or not to let loose with a downpour.

Randy was fussing and Joly knew all the traveling had to be hard for him. She wanted to tell him about Duncan, but knew it was too soon. What if she failed in her search? Failure was not an option in her mind, but she knew in her heart it was a possibility. Ten years was a long time. Maybe he didn't even live in this area. Maybe he had just been passing through when Morag had picked up his presence. *North.*

"Morag... what is it about going north? I keep feeling I'm missing something, but I can't for the life of me think what it might be."

"I don't know, dear. Nothing comes to mind."

Sara had been sitting back with her eyes closed, thinking of another time, another place. She sat up and frowned. "Wasn't there something about the north in your riddle?"

Joly hit the brakes. A car behind them almost rear-ended the rented vehicle. The driver laid on his horn and sped around them, waving his fist in the air. Joly pulled over to the side of the road.

Joly and Morag stared at each other. Morag found her voice first. "*Damn!* How stupid." She dug in her purse for the worn piece of paper.

"The gift to summon is abandoned in Polaris. The ability to invoke is left behind, not in the northern sky, but in the north."

"Couldn't abandoned mean lost?" Sara wasn't particularly good at riddles, but she had a quick mind and with being an artist, her concept of words and their meanings was broader than most.

Joly tried it out. "The ability to summon or invoke or call forth is lost in the north. *Oh my Gods! Oh my Gods!* Morag, it's about Duncan, the riddle is about Duncan. He's lost his memory... isn't that what it's saying?" She was shaking with excitement.

Morag was smiling and nodding her head. "Yes, my dear. I do believe you could be right."

A voice whispered in Joly's mind and she smiled at the two women. "You know what else Alyce said to me? She said 'All waiting is long.' She knew and was trying to tell me, without telling me."

Joly pulled back on the highway, the three women discussing the riddle and what else it was trying to tell them. Randy had picked up on the excitement and had quit fidgeting, seemingly content to listen to his favorite people, who all had smiles in their voices.

After checking in at the new hotel and having a bite to eat, Sara and Randy went back to the room, while Morag and Joly headed out to start their search. With a map of the area that showed all the side roads, they opted to start at the southeastern section. They spent the afternoon driving up and down back roads, side roads and through numerous villages and hamlets, with names like Stillingfleet, Osgodby, Thirtleby and Holme On Spalding Moor. Morag sensed nothing, her crystal showed nothing and Joly's heart kept up a staccato beat in her chest.

The rain, although it never poured, let them know it was there. The intermittent drizzle kept up all afternoon, just enough to irritate Joly with having to constantly turn the wipers on and off.

On the second day of their search, they headed east, driving through places named Fangfoss, Musley Bank, Thwing, Wetwang and Primrose Valley. The rain came down in earnest for most of the afternoon and they could hear the thunder overhead. Headed back to York that evening, Morag suggested they give it two more days and then they really had to leave. Joly nodded in agreement, unwilling to speak aloud that she may have to leave Duncan behind after all.

Randy sensed the sadness in his Mother and tried his best to cheer her up. When it didn't work, he settled for cuddling with her. They were in bed early and in the dark, the tears slid silently onto her pillow.

The two pinpoints of light glowed in the distant darkness. Joly waited impatiently for Duncan's eyes to approach. The garbled noise grew louder with the never ending..."You dum-de dum, you dum-de dum."

The eyes stopped, unblinking, they accused her again and again. "You dum-de dum, you dum-de dum."

"Duncan, this is crazy. Where are you? Can't you see I'm trying to find you? Help me... please... help me." She cried and tried to look away, but her head wouldn't turn. She tried to close her eyes, but they remained open, looking at the vivid blue eyes. "Duncan, I don't want to do this anymore. Damn it Duncan! You're pissing me off!"

The eyes blinked closed. The darkness consumed her. "You did-de dum. You did-de dum. You didn't dum. You didn't dum." The eyes opened and they were filled with pain.

"Duncan? I don't know what you think I did, but I didn't do it. Honest. All I have ever done is love you. Honey... I will always love you."

The eyes blinked closed. You didn't dum. You didn't dum. You didn't wa..."

"Joly... wake up. Come on Sweetie... wake up now." Morag's voice was firm. When she saw Joly's eyelids flutter, she breathed a sigh of relief. She knew this couldn't go on. One could only make so many trips into the veil between the worlds before they were unable to return.

Sara sat wide-eyed from her bed on the sofa, wondering if the dreams, nightmares, whatever they were, were ever going to end. She pictured herself having to sleep in Joly's room back at the house, just in case.

Joly opened her eyes and swore. "Damn it Morag, he was just telling me what I'm supposed to have done."

Morag shook her head. "You know how dangerous these trips are. I don't really give a rat's ass at the moment if you never find out. You are just so damn lucky I have been able to pull you back." She returned to her side of the bed on the other side of Randy, who had slept through the whole episode. Without another word, she climbed into bed and tucked the covers around her neck.

Joly lie there, torn between being upset at almost knowing what Duncan was trying to tell her, and yet knowing that Morag was right.

There had been a young witch in Vancouver several years before who had been unable to make it back. Her body was taken to some long-term care facility, where they fed her intravenously and her heart continued to beat. Of course the doctors didn't believe the wild story that had been told to them. That she had gone away in a dream and been unable to return.

Joly thought of Randy and turned to hold him. Yes, she needed to come back. She couldn't stay with Duncan in that world that lay between the Otherworlds.

"I'm sorry, Morag. Of course you're right. I didn't mean to be a bitch."

The only answer was silence.

The next morning Joly went to Morag and gave her a hug, apologizing once again. Morag was tired and also disheartened. She patted Joly on the back and murmured that it was okay. Joly knew it wasn't and felt terrible, but she didn't know what else to say.

Breakfast was a quiet affair, and afterwards Morag informed Joly that she was staying at the hotel to rest.

Randy balked at being left behind, so he and Sara joined Joly in the car and headed west. She had decided to check the area between the M1 and York. This took them through towns called Helperby, Cattal, Cowthorpe and Appleton Roebuck. By early afternoon Randy was ready to go back to the hotel, as were the cats, so she dropped them and Sara off, checking on Morag at the same time. Morag was in a better mood and said she would go with Joly and they set out heading for the northeast.

The weather had gotten progressively worse and the rain came down steadily. The windshield wipers lulled Joly into a stupor. She was disheartened and tired. The strain of the previous night and peering through the spotty window was wearing her down.

They were in a town that bordered on a national park, driving up and down the streets, automatically glancing down the side streets as they crossed them when Joly suddenly realized she had seen something. She hurriedly parked the car, telling Morag to wait. She ran back to the corner and looked down the side street. There, limping away from her was a man with white hair.

Her heart racing, she began running, calling out, "Duncan... Duncan. Wait up, Duncan."

The man was a block away and appeared not to hear her, as he continued on his way.

Joly ran through the puddles, oblivious to how wet she was getting, oblivious to the people looking at her, her breath coming in ragged gasps.

"Duncan... *wait!*" She screamed again as she closed in on the man ahead. She had no idea how shrill her voice had gotten. When she was about ten feet away, the man stopped and turned around.

She was running full out and had trouble stopping, almost pushing the man over, as she put her hands out to keep her balance.

The man looked at Joly in something akin to awe.

Jimmy Smith had not been having a good month. The weather had been damp and cold, so there weren't many cans or bottles laying around. Business was slow at the shop, so Hans didn't need him for anything. Gisela was tired of him being under foot, so she would chase him outside to get some fresh air.

Jimmy hadn't been sleeping well the past while either, so he felt more tired than usual. He'd been having a weird dream. The same one, night after night about the denim clad woman. The scent of magnolia blossoms was always strong right after the dream and he wondered why. In the dream he kept telling the woman, "Part of me is missing, part of me is missing," but she didn't seem to understand..

He wanted to talk to the woman, but he couldn't. He couldn't find her again. She had disappeared like the other thing he had lost. He was tired of losing things; losing people. It had been better before, when he hadn't almost found what he was missing. Back then, he had at least been content. Now, it was like he had ants in his pants. He was always looking, searching, sniffing the air.

He had been in his bedroom looking at the picture frame when Gisela spotted him. Even though it was raining she told him to go and get some air. He walked over to the shop and see if Hans was busy. Hans had no work for him, so he went out in the rain again and decided to go to the coffee shop. At least it was dry there and nobody would chase him out, at least not for a while.

He was walking down the street, deep in thought, when he became conscious of somebody yelling. He couldn't figure out what they were yelling, but it was sure getting loud. When it sounded very close, he turned around to see what the hollering was about.

Jimmy was shocked when he saw the woman running toward him. He thought she was going to knock him over, but she finally stopped inches from him, throwing her hands out to keep her balance.

He looked at the lady in total shock. *It was her.* He had found her at last and he was terrified he would lose her again.

"H-h-ello. M-my name is James Smith."

Joly's mouth opened and closed looking much like a fish out of water. She was suddenly very embarrassed.

Morag could feel Joly's excitement, could feel her heart pounding, and knew that Duncan must be near. Why she couldn't feel him she didn't understand, but she decided she had better go and see what was happening. She got out of the car and walked to the corner, the raindrops splattering on the concrete around her. She crossed the road and continued on, seeing Joly at the other end of the block. She appeared to be talking to someone and Morag's heart stepped up a notch. *Oh, to see my beloved son again.* She quickened her pace, hurrying to catch up.

"Uhh… hello." Joly didn't quite know what to say.

Jimmy was determined that the lady would not get away from him this time. He smiled his gentle smile and asked, "C-can I buy you a soda?"

Just then, Morag puffed up to the two of them, and her eyes wide, she opened her mouth to speak, but Joly spoke first. "Morag, this is James Smith. He's just invited me for a soda."

Morag's mouth stayed open.

Jimmy smiled at her and said, "I-I know who you are. You're her Mother."

Morag was still speechless, so Joly answered. "Yes, she's sort of my Mother." She smiled back at the incredible blue eyes, the only blue eyes she had ever loved.

The gift to summon is abandoned in Polaris. The ability to recall is lost in the north. Her Duncan had no memory of her, didn't know his own Mother. She wanted to hug him, to hold him, to kiss him, but all she could do was smile politely and agree to go for a soda with him.

Morag looked at her son and finally realized why she could not feel him. He was somebody else completely; there was no memory, no sense of her son at all.

Jimmy looked around, and then back at Joly. "W-where is your little boy?"

Both Joly and Morag's mouths dropped open. Morag finally found her voice. "How do you know about Randy?"

Jimmy smiled again. "I-I saw you in the city, at the airport. Y-you had a little boy with you. H-he is very cute."

They were getting soaked standing in the rain, but no one seemed to notice.

Joly answered, still amazed, "Yes, he's with his nanny, in York."

Jimmy shook his head, confused. "Y-york? Y-you live in York?"

"Uh no… we live in Canada, in Mission."

Jimmy's eyes lit up. "M-mission… I know Mission." Then he ducked his head down and when he brought it back up, the light was gone. "I-I don't know how, but I know Mission."

The moment his eyes lit up, Morag felt him. It was only for a split second, but it was there. She knew then, that he had momentary flashbacks. He must have had one the day they were heading to Hadrian's Wall. He had been at the airport on one of their trips. He had seen them, but obviously had had no flashbacks. Then she remembered sitting in the plane and the kaleidoscope of pictures that had swirled around and she knew when he had been at the airport.

She smiled brightly and said, "Do you mind if I join you for a soda?"

"N-no." He suddenly noticed how wet they all were and was embarrassed. Gisela would not be happy with him if she knew how bad his manners were. "C-come with me." He turned and led them another half block or so to a coffee shop.

As they entered the waitress called out, "Hi Jimmy, awfully wet out there today."

He answered, "H-hi Sophie, yes, it's not very nice." He remembered his manners. "S-sophie, I have friends with me today." And then he realized he didn't know their names. He led them to a booth and he sat on one side. The two women sat on the other side both still feasting their eyes on the one who had been lost for so long.

When Sophie approached the table, Jimmy looked at the white haired lady and knew she was a tea drinker. He studied the one from his dreams and decided that she too, drank tea. "S-sophie, we'll have two teas and… n-no. M-make it three teas, please."

Morag again felt the split second familiar feeling. She wondered how long it would take for him to remember everything.

Jimmy looked at Joly in puzzlement. She smiled. He decided he had to ask. "W-when I dream about you, I smell magnolia blossoms. W-why?"

Joly laughed. "Every spring at home, I used to go up to the next block and ask for some of their flowers. I would make a bath oil from them. You always said I smelled so good afterwards." She saw the look of confusion on Duncan's face and realized what she had said. "It's okay Dunc… umm… James. I know you don't remember, but it's okay." She reached across then and touched his hand. She laid her hand on top of his and he felt the warmth.

He looked at the hand laying over his. He wasn't sure why, but it felt, not just good, but somehow, it felt right. He turned his hand over, palm up and closed it over the lady's smaller hand. He looked up then, afraid of what he might see in the lady's eyes. What he did see, startled him. She had two big teardrops perched on her lower lashes and as he watched, he saw them fall slowly down her cheeks.

Morag watched the interplay between the two of them. She saw that even without his memory he loved Joly, as he always had. She wondered briefly what would happen next and then said screw it. The Gods had brought them to Duncan for a reason. They would let her know what the next move was.

She was more than content to just sit and look at her son. The white hair was the hardest thing to get used to. Her contact with the demon had turned her hair white and she supposed that's what happened to Duncan also. He was ten years older, but he hadn't really changed. His speech was completely different, very slow, hesitant... not quite a stutter, but he seemed to have trouble getting his sentences started. He had a very slight English accent. She wondered why the accent wasn't more pronounced. Ten years was more than enough time to pick up a new speech pattern. There seemed a maturity about him that hadn't been there before, and yet there wasn't. She had yet to hear him laugh. It was funny. He was always laughing before, and now, he was quietly sitting like some old grandpa holding on to some old grandma's hand. She smiled at the picture in her mind.

Jimmy was lost in the lady's dark eyes. He thought he would never get tired of looking into them. He still was having trouble believing that she was sitting across from him, letting him hold her hand.

Joly looked into the eyes of the man she had loved forever and saw no accusing look. She wondered again about the dream. He must have retained a partial memory of something and maybe that was why he was accusing her. She didn't know and at that point, she didn't care. She was holding her beloved and that was all that mattered. Without conscience thought, she raised their joined hands and kissed the back of Duncan's hand.

He kept looking into her eyes and drew their entwined hands to his side of the table and kissed the back of the lady's hand.

There was a terrible roaring in Jimmy Smith's head. He had to let go of the lady's hand and hold his head so it wouldn't blow off.

Joly could only watch, not knowing what else to do.
Sophie saw what was happening and picked up the phone.

Less than three minutes later, Hans came puffing into the coffee shop. He saw the two women and knew his worst fears had been realized.

"Jimmy... ve need to go home now, ja?"

Jimmy stumbled to his feet, the whirling of the colors and scenes coupled with the roaring, had sent all thoughts of anything or anyone else from his mind.

Joly arose and put out her hand. "Please," she whispered, "He's my husband."

Hans nodded, "Come."

Morag stopped at the till and paid for the tea, and then followed the other three outside. The kaleidoscope of colors and pictures had ceased swirling around her mind. It was the same thing that had happened on the plane. Duncan was remembering, if only for a moment.

Hans was doubled parked on the street. "Get in." He opened the front door, eased Jimmy in, and carefully shut the door again. He walked around to the driver's side and got in.

"Where are you parked?" he asked, looking at Joly in the rear view mirror. She pointed up the street and said, "Around the corner."

"Facing which way?"

Joly looked around to get her bearings. "That way." She pointed.

Hans went around the block and stopped when Joly pointed out the car. "You follow me," he instructed.

As soon as they were in the car, Joly said, "My Gods, Morag. Now what are we going to do?"

"We wait and see. There's a reason we are here. It will be made known to us sooner or later."

Joly followed the older model car for several blocks until it pulled into the curb. She followed and parked behind it..

Jimmy got out of the car on his own and when he would have headed toward Joly, Hans grabbed him and led him to the house. Opening the door, he walked in and looking over his shoulder said, "Come."

Joly and Morag walked in, closing the door behind themselves. They heard the murmuring of voices down the hall and waited.

Shortly, a very large woman came bustling around the corner. "Velcome to our home. I am Gisela Verner. Come and sit. Hans says you are Jimmy's vife?"

Joly nodded. "Yes, my name is Joly…" she paused. She had her husband back. It was time to resume using her married name. "Joly McEwan. This is Duncan's… umm… James' Mother, Morag McEwan."

"James…" Gisela laughed a great booming laugh. When she was finished, she had tears streaming down her face. She blew her nose and chuckled again. "James… such a grandiose name, ja? He is Jimmy… everyone calls him Jimmy."

Joly asked, "Where did the name come from? When he umm… lost his memory, how was a name picked?"

"He picked Jimmy. The doctor I think, give him last name."

"But how did he pick the name Jimmy? Out of a book, how?"

"I think doctor read names out of book, when he say Jimmy, Jimmy say ja… that's my name."

Morag spoke up. "I assume the doctor said James, not Jimmy."

Gisela looked at her. "Ja, I think so."

Morag nodded. "He picked James because it was his wife's maiden name. It was a name familiar to him. Have you noticed he prefers James over Jimmy?"

Gisela looked at Joly. "It vas your name? Ja... he alvays say his name is James, but ve are common people. Ve have no airs. Ve call him Jimmy. I'm sorry. Ve didn't know."

Joly nodded. "It's alright. May I see him please? Can you tell me what happened in the coffee shop?"

"Ja... of course. Come. You too." She motioned to Morag to follow. "He has spells. I think he is remembering, but it hurts his head very bad. He vill be okay tomorrow."

Gisela led them into the small bedroom.

Morag noticed the radio immediately. Duncan had always had one by his bed when he was at home. Joly's gasp was heard by all, and everyone's attention was directed by her eyes, to the empty picture frame on the dresser. Morag's intake of breath was heard next. The frame was the exact same one, only smaller, that held their wedding picture.

Joly walked over to the bed and sat on the edge of it. She placed her healing hands on either side of Duncan's head. The frown soon disappeared of his face and ten minutes later he opened his eyes. He looked at Joly and smiled. She smiled back, keeping her hands where they were.

A few minutes later Duncan reached up and took her hands in his own. "Jo... you are Jo, right?"

"Close honey. I'm Joly."

He tried the name several times and eventually seemed happy with it. He sat up and Gisela bustled over, all concerned.

Jimmy looked at her. "I-it's okay Gisela. M-my head is good now." He looked at Joly. "I-I'm sorry. M-my head gets these pictures, all jumbled together. I get dizzy and my head hurts."

"It's okay." She took his hand and held it.

Gisela waved to Morag, "Come vith me. I vill make coffee and ve can talk." They headed out of the room.

Jimmy yelled after her, "G-gisela... they drink tea."

The two sat there for several minutes, holding hands and not saying anything.

Finally Duncan looked at Joly and smiled. "C-can I say something, without you getting mad?"

"Of course. Anything at all."

"Y-you sure?"

"Yes, I'm sure." She smiled.

"I-I see you, sometimes in my dreams, sometimes I just think about you. I always have this one thought when I think of you. C-can I tell you what it is?"

"Yes."

"Y-you won't get mad."

Joly smiled. "No, I promise I won't get mad."

Duncan looked down at his hand connected to the hand of the woman beside him. He spoke so softly, she wasn't sure she had heard correctly.

"Say it louder please, James."

"I-I love you."

She could feel the tears again and willed them away. She looked at Duncan and repeated the words. "I love you, too."

She wondered how much he really did remember. "What else do you think of, when you think of me?"

"S-sometimes… it's like… I-I don't know. It's like… p-part of me is missing." There, he had said it. He hadn't told anyone that, ever. Not even Gisela. He waited for the laugh. It didn't happen, and he chanced a look in Joly's direction.

She sat there with tears running down her cheeks. Jimmy was horrified. "I-I'm sorry, Joly. I-I'm sorry Joly. I-I didn't mean to make you cry."

Joly turned to him and put her arms around his neck, burying her head in the curve of his neck. "Oh Duncan… I know that. Part of me has been missing too. But we're back together, we're whole now."

"Y-you call me Duncan. Why?" He hesitantly wrapped an arm around Joly's waist.

"Because it's your name. Your name is Duncan McEwan. The lady with me is Morag McEwan. She's your Mom. My name is Joly McEwan. I am your wife."

"Y-you are my wife?"

"Yes."

"T-that means we're married?"

"Yes."

"S-so it's okay for me to love you."

"Oh yes, Duncan, it's more than okay."

In the kitchen, with Gisela bustling about, making tea and coffee, putting out a plate of cookies, Morag filled her in on some of what had happened. Gisela asked many questions, some of which Morag had trouble glossing over, but eventually Gisela seemed satisfied.

Hans walked in and sat at the table. He stared at Morag for a minute and finally asked the question that had been bothering him for years. "So now you have found Jimmy, what will you do?"

Morag shook her head. "I'm sorry. I'm not sure what you mean."

"This is the only home he knows. This is the only life he knows. He is happy here. You will go back to your home and leave him here, ja?" He really didn't want to hear the woman's answer.

Morag was glad she hadn't been in the middle of taking a sip of tea, because she knew she would have choked on it. She smiled at the brusque man, and knew why he asked. She just wasn't sure how to answer. Would Duncan want to stay with Joly? Would he go with an almost total stranger to what would be a strange land? He would need a passport. Would Joly be able to drag herself away, if he chose not to go? She gave Hans a sad little smile and stated, "I think that would be up to Duncan, or Jimmy, if you prefer."

"Duncan." Hans tried the name for the first time and decided he did not like it. It was too formal. "I think I prefer Jimmy." He saw the look on Morag's face and added, "For now."

The aroma of something wonderful cooking, Gisela was keeping busy, as she spoke to Hans. "Go get Jimmy and his vife. Tea is ready." She smiled at Morag. "I still call him Jimmy. That is who he is to me."

"That's fine. I understand."

Hans walked down the hall and poked his head in the bedroom door. What he saw took his breath away, and he knew things were about to change in their lives.

Jimmy and the woman had their arms wrapped around each other and Jimmy had just given the woman a kiss on the side of the mouth. As he watched, she moved her head slightly and kissed Jimmy's lips. Jimmy's one arm tightened around the woman and his other arm slid up to the back of the woman's head. His mouth open slightly; his lips headed unerringly straight for the woman's mouth and as they connected, she moaned.

Hans quietly turned and walked back to the kitchen, wondering how Gisela would handle not having anyone around to mother.

Jimmy Smith felt something happening and was suddenly terrified. He pushed Joly away and placed his hands between his legs, his fingers clasping and unclasping. He appeared to show a great interest in his busy hands.

Joly, once over the shock of being pushed away, watched Duncan closely. She spotted the tell tale bulge at his crotch and wondered if this was something uncommon for him. Or was something else bothering him?

"Duncan…? Look at me please. Duncan?" She put her hand over his arm.

Duncan raised his head, tears evident on his eyelashes. He shuddered and drew in a deep breath. "I-I'm sorry, Joly. I-I… t-this…" He looked back at his hands as a tear slid down his cheek.

"Duncan honey… it's okay. Can you listen to me for a minute?"

He nodded, still watching his hands.

"Duncan… Jimmy… James. I don't know what to call you."

He said nothing.

"You and I played together as small children. We went to school together. We have always been together… always. We came to England ten years ago, you and me, your parents and my parents and another couple, Raoul and Bettina."

There was no sign of recognition at the names, so she continued.

"There was a bad accident, a very bad accident. Both my parents died, Bettina and Raoul died and your Dad died."

He looked at her then. "W-what did my Dad look like?"

"Duncan… do you remember your brother, Stephen?"

"S-Stephen? I have a brother… or is he dead too?"

She smiled at that. "No Duncan, Stephen is very much alive. He's back in Canada. He's married to a woman named Elise. Does that ring a bell?" Duncan had disliked Elise from the moment he met her. He was all laughter and fun. She never laughed, rarely smiled and was far too prim and proper.

He shook his head again.

"The reason I mentioned Stephen is because he and your Dad looked so much alike. Your Dad had red hair and blue eyes. He was probably about six feet tall. He had a nice build. He was quite serious. You would always try to get him to laugh more."

"I-I don't remember. J-Joly… if we're married, doesn't that mean we should live together?"

It was her turn to look away. She needed time to think, but she knew she never wanted to let Duncan out of her sight ever again. What was going to happen? She was a *Sister of the Triple Moon*. She had an obligation to the world. She had Randy to think of.

"Yes, it does mean that. Does that idea bother you, or maybe scare you?"

"I-I don't know. I-I think I need to think."

She had to force the next words out of her mouth. "Do you want me to leave, so you can think?"

"*No!*" He grabbed her hand and tucked it into his lap.

Gisela heard the shout and rushed into the hall. Hans was one step behind her. He grabbed her before she got to the door and stopped her, shaking his head. He led her back to the kitchen. "He has to work this out, without you or me." He went and sat down again.

"Would you like me to just go in the kitchen and have a cup of tea?"

"No!" He looked up at the ceiling as if the answer might be there. "C-can you just lay down with me? J-just hold me, while I think?"

Joly took his face in her hands and gave him a light kiss on his lips. "Yes, Duncan, I can do that."

They lay down and Joly watched Duncan's eyes. He looked back at her. She thought about the mind meld she did with the cats and wondered if it would work with Duncan. She decided to try. Duncan didn't seem inclined to look away, so she said nothing. She concentrated on his breathing, matching her breath to his.

When the meld happened, she wasn't prepared. The pain was so intense that she closed her eyes against it. The contact gone, she looked at him. "Duncan, your head is hurting something fierce."

"N-no… it's okay now."

"But honey… there is still lots of pain there. I felt it."

"Y-you did? N-no, it's okay. I feel fine."

Joly thought about that. If he always had that much pain and he thought it was normal, no wonder he had trouble with flashbacks and trying to remember. She decided to try the meld again, now that she knew what to expect.

She looked back into his eyes and he seemed content to look into hers.

When the pain hit she was prepared, but it was still a shock. It was like a kaleidoscope of grays and blacks, smashing against one another, almost as if she were watching a stormy sky. Periodically, what appeared to be an electrical charge flashed through it all, like a mini bolt of lightening. She concentrated on getting past that and soon reached a calm area, deep within his mind. There, it was mostly blues and greens with some purple streaks. She felt the calm and waited. It wasn't long before she found she was right. A fuzzy picture came to her mind. It was Duncan and her in their bedroom. She heard him speak the words that had flashed through her mind not many weeks before.

"Joly, I love you so damned much. When we're apart, I feel like part of me is missing and I'm never whole again, until I am back with you. I can never get enough of you; you're like an addiction to me. Tell me you'll never leave me; tell me you'll never go away without me."

Okay... time to back out. She returned to the pain and concentrated on getting past the pain to his current thoughts.

I love you, I love you, I love you. Part of me is missing, missing, missing. James... can you hear me?

Duncan blinked.

No, don't close your eyes. Listen to me; come with me on a trip. Don't move. Don't close your eyes.

She gently led him to the house he had grown up in. She showed him her home across the street. She envisioned his parents on their front steps and her parents on theirs. She let Stephen in for a moment. She took him to the places they liked to go. She took him to their bedroom and showed him his vague memory. She kept it up as long as she could, but the pain was horrendous and she knew she would have to close hers eyes soon. Just as she was about to back out, Duncan sent her a picture.

She didn't think he did it purposely. His mind was a mess of thought patterns that had no rhyme or reason, but the picture was clear and it wasn't very nice.

They were in the airport. Duncan was watching them, watching Randy, following them and when they split up, he followed her. When Morag returned with Randy in tow, and she hugged him, Duncan's thought pattern turned gray. He was filled with anger and sorrow, but it didn't seem to be directed at Randy. It was directed at her. And then she heard the garbled voice from her dream. *You didn't wait. You didn't wait. You didn't wait.*

She was losing her strength. Did she have time to take him to India? She had to try. She tried to lead him, but he would not follow. She decided to talk to him.

Duncan... I adopted the little boy. When I was in India. He was starving and he had no family. I brought him home with me. Duncan, I have always waited for you. Always. I will wait for you forever. Do you understand me? Forever!

She had to close her eyes. She needed to go and ground herself. She was exhausted. She lie there trying to gather the strength to get up. Duncan placed his arm over her, as if he knew. He snuggled in closer and she looked at him. His eyes were closed. He looked at peace.

She closed her eyes and slept.

In the kitchen, Gisela asked Morag to stay for supper. She accepted. Gisela walked softly down the hall and peeked in the bedroom. She looked at the two still figures on the bed, arms and legs entwined. She shook her head. She had let her children go when the time was right. She would let Jimmy go also, but first, the time had to be right. She went back to the kitchen and served supper for three.

The blackness appeared and then the eyes. Joly waited, wondering what would happen this time. As the eyes approached, she watched for the accusing look in them. They stopped when they were still a distance away. She wondered what was happening. Suddenly she realized that there was no noise, no booming, no garbled voice... no anything. It was dead silent. Slowly the eyes resumed their approach. When they were close enough, she saw no accusing look, no anger. In fact, they looked sad.

"Duncan? Are you okay honey?"

A teardrop welled up in one of Duncan's eyes, spilled over and fell into the nothingness.

"Duncan? It's okay honey. You didn't know. I love you Duncan. I'll always love you. Rest now honey. We'll work it out. We've always been able to work things out. That hasn't changed. Sleep now my love; sleep in peace. I'm here and I'm not going anywhere. I love you."

The eyes closed. Joly slept at peace, as did Duncan.

They both woke at the same time; the first thought in each one's mind was how right it felt to be wrapped around the other. Their eyes opened and they smiled at each other. Duncan gave Joly a squeeze.

"I-it was good to sleep with you. I-I liked it. It felt... right."

"Yes, it did, didn't it?" She leaned over and whispered, "I have to pee."

Duncan looked startled. He whispered back, "D-did you talk to me like that before? You shouldn't say that."

Joly giggled and whispered, "Yes."

Duncan looked thoughtful. "W-we lived differently, you and me, than I do now. T-that could be a problem, couldn't it?"

"I think that if I don't find a bathroom soon, you are going to get wet." She giggled again.

Duncan could move fast when needed. He was up and off the bed in a flash, a look of consternation on his face. "I-I'll show you." He left the room.

Joly got up smiling, and followed him out into the hall. He was waiting by a door and when Joly came into view, he pointed and headed to the kitchen.

Duncan smiled at Gisela. "I-I'm hungry, Gisela."

"Ja, you sit down. I get for you."

Duncan sat and looked at Morag. "Y-you're my Mother."

She smiled at her favorite son. "Yes, I'm your Mother... but you always called me Mom, not Mother."

He tried it out. "M-mom." He frowned and looked hard at Morag. "I-it doesn't feel right."

Damn! Oh well, she had tried. She nodded. "You're right. Actually you had the terrible habit of calling me Maw."

He tried it. "M-maw."

He nodded his approval and Morag knew one thing wasn't about to change.

"Did you and Joly talk?"

He nodded and then remembered his manners. "Y-yes."

"Do you have any questions?"

He shook his head. "N-no."

Joly walked into the room. Gisela smiled at her and asked if she was hungry.

"Actually, yes. Thank you." She went and sat beside Duncan and reached for his hand.

He slid his chair closer to hers and put his arm around Joly. "C-can you tell me something, Joly?"

"Sure honey, what?"

"H-how did you do that thing to show me the pictures of my Dad and my brother?"

Morag leaned forward and scowled.

"Here's supper honey. I'll tell you later, okay?"

Gisela put their food on the table and looked at Joly. "You have pictures of Jimmy's Dad and brother. Can I see, please?"

Joly choked on her first bite.

Morag reached into her purse and pulled out her wallet. She fiddled for a bit and finally brought out two pictures. One of her and Brody and one of Duncan and Stephen. She handed them to Gisela, frowning the whole time.

Joly was watching her and knew something was wrong, but she wasn't sure what and she was afraid to ask in front of these people.

It was getting late. She needed to get back to Randy. Her appetite suddenly gone, she pushed her plate away. She thought she was going to cry and didn't want to embarrass herself in front of this woman who had looked after her beloved all these years.

Gisela finished looking at the pictures, nodded and handed them back to Morag. "Good looking family. Ja... very good."

Morag sat back, the frown gone. Joly smiled to herself. Now she knew what had happened. Morag didn't carry pictures of her family, any more than she did. She'd had to do a quick bit of magic there. No wonder the frown.

Duncan ate like he had never seen food before. Joly watched him with a smile on her face. Some things, even memory loss couldn't erase. Duncan had always loved food.

He noticed Joly had pushed her plate away and he frowned. "Y-you have to eat to keep up your strength." He pushed the plate back in front of her. "G-gisela gets upset when you don't finish your food."

Joly picked up her fork and resumed eating. She didn't want to offend Gisela and Duncan seemed to have a new set of rules to live by.

When Joly had finished picking at her food and Duncan was finished polishing off his plate, he grabbed her hand and pulling on it, he said, "C-come with me, Joly.."

She followed him to the door, he opened it and they went outside. The rain was still coming down, but there was a roof over the entry and the steps. Duncan went and sat on the top step and patted the space beside him. Joly sat down. The concrete was dry, but felt damp.

"Y-your little boy, what was his name?"

"Randy."

"R-Randy will be wondering where you are."

"Yes. Your Mom said she phoned and told Sara we'd be late." She saw his look and continued. "Sara is his nanny."

He nodded. "I-If you leave, will you come back tomorrow?"

She ducked her head down, the tears threatening to fall. She had a lump in her throat, the size of a baseball. She couldn't answer.

Duncan looked at her and coaxed her chin up. "D-don't be sad, Joly. I-I love you. Y-you love me. W-we'll work it out."

"Duncan… I don't know if I can walk away tonight without you. I know I have to go to my… no… to *our* son, but I don't want to leave you behind. Even knowing I will see you tomorrow, doesn't change that I don't want to leave you. Not now, not ever!" She cried in earnest.

Duncan wrapped her in his arms and held her until the sobs lessened. "D-do you want me to come with you?" The thought of going with this woman terrified him, but it excited him too. He wasn't sure what he wanted her answer to be.

Joly thought of the sleeping arrangement. She, Morag and Randy in one bed. It wouldn't work. She could rent another room for the three of them… or the two of them. She wasn't anxious to make love. She just wanted him in her arms.

Morag came outside and stood behind them. "This old girl is ready to head for bed. What are we doing, Joly?"

Duncan stood and faced his Mother. "I-I'm coming with you, is that okay, Maw?"

Morag smiled. "I thought you might be. You'd better let Gisela know."

"Y-yes." He went inside.

"Joly, are you okay?"

She looked up and smiled. "I am now."

Morag sat down beside her. "Dare I ask what you did in there, that I had to cover for?"

Joly grinned and then laughed. "Oh… thank Gods you were there. I damn near filled my pants when she asked to see the pictures."

Morag smiled back. "Did you do a mind meld?"

"Yes."

"What did you find?"

"Oh Gods, Morag. The pain. He is in such incredible pain, constantly. Yet when I asked him about it, he said, he was fine. There is memory, but it's buried deep beyond the pain. When he tries to bring it forward, it's too much for him."

"You can heal him. It may take time, but you have the power."

"Morag, what about the riddle? Don't you get the impression that something else is supposed to take place?"

"Possibly, but what… and when?"

"I don't know."

Duncan walked out with a small suitcase. He smiled nervously. "I-I'm ready."

Morag looked at Joly. "We need to thank our hostess."

"Yes." She got to her feet and followed Morag in.

They found Hans with his arm around his wife. Morag and Joly thanked them for their hospitality and assured them they would return the following day. They said their goodbyes and walked out to the car.

Morag climbed in the back seat and Duncan sat beside Joly, his hand on her knee. In the dark, she smiled. He had always done that when she was driving.

"Are you going to get another room, dear?" Morag asked from the back seat.

"Yes. You can have the bed to yourself. Won't it be nice to stretch out?"

"You're taking Randy with you?"

"Yes."

They completed the drive in silence, Joly and Duncan taking turns squeezing each other's hand.

Duncan was nervous. He wasn't stupid. He knew what married people did in bed. He guessed he and Joly had done *it* when they were together before, but he didn't remember. He wasn't even sure he knew how. He tried to think about the past and his head started hurting, so he quit. Maybe Joly…no… his wife, wouldn't force it.

At the hotel Joly spoke to the desk clerk and got another room two doors down from where they were. They went up and as she opened the door, a small figure threw himself into her arms. Joly picked Randy up and walked in the room, Duncan one step behind her and Morag bringing up the rear.

"Sara, this is my husband Duncan, Honey, this is Randy's nanny, Sara."

Sara smiled at the man and got up to shake his hand. "Hi Duncan. I've heard all about you. It's nice to finally meet you."

"H-hi Sara."

"And this is Randy. Randy, can you say hi to your Daddy?"

Duncan spoke first. "R-Randy, c-come and see me. " He held his hands out. Randy hesitated.

"I-it's okay. Y-you don't have to." Duncan looked crushed.

Randy looked at Joly. "Dad-dy?"

"Yes, Baby Cakes, Daddy." She knew he didn't understand the meaning of the word. At the moment, it was just a name that belonged to this new person.

Randy took a long look at Duncan. He struggled out of Joly's arms and went to Duncan. "Hi Dad-dy."

Duncan struggled down to his knees. "H-hi Randy." He held his arms out and Randy hesitantly walked into them.

Joly grabbed a few things for the next morning and after Randy said goodnight to Sara and Morag, the three left for their room.

Once in the room, Joly got Randy's bath ready. Duncan joined them, watching the interplay between child and mother. After the bath, with Randy tucked in, Joly picked up a book to read to him.

Randy took the book from her hands and handed it to Duncan. "Dad-dy read."

Duncan's expression made Joly laugh.

With his slow speech, the reading took longer than normal and Randy fell asleep long before the end of the book.

"Come here." Joly walked over to the sofa and sat down. Duncan joined her and put his arm over the back of the seat, his hand on Joly's shoulder. She rested her hand on his knee.

She knew he had questions, but some she couldn't answer yet. He had no memory of the craft and he had almost blown it at the table. Thanks to Morag, that had been salvaged for the moment, but he would ask again. She wasn't sure what he would think if she performed a healing on him. A massage should be acceptable. She decided she would start there.

"Duncan, you said your head was fine, but I think you still have a lot of pain. You're used to it, but it's there. Can I give you a head massage?"

"S-sure. W-what do you want me to do? M-my head's fine though."

She smiled at him and had him lie down with his head on her lap. She gently massaged his head and temples, while thinking about the riddle. They had the first line figured out. Did the rest apply to Duncan too? *The mirth is secure in the psyche.* Mirth, enjoyment, happiness, joy, is safe in the soul. She decided that it did mean Duncan. His memories of their good times were safely tucked away in his soul. *Widdershins and fire releases the void.* Widdershins meant counterclockwise and was used in banishing spells. Fire, what kind of fire? Releases the void… lets go of the nothingness. She pictured the nothingness from her dream. Did it mean she could banish his memory loss? A banishing spell with some kind of fire would get rid of the blockage? Maybe. It made sense, but it was so generalized. What kind of fire… a bonfire, fireworks, something as small as candlelight? She shook her head. She would talk to Morag and see what she thought about it. *Gemini becomes the nucleus.* Gemini was the twins; it was also a constellation, a group of stars. Nucleus meant core, center… what else?

Duncan was almost lulled to sleep. The massage felt good. Did his head hurt? He didn't think so. He wasn't sure why Joly kept insisting it did. They would have to go to bed soon. Randy was sleeping with them. He was glad. He still didn't want to think about the other thing. Then he had another thought. *I have to get undressed.* He sat up suddenly.

Joly looked at her husband, saw his wild eyes and knew something was wrong. "Honey, what is it?"

He remembered the bathroom and his pajamas. The wild look disappeared and he relaxed. "N-nothing. I-It's okay now."

Joly stood and wrapped her arms around him. He held her tightly, wondering what was going to happen. His universe had been turned upside down and inside out. The orderly life he knew was gone. He was suddenly very afraid. He looked down at Joly and wondered if she was ever afraid. He decided no. His Maw… he didn't remember her, or a dad or a brother. He didn't really remember Joly, but being with her felt right. She had shown him those pictures. He didn't know how she did it, but he didn't remember any of the places he had seen. He wondered if it was make-believe. Maybe that's what it was. Maybe she wasn't his wife. Maybe he just wanted her to be. Maybe he was just dreaming and when he woke up, none of it would be real. It was too much for him to think about. His head was starting to hurt.

"I-I think I need to go to bed, Joly."

She released him and smiled. "Okay honey. You can use the bathroom first."

He picked up his suitcase and went into the washroom. She heard the click of the lock and smiled. This new Duncan would take some getting used to. She grabbed her nightshirt and stripped down. She waited… and she waited some more.

Duncan had changed into his pajamas, washed and brushed his teeth. He had combed his hair and gone to the bathroom. He stood staring at the door, afraid to open it. He waited and waited, wondering what he could do next.

The knock startled him. "Duncan… you okay?" He had no choice. He had to open the door. He fumbled with the lock and taking a deep breath, he pulled the door open.

Joly lowered her face so he wouldn't see the smile. Duncan in pajamas? That was just too much. He had been sleeping nude since he was about twelve according to Morag, and he hadn't even owned a pair of pajamas. When they were married, he wandered around their apartment nude most of the time.

Duncan left the bathroom and Joly went in, closing the door behind her. She thought about his earlier erection and his behavior. She appeared to be married to a complete stranger. She completed her ablutions and opened the door.

Duncan was in bed, the covers pulled up to his chin, his eyes tightly closed. She turned off the light and slid in on the other side of Randy. He let out a small moan and she turned on her side, wrapping him in her arms.

Duncan lie there, afraid to breathe. He had never, never slept with anyone before. He was wide-awake, all thoughts of sleep, far from his mind.

Joly could sense his fear and she reached one hand over to him, resting it on his chest. She felt his intake of breath and wondered if he thought she was going to rape him. She moved her hand until it was over his heart and she sent calming energies to him. Within ten minutes, Duncan was fast asleep. Joly left her hand where it was and sometime later, she too, dozed off.

Duncan woke abruptly, as he always did. His first thought was where was he? His second thought was who was in his bed? His third thought was of Joly. He turned his head then, almost afraid to look. The little boy, Randy, was snuggled up against him and on the other side... there she was.

It hadn't been a dream. He was married and sleeping with his wife and son. He laid his head back on the pillow and stared at the ceiling. She said she lived in Mission. If they were married, he should go there with her. Married people lived together. Would he have to go on a plane? He didn't know if he could do that. They were noisy and big. He would miss Hans and Gisela. What would he do for money? They must have bottles and cans in Mission. He could recycle there. He wondered what his brother did. Maybe he could help him, like he helped Hans.

Duncan felt a tickling on his side. He moved away from it. It followed him. He lifted the covers up and looked. Randy's fingers were making scratching movements against his pajamas. He thought it was strange. He quietly got out of bed and had just stood up, when Joly leapt up and over Randy yelling "Boo." Randy shrieked and Duncan almost wet himself.

A wrestling and tickling match ensued. Once Duncan's heart settled back down, he stood and watched, smiling. That would take some getting used to.

"Daddy, come play." Randy looked at Duncan, grinning from ear to ear.

Duncan wasn't sure how to play, but he went and sat on the edge of the bed. He had no sooner sat down and a pillow hit him across the face. He leapt to his feet again. "W-why did you do that?"

Joly was at a loss. Duncan couldn't remember how to pillow fight? This was going to be a lot harder than she had thought.

Instead of answering him, she smiled at him and hit Randy on the side of his head with her pillow. Duncan was horrified until he saw that Randy was hitting Joly back with his pillow. Randy turned around and hit Duncan across the shoulder and giggled, waiting for the retaliation. It didn't happen.

"Daddy... play."

Duncan, overwhelmed by everything, started to cry. He sat on the floor and brought his knees up under his chin and buried his face in his hands, the wracking sobs frightening Randy and surprising Joly.

She quickly reassured Randy that it was okay for Daddy to cry. She walked around the foot of the bed and sat beside Duncan, placing her hands on the sides of his head, sending her healing, calming energies to him.

When the sobs became sniffles, she took him in her arms, holding him tightly. A minute later, he turned and wrapped his arms around her. When she knew he was back to normal, she got up saying, "I'll be back in a sec."

She took Randy and walked down the hall to their other room knocking softly on the door. Morag answered and called Randy in. She could sense Joly was having problems.

"I'll be back in a bit, Sweetie," she called as she turned to go back to Duncan.

"You okay?" Morag asked.

"Yes, I'm fine. Duncan's a little overwhelmed, I think." She walked down the hall conscious of Morag scrutinizing her. Only then did she realize she was wandering the hallway in her nightshirt. She quickly reached her room and went in, firmly closing the door behind her.

Duncan was where she had left him and she went over and gently pulled him up to the bed. She lay down beside him, taking him in her arms. He seemed content to let her do the holding. They lay like that a long time.

Veronika was mad! The energy field was back and stronger than ever. She went in and clomped down the stairs to the basement. She rapped sharply on the door of Polina's room.

There were sounds of stirring and a mumbled "What is it?"

"Polina, come with me."

"*Babushka*... look at the time."

"Come... now."

A minute later the door opened. Half asleep, Polina followed Veronika outside. She felt it immediately. "What is it?"

"I would like to know that too."

The darkness swirled around them, as they decided what to do.

"Let me do the circle, Grandmamma. I want to try something."

"*Da*, okay."

An hour later, the air was again clean, but Polina was careful not to gloat. She knew she had been too hasty the last time. She would wait.

Duncan had so many things going through his mind; he was having trouble figuring out what was what. He was no good at playing, he was afraid to sleep with his wife; he didn't know if he could go with her to Mission, He decided he didn't know anything. That being the case, he figured maybe he should go back to Gisela and Hans. He wondered if Joly would come and visit him once in a while.

His mind made up, he sat up. "J-Joly, I need to go home. I-I don't know how to play; I-I don't know how to be a husband. I-I don't know anything, anymore. C-can you come and see me sometime, maybe?"

Joly wasn't prepared for that statement. She wondered how to answer. Her mind a whirl of emotions, she thought for a minute. "Duncan honey, what did you say to me last night when we were on the steps?"

He thought about it, but he couldn't remember. "I-I don't know."

"Duncan, can I take you on another trip?"

"I-I don't think so. I-I don't think you should do that. S-something about it isn't right."

"What's not right about it, Duncan? Is it wrong to see pictures of different places in your mind? Can't you see the airport, when you think about it?"

He thought about it. "Y-yes."

"This is the same thing, only I'm showing you some of my pictures. It's nice to share things, right?"

He thought about it. "Y-yes."

"So come with me for a little while, and then... if you still want to go... I'll take you back."

He hung his head and thought about what she had said. He decided it made sense. "O-okay."

The melding went quicker this time, but Joly still almost lost her concentration when she hit the pain. She couldn't understand how he could think it was normal. What she was about to do was very stupid, but she had to try it.

She started the memory on the airplane, when they were all flying to England, Morag and Broderick, her parents, Bettina and Raoul and Duncan and her. She let him see the laughter, hear his own goofy jokes, watch the camaraderie of their group. She showed him their arrival in London, his complaining about the rain. She let him listen to her silly ditty. She took him to their hotel room, showed him the two of them putting on their robes.

She felt his heartbeat quicken and wondered if she should continue. She needed to take him a little farther. She showed him their arrival at the clearing, the drawing of the circle, how serious everyone was. His heart was pounding, his breathing ragged. She knew she had reached the critical point. She should back out, but she had to take him one step farther. She allowed him just the briefest glimpse of the evil they had fought that day. No more than a second or two, just before he had tossed her out of the circle.

Duncan bolted upright. *"No! No!"* He wasn't there in the hotel room. He was in the circle fighting the demon. His eyes were wild and his head whipped around. *"Go, Darlin', now! Get out of here!"*

"Duncan, come back to me honey. Duncan, come on." She put her hands on his head, but he shook them off, still yelling.

Shit! Now what? She wondered if maybe she could join him. She yelled. *"No! Not without you!"*

He turned and grabbed her, his eyes not seeing anything but the event of the past. She wrapped her arms around him and hung on for dear life as he tried to throw her again and again. He no longer worked out and she had been working out for over nine years. He couldn't dislodge her. They fell off the bed and he struggled to his feet with Joly still hanging on. He swung her around until he was dizzy and his strength gave out. The volume of his cries lessening as the violent thrusts weakened. He finally let go of her and sat on the edge of the bed softly weeping.

"Honey? It's okay now. You're here and I'm here. Everything's going to be fine. Remember… we can work it out, together." She went to put her arms around him and he grabbed her and threw her down on the bed and lay on top of her. His mouth savagely attacked hers, bruising her lips. He was rough, his tongue searching out every part of her mouth. She let him have his way, returning his violence with her softness. Her love came through; tempering his anger and he lightened the pressure.

He couldn't get enough of her. He couldn't get close enough to her. His lips never left hers, but his hands were everywhere. He kneaded her breasts, tweaked her nipples, slid down her ribcage, stroked her hips, ran his fingers down her arms. He got tired of the clothing between them and tore his pajama top off, popping the buttons. He grabbed her nightshirt and ripped it down the front. When his chest finally touched hers, the madness left him.

Still without leaving her lips, he pushed his pajama pants down and kicked them off. He lowered himself onto Joly. With his hardness pressing against her, she moaned. Her hands were dancing a tattoo across his back, her nails digging in, releasing, moving and digging in again. He rubbed himself back and forth over her mound, until she could no longer stand it. She reached down and guided him home. Their mating was violent; ravenous; their primal urges unsatisfied for too long. There was no tenderness. He slammed into her again and again. She matched him stroke for stroke and amidst the moans and panting, they peaked as one, teetering momentarily at the pinnacle, and then spiraling back down to earth together.

Their slick bodies still attached, they lay gasping and kissing in between breaths. Through it all, not one word had been spoken. When their hearts quit pounding and their breathing became normal, they still lay there, their mouths still touching, butterfly kisses being passed back and forth.

Much later, Duncan lifted his top half up and he looked at Joly. "*Gods woman!* That has to be the stupidest thing you have *ever* done."

She frowned. "I know… but I didn't know what else to do."

He rolled off her and headed for the bathroom. "What if it hadn't worked? Did you ever stop to think about that? Gods… you're crazy."

She sat up. "But it did work. It had to work… don't you see… if it hadn't… I would have lost you… *again*." Her sentence ended in a wail.

Duncan sauntered back into the bedroom, his one leg slightly dragging behind, totally comfortable in his nudity and reached for his wife. He pulled her up off the bed and held her, rubbing her back and kissing her neck.

"I love you Duncan."

"I know that, Darlin'. I love you too." He held her for a while longer and suddenly pushed her away from him. "Hey pretty lady, let's go have a shower."

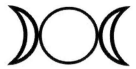

14. Big Magic

A long time later, they knocked on the door down the hall. Morag opened it and saw the misty sparkle in Joly's eyes. She knew what it meant. She had always known when the two of them had made love. Joly's eyes had always given it away. She smiled and stepped back wondering what else had happened. She had been so busy looking at Joly's eyes; she hadn't even glanced at her son.

"Hey Maw, how's it hangin'?" He grinned at her shocked face and leaned forward to give her a bear hug. "Damn it's good to see you. I like the white hair; kinda looks like I take after you." He kissed her cheek and turned to Sara. "Hey Sara, nice to see you again." He looked at Randy and walked over to him, squatting down when he was beside him. "Guess what Randy? I remember how to play." He tousled Randy's hair and walked to the window.

"York? Don't think I've ever been here. Don't think I even wanna visit." He turned around. "Ladies, I would dearly like to go home." He smiled at them all and then realized something.

He walked over to his Mother. "Maw... one of these cats' grab your tongue?"

Morag, with tears in her eyes, wrapped her son in her arms. "Duncan... I don't know what happened this morning, but the Gods will be getting a special thanks from me."

"Maw... you don't even wanna know what happened. My wife... my wife... oh hell! I love my wife." He grabbed Joly in a bear hug, making her laugh.

"By the way *Mom*... what was that all about? *Mom?* Shee-it. Even Jimmy Smith knew you weren't called Mom."

"I just thought it would be nice to be called Mom. You with that horrid Maw and Stephen with his prissy Mother." She sighed loudly, making everyone chuckle, except for Duncan who only smiled.

Duncan looked at the cats. He knew they weren't his Mother's and he didn't think they belonged to the nanny. And he knew how much his wife had always loved cats. He eyed the Persian. It wasn't really Joly's type. He wondered where it fit into the picture. He looked at the large black shorthair and decided it looked to be okay. He watched the smaller one and decided it too was all right.

He nuzzled Joly's ear. "Who're your four legged friends?"

She smiled. "Nefertiti is in the window. She saved my life ten years ago. That's Salem by your Mom. He saved my life about six years ago and the little one is Pip."

"Pip hasn't saved your life?"

"She woke me when I fell asleep driving, so she helped to avert a bad accident. She also talks to Randy and translates anything he doesn't understand."

"Ahh… then you are earnin' your keep. Good show. Darlin'… I have worked up one heck of an appetite." He nuzzled her neck again, tickling her. She squirmed out of his grasp.

"Me too. How about everyone else?" She was blushing and she turned to fiddle with Duncan's shirt collar.

Morag smiled. "We got tired of waiting for you two. We went and ate a while back. So go ahead. Fill up and then we had better make some plans for leaving."

"Leavin'! Man… that sounds so good. I don't suppose you've got my passport with you."

"No honey. Until three days ago, we weren't even sure you were alive."

"*Whoa!* That sounds scary. Let's go eat. You can start fillin' me in on the last ten years and what I've missed."

He hugged his Mother on the way out and they went downstairs to eat.

Duncan couldn't believe Joly had spent nine years living alone in the Yukon.

He listened with horror to the story of their failure ten years prior. He hadn't realized his Mother had been injured and again, he knew how blessed he was to have Joly and her healing skills. He mourned the passing of his Father and Joly's parents and Bettina and Raoul. And he discovered he had the Persian to thank for rescuing Joly.

He smiled at the story of Stephen searching for their Mother. Some things never changed. Stephen had always been a stuffed shirt. Duncan was surprised to hear he was still with Elise. She was even stuffier than Stephen was.

Joly told him about the past year, about the calling and the traveling, about the evil that had been let loose in the world. And that they figured the *Sisters of the Triple Moon* were being called together.

She told him about Randy and how Pinga had tried to take him away from her, about Morag saving her butt in Mission when she stupidly went to the temple. She told him about Randy's insecurities, and how he always slept with her.

Duncan said, "We'll work it out, Darlin'." He said he hoped he would be a good father, and Joly said she had no doubts on that issue.

Duncan told her about his simple life, how good Hans and Gisela had been to him. He didn't remember leaving the circle and had no knowledge of how he came to be so far north in England. His first vague recollections were of being in a hospital. From there they had put him in some old folk's place that he hated. Hans and Gisela had rescued him from there. He smiled when he told her about collecting cans and bottles and how the day before, he had decided he would do that same thing in Mission. He told her that through Hans, he had discovered he was good with electronics, something he hadn't known.

He told her about the dreams and the sporadic memories that plagued him, but he truly had no knowledge of a previous life. He only knew he was missing something. He briefly mentioned the pain, saying he had gotten so used to it that it never bothered him, unless he was having a flashback.

Joly told of how Morag had sensed him three months prior when they were there, and he told her he'd felt the connection, had tried to maintain it, but the pain wouldn't let him.

He told of seeing her in the airport, of not knowing who she was, but that he knew he needed to talk to her. He had lost her in the crowd. He told of seeing Randy and being upset, but he didn't know why, of watching the plane on the tarmac and having a major flashback. Hans had needed a wheelchair to get him back to the car.

She asked about his leg and the limp. He said he didn't know. He'd heard he'd been born with it, which he had believed at the time. He assumed the demon had done it.

She told him about Rhiannon and Maddie and how from that little bit of information, they had come to York and that they would have left that very day, if they hadn't found him.

He squeezed her hands so tightly it hurt. "Gods Joly, I am *so* thankful you saw me. Those flashbacks sometimes only happened every two or three months. Maw could have waited a long time to sense me again." He kissed her hands and knew it would be a long time before he let her out of his sight.

Three hours later they went back upstairs. Duncan headed straight to Nefertiti.

"Miss Nefertiti, I understand I have you to thank for savin' my wife's life ten years ago. I do thank you wholeheartedly. You have no idea what it means to have her back in my life. Thank you Ma'am." He executed a bow that would have done the Queen proud. Nefertiti dipped her head in acquiescence.

"Alrighty then... what now?" He looked at the women expectantly.

Morag answered. "You need a passport. You can have one in twenty-four hours in London. We're booked out of London three days from now. You need to go back and settle your affairs. You should do that today. I don't know if you want to head to London tonight or wait until the morning."

Duncan thought about it. "Tomorrow, I think. Yeah, we should head back so I can pack and clean out my bank account. That'll throw 'em. I have been in that bank every Monday since the beginning of time, putting money in. Never took any out. Too bad I can't save like that in this life." He smiled.

"I'll let the desk know. I told them I thought we would be staying. Okay, away you go now. We'll see you when you get back." Morag gave her son a hug.

"Me go Mommy." Randy headed for his jacket. Duncan helped him put it on and the three of them left.

On the drive to the village Duncan said he would have to pretend to still be slow-witted. The people were simple people and they wouldn't understand how he could be so different in less than twenty-four hours. Joly agreed with him.

She gave him an A for effort, but he didn't pull it off very well. He walked straighter, talked faster, kept forgetting to stammer his first word of a sentence, kept reverting to his Canadian slang and style of speech. She noticed Gisela look at him funny several times and she was glad they had Randy with them. He provided a distraction for Gisela, as she obviously loved children. Still, she was glad when they were able to say their goodbyes. Both Gisela and Duncan had tears in their eyes when they hugged and Gisela watched them walk to the car, stow his two boxes of things and drive out of sight. He didn't do much better with Hans at the shop, or at the bank.

As they drove out of town, Duncan thought about Jenny Hallett. He'd have liked to say goodbye to her, but he knew it would only raise more questions. She had always treated him as an equal and he knew now why he had always been drawn to her. She and Joly could have passed for sisters.

"Well Darlin', thank Gods that's over with. I'm no good at pretendin'."

When they got back to the hotel they all went for supper. The conversation was lively, but Duncan noticed Sara was fairly quiet. He asked Joly about her when they were back in their room. She told him about running into Jesse in Greece and what had happened.

"They seem to love one another, but they both have issues that need to be resolved first, I think."

"Hey Darlin', shall we conjure up some magic and get them on the right track?" He wiggled his eyebrows and both Randy and Joly laughed.

She ran the water for Randy's bath and was tossed out of the bathroom. "This is guy time," she was informed.

She sat on the bed, her arms resting on her knees, listening to the sounds of laughter coming from Randy. Quickly she sat up, an alarm going off in her head. She shouted to Duncan that she would be right back. She ran down the hall and Morag opened the door as she got to it. Joly rushed in.

"Morag... something's not right... not yet."

"Slow down dear. Catch your breath. I'm not going anywhere."

"Morag... have you heard Duncan laugh? He hasn't laughed. He smiles lots and jokes and grins, but he hasn't laughed."

Morag was silent for a moment and agreed. "It'll come dear, just give it time. Look how far he's come since last night. Don't be in such a hurry. You have the rest of your lives together."

"Yes, I suppose you're right. It just seems so strange. Sorry I barged in. Good night." She turned to leave, Morag and Sara returning the good nights.

She walked slowly down the hall thinking. Morag was wrong; she could feel it. She thought about the riddle again. The mirth is secure in the psyche. Mirth could be laughter. *The laughter is safe in the soul.* Widdershins and fire releases the void. Counterclockwise and fire lets go of the nothingness. *What fire?*

She walked in their room to find Duncan and Randy on the bed. Randy was still wet and Duncan wasn't much drier. "Hey guys... no wet bodies on my bed, thank you very much."

Duncan grinned. "Aww Mom, we're just playing."

They got Randy tucked into bed and they went and sat on the sofa. Joly began the healing of Duncan's leg. It wasn't misshapen like Morag's had been, but again, the muscle tissue had been melted together in his thigh. She thought he would be walking normally within the month.

When they went to bed, they cuddled close to Randy and wrapped their arms around one another over their son.

The next morning Morag surprised everyone with the announcement that she wasn't going with them. Her Grannie had called to her and she was needed in Scotland. A serious problem there needed immediate attention. Joly and Duncan wanted to go with her, but she said no, it was something she could handle.

"You need to get back to Canada. I sense something happening there, but it's not clear what it is yet. You will be needed there, and soon. The two of you can deal with whatever it is. I'll be back when I'm finished here. I'll take a taxi to the bus depot later and I'll cancel my plane reservation before I leave."

They had breakfast together and then the four of them loaded the car and they headed south. The trip back to London was uneventful. Sara kept Randy occupied while Joly and Duncan discussed their itinerary for the day. Nefertiti was in her usual place up in the back window. Pip was next to Joly and Salem decided to check out Duncan. He curled up on Duncan's lap and was pleased when he was allowed to stay there. Duncan absentmindedly petted him.

Morag sat on the bus thinking. She did a lot of that when she traveled alone. Others read, but she liked to use the time to think, plan and review.

She thought about Duncan and the sudden return of his memory. She wondered how it had come about. She had watched him and felt him. His memory had been buried so deeply she couldn't even pick up on it. There was one way… *Gods! Joly wouldn't have… would she?* It was far too dangerous. What had Duncan said? '… *You don't even wanna know what happened.*'

Morag bowed her head. If Joly had taken Duncan back to when he lost his memory, then they were damned lucky. She thought about two others who had tried the same foolish stunt. One had had a fatal heart attack upon remembering, the other had a seizure, and as far as she knew, the woman still lay in a vegetative state. She had heard there were others, all with the same results. The shock of being forced to remember everything all at once was just too much.

She thought of Joly and Duncan and the bond they shared. It had been there even when he had no memory. Perhaps that was what was needed to succeed. She didn't know. She was just thankful to have her son back. Whatever Joly had done… it had worked and there was no point in dwelling in the past. She looked out the window at the trees rushing by and thought of her childhood home.

She had been five when her parents decided to uproot the family and move to Canada. Her brother had been excited about the move, but she had not. Her Grannie was staying behind and she hadn't wanted to leave her. There was a bond between the two of them and her Father had had to wrench her out of Grannie's arms on the day of departure.

Her brother… she seldom thought about him anymore. He had hated Canada, and had grown into an angry young man. As soon as he was old enough, he had moved back to Scotland. Less than two years later, he was dead, killed in a brawl of some sort… she had never heard all the details.

She had missed her Grannie something fierce, but Canada had taken hold of her and she had never been back to Scotland until now.

She had always maintained a sporadic connection with her Grannie, even after she had died, but this was the first time she had demanded Morag's return. She wondered what the problem was. She smiled as she thought of Grannie telling her about the *Sisters of the Triple Moon*.

Her thoughts returned to her youngest son. Yes, she had noticed he never laughed. She had glossed over Joly's concerns the previous night, because she needed Joly to concentrate on the world problems, not her personal concerns.

She thought about the riddle. *The mirth is secure in the psyche.* Mirth could be laughter. Well, whatever Alyce had meant by it all, she was sure that when the time came, it all would be sorted out.

Morag's head nodded with the movement of the bus, her eyes closed and she slept.

After checking into their hotel and eating, Joly and Duncan went and got his passport ordered. He had to apply for it under the name of James Smith, as that was the only identification he had. He would get his real one updated when he got back to Canada.

Then they went shopping. Gisela had bought him nothing but cotton chinos and he desperately wanted a pair of jeans.

Back at the hotel, Duncan emptied his two boxes and sorted through the contents, opting to keep two shirts, some underwear, socks, his telescope and the picture frame. The rest he packed up to donate to a thrift shop.

Joly asked him about the frame.

"I don't know. I saw it in a store window one day and I just knew I had to have it. You have no idea how often I would stare at it, trying to visualize the picture that belonged in it."

Joly made sure they were booked into a suite and she'd hoped to convince Randy to sleep with Sara, but he wouldn't have any part of it. After his bath and story, and once he was asleep, Joly and Duncan went into the living room.

Sara called to Joly from her doorway. Joly went over and Sara asked her if she wanted to switch bedrooms. "I'll sleep with Randy. He won't notice until morning. I know you two need your privacy."

"You don't mind?"

"If I did, I wouldn't have offered." She smiled.

"Thank you, Sara." Joly gave her a quick hug.

They quietly grabbed a few things for the next morning and saying good night, they traded places with Sara.

Duncan shut the door and leaned back against it watching Joly as she organized their belongings. When she was done, she turned and looked at him. The game they had played so many years before came automatically to her.

"Like what you see?"

"I'd like it better if you weren't wearing all those clothes."

"Hmm… well…" She unbuttoned her shirt, taking care to open it, as each button was undone. "Better?"

"Some."

She smiled and removed the shirt. Reaching behind, she unclasped her bra and bringing her hands forward again, slid it off her arms, letting it drop on the floor. "Now?"

He shook his head, "Not yet."

Joly undid the button on her jeans, unzipped them and slid out of them.

"Now?" He saw her eyes look at his groin, knew she saw the bulge and watched as she shivered.

His throat was dry. He couldn't answer. It was all he could do to force himself not to rush over, grab her and throw her on the bed. Gods, he wanted her. He shook his head.

She smiled and it was almost his undoing.

She reached down, slid her thumbs inside the elastic of her panties, and slowly slid them down. With her dark thatch still half hidden, she stopped. She went to speak and had to clear her throat. Her voice came out a throaty whisper. "I can't reach down any farther."

Duncan moved then. He was across the room in an instant, his limp barely perceptible. He went on his knees in front of her, his hands on her backside and his face buried in the dark curls that were peeking over the pink elastic. He was shaking and he knew he was losing control. She had always had this effect on him, but it had been so long. His fingers, soft and smooth from years of little physical labor, clenched and unclenched her firm buttocks. He tried to control his ragged breathing without success. Running his tongue up her smooth skin, he felt her intake of breath. He circled her belly button with his tongue. He was rock hard and being confined in the new jeans was painful. He tried to ignore it and concentrated on the woman in front of him. He reached inside the pink panties and slid his hands down the silky skin, dragging the skimpy material with them.

Joly wondered how long before her legs would give out on her. They felt like two bands of rubber that had somehow attached themselves to her torso. Her fingertips kneaded Duncan's scalp as she arched back, savoring the tremors pulsing through her body. Senses she had thought she would never feel again had come alive, and she gloried in the feeling of each and everyone of them.

Duncan wondered at her stamina as he nuzzled the pink nub that peeked out of the curls. His legs felt like jelly and he was on his knees. He flicked his tongue over the soft folds and almost lost it when she moaned. He moved his hands from her backside to spread her apart and he sucked and licked, savoring the taste of the only woman he had ever known. Her moans changed into whimpers and then into gasping cries. He needed release in the worst way, but his beloved came first. Her hips were thrusting and twisting, her fingers were wrapped in his hair so tightly he wondered if he might be bald before they were done. He wiggled his tongue up as far as he could reach and then slid it back to tickle that most sensitive part hidden in the folds. He felt her quiver, felt her muscles contracting and he took her full in his mouth as he suckled her velvet folds, and he sent her spiraling over the crest. He felt her legs give out and as she crumpled, he rested on his heels, reached up and guided her onto his thighs. He gathered her into his arms and held her tight, burying his face in the curve of her neck, breathing in her feminine scent.

They stayed like that until Joly's ragged breathing had calmed somewhat. Then Duncan lifted her up and he got to his feet. He winced as he stood, the blood rushing back into his lower legs.

Joly cocked her head and looked him up and down.

He grinned. "Like what you see?"

"I'd like it better if you weren't wearing all those clothes."

He pulled his T-shirt up slowly and lifted it over his head, tossing it on the floor.

Joly sat on the edge of the bed and stretched her arms out behind her, leaning back on her hands. Her firm breasts jutted out, the dusky nipples hard and Duncan wondered if he had enough stamina to play out their game.

"Better?"

She gave him a half smile and replied, "Some."

He struggled to undo the button on his jeans and then quickly unzipped them. He wiggled his way out of them, hoping to elicit a laugh. Gods, he needed a distraction. She remained silent. His manhood struggled to break free of the remaining material that covered it.

He went to speak and nothing came out. He swallowed and tried again. "Now?"

"Not yet."

He put his thumbs inside the elastic and slowly lowered his shorts. When they hung up on his swollen member, he stopped. "I seem to have hit a snag."

Joly sat up. "Come here." Her voice was husky with desire.

Duncan walked to the bed. Joly reached out and unhooked the shorts giving freedom to the weapon within. She wrapped her hands around his length and kissed the tip of it. He shivered, goose bumps appearing on his arms and legs. She softly stroked him as she nibbled and kissed the tip.

She knew he wouldn't be able to take too much of this. Still, she would try her best to make it as good for him as he had for her. She grasped his balls and gave them a gentle squeeze as she took him in her mouth. He moaned loudly and shuddered.

Damn! He wasn't going to be able to hold it. He unconsciously thrust and withdrew, his hands wrapped tightly in her hair. Joly squeezed his balls harder. Duncan stilled. *Shit, that had hurt.*

She smiled to herself and continued the sucking, nibbling and licking of his shaft. She moved her hands up to his groin, her fingers causing a tickling sensation. She flattened her palms and slid them across the smooth skin to his behind. She clenched his cheeks and kneaded them, placing little butterfly kisses along his length. He bucked again and she knew the time had come.

She moved her mouth up, running her tongue along the fine hairs that led to his belly button. She gripped his waist and continued up to his ribcage. She eased herself off the bed and continued kissing and nipping going up to his nipples. First one and then the other received kisses and sucking.

Duncan had his arms around her and when he could take no more, he guided her back down on the bed. He mounted her and eased his shaft in between the slick folds and guided it home.

He lay still for a moment, savoring the tight warmth that encased him. He slowly raised himself until only the tip still penetrated and he lowered himself once again. She met him half way, wiggling her hips as they met. He felt a tremor and knew he couldn't last much longer. He reached down and took a nipple in his mouth, gently nibbling, stroking, and coaxing. He switched to the other one, reveling in their pebble-like hardness.

She welcomed the fullness and wondered how she had lived for so long without him and she realized that she hadn't lived at all. She had only existed for all those years. She had been half of a whole, half-alive, half not. She wrapped her legs more tightly around Duncan's hips and squeezed. She felt his tremor and marveled at his stamina. She knew he had to be hurting something fierce.

He looked into her eyes and saw the love she had for him and he became more determined to make it last. He kissed her then, with all the sweetness and tenderness that he felt for her. Their tongues danced a duet in the dark, moist recesses of their mouths. Almost lazily, they pushed together, pulled apart and pushed together again. He moved his hips in a circle, thrilling at the low moan he elicited. Gods, he was hot! His heart hammered against his rib cage, the staccato beat echoing in his head. He felt the blood coursing through his veins, and with no conscious thought he picked up the pace.

She felt his muscles as they rippled with their movement. She looked at the face of the only man she had ever loved and felt herself grow even hotter. She matched him thrust for thrust, her breath coming in small gasps. Their skin grew slick as their burning need increased and soon they were bucking like two bronco riders. Her nails raked his back as the fire intensified inside her belly. The fire turned into molten lava and just when she thought she couldn't get any hotter, she felt the pressure build even more as it rose up the narrow chimney of the volcano that was building inside her. She threw her head back and whimpered for release.

The mewling sounds coming from Joly were his undoing. He knew she had reached the peak and his seed and his shout erupted at the same time. He slammed himself to the deepest depths of her silky sheath, and through the roaring in his head, he faintly heard her cry out. The pleasure and the pain combined and he vibrated from the release, his manhood spasming uncontrollably and his seed spilling over.

Joly's explosive climax left her with no conscious thought, just the sense of being whole again. She drew in deep breaths of air, as her muscles squeezed again and again, wringing the last drop of seed from him.

Duncan lowered himself on shaking arms to the damp, quivering body below him. He buried his face in Joly's hair and kissed her neck. He tasted her tears and felt his own fall. Turning his head, he was finally able to draw in a full breath of air.

Joly's hands were resting on his shoulder blades and sometime later, Dun-

Duncan felt little circles being drawn on his back. He smiled and lifted his head to give her a gentle kiss. She devoured his mouth, her hips undulating in an age-old rhythm and her hands moving in between them to tease and coax. And for the second time that night they took each other to that highest of peaks.

Sara slowly became aware of a small voice and then she remembered she was sleeping with Randy. Was he dreaming? She forced herself awake to find Randy sitting up in the bed.

"Hey Sweetie, it's not time to get up yet. Come and lay down." She patted the space beside her.

"Where Mommy?"

"She's sleeping in my bed. Come on now, come lay down."

"I want Mommy." Randy was adamant. He got out of bed and headed to the door.

"Randy, no!" Sara jumped out of bed and raced to catch up to him, but he was out of the room and at the door of the other bedroom. He opened the door and scampered over to the bed, climbing in.

Sara stood at the doorway wondering what to do.

Joly and Duncan were entwined around each other and Randy clambered on top of the two them, burrowing his way in between. Joly awoke wondering what was going on, and then she felt Randy snuggling against her. She smiled ruefully to herself and threw her arm over her son to rest her hand on her husband.

Sara smiled and gently closed the door.

Randy slept dreamlessly the rest of the night in his cocoon of warm, bare skin, surrounded by the rhythmic thumping of two hearts that beat as one.

Morag spent the night in Edinburgh and was on the train at seven the next morning. She looked out the window with interest, wondering if she would recognize anything on the three and a half hour trip to Tyndrum. It had been over fifty years, so she didn't expect to recognize much, nor did she expect to see anyone that she knew.

She had booked a room at a small hotel and after freshening up; she wandered through the small village. There seemed to be a lot of people around for the size of the town and after talking to a shopkeeper, she discovered the area had become a popular tourist destination.

Listening to various conversations on her walk, Morag kept hearing how the animals to the south of the village were all behaving strangely. Cows and ewes had quit giving milk, hens had quit laying, dogs were walking around with their tails tucked between their legs, cats were refusing to set foot outdoors and no wildlife or birds had been spotted for some time. Her childhood home was to the south.

After having lunch at her hotel, she headed out to her old home. She wondered if anything remained of the cottage, or if perhaps someone still lived there. She hadn't bothered checking her crystal ball, preferring to see the real thing, whatever it might be. She had no trouble deciding which way to go, an inborn instinct led her in the right direction. The spongy ground told her that there had been some heavy rainfall, but the day was sunny and warm.

The old crofter's cottage she had been born in was still standing. The croft appeared to be abandoned, the only sign of life being a few sheep grazing in the nearby field. She made her way to the door and found it was open a couple of inches and when she pushed against it; it quietly swung inward. Morag took a deep breath and entered. She wasn't sure what she had expected, but it wasn't what she found.

What she found was... nothing. There was no sense of anything. It was as if the entire place had been wiped clean of all human contact. She wandered from one end to the other, touching the walls, the few sticks of furniture that remained, the floor, the cupboards, but she couldn't feel anything. She touched the wood of the windowsills; she touched the stone of the fireplaces that were built into each end of the cottage and again she felt nothing. This was *not* normal. Every home left something of its previous occupants. She should have been able to sense something of her family, even though they hadn't lived there in over fifty years. She should have been able to sense something of the families that had lived there since. There was nothing. She tested the bottom two steps leading upstairs and decided it was safe to climb. She went into her bedroom first and then her brother's. Although there was no furniture, she could picture their box beds as clear as if she had been there yesterday. She touched the wood. Nothing. She walked into her parent's room. Again, there was nothing.

She went back downstairs and walked outside. She walked around the perimeter. Everything looked and felt normal. She touched the outside of the house. Nothing. Shaking her head, Morag walked toward the sheep. Halfway there, she was suddenly assaulted by a bizarre feeling that left her weak. The sheep were bleating in terror, as their hooves pounded into the ground, carrying them away from the cottage and toward the distant tree line.

Morag stood still, trying to figure out what had just happened. She looked around and shook her head. She appeared to be several feet from where she had been walking. Squatting down, she checked the damp ground and saw no sign of any footprints. She walked fifteen or twenty feet to her left and saw where her footprints ended.

Looking around, she saw no sign of any wildlife. There was total silence. She had a terrible sense of impending doom and knew she had to get out of there, fast. She started running toward the path, knowing that nothing was there at the moment, but also knowing that something big and bad was about to happen.

She ran down the hill toward the tree line and the river. As a child, the river had seemed close, but now it seemed as though she would never reach it. She was gasping for air when she finally reached the tree line. She stopped and bent over, sucking in the cool air. After several deep breaths, she stood and laid her hand on the trunk of the tree. She could feel the vibration from within. There was something terribly wrong. Trees normally only showed fear before a major earthquake or a volcanic eruption. There were no active volcanoes in Scotland and she was sure that no earthquake was underway.

She looked back up the hill at the cottage and as her eyes lit on the doorway, she was again assaulted by the alien feelings. She had been holding onto the tree when the sensation of displacement hit her. As it passed, she found she was clutching onto a large piece of bark, which had obviously been ripped from the tree. She looked around and was startled to see that she was less than ten feet from the river.

Fear coiled in her stomach as she thought about the distance from the tree line to the river. She knew it had to be at least a quarter mile, if not more. *What in the Gods' names is happening?* She started running again, this time keeping to the bank of the river.

When the third assault hit her, she was a mile from her childhood home. The displacement moved her from her side of the river to fifty feet beyond, on the other side.

Morag looked back at the direction she had come from. Her lungs heaving, she said aloud, "Screw it!" and she sat on the damp knoll, pulling her knees up under her chin.

Thirty minutes later, with nothing else happening, she got to her feet and walked back to the village, having to follow the river to the railroad, in order to cross the bridge.

In her room, she undressed and climbed into a hot shower, letting her mind wander as the spray cleansed the grime from her. When the water began to cool, she turned the taps off and dripping her way across the carpet, she went and lay down. In minutes, she was fast asleep.

When she awoke, she dressed and went to the restaurant for supper. When she was finished, she returned to her room, undressed and went to bed. She slept through the night.

The day was a lazy one for the four in London. It was still raining, so except for picking up Duncan's passport and eating, they stayed in their room. They discussed the things they needed to do once they were home and they played with Randy. Sara doodled, more than sketched, every doodle ending up looking suspiciously like Jesse.

That night Randy giggled when Joly and Duncan tucked him in. "Me find you."

They assured him that he wouldn't have to find them, that they would all be sleeping together.

The next day everyone eagerly anticipated the return home, but most of all, Duncan. He felt sick to his stomach as they boarded the plane and Joly held his hand to calm his frayed nerves. As the plane lifted off the runway, he looked out the window and softly said, "So long England... can't say I'll be missin' you."

Joly heard and squeezed his hand. They were going home as a family and her heart was singing.

Emilia felt her wards being breached. It was early afternoon and she wondered what was going on. There had been an uneasy peace between her neighbors and her for several months. She was in the north field and the breach had come from the west. She jumped in the jeep; made sure her rifle was ready and headed in the direction of the problem.

She felt a stab of pain along her shoulder and reached up to hold it. She felt blood and drew her hand back to look at it. There was nothing. *Diosa, protect me and mine.*

She heard a scream and knew it was Jacinta. She drove faster, terrified of what she was going to find. She came over the crest of the hill and saw several men surrounding her *niña*. Jacinta was on her horse which was rearing in terror, as the men were trying to get close enough to pull Jacinta off. *Where's Viento Blanco?* She saw a speck of white lying on the ground and knew the dog was hurt.

She slammed the brakes on and aimed the rifle. *Diosa be with me.* She fired. A puff of dust rose at the feet of one of the men. The loud report had them looking around for the source. She fired again and saw one of the men fall to the ground, leap to his feet and take off with a faltering gait.

Bueno! She had hit him. The other half dozen men were running to their vehicles, jumping in them and driving away.

She threw the jeep in gear and rushed to where Jacinta was slowly bringing Estrella under control.

"*Madre*, they shot *Viento Blanco*."

"*Si, niña*, I know." She jumped out and ran to the dog. He looked at her as she crouched down at his side.

The red of the blood looked obscene on his white fur. She found the bullet had gone into his shoulder. She drove the jeep up beside him and she and Jacinta carefully loaded him in the front seat.

"Take Estrella home and lock the door. I'll be back as soon as possible."

The drive into town seemed to take forever. When she reached the veterinary clinic, she was surprised to see the dog was still conscious.

Ninety minutes later the bullet was removed, the shoulder bandaged and she was on her way home.

She had gone by the police station and filed a report. They knew the man she hit would need medical attention.

At home, Jacinta helped carry White Wind into the house where they laid him on his blanket.

Emilia lit a candle. "We must pray for *Viento Blanco's* recovery and thank the Gods who watched out for you today."

"And we need to thank them for letting you know we were in trouble," Jacinta said as she lit another candle.

As she lay there, Morag stared at the ceiling and soon it began to waver in the diffused light coming from the window. As she relaxed her eyes, her vision grew fuzzy. Mists appeared from the corners of the room and swirled around, growing thicker until the ceiling disappeared. She asked, "Grannie? Are you here?"

"*Tha mi*, lassie."

Morag dredged up a tired smile. "Grannie, you know I haven't spoken Gaelic in fifty years."

"*Fad leth-cheud bliadhna?* Ye sud be ashamed o' yersel'! '*S e Albannaich a th' annainn.*"

"Grannie, I may be of Scots descent, but I *am* Canadian."

"Ochhh, *Canèidianach...* ye *sud* hae coom haime tae tha *Ghàidhealtachd.*"

"Grannie, I'm tired. I don't know what the hell is out there. And all you can do is bitch at me. Now either help me or go away."

"*Bu àill leat?* Sin' whan did ye stairt takkin tae ma like tha'?"

Morag lowered her eyes, ashamed. "*Tha mi duilich* Grannie. I'm sorry."

"*Do leisgeul gabham.*"

She was thankful her apology had been accepted. And that her Gaelic, although extremely rusty, had been passable enough not to elicit any comment. She sat up on the bed. "What is it, Grannie? I've never seen anything like it before and what am I supposed to do about it?"

"Tis a voortex... an ye wunt tae get red o' it."

"*That's a vortex?* There are vortexes all over the world, but they sure as hell don't behave like that!"

"Aye... an ye dinna wunt this wan tae git ony stronger noo, dae ye?"

"Damn!" Morag thought for a moment. "Any suggestions Grannie? I haven't dealt with anything like this before."

"Ye'll feegur it oot. Yer *air lethglic.* If a dinna thin' ye cuud handle it, I wad nae hae caa'ed ye."

Morag heard the smile in her voice, but could not reciprocate. "I should have brought Joly and Duncan. I was under the impression it was a *minor* problem."

"Dinna fash. Ye'll nae be awuntin halp."

Morag got out of bed and walked to the window.

"*Duine caol.*"

"I'm sorry, Grannie... what did you say?"

"Ochh! Yer skinny lass. Ye wunt tae eat mair."

Morag looked down at her body. The past six months of activity had toned and firmed her muscles. She was in good shape for her age. She looked at her legs and smiled. *They* were in great shape. She walked over to her suitcase and removed some clean clothes.

"Grannie, I'm not skinny, and if I was fat I wouldn't be able to do all the running around that I've been doing, and you know that."

"Aye lass, yer nae settin' roond waiting tae grow auld an' *is math sin!*"

"In case you haven't noticed, Grannie, that's happening whether I'm sitting or not." Morag smiled and took her bottom lip in her teeth while she thought.

"Okay... so we have a *minor* problem of a vortex that can move someone across a river who is a couple of miles away from the epicenter. You said it will get stronger. When?"

"*A h-uile latha* it gains pouer. *A h-uile latha* it tests itsel'. Yestre'en it wis muckle mair pouerful than afore. T'dey cuud be too late."

"Too late for what?"

"A dinna ken, lass. *Canaidh mi seo riut*, a think tis awmaist duin."

"Alright Grannie... I'll get to work on it... I don't suppose..."

"A canna' hel' ye Morag. A tauld ye tha'."

"I know. I thought maybe a hint." She smiled again. "It never hurts to try."

"Aye, an ye ay cuud wrap me aroon' yer wee finger." There was laughter in the voice.

Morag chuckled. "I love you Grannie. It was hard growing up without you nearby."

"A ken. A was ay pairtial tae ye. A ken a sud no hae a fa'rit, but a cuud no hel' masel'. Ye wis a Sister o' tha *Tri-fillte Gealaich*, a speicial *gheasaibh*, an ye wis a bonnie lass. Twas easy tae loue ye."

"Jeasaibh? Witch... right?"

"Ochhh! If ye cinna pronoonce it richt, ye micht wunt tae haud wi' speekin' tha English. Aye... a witch."

Morag laughed. The smile remained as she finished dressing and then slipped into her shoes. "You still here Grannie?"

"Aye. *Cùl nan cóig riut!* Tis a fine braw dae fur a wauk. *Dealaichidh mi riut an-dràsda.*"

Morag smiled. "Aye Grannie, that it is. I'll talk to you later." She grabbed her room key and wallet and headed out the door.

She had a quick bite to eat and two cups of tea. As she walked back to the croft, she thought about what her Grannie had said. Every day it tested itself. Yesterday it had hit her sometime after two. She hoped it kept to the same schedule every day. Everyday it grew stronger. *Gods!* What was trying to come through? All vortexes were either an entrance or an exit. She assumed this was an exit, a place for something from another world to enter into their world. An entrance would be for something that was already there to leave by. She didn't think anything was roaming about that needed or wanted to leave. That took her back to her original thought. What was trying to come through? What would need a vortex that powerful? Most vortexes were fairly tame. She had heard of vortex displacement happening with movement of several feet, but never had she heard of one powerful enough to move somebody hundreds of feet.

Her thoughts turned to the various types of travel and all that she knew about them. Soul travel, light travel, shadow travel, teleportation, astral travel. Then there were the breakdowns of each of those, some of which were remote viewing, metaphysical projection and travel and astral projection.

Her mind awhirl with all the variables, she found she was soon back at the croft. Her thoughts turned to the task at hand. She spent the next two hours combing the area with all her senses on high alert, looking for any sign at all, of what was in the making.

Once she was satisfied that she hadn't missed anything, she walked back to the house. She was carrying a rusty nail she had found. Walking inside, she went over to the stairs and taking the nail, she proceeded to scratch out an area of about four by six inches. She blew the wood chips away from the area and placed the palm of her hand flat on the clean surface.

She was assailed by visions of people and animals. Amongst them were her parents and brother, her Grannie, and a dog that she had forgotten about.

She sat down on the step and thought about what she had learned. The displacement only seemed to move people and animals. Anything with its roots in the ground seemed to be safe. The clean sweep of the removal of all signs of the previous inhabitants was only on the surface, which said to her that the vortex's strength was not really as powerful as it seemed.

Her next problem was what would be the best way to shut it down permanently. Regardless, she was going to need a wand. Running the different woods through her mind, she decided she needed one made of alder. She got up and walked down to the tree line. It was cooler in the shade of the trees and she quickened her pace as she walked down to the river. The alder trees grew close to the water and as she made her way toward them, she thought about what else she might need. When she spotted the tree she was looking for, she walked over to it and laid her hand on the trunk. She could feel the gentle quiver emanating from within and knew that it too was afraid.

"My friend... I sense your fear and I would like to help you. If you would willingly part with just one straight branch, I will get rid of the evil that has come to this part of the world." She waited. The quivering lessened and finally stopped.

"Thank you." Morag reached up but couldn't reach the lowest of the branches. She walked down to the riverbank and mentally called for the help of the birds. She had not seen any birds and wondered if any would respond to her plea. She sent the same message to them that she given the tree. Again she waited.

The water sparkled in the sunlight and the sound of the rushing water calmed and relaxed her. She remembered her brother fishing just around the bend, and she smiled as she thought of how annoyed he would get with her incessant babbling. He was always telling her. "*Shhh... haud yer wheesht, lass. A canna git a wee bite wi' yer steidy takkin.*" She remembered the time she had fallen in. She had been wading in the shallows and ventured out too far. The current grabbed her and she'd lost her footing. Her brother had pulled her out and taken her home. She had received a severe tongue-lashing from her Father and her brother was treated like a hero for weeks afterward.

What's that? She shook her head and dragged herself back to the present. The noise repeated itself and she looked around. The trees were filled with birds of all sizes, from large golden raptors to tiny wrens and titmice. They were all watching her.

Morag laughed. *Gods!* How she loved the birds.

She sent them the message that she needed them to lower a tree branch down to her. The sound of wings beating filled the air as they flew down to do her bidding. The large eagles and crows lit on the limb first, and then the smaller birds squeezed in between and perched on the smaller branches of the limb. Morag watched as the branch lowered with the weight. She reached up and grabbed the tip. The birds sat and watched her, unafraid of the woman who spoke their language. She reached out and stroked the backs of several, as she thanked them for coming to her aid.

One by one, the birds took flight, but only as far as nearby branches. They watched and waited.

Morag rang her fingers along the different branches until she felt one vibrate under her fingertips. She realized she had nothing to cut it off with.

"Damn!" She let go of the branch and searched the ground looking for a sharp edged rock. Finding none, she wandered farther along the river's edge. She soon found herself at her brother's old fishing hole. She stood quietly for a moment, letting the memories wash over her.

"*Confoond I', Morag! Ar ye takkin ma on? Ye dinna lose ma knife!*"

Morag laughed and headed into the trees. She hadn't lost Iain's knife. She had decided she didn't want to see the fish die and get cut open, so she had hidden it. It hadn't helped. Iain had angrily taken the fish back to the house and gotten another knife from their Mother. Their Father had arrived home that night with the news that they were moving to Canada. The knife had been forgotten.

The trees had grown and everything looked different. She remembered there were several large rocks in a group. As she wandered through the underbrush, she was struck by a thought. The rocks that had been large to a five year old would not be large to an adult. She shook her head in frustration and walked back the fishing hole. Once oriented, she walked back into the trees. She spotted them right away. They were much smaller than she remembered. She laughed; her voice the only sound in the silent woods. She rolled some of the stones away from their place in the grouping and reached her hand under the hollowed out place beneath. Her fingertips touched several places before finding what she was after. She withdrew the knife and replaced the rocks, thanking them for keeping the knife safe through the years.

She walked back to the river and rinsed it in the water. The blade was rusted, but she thought it would still make a clean cut. Walking back to the alder, she wondered if Iain was buried in Tyndrum, or elsewhere.

At the alder the birds all waited. When they saw Morag returning, they again flew to the limb, weighing it down until Morag could reach it. She found the branch and with one clean cut, it was hers. She thanked the tree and then she thanked the birds. The birds darkened the sky as they rose as one to fly to where it was safe, until the evil had been dispensed with.

Morag walked back to the cottage and sat on the stoop. With the sun warming her, she trimmed the branch until she was satisfied with the wand. Rising, she stretched and walked back to the hotel.

She hadn't brought much in the way of supplies with her, so as she sorted through what she had, she wondered if she could find the things she still needed in the small village. She didn't need to search very far. She found a store that carried an assortment of miscellaneous items and made most of her purchases there. Next door, she found the rest of the things she needed.

She went and ate a light lunch and then packed up everything she would need for the closing of the vortex. Then she headed back to the croft.

As she walked along, she thought about the dozens of spells she had cast through the years. Of the banishings, reversals, reflections, deflections, revocations, invocations, evocations, unbindings, protection, summonings, divinations and more. She had never had a mentor or anyone to show her how they were done. In the beginning, she would panic at first until she thought it through and figured out what was needed. She chuckled to herself. She couldn't remember the last time she'd had a panic attack. It had to have been over thirty years ago. She'd hoped that Grannie would give her a hint, but it really wasn't necessary. She'd figured it out fairly quickly.

She didn't envy Joly and her super powers. She was quite content to just have the knowledge. A soul witch, her Grannie had called her years earlier. It was a good title.

Her powers defined her as someone special. She had never thought of herself as being special or different. And the disaster that had taken her husband and friends hadn't been prevented, even though she was one of the Sisters.

She had been careless. Plain and simple. She understood it was her fault the demon had damned near won. They had fought too many that were similar. Their successes were known worldwide by those who monitored demon movement. She hadn't checked the area out thoroughly. If she had, she would have realized the demon was not one of the many, but a mutant that was far more powerful. The rest of the group had trusted her and now they were all gone, except for the two young ones. When she'd had Stephen take her back to the site, she checked then and saw that all the signs were there. She had screwed up and because of it; she had paid the price. She was a widow, her children were fatherless, Joly had lost her parents and two other dear friends were no more. It was a hard lesson learned, but she wouldn't make that mistake again. And no matter how tired she felt, no matter how much she wanted to just give it all up, she wouldn't. She owed Joly and Duncan her services for the rest of her life and she would not shirk in her duty.

Morag realized that she had reached the croft and had been standing in one spot for some time. *Gods!* What a time to be woolgathering. She noted where she was standing and moved away from the area. When she looked back, she realized the air in the spot she had been standing in looked somehow different. It wasn't anything really definable. It just seemed different. She walked back and looked closely around. There appeared to be nothing different. She walked away again and looked back. Yes, there was something there. It had to be the portal opening. The vortex had grown so powerful that even when it closed, it left something of itself behind.

Good! That made her job easier. She looked around. As she had thought, the cottage was too close. She would have to include it in the circle. She emptied the bag and laid everything out. Then she went into the house.

She wandered through the rooms and went upstairs. She stood in her old bedroom and thought about her brother. He had been seven years older, so they had never been really close. He had watched out for her when she was small and she had pestered him with always wanting to go with him, whether it was fishing or herding the sheep. After the move to Canada, he had distanced himself from the whole family, so when he returned to Scotland she hadn't really missed him. She was only thirteen when her parents received word that he was dead.

She walked back downstairs, pleased that she had his knife. She would give it to Duncan. She thought Iain would have liked that.

Back outside, she said goodbye to the cottage. When she was done, it would be nothing but a pile of rubble.

Morag picked up a roll of string and tied one end of it to Iain's knife. She pushed the knife into the ground and walked away, unwinding the string as she walked. When she reached the end of it, she marked the spot with a piece of bright wool, which she weighted down with a rock. She repeated this several times, until she needed to mark the far side of the cottage. Walking around to the back of it, she looked at her markers on either side. She had a distance of roughly twenty-four feet. She picked up several fist-sized rocks and laid them out, and then she walked to the corner of the house and eyed them. Not quite a semi-circle, she decided, and she went and rearranged them. Once she was satisfied, she took her athame and drew her circle, following the brightly colored bits of wool and rocks. It was the largest one she had ever done, with a diameter of seventy-eight feet. She drew in the pentagram around the area where she thought the portal door was located. She walked around the circle one more time drawing in various magical symbols.

She set up her alter on a flat area of ground well back from the edge of the circle. She drew a doorway in the circle, as she was going to have to exit it during the ritual. Once that was done, she undressed and took two bottles of water to which she added a mixture of oils and poured them over herself. She found it awkward trying to bathe and pour the water at the same time. It worked much better when Joly was with her.

She slipped into her shoes and drip-dried as she continued with her preparations. She was almost out of time. She took four silver candles and placed them at the four quarters of the circle, lighting them as she went.

She lit the two purple candles on the altar and dipped her athame into the water, blessing it. She called out,

"In the name of the God Janus, I cast out from thee all impurities and unclean spirits."

She dipped the athame into the sea salt to purify it, and called out,

"Blessed be this salt, in the name of the God Janus, that which would malign or hinder shall be cast out and all good shall enter herein."

She poured the salt into the water and set it in the center of the circle and then she retraced the pentagram with the athame. Next, she took a bag of sea salt and carefully poured it all around the edge of the circle.

A sense of urgency overtook her. She knew she had only minutes left before the vortex opened the portal. She hurried to the circle and raised her arms.

"I call upon you Gods and Goddesses of old,
I call upon you Gods and Goddesses of new.
I call upon the Four Quarters
For that which is right, to be done.
I pledged to honor you in all ways,
I vowed to work for the good of all.
The universe maintains a balance.
The balance has been disrupted.
The netherworld has opened a door.
Help me to close the portal and protect this earth."

Morag left the circle and ran to the altar. She picked up the orange candle that had been rubbed in rue and olive oil, and lit it. She faced the center of the circle and called out,

"Earth and Air, Water and Fire,
Hear me! Close, by my desire!
Build me walls stronger than steel,
Build me a roof to complete the seal.
Take the seal deep into the ground
And build a floor so the seal is bound."

She picked up the bowl of pine incense mixed with charcoal and the lighter. She was shaking and she dropped the lighter. She picked it up again and lit the incense. A thin stream of smoke rose from the bowl.

Morag carefully held the bowl of incense and the candle as she ran back into the circle. She lifted the bowl and called out,

"Father Sun with glowing light.
Hear me and aid my plight.
As I send this earthly smoke to you,
Please send your power down here too.

Hear my spell and help me send
The evil back, the earth to mend.
Then let nothing pass your fiery wall
Nae, nothing, nothing at all."

She blew on the incense causing a puff of smoke to rise up.

"Janus, God of portals, hear my plea,
Close the doorway that you see.
With incense smoke and candle flame
Away from here, send all bane.
With pure water and earthly salt
Let any harm come to naught.
What has come must return.
Close the door and let it burn."

Morag picked up her wand and the bowl of salted water. She turned the bowl upside down and let the contents drizzle to the ground. She poured the incense mixture on top and set the orange candle on top of the pile.

She stood up and quickly ran back, until she was ten feet outside the circle. She closed the doorway and pointed her wand at the circle and shouted,

"Evil sent, must go to rest
Back to the world that it knows best."

The final words were barely out of her mouth when she sensed, more than saw or felt the first tremor. She picked up the bell. She walked around the large circle quickly, ringing it in three-ring successions. She had just reached the altar again when she felt the second tremor beneath her feet. She watched her circle, but neither saw nor felt anything else. She saw movement from the corner of her eye and as she turned her head, the wooden window and door frames fell off the cottage. The roof sagged in the middle. The ground beneath Morag trembled and shook so hard that she had trouble keeping her balance. She could hear the creaking of the cottage as it struggled to remain upright, the earth moved and cracked by her feet. It grew hot. Hotter than Scotland had ever seen. The sweat poured off Morag's face and dripped onto her chest. Her hair clung to her scalp. She pointed her wand and continued.

"Go back now! You must leave.
To this world, you cannot cleave."

She felt the vibration in the wand and as she saw the tip of it spark, her world went black. Morag crumpled to the ground.

She didn't see the little cottage explode, nor did she hear the banshee shrieks that came from within the walls. She was not aware of the implosion that caused the earth to sink twenty-five feet down within the Sacred Circle, nor did she know that second-degree burns covered the entire front of her body.

Veronika felt the shift from the kitchen and rushed outside. The heaviness of the air took her breath away. She stumbled to the piece of earth where the energy field had been. It was gone.

She felt the invisible cloak of air swirling around, hovering, pushing and wondered, "Now what?"

Polina had been disappointed when she'd discovered she had failed to remove the evil thing. Veronika wondered what she would think of this new horror. She took a deep breath and went back inside, wondering what her next step was.

Morag's first semi-conscious thought was that her throat burned and she needed a drink. She licked her lips and found a drop of moisture on them. She felt the cool breeze and she licked her lips again. She found another drop of moisture. She opened her eyes.

Dozens of small birds flew in holding patterns, fanning her dehydrated body. Larger birds were flying to and from the river, delivering life saving drops of water to the lips of the woman who had saved them. Yet other birds, the large raptors and the crows encircled her body, covering it with their out-stretched wings, protecting it from the summer sun.

Morag tried to move and a million needles of pain stabbed the front of her body. She lowered her head and looked down. The front of her body was bright red. *Damn!* She had a major case of sunburn. She needed to get to the river, but she wasn't sure she could manage it. She thought of the time when she dragged both Joly and herself to the road. Yes, she could do it, but it would take time.

First, she needed to close the circle. She moved her head to see what was left of the cottage. She blinked. She saw nothing. *What?* She raised herself up and took another look. She saw the hole then. *Gods!* She wanted a closer look. She slowly dragged herself to her knees. *Ouch...* that hurt. She pushed herself to her feet. The birds sat and watched.

She could feel her skin cracking, but she forced herself forward. The hole was massive and at the bottom, she saw the remains of the small cottage. She shook her head. *Damn!* She had thought she was going for overkill with the spell, but it looked liked she had done it right.

She closed the circle and turned to the altar. She slowly and painfully put everything back in the bag, picked up her clothes and began the long walk to the river. The birds followed her, some walking along side of her, others flying back and forth, watching. She wondered where the entrance of the vortex was located.

It took Morag more than an hour to walk the half mile. She wanted to sit and rest, but knew that if she sat down, she would never get up again. She pushed on until she could hear the rushing water. She slowly walked into the cold water, the wetness easing the parched skin. When it was up to her knees, she squatted down, shivering with the cold.

She sat until her teeth were chattering and her body was numb. She eased herself up and walked back to the shore. She gingerly put her blouse and skirt on, leaving her underwear off. These she placed in the bag, and she slowly began the mile and half walk back to the hotel. The birds went with her, making sure that she made it without crumpling to the ground along the way.

She was thirsty, but she knew she could not stop for tea. She went straight to her room and ran a warm bath. While the tub was filling, she picked up her crystal to find Joly. Morag found her sleeping on the airplane returning to Canada. She quickly backed away and put the crystal down. She wouldn't ask Joly to do a healing from the plane. She would have to wait. She went and sat in the tub and soaked. When the water grew tepid, she climbed out and crawled on top of the covers. She slept.

Rauna stared at the thing in front of her. She searched for information from the world around her, but all she got was darkness, a great cry of fear. If the world itself couldn't deal with this, how could she? For the first time in her life she started to feel doubt. She was afraid. She heard the cry of horror in her ears and she didn't know what to do. She didn't like the feeling, so she got angry. She closed her ears from the atrocious wail and took the fight posture, kicking her heels to the ground and filling her lungs with the air. She didn't like being afraid for one bit, so she ignored the feeling. This was not the time or place.

"I don't know what you are, but there is nothing more than a human being. I am a limitless spirit in a limited body, you are nothing."

"I am nothing," said the thing and bounced over her.

Rauna let her senses dive into this nothingness around her and was met by nothingness – she remembered Nietzsche's words. "And if you gaze for long into an abyss, the abyss gazes also into you."

"Yes, you are searching through me, but you won't find anything you can use," she said.

"You find nothing," said the thing.

"I have found it already," laughed Rauna. "You will return to where you came from, you will return to what you were."

She moved on, and the void moved with her.

She felt the earth and air sigh of relief when the weight of nothingness was removed from it.

She moved her hands to aid her mind to better reach the borders of the darkness, her hands sailed through the air in the silent, slow dance when she gathered the thin edges of nonexistence and forced it to become more compact, her golden eyes stared beyond everything visible.

The darkness got harder and harder, as it was forced back; it got more and more difficult to walk, but Rauna continued. She had seen the trace of emptiness left behind this thing and she intended to see that the scar was removed.

15. Thunder and Lightning

Duncan's first view of Vancouver through the small window of the plane, brought tears to his eyes. He squeezed Joly's hand and she squeezed back. His heart was pounding like a jackhammer with excitement and fear.

Ten years was a long time to be away. Things would be different. He had so much to catch up with. He knew Joly would help to make the transition go smoothly, but it was still going to be a major adjustment for him.

After going through customs and walking outside into the damp air, Duncan awkwardly lowered himself to the concrete, oblivious to the looks from the people around. He kissed the cement and stood up again. He raised his arms and spoke to the skies.

"Thank you my Gods and Goddesses, for bringin' me back home."

He turned to Joly. "So... how do we get home? Walk?"

She laughed. "You go and wait for the luggage and cats. I'll get the truck."

"*Truck?* You never told me you had a truck."

"No... I guess I didn't."

He tried to picture her behind the wheel of a pickup and couldn't. He shrugged his shoulders and grinned. "Okay pretty lady. You're the boss."

He turned and picked up Randy. "Come on bucko, let's get the cats." He found Sara waiting by the carousel.

As they stood there, he whispered in Randy's ear. "Let me guess. Mommy's truck is green, right?"

Sara overheard and laughed, but said nothing.

Randy, still not fluent in English understood enough. "Mommy geen tuck."

Duncan smiled. "Yeah... I kinda figured that."

They retrieved the bags and went to get the cats. By then, Joly was back and they loaded up the truck and headed for Mission.

Duncan's first glimpse of the street was overwhelming. His heart was pounding so hard he wondered if he'd returned only to have an immediate heart attack. *Better to die at home than abroad.* He jumped out of the truck with Randy still in his arms.

Sara climbed out and took Randy from him, knowing he needed some time to orient himself. She put Randy down, grabbed her suitcase from the back of the truck, and went to unlock the door. Randy wanted to stay with his parents, but Sara said no. She took him by the hand and went inside, leaving Joly and Duncan alone. Moments later, she reappeared to grab the carrier with the cats, taking it into the house and shutting the door.

"Welcome home, my love." Joly put her arms around him and kissed him gently on the lips.

"Yeah." He buried his face in her hair and squeezed her hard. Her uncomfortable gasp, made him release the death grip he'd had on her. "Sorry, Darlin'… didn't mean to squish you.

Walk with me," he demanded, as he took her hand and headed up the sidewalk toward the other end of the street.

She knew where he was going. When they were young, they had always said they would someday buy the house around the corner. It was a big old place, much like an old farmhouse, two stories high, with a wrap-around veranda and lots of windows. It had been in an extremely run down condition, with old weathered wood siding and the window frames hadn't seen a coat of paint in many years. The large yard was over run with weeds and none of the bushes had been tended to for a long time. They had talked about the different things they would do to fix it up with her Father's help. They hadn't known the recluse who lived there, so they had never seen the inside and their imaginations had run wild with the different interior layouts and number of rooms.

She had only been by the place once, since her return. She knew Duncan was in for a surprise. They turned the corner and walked up the hill. She felt more than heard his intake of breath. Ownership had obviously changed hands. The house had a sparkling coat of white paint on it. The trim was all dark green and the roof was sporting new black shingles. The lawn was green and freshly cut and the bushes were trimmed and neat.

"Different, eh?" She commented.

"Wow! Yeah. Guess somebody else got to it before we could."

"Mmm. Well, we have Mom and Dad's house anyhow. I guess we don't really need two."

"No, I guess not." He sounded disappointed.

Joly wondered if he was going to have a problem with living in her parents' home. She hadn't given it much thought, assuming that he would be fine with it.

They walked back to the house and went inside. Randy ran to Joly and led her to the kitchen. He was hungry and wanted a snack.

Duncan roamed through the house, going into each room and thoroughly checking them out. When he was done, he went into the kitchen.

"Darlin'… there seems to be a problem here." He looked perplexed.

Joly shook her head. "What kind of problem, honey?"

He took her by the hand and led her to the living room. "Look."

She looked, but saw nothing out of place. Before she could respond, Duncan dragged her through each room, saying the same thing. Then he took her up the stairs and through the bedrooms, bypassing Randy's room. He led her up to the third floor, stood silently while she removed the key from around her neck, and unlocked the door.

He marched in, glanced around and snorted. "I figured as much."

He walked out and limped back down the stairs. Joly quickly locked the door and ran after him. When she caught up to him, he was back in the living room.

"Honey, what's wrong? What are you seeing that I'm not?" She looked around again. She shook her head. "Everything's the same as it always has been. Nothing's changed."

He whirled around at that and pointed his finger at her nose, startling her. "And that pretty lady, is the *whole* problem here."

Joly looked at him as if he'd lost his mind.

"You said nothin's changed, right?"

She took another look around the room. "Right."

"So tell me, Darlin', are we to spend the rest of our lives livin' with your parents things? What's happened to *us*? Where's *our* stuff? The only thing I saw that was actually yours in this place was a couple of things on the dresser and Bast. And then there was some cheap imitation sitting beside her."

Joly took another look around the living room, stunned at what he had said. Having grown up in this home, she hadn't even thought about *their* things.

"You're right of course honey. I haven't changed anything. Our stuff is in the basement. When I came home ten years ago, I made one quick trip to the apartment and grabbed a few things. Kyle Devon was instructed to have the apartment cleaned out, the furniture sold and the personal belongings brought over here to be stored. I haven't had a chance to really think about unpacking or sorting... and I wasn't ready to face your stuff... our stuff." The tears spilled over onto her cheeks, as she again relived her years alone.

Duncan wrapped his arms around her and laid his chin on top of her head. He looked around at the spotless, but outdated room. He was being over sensitive. There had been too many changes in too short of time. He kept forgetting that Joly's world had also been turned upside down with his return.

"I'm sorry, Darlin'. I wasn't thinkin'." He kissed her, deeply and passionately. They had always worked through everything together. It would be okay.

Later, in the master bedroom, Duncan picked up the small statue of Bast. "So just where the hell did this impostor come from?"

Joly laughed and told him about her birthday and Stephen's good intentions.

Duncan was amazed. His brother had actually bought something that had to do with the craft. He replaced the statue back from where he had taken it.

"So what do you think? Should I phone him? Should I just show up on his doorstep? Should I wait and let Maw break the news to him?"

"I don't know." Joly explained to him the reaction she had received from him with the arrival of Randy.

Duncan thought about it. It sounded as if Stephen had been hitting on Joly and had gotten really pissed that she had decided to adopt, without informing him. If that were the case, he would have no reason to stay angry, once he knew she wasn't available any more. He looked at his wife and wondered at her innocence. She didn't seem to be aware that anything odd had happened. He knew that he had gotten the far better deal in a wife. He thought about Elise and shuttered. *Gods!* To be married to that harridan would be a fate worse than death. He wasn't surprised that Stephen had been sniffing around the young *widow*.

"Yeah, well... maybe I'll leave it to Maw. I've got enough to keep me busy here anyhow, and it's not like we were ever close."

He looked at the small statue again and realized that he hated seeing it beside the one he had gotten for her. *Jealousy?* He'd never been jealous in all of his life. He had always known that Joly was his. He thought about seeing Joly with Randy in the London airport and knew he had felt jealous once before. He remembered the hatred he had felt for the unknown father of Randy, the absolute despair that had overtaken him at the thought of someone else sleeping with the woman he didn't even know was his wife. Yeah... he had known the green-eyed monster and it was time to get rid of it.

Joly stood and watched the various expressions on her husband's face. She had never forgotten any of them and she knew he was having trouble with something. She saw the eyes... the almost accusing look and knew he was back at the airport. *Gods!* He didn't think she and Stephen... she couldn't even finish the thought. It was too ludicrous.

"Where should I put the little one honey? I know it doesn't belong in our bedroom. I just had such a horrid evening that night and I sat it there and forgot about it. I haven't really been home too much since my birthday. It was a sweet gesture on Stephen's part and it must have cost him dearly to set foot in a place that sold such an item."

"Wherever you think it would look right, darlin'. Maybe in the craft room?"

"Yes! Good idea. I'll run it up now and maybe tomorrow, we can start hauling out our things and decide on the changes here." She picked up the statue and left the room with it.

Duncan looked around the master bedroom. He liked what she had done with it. There was nothing of her parents stuff in there except for the furniture, but there was really nothing of hers... theirs, either. It would be a good place to start. The first thing that needed to be added was their wedding portrait. He thought of the small frame in his bag. It was time for an updated picture of them. Their tenth anniversary had just passed.

Morag stirred and the pain was instant. Her eyes flew open. Damn, but she was stiff. She could feel the skin crack as she eased herself out of bed. She wondered what time it was in Mission. She hung on to the edge of the desk while she tried to think. She finally decided it was the middle of the night over there. She went and ran the tub full of warm water and had another soak. She couldn't dry off, so she waited until she was mostly dry and then she put on a skirt and blouse and her shoes. She slowly walked to the restaurant and had a hearty breakfast.

Afterwards, she walked to the store and bought some vinegar, whole milk and a box of tea bags. Back in her room, she undressed and soaked in a tub of water with vinegar. When she got out, she applied milk soaked towels to her skin. After twenty minutes, she climbed back into the tub and rinsed it off. She filled the sink with hot water and tossed six tea bags in it. Thirty minutes later she soaked her towels in the solution, damp wrung them out, and went and lay down, placing the towels over her body. She felt better.

Every two hours she repeated the process. She wondered if she would ever do another spell sky clad. She chuckled to herself. She knew she would.

She realized she would have to wait until late afternoon to try to reach Joly. She knew by that time she would be mobile and decided not to bother her. She would spend another day recuperating before heading to London.

The next day Sara kept Randy entertained while Joly and Duncan started sorting through the boxes in the basement. True to his word, the wedding picture was the first thing to go in their bedroom.

As he placed it by the statue, he thought about all the wasted years and was overwhelmed with sorrow. He pictured his slender wife working a gold mining operation alone, building a cabin alone, living isolated from everyone. He had had the better end of the proverbial stick. He hadn't been able to remember, and he had had loving people to care for him. Joly had had no one except for the cats and her memories.

He went in search of Salem, who was in the kitchen window. "Salem... a little overdue I know, but I just wanted you to know I appreciate your lookin' out for Joly." He stroked the cat, wishing he had the ability to talk to him. He could feel the rumble of the cat's purr through his fingers and knew Salem was okay with his overdue thanks.

He tracked down Pip in Randy's room and thanked her too, for being there when he wasn't.

He went back down to the basement and smiled at Joly. She had a smudge of dirt smeared across her cheek and all he could think of was making love to her.

He walked up to her and leaned forward, not touching her. He kissed her with little butterfly kisses. Then he ran his tongue around her lips. Her mouth opened and he teased the inside of her lips. She leaned into the kiss and lengthened it, giving him an instant erection. They still didn't touch, except for the lips. He ran his tongue down her chin and she giggled when he tickled her throat. "Love you pretty lady."

Her eyes sparkled. "Love you too, honey... forever."

He grabbed her to him then, and undid her jeans, lowering them down below her hips. He squatted down and ran his tongue around her belly button, and then trailed his tongue down to her triangle of curls. His tongue searched out the nub and then his mouth claimed it. He licked and suckled until her moans had turned into breathless gasps. He stopped and stood up, his legs almost buckling under him, as the circulation returned.

He quickly undid his jeans and slid them down. He lifted Joly and sat her on the edge of the worktable. She leaned back on her hands, allowing him easier access. He entered her with no hesitation and then he picked her up, holding her buttocks in his hands. He squeezed her cheeks as he slowly withdrew and thrust inside her again. In return, she kissed and bit his neck, making the most sensuous sounds as she did. They lost track of time, of where they were, until they climaxed amidst a universe filled with fireworks.

Still breathing hard, Duncan smiled at Joly, "Gods woman... you have an awful effect on me."

"Hmm... I don't know. I kind of like it." She waited for the laugh that never came, settling instead for a long lingering kiss.

They pulled their jeans back on and continued going through the boxes, commenting on different things they discovered.

"You know what? I think we're doing this backwards. I think we should start by emptying the living room." Her mouth dropped.

Duncan watched the startled look cross her face and knew she hadn't planned to say that. "Are you ready to do that?"

"Umm... I ... don't know." She bit her lip, frowning.

"Come with me, Darlin'." He grabbed her hand and led her to the living room.

"Okay pretty lady, one wall at a time." He led her to the back wall. "What do you like about this wall?"

She looked at it, but didn't answer.

"What don't you like about this wall?"

She shook her head and turned, burying her face in the curve of his neck. He felt the sigh, but didn't sense any tears.

He took the sides of her face in his hands and pulled her back so he could see her eyes. He kissed her forehead. "You're not ready. But you know this will never truly be *our* home, don't you? Not until you are ready to make it so." He kissed her forehead again, and walked out the door and back downstairs.

Joly went to the sofa and curled up in the corner of it, wishing more than ever that all her family could be there. She looked around the room at the prints, the plates, the pictures. Her eyes swept over the buffet, the coffee table, the end tables, and the entertainment center. She remembered where all the plants used to be located. She eyed the knick-knacks and ornaments. It was definitely her Mother's room, not hers. Her Mother had loved clutter. Joly's idea of the perfect living room was far different, no less homey, just very different.

She jumped to her feet and ran to the top of the stairs. She yelled at Duncan. He came up the stairs looking concerned. "What's up, Darlin'?"

"It's okay. I just need to do something and I need you here with me." She turned and walked back into the living room.

"I need to talk to Mom and Dad, but I'm afraid to stay away too long. Can you watch me... make sure I'm okay? Keep Randy and Sara away?"

"Is this wise?"

"Yes... yes it is. I've gone before, but only for a hug. I need to talk to them. Can you understand?"

He thought about how close she had been to her parents. He would never stop her from going, but he worried about her crossing into the other dimension. Too many things could happen.

"Let me run up and talk to Sara. You prepare and I'll be right back, okay?" He kissed her and left to go upstairs.

She relaxed and grounded herself. She began a brief meditation. She heard the three of them come down the stairs and heard the outside door open and close.

Duncan walked in and sat beside her. "Sara took Randy out so there will be no disturbance. Where do you want to do this?"

"Right here." She was sitting on the floor, her back against the sofa.

Duncan sat on the coffee table, but was careful not to touch her or disturb her in any way.

"Whenever you're ready, Darlin'."

She smiled softly and closed her eyes.

She took herself back in time, to the way the house had looked ten years before.

She walked up the front steps and opened the door. The smell of freshly baked bread made her mouth water. She walked forward through the entry hall and looked into the living room. Her Father was sitting on the sofa. Her Mother was on the floor, sitting in between his legs. He was brushing her hair.

"Hi Mom, hi Dad."

They both turned with smiles on their faces. Her Mother rose and rushed to Joly, wrapping her arms around her. Her Father was right behind her and he enveloped them both with his arms. The hug lasted only moments, but Joly knew complete peace in that small period of time.

"I hope you'll stay longer this time." Her Father's voice rumbled over

and around her.

"Yes, I will. I need to talk to you."

"Would you like a cup of tea, Joly?"

"No Mom, it's okay. I'm fine."

"You sure? The kettle is hot."

"Yes, I'm fine."

"Well, come and sit down. Tell us something we don't know." Her Dad laughed and led her to the sofa, pushing her down onto it.

"Do you mind if I run upstairs. I just need to see something."

"Go ahead. This will always be your home. You don't need to ask to wander about in it."

Joly ran lightly up the stairs and headed for her bedroom. She peered around the door and was relieved to find that it hadn't changed. She walked to her parents' room and found it also had remained the same. The pinkish brown walls and yellow trim were still there. It hadn't turned green when she repainted. She breathed a sigh of relief and ran back downstairs.

She rejoined her parents in the living room. Her Mother had been busy in her absence. A cup of tea awaited her, along with two slices of freshly baked bread with blackberry jam.

She felt the urgency to return, but she knew Duncan was watching out for her. She willed herself to relax.

"We're living in the house now."

"Yes. We're pleased to see that. I see Duncan still had thoughts about the place around the corner." Her Father took a sip of tea.

"Yes, but someone else seems to have beaten us to it."

Her Mother smiled. "I like what you did with the bedroom. It looks wonderful. Not really my thing, mind you, but it is very much you."

"I was worried. I thought that maybe what I did, would affect you."

"Silly girl. Of course it doesn't affect us. You go right on making changes. Make it yours and Duncan's. We enjoy seeing the changes. Get rid of anything you don't like. Goodness, there's no need to hang on to things that you have no use for. I will always have my knick-knacks and pictures. Your being happy makes us happy and that's all that matters. You know that."

"I guess I was being silly. I just sometimes feel so guilty."

"Nonsense Joly. Never feel guilty. You need to live, to enjoy life… every day of it. You don't have time to allow guilt to come creeping in. When I say you don't have time, I mean nothing ominous. You have a husband and a son to care for. That's a full time job. Don't be a slacker."

She grinned. "Thanks for the pep talk, Dad. I miss them, even though I always hated them."

He laughed, his smile lighting up his whole face. "I know you did. That's why you got so many. They will stand you in good stead over time."

"I know." She finished her tea and wiped the jam off her fingers.

"I have to go. I've been gone too long." She jumped to her feet, suddenly very anxious.

"Yes, you do. One last hug for your old man?" He held his arms out to her and she rushed into them, the tears welling in her eyes.

"Don't cry, Baby Girl. We'll always be here, waiting for you."

"I know." She turned to her Mother and hugged her hard.

"I love you, Mom. I love you too, Dad."

"We love you too, dearling."

Joly opened her eyes, the sense of panic very real. Duncan was nowhere to be seen. She jumped to her feet and rushed through the door into the hall.

"Duncan? *Duncan?*"

She heard the screaming and ran to the door. Duncan was carrying Randy who was covered in blood. Sara was crying and running along behind Duncan. Even with his limp, she was having trouble keeping up.

Joly ran down the steps toward them.

"Get the keys. He needs to go to emergency. Sara, grab a blanket, somethin' to stop the blood from drippin' everywhere." Duncan stood by the truck door, waiting. He held Randy tightly against him, trying to tell him everything would be all right.

Joly ran to Randy. "Where's he hurt?" *Gods!* There was so much blood.

"His leg, I think, and his hand. I told you to get the keys!"

Ignoring Duncan, Joly pulled her T-shirt off and wiped it down Randy's leg. Randy screamed louder. She looked closely and saw the glint of glass. She reached carefully for it and when she felt that she had a good grip, she pulled. The blood gushed out of the hole in the side of his shin. Joly lay her hand on top of the flowing blood and sent her healing energies to it. Within a minute, the blood flow had slowed to a trickle. She kept her hand there and took Randy's hand in her own. There wasn't as much blood, but as soon as she gripped his hand, he screamed. At the same time, she felt the glass cut her finger.

Sara returned with a couple of towels only to find that they were no longer needed.

"Bring him in the house," Joly commanded.

She turned and led the way, stopping at the bathroom for some tweezers.

Duncan followed her, amazed at what he had just witnessed. He still thought stitches would be necessary, but at least she had stopped the bleeding. Duncan sat Randy on the kitchen counter and turned the light on. Joly ran cool water and gently ran it over the injured hand to remove the majority of the blood. The whole palm of his hand glinted in the light.

Sara peered over and threw her hands up to her face. *"Oh my God... oh my God!* I am *so* sorry... so sorry." She burst into tears again.

Joly looked up from what she was doing. "For Pete's sake Sara... get a grip. What would you do if this happened when we weren't around? If you're going to fall apart like this when something happens, maybe you're not suited to be a nanny."

Joly stood holding Randy's hand with her eyes closed. She grounded herself and then she concentrated on sending healing energies to Randy's hand. When she was satisfied that he would feel minimal pain, she picked up the tweezers and started removing the many small shards of glass. Randy winced a few times, but there were no more tears. Pip sat beside him and Joly figured they were communicating. When she was satisfied all the glass had been removed, she washed the hand with soapy water, rinsed it and dried it off. Again, she sent her healing energies to the hand. Some time later, she let the hand go and picked up Randy's leg. It had been a large piece of glass that had entered his leg. She checked carefully for more glass, finding some small shards. When it was cleaned out, she washed and rinsed it and sent more healing energies to it.

She looked around and realized Sara had disappeared. "Honey, can you get me some bandages out of the bathroom, please?"

"You bet." He disappeared around the corner, only to reappear moments later with the bandages.

Joly wrapped the leg and the hand and when she was done, she picked Randy up and gave him a hug. "You were such a good boy. Do you need a drink?"

He shook his head and lay it down on his Mother's shoulder, content to be held.

Duncan put his arms around the two of them. Joly thought about her Father, and how he always did the same thing.

A few minutes later Joly softly said, "I think he's asleep, as is my arm." She grinned at Duncan. He took the sleeping child and carried him upstairs to his bed.

Joly shook her arm to get the circulation moving again, and then she walked upstairs to see Sara. After a lengthy discussion, Joly went to see Duncan, who was up in the magic room.

"Everything okay, Darlin'?"

"Yes, I think so. Sara feels she lost it because it was the first accident with Randy. She said she's usually good around blood and doesn't have a problem with tending to wounds. I think she'll be all right."

"Did she say what happened?"

"Yes. They were walking up the next block on the far side of the street. She said she saw the glass, that she had hold of Randy's hand and that they were moving away from it to go around, when Randy tripped on something… she's not sure what. Because she had a hold of his hand, only the one landed in the glass, along with the one leg. She said it happened so fast, she didn't have time to jerk him up to try and keep him out of it."

He nodded. "The far side of the next block? I think I'll take a broom and dustpan over there and clean it up, before some other kid falls in it."

"Take a garbage bag too honey." She kissed him, and they walked down the stairs together.

At the bottom of the stairs, Duncan paused. "That was some pretty powerful healin' you did. I know you said you healed Maw's legs, but to be honest, I really didn't have any concept of what you were capable of doin'. I won't be makin' that mistake again. I suppose gettin' a medical card is a moot point with you around."

Joly laughed. ""Well, I have one for Randy and me. And yes, I think you need one. What if I wasn't around and you hurt yourself?"

"Point made. I'll get a card." He smiled and headed for the kitchen to get the broom and dustpan.

After Duncan left, Joly went back into the living room, this time with two empty boxes. The things of her Mother's that she didn't care for went into one box and other things that she might or might not use went into the other. By the time Duncan returned, she had two bare walls and several bare table-tops.

Duncan was amazed at the transformation. "What brought this on?"

She smiled at him. "I talked to Mom and Dad. They said to go for it, so I am. What color do you think we should paint the walls?" Her Mother had opted for a basic beige color with chocolate brown trim. The area carpet was a print of browns, beiges, dark greens and some white. Joly had always hated it. *They're good honest earth colors. Why do you dislike it so?* Boring was the only thing that Joly could ever think of for a response.

"Do we have any paint chips?"

"Yeah. In the basement, over on Da... the workbench. They're sitting in a jar."

He walked downstairs and picked up the chips. While he was down there, he wondered about changing the shop around. Colin had everything laid out the way he had wanted it, but Duncan knew he would prefer things differently. He went back upstairs to find Joly still busy removing things.

"Hey, Darlin', do you mind if I change the shop around?"

Joly put down the picture she was looking at. "Honey, Mom and Dad said we are to make the house ours, that they are enjoying seeing the changes we make. So go ahead... do your thing... *darlin'*. She laughed and gave him a peck on his nose.

That evening, after Randy was tucked in their bed and they were back downstairs, Joly working her healing magic on his leg, Duncan surprised her with a request.

"Hey, Darlin', I'd really like to go firewalkin'. I realize the island's out because of the time of year, but would there be somewhere else we could go?"

"Gee, I'm not sure honey. I can't think of anywhere off hand, but maybe call Kyle Devon in the morning. His group is still active and he might know someone or maybe know of a place we can go."

"Good ol' Kyle Devon. I'm surprised he's still practicin'. Have you seen him lately?"

"Just before we went to Greece. Oh, *damn!* I need to change my will again. I had it changed because of Randy, but now you would become his guardian. You need to make a will too, just in case."

"Okay, I'll set up an appointment and we can ask about the firewalkin' at the same time."

"Something else I need to do is a change of names for Randy and me. Mine will be easy enough. I am legally McEwan, but Kyle will have to get Randy's changed. I wanted to make his last name McEwan, but because the only I.D. I had on me in India was James; Kyle said to do Randy's in James too."

"Well, we can take care of that at the same time."

Joly was the one that phoned the lawyer the next morning. She thought it would be too much a shock for Kyle if Duncan called him. As it was, he was tied up with a client, so Joly made an appointment to see him two days later.

They poured over the color chips and decided that whatever color the living room was painted; they wanted to leave the hardwood floor exposed. A small rug in front of the sofa was all they wanted on the floor.

"Do you think we should buy a new sofa? That one of Mom's is kind of gaudy, and if we're painting, won't it look out of place?"

Duncan looked her. She didn't seem to be having any trouble now, getting rid of her parents' presence in the house. He was glad she had gone and talked to them. He just hoped she wouldn't ask to go too often.

"You know… a sectional would look good along those two walls. Maybe get a square coffee table and matchin' end tables."

She smiled. "Yes. I like that idea. You know… maybe a display cabinet or something on the far wall. I'd like to keep some of Mom's little knick-knacks, but I don't want them covering the tops of everything."

"That works for me. When we go and see Kyle, we can go on a shopping expedition too."

"Do you think we should pick the paint to match the sectional, or find a sectional to match our paint?"

They narrowed the color selection down and were close to choosing the final colors. "It's not really going to matter that much. We basically know what we want, so we might as well decide now. Then we can get the paint and have the room painted before the furniture arrives. Hey… do you have any paint left over from our bedroom?"

"Which color, the light or the dark?"

"Either. I like both. I was thinkin' for the trim and maybe this, for the walls." He picked up a paint chip and handed it to Joly. It was a salmon color.

She looked around the room, visualizing it in the new colors. "Too much. Maybe we could do one wall in the cyan too."

Within minutes, they were heading out the door to buy the paint. When they returned home, they washed the walls, removing the furniture as they went around the room. Sara joined them in scrubbing and Randy watched in amazement at what was happening.

By the end of the next day, the painting was done. Three walls were painted in the salmon, with the fourth wall done in the light cyan. All the trim around the windows and door was done in the dark cyan. The hardwood floor had been scrubbed, waxed and polished to a brilliant shine.

They stood in the empty room looking at the results of their work. Randy clapped his hands in delight, making Joly and Sara laugh.

Duncan grinned. "Well, if it meets the approval of the youngest one here, it must be good."

After two nights of Randy sleeping with them, Duncan decided that stronger measures were called for. After his bath, Randy ran into the master bedroom and jumped on the bed waiting for his story. When Duncan never showed up or answered his calls, he climbed down again to go and find him.

"Daddy? Daddy?" He went down the hallway toward the bathroom. As he walked by his bedroom, he saw Duncan lying on the small bed. He giggled and ran in the room.

"Come Daddy, come." Randy tugged on Duncan's hand.

"No Randy, Daddy's going to sleep here tonight."

Randy frowned. "No Daddy, Randy bed."

Duncan propped himself up on his elbow. "Randy doesn't sleep in his bed. Randy sleeps in Mommy and Daddy's bed, so Daddy's going to sleep in Randy's bed."

"*No!* Randy bed. You go Daddy bed." He tugged on Duncan's arm.

"No Randy. You go to Daddy's bed. Daddy sleep here." He lay down again, trying desperately not to smile.

"*No!* Randy bed." He climbed over Duncan and sat against the wall. He put his feet in the middle of Duncan's back and pushed.

"*Go.* Randy bed. Randy sleep." He began to kick Duncan's back and started to cry.

Duncan sat up and gathered Randy into his arms. "Hey buddy… shh. It's okay." He cuddled Randy until the tears stopped.

"Okay… you're going to sleep in your bed, right?"

Randy sniffled and nodded his head.

"And you're going to stay in your bed all night, right?"

Again the head nodded.

"Okay, let me go and get your book." He walked to his room and picked the book up from the side table.

At the bottom of the stairs Joly smiled. She had heard the commotion and gone to see what was happening. From the bottom of the stairs she heard what Duncan was doing, so she stood and listened. A few minutes later she went up to say goodnight and pretended not to see Randy in his room as she walked past.

"Mommy! Here."

She turned and peeked in the door. "What are you doing in here?"

"Randy sleep Randy bed, 'kay?" He grinned at her and her heart melted once again.

"What a big boy you're getting to be, Sweetie. Wow! That's great." She leaned over to hug and kiss him.

Duncan watched the two most important people in his life and felt blessed. He knew how lucky he was. When Joly stood, she walked over and rested her hand on his shoulder while he finished the story. Duncan stood and snugged the covers around the sleeping child and together they left his room hand in hand.

They went to bed early that night, but when morning arrived, it found two extremely tired people stumbling to their feet to greet the day.

Duncan looked at Joly, sitting across the table from him as they ate breakfast. "You're positively glowin', Darlin'. I wonder why." He smiled.

Joly ducked her head in embarrassment. "Sure you do."

She could feel herself blushing all the way to her toes. She was sore and stiff and she was not looking forward to the drive into Surrey to see Kyle Devon.

They left right after she did a healing on Randy's leg and hand. The many small cuts on his hand were almost healed and the leg injury had a good clean scab on it. Joly thought that in another two days the scab should fall off.

Duncan was amazed at the changes everywhere he looked. Even Mission had grown, with a new shopping center over in what he had known as the industrial area.

They went to the lawyer's office first.

When Kyle stepped out of his office to escort Joly in, he was surprised to see her with a young white haired man, but he didn't say anything. He had thought that she was completely devoted to her dead husband's memory. Maybe he was wrong.

"Joly, come in please. I'm surprised to see you here, though. I thought you and Morag would be off in Quebec checking out the development there."

"Morag's in Scotland. What development?"

"You haven't heard? You should turn the news on occasionally. How did you make out in Greece?"

"It went well. We were pleased with the outcome and we saw some wonderful sights. What development?"

"There's some pretty weird stuff going on not far from Quebec City. I think the area is called Charlevoix. It's taking place up in the hills there."

When they were seated in the office, Kyle looked at the young man, but it was Joly who spoke first. "Kyle, you obviously don't recognize Duncan."

"Duncan?" Kyle leapt up from his chair and leaned over the desk. "What the Sam Hill have you done, Joly? Tell me you didn't resurrect him, please tell me you didn't."

Duncan grinned. "No, not in the sense you're referrin' to. I had lost my memory, but I was always very much alive."

Kyle expelled a large breath. "Oh, thank the Gods! You had me worried."

Joly was angry. "I'm surprised you would think I would do such a thing, Kyle. When have I *ever* given you any reason to think I would try to resurrect the dead? I have *never* led you to believe that of me!"

Kyle moved around the desk and squatted down in front of her. He took Joly's hand in his and looked her in the eyes. "No… no, you haven't, and I apologize for jumping to the wrong conclusion. You might have given me some warning though."

He turned to Duncan, rising and holding out his hand as he did. "Welcome back, Duncan. I would love to hear your story sometime. Maybe I can take the two of you out to dinner one evening."

"That would be nice, Kyle. Thank you. It's a pretty borin' story though. I've been holed up in a small English village, livin' with a German couple."

"So I can guess what brings you here. You need to update your wills. How did you feel when you found out you were a Father?"

"Great, once I discovered he was adopted."

Kyle laughed and nodded his head. He looked at Joly. "I suppose you'll want to change the name on Randy's birth certificate." He looked back at Duncan. "She was adamant that Randy's name was to be McEwan, but it couldn't be done while she was in India."

"So I heard, and yes… we do want his name changed. Is there goin' to be a problem with Joly changin' her name after all these years?"

"I shouldn't think so. There was a time when she may have had some problems, but I can do it all from here if you like. Save you running around, my dear."

"Thank you, I'd appreciate that."

"We have another request, Kyle. I would really like to go for a firewalk. Kinda get back into the swing of things. I know it's the wrong time of year for it, but we thought you might know someone."

Kyle looked long at Duncan. He obviously hadn't known he was a witch when he'd had no memory. These two people had a challenge in front of them. He knew they had always been very close, and he hoped they were up to the task.

"I think I can help you. One of our group has some acreage out in the valley. I'm sure he wouldn't mind you setting up out there. Let me give him a call and I'll see what I can arrange."

"Thank you."

"By the way Joly, how's young Sara making out?"

"She's been doing really well. We had a bit of a test two days ago, but I think it will be okay. Thanks for asking. She's become an integral part of the family."

The small talk continued for several minutes, while Kyle made notes on the things he needed to do. Finally he stood up. "I hate to rush you out the door, but I have another appointment. I really wish you had told me what was up. I would have booked you in for a longer time."

"It's okay Kyle. We need to get going anyhow. We're redoing Mom and Dad's house... making it ours, you know? We're going shopping for living room furniture today."

"Wonderful! Well, you two have fun and... Duncan... I'm really pleased to see you. This was one lonely lady while you were gone."

"Thanks." He put his arm possessively around his wife. "Yeah... she seems kinda happy to have me back." He grinned.

They said their goodbye's, with Kyle reminding Joly to check out what was happening in Quebec.

Morag opted to catch a small plane from Edinburgh to London. She would have preferred the bus, but she was still pretty sore. The train ride to Edinburgh had been rough on her.

Once she was back in London, she got a small room at the hotel where they usually stayed. She booked the room for three days, having decided she needed more healing time. She was feeling better, but she didn't want to arrive back in Canada looking like a lobster.

Duncan and Joly spent most of the day wandering through furniture stores. By the time they were done it was supper time. Joly called Sara and told her they would be eating out and would return later that evening. They went to a restaurant that they had loved to go to before. They talked about their purchases and other changes that they wanted to make to the house.

"Honey, I sort of got the impression that you weren't really happy with the thought of living in Mom and Dad's house forever."

Duncan took her hand and kissed it. "Darlin'... I would live in a dog-house, if that was where you wanted to live. I don't have a problem with it at all, just as long as we keep makin' it ours."

"You seemed disappointed though, after we went and looked at the farm-house."

"You have to remember Joly; you've had ten years to get the dream out of your head. I've had less than a week. I'm okay with it. There are a lot of things I'm going to have to adjust to. That was just one of many." He kissed her hand again.

"Yes, you're right. I'm sorry honey. It's easy to forget that you're brand new at being you. I love you, Duncan."

"And I love you pretty lady."

They arrived home just in time to read Randy his story and say goodnight to him.

Sara asked about their day and they told her about their purchases. The next day should see several trucks dropping various items off.

Exhausted from the busy day and lack of sleep, it wasn't long before they were in bed fast asleep, the two bodies so tightly entwined, that at a glance there appeared to be only one.

The following day was a busy one, as truck after truck arrived with different pieces of furniture. Joly left Duncan in charge of supervising the unloading of each one and making sure that each piece had arrived in the same shape as it was purchased. She was still concerned he might not be feeling too good about living in her parents' home and she was hoping that if he put the living room together, he might feel more like it was their own place. While he was busy doing that, Joly investigated what was happening in Quebec.

She didn't like what she found.

She went up to the magic room and began searching through the Book of Shadows for any mention of Manifest Thought Forms. It was almost an hour later when she found her Mother's notes. The page actually had grabbed her attention before she realized it was the one she was looking for. The attention getter was at the bottom of the page. Instead of her normal wild writing, her Mother had printed in large capital letters that were underlined: <u>AVOID WHEN POSSIBLE – THEY CAN CAUSE TEMPORARY PARALYSIS AND WILL ATTACK WHEN THREATENED</u>

Joly read her Mother's notes and sat back to digest what she had read. She wondered briefly if she should contact Morag, but decided against it. She needed to start making her own decisions. Morag wouldn't always be there for her. She shook the depressing thought away.

She had an idea but needed more information. She went back to the book looking for anything else she might be able to use. She was so focused on what she was doing she never heard Duncan.

He stood in the doorway watching her. He would never get tired of looking at her. *Damn!* He loved her *so* much. Ten years gone... never to be recovered. He'd missed seeing her turn into a woman... he'd missed so many things.

She was suddenly aware that Duncan was near. She was frowning when she looked up from the book, but smiled when she saw him. "Hi honey, come here and look at this."

He walked over and put his hands on her shoulders. He read the page she had open. She turned to another page that she had a pen stuck in. He read the large print at the bottom first, and then he read the rest of the page. *Nasty!*

<u>Manifest Thought Forms</u> - An electromagnetic energy field created by someone who projects their anger and negative emotions into a single area of their mind. As the negativity grows, it becomes an entity that can be controlled. When it gets large enough, it starts to feed off of the negative emo-

tions and fear of others and it eventually tries to produce more negativity with acts of aggression.

"This is what we're dealin' with in Quebec?"

"That's what they say. I've looked for more information, but Mom doesn't seem to have anything else on them."

"Yeah... I can see why. What do you think, Darlin'? Can we vanquish this enemy?" He grinned at Joly to cover up the doubts that had crept into his mind. He had hoped to get back into the swing of things slowly, not be thrown to the lions on his first time out.

"I think so. I think rather than face them head on; we should try to find out if they're all coming from one place. It would be easier to annihilate the cause, than wipe out how ever many of them that there are."

"Not going to happen, pretty lady. Didn't you read this?" He pointed out a passage to her.

'The Manifest Thought Form can become independent and it will take command of its own actions. The programmer will no longer have the power to control it.'

"You're saying that you think these things are that far advanced?"

He rubbed her shoulders absentmindedly as he thought. "It sounds like it, don't you think?"

"Yes, I suppose you're right." She wasn't doing too well on her own after all. Maybe she really did need Morag in on this. She thought it was strange that Duncan would pick up on that, after being away for so long, but perhaps that was why he did notice it. He had a fresh view on things. Between the two of them, she decided they would make out all right.

"So? Tell me your thoughts, my wise lady."

She stood and put her arms around Duncan's waist, leaning her head on his chest. She listened to the beating of his heart and discovered her thoughts had cleared. Love was a wonderful thing!

"First... they feed on negative energy, so we must approach them with absolutely none. Positive thoughts only. Do you think we can do that?"

"Darlin'... we can do anything at all, when we're together. Yes, we can do that." He hoped he sounded more positive than he felt.

"Second... they have an electromagnetic energy field, not just the manifestation that we will or will not see. So we will have to deal with the whole, not just the part."

"Understood, Darlin'."

"Third..." she paused.

"Third?"

She looked him in the eyes. "No wands."

"*Say what, Darlin'*, you can't be serious. That's my forte." Now he was concerned. *I'm damn good with my wand. What the hell am I going to work with, if not that?*

"They will feel threatened if they see anything in our hands. We don't want them attacking us."

"Tell me pretty lady, how are we supposed to fight them?"

"Do you trust me?" She looked intently at him.

"With my life, Darlin', but that doesn't answer my question."

"We're not going to fight them. I… we… are going to heal them."

Duncan looked at her as if she had lost her mind. "Joly McEwan, tell me I didn't hear that. Tell me you're jokin'; tell me anythin' at all. Just please tell me you're not serious."

"I am serious. Look at what Mom wrote… here." She pointed to a short passage above the large printing.

He read aloud, "Remote healing is the only safe way to deal with these entities."

She turned to another page. "Here." She pointed to another passage.

"Everything you can see and think of was created by a thought form and everything you can see and think of can be changed by a thought form."

She looked at Duncan. "So if you put the two concepts together, it should work, right?"

He shook his head. "I don't know. I think we need to delve a little deeper here, and see what we come up with."

"Oh, I agree. I haven't got the details worked out. I was just researching when you came in."

"Oh yeah. Hey, come with me pretty lady, I've got something to show you." He took her by the hand and led her down the stairs to the living room. Her soft "Ohhh," told him all he needed to know.

She was speechless. The living room looked like it belonged on the pages of one of those fancy magazines. Duncan had even hung the new pictures. The teal blue/green sectional was against the two walls to the right of the doorway, with the square oak coffee table in front of it. Square oak end tables sat at each end, with funky contemporary lamps with a clear glass outer shell shaped like a giant brandy glass vase that rested on a nickel colored base. Inside the clear glass was a nickel post on which rested a bullet shaped glass shade of different shades of green. A matching torchiere floor lamp was across the room. The small area carpet in various shades of salmon and green fit perfectly underneath the coffee table. A new oak sideboard had been placed in front of the bay window and a glass-fronted cabinet was placed against the far wall, to the right of the small window, ready for some of her Mother's things. To the left of the window, was a new entertainment center, also in oak. The entertainment center had been a spur of the moment purchase, as neither of them were big fans of television, but it had been a perfect match to the display cabinet. Two large Andre Orpinas prints were above the sectional and three smaller prints were hung on the adjacent walls.

"Oh honey… it looks awesome! I love it!" She threw her arms around Duncan and gave him a deep passionate kiss, which he returned wholeheartedly.

When he could breathe again, he grinned at her. "Yeah... I like it too."

Joly phoned and made reservations on a flight to Montreal for two days hence. Sara and Randy would stay behind, as would the cats. She wasn't taking a chance on the entities grabbing one of the felines.

The following day, after registering Randy for kindergarten, they worked out their plan for getting rid of the manifest thought forms. Duncan still wasn't happy with it and told Joly so.

"It'll be fine, honey. You'll see."

"Maybe we should get a hold of Maw and ask her."

"You don't trust me." She could feel the tears coming and left the room, walking up to the magic room and touching different things of her parents. She was hurting. It was hard getting to know Duncan all over again. He was so much more serious; not like he had been. Before, he wouldn't have given two hoots. He would have been the first one on the plane, laughing as he went aboard. That was hard to get used to, too. He never laughed, not as much as a chuckle, ever.

Duncan climbed the stairs slowly. She didn't understand. He had just gotten her back. He had just gotten his memory back. He wasn't ready to take a chance and lose her again. *Damn!* Sometimes love hurt so much.

He stood in the doorway and watched as she held a statue of Isis to her breast. It had been her Mother's. He could see the tears on her cheeks and knew she was hurting too. He stepped into the room.

"Darlin'... I told you before and I'll say it again. I trust you with my life. I've had you back a week. I'm having trouble with the time frame, not with you. I'm sorry." He bowed his head and stared at his shoes. He'd screwed up bad. He could feel the hurt emanating from her. She was really torn up.

Joly said nothing, turning and placing Isis back on the desk.

She finally looked at him. "Before we go, I need to talk to you." She sat down.

"Darlin'... you sound way too serious. What's up?"

"Come and sit down. It is serious, but I'm hoping it's not a problem."

Duncan joined her at the desk, reaching across to take her hand in his. "Darlin', this is us. We don't have problems. *Yeah, right!* "What's up?"

"I just need to be sure of something." Joly looked in his eyes and saw the love and the sorrow. She gave him a small smile and looked down at their entwined hands. She knew she was being overly sensitive. She wondered how to begin.

"Honey, in the past year, I've discovered I have some pretty incredible powers. Powers I wish I'd known about when I was eighteen." She drew in a shuddering breath.

"Darlin', you know we can't undo what's been done. We can only try to ensure that nothin' like that ever happens again." He squeezed her hand.

"I know. But my concern is..." She hesitated.

Duncan raised an eyebrow. "You're having trouble with this, honey. That's not like you. Come on now. Spit it out." He stood up and pulled her to her feet. He wrapped his arms around her, gently rubbing her back with one hand.

"Tell me."

She buried her face in his shirt and hugged him tightly. "Honey, I need to know that you won't ever try to throw me out of another circle. That you understand no matter what happens... I need to be able to deal with it myself, my way." She didn't mention that he had compromised the circle when he'd thrown her out of it.

She looked up at his face then, afraid of what she might see. She already knew that if he couldn't promise to do this, she would have to go alone and she didn't want to do that.

He continued rubbing her back, and watched her eyes. He could see the concern, the fear that he might not agree with her. He would do anything, absolutely anything, to keep her safe. He knew she would go without him. He understood she would have to, and he liked that option even less than the one she had just presented to him. He leaned forward and kissed her forehead.

"Darlin', I would fight the whole world single-handedly, to keep you safe. You know that. I also know I will not be left behind, to sit here wondering what the hell you're up to, what you're facing." He kissed her forehead again. "You have my word pretty lady, whatever plan we implement, whatever happens, we're in it together... to the end."

She smiled then and as he watched her face light up, he wondered if he would be able to keep his word.

"Your apology will be accepted, only if you accept mine. I'm being too sensitive. I know this. If you want to call your Mom, go ahead. I don't have a problem with it. I just thought that she's probably busy and really doesn't need us bugging her."

"You're right. She doesn't... and we can do this on our own. You have been working with her for the past year. I'm sure you know what you're doing. I'm just being a worrywart." He kissed her forehead one more time.

Joly laughed. "I haven't heard that expression for..." She realized the last time she had heard it was the night that everything went wrong. "... A long time," she finished lamely, knowing that he would be remembering too.

They had been setting up at the site. Broderick was fussing over some minor thing. Bettina had given him a playful punch on the arm. "Oh Broderick... don't be such a worrywart." It was the last words that she had heard Bettina say, other than the chanting inside of the circle.

"Yeah..., sorry, I didn't mean to ..."

"I know." She kissed him then, long and hard. They ended up staying in the magic room for quite some time.

They spent the evening with Randy and went to bed early. They had to leave for the airport at eight the following morning.

They said their goodbye's to Sara and after numerous hugs and kisses from Randy, along with a few tears; they managed to get into the truck and head for the airport. They were flying to Montreal and from there; they would rent a car to drive to the small town of Petite Riviere St. Francois.

Duncan was fine right up to the time he boarded the plane. Then he slowly lost control. He was squeezing Joly's hand so tightly, she lost all feeling in it. All he could think about was that after ten years of being away, he had been home only seven days and he was leaving again. He knew the fear was irrational, but he couldn't control it.

Joly sent all her calming energies to him, but it was still a long time before he finally grew quiet. She wondered if she should have left him at home and knew that wouldn't have worked any better. At least when he was with her, she could help him control his fears.

Once he was off the plane again, he was fine. He knew he was still in Canada. He knew he still had his memory and he knew his beloved wife was with him. He wondered about the fear and hoped it wouldn't continue. They usually did a fair amount of traveling. He didn't need to be acting like an idiot every time they went somewhere.

Morag laid her head against the back of the lawn chair. Damn, she was glad to be home again. She had gone over to Joly's and found out from Sara that their two flights had crossed paths in the sky. She had brought Randy a small toy and visited for a short time.

She had fed the birds and was enjoying relaxing and listening to them. She thought about getting her crystal out to see how Joly and Duncan were doing, but decided to wait until the following day.

Now the darkness was only an armful, but hard as steel and cold as ice – Rauna could feel the fury and hate flowing from the globe, blacker than black. Her hands couldn't feel anything anymore, they were frozen, but she continued. The trace was almost over swept and she could see where to put the thing. Everything was happening in slow motion, so slowly that the movement was hard to notice, but still she moved forward. Millimeter after millimeter she forced the thing to become more and more compact, smaller and smaller, to fit in the hole the size of a pinhead.

The last meter took an eternity to pass over. The energy collected to the corn of darkness made her hands shake. She was tired, so tired, but she knew that if she let go now, she would never be able to do this again. She forced the speck into the hole and the speck imploded. It collapsed through itself and turned over and exploded in the other side of the hole. The implosion had closed the hole, but the impact was still strong enough to knock Rauna down.

Joly rented a car and they headed for Quebec City, three hours away. They spent the night there and early the next morning they were on their way to the village. They reached Petite Riviere St. Francois shortly after nine in the morning. The mist lay thick in the valley. The day was a gloomy one and the thunderclouds hung heavy overhead.

The area was beautiful with the beginnings of autumn in the air and on the trees. The leaves had started putting on their fall coats of golds, reds and oranges. They were in a World Biosphere Reserve, one of twelve in Canada. The Charlevoix area owed its incredible geography to the fall of a fifteen billion ton meteorite, three hundred fifty million years before. The high mountains with valleys slicing through them sat along the edge of the St. Laurent River. Le Massif was a ski area with the highest vertical drop east of the Rockies.

They had reserved a room at a small Bed and Breakfast. After checking in, they sat in their room having a cup of tea while discussing last minute details. They knew they would not be able to have a trial run through the area. It was too dangerous. One small negative thought and they could be finished before they even got started. They needed to begin the fire spell at noon.

Joly knew she was more than capable of clearing her mind of negativity, but she was concerned about Duncan. He was already having doubts about what they were doing. She was going to have to fix that before they did anything else. She knew she could make him stay in the town while she went to the site, but that would solve nothing. He needed to see her in action to understand that she was fully capable of doing what she said.

They began a meditation, one they had used many years before. When Duncan had calmed and completely relaxed, Joly took his head in her hands. She did a small mind meld, just enough to connect the two of them, so she could send her positive, calming energies to him.

They packed the few things that they would need and headed to Charlevoix Field, where the entities were located. Why the Manifest Thought Forms had decided to congregate there, they would probably never know. Perhaps the person or persons who had given them life, lived in the area, although Joly thought it was doubtful. It took incredibly evil people to conjure up these entities and the population in this area was too small to hide anyone like that for long. Maybe they lived in Quebec City. It wasn't too far away.

With her mind still connected to Duncan, they got out of the car. She grabbed the bag and took his hand in hers. They slowly walked up to the admittance gate, which had a closed sign on it. They went through and followed the pathway. The path branched out in several places, but she had looked at a map, and knew where she wanted to go. There were two waterfalls on the far side and she wanted to be within hearing distance of them. Not close enough so they would interfere, but close enough that the sound of the falling water would be a soothing background melody.

As they walked, she was conscious of the evil around them. She saw movement several times out of the corner of her eye, and she thought about the Shadow Beings. These were not them, and the malevolence that was being thrown at the two of them was very powerful. The Manifest Thought Forms were trying to get them to think negative thoughts in order to feed and gain strength. Joly smiled and gripped Duncan's hand tighter. She glanced at him and he calmly smiled back. As they walked, the forms grew bolder and darted back and forth, trying to frighten them. Joly and Duncan continued to smile, made small talk and ignored them. One Form came in low and reared up in front of them, startling them both. Joly laughed and squeezed Duncan's hand. He smiled. He was doing okay.

When they reached the area she had placed in her mind, she put the bag on the ground. She took Duncan's other hand in hers and they stood looking into each other's eyes. She sent her energies to him, willing him to be strong and positive. His mind was completely open to her and he was calm. He smiled at her and she squeezed his hands. He returned the squeeze and leaned forward to give her a light kiss on her lips. She let go of his hands, totally attuned to his mind as she went to the bag and began her preparations.

She was humming as she drew her circle.

As Duncan placed the white candles at the four quarters, the Manifest Thought Forms began to get extremely agitated. They started to make audible sounds that varied from low growls to high-pitched squeals that were hard on the ears. They began floating in, almost attacking the two humans but stopping just short of touching them. The humans had done nothing to challenge them and had showed no animosity to them. They could not touch them; only try to scare them into thinking negative thoughts or doing something that would provoke them.

Joly sensed Duncan's mind falter and turned to grab his hands. She looked into his eyes and sent him her strength. A Manifest Thought Form seemed to know something had almost happened and it swirled around them, the dark ugly mass sending vibrations of impending doom and horror to the two of them. They ignored it, maintaining their positive thought patterns.

Duncan regained his meditative state and squeezed Joly's hands to let her know that he was fine. They continued with their preparations, setting up a small altar and then undressing. They washed each other with the oils and bottled water. As they finished, a bolt of lightening shot across the dark sky. A loud clap of thunder followed. The skies opened up and the rain came down.

Joly drew in a spiral pentagram in the circle. It resembled a flower with five petals. In each of the five small petals that circled the center of the large pentagram, she placed a white candle. They had chosen the spiral pentagram as it did not work the same as the pointed one. The pointed pentagram kept things out. The spiral pentagram drew things in. Duncan lit the candles. They'd had trouble with the opening prayer. They needed to make their wishes known to the Gods and Goddesses, but they couldn't say anything against the Manifest Thought Forms. They stood in the middle of the circle and raised their arms.

The Manifest Thought Forms were gathering around them. They were angry and were darting about trying to upset the two people who didn't seem to have any negative thoughts to feed from. They whirled around the circle, some trying to put out the candles, others trying to stir up the soil to erase the circle. The ground had become too wet and they were unsuccessful. The candle flame swirled around from the breezes, but remained lit. They grew angrier and their shapes changed from gray to black, from blob like figures to horrid fiendish shapes.

The rain was falling harder and the lightning continued to light up the sky. The thunder rumbled and growled.

"We call upon you Gods and Goddesses of old,
We call upon you Gods and Goddesses of new.
We call upon the Four Quarters
To aid us on this day."

Joly went to the altar and lit the incense. She walked around the circle, the small wisps of smoke disappearing in the wet air. She walked back to the middle and raised the bowl.

"Firedrakes and salamanders
Send us your healing light
With cleansing fire and dragon's blood
Help us to set things right."

She went and sat the bowl on the altar and returned to the center of the circle, taking Duncan's hand in hers. They raised their hands to the sky.

"Allow your power to move within our hands.
Lord of the sun, feel our love.
In our circle of light
Send us your fire from high above."

Joly released Duncan's hand and assumed the Goddess position to ground herself. She had done so earlier, before connecting to Duncan, but she knew reinforcement wouldn't hurt. Then she visualized the white healing light entering her body and she felt it filling her. When her fingers began to tingle with the healing power, she turned and held her arms out to Duncan.

He reached out and took her hands. He had felt the power before, but never this strongly. He smiled at his wife. She smiled back and then they turned with their backs to one another. They linked their arms at the elbows and stood with their palms open.

Joly opened her mind, slowly at first. She had never done this before, even though she knew she could. Her powers were still too new and she wasn't in any great hurry to try them all at once. Also, she knew she had to be careful because of Duncan. They were still joined in their minds and her power as a *Sister of the Triple Moon* was so much greater than his. She knew he could hold her power and use it with her, as long as she didn't overwhelm him with too much all at once.

Duncan could feel the healing energies entering him and was amazed at the strength of it. He realized that his wife really did have super powers and he knew he had no need of being afraid for her. He understood finally, that she could indeed look after herself.

As her mind opened and the healing energies filled the two of them, they sent the power out from them and toward the Manifest Thought Forms. Joly and Duncan were bathed in a bright glowing white light.

It was raining harder, and the thunder crashed in waves as the lightning forked around them.

The Manifest Thought Forms were caught by the healing energies. They tried to flee, but they had waited too long. Thin, ribbon like tentacles extended out from the white light, attaching to each nightmarish shape that surrounded them. The ribbons wove their way through the nearest ones and attached to the ones farthest away. The grotesque figures fought against the ribbons, trying to escape. Then they tried to attack Joly and Duncan, but could not. The ribbons would not bend back toward the two that had sent them out.

Joly continued to open her mind.

Duncan wondered briefly how much more power there could be. He had never felt anything like it. He felt as if he were lighter than air and wondered why he wasn't floating. He felt the muscles in his leg moving, separating and rearranging themselves. He knew without a doubt that he would leave this place walking normally. He had seen the white light before, surrounding others, and now he knew what it felt like. He felt a sense of awe that he could be part of this.

The Manifest Thought Forms continued their struggle against the pure beings in front of them. The smaller ones had already succumbed to the healing energies. The pure negative emotion that had brought them into existence was slowly erased from them. As the pure healing energy consumed them, their shapes turned from black to gray to white and then they slowly vaporized until there was nothing left.

The white light continued to grow until Joly and Duncan could no longer be seen. The Manifest Thought Forms slowly disappeared, until all that was left was the glowing white light.

Morag picked up the crystal and thought about her son and daughter-in-law. The crystal misted and cleared. She saw the white light and watched as it grew. From the size of it, she knew both were inside of it. She shook her head as she smiled. She had wondered if Joly would figure out that she could empower Duncan with her powers, as long as they were connected. She was pleased with what she saw. Morag put the crystal down.

She called Stephen's office and left a message for him to phone her. She knew he would immediately panic, as she never called him, but with the way he had been acting the past while, she decided the moment of extra stress wouldn't hurt him. She hoped it might shake him out of whatever the blue blazes was bothering him.

The thunderclouds rolled in waves toward the hill where the pure energy was centered. The lightning followed.

The white light slowly dissipated to reveal the two nude figures standing there. Joly unlocked her arms from Duncan's and turned to face him. She wrapped her arms around him and hugged him. He was still, and with concern, she looked up to see a small smile on his face. Slowly, almost hesitantly, he moved his arms and he embraced her, their lips locking together in a deep kiss.

The thunder crashed directly above them, startling them out of their embrace. They looked up and as they did, five bolts of lightning zigzagged toward them. They watched in awe as the five candles surrounding them were neatly snuffed out.

Another loud clap of thunder rolled over them and they looked skyward once again. A dozen lightning bolts zigzagged toward one another and as they collided, the sky lit up in an unearthly glow. The thunder was so loud their ears were ringing. From the center of the maelstrom appeared glowing orbs of light that hurtled toward the earth. As they came closer, the ball lightning slowed and descended to circle around them, almost seeming to dance as they undulated up and down, in and out.

What happened next happened so fast that Joly didn't have time to scream, she didn't even have time to suck in her breath.

One of the lightning balls separated from the others, and with the speed of light, it headed for Duncan, hitting him squarely in the chest. He was knocked backwards ten feet and landed on his backside, the glowing orb disappearing inside of him.

Veronika found the woman lying face down in her back yard. She checked her carefully, didn't see any back or head injury, so she turned her on her side, and saw her frost burnt hands. The woman was otherwise unharmed and breathing.

Veronika knew she was a *Sister of the Triple Moon* because of the feeling of oneness, but she didn't understand what had happened. What would cause an unknown Sister to be unconscious with such horrible wounds to her hands in her backyard, and why hadn't she noticed anything? She would have to check her wards again.

She wasn't sure what to do, so she sent out a call to Sergei and Polina.

She couldn't move the woman on her own, so she got a blanket and covered her. Then she filled a basin with warm water and soaked the frozen hands. When they felt warm to the touch, she carefully broke open the blisters and let them drain. She soaked the hands again, and then dried them and wrapped them loosely in white cotton. She tucked them under the blanket, all the while talking softly to the woman.

While she waited for the grandchildren, she realized the air felt different. She opened her senses and discovered the heaviness was gone. There was no more swirling darkness. She looked at the woman and nodded. Somehow, the woman was responsible for the clean air.

As she looked around she noticed a strange bird in the apple tree. The large black and white crow appeared to be watching her.

"*Vorona*, is this your *prijate*'? If it is so, you don't worry. I will *popechenie* for like she is my own. *Da*, I will."

She closed her eyes and quietly prayed to the Goddess of healing.

Joly ran to him, her mind blank. She could not fathom Duncan being taken away from her again and her emotions shut themselves down. Duncan was still in a sitting position and as she reached him, she grabbed his shoulders, unable to speak.

He looked up at her, smiled a little cockeyed smile and then he laughed. The laugh that she hadn't heard for ten years rolled over her and around her and as her heart began to beat once again, she chuckled and then she too, began to laugh. He pulled her down beside him on the wet ground. They sat in the pouring rain with their arms around each other, and they laughed and they laughed.

Joly sensed when Duncan's laughter changed and she knew he was crying as he laughed. She reached up and held his head as she sent her calming energies to him. Slowly, the laughter died and he looked at her, the tears indistinguishable from the raindrops.

"You okay honey?"

He nodded and looked around. "You know Darlin'... I think I'd like to see this place when my bare ass isn't covered in mud." He looked back at her and laughed. He jumped to his feet and pulled Joly up. They walked back to the circle.

She knew she had to close it and she thought about the riddle. *Widdershins and fire releases the void...*

Joly led Duncan to the center, knowing that he had to be in it. She then walked counterclockwise around it thanking the quarters. On her second time around, she thanked the Gods and Goddesses for their help. On her third pass, she closed the circle.

"Circle of power, we release you.
All that entered herein
May you depart in peace.
The circle remains open, but unbroken."

She returned to the center and together they grounded themselves and sent the excess energy that they had raised, back into Mother Earth. They dismantled the altar and dressed, most of the mud having been washed off by the rain.

When Joly would have taken Duncan's hand, he laughed and took off, skipping, jumping, hopping and running. His leg was back to normal. She smiled as she walked. Her beloved was whole again.

That night after a lengthy spell of lovemaking, as they were dozing off to sleep, Duncan murmured something that Joly didn't quite hear. "What honey?"

"I said... you and me... we're kinda like Siamese twins, separate, but joined."

Joly snuggled in closer to him. She fell asleep smiling, thinking about Gemini, the two, being the nucleus, the one.

16. Walking on Fire

Morag heard the phone ringing and knew it was Stephen. She smiled as she answered. "Hello."

"Mother, is everything all right?"

"Everything is fine, Stephen. How are you doing?"

"I'm fine, Mother. What's wrong?"

"Stephen, have you ever thought that I could be calling with some pleasurable news? That I'm not always filled with doom and gloom?"

"Mother, you never phone me. When you do, I worry."

"Well, you don't need to worry right now. I actually called to tell you some good news."

"What is it, Mother? You know I'm busy. Not everyone has time to sit and talk."

"Maybe you should make the time, Stephen. Life is good when you take the time to enjoy it. I just got back from a trip..." She was interrupted.

"I gathered that. I did try to call you a couple of times. Why didn't you call me to take you to the airport? You know I would have done that."

"Stephen, you have been acting like an complete ass the past while. I didn't need to sit in your car for an hour with you staring stonily out the window."

She heard him sigh and felt a brief moment of guilt. "Stephen, are you sitting down?"

"Yes, Mother, I am."

"Where are you?"

"I'm in my office. Why?"

"Are you alone?"

"*Oh for...* yes, Mother, I am alone."

"Stephen, your brother is alive."

"*What?*"

"Duncan is alive, Stephen. He's here, with Joly. No, not here, as in Mission. They're in Quebec right now. They should be back in a day or two."

There was no answer.

"Stephen? *Stephen?*"

"I'm here. I… don't know what to say. Where was he? How is he? Is there any hope that any of the others are alive?"

"He was in England. He suffered a complete memory loss, but he's okay now. He's fine. And no, the others are gone for good. We've been to the graves." She knew there was no point in trying to explain to him about his Father and Colin. He would never understand.

"I see." His mind was whirling. He felt sick. He needed to get off the phone. "Mother, will you call me when Duncan returns? I'd like to see him. I have to go now. I'm on my way to a meeting."

She shook her head. He was lying again. Why couldn't he understand that it was okay to show emotion? "Of course, Son. You have a good day now, and Stephen… don't work so hard."

"Yes, Mother. Goodbye."

He hung up the phone and dashed to his private washroom. He barely made it, before throwing up. The roaring in his head subsided and he washed his face. He went back to his desk and sat heavily in his chair.

Duncan's alive! It was too much to comprehend. *How long's it been? Something like ten years. What's he been doing all these years? How did Mother find him? He was with Joly? After that long apart, what would they have in common? What did he think about Joly having that kid? Hell, he's probably married to someone else and got kids of his own.*

Stephen pictured Duncan as he had been, always goofing around, with never a serious thought in his head. He pictured Joly as she was, quiet and serious, but with a ready smile.

He thought there was a good future for the two of them. She was a pretty woman and would look good dressed in the right clothing. Of course she would have to do something with that hair of hers… and give up the damned craft. He couldn't have a wife who was running all over doing whatever. Stephen rubbed his eyes. He had enough crap happening in his life without this. Why couldn't Duncan have stayed missing for another year, until he and Joly were married? He and Elise had discussed their divorce. They were trying to work out the details.

His thoughts turned to the kid. That was where the problem lie. He would not have some Indian kid running around calling him Father. His Mother said he was prejudiced. He was not. He had no quarrel with anyone who wanted to adopt from a Third World country. In fact, he gave credit where credit was due, and he wished them well with their endeavors.

However, for himself, there was just no way. He was not going to have his business partners looking at him as if he was some kind of aberration, unable to have children of his own. He had always worn protection when having sex. He did not want children and although he knew that Elise had never wanted any either, he was not about to leave something like that to chance. He knew she was on the pill, but things happened. Well, they weren't happening to him.

He decided he was going to have to move faster than planned. He'd wanted to wait until the divorce papers were filed, but now he thought about it, maybe it wasn't such a good idea. He didn't need Joly becoming attached to the kid. The sooner she knew of his intentions, the sooner she could send the kid back to India, or wherever. He didn't really care where, as long as he wasn't in Canada, or anywhere he could interfere. He wondered how long the adoption process took before it became final. He thought at least a year. What was it she had said? *Would you like to see his birth certificate?* That was impossible. She couldn't have one that said he was a McEwan already.

When he went out to see Duncan, he would set up a dinner date with Joly and go from there.

Damn! The time had flown. He needed to get some work done. He paged his secretary and asked her to bring him a file.

Morag got out her crystal and scryed to the southeast. It was still okay. They still had some time before they needed to head down that way.

She thought about Duncan and Joly and smiled. The two lovebirds. She shook her head. They had always loved each other, even more so than she and Brodie. No, that wasn't exactly true.

There had never been anyone else for her. She was sixteen when she had first laid eyes on him and she had known in that instant he was the only one for her. It had been the same for Brodie. Damn, but she missed him.

Joly and Duncan had just found each other much earlier in their lives. She thought about the ten years that were lost to them forever, and decided that that was why. They had needed the extra time as youths, to make up for the time apart.

Randy had shown her the revamped living room. They weren't wasting any time, those two. She chuckled to herself. It was good to see Joly moving on with her life. She seemed to finally accept that Morgana and Colin were gone and now Duncan was back, she should soon be able to realize the full extent of her powers. Maybe she already did. They hadn't had much opportunity to talk the past couple of weeks.

She allowed the crystal to take her where it would. There was so much evil and unrest in the world. Sometimes she wished she could just wiggle her nose and be at each place, do her magic and head on to the next one. Well, that wasn't exactly the way of it. She was quite capable of traveling through space, but she preferred to travel the normal way. Besides, she was obligated to Joly and Duncan. The three of them would conquer the worst of the evils with the help of any other *Sisters of the Triple Moon* that were scattered throughout the world. There were other witches who were quite capable of taking care of the small stuff. She neither saw nor felt anything happening at the moment so she put the crystal on its stand, and went to feed her birds.

She thought about the Sister in India. She understood there was good and evil in every walk of life and just because you were picked by the Goddess, didn't mean you would do right by it. She wondered if there were any more bad ones and fervently hoped not. She wondered again how many of them there were. She still thought either seven or nine.

Joly and Duncan left the small town and drove back to Montreal. The sun was shining and they took their time, stopping to sightsee along the way. Their flight back home wasn't until the next day, and they made the most of the little time they had alone. They were in bed early, but it was hours later before they slept.

Duncan was himself again and he bounded onto the plane, dragging Joly along behind him. He cracked jokes with the flight attendants and laughed all the way to their seats. Joly watched for any signs of fear, but there were none. She snuggled up against him and except for meal and bathroom breaks, they cuddled for the entire five and half hour flight.

It was almost six when Joly parked the truck in front of the house. Sara knew their approximate arrival time, but she hadn't told Randy. She didn't want to take any chances that something might happen, as it had in Greece.

Duncan was through the door first. He turned and bowed low as Joly came in behind him. She laughed and playfully punched him on the shoulder. He grabbed it and yelling, "Ow, ow, ow," he flailed about, eventually falling on the stairs.

Randy had been sitting at the table eating his supper, when he heard the door open. He had jumped up and ran to the doorway in time to see his Father's performance. He ran down the hall giggling and threw himself in Duncan's arms. Duncan was laughing as he wrapped his arms around Randy and stood up.

Sara, still sitting in the kitchen, heard the strange laughter and got up to see what was happening. As she walked around the edge of the doorway, Duncan and Randy careened into her. Duncan roared with laughter again and Randy laughed with him. Joly brought up the rear, grinning from ear to ear.

"Hi Sara, in case you haven't figured it out, the riddle's been solved and I have my husband back in his entirety. I'm sure it will take you awhile to get used to him. He's a bit of a goof." She smiled and reached for Randy.

Morag was in her back yard when she sensed that Joly and Duncan had arrived home. She wanted to know how they made out in Quebec, but decided to wait until the following day to go over.

Sara was happy for Joly and Duncan. She noticed the limp was also gone. She did up the few dirty dishes and went to her room. Duncan had made her laugh several times, but she really didn't want to join in the playfulness. It reminded her of another time, another place. She lay on her bed with Jesse's voice whispering in her mind. She felt her tears begging for release and allowed them to fall.

The three cats knew immediately that things had changed once again. Nefertiti sighed. It wasn't bad enough that there had been one noisy human in the house, now there were two. It was good to see the Mistress happy, though.

Salem watched the Mistress, saw her glowing eyes, heard her laughter and knew her time of healing had ended. She was whole again. He wondered if it was time to be moving along. He wasn't that young anymore and he would have to leave soon, if he was going to search for someone else that might need him.

Pip also watched the Mistress, sensed her heart and knew that she was almost healed. She only had one more hurdle to cross.

Stephen grabbed his jacket and was tempted to slam the door as he left. He couldn't take any more of Elise's screaming. He got into his car and carefully backed out of the garage. Once he was on the highway, he accelerated and let the swiftly moving vehicle carry him away. He still couldn't believe it. She wanted his car. It wasn't enough that he was giving her the house, her car and several million dollars. She had demanded his car in addition to the rest of it.

He had no destination in mind and had driven for about an hour when he realized he was headed to Mission. He braked and pulled off to the side of the road. He wondered if Joly was back. He was only about twenty minutes away. He might as well go and see. If she was home, maybe she would invite him in for a cup of tea. He hated tea, but would drink it when he had to. Then he could ask her out. He would go over and see his Mother and Duncan some other time. He was in no mood for his Mother's scrutinizing.

He turned the corner and saw her truck parked in front of the house. He felt his mood lift and smiled to himself. Maybe the day wasn't a total loss after all. He pulled in behind the truck and parked. The truck would have to go. He couldn't have his wife driving around in something like that. Maybe he would buy her a Mercedes for a wedding gift. He climbed out of the car, walked to the door, and rang the bell.

Joly and Duncan had been in the living room with Randy. He hadn't wanted to go to bed after his bath, so Duncan brought him downstairs. They had been sitting and quietly talking when Randy finally fell asleep in Joly's arms. They were on their way to the stairs when the doorbell rang.

Duncan reached out his hand and turned the knob, his other arm around his wife. He swung the door inwards.

The smile on Stephen's face slowly disappeared. He couldn't believe what he was seeing. The white hair surprised him, but it was his brother's face looking back at him. He hadn't expected to find Duncan there, never mind with his arm wrapped possessively around Joly and the kid.

"*Stephen!* Gods Bro'... it's good to see you." Duncan let go of Joly and embraced his brother. "Come in... come in. Sure wasn't expectin' to see you at this hour." Duncan dragged his brother in and shut the door.

"Hi Stephen. Will you excuse me for a moment? This little guy needs to go to bed." Joly turned toward the stairs.

Duncan rushed to her side. "Here, Darlin', let me take him up. Maybe you can put the kettle on for tea. Do we have any instant coffee?" He carefully took Randy from her arms.

She leaned over to give him one last kiss and automatically reached up to give Duncan one too. "I don't think so. Hurry back honey."

She turned and sensed something wrong with Stephen. "Are you okay? You look funny. Come and sit down." She took his arm and led him into the living room. Once he was seated, she went to the kitchen and put the kettle on.

Stephen could smell the fresh paint, the newness of the furniture, the wax on the floor and he bowed his head. He was such a bloody fool. Thank God, he had no close confidants, so he had told no one of his plans. He would have been laughed out of town. He felt sick to his stomach again.

Duncan returned and sat down beside him. "Hey Bro', you okay? You look a little pale."

"Yes, I'm fine. I'm under a lot of stress at work and I probably should be getting more sleep. Needless to say, I was shocked when Mother told me you were alive. How on earth did she find you after all this time?"

Duncan was watching him closely. "Uhh... she didn't. Joly found me. That connection of ours led her pretty much right to me." He grinned.

Stephen's eyes opened wide. "Joly was looking for you? Even after all this time? That's pretty far fetched wouldn't you say?"

"Nah. I was reaching out to her in her dreams, and before I got my memory back I kept having flashbacks about her. You've got to realize Bro', Joly and I... we're connected... here." He thumped his fist against his chest. "You know she and I were always together. It was meant to be. You have no idea how much I love that woman."

Joly came around the corner with a tray in her hands. She smiled as she heard the last remark. She set the tray down and leaned over to Duncan, but looked at Stephen. "And you have no idea how much I love this man." She gave him a peck on the lips and sat down beside him. Duncan put his arm around her shoulders.

"Excuse me, please." Stephen was going to be sick; he leapt to his feet and rushed out the door. As he turned the corner to head for the bathroom, he slammed into Sara, knocking her to the floor. She cried out as she landed.

Duncan and Joly ran into the hall just in time to see Stephen disappearing into the washroom. Sara was still on the floor, staring after him.

"Are you okay?" Joly knelt down to touch her arm. She appeared none the worse for wear, but had had the breath knocked out of her.

"Who the hell was that rude imbecile? He ought to be shot."

Duncan roared with laughter. "That dear Sara, was my big brother." He laughed again, as he helped her to her feet.

Joly sensed that Stephen was throwing up. She wondered why. She hadn't felt any illness around him. She walked down the hall and knocked lightly on the door. "Are you okay, Stephen?"

She heard a muffled reply which she took to be an affirmative answer, and she went back to the living room. Duncan had seated Sara and poured her a cup of tea.

"Honey, Stephen's not well. It's his stomach. I know he won't let me near it. Should I run over and get Morag?"

"I'll go, Darlin'. Back in a flash." He jumped up and hurried out the door.

He and Morag were back before Stephen left the security of the bathroom.

Morag reached for Joly and they hugged. "I missed you."

"Missed you too, but I was in good company." Joly smiled.

They heard Stephen coming down the hall and Morag went out to meet him.

"You look like hell, Son. I think you better come home with me. You can sleep in your old bed."

"I need to go home, but thanks for the offer, Mother."

"You won't make it. Look at yourself. No, you're coming with me." She turned and said goodnight to everyone and led Stephen out the door. He never said another word.

They all looked at one another and then Duncan laughed.

"That was about one of the weirdest things I've ever seen. Gods, did you see him? He was actually green." He shook his head and laughed again.

Joly looked perplexed. "Why would he have driven out here, when he wasn't feeling well? It doesn't even make sense."

"Oh yes, Darlin', it makes perfect sense. He was probably fine up until he walked through that door." He snickered and started cleaning up the dirty cups.

Joly raised her eyebrow, looked at Sara and shrugged.

Sara shook her head, not understanding anything that was going on. She got to her feet, said goodnight and headed up to bed.

When they were curled up in bed, Joly said softly, "Are you going to let me in on your little secret?"

Duncan snickered again. "Gods, Darlin', you have no idea how much I love you."

"I love you too honey, but that doesn't answer my question."

"Well, Darlin', it's this way. Stephen arrived tonight to see you, not me. When he saw us together, well, he just kinda lost it." He chuckled again.

Joly bolted upright and turned on the bedside light. "Duncan...you *can't* be serious?"

"Very serious, Darlin'. I figured he had the hots for you when you told me about him giving you that Bast statue. Tonight just confirmed it."

"*You've got to be wrong!* He's married... I'm married. For Pete's sake. It doesn't even make any sense."

"Turn the light off, Darlin' and come here."

Joly reached over and turned off the light. She snuggled into Duncan's arms.

"Darlin', he thought you were a widow and think about it. Would you want to be married to Elise forever? I bet they're in the midst of a really nasty divorce."

Joly thought about the times she had seen Stephen. He had acted a little weird, sometimes stuttering and being almost shy at times. *Gods! We're nothing alike.* Why would he even think that the two of them might get together? He *had* kissed her several times, usually on the cheek or forehead. *Oh my Gods!* Had he been trying to let her know he was interested?

"I didn't know honey, I honestly didn't know. You were the only one I ever thought about." She felt badly and as she thought about the different times she had seen him, she remembered his reaction to Randy. Was *that* why he had been so upset? Now it made some sort of weird sense.

"I love you honey."

"Love you too pretty lady."

Morag led Stephen across the street and into the house. He protested all the way, but once inside he quietly went and sat down, his head lowered so he wouldn't have to look at his Mother.

Morag heated some water and made Stephen a cup of peppermint tea to settle his stomach. She was quiet as she did this, wondering how to talk to this man-child of hers.

As he drank the tea she looked in his eyes. "You and Elise are finally calling it quits." It wasn't a question. He nodded his head, but said nothing. "It's going to cost you a bundle to get rid of her, but you'll be better off. Maybe you won't work as hard. Maybe you'll take some time for yourself." He nodded again.

"Stephen, you don't love Joly, you know that, don't you?"

He looked at his Mother then. "Love? What's love, Mother?"

She sighed. "Love is what your Father and I had. Love is what Joly and Duncan have always had. Love is what Morgana and Colin had. You have been around love all your life. All you have ever had to do is lift your head out of your damn machines and you would see that love is all around you. When you took up with that twit, how did you decide that she was the one for you? You certainly didn't love her. Was it the way she dressed?"

"Mother, leave Elise out of it."

"So what was the plan, Son? Divorce her and marry Joly? Do you really think Joly would have had you?" She chuckled. "Joly would be horrified to know what you had planned for her. I suppose the craft would have been out too?"

Stephen appeared to be very interested in his cup.

She sighed again. "Stephen... once more I will tell you this. You have become too powerful. You figure you can bulldoze your way through life, taking what you want. It doesn't always work that way."

She stood and walked around to the back of his chair and began massaging his shoulders. "You know... the thought had crossed my mind on more than one occasion that maybe the two of you *would* get together."

He turned and looked her. "Really?"

"Yes, Son, really. However, it didn't take me long to realize it could never work. A Mother only ever wants the best for her children. My original thought was that Joly would make you a lot happier than that twit. But then I realized you would be Joly's downfall."

"Why?"

"You would have smothered her, Son. You wouldn't have allowed her the craft and that is who she is. You would have made her dress differently... no more jeans, right? What else would you have done?"

Stephen bowed his head. "No truck."

"Uh-huh... a big fancy car and what else?"

"Her hair."

"Ah yes. Her hair bound so tightly against her skin that she would have a headache at all times. A wonderful life you had planned for her. Stephen..." She went around to his side and squatted down, looking into his eyes.

"She's a butterfly, Stephen, a beautiful butterfly and you would have caged her. She would have died, Son. If you had managed to trap her, you would have killed her." She stood. "Now... go to bed. There's a new toothbrush in the bathroom closet on the second shelf. I'll see you in the morning."

Morag took the cup over to the sink. She heard Stephen stand and was startled when she felt him wrap his arms around her.

"Thanks Mother..." He kissed her neck and turned to go.

"Stephen?"

He stopped at the door and turned.

"I love you, Son. I always have."

He nodded and left the kitchen.

Morag washed the cup and saucer and put them away. She had been waiting for Stephen to comment on the colors she had painted his room, but all was quiet. She decided he probably hadn't turned on the bedroom light.

She turned off the lights, washed and brushed her teeth and went to bed. She was a long time going to sleep.

In the room next to hers, Stephen was also a long time going to sleep. He finally allowed himself a really good look at who he had become. He didn't like what he saw. He decided once Elise was out of his life, he would have to change some things, maybe a lot of things.

He thought about Joly and the things that had drawn him to her. He came to the conclusion that it was the very essence of who she was that he would have taken away. His Mother was right. She was a beautiful butterfly and he knew he wanted to see her stay that way.

He pictured the way the three of them looked, as the door had opened. They'd looked like a happy family. He wondered if he would ever find that kind of happiness. He didn't think so.

He smiled to himself. He really did love his brother. *A frog?* Sure. Whatever.

His pillow felt damp and he reached up to see why. He discovered he was crying. Real men didn't cry. He was horrified, but the tears didn't stop, and he finally accepted them for what they were. It was a time for new beginnings. He was being reborn. He finally slept.

It was the final day of the Labor Day weekend. Joly and Duncan were still in bed, discussing what they were going to do for the day when the phone rang.

"Hello?"

"Good morning."

"Hey, Maw! How're you doing? What's it like outside? Is it as nice as it looks from the comfort of my bed?" He laughed.

Morag was silent.

"Maw? You still there?"

"Yes. Duncan, did I just hear you laugh?"

He laughed again. "Oh yeah. That you did. Can't wait to tell you all about it. What's up?"

"I thought you all might like to come over for breakfast. And yes, it is beautiful outside."

"Uhh... do you think that's wise?"

"Perfectly. See you in about an hour."

She hung up and rejoined Stephen at the table.

"Just like that."

He smiled at her. "You're something else, Mother. You know, I never could figure you out, not when I was growing up, not as an adult, never."

"That's one of your problems, Son. You try to analyze everything to death. What's to figure out? I am who I am. Why is that a puzzle?"

"What do witches do?"

Her eyes opened wide. "Are you serious?"

"Yes."

"Come with me." She led him to her craft room. They spent the next forty-five minutes there, as Morag explained different facets of the craft. She didn't go into great detail and she didn't touch on the more serious aspects of what it was that she did. When they walked back out to the kitchen, Morag looked at Stephen.

"Were you aware, Son, that you do have some witches blood in you?"

He smiled. "I don't think so."

"Do you remember when I was missing? You picked up my crystal ball and tried to find me, but you were afraid. You didn't give the crystal enough time."

She laughed at the expression on his face. "Oh yes, my Son. You had found me. You just didn't know it."

She turned her head. "Do you want to get the door, or do you want me to?"

"But no one's…" The doorbell rang. He shook his head. "It's all right Mother, I'll get it."

He had butterflies in his stomach, as he walked to the door. For someone who was in control of a multi-million dollar empire, he wasn't used to the feeling. He swung the door open.

The three adults standing there all looked a little apprehensive. The youngest member of the family had no such problem.

"Hi Unca Sea-ven."

"Hello Randy." This was a child, it really didn't matter what color his skin was. He reached out to take him from Duncan's arms. "Good morning, *Bro'*. Hi Joly, come on in."

He turned to Sara as she entered. "You're Sara. My sincerest apologies for knocking you down last night. I'm Stephen, Duncan's rude imbecile of a brother." He smiled and held out his hand to shake Sara's.

Embarrassed, she ducked her head. "I'm sorry. I didn't mean to be rude."

"You weren't rude. You were right."

Randy squirmed to be put down. "Where Gra-Morg?"

Stephen put him down. "She's in the kitchen."

Stephen lowered his head and took a deep breath. He looked at Joly and Duncan. "I want to apologize to the both of you. I was out of line last night. I have no excuse, other than I'm too used to getting my way. I'd like to try again, if you'll give me a second chance."

Duncan reached for his brother and hugged him. "You're an idiot, but I still love you." He stood back, grinning.

Stephen had tears in his eyes again. He really needed to get some control over himself.

Joly saw the tears, felt his shame and embarrassment. She stepped forward to hug her brother-in-law. "Stephen. You're a good person inside. You just need to learn how to release it."

They headed for the kitchen, where the smell of freshly baked buns and crisp bacon drew them.

With the events of the night before out of the way, the conversation became lively and at times noisy. They decided to spend the day together, finally deciding to go to Stanley Park.

Morag decided she had waited long enough to hear about the events in Quebec. She was about to ask, when Joly turned to her.

"How did you make out in Scotland?"

"Good. Everything went without a hitch." She smiled.

"I didn't realize it got so hot over there that you would get such a great tan. You almost look like you got burned."

"Yes... well, it did get a little warm all right." She chuckled as she thought about it.

"And Quebec? How was it?"

"The colors were pretty. It was pretty easy, overall. We saw ball lightning. I know it's a rarity, so we were blessed. Alyce's riddle finished playing out there. The ball lightning was the fire."

"Ahh. Well, it's nice to see you back to your old self Duncan."

"Do you know yet where we are going next?"

"No. But I'm sure we'll know very soon."

Stephen had been following the conversation with interest. He was totally lost, but decided if he started paying more attention, he might find out more about the craft and his family. "Why would that be?" He asked.

Morag looked at him, a smile playing at the corner of her mouth. "Well, Son. There is a lot of evil happening in the world just now. Something transpired last All Hallow's Eve that is causing many more problems than normal. Things seem to be happening at a faster pace now, so we'll probably only be home a week or so, before we have to head out again."

"Is this evil dangerous?"

"It depends in what context you would classify dangerous."

"Compared to what happened to you two and Dad."

"Oh... about the same I suppose. And it was us three and your Dad."

"Right. I forgot Joly was there. Sorry."

"Mommy, come... look." Randy stuck his head in the kitchen. Joly followed him to the living room. Randy walked over to the coffee table and gently put his hands around Morag's crystal that was sitting on its stand.

"Where Pip?"

Joly watched as the mists appeared and receded. The crystal took Randy to their home, and to his bedroom where Pip was stretched out on his bed.

"See Mommy. Pip in bed."

"I see, Sweetie. You're very clever. Shall we show Gra-Morg?"

"Yes." He ran to get her, dragging her back with him, his tiny hand clutched on to hers.

Again, he put his hands around the crystal. "Where Pip?"

Once again, the crystal took him to Pip.

Morag nodded her head. "I thought as much. Very good, Randy. Soon, we'll have to start teaching you the ways of the craft."

She smiled at Joly. "No wonder you two bonded so quickly. He is definitely one of us. I thought so when he started talking to Pip, and in Greece, he saw things in the crystal when I was scrying." She hugged Joly.

Joly and Sara cleaned up the kitchen, leaving Morag to visit with her two sons, something she had not been able to do for many years. Even as they talked, Joly remained conscious of her husband's laughter. Once they were finished, they got ready to head for the city and Stanley Park.

Stephen felt guilty. He knew he should be at the office catching up on some paperwork. He hadn't called Elise since he had stormed out of the mausoleum either. *Screw it.* He was going to relax for just one day and try to enjoy himself. Something that he really couldn't remember doing.

Morag and Sara went with Stephen, leaving Joly, Duncan and Randy to follow. Joly soon gave up trying to keep up to Stephen as he wove in and out of the traffic, slowly widening the distance between the two vehicles. They had agreed to meet at the aquarium.

Emilia, Jacinta and White Wind were in the jeep, driving home from town. They had planned on making a day of it, but something told Emilia to get home fast. The dust cloud rose behind the vehicle as she expertly took the curves, traveling much faster than usual.

White Wind began whining and then he barked.

"Silencio, Viento Blanco." The dog grew more excited and lunged into the front seat, his nose glued to the windshield.

Emilia felt it then. Something bad was happening and she opened her senses. In her mind she smelled the smoke and saw the flames. *"Gods, no!"* She floored the accelerator. The jeep slewed and righted itself as she turned onto her land. White Wind's barking was deafening them, but she knew he smelled the fire.

The house came into sight. She saw no smoke or fire and slowed. "What...?"

She braked hard and threw the door open. White Wind scampered over top of Emilia and ran. She followed, with Jacinta bringing up the rear. They ran around the side of the house and saw wisps of smoke seeping out of the barn.

Jacinta screamed. The horses were inside.

Emilia opened the barn door, but it was the wrong thing to do. The fresh air turned into a fireball and with a mighty whoosh, the entire barn was burning.

White Wind ran past them into the flaming inferno.

"Viento Blanco... no! Madre, help them."

Emilia knew her greatest gift of magic would only make things worse. She listened for the dog, but only heard the frightened screams of the two horses. She knew she would kill whoever was responsible.

The heat pushed them back and Emilia held her daughter as they cried.

There was movement at the door and Estrella galloped out into the fresh air. Vito was right behind her and White Wind was nipping at his heels.

Jacinta ran for her horse and Emilia went to the dog.

He lie down and let her check him over. She found nothing wrong with him. There wasn't even a singe mark on his fur.

He looked at her with laughing eyes and she chuckled. "Goddess, thank you. *Viento Blanco,* you've been keeping secrets." She ruffled his fur and laughed again. She hadn't known he was a familiar.

Stanley Park is an area of one thousand acres located less than one mile from downtown Vancouver. Its evergreen forest of majestic cedar, hemlock and Douglas fir trees is home to a variety of wildlife, birds and plants. The Vancouver Aquarium is one of the many attractions, along with a children's farmyard, miniature railway, heated swimming pool, water park, tennis court, pitch and putt golf course, Theatre Under the Stars, and a five and one half mile perimeter seawall and promenade. At one time there had been a zoo, but due to public pressure, it had been closed down. Lost Lagoon, also part of the park was home to a variety of birds including swans, Canada Geese and ducks.

Morag was looking forward to seeing it again. It had been eleven years since Brody had taken her.

They were walking along a path when Duncan yelled over to Morag, "Hey, Maw... wanna go firewalking?"

She raised her eyebrows. "And what brought this on?"

"Oh, Kyle Devon's checking out a place for us to go. I just really want to walk through the coals again."

"Sure, I'd love to. How about you, Stephen? Would you like to join us?" She smiled and hooked her hand around his elbow.

"I don't have ti...uh... well; let me know when you're going. If I'm free, I'll come and watch. Just don't expect me to participate."

"Way to go, son." Morag squeezed his arm. He really was trying. She was proud of him. If only he could keep it up. He was what… thirty-six. He wasn't too old to learn a new way of living. It would be hard for him, but he could do it.

They had an enjoyable day. Stephen drove his Mother and Sara back out to Mission, but he didn't seem to mind. Morag asked him what he was going to do.

"I don't know, Mother. I'm letting Elise have the house."

"I don't suppose you would want to commute from Mission."

He smiled. "Not too likely Mother, but thanks. I might come out and spent the occasional weekend though."

"I'd like that. I don't suppose I can interest you in doing some painting."

"Mother! What is it with you and the painting? I told you I'd hire someone. You turned him down. I still had to pay him, you know. By the way, my room looks like you're setting up to move a girl into it."

"Stephen, those are not necessarily girls' colors. Not every man wants everything to be brown. That's possibly one of the reasons you were always so somber. Perhaps I should have painted that room a different color, years ago. We will paint when you come out to visit. I'll show you why."

He shook his head. "Yes, Mother."

Rauna felt the cold and opened her eyes, but it felt as if she hadn't opened them at all. The darkness was absolute.

She felt something slash at her, and then a deep voice, colder than ice, spoke. "Who are you?"

"Who are you?" she asked in response.

"I am the Lord of the Abyss," the voice thundered, "and you do not belong here."

"Abyss? No, I don't belong here."

"Who are you?"

Something slashed at her again and she was hit on the back from behind.

"Leave," whispered a voice.

"Don't leave," whispered another. "I'm hungry, you're light."

And they were all over her, biting, hitting, scratching, screaming… and Rauna screamed with them.

After a while; it felt like an eternity or maybe it was just seconds… Rauna couldn't tell, she started seeing what was in the darkness, and she closed her eyes wishing she hadn't seen anything. This was the Abyss… where pain, fear, anger in the flesh, black forms, sharp claws and overwhelming anxiety ruled.

The things attacked her all the time and it felt as if they were eating her alive. Her mind tricked her and she had nightmares, knowing that all that had happened was to her … and it was for real.

The next morning was Randy's first day of kindergarten. Duncan and Joly walked him to the school, which was located two blocks away. Joly had concerns with Randy's limited English, but the principal assured her they would make out fine. She had enrolled him in a French Immersion School, believing that his knowing Canada's second official language would be of help to him in the future.

When they returned home, Sara informed them Kyle Devon had called. Duncan returned his call. He had a location for their firewalk. Kyle gave him the name and number to call. He also told Duncan he had mailed some papers on the previous Friday.

Duncan called the number and set up a time to go over and check out the site.

At lunchtime, they walked back to the school to pick up Randy. He talked non-stop all the way home and couldn't wait to take the papers out of his back pack to show them the work he'd done that morning. Joly proudly hung the artwork on the fridge.

Early that evening they drove out to Sumas Prairie to check out the firewalk location. The farmer who was also a witch, was quite excited at the prospect of hosting a firewalk. He was talking about inviting several covens to come and participate. Duncan hated to burst his bubble, but had to tell the fellow they just wanted to do a small personal walk. The farmer was not too happy with that piece of news. Joly informed him they would be glad to pay him and this further upset him. It became apparent that he didn't want the money; he wanted the prestige that went with hosting such an event. Duncan asked why he couldn't host his own event after they set it up and did their private walk. He thought about it for a few minutes and decided he could do that.

They picked out an area that was away from the highway and the publics view. They would order in the firewood and set it up for the following night. Duncan knew they could be called away anytime and he wanted to do the walk before leaving again.

The following morning after walking Randy to school, Duncan ordered five cords of birch wood to be delivered that afternoon. Joly dug out the cassette tapes and the battery operated cassette player.

They told Morag, who in turn called Stephen. He had finally given her his cell phone number, so she no longer needed to go through his secretary. He tried to make excuses but Morag interrupted him and told him he was once again being an ass. After a moment of silence he agreed with her, and said he'd pick her up.

That afternoon Duncan and Joly went out to the field. It was one that had lain fallow that summer. They raked it smooth and made sure there were no rocks or any sharp objects they could cut their feet on. The actual fire pit was about six feet wide and around twenty-two feet long. They cleared and raked an additional five feet around the pit area for walking. At the east end they cleaned and raked a six foot circle, as well as a pathway to the fire pit. The truck arrived with the wood. They unloaded it and then stacked it in the pit. When they were done, the stack of wood was four feet high. The wood was dry and Duncan was pleased.

They drove home to find supper waiting for them. Sara had prepared marinated chicken breasts, spaghetti and a green salad. It hadn't taken her long to realize she needed to triple what she and Joly ate, to accommodate Duncan's enormous appetite.

After supper, Duncan gave Randy an early bath and read him a story. Sara entertained him while Duncan and Joly went to prepare for their evening.

They showered together and after drying off, Joly went to the closet. She eyed the beautiful rose gown that Morag had given her. She decided against it. They would be covered in soot and ashes when they were done. She reached in and took out the green one. Duncan's blue robes had been unpacked and he was almost dancing as he threw the gown over his head.

"Excited honey?"

He laughed. "Oh yeah! I can't wait."

Across the street, Morag was putting on her purple gown. Stephen arrived grumbling about the things he needed to be doing. Morag told him to quit worrying so much. His empire was not going to fall if he took some time away from it.

They drove out to the field, Stephen having to follow Joly. He chafed at having to drive so slowly and again Morag reminded him that he needed to slow down in all parts of his life, driving included.

Upon reaching the field, Duncan removed a tiger torch and a cylinder of propane from the back of the truck. He connected them together, opened the valve, struck a match and lit the end. He then shoved the end into the wood near the ground until he had a good blaze going. He repeated this every few feet on both sides, until all the wood was burning and crackling. He put the tank and the torch back in the truck. Joly had taken the portable cassette player and placed it a little ways back from the circle. Morag had laid out a blanket beside it.

Morag had convinced Stephen to join them in the circle. He didn't have to firewalk, but she wanted him to be a part of the festivities.

He took his shoes and socks off, complaining the whole time. He looked at the long gowns that the others were wearing. "Uhh... what do you do? Pick them up as you walk through?"

"You can, but it's not necessary. They won't burn."

While the wood burned, they sat on the blanket and listened to a meditation tape. The tape transported them to a place of brilliant sunshine, flower filled meadows, singing birds and babbling brooks. Joly didn't need the meditation but she joined in, her one hand clasped with Duncan's, the other with Stephen. She was a natural firewalker. She could walk through fire at anytime, in any place. There weren't many who could do so without the preparation. She always thought Morag could probably do the same, but she didn't know for sure. Duncan loved the meditation part of the ritual and wouldn't even consider walking without it. Stephen sat between Morag and Joly, quietly listening.

Morag could feel his heart beat slow and knew he had relaxed, probably for the first time in many years.

It took close to an hour for the fire to burn down to the ground. The bed of coals glowed red in the evening darkness. It was time. They gathered in the circle. Morag called the quarters and then said a short prayer. Joly went to the player and pushed the on button. The new age sounds of drums, pan pipes and ravens filled the air. They joined hands and walking clockwise around, they began to chant their firewalk mantra. They had only gone around twice, when Duncan let go and headed for the bed of coals. He never faltered, but walked straight through them. When he got to the far side he jumped in the air. *"Yes!"* He did a little dance back to the circle and joined hands again. Shortly after, Joly and Morag both let go at the same time. They laughed and clasping hands together, they walked through the coals. After that they walked, they danced, they twirled through the embers.

Stephen stood in the circle feeling alone and stupid. He couldn't take his eyes off the hems of the gowns. He watched them drag through the coals and waited for them to burst into flame, but it never happened.

Duncan sashayed up to him and grabbed his arm. "Come on, Bro', you gotta try it."

"I don't think so."

"Yeah, come on now. It's easy." Duncan took Stephen's hand in his.

Joly saw what was happening and walked over to them, smiling. "Hey, come here." She took Stephen's other hand and they led him to the end of the pit. She and Duncan resumed chanting quietly.

"All of Mother Earth is sacred,
Every step I take is sacred."
Stephen's voice hesitantly joined theirs.

When Joly sensed Stephen's heartbeat had slowed, she and Duncan took a small step forward, each with one foot on the embers.

Stephen could feel the energy pulsating through him. He wanted to step forward. He was frozen and couldn't move. He wiggled his toes. Then he moved his foot. He touched the edge of the coals. He sensed they weren't burning him. The corner of his mouth turned up and he took a full step forward. Joly and Duncan took another step and Stephen followed. When he was five feet in, Joly sidestepped out of the pit, allowing Stephen and Duncan to go alone.

Stephen made it half way. Suddenly he realized that what he was doing was impossible, and as that thought hit him, his foot burned. He leapt off the coals and sat down to check the bottom of his foot. Joly squatted down beside him and saw two small red marks. She laid her hand over them and within a minute, Stephen could feel no pain and when he looked, he couldn't see any marks.

Leaving Stephen, Joly went and grabbed Duncan's hand. They stood in the middle of the pit and scooped up handfuls of burning coals, throwing them up to the sky and watching the embers sparkle in the night air as they fell back to the ground. Duncan was laughing the entire time. Morag picked up a large smoldering coal and holding in her hand, she gently blew on it until it burst into flame. She laughed and threw it back. She went and sat beside Stephen and pulled two ribbons out of her pocket and handed him one of them.

"What's this for?"

"I thought you'd like to try your hand at some magic."

"Sure." He didn't sound convinced.

Morag moved to the side of the pit. She waved her ribbon over the coals and let the one end fall in. Nothing happened.

Stephen moved forward, his eyes never leaving his Mother's ribbon. "That should have caught fire."

She nodded. "Yes, and if I let go of it, it will. As long as I'm holding it, it won't. Throw yours in."

He did… and nothing happened. He decided the ribbons had been fireproofed, so he let go of his. It burst into flame immediately. His mouth dropped open.

Morag laughed and handed him her ribbon. He dragged it through the coals, took it out and examined it, and laid it back in them. He was astounded.

Morag smiled at him. "It's magic, Son. I told you, you had witches blood in you." She stood up and walked back into the slowly dying embers.

When the coals began to cool, Joly went and got a basin, some towels and a jug of water from the truck. After they thanked the quarters and dismissed them, they took turns washing and drying their feet. Duncan raked the coals again, ensuring they would burn out safely. They packed up all their belongings and headed for home.

Morag insisted Stephen spend the night and without much fuss, he agreed to stay. He showered first and Morag heated water for tea. She made a cup of instant coffee for Stephen. When he was done, Morag quickly showered and joined him. She noticed he looked more relaxed than she had seen him in a long time. He drank his coffee without fidgeting and did not rush off to bed, but seemed content to sit and talk.

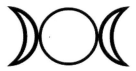

17. Hexed

The next morning a large manila envelope arrived from the lawyer's office. The first items they found inside were Randy's new birth certificates. Kyle had gotten them both the small laminated one as well as the large parchment one that included all the details. The name on them was Ranjit Duncan James McEwan. Duncan was adamant that Joly's maiden name remain part of Randy's name. Joly ran her finger over the name as if she was afraid it might disappear. He teased her about it, but she noticed that when he held the large certificate, his knuckles were pinched white. Beside Name of Father, it read Duncan Fraser McEwan.

The second item they pulled out was Joly's new passport. She looked at the name Joly Anne McEwan. It had been a long time since she had seen her name written as McEwan. The tears welled up in her eyes, but she held them in check.

The third item in the envelope was Duncan's passport. Duncan could safely travel again under his own name. All he had to do was get his picture taken. He went and got the James Smith passport and walked out into the back yard. He struck a match and set it on fire.

Joly stood quietly and watched him. She saw his tears and knew he was crying for all the missing years. She waited. He finally walked to her and buried his face in her neck. She held him as he cried, his tears releasing the anger and sorrow, knowing that when he was done, he would be finished with his last life.

It was some time later they went back inside and opened the final piece of paper. It was the deed to the James' home. The property now belonged jointly to Joly and Duncan McEwan.

They had already gone to the Department of Motor Vehicles where Joly produced their marriage certificate and her new driver's license was on order. Because Duncan had been so long without one, he needed to redo both his written test and his driving test. His appointment for the written test was for the following day. Joly had also ordered her new social insurance card and she had replacement credit cards on order. The only other thing they were waiting for were the three new medical cards.

Duncan had been surprised when Kyle told him his bank account was still in tact. Kyle had put the money in trust for Joly, but she had never enquired about it and her parents had left her financially secure. Kyle would be mailing him a cheque for the funds with interest.

Duncan had worked as a trainer before the accident and wanted to get back into it, but he knew there was no point in doing so until they were finished with what was currently happening in the world.

They discussed the truck and its usefulness. They decided to keep it, but they needed to get a vehicle with more seating. They decided to look at some vans.

Morag spent the afternoon puttering in her back yard. Toward supper time she started feeling odd. She felt a vibration going through her. She thought at first some heavy machinery was running close by, but after opening her senses and listening, she knew that wasn't it. She wandered through the yard and decided it was more distinct near the house. She went inside and the feeling grew stronger. She could definitely feel a hum. Somehow, it felt familiar and yet it wasn't.

She went to the sink, filled the kettle and plugged it in. She turned and saw a strange green pulsating glow coming through the living room doorway. *What the heck?* She approached the door slowly and as she came closer to it, the glow deepened, the humming intensified. She peered in, completely mystified.

She laughed. She had always known her crystal ball was special, but she had never thought it would actually *summon* her. It sat on its stand on the coffee table where she had left it, the green crystal pulsating. It reminded her of a heart beating rhythmically as it appeared to have a life of its own.

She sat down and still smiling, she picked it up. There were no mists this time. It took her across the ocean to a vast desert area. Morag saw the people lying where they had fallen. There appeared to be at least a dozen of them. The crystal took off again and not far from the previous place, more dead lay strewn about. Morag got a sense of something terribly powerful and extremely evil. Looking at how they lay on the sand, she got the impression the attacks had come as a complete surprise.

She waited to see if the crystal would take her elsewhere. It did, three more times. Each time it was the same scenario. The dead ranged from the largest group of about twelve down to the smallest group of five. She zoomed in on some of the dead, but could see no cause of death. There appeared to be no marks on the bodies, nor was there any sign of blood.

This was the Australian Outback. Families were spread out with some living in close proximity to their neighbors, others living very much on their own. The deaths were happening in remote places, but how soon would they begin happening in a village or town?

Morag wondered how fast they could get there. She headed to the phone to call her travel agent. There were no flights the next day. They would have to wait until the following afternoon and it took two days to get there. She could not go on her own. She could tell that the force was at least as powerful as she was. She needed Joly. She thought about the two lovebirds across the street and decided the next day would be soon enough to tell them they had been summoned.

That night Joly dreamed, not so much a dream as a nightmare.

She was a rag doll being thrown hither and yon. There was sand in her nose and her mouth. She had no control. She was a puppet, with some invisible force pulling her strings. One second she was in the air; the next, she was flopping on the ground. She had no control. Duncan appeared in front of her. He split in half, becoming two, both halves reaching out to her, calling her name. One of the two evaporated into nothingness. The other Duncan shape shifted into something evil. She could not respond. She had no control.

Duncan awoke when he was hit by a flailing arm. He turned the small light on and saw the terribly distorted face, the mouth opening and closing, the arms and legs moving, each at odds with the others. Joly was bathed in perspiration. She made no sound.

He called her name softly and reached out to hold on to her shoulders. Her arm came up and batted him away. He reached down and grabbed her around the waist. Her wrist smacked him across the nose. It was a hard hit and it brought tears to his eyes. He hung on and awkwardly lifted her into his arms. After struggling, he managed to get one arm confined. He was trying to grab her other arm, when she suddenly went still.

She lay limp in his arms and she reminded him of a rag doll. He enfolded her into his arms, carefully placing her head on his shoulder. He sat there for a long time, just holding her, softly saying her name and telling her how much he loved her. He kissed her shoulder and gently rocked backed and forth. Finally, he lay her down again and covered her. He curled up under the covers and held her tightly, wondering what she had just experienced and if she would remember the dream in the morning.

Joly stirred and licked her lips. Her mouth was dry. She felt Duncan snuggled against her and she opened one eye. He was watching her.

"Goo… ahh." She tried to clear her throat. She shook her head and sat up. She swallowed and tried again. "Good morning." It was a whispered, rasping voice.

Duncan sat up, concerned. "I'll get you a drink." He jumped out of bed and rushed to the washroom, returning seconds later with a glass of water.

Joly drank the entire glass without pausing to take a breath. "Thanks honey."

Her voice was stronger, but still very raspy.

Duncan looked around. Where was Pip? He thought she never left Joly's side in the night. He thought about the dream and realized that Pip hadn't been around then either.

He went and got dressed, aware that Joly was still sitting in bed. He went over to her and sat beside her.

"I think maybe you should stay in bed today. You don't sound too good."

She went to speak and had to clear her throat again. "I'm fine. Just need a cup of tea." She went to stand up, and would have fallen if Duncan hadn't been there to grab her. He sat her back down.

"You will stay in bed. I'll bring you some tea. I mean it. Stay put. Don't try to be some kind of hero." He leaned over and kissed her, then helped her back under the covers.

He went down stairs and headed to the kitchen. Salem was sitting the window. "Salem buddy, where's Pip? Somethin's wrong with Joly."

Salem jumped down and vanished around the corner into the hallway.

Duncan looked through the cupboard wondering which tea would most benefit her throat. He finally decided on chamomile and ginger. He put the kettle on and looked at the time. He still had half an hour before getting Randy up.

While he was waiting, he suddenly realized Nefertiti wasn't around either. Joly had installed a cat door so they could go outside whenever they wanted, so he knew they hadn't inadvertently been locked outside. He walked down to the basement and called for them, but got no response.

Salem dashed by him as he was heading back up the stairs. He let out a horrid yowl and loped to the door that led to the back yard.

Duncan went and opened it. Salem ran outside and disappeared in the darkness. Duncan stood outside listening. He heard nothing at first, and then he heard a low growling.

He walked over toward the hedge that separated their property from Joan Ardell's. He heard a shuffling sound and peered down. He walked along the hedge until he saw movement. *Damn!* He should have grabbed a flashlight.

He found the three cats together. Nefertiti had Pip by the scruff of the neck and was slowly dragging her along. Salem kept trying to help and Nefertiti would growl at him, telling him to back off. When she knew Duncan had found them, she let go of Pip, who lay still.

Duncan reached down and picked her up. At first, he couldn't feel a heartbeat, but then he found it. It was very weak. He rushed back in the house, the other two cats on his heels. He ran up the stairs to the bedroom.

Joly looked pale against the sheets and he wondered about disturbing her. He called softly to her. She didn't move. He ran back downstairs and out the front door, heading to his Mothers.

He rang the doorbell and she answered immediately.

"What's wrong with Pip?"

"I don't know. Joly's sick. I thought maybe you could help her."

Morag took the cat and went into the kitchen. She laid Pip on the table and turned the overhead light on. She ran her hands up and down Pip's body. She found no broken bones. She opened her senses and allowed Pip's spirit into her.

"She's been poisoned." Morag went to the cupboard and removed several bottles of herbs, searching for one in particular. "Put the kettle on. It should still be hot." She found what she was looking for and went to another cupboard. She removed a bottle of vinegar.

Duncan plugged it in and went back to Pip.

Morag mixed a small amount of vinegar and water together. She opened Pip's mouth and poured a small amount into her throat. The swallowing reflex did not happen. Morag turned Pip's head and let the concoction drain out.

"She's too far gone." She stuck her finger down Pip's throat, forcing the muscles to contract and open. She again poured a small amount of the vinegar mixture into the opening. Again, nothing happened.

Morag laid her down and wrapped her hands around the small cat's stomach. She began a kneading movement. "Unplug the kettle and make a very weak ginger tea. I don't know if she'll respond, but if she does, we'll need it." She continued her kneading.

"You said Joly was sick?"

"Yeah. She had some weird dream last night. She was thrashin' all over the bed. Then this mornin' her throat was all dry and scratchy. She almost fell when she tried to stand."

Morag thought about the desert sand in Australia. *No, it couldn't be! Damn! Come on Pip.*

She had been doing the gentle kneading for almost fifteen minutes, when Pip's stomach contracted and she threw up. The smell of the contents from her stomach, mixed with the vinegar solution, was vile.

Duncan grabbed some paper toweling and cleaned it up. As he was walking to the garbage can, Morag stopped him.

"No... don't throw it out. We need to know what it is." She was still kneading Pip's stomach. It wasn't long before another retching brought up some more.

Pip coughed and drew in a deep shuddering breath.

"Bring me the tea." Morag took it from Duncan and poured a small amount down Pip's throat. She swallowed it. Morag poured a bit more and satisfied it was going to stay down, she picked up the cat.

"She should be fine now. It was very close. That stuff had been in her for quite some time." She handed Pip to Duncan and went to check the contents of the paper towel. She searched through the mess of half digested food, mucous and grass. At first, she couldn't find anything. She was going through it a second time when she found what she was looking for. She knew Joly would never feed the cats' raw meat, but she found a very small amount, mixed in with everything else. She carefully removed it, went and got a small vial, placed the meat in it and snapped the lid on it.

"We need to know who did this. Make sure when Pip's well enough she takes you to where she found it."

"Now, let's go and see what's wrong with your wife."

They walked across the street, where Duncan carefully laid Pip on the sectional. Salem and Nefertiti went and sat beside her.

Duncan heard Sara and Randy in the kitchen and yelled at Sara to take Randy to school.

Morag headed up the stairs, afraid of what she might find. She had several scenarios' going through her head, and none of them were good. She walked into the bedroom and saw how pale Joly was. She walked over and laid her hand on her forehead. There was no fever. *Damn!* She'd been hoping there would be. She drew the covers back and began a careful inspection of Joly's nude body.

Duncan walked into the room, and was shocked when he saw what his Mother was doing. "What the hell you lookin' for?" He walked over and leaned down to see what she might be seeing.

Morag pointed. "Here, here, here. Do you see them?"

They were faint, but there were bruises covering most of Joly's torso, with more on her legs and arms.

"Maw? What is it?" He reached out and ran his fingers along Joly's cheek.

"She'll be fine, Son. Not to worry. You said she was thrashing around?"

"Yeah. Kinda reminded me of a rag doll. It was real weird, Maw. When she went still, it happened real sudden like."

"She was attacked by a witch…"

"What? Why?"

"Most likely the one we have to go and fight. I was going to tell you this morning. We're going to Australia. Go and get the tea you were brewing, she needs fluids. What kind were you making?"

"Chamomile and ginger."

Morag nodded. "Good choice." She sat on the bed and lifted the still figure into her arms. Joly moaned and opened her eyes. She tried to speak, but nothing came out.

"Be still child, Duncan's bringing you some tea."

Joly nodded and let her head fall against Morag's shoulder.

Morag heard Randy coming up the stairs. "Mommy sick. My Mommy sick."

Morag covered Joly as he ran into the room. He quietly walked to his Mother and touched her arm. "Mommy sick?" He looked at Morag.

"Mommy'll be fine, Sweetheart. She just needs some sleep."

"Oh."

Joly opened her eyes again and tried to smile at her son. Randy reached up to touch her face. "Mommy." He laid his head on her arm.

Duncan arrived with the tea, put it on the table and took his son down to Sara.

Morag put the cup to Joly's lips. She drank thirstily. Duncan arrived with another cup and Joly drank it too. She lifted her head.

"I feel like I've been run over by a truck." Her voice was still raspy, but stronger.

"Duncan, help me get her on her feet."

Between the two of them they got her standing up. "Sweetie... you need to concentrate. I want you to ground yourself. Son, we'll ground also."

Morag and Duncan, each with one arm around Joly, grounded themselves.

Joly put her palms out and tried to concentrate. She could feel the energies from the two beside her. She let herself absorb them and as she felt some of her strength returning, she grounded herself.

"Okay Sweetie, now you need to begin healing yourself." They sat her on the edge of the bed.

"Heal what?" She looked confused.

"Just a general healing, dear. Your entire body needs one."

"Okay." She still looked confused, but she did as she was told.

Ten minutes later, she smiled. "That feels better." Her voice was almost back to normal. She shook her head. "I don't understand what happened."

"I know you don't. I'll explain it later. Right now Pip needs you. She was poisoned. I got the crap out of her system, but now she needs your healing energies."

Joly stood. Duncan grabbed her robe and helped her put it on. They went downstairs, Morag and Duncan on either side of Joly. She still appeared weak.

Joly sat on the sectional and picked up Pip. Cradling her in her arms, she allowed her energies to flow.

Morag and Duncan went to the kitchen. "She'll need more tea. Healing Pip will help to heal herself. She will bring more energies to the fore because she's not doing it for herself."

"This witch in Australia. He or she is very powerful, right?"

"Yes. I suspect it is a *Sister of the Triple Moon*, one who has turned against the right path."

"Shee-it! That happens?"

"Son, there is good and bad wherever you go, whatever you do. You know that. Being a Sister is no different. For as much as we want to make the world a better place, there will always be those who want to destroy it."

"Can we defeat this witch?"

Morag smiled. "Of course we can. We have the Gods and Goddesses on our side. And we are three."

He nodded his head. "Do you think there's only one?"

"I dearly hope so."

"You can't tell?"

"It seems to be the work of only one, but I won't know for sure until we're there." She told him what the crystal had shown her.

"That's really nasty."

"What's really nasty?" Joly came around the corner and went and sat down. The color had returned to her face and her voice sounded normal.

"We leave for Australia tomorrow night at seven-thirty."

Her mouth felt gritty again and she wondered why. She got up to go and brush her teeth and rinse out her mouth. "I'll be right back," she croaked.

Morag noticed the facial expressions, as well as the voice change. She knew that Joly remembered nothing of the dream. That was the witch's doing. She knew the reason she hadn't been attacked was because she had her wards in place. Whoever it was, knew they were coming and was letting them know that he or she knew.

While Joly was in the washroom, Pip came into the kitchen. She looked weak and bedraggled, but at least she was up and walking. Duncan picked her up.

"Hey little girl. Nice to see you up and on your feet. When you're feelin' better, I need you to show me where you got that meat." Pip appeared content to be held and cuddled.

Joly returned and drank another cup of tea. "So tell me what's in Australia." Her mouth got the gritty taste in it again.

"What the heck?" Her voice croaked. She went to the sink and drank a glass of water. "That is so weird."

"

Morag now knew what was happening. Joly had been hexed. This particular one seemed to be behaving similar to a post hypnotic suggestion. Every time Joly heard the word Australia, something happened to her throat or mouth.

"Tell me what's happening in your mouth."

"It keeps getting this gritty feeling, like I've swallowed a bucket of sand."

"Ahh... okay. We can fix that. Then we'll discuss the trip."

Sara returned from taking Randy to school and Duncan filled her in on Pip's poisoning. He went to tell her about leaving and Morag shook her head. He raised an eyebrow, but kept quiet.

"How are you feeling Joly? You look okay."

"Much better, thanks. It's just my mouth now."

"You've been hexed, my Dear." Morag knew she wouldn't take kindly to that bit of news.

"*What?*"

"Yes, that's why the thing with your mouth keeps happening. It's an easy fix. I need to go and feed the birds. Give me a half hour, and then come over. I should be ready for you then. Oh, and either wear or bring a gown." She headed down the hallway.

Joly looked at Duncan with a frown on her face. "I don't understand. Hexed? How? When?"

"Darlin'." He placed Pip on the chair and walked over to her. He enfolded her in his arms. He loved her so much and to know that this was done while he was sleeping inches from her, really bothered him. He should have been able to protect her, and he hadn't. He'd grown lax in his duties. It wouldn't happen again. He kissed her softly, gently. "I love you pretty lady. We need to wait to discuss it, okay?"

"Honey, I don't want to wait. I don't understand what's going on. You're keeping something from me... *why?*"

"Darlin'... you need to wait."

"I'm sorry honey. I just really need to know what's going on."

"And you will, Darlin'. But later, okay. Please?"

She knew he wouldn't ask, if it wasn't something that needed to be done. But this was her that they were talking about. *Hexed?* No, she didn't think so.

"No, I want to know now. Damn it Duncan, *tell me!"*

"How's your mouth?"

"It's fine, now quit changing the subject."

"Australia."

Her mouth filled with the feel of grit. Her eyes opened wide and she looked at Duncan with her mouth half open, the choking sensation overwhelming.

"Yeah Darlin', now you know. Go rinse your mouth out. I'll make you some more tea." He turned to the stove, silently cursing her stubbornness.

She gargled with the mouthwash. Hexed? How had that happened and when? She thought about how weak she had been, about Morag telling her to heal herself, how battered she had felt. Okay, she knew when. Sometime while she was sleeping, but why? And why Australia?

Shit! She couldn't even think of the word. She gagged and retched into the sink. She swallowed another glass of water. *Gods!* She was going to float away.

She finally managed to drink her tea, and then she went up to get a gown. It had been advertised as a nightgown in the store where she bought it, but she used it for a ritual gown, when she wasn't with a group of people. It was a semi-transparent, silky mint green material and she loved the way it clung to her skin. She hadn't worn it in ten years.

She did another quick healing on Pip, told her she would want to know where she had gotten the poison from, when they came home again.

They crossed the street to Morag's. She led them to the back yard. In amongst her flowerbeds she had left a circular area of ten feet. It was there that she performed most of her outdoor rituals.

She handed Duncan a bowl of water. He sniffed it and recognized the scent of sandalwood, mixed with something else.

Morag led Joly to the center of the cleared area and told her to sit down. She lowered herself to the ground, folding her legs to the side. She knew what ritual she would do if she was alone, but Morag seemed to be doing something different. She was still learning. She smiled at Duncan, who was standing with the bowl, watching his Mother.

Morag finished setting up her small altar and turned around. "Duncan, I'd like you to wash Joly's face and neck… and don't forget to do behind her ears."

He smirked, and then he laughed. "Alrighty then."

He knelt down beside Joly and dunked his hand into the solution. "Why am I doing this?"

"The ritual we're about to do involves her face. It's no different from doing a complete body wash for many of our spells. For this one, it's all that's required."

He leaned forward and kissed Joly on the lips, then dribbled water over them. He kissed her on the forehead and splashed water on it. He kissed both ears and drizzled water over them, running his finger along the crease at the back. Joly shivered. He was making it hard to be serious. She tried not to smile, but failed, the small grin creasing the corners of her mouth. Duncan dripped water on her nose, grinning at her.

Morag looked on. "We might be here all day at this speed." She smiled to take the harshness out of the words.

"Sorry, Maw." He quickly finished with the washing process and Joly smiled at him, feeling the slight breeze cooling her damp face and breasts. Duncan had spilled the water across her shoulders and chest.

Duncan stood and looked down at his wife. The wet material of her gown left nothing to the imagination and her breasts appeared to be shimmering through the sheer fabric. He felt himself start to harden. *Mandrake! Down boy!*

Morag took the bowl from him and set it outside the circle. She went and stood on the left side of Joly. Duncan moved to her right.

Morag raised her arms.

"I call upon you Gods and Goddesses of old,
I call upon you Gods and Goddesses of new.
I call upon the Four Quarters
To aid me on this day.

I pledged to honor you in all ways,
I vowed to work for the good of all.
The universe maintains a balance.
The balance has been disrupted.
Evil has been found in our midst.
Help me to banish it from our presence."

Morag went to the altar and picked up her bell. She rang it three times.

"By Earth and Air, Fire and Sea,
Let no harm touch those close to me."

She lit two white candles and two black candles. She dipped her athame into the water and raised it in the air.

"In the name of the Goddess Bastet, I cast out from thee all impurities and unclean spirits."

She dipped the athame into the sea salt to purify it, and called out,

"Blessed be this salt, in the name of the Goddess Bastet, that which would malign or hinder shall be cast out and all good shall enter herein."

Morag picked up a magenta candle and handed it to Joly. She lit it and went back to the altar. She lit a smudging stick and handed it to Duncan. He walked around Joly letting the sandalwood smoke cleanse her. While he was doing that, Morag lit another black candle, which she placed in a small cauldron. She filled the cauldron with water, the candle flame burning brightly above it, and placed it on the ground in front of Joly.

She raised her arms and spoke.

"As above and so below
The sky, the earth, the universe aglow.
As without and so within
The universe our home, all veils so thin."

She returned to the altar and picked up a small bowl. She faced the east and dipped her index and middle fingers in the contents of the bowl. She raised the fingers and drew the sign of the pentagram in the air.

"Bastet, I have been with you from the beginning. Hear me this day. Help me to banish the evil that has been placed upon the one in our sacred circle."

She returned to Joly and taking her athame, she dipped the tip of it in the mixture. Withdrawing it, she traced a pentagram on Joly's forehead.

"I consecrate you, Joly McEwan, in the name of the Goddess Bastet."

Joly could smell the basil and garlic. Her stomach flip-flopped. *Gods!* Her mouth filled with saliva and she swallowed.

Duncan lit the incense. The smoke from the red peppers burned his eyes. He picked up the container and began walking around the circle, chanting quietly.

"Fire and air, earth and sea.
Hear me, hear my plea.
Earth and fire, sea and air,

Hear me, hear my prayer.
Air and earth, sea and fire
Hear me, hear my desire. "

Morag reached into her pocket and withdrew a stone. Joly recognized the tiger's eye and was pleased. She would have used the same.

Morag held the stone in the air.

"In the name of the Goddess Bastet I ask for protection,
In the name of the Goddess Bastet, I ask for deflection. "

She placed the stone against Joly's forehead. Joly felt the coolness and leaned into it. The stone was removed.

"Open your mouth my dear. "

Joly complied. Her stomach was still roiling. She had her eyes closed as she concentrated on not disgracing herself. She felt the coolness of the stone as it was placed on her tongue. She closed her mouth around it and felt her stomach settling down. She felt the tip of the athame retracing the pentagram on her forehead.

Morag began chanting.

"Protect, deflect.
Protect, deflect.
Protect, deflect. "

Joly gagged and swallowed.

"Protect, deflect.
Protect, deflect. "

The gritty taste returned and she felt a dry, choking sensation in her throat.

"Protect, deflect. "

She was sure she could actually taste the sand. The stone also seemed to be covered in grit. She started to gag.

"Protect, deflect. "

She choked and leaned forward to open her mouth. The sand poured out, it snuffed the candle in her hands and pooled on her knees and the ground. She retched and when there was no more sand, she vomited.

Duncan was still chanting, the tears streaming down his cheeks. He watched as the sand poured out of her mouth, and he saw her throw up. He wanted to go to her, but the spell wasn't done yet. He sent his love to her on the wings of the air currents.

Morag rested her hand on the top of Joly's head. As she did so, the candle that was burning in the cauldron of water spluttered out.

"The sand is gone, your throat is free.
By earth and air, fire and sea.
The pentagram upon your forehead lay
To protect you both night and day.
The stone I give will cause deflection.

You are safe, you have protection. "

She reached into her pocket and brought out another stone. She bent down and folded Joly's hands around it. She stood, walked to the altar and picked up the bell.

Duncan returned the incense to the altar and went to stand by his wife; he placed his hand on her shoulder. Morag rang the bell three times.

"Thank you my Gods and Goddesses for being with us today. Thank you Bastet, for answering my call."

She walked to the east.

"Guardian of the East, thank you for attending our Circle. I release you. Return to your home and harm none on your journey."

She walked counter clockwise to the north, then to the west, then to the south, thanking each Guardian and releasing them. She returned to the east and then continued to the altar. She blew out the white candles, leaving the black ones to burn down.

She returned to the circle and raised her arms.

"The circle is open, yet unbroken."

Morag went into the house and returned moments later with a towel. Duncan took it from her and knelt down to clean up his wife. He took his finger and wiped a bit of vomit from the edge of Joly's lip. He leaned in and kissed her. He tasted the vomit and sand.

He smiled at her. "I love you, Darlin'." He continued wiping her gown.

"I love you too honey." She opened her hands and looked at the Apache's Tear stone. She clasped her hand around it as Duncan helped her to her feet.

Morag wrapped her arms around Joly and hugged her. She smiled. "Go and get cleaned up. I'll come over in awhile and we'll discuss the trip."

Joly smiled back. "Yes, the trip to Australia." Her mouth remained clear. She took Duncan's hand and they walked around the side of the house and across the street.

They showered and dressed.

While Joly made something to eat, Duncan went outside to place some wards. He saw where Joly had placed the previous ones, so many months before. He shook his head. She might have more powers than he did, but she was lax in her everyday duties. It was okay. He didn't mind looking after the mundane things.

He had missed his drivers' exam, but it didn't really matter. He would re-book it when there was more time. They had looked at a few vans the previous day, but Joly was unhappy with what they had seen. He knew she wanted one in green and the only green one they had found, was a dark green that she didn't care for. He'd noticed that almost all the interiors, regardless of the exterior color, were gray or tan. He knew Joly would not buy anything with a gray or tan interior. She liked and needed color in her life. That was something else they would do when there was more time.

Joly joined him in the yard. "It's time to pick up Randy honey."

"Just a sec'." He finished placing the last ward. He would ward the house when they returned.

He took her hand and they walked to the school. Randy came bursting out of the doors grinning from ear to ear.

"Mommy, Mommy… you not sick. *Yaaay!*" He threw himself against her legs and wrapped his arms around her.

They each took a hand and walked home, content to listen to Randy chatter about his morning.

Over lunch Joly and Duncan shared the news that they were leaving the following night for Australia.

Sara wondered how long they would be gone. They weren't sure. They told her they would be discussing it in more detail with Morag that afternoon.

After lunch was over and Joly had cleaned up the mess, she went to the bottom of the stairs and called Pip.

Duncan was placing more wards and she let him know she was going to do a mind meld with the cat.

Pip and Joly went into the living room and Joly lay down on the floor. They began the meld. Joly noticed it went quicker and was pleased. She thought possibly the more it was done, the easier it became.

"So tell me wee Pip, just what happened yesterday."

"I'm sorry, Mistress. I know better. I wasn't even hungry. I don't know why I took the meat, Mistress. Can you please thank the Lady Morag for saving me?"

"Yes, Pip, I can do that. Now… tell me. Where did you find the meat?"

"Next door Mistress. I know you said we should never go over there, but I smelled it and I just wanted to see what it was. It was dark. I knew I was safe from the old woman. I'm sorry Mistress. I was bad."

"You found the meat over at Joan Ardell's?"

"Yes, Mistress."

"I'd like you to show me where, please."

"Yes, Mistress. Right now?"

"Yes, please, and Pip?"

"Yes, Mistress."

"I'm very glad you're okay."

"Thank you, Mistress."

"Pip? One more thing."

"Yes, Mistress?"

"How are Salem and Nefertiti getting along these days?"

"They mostly try to ignore each other. Nefertiti would get rid of Salem, if she thought she could get away with it. He knows this, so is very careful."

"Good. Thank you, Pip. Now let's go next door shall we?"

Joly called Duncan and they followed Pip out the basement door. They walked next door and Pip led them to an opening under the back steps.

Duncan could smell the rancid meat, before he saw it. Joly handed him a sandwich bag and he scooped up the poisoned delicacy.

They walked around to the front door and rang Joan Ardell's doorbell. While they stood waiting Duncan reached in his pocket and pulled out the little vial his Mother had given him, which contained the small sampling from Pip's stomach.

The door opened. Joan Ardell looked startled to see Joly standing there. She frowned at Duncan and scowled when she spotted the cat with them.

Duncan spoke. "Miz Ardell, I don't know if you remember me, Duncan McEwan. It doesn't matter. We have something for you."

He went to hand her the baggy. She looked at it and took a step back, the fear evident in her eyes. Duncan held out the vial.

"This, Miz Ardell, was removed from that cat's stomach. That cat, Miz Ardell, is a valued member of our family. We were not too pleased needless to say, when she told us you were the one that poisoned her."

Joly sucked in her breath. *Not a wise thing to say, Duncan.* She decided she had better interrupt. "Well, she didn't really *tell* us, Mrs. Ardell, but she did lead us right to your stash under the steps. Why would you do that? Why would you want to harm an innocent animal? And what if a child had found it and eaten it? Would you feel any guilt then?"

Duncan could tell Joly was about to lose it. He put his arm around her. "Miz Ardell, if I ever find, or even hear of any poison being outside on your property again, I swear you will be sorry." He tossed the baggy of meat through her door, into the living room. He placed the vial back in his pocket.

He turned Joly around. "Come on, Darlin', come on, Pip. Let's go home." They went down the stairs.

Joan Ardell watched them leave. The fear went all the way to her stomach. She started cramping. She shut the door and widely skirted the bag of tainted meat. She moved as fast as she could toward her bathroom, her cane thumping across the expanse of hardwood floor.

She didn't make it.

As she stood there soiling her underwear, she knew she would never put tainted meat outside again, regardless of how much cat crap she found in her flower beds. Nor would she ever say a harsh word to that Indian kid, regardless of how much she hated him and all of his kind.

She kept seeing the James girl as a child on her stomach, staring into the cat's eyes. ...*she told us you were the one that poisoned her.*

She awkwardly walked to her bathroom and began filling the tub. She wondered if it was time to sell her home and move into one of those seniors' complexes.

Morag walked outside and saw the three of them coming out of the Ardell property. She knew where the poisoning had come from. *Miserable old woman anyhow.*

"Hello! I was just on my way over. How are you feeling my dear?"

"I feel great, Morag. Thank you. Come in. I'll put the kettle on. Or would you rather have a glass of iced tea? It's gorgeous out today."

"Iced tea would be nice. I see you were next door. Everything all right now?"

Duncan snorted. "It damned well better be! Stupid old woman. I'd like to have wrapped my hands around her neck and squeezed."

"*Duncan!*"

"Sorry Maw, she just really pissed me off. What you got there?"

"A map." She fanned herself with it, making Joly smile.

They sat in the kitchen and made their plans for the trip. Randy interrupted numerous times and Sara finally took him out for a walk.

They laid the map out on the table. When they saw how remote the area was that they were headed to, Duncan suggested they rent a camper or motor home of some sort, so they wouldn't have to travel back and forth. Morag thought it was a good idea. It would also give them more room to store extra water.

That evening Morag called Stephen to let him know they were leaving the next day. He wanted to give them a ride to the airport. She agreed. Anything to get him away from the office.

Nefertiti was horrified to learn the Mistress had been attacked while sleeping. She informed Pip the next time she did something stupid, she was on her own. Nefertiti was not going to leave the house again, and leave the Mistress unprotected. She saw the Mister had placed wards and she went to check them out. She was surprised. He had actually done a good job.

She discovered the humans were leaving the next day and leaving the felines behind. She was not happy with this news, especially with it coming on the heels of the attack. She wondered if there was something else she could do.

Salem was also unhappy at being left behind. As much as he loved the big house, he knew his place was with the Mistress. All thoughts about moving on were gone. She had been attacked in her bed, while he was sleeping downstairs. He was still waiting for Neffy to tear a strip off him for not being aware of what had been happening. He knew he was still needed and resolved to start sleeping in the Mistress' bedroom.

Pip was still feeling very stupid for eating the bad meat. She was trying to stay out of everyone's way. She wished the Mistress wasn't leaving. With Randy in school the mornings were pretty boring. She decided she would sleep with Randy while the Mistress was gone.

Joly and Duncan waited until Randy was in bed to start packing. They had wanted to spend every possible moment with him before they left.

The next morning they walked Randy to school and then they went home and puttered in the yard. Joly weeded while Duncan mowed the lawn and edged around the flowerbeds and trees. The first time he felt the eyes staring at him he ignored it, but the second time, he decided he'd had enough of the old biddy next door. He put the edger down and faced the old woman's house. He raised his arms straight out in front of him and wiggled all of his fingers. Let her think he was putting a hex on her. She deserved it. *Bitch!* He never felt the eyes again.

They picked Randy up from school, had lunch and played with him until it was time to leave.

Stephen arrived just after three and they loaded the suitcases in his trunk. Both Randy and Joly were crying. Duncan also had tears in his eyes. Stephen watched the tearful parting in amazement. He couldn't ever remember crying over his parents leaving. He wondered if there was something wrong with him.

The drive to the airport was noisy with everyone chatting. Stephen was in better spirits than Morag had seen him in a long time. She wondered if he had moved out of the house yet, but didn't ask. She didn't want to put a damper on his good mood.

They had a long wait at the airport and when they were finally able to board the plane, they did so with a sense of relief.

Duncan watched as Vancouver disappeared from sight. They were off on another adventure. He wished his Dad was with them. He thought of Joly and her parents and realized he was lucky. He still had his Maw. He reached over and squeezed her hand. Morag gave him a quizzical look. He smiled back and put his arm around Joly.

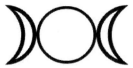

18. Death in the Desert

They changed planes at Sydney and arrived at Alice Springs at twelve thirty in the afternoon. They had been in the air for almost twenty-four hours and the time zones had shot them ahead by seventeen hours. By the time they cleared customs and got their baggage, it was almost two. They took a taxi to their hotel, and then Joly and Duncan went in search of a motor home to rent.

They found what they were looking for within the hour. It was a small unit, but came with everything they would need. There was a tiny washroom, a kitchen with a small fridge, a three-burner cook top, and a table with two bench seats, which made up into a single bed. Over the two bucket seats in front was a double bed. There was also a small closet tucked in between the table and the washroom. They were given a complete run down of how everything worked, things to be on the look out for and many other instructions. By the time they were allowed to leave with the vehicle, Joly felt like they should own it. They didn't get back to the hotel until supper time.

As they were only staying the one night, Morag hadn't bothered getting them a suite. She knew that if Joly and Duncan wanted to be alone, they would find a way. She thought about the small motor home in the parking lot and knew where they might spend part of the evening. She smiled to herself.

That evening when Joly was in the washroom, Duncan asked his Mother to lend him a hundred dollars. She never questioned him; she got her purse and handed him the hundred. He said he would be back shortly.

He yelled at Joly. "Hey Darlin', goin' out for a minute. Be right back."

She yelled back, acknowledging that she heard him.

The hotel they were staying at had a casino. Duncan had always been lucky where gambling was concerned. He wondered if it still held true after ten years. He headed to the cashier and exchanged the hundred dollar bill for five dollar chips. He headed to the blackjack tables and watched for a few minutes. There was either five or ten dollar betting with a maximum of either four hundred or five hundred dollars depending on which game one was playing. He started at a five dollar table.

Within twenty minutes, he had turned his one hundred dollars into three hundred fifty and he moved to a ten dollar table. Fifteen minutes later, he walked out with eleven hundred dollars in his pocket. He got back to the room and gave his Mother her one hundred dollars.

Joly was lying on their bed with Morag's crystal in her hands. "Hi honey. I was just checking in with Nefertiti." She watched Duncan hand Morag the money and smiled. "Were you lucky tonight?"

"Always, Darlin', always." He grinned at her and jumped on the bed.

Joly squealed and Morag jumped to her feet. "*Here!* Give me the crystal before you smash it to smithereens." She took it from Joly and as soon as she had, Duncan threw himself on top of her. She squealed again and a tickling contest ensued. Soon after, a pillow fight started. They got Morag involved and it wasn't long before she was throwing and hitting faster than the other two. When they were done, everyone was gasping and laughing.

After a few minutes, Duncan got off the bed and headed to the washroom. "Come on, Woman," he called, as he closed the door.

Joly grabbed some clean under things and joined him. He turned the shower on and climbed in. Joly heard him sucking in his breath and smiled. Seconds later, he stuck his hand out and waved for her to join him.

She climbed in the tub and Duncan grabbed her to him. He kissed her long and hard. She felt his erection throbbing in between them. She raked his back with her nails as he kneaded her breasts and rubbed himself to her. He lowered his head and sucked one nipple and then the other. Goosebumps covered Joly's arms. He slid down and buried his face in her damp curls.

Morag turned the television up. She heard the bumping, thumping and all the little noises that went with making love in a shower. She recognized them. She and Brody had been there, done that. She was smiling to herself when a news bulletin flashed across the screen.

Three more bodies had been found south of the Walungurru area. Once again, there were no marks on them. This brought the total number of deaths to thirty-two.

Some of the isolated aboriginal families were temporarily moving into communities. People were afraid. The superstitious nature of the aboriginals was running high. They said an evil witch was among them and that he was responsible for all the deaths. The police were trying to convince them that it wasn't a witch, but they were having no part of it.

The autopsies showed that they had all died from asphyxiation. Without any marks on the dead, it was as if they had been starved of oxygen.

When Joly and Duncan came out of the washroom, Morag told them what she had just heard. There was nothing they could do. They were trying to get there as fast as possible. They placed a sealing spell around the room, ensuring a safe nights sleep.

Joly and Duncan climbed into bed and Morag went to the washroom to change into her nightie and wash up. When she came out, her first thought was that one of the two had gone out, and then she realized they were both there. They were wrapped around each other so tightly, it looked like only one person was in the bed. She shook her head as she lay down and turned the light off. She would have smothered trying to sleep like that. As much as she and Brody loved one another, they had both needed their own space to sleep. At times, their queen size bed hadn't seemed big enough. She smiled as she thought about the two across from her. They could have slept on a single cot and still had room for another person.

They were up early. After a quick breakfast, they loaded up the minihome and drove to the mall. Morag went shopping for a few things she felt would be needed for when they met up with the evil one. Joly and Duncan bought groceries and several cases of bottled water. They drove to a gas station and bought extra gas to take with them, as well as extra oil and other necessities needed for when gas stations are far apart. Duncan insisted on getting an extra fan belt as well as some hoses. They also purchased a five gallon container, which they filled with water for the radiator.

It was already twenty-one degrees Celsius and the sun was shining in a cloudless sky when Joly headed north on the Stuart Highway. She had traveled less than fifteen miles when she saw the Yuendumu Road turnoff. She turned left and relaxed in her seat. According to the maps, she would be traveling west from this point on. The road was asphalt and she made good time An hour and a half later, she found the next turnoff with no problem.

She had to change roads twice again. The second time, she turned when she should have continued straight through. She realized she was headed the wrong way when the sun was on the wrong side. She turned around and went back to a place called Bunghara. She stopped and got out to stretch. Joly got some fruit from the fridge, while Duncan opened fresh bottles of water. Joly had another look at the map and they took off, again heading in a westerly direction. The road wasn't as smooth and she had to slow down. When she passed 5 Mile Bore and reached Papunya, she knew she was past the worst of the confusing roads and trails. The gravel road became rough and poorly maintained. Joly slowed down and proceeded with caution.

The land around them was red, the soil was red, the hills were red, and the rocks were red. It was an unusual and impressive landscape. The heart of Australia, the area was commonly known as the Red Center. It was a harsh, ancient land inhabited by various Aboriginal tribes. The tribes, although different, shared similar customs and ceremonies, and all traveled extensively through the vast land to meet their ceremonial obligations. This was the land of their ancestors and sites of ceremonial significance or dreaming places were extremely important to their way of life.

The Pintubi people were not discovered until nineteen sixty-three. Until then, they had maintained their traditional way of life, which had been unchanged for thousands of years. They were taken from their land, moved into a community, given clothes and had to adapt to a way of life completely foreign to them. In nineteen eighty-one they moved back to the land and the small community of Walungurru was founded. Approximately four hundred people lived there. The community had a school, a clinic, a women's center, store, art center and a council office. As well, there was a small air strip with weekly service to Alice Springs. A doctor and two nurses lived on site, as well as health workers and teachers.

Not all of the Pintubi people wanted to continue with the community life style. Several families returned to live on the land. The Walungurru council took responsibility for these families, and serviced the several outstations where they lived.

It was south of this community that Morag, Joly and Duncan were headed. It was getting dark when Joly arrived at the Sandy Blight Junction. They were thirty minutes from Walungurru. She turned left onto another rough gravel road.

"How much farther do you want to go tonight?"

"Stop when you're ready, dear. There's no point traveling in the dark."

She pulled off the road onto the desert floor.

Morag made up large tuna salads for supper, and after they ate Joly scryed home. All appeared to be well on the home front. When Joly was done with the crystal, Morag checked out the area to the south, but she found nothing. A sealing spell was placed around the mini-home.

They went to bed early, were up and ready to go when the sun rose at seven the next morning. The road soon became a track and they bumped along at an extremely slow pace. They had been traveling for three hours when they arrived at an impressive outcropping of red hills and rocks.

Joly parked by the rocks, pulling into the shade as far as she could. Duncan stretched and went to check out one of the large rocks. Joly went into the fridge and got a bottle of water.

Morag grounded herself and did a bit of exploring. She sniffed the air, but sensed nothing out of the ordinary. If they were in fact chasing a Sister, she would have an incredible power or powers. She could be anywhere with a barrier up to block the sensing. Morag didn't like it, but there was nothing to do but hope for the best. The three of them had tried to put a plan together, but not knowing what powers the witch possessed made it difficult.

Duncan had had his wand ready since getting off the plane. Morag noticed he'd done a meditation in the van. He was no match for what they were facing, but as long as the witch was concentrating on Joly and her, he should be able to do some damage from the rear.

Joly had grounded herself earlier and Morag could see she was doing another one. She was ready with her kinetic abilities and her wand.

For herself, she was as ready as she would ever be. Any knowledge that she had on the Sisters had been gone over in her mind. There wasn't much. She would have to depend on Joly for the power. She would simply treat the witch as a demon and act accordingly. She too, had her wand ready, as well as a small bag of sea salt.

Morag went to the van and got a bottle of water. "I'm going to climb up a bit and have a look around." She sidled in between two large boulders and vanished from sight.

Duncan took Joly's water from her and took a drink. She playfully punched him on the arm. "Thief! Get your own water. It's so hot out here this one won't last anytime at all, as it is."

"Yes, boss." He bowed, and laughing, he walked toward the van, which was thirty feet away.

Joly watched him, her eyes on his backside. She called out, "Nice buns, Hon."

He began walking with an exaggerated wiggle. She threw her head back and laughed.

The explosion was deafening. She jerked her head forward to see the van erupting into a fiery mass of flames. The blast blew Duncan off his feet.

"Run Duncan, run… it's going to blow." Absolute terror replaced any lucid thoughts; *the heat had to go.* Her body cooled and the air around her shimmered as the incessant heat waves fought with the cooling vapors that were being emitted from Joly's rapidly cooling body. She threw out her arms, pointed her fingers and directed the icy jets of air in Duncan's direction.

He got to his feet and began running toward her. The fuel tank ignited. The explosion blew apart the flaming vehicle, chunks of metal and debris flying in every direction like lethal shrapnel. Duncan landed face down in the sand. He got to his feet again and kept on running. Secondary explosions from the extra gas cans they were carrying continued the bombardment of flying debris.

Joly saw the jagged edged piece of metal flying toward him and knew it was being directed by something other than the explosion. She looked at her beloved and her heart melted, the ice evaporated, and she was filled with heat. She watched the piece of metal as it closed in behind Duncan. As she pictured herself on fire, she reached behind and grabbed her wand. In one fluid movement she brought it out in front of her and pointed it at the flying shrapnel. She felt the fire rising in her, felt it rush down her arm and felt the wand vibrating. She directed the heat across the open space. The metal incinerated less than two feet behind Duncan's head.

Morag heard the initial blast and opened her senses. There was only the faintest hint of something evil. She heard Joly yell, but couldn't make out what she said. She turned around to head back down to the ground. Seconds later, she heard the second explosion. She knew what had blown up. She cursed herself for leaving the two young people alone. She muttered as she scrambled down the smooth surface. "Hold on kids, I'm coming."

One second Joly was standing and pointing her wand, the next, she was flat on the ground. *What the...* She went to stand and her legs started twitching. She watched them, her mouth hanging open. She reached down to grab one leg and her arm went flying up in the air. Then the other arm did the same. Soon, all her limbs were twitching and flopping around, each independent of the others.

Duncan watched in horror and knew he was seeing the same thing he had watched in their bed. He looked around in vain for the one doing this, but could see no one. He ran toward Joly. He had almost reached her, when she lifted into the air and slammed face down several feet away. He thought about her throat and knew sheer terror. He heard a sound from the direction of the rocks. He turned to see his Mother standing with her arms out. As he watched, she slowly disappeared.

He ran toward Joly and once again, her body was picked up and carried away from him. Again, she was thrown face down in the sand. He had seen her eyes were open, but she made no sound. She lay where she had landed, her arms and legs spasming uncontrollably, her face buried in the red sand. He knew she couldn't breathe. As he watched, unseen hands turned her over. *Thanks Maw!*

A scream of rage came from the far side of the rocks.

Morag felt her then. She had let her guard down. *Bad mistake on her part.* She headed toward her, still invisible.

He sensed her as she closed in on him and tried to direct his levitating abilities toward her, but he missed. She swept in beside him and reached into her pocket. She withdrew a handful of sea salt and threw it in his eyes.

Again came the scream of rage, this one combined with agonizing pain. He wiped at his eyes frantically. Morag stood and watched calmly. When he had finally quit rubbing them and the tears had lessened enough that he could once again see, she threw another handful of salt at him. Then she withdrew her wand. The bloody murdering bastard would kill no one else. She allowed herself to become visible.

Duncan had reached Joly and lifted her in his arms. He ran in a zigzag pattern to the protection of the rocks. He gently laid her down and turned to go and help his Mother. He heard the guy screaming in pain and knew she was responsible for whatever agony he was suffering. *Whatever she was doing, it's not enough. The asshole's going to pay for what he did to Joly.*

Morag pointed the wand and spoke the words. The end of the wand vibrated and the man fell to the ground. He moaned, still attempting to clean the salt from his eyes. She went to hit him with a second charge, when she became conscious of movement behind her. She whirled around, the wand pointed in front of her.

Joly shook her head. She had sand in her nose and mouth. She desperately needed a drink. She gingerly moved her arms and found that other than being sore, they were okay. She tried to stand but her legs refused to cooperate. Every bone in her body was hurting. She looked for Duncan and Morag. From her spot in the rocks, she could see neither, but a sparkle on the ground caught her eye. It was her bottle of water. *Oh, Gods...* she needed it. She stuck her head out and looked around. She saw nothing. She started crawling toward the bottle that lay twenty feet away.

Duncan stood with his wand pointed at the downed witch's legs. Morag lowered her wand and stood back. Duncan sent a charge that hit him in the kneecap. The guy screamed. Then Duncan hit him in the hand, first one and then the other. The man's screams were deafening. Duncan pointed his wand at the second kneecap and let go with another charge. The evil witch passed out. *"Bastard!"* Duncan turned to go back to his wife.

Duncan saw Joly crawling out in the open. He wondered what she was doing when he spotted the bottle lying in the sand. He jogged out toward her.

Morag didn't hold with torture, but understood her son's rage. She approached the unconscious witch with caution, her mind awhirl. This was a male, not a Sister. What was going on? There was no way he could have such strong power. *Gods! There were two of them!*

She whirled around. *"Duncan...* there's another one. Watch out!"

Her warning came too late.

Joly heard Morag yell and turned in the direction of her voice. She saw Duncan and started to smile.

Duncan shimmered on the sand.

Joly blinked and thought she was seeing things. The shimmer remained. As she watched, Duncan walked away from himself. The shimmering stopped. Two very solid Duncan's stared at each other.

They both shook their heads and looked at Joly. The one on the right spoke. "Uh... Darlin', you want to do something about this."

The one on the left pointed to the other. "He isn't me, Darlin'. You might want to get rid of him."

Joly shook her head. *Which one was her Duncan?* She sat on her backside, and realized that she still had her wand tightly gripped in her hand. She wrapped both hands around it, finding a small amount of comfort with something familiar. She rested it on her legs, the thought crossing her mind that the world had gone crazy. She needed a drink. She was having trouble thinking. Gods, she was thirsty. Her mouth was still gritty from the sand and every time she breathed in, she could feel granules of sand disappearing up her nose.

She listened to the two Duncan's arguing over which one was the real one.

"Joly, for the love of the Gods… *do something!*"

"Joly, I love you. What the hell you waitin' for?"

"Darlin', he can't possibly look that much like me."

"Yeah, surely you can tell us apart."

She looked like she was about to pass out. She knew this and was content to let the evil Duncan think that. She wasn't sure what she was waiting for, but she would know it when it happened. *Where's Morag? I'd kind of like some help here.* Her wand appeared to be lying loosely in her hands. It was not. She had complete control of it, and it was ready and waiting for the power within to be released.

The Sister had the power to shapeshift. Morag knew there were those with the ability, but she had never seen one before this. She knew she had to take extreme caution. Even invisible, this Sister was sure to sense her. She wasn't ready to die yet, and she definitely wasn't about to die by the hands of another Sister. She began the process of blocking all of her senses. It wasn't something that could be done with any speed. She needed to block each sense separately. She began with becoming invisible again. Once that was done, she needed to remove her scent.

The one Duncan turned to the other. *"Enough of this bullshit!"* He attacked the other figure.

Joly raised the tip of her wand.

The two figures tussled for a minute, then the one threw the other away from him. *"Now Joly!* Kill him."

Still she waited.

The one on the ground picked himself back up. "Thanks Darlin', had me worried for a second."

Morag was ready. She advanced slowly. She checked for footprints in the sand. There were none. She approached the two from behind. The only trouble with what she was doing, was that with all her senses blocked, she couldn't sense which of the two was the real Duncan. She could only observe, and hope to see something that would tell her who was who.

Joly knew the impostor would only play the game until she tired of it. What she would do then, she wasn't sure. *Gods!* She needed a drink. She wondered how long they could last in this heat.

"Darlin', I don't know what you're waiting for, but I've had enough of this B.S." Duncan on the right reached in the back of his jeans.

"Yeah. Enough is enough!" The other Duncan reached in the back of his jeans.

They both pulled their wands out and pointed them at each other.

Joly raised hers.

Morag saw what was happening. Joly's wand was pointed directly at herself. She had to move fast. She let her guard down as she turned to get out of the line of fire.

The evil one sensed the movement and she whirled around, her wand already vibrating.

Joly sensed the movement almost before it happened. Her wand vibrated and sparked at the same time as Duncan's did.

Shelley Sawyer knew she had lost this round. As the two lethal charges approached her, she twirled to her left and vanished into nothingness.

The two charges hit the sand and blew a hole five feet deep into the earth.

Joly watched Duncan, afraid that he would again split into two. She glanced at the bottle still laying ten feet away. Looking back at Duncan, she got to her knees and began crawling toward it.

Duncan watched Joly, waiting to see if she would start flopping around again. Not taking his eyes off her, he started walking toward her, every nerve ending in his body tingling. He was terrified the bitch would come again, just as he reached her.

Morag, still invisible, stood with her back against the rocks, watching and waiting. She watched them both, all her senses wide open and on high alert. She might be gone for the moment, but she knew without a doubt, the Sister would be back. The fifty thousand dollar question was when?

Joly felt the hot plastic. Still watching Duncan, she removed the cap and guzzled down half the water, some of it spilling out of the sides of her mouth.

"Darlin', you wanna save a bit for Maw and me?"

She removed the bottle from her mouth, gasping for breath as she did so. She held it out to him, with no apology. She knew they were all thirsty, but she was the one that had had half the desert shoved down her throat.

Duncan took a mouthful, swirled it around in his mouth and swallowed. He reached for the cap. Joly handed it to him and watched as he carefully screwed the lid back on.

"Help me up?" Her voice sounded scratchy.

Duncan reached for her. As soon as he felt her hand in his, his eyes filled with tears. He pulled her to her feet and held her tightly against him.

She could feel his body vibrating and knew that hers was vibrating also. They clung to each other, both wondering when the next attack would come.

"Come on." Duncan turned and keeping his arm around her, he led her toward the rocks. Once they were in the shade, he told her to ground herself. He grounded with her.

"'Okay Darlin', you better do a healin' while you can. I'm gonna go find

Maw." He took the water with him.

Joly assumed the Goddess position and grounded herself again. She was still feeling the effects of the sun. She welcomed the healing light into her body.

"Maw? Where are you?"

Duncan walked along the edge of the rocks, looking around for something, but unsure whether he would even know it if he saw it.

Morag materialized several feet in front of him. He wrapped his arms around her and she returned his embrace.

He handed her the water.

"Is this it?"

"Probably. We need to check the wreckage, see if there's anythin' to salvage."

She took a drink. "I still had some water when I heard the explosion. The bottle should be up in the rocks."

"I'll get it later."

They walked back to where Joly was waiting.

Morag smiled and held out her arms. Joly walked into them and they hugged. Joly could feel the tears but knew she didn't dare cry. Their bodies needed all the moisture they could conserve.

It was a somber threesome that walked out to the wreckage. They knew their chances of survival were minimal at best. A full bottle of water wouldn't last a day for one person, never mind three. In Alice Springs, they had been told that each person needed to carry a minimum of five liters of water per day. That amounted to three and a half gallons for the three of them for one day.

They no longer had the area maps and unless they walked in the heat of the sun, they had no way of knowing which way to go. None of them were familiar with the stars of the southern hemisphere.

They began the disheartening task of searching through the bits of aluminum, fiberglass and steel.

Morag sensed it before she found it. She lifted several chunks of fiberglass and bits of wall paneling away, and underneath, her crystal sat unscathed. The green brocaded box it had been sitting in, appeared to no longer exist. She picked it up and smiled.

"Look what I found."

The other two both looked and were amazed to see what she was holding. Their moods brightened with the discovery, and they resumed the search through the rubble with lighter hearts.

They found enough scraps of material that they were able to fashion kerchiefs to wear over their heads for protection against the merciless rays of the sun. Joly decided that Duncan looked like a pirate. All he was missing was the eye patch.

An hour later they surveyed the small pile of items they had salvaged. There wasn't much. Two cans of tuna and three cans of beans were all that remained of their food supplies. They had found two bottles of water, the plastic melted, but in tact. The other major discovery was Joly's handbag, which had been wedged in behind her seat. Her and Duncan's passports were safe, for all the good they would do in the middle of the desert. They looked in vain for Morag's purse, but could find no trace of it

"Is there any point in continuing with this?" Joly wiped the perspiration off her brow, with her arm. It was well over thirty degrees Celsius in the sun. She went and sat in the shade of a rock, wondering how they were going to get out of this mess. She knew Morag was good with her magic, but she couldn't fathom how she could utilize it in the middle of nowhere.

Duncan had found the small fridge but the door was melted shut from the heat of the blast. He had tried with various pieces of metal to unseal it, but had no success. He knew there were several bottles of water inside it. He was wondering if he could open it with his wand, without damaging the bottles.

"Hey Maw… come here." Morag straightened from the pile of debris she had been sifting through. She rubbed the small of her back and walked over to where he was standing.

"Can we get into this without damaging the bottles inside?"

"A piece of cake, Son. Let's finish here first. The water is safe where it is."

Duncan saw Joly sitting in the shade and walked over to her. "You okay, Darlin'?"

"I'm okay." She smiled, her teeth glistening white through her red, dirt encrusted face.

"Come on then, no slackers allowed." He reached down and pulled her to her feet.

She looked at his red arms and legs and was thankful that she could at least heal the sunburns that they were getting. Morag was wearing a loose cotton skirt that had been covering her legs, when she was crouched down searching, but the short sleeved cotton blouse offered no protection for her arms. Duncan was wearing shorts and a T-shirt and had the most skin ex-posed of the three of them. Joly was wearing cotton slacks and a T-shirt.

They sifted through the rubble for another hour, their only finds, a can of salmon and one of carrots.

Morag desperately wanted a piece of the material from her crystal ball box. She knew it was a silly thing to be looking for, but nonetheless, she looked. She found nothing, not so much as a small scrap of it which she thought was strange, with the crystal itself being in tact.

A fragment of a thought skittered across her mind and was gone. *What was it?* She tried to bring it to the fore and could not. There was something she was missing. *Damn!* She hated it when she had incomplete thoughts. She needed a drink.

She walked over to the shade, picked up the partial bottle of water and opened it. She took a small mouthful, swirled it around and swallowed. She recapped the bottle and put it down.

"Duncan, I think we're done here. Do you want to go up and get that other bottle of water? I'll open the fridge and then we should rest in the shade for a bit. The sun should be down in another two or three hours. We'll need our strength if we're going to try and walk out tonight."

"Okay." He headed to the rocks where hours earlier, he had watched his Mother disappear from sight. He squeezed in between the two boulders and vanished.

Morag walked over to the fridge and removed her wand. She envisioned a small welding torch, the tip glowing with a blue flame and touched it to the spot where the door joined the body of the unit. She was rewarded with the sounds of melting metal. She carefully went across the top and around the top edge, repeating the process several times. She had broken through in one small area, when she became aware of the scent of evil. She whirled around, but there was nothing. She turned back to the fridge.

Gods, no! She turned and ran. She had gone less than ten feet when the fridge blew. The door hit her solidly in the middle of her back and knocked her to the ground. She lie there with the breath knocked out of her, conscious of silent laughter emanating from somewhere up in the rocks.

Joly had gone back to the shade with the two cans. She sat with her back against the rock and closed her eyes. The explosion startled her and by the time she focused on Morag, the door had already hit her. Joly jumped to her feet and ran to help her. As she leaned down, Morag looked toward the rocks.

"I'm fine child. Get Duncan. He's in danger." She lifted herself onto her arms.

Joly pushed the door off Morag's back and lit out running for all she was worth. She reached the crevice in between the two rocks, sidled through and scampered up the uneven incline. She wanted to call out, but knew she needed to be quiet. Her rubber soled jogging shoes made little noise as she ascended the twisting pathway.

She hadn't gone far when she saw the bottle, the lid beside it and the water already evaporating from where it had been dumped. *Shit!* Where was Duncan? She picked up the bottle and upended it over her open mouth. She was rewarded with one drop of moisture on her tongue. She quietly placed the bottle back on the ground and continued climbing. She had her wand in her hand, and wondered what she was going to find.

Morag had managed to get to her feet. Her back was injured, but there was time enough later to get Joly to do a healing on it. She thought that a couple of ribs were broken. *Damn!* She really needed to quit breaking ribs. She looked at the interior of the fridge. Everything that had been inside was melted to a blackened crisp. The witch had put a spell on it. She sent a quick prayer of thanks to the Gods that Duncan hadn't succeeded in opening it.

Joly was fast running out of breath. Her mouth was dry and she felt light-headed. She realized none of them had had anything to eat since before seven that morning. She paused and leaned against a rock to catch her breath, and became aware of a strange clinking sound coming from behind her. *What is that?* She wondered if she should go back or continue climbing.

Duncan came first. She continued up and around another boulder. *No! No! No!* Duncan was directly ahead of her. He was bound with rope, his knees bent and his ankles and hands tied together behind his back. There was no movement.

Her nostrils flared as she opened her senses. She didn't feel the evil one, but she knew that meant nothing. She thought about the noise she had heard. She felt the evil one had been there and she wondered what was next on her agenda.

She hurried to Duncan, skirting around him to see his face. Her gasp of horror turned into a moan. He was awake, but just. A gag was shoved in his mouth, held in place with duct tape. There was dried blood across his face and one eye was swollen shut. She saw the bruises on his arm. She laid her hands on his face. She did a quick healing, just enough to take away the pain. She carefully peeled back the tape and removed the silky material from his mouth. She automatically shoved it in her pocket, always conscious of not littering. She went around behind Duncan and untied the rope. She rubbed his legs, getting the circulation going, and then helped him to his feet.

He tried to say something, but nothing came out.

"Hush honey. Save your breath." She wrapped her arm around him and started down the slope. She knew Duncan was dehydrated, but the urge to get back to Morag was overwhelming. They mustn't separate again. It seemed to be what *she* was waiting for.

Morag knew she wasn't safe alone, so again, she became invisible. She removed all of her senses and stood still, unsure what she was waiting for.

Joly and Duncan slowly made their way around the rocky outcrops. They came to a dead end. Joly shook her head. She was sure there had been only the one path when she went up. They turned around and climbed again. When they reached the spot where the empty bottle lay, she felt a terrible foreboding. They were on the right path. The damned woman had blocked the way down. She led Duncan over to a shady area of the rocks and eased him down. *Gods! We need water.*

She had the ability to make ice. Would *she* give her the time to do it and would it be enough for the two of them?

Nothing ventured, nothing gained. Her Father's voice filled her head. She smiled. "Thanks Dad."

Duncan looked at her. He was completely done in. He wondered why Joly was talking to her Dad. He hoped she wasn't hallucinating. He knew they really needed a drink.

She opened her arms and prayed to her Goddesses and Gods. She grounded herself. She found two small rocks and thought about ice forming on them. *Gods... I'm so tired... no, not tired... weak.* She tried to bring forth the cold and nothing happened. She looked at Duncan and knew she had to do this or he would die.

No! I won't let that happen! The anger bubbled up inside of her. She felt the coolness build and she slowly brought it to the surface and concentrated on the two stones in her hands.

Duncan felt the air around him cool. He knew he must be dying because he could tell it was still hot. He could see the shadows from the sun. He thought it was a terrible waste. Joly had just found him, and now she was going to lose him again. He felt his eyes tear. *I love her so much.* He wished he had been able to protect her, to save her. He thought about his Mother, alone down below and wondered if she was still alive. He hoped so. Joly would need one of them to keep her company to the end and he didn't think it was going to be him.

He felt the cold against his parched lips and automatically opened his mouth. The icy stone was a shock. His good eye flew open and he jumped when he saw Joly so close to him. She was sucking on something and smiling at him.

"Hi honey. You okay?" The low, gravelly voice didn't sound like her at all.

The moisture trickled down his throat. He didn't trust himself to speak. He'd thought he was dead, and there was his wife smiling at him like nothing was wrong. He nodded his head, tears welling in his eyes. She would never know how much he loved her. He hadn't known how strong she was. That she could smile at all, given their current circumstances, amazed him.

"I need to go and see if I can find a way to get us out of here. Will you be okay for a couple of minutes?"

He nodded again and closed his eyes. He didn't want to watch her walk away. He pictured her smiling face and knew he would die a happy man. He had been so blessed to have such a wonderful wife. He wondered how long he would have to wait before he would find her in another life, another time.

Morag heard something to her left. She didn't move. She didn't breathe. She slowed her heartbeat, so it barely was pumping enough blood to keep her alive. She waited. She heard nothing.

Wait! There it was again. Whatever it was, it was closer now. In one hand, she held her wand. In the other, a handful of sea salt. She held her breath.

She almost gave herself away when she realized what it was that she was hearing. The Sister was dragging her hand along the rock face as she took a step and paused to listen.

She was close, very close.

Morag waited.

Shelley Sawyer's every sense was on high alert. She'd blocked the other two up above and knew they would die soon. The one down here was the one she was concerned with. The crone still had tucker and water. She didn't think the ratbag could get back to civilization, but not knowing what powers she had, the possibility was there. She was as cunning as a shithouse rat and she was dangerous. The bitch had killed her baby brother, and now she was going kill her, slowly and painfully. She hadn't realized the crone's powers were so strong.

She had made the mistake of thinking it was the young one who was the most dangerous. That she put that pathetic drongo ahead of her own safety only emphasized how weak she was.

She smiled as she thought of the look on the idiot's face as she had dumped the bottle of water on the ground. She had enjoyed kicking the crap out of the bastard. Her kick boxing had always come in handy. She should have killed him, but the sun would do that soon enough.

She wondered again, how many more of the Sisters were out there. Her plan to annihilate them all and reign supreme over the world was working well. It had taken her a long time to figure out how to make the boxes with no air, too long. Each one she built was bigger than the previous. Soon, she should be able to cover small towns, asphyxiating all within. Then she would start on the cities. That they didn't work on the Sisters had slowed her down. She hadn't thought she would have to kill them separately.

She had killed one Sister in Asia and someone had done her a favor and gotten rid of the one in India. Soon, these two would be history. She thought about the magical number thirteen and wondered if that was how many there were. If that was the case, she had eight more to get rid of. She had discovered two more in Florida and she would take care of them next. She had started things rolling over there that she would personally finish up, as soon as she was done here.

She needed money. She would have to box in a bank and rob it.

Then there was still the damned sorcerer to deal with.

Where the hell is she?

Shelley took another step forward.

She was directly to Morag's left. Her next step would have her bumping into Morag. Morag raised her hand and threw the salt. As she threw it, she was on the move. She knew she had worn out her welcome at that particular spot.

As she had brought her arm up, the evil one felt her and sent a charge of electricity that would have downed an elephant. It blasted a hole in the rock face, spraying splinters of glass like rock shards in every direction.

Morag's aim was true and the salt hit the other woman's eyes.

Her concentration gone, Shelley rubbed at her eyes, cursing a blue streak. Rock chips had also found their way to her face, cutting her skin, and the blood ran in rivulets from her forehead into her eyes.

She was an idiot. She could have killed them all at any time, but she thought she'd show them some real power. She liked playing, flaunting her abilities.

Morag watched as she became visible. Still invisible herself, and unconcerned with the current state of the other one's senses, she walked to her and slammed her foot into the other one's knee. As she connected with her, she felt the familiar oneness. She heard the bone snap. The Sister fell to the ground, without uttering so much as a whimper. *Tough bitch, this one.*

She looked at the hole in the rock. Damn, but they had been lucky. If she hadn't been so busy trying to impress them with how powerful she was, she could have killed them all in a heartbeat. Her main ability appeared to have been electrokinetics. Had she and Joly met on a fair field, it would have been a fight to end all fights.

She wasn't about to screw around with this one.

Shelley felt the oneness and was amazed by the feeling. Then she felt her knee snap and she was falling. She landed hard.

The oneness… this is my Sister. What have I done?

She pointed her wand and killed her. She pushed the body over with her foot. The woman appeared to be in her mid thirty's. She had a hard look to her face and her muscles showed she worked out regularly. Yeah, this was a tough one. The world was definitely better off without her.

She went to their small pile of goods and picked up a full bottle of water. She unscrewed the cap and took a drink. She recapped the bottle and walked to the crevice. She didn't know what she was going to find, but she prayed that the Gods and Goddesses were looking out for the other two.

Joly checked the dead end. It seemed to be one solid piece of rock going all the way around. She knew it wasn't. She stood back and pointed her wand. It quivered and a large chunk of rock broke away.

She walked around the bend and checked on Duncan. His eyes were closed. She was worried. He needed more moisture. *Damn it!* She allowed the anger to build again and she picked up two more small rock chips.

Duncan felt his lip being pulled down. He didn't care any more. If something wanted to eat him, so be it. *I love you, Joly.*

I love you too, honey. Now come on. Open your mouth for me.

He tried to respond. It was too much effort. He felt fingers force his teeth open. The stone in his mouth was removed and another took its place. Without any conscious thought, he sucked. He was still sucking on it when the fingers inched their way back in and took it from him. *No!* Another one took its place. He resumed sucking.

He managed to open his good eye. She was there, watching him. When she saw his eye open, she smiled. *Oh Gods, I love you so much.*

"A little better?"

He nodded. He noticed something was wrong with her voice. What was it? He couldn't think. It took too much effort. He closed his eye again. The light was bothering him.

Joly stood, weaved a bit and found her balance. She needed moisture too, but first Duncan. She needed to get them out of there. She walked back to the blockage and raised her wand. Before she could give it instructions, there was a blast from the other side. The whole rock face shook.

She stepped back, almost falling. She held on to the rock beside her. *Morag? It has to be Morag.*

"Morag!" She thought she shouted. She didn't know her voice was gone.

Joly slid to the ground, too weak to stand any longer.

Morag let go with another blast from her wand. *There!* She could see a glimpse of daylight on the other side. One more should do it. She raised her wand again. *What was that?* Something moved, blocking the sliver of light. She opened her senses and felt Joly on the other side. *Damn!* She would have killed her with the next blast. She got as close to the tiny crack as she could.

"Joly, can you hear me?" There was no answer. "*Joly?*"

Joly heard someone calling to her. The roaring in her head almost drowned it out. *What? What are you saying? Does it even matter?* She was too tired to think.

Morag listened with her senses, as well as her ears. There was no answer. She needed to get water to them. *Where's Duncan? Did Joly find him?*

There was no alternative. She had to get to the other side. She had not ventured through anything solid in years. She hoped she could still do it. She took another drink and carefully tucked the bottle and her wand in the deep pocket of her skirt.

She grounded herself and called upon the element of air to assist her. She willed her body to become one with the air. She felt it in her toes first. The feeling of pins and needles always bothered her. She looked down and saw that her toes were gone. *Good!* It was working. She concentrated and soon felt her fingers disappearing. It was a long slow process, breaking ones body down into individual molecules. She felt herself come completely apart.

She moved toward the crack, the molecules moving as a mass toward the rock face. The feeling as she went through the rock was a strange one. It was like she was being hit with a million tiny grains of sand. It didn't hurt; it just felt strange. She was through. The process of putting herself back together went much quicker. She saw Joly lying at her feet and grabbed the water out of her pocket. She removed the cap and trickled the water through the parched lips.

Joly gagged and coughed. She opened her eyes. Morag put the bottle to her lips and she drank deeply. Joly turned her head to the side. Her lips moved but nothing came out.

"What, dear?"

Her lips moved again. *Duncan.*

"Where is he dear? Is he near?"

She nodded her head once.

Morag went around the corner. She saw him leaning against the rock, his head on his chest. *Gods, no!* She lifted his head and gasped. The black eye was swollen and the rest of his face didn't look much better. She forced some water through his teeth. He coughed, a small rock falling out of his mouth. *Thank the Gods!*

She put the bottle to his lips, tipping it up. He swallowed. *Good!*

She ran back to Joly and gave her another drink. Joly lifted her head. She croaked out Duncan's name.

"He'll be fine dear. Not to worry." She ran around the corner and gave Duncan another drink.

He opened his mouth. Before he could say anything, Morag said, "She's fine, not to worry."

He relaxed.

The sun was going down and already the air felt cooler. They would be cold through the night. Morag knew the other two were in no shape to make the trek to the bottom and she wasn't sure what crawled or walked on the desert floor in the dark. She would have to go and bring up what remained of their meager possessions.

She decided it would be easier to drag Duncan down to Joly, so she wrapped her hands under his armpits and pulled.

Shit! She'd forgotten about her ribs. She couldn't drag him.

"Duncan? Listen to me. Joly is around the corner. Can you crawl down to her? She's worried about you."

He pushed himself over onto his stomach and lay there.

Morag reached down and gave him another small drink.

She walked to where Joly was lying and gave her another drink. "Joly, listen to me. Duncan is worried about you. Can you get yourself up to him? I have to go and get our supplies."

Joly turned herself over onto her hands and knees and began crawling.

Good! Morag pulled out her wand and pointed it at the rock wall. One more blast and she had her pathway through. She kept her wand ready, unsure what she might meet on her way down. She made it to the bottom and walked to their small pile of belongings.

She opened Joly's handbag and placed her crystal inside, along with the three cans of fish. She tucked the beans and carrots in her skirt pockets and picked up the handbag. She reached down and picked up their last full bottle of water and the one that still had a few swallows left in it. She kept her wand ready as she made the trip up the winding pathway.

She found Joly and Duncan wrapped tightly around each other. "Alright you two. We need to move up to higher ground. Are you ready?" She knew she sounded too chipper, but she was ready to collapse and knew she probably would if she didn't keep moving.

Joly lifted her head. Morag went to her and gave her another drink.

"Come on dear. You need to pull yourself together. You need to heal Duncan... and I also have need of your gift."

"Sorry. Didn't mean to pass out." The voice was a harsh whisper.

"It's alright dear. Here, let me help you up." Morag reached out her hand.

Joly slowly got to her feet and once she was up she leaned against the rock wall. She assumed the Goddess position and grounded herself, and then she opened herself to let in the healing light.

Morag was going to drop. She could feel herself getting far too light headed to continue on. She slumped against the rock opposite Joly. Her legs felt like jello.

Joly finished her self-healing and saw Morag slowly slipping to the ground. Two steps and she was beside her. She lowered her down gently and ran her hands around Morag's body. She found the damaged ribs in her back and sent her healing energies to them and then did a general healing on her friend. She picked up the almost empty bottle of water and insisted Morag have a drink.

She turned her attention to Duncan. She laid him out flat and started with his face. Ten minutes later, she had done all she could for the moment. She was still weak herself and she needed to rest.

"Morag, do you still want to go up?" Her voice was stronger, but raspy.

"I'm not sure we can make it. What do you think?"

"We should try." She went to Duncan and helped him to his feet. He still looked terrible, but he was mobile.

"Come on, Maw." He weaved his way over to her and gave her his arm. They held on to each other as they slowly made their way to higher ground. They didn't want to go all the way to the top, as they would get the first blast of heat when the sun rose. They found an area that would give them shade and also gave them a view of the pathway back down.

The Sister and her cohort might be gone, but they didn't know what other evil might lurk around the corner.

Duncan managed to get a can of beans opened with the small pocket knife he carried, and they hungrily ate their portions, washing it down with the last of the opened bottle of water.

They huddled together on the ground, their arms around each other. They slept from sheer exhaustion, the unfelt cold creeping in and wrapping itself around their bare flesh. Sometime in the darkness of the night, each woke up shivering, curled in tighter to the others and slept again.

By early morning, unable to ignore the cold any longer, they stirred and awoke. Their teeth chattering, they knew it was time to get moving.

Duncan opened a can of tuna which they shared, and then they began the trip down the rocky hill. They moved slowly in the blackness, the predawn light not yet reaching in amongst the rocks. They listened for any nocturnal animals that might be there, but they heard nothing. They reached the bottom and squeezed through the crevice. They knew which way they had to go. They discussed whether they should stay where they were and hope for another traveler to come along, or whether they should take their chances out in the open.

"I think Joly should do another healing on us and by then it should be light enough for me to check with the crystal." Morag knew they needed rest, but she also knew that without water, it really didn't matter whether they stayed or went. She thought about the protection of the rocks and knew that would be her choice, but she would do whatever the other two decided.

She was well aware that she could get herself out of there. She had the ability to travel through space, but she knew she wouldn't do it. She would not leave the other two behind and she didn't think she could take the two with her. One, possibly. She was too weak. No, she would stay with her two charges and hope for the best.

Joly did the healings on them, concentrating on Duncan's battered face, Morag's ribs and the burnt skin. When she was done, they all felt better and even somewhat positive about their predicament.

Morag knew if there was another witch in the communities to the north, she could contact them and let them know their whereabouts. She tried, but received no answer.

She walked toward the end of the hill, her crystal in her hands. The sun was throwing a low light in the distance. She thought about going back up to the top of the outcropping where the sun would already be shining. No, she wanted to conserve what energy she had.

Joly and Duncan had told her about the ice crystal rocks and she knew that would work for a while, but not indefinitely. The sun would sap their strength and Joly would eventually become too weak to perform even that touch of magic. Joly could also cool the air around them, but again, she would only be able to do it for a short while.

She walked by the first body that she had killed. It already smelled bad and she skirted it, holding her breath.

Again, a thought skittered at the edge of her consciousness, only to vaporize into nothingness. *Damn! What is it?*

Joly and Duncan sat with their backs against a rock, holding hands. They had discussed what they should do, and both knew they could not try walking out. The sun would burn them to a crisp before lunchtime and the darkness would confuse them. They could end up farther out in the desert. Morag's crystal could not lead them in the darkness. They knew they would probably be okay for one more day, but the following day would not be so kind to them. The one bottle of water that remained, along with icy stones would only last so long.

They talked about Randy, Sara and the three cats. They talked about the things they had always wanted to do together and they talked about finding each other again.

"You know I'll always find you, no matter what."

"I know that honey." She leaned over and kissed him gently on his lips.

He put his arm around her and they sat quietly, both lost in their thoughts. Joly laid her head on his shoulder and placed her hand over his heart.

Morag had enough light. She sat on the desert floor and held the crystal in front of her. She went first to the north and then to the south to see if there was any vehicles traveling toward them. There was nothing. She then scryed the area around them, not looking for anything in particular. She felt the crystal hone in on a spot somewhere near the rocks. She didn't see anything, nor did she recognize the particular area. She backed out and when she could see the whole of the area they were in, she saw that the crystal had taken her to the other side of the outcropping. It was still cool enough for walking. She went back to the others and told them what she had seen. They got to their feet and began to walk around to the far side. They were quiet, not only to conserve their energy, but also because there was nothing to say. It had all been said and all that remained was for the ceaseless sun to finish them off.

By the time they reached the far side, the sun was beating down on them, its rays already burning their tender flesh. They each had a drink and Joly cooled three rocks, the moisture lasting longer in their mouths than the after effects of the water.

They rested while Morag got the crystal out and again, it took her to a place not far from where they were. She noticed the sand seemed to be disturbed in places.

"We're almost there. Do you want to rest awhile first, or carry on?"

Duncan pushed himself to his feet and pulled Joly up. "Let's go. Time's a wastin'." It was left unsaid that they had nothing but time. They continued walking. There was still shade on this side of the outcropping, although the heat was just as intense. Duncan and Joly were leading with Morag a few steps behind.

"*Hey!* What's that?" Duncan released Joly's hand and sprinted out toward the desert, avoiding the prickly spinifex grass that grew in tufts across the desert floor.

Joly spotted the footprints that led out to where Duncan had run. She followed them in the other direction and realized quickly that they were leading around the outcropping to the far side, where they had just came from.

The witches! Morag suddenly knew what it was that had kept niggling at the back of her mind. How had they had gotten there? She felt a burst of excitement flowing through her, the first in many hours.

"*Hey, here!*" Duncan had his arms out in front of him, feeling the air.

Joly and Morag headed out toward him, both wondering what he was doing.

"Look! Feel this." He kept running his hands through the air. Joly and Morag reached out and did the same. They felt it instantly.

There was something solid there. The vision of a vehicle shot through Morag's mind. *Damn!* The bugger's had concealed their transportation inside an invisible dome.

Duncan laughed and Joly joined him. Morag was smiling as Duncan picked up Joly and swung her around.

"*Woohoo!* We're gonna make it after all." He put Joly down and grabbed his Mother by the hands, swinging her around. Morag laughed and they had a group hug.

They would need to cast a spell to get rid of the invisible barrier. If it had been put in place by a common witch, they would have no trouble removing it. But because it had been built by a Sister, it would either be impervious to the powers of other Sisters, or it would take every ounce of strength that the three of them had left to give.

Morag knew they didn't need anything but themselves to perform a ritual, but she was so used to having the embellishments that for a moment she wondered if they would succeed. She shook her head. *What a goofy thought.* She knew better. The first rule for performing magic was that one needed oneself... nothing else.

Once the excitement died down, Morag moved forward to draw a circle, but Duncan raced in front of her. "Maw, can I? Please! Come on... *please?*" He grinned at her.

She smiled at him, knowing his chance of success was slim to nil. "Think you can remember how?"

"Oh yeah."

He walked to the center and put his head down.

Morag watched, her eyes twinkling. She was going to enjoy this, even if he didn't succeed.

Joly's eyes were also sparkling. She loved to watch Duncan in action. He always did his rituals with such pizzazz.

Duncan whirled around, raised his arms and looked to the sky. His normally exuberant voice deepened and with all playfulness gone from it, he loudly intoned,

"In the name of the Gods and Goddesses and all ye Great Spirits,
I call upon ye to bear witness to the events that have happened here.
Protect us and know that we are thy devoted servants."

Duncan stood for a moment with his arms raised. He could feel the energy flowing into him and then he walked around in a large circle releasing the energy, allowing it to flow through his fingers, as he drew in the circumference of the Sacred Circle.

He walked to the center and faced the east.

"Guardians of the East, I do summon and call ye to witness this rite and guard this circle.

I call upon the Element of Air, whose very breath helps us to communicate and gives us life."

He turned and faced the south.

"Guardians of the South, I do summon and call ye to witness this rite and guard this circle.

I call upon the Element of Fire, whose very breath controls our passions and gives us warmth."

He swung around to the west.

"Guardians of the West, I do summon and call ye to witness this rite and guard this circle.

I call upon the Element of Water, whose very breath gives us new beginnings and cleanliness."

He turned to the north.

"Guardians of the North, I do summon and call ye to witness this rite and guard this circle.

I call upon the Element of Earth, whose very breath helps to ground us and gives us strength."

He turned back to the east, his hands at his side and his face raised to the sun. For a moment he was still, and then he raised his arms again.

"I call upon Zeus, God of Thunder.
Father to all, both immortal and mortal.
With thy stormy skies and lightning bolts
And with thy sense of justice and fairness for all."

Morag raised an eyebrow. *Zeus? Nothing like calling out the big guns!* She shook her head, smiling.

"There is magic in the air,
There is sorcery everywhere.
There is good and there is bane.
Two lives were taken, but not in vain.
I am thy servant; hear my prayer.
I will protect thine earth, on this I swear.
We could not let the terror reign.

Vengeance was ours, for so many slain."

Joly envisioned him wearing his robes. She pictured them swirling around as he moved back and forth asking to be heard. *Gods, but I love that man!*

"Zeus, Father of wisdom,
Look with thy kind eyes upon my Mother,
She has served thee as well as any other.
Zeus, Guardian of the poor and forsaken,
Look with thy kind eyes upon my wife,
She..."

He faltered, his voice cracked, he stumbled and regained his balance. The heat and lack of food and water were taking their toll. He lost his train of thought. *What rhymed with wife?*

"Zeus... she is everything, she is my life."

Yeah, it's not great, but it's certainly true. He regained his stride and continued.

"Zeus, hear me, we are in trouble.
Our very lives depend on the breaking of this bubble.
Zeus, great Father of the Light of Day.
We, thy humble servants would like to go home.
Please, assist us and remove the invisible dome."

Duncan sank to his knees, resting on his heels. His arms hung at his side, the palms open and facing upwards. His head was thrown back.

Joly took the bottle of water and walked out to Duncan. He hadn't built a door, but he needed a drink. She handed it to him. He took it, poured some on the parched earth and took a small drink. He smiled and handed the bottle back to Joly.

The intense blue sky above them showed no sign of anything unusual happening. They watched and waited.

Duncan, rested and revived by the drink, knew he had to get out of the sun. He could feel his skin blistering. He got to his feet and closed his circle.

"I thank ye Gods and Goddesses and ye benevolent Spirits for being here today.

I thank thee Zeus, for allowing me the privilege of being able to call upon thee."

He walked to the east.

"Guardians of the East, I thank ye for attending my Circle. I release ye. Return to thy homes, harming none on thy journey."

He walked to the south, to the west, to the north, thanking his Guardians and releasing them.

He returned to the center and raised his arms.

"The circle is open, yet unbroken."

His head down, he walked slowly toward Joly. He had never had a spell fail before.

Morag saw the dejected look. She knew he had cast the spell perfectly, but she wasn't surprised. They would rest a bit and try again.

He was wondering what he had done wrong, when he heard what sounded like the crack of a whip. He turned in time to see the lightning bolt hit the invisible barrier. The dome silently vanished and in front of them sat an old battered jeep. It was painted a rusty red with blotches of green, a camouflage of sorts for when the two had carried out their dirty deeds.

Duncan let out a whoop that should have woken the dead. Energy that hadn't been there a moment before materialized, and he bounded out to the jeep. He hadn't yet come to a complete stop when he let out another yell.

"Hey! Look at this!" He reached in the back seat and turned around with bottles of water in both hands.

Morag and Joly reached the jeep and they each took a bottle of the life saving liquid. No one cared that it was warm. It was wet and that was all that mattered.

"Don't drink it fast," Morag admonished. They didn't need to deal with cramps on top of everything else.

They checked out the jeep. The keys were in the ignition, saving them a trip back to search the pockets of the rotting corpses. There were two cases of water and an assortment of canned food. In the back were two insulated jerry cans of fuel. There were also two hats laying on the front seat. There were no identifying papers of any kind in the jeep, and Joly prayed that the Goddess would be with her as she drove it back to Alice Springs. There was a mess of garbage on the front and back floors, empty cartons, bags, cans and bottles. They emptied a box of food and cleaned up the litter.

Both Joly and Duncan insisted that Morag wear one of the hats. The two of them would take turns wearing the other one. Joly insisted that Duncan go first, after being out in the sun while casting his spell. The jeep had no roof, so they would have the sun beating down on them until it set that evening.

There wasn't much shade to be found, but they sat against the rocks where they each had a can of pasta and a bottle of water.

They climbed into the filthy vehicle and Joly turned the key. The engine caught immediately. She put it in gear and it rolled ahead.

She drove until she reached the main road, where she stopped to take a short break. They were tired and both Duncan and Morag had been dozing. Joly did a healing on their red and blistered skin.

"You want me to drive, Darlin'? You look about done in."

"Would you? I could use forty winks and I really don't want to spend another night out on the desert."

"Yeah, it should be safe enough out here. If they stop us, we're dead in the water anyhow, won't matter whose drivin'."

"True. If I'm sleeping, wake me up before we get to the city."

"Sure thing pretty lady." He reached over and pulled her to him. They embraced for a moment and then got back in the jeep.

Duncan stalled it the first time he let out the clutch. He was successful the second time and they lurched along for several feet, before he managed to get the speed and the transmission synchronized.

Joly giggled and Morag laughed out loud. Duncan joined them. He went to shift into third and again they lurched along.

"Gee... am I keepin' you ladies awake?" He laughed again. It felt good to laugh. For a while, he had thought the laughing was over forever. *Screw that. I'm not ever gonna quit laughing. It is so good to be alive!*

He drove until he was about an hour from Alice Springs and then he pulled off to the side of the road. Joly stirred when the vehicle stopped.

"Darlin', you awake?"

"Mmmm..."

"Uh... you want to take the wheel into town?"

"Mmmm..."

Shit! Now what? He sat with his fingers tapping on the wheel.

She was cold and her neck hurt from the way she had been sleeping. She forced her eyes open. They were parked somewhere. It was pitch dark, except for the dash lights. She could hear the rhythmic tattoo of something. She struggled to sit upright, groaned as she straightened her head and neck.

"Darlin'?"

"Hi honey. My neck hurts. Just a sec." She moved it around, working the kink out of it.

"Where are we?"

"Almost to town. You okay to drive in?"

"Already? Wow! Did I die or what? What time is it?"

"I don't know. Late I guess. Maybe close to midnight."

"Oh. I need a drink." She felt around for the bottle she'd had in her hand before she had fallen asleep. She found it and took a long drink. "Mmmm, that's better."

They traded places and Joly drove into town. She wasn't sure what time it was, so she drove to the Woolworth's store. It was still open.

Good. It wasn't midnight yet. She knew she looked a mess, but she didn't want to search for a public washroom and then miss the store. She would never see these people again, anyhow. She parked in front.

The lights woke Morag and disoriented for a moment, she wondered where they were. The memories of the past three days suddenly flooded her mind and she sat up. She realized they were back in the city.

"Going shopping?"

Joly laughed. "Seems kind of stupid doesn't it, but I can't bear the idea of putting these clothes back on again in the morning. You want to join me?"

It was cold in the jeep. She would welcome the warmth. "Sure, why not?"

They went into the store. It was quiet and they attracted some attention.

None of them really cared. They were all happy to be back in civilization.

As Joly was the only one with a credit card, she paid for everything. They bought two small bags, toiletries and clothing enough to get them back home. When they left the store, she drove to the bank and withdrew some cash for incidentals.

Returning to the jeep, Joly drove back to the hotel they had stayed at before. Checking in went smoothly, other than some strange looks from the desk clerk. She was glad it was late and no one else was around. Once they reached the room, they breathed a collective sigh of relief.

"Maw, you go and shower first."

Morag didn't argue. She took the new nightgown and disappeared into the bathroom.

"Maw... just one request. Don't be usin' all the hot water."

Morag laughed as she closed the door. While she showered she thought about Duncan's spell. That it had worked meant the original spell of invisibility had to have been cast by the male witch. Gods, but they had been lucky. The Sister had to have been training the male. He had way more power than was usual for a common witch.

She thought about the invisible dome and the box that Pip had almost died in. She wondered if somehow, the two were related. It was an unusual ability. All witches were capable of building invisible domes, but most didn't bother, as the solidness remained for any unsuspecting person to walk into. The box was the exception. Had it been built by a Sister, and if so, why?

Duncan reached for Joly and took her in his arms. They stood holding each other, happy to be alive. It had been an experience they didn't want to repeat any time soon.

When Morag came out of the washroom, Joly and Duncan went in. There was no playfulness. They showered and with their towels wrapped around them, they headed for bed.

Morag was already tucked in. They said goodnight to her, and soon all that could be heard were the soft sounds of three extremely exhausted people.

The following morning they were up early. They were hungry and couldn't wait to go and eat their first decent meal since leaving Alice Springs three days prior. After Joly did healings on their sunburns, Morag's ribs and Duncan's face and arms, they headed to the restaurant and ordered large breakfasts, which they consumed with little fanfare.

While they were eating, they discussed Morag's options for getting home. Joly and Duncan thought she should just will herself there, but she declined, telling them that it was too great a distance and she was out of practice.

It wasn't the real reason why. She refused to leave them. She had sworn to watch out for them both until she could no longer do so. The worst that could happen to them on the plane was either a drunken pilot or a hijacker. It didn't matter.

She could call Kyle Devon and have a new passport couriered to her, but she didn't want to wait. Time was of the essence and she knew they had to return home as soon as possible. She could make the trip traveling invisible, but it was too dangerous. There was not a lot of elbow room on a plane and she knew the chances of discovery were too great.

She decided that the only feasible option was to do what she had done with the pictures for Gisela Werner. She would use telepathic suggestion along with some sort of paperwork, and hope she could pull it off.

"Does anyone know what day it is?"

"No. Let me think. Is it the fourteenth? I'm not sure."

Joly reached in her bag and pulled out the receipt from the previous nights shopping trip. "Yesterday was the fourteenth. Aren't our reservations for the fifteenth?"

Morag nodded. "Yes they are. I guess we're supposed to be on the plane this afternoon. I would say we cut that pretty fine."

The other two agreed with her.

When they went back to the room, Morag took her crystal to the window. Several minutes later she commented, "All is as well as can be expected with the world. Would you like to let the cats know you're alive and well?"

"Umm, isn't it still yesterday there? I think I'll just phone. I need to hear Randy's voice. For a while there, I didn't think I would ever hear it again."

She picked up the phone and called home. Sara had been frantic, having heard nothing since their arrival. Her concern had been picked up by Randy, who had been crying and acting up for the last two days. Joly assured them both all was well and that hopefully, they should be back home in a couple of days. Duncan talked to Randy as did Morag. Once Randy was satisfied that all his people were okay, he settled down.

Joly asked Sara about the cats, and was told that Nefertiti had been making life miserable for the other two. She had had another fight with Salem and both of them were missing patches of fur. She had also been seen smacking Pip for some unknown reason.

Joly asked to speak to her. Sara called Nefertiti and put the phone to her ear.

Nefertiti was pleased to hear the Mistress' voice. Although Joly assured her that all was well, she could sense the stress in the Mistress' voice. That there had been trouble was obvious.

"… and Nefertiti, please try to get along with the other two."

Later in the morning, Morag asked Joly if she would mind driving her to the store. She wanted to find something that she could use to help convince the airport authorities that she was carrying a valid passport. A blank piece of paper had worked for Gisela, but this next bit of tomfoolery would be in a very public place, with many eyes and curious people.

Morag purchased several small items and back in the room, she kept busy for an hour cutting, coloring, and with the help of a borrowed stapler from the front desk, she soon had an imitation passport. She had fashioned it from colored craft paper and white paper. She had neatly printed on the front of it and colored it in. From a distance, it looked like the real thing. Now all she had to do was convince the person she handed it to, that he or she was in fact looking at the genuine article. She put it in the new purse she had bought the night before.

They checked out of the hotel and drove out to the airport. Joly parked the jeep and paid for three hours parking. They walked away from it. It had served them well. The motor had been well looked after, even though the rest of it had been badly abused.

They checked in, handed over their luggage, and then went to eat.

They were anxious to get back to Canada. This had not been a good trip and Morag knew it was going to get worse.

They lined up for customs, Morag in front with Joly and Duncan flanking her. She was going to have a hard enough time concentrating on the officer ahead, without having to worry about some stranger behind her peering over her shoulder, wondering what she was holding.

Morag was up next. She was frowning as she held her fake passport in her hands. The officer reached for it and asked if she had anything to declare. She shook her head and answered, 'No."

He flipped open the pages and looked at a couple of them, a frown crossing his face.

Neither Joly nor Duncan had breathed. Suddenly Joly elbowed Duncan hard.

"*Hey!* What was that for?"

"Because you're such an *ass*." She responded loudly.

Duncan caught on. "I'd rather be an ass, than a *bitch*."

"Yeah, well… a bitch is man's best friend. Nobody likes an *ass*."

"Man's best friend all right. That's because you're a bitch in heat."

The customs officer was watching them, Morag's passport forgotten in his hands.

He wondered if he should let them on the plane. He could tell by their accent that they were Canadian. Well, he didn't want them hanging around in his country. He grabbed his stamp and slammed it down on Morag's papers.

She was through.

Joly handed him her passport.

"Anything to declare?"

"Just the deadbeat behind me."

He slammed the stamp down on her passport. "Proceed."

He took Duncan's passport, stamped it and forgot to ask if he had anything to declare.

Their return flight had two stops and they would be thirty-five hours traveling. With the time difference, they would actually be home on the following day.

Stephen was at the Vancouver airport waiting for them.

When Morag walked through the doorway and saw him, she stopped abruptly, and a fellow traveler behind her, bumped into her. After a hurried apology, she walked toward her son, a smile lighting up her face.

After a hug, she stood back and looked at him. "Stephen, you're not wearing a tie."

He looked embarrassed. "Uh… no, I actually haven't been in to work yet today."

"Oh, how come?"

"Uh… I'm moving."

"I see. Well, I'd offer you a hand, but right now I need to get home and find my bed."

Duncan hugged his brother, causing Stephen to turn red. Joly laughed and also gave him a hug. They waited at the carousel for the two small bags.

Stephen raised an eyebrow when they were retrieved. "That's not what you left with."

"No, it isn't. We ran into a small problem and lost the others."

"A *small* problem?" He knew better. His parents had been traveling for as long as he could remember, and they had never lost their bags before.

"Well, maybe not so small, but it doesn't matter now. We're here, and in one piece as you can see."

It was three very relieved people who climbed into Stephen's car that morning. They were all looking forward to being home in an hour's time.

Rauna thought the attacks were growing less fierce, or maybe she was getting used to the pain and fear. Perhaps she was becoming part of all this… part of the Abyss, as dark as the rest, as they ripped her light and soul apart, piece by piece.

Veronika looked in on the unconscious woman. There was still no change. She had not moved in the two weeks she had been there. Her hair appeared to be changing color. It had been a tawny gold when she was discovered in the yard, but now there were streaks of white scattered throughout it. She understood it was a magical sleep, but she had no idea how to bring her back from it.

The grandchildren had come and she suggested they take her to the hospital, but Polina said no. The woman was one of them and they needed to look after their own. Besides, the unconsciousness was not of the earth and therefore the doctors wouldn't understand it. Sergei had asked how she knew this.

Polina had shaken her head. "I can smell the scent of another dimension on her clothes."

They had taken her in the house and put her in the spare bedroom. Polina and she had stripped the woman and cleaned her, and then Polina had sat holding her hands as she sent her healing energies to the raw flesh. Polina wasn't a strong healer, but twice a day she faithfully came and held the hands. They looked better now.

Veronika was familiar with frozen extremities, as she had seen such things many times before, when she still lived in Russia.

Russia… the Gods knew how much she missed her homeland, but she could never go back. She prayed to the Goddess that she could return there in her next incarnation.

Veronika took a sliver of ice and pushed it between the woman's lips. She stroked the wispy hair and spoke softly. "Come back to us soon, *Tsipotchka.*"

She turned and went to the kitchen. Cutting up an apple and putting it and a handful of peanuts on a plate, she went out to the back yard. She looked in the apple tree and the magnolia trees.

"*Vorona*, come… eat." She searched for the black and white crow, but didn't see it. She put the plate on a low table in the yard and returned to the house.

19. Cor Blimey!

Stephen parked in front of Morag's house and Duncan removed the bags from the trunk.

Sara was returning from school with Randy. Sara spotted them first and waved. Randy saw them and began to run.

"Mommy, Daddy, Mommy, Daddy, Gra-Morg!"

Duncan ran across the street to stop him from crossing the street alone. He was too excited to think about the traffic. Randy ran into his arms. Duncan swung him up and walked back to the car.

After everyone had received their hugs and kisses, Joly, Duncan and Randy headed home. Stephen agreed to visit his Mother for a few minutes.

Sara stood waiting at the door. "Welcome back, you two. As you can see, you were missed."

She put the kettle on and made sandwiches for all. Randy couldn't get enough of them, jumping from one lap to the other and back again.

Nefertiti walked past, disdainfully ignoring everyone. Joly saw her and saw the tufts of fur that were missing.

"Nefertiti, come here please."

She turned.

Joly picked her up and examined her. She didn't seem to be injured other than the missing fur. She silently did a healing on her, wondering what the problem was with the cats. When she was finished, she put her down and Nefertiti left the room.

She thought about Salem and realized that she hadn't seen him.

Pip was sitting on the mat in front of the sink, watching the interplay between Randy and Duncan.

"Pip, where's Salem?"

Pip jumped to her feet and headed down the hall toward the stairs. They went up and Joly found Salem lying on their bed. She thought that was odd, as he usually never went in the bedroom during the day. She couldn't believe her eyes as she walked closer to him. There were great patches of fur missing everywhere; there was a slash across his face and another one on his neck. She gently picked him up and did a healing on him. When she was done, she put him back on the bed and she went in search of Pip.

Pip had gone back downstairs and Joly called her into the living room. "I need to talk to you, Pip."

She lay down on her stomach and began the meld.

"Pip, I'd like to know what's going on between Salem and Nefertiti. The scrapping seems to be happening oftener now. Why?"

"Mistress, it's Nefertiti. She says she's the boss and whenever she doesn't get her way, she gets mad. She really doesn't like Salem and she's trying to figure out a way to get rid of him. Not just get rid of him, she wants him dead."

"*What?* Pip, you're not serious?"

"Yes, Mistress. Very serious. She doesn't much care for me, she says I'm useless, but she really hates Salem, Mistress. Salem has to watch his every move, as she is always there and you can see she's just waiting for a chance to do something bad to him."

"I see. Thank you, Pip."

"You're welcome, Mistress."

"Pip?"

"Yes, Mistress?"

"Are you all right? I mean, does she try to hurt you too?"

"Not really, Mistress. She takes a swing at me every now and then, just to keep me in line I think, but she doesn't beat me up like she does Salem."

"Thank you, Pip. Go in peace, my dear."

"Thank you, Mistress. And Mistress?"

"Yes, Pip?"

"It's good to have you home again."

"Thank you, Pip. It's good to be home again."

Joly lay her head on her arms. She wondered what she was going to do with Nefertiti. Gods, but she was tired. She needed a drink. She slowly got to her feet and headed to the kitchen.

"Mommy, Mommy, where you go?" Randy ran to her, throwing his arms around her hips.

"Hey, Punkin. I went to talk to Pip." She swung him up on her hip as she went to get a glass of water.

She and Duncan spent the next two hours playing with Randy. They all ended up falling asleep on the big bed. Randy woke them up at supper time. Sara had supper ready and both Joly and Duncan were thankful to have a home cooked meal.

They spent some more time with Randy, and then Duncan took him for his bath and bedtime story. Joly joined them before Randy fell asleep.

"Love you, Mommy."

"Love you too, Sweet Pea." She leaned over and kissed him goodnight.

Duncan finished the story, tucked the covers around him and they left the room.

"Ready for bed?"

"Yes, but I need to talk to Nefertiti first. I should have done it earlier. She's become a bit of a problem. I just don't know what to do about her."

"Give her options, Darlin', just give her options. Lay the onus on her. She's a big girl."

"Yes, of course. Thanks honey." She reached up to kiss him. He put his hands on her cheeks and returned her kiss.

"Hurry back pretty lady."

"You know it." She smiled at him and went in search of Nefertiti. She found her in the living room. She thought that was an odd place for her, but then she remembered Salem was in the master bedroom.

"Nefertiti, I would like to talk to you."

She began the mind meld with some trepidation. She was angry with Nefertiti and was unable to completely relax. Nefertiti's thoughts sorted themselves out and the first words to come through clearly were, "You're upset with me."

"Yes, I am upset, Nefertiti. I fail to understand why you keep picking on Salem."

"Mistress, he's a born loser. I have tried my best to teach him to be better than he was when he came to us. It's no use. He has no desire to improve. I cannot put up with his lackadaisical attitude."

"I'm sorry you feel that way. Not everyone, human or feline comes from royalty. Most of us are commoners Nefertiti, me included. You seem to be getting more crotchety as you age. That's unfortunate. We've been together a long time. I have no desire to ask you to leave, but…"

"*Leave, Mistress?* Why would you ask me to leave? I have done *nothing* wrong!"

"You don't feel that continually harassing Salem and Pip is wrong? I'm sorry Nefertiti. It *is* wrong, very wrong and I won't put up with it anymore. I'm really sorry I have to say this, but you have two choices. Either come down off your high horse and be family, or find yourself another home."

"*Mistress!* I can't believe you're thinking this way. I saved your life. I watched out for you in the cabin. I have been here for you ever since the Bad Time. Mistress, if anyone should leave, it should be that good for nothing Salem. What has he done the past while? Nothing, except eat everything in sight and take up space."

"Nefertiti, you're forgetting something. Salem also saved my life. He has also saved me from having several bad accidents and he also watched out for me in the cabin. Tell me, what have you done the past while besides eat and take up space?"

"Well, I've… I've… I've been watching out for you when you're here. When you're away, I watch out for the other humans."

"As do Salem and Pip. Nefertiti, in this home, you are all equal whether you like it or not. Accept it, live with it... or leave. I love you Nefertiti, but I won't put up with your behavior. If you choose to stay, I would suggest you guard Salem's life as you do mine. If anything happens to him that looks suspicious, you will be very sorry. Have I made myself clear?"

"Yes, Mistress."

"You may go, Nefertiti. Be well." Joly laid her torso on the floor and buried her head in her arms. Gods! She hoped Nefertiti wouldn't leave, but if she did, it would be for the best. She needed to go and do another healing on Salem. Some of his skin had been literally torn out along with his fur.

She got to her feet and slowly headed up the stairs.

The following morning Duncan and Joly both felt more human. The uninterrupted night's sleep had helped immensely.

As soon as she knew the lawyer's office was open, Joly called Kyle. She managed to get him before any clients had arrived.

"Kyle, I need your help. I rented a small motor home over in Alice Springs and it was blown up."

"My Gods, is everyone all right?"

"Yes, we're all fine, just tired. I don't have the rental papers; they were in the glove box. I do have the name of the company though."

Kyle wrote down the information and asked her if there was anything else she needed.

"I don't think so. You might want to give Morag a call. She lost her passport in the explosion."

"*What?* How did she get back home? She is back here?"

Joly smiled. "Yes, she's back here. She used her powers of suggestion and a few pieces of paper stapled together."

"You do like to live dangerously, don't you? I don't suppose you'd consider the nice quiet life I lead. I'm sure our coven would accept you as members."

Joly laughed. "I think not, Kyle. Thanks just the same. I don't suppose you'd like to spice up your life a little? Live large and that kind of thing."

She heard him spluttering on the other end of the phone. "Spice up my life? Exploding motor homes, lost passports, sneaking children out of foreign countries, misplacing husbands. No, no, Joly, I think I will just stay here and live my perfectly quiet, perfectly safe life. Thank you just the same."

They talked for a few more minutes and Kyle assured her he would take care of getting the bill for the motor home.

She cleaned up the dishes from breakfast and decided to do a couple of loads of laundry.

Doing laundry was a menial chore, but Joly relished the normalcy of it. She was thinking about how happy she would be to see the end of all the traveling. She knew they would still be called, but at least there would be time in between the trips to stay at home and just enjoy being together as a family. She had been checking all the pockets, removing rocks and other unidentifiable items from Randy's pants, when she felt a soft lump in the slacks she had been wearing in Australia. Reaching in the pocket, she pulled out a scrap of material. She frowned, wondering where it had come from, when she remembered the gag that had been in Duncan's mouth. She went to throw it in the wastebasket, when it dawned on her that it looked familiar. She took a closer look at it. *Where have I seen this before? Wait! Isn't it from the box that held Morag's crystal?* She ran upstairs and across the street.

Morag answered the door smiling. "Hi dear. I was just thinking about you."

Joly held out the scrap of material.

Morag reached for it with a look of wonder crossing her face. "Where on earth did you find this?"

"It's from your crystal box, right?"

"Why yes, but how did you get it?"

Joly shook her head. "When I got to Duncan up in the rocks, he was gagged. It was in his mouth."

"*What?* That's impossible!" Morag turned. "Come in dear." She led the way to the kitchen. Once there, she laid the scrap of material down, trying to smooth it as best as she could. Because of the type of material it was, it kept wrinkling back up as soon as she let go of it. Morag finally went to the sink and ran some warm water. She wet the material, squeezed the moisture from it and went back to the table. She spread the material out again, stretching it with her fingers.

Joly gasped. "My Gods, look at it."

Morag *was* looking at it. The four sides had been cut precisely down the edges of the box. There was not a ragged edge to be seen. What was puzzling her most was how had the woman managed to do this? They had been out of the van ten minutes, twelve minutes at the most. The van had never been out of the sight of Joly and Duncan. True, she had been able to make herself invisible. Had she gone in the van as soon as they were all clear? It was the only plausible answer. The knife she used had been incredibly sharp.

She turned and left the room. Joly eyed the material. It was very pretty, but there was something. She didn't know what it was, but something about it was giving her the heebie-jeebies. It was weird. She didn't remember feeling bad vibes from it before.

Morag returned with the crystal in her hand. The crystal began glowing. Morag and Joly watched it, as it became brighter. The clear glass misted and cleared. The crystal gave them a memory. It showed them the Sister inside the motor home. The crystal had been removed and was obviously laying on the floor. The view was from the floor looking up. They watched the evil one slit the cloth with a knife that looked suspiciously like a physician's scalpel. When she removed the material from the box, she wiped it across her brow, catching the drops of perspiration in it.

That's what she had sensed. The evil still clung to the cloth.

"You need to wash it, wash it really well."

"Yes, I will. Damn woman anyhow." She shook her head. "I'm glad to have the material back just the same. I wonder if I can find another box."

"I'm sure you will." Joly smiled at her and she smiled back.

"Thank you child." She reached over and hugged Joly.

Joly skipped across the street, pleased that Morag was happy.

The next day, Joly and Duncan went shopping for a van. There was nothing that Joly liked, but she knew they had to buy something. "You pick one honey. I don't care. They're all ugly."

The salesman took offense at that remark and Joly finally told him to get stuffed. They went elsewhere.

Duncan tried to talk to her. "Darlin', if it was green outside and inside, you'd love it, so you can't be sayin' they're ugly just because you don't like the color."

"Honey, they are ugly, though. Every interior is either grey or tan. How gross is that? There are some that the exterior is okay, even if it's not green, but it's the interior we have to look at every time we get in the damn thing."

"Tell you what, Darlin'. We'll pick up the next one we see, whatever color it is. That way we have it. Then we will custom order you one, in the colors you want, okay?"

She raised an eyebrow. "Can we do that?"

"Of course we can."

The next van they found was not only tan inside, but tan outside as well. Joly hated it, and told the salesman so. Duncan tried his best to shush her, but she would have no part of it. Duncan didn't care for the tan exterior either, so he finally decided on one that had a burgundy exterior and a grey interior. When the papers were signed, she walked back to the truck and threw her arms around the hood.

Duncan walked up behind her. "Tell you what, Darlin'. You just drive the truck and I'll drive the van until your new one gets here, okay?"

He couldn't believe it. She had tears in her eyes. "Hey, what's this?"

"Its just so depressing. It's so ugly."

"Okay, Darlin', its ugly, but its ours and we'll all fit into it. That's what's important, right?"

She nodded as she wrapped her arms around him. *Gods, but I hate it. Grey... yuk.* What was the world coming to anyhow?

Duncan made another appointment for his driver's test. He wondered if he'd still be there for it. He was, and he passed his written exam with no problems. He made an appointment for the driving exam and was pleasantly surprised when he was still there to take it. He also passed it and was secretly pleased to be able to drive again. He hadn't missed it. As Jimmy Smith, he hadn't remembered, and so much had happened since coming home, there hadn't been time to think about it.

He convinced Joly to drive the van, telling her she would need to get used to it, for when her own arrived. She found she enjoyed driving it, as long as she didn't think about the depressing lack of color that surrounded her.

Duncan said he wanted to drive into the city. Joly thought he was crazy. He didn't even like the city.

"Why don't we go to Surrey instead? That way you still get to drive in amongst all the crazies, but we don't have to go quite so far for you to do it."

He laughed and agreed with her. They took Morag with them and drove over to Abbotsford to jump on the freeway. Duncan drove skillfully, the years of not driving melting away with the miles. He slowed down once in Surrey, looking for the exit to the big mall.

Morag was looking out the window, when she thought she saw a familiar face. She turned quickly to get another look. He had turned, but she was sure she knew who it was. If it wasn't Jesse Alexander, then he had an identical twin hanging out in his old stomping grounds. She smiled to herself. Life could get a little more exciting in the near future.

Joly had also spotted the familiar face. She wondered if Jesse had called Sara. He didn't have their phone number, but she didn't think that would slow him down. She smiled, wondering how Sara would feel about him being back.

They were wandering through the mall when Duncan said he needed to go and do a couple of things. They agreed to meet back at the same place an hour later. He left, his long legs carrying him quickly out of sight. Joly watched until he vanished and then turned to Morag, to find her watching her.

"Something wrong?"

"No, I was just watching your expression. You looked apprehensive, like he might not come back."

Joly laughed. "Sorry, I guess I still don't like him out of my sight."

They went into a few stores and looked around. Their purchases were few, as neither had any real need for anything. When the hour was almost up, they headed back to the agreed upon meeting place.

Duncan loped into sight. Morag again watched Joly, saw her eyes light up and heard her release her breath.

"Hey, Darlin', I missed you." He hugged her and gave her kiss on the tip of her nose.

Joly was surprised he didn't have any bags or packages. She thought he had gone to do some shopping.

They made their way back to the parking lot. Duncan slid open the side door for his Mother and Morag got in. He then opened the passenger door for Joly.

Her intake of breath was quite audible. "Aww honey." She turned and wrapped her arms around Duncan, burying her head in the curve of his neck.

He held her, whispering in her ear.

"It's not great, but it's better. I tried to find green floor mats, but they have to be special ordered. Is it okay?"

She had tears in her eyes once again. *Gods, but I love this man*. She turned around and looked inside the van again. He had covered all the seats with green seat covers and even the steering wheel was sporting a green leather cover.

"Yes, it's much better honey. Thank you." She still hated the interior, but she knew she would have to make the best of it. Duncan had tried to make it more to her liking, so she would show her appreciation by not doing anymore complaining. As she climbed in, she spotted something else. There was a small plush emerald green cat hanging from the rear view mirror. She grinned. Yes, she could live with it.

Daily, Morag would scry to the southeast. It hadn't returned yet, but it was almost time to be leaving. There would be preparations to make. This wasn't a normal demon that was loose, but an extremely powerful one. She needed to set a date for their leaving. She had made a large batch of holy water on the last full moon. She had lots of sea salt. There were a few other things that she wanted to get, but they were common things and could be purchased anywhere.

Her birthday was coming up. She didn't want a big shindig for it. Maybe they could leave before it arrived. She would rather it was pushed to the background. Not that she felt her age, because she didn't. In fact, since her trip to Scotland, she had been feeling great. The tiredness that had been plaguing her seemed to have vanished and she had energy to spare.

She hated to drag the two kids away from Randy again. That was the main reason they still hadn't departed. They had been back from Australia for a week now. She would give them a few more days. She would be glad when this final battle was over. There would still be trips abroad, but not nearly as many.

Sara wasn't feeling well. She hadn't been sleeping and she was tired, but every time she closed her eyes she would see Jesse's face grinning at her. She had banished his ghost and most of her memories before seeing him in Greece. Now the hurt was back as strong as it had been when he had first disappeared from her life. She was still haunted by the statement from Joly that he had their sketch on his wall. Why? Why would he have taken it with him?

She thought about running into him in the lobby of their hotel. She had forgotten he knew of her habit of going for a walk when she was upset. He had tried to apologize, but all she had wanted was to get away from him. If she hadn't run, she probably would have embarrassed herself by throwing her arms around him. She loved him so much! She sometimes wondered if she would ever meet another who would turn her heart the way he had. She didn't think so.

She wondered if she should go to the doctor and ask for some sleeping pills. No, a better solution would be to ask Joly to make her a special tea to help her sleep. She just didn't want Joly thinking she couldn't look after Randy. Maybe she could ask Morag.

The silence of the early morning was shattered by a loud crash, much cursing and the sounds of someone flailing about in the darkened room.

Startled out of a sound sleep, Duncan and Joly sat up. Duncan reached for the knob on the light with one hand; the other held his wife's wrist. They looked but saw nothing. Duncan, with a frown on his face, climbed out of bed and slipped into his jeans.

The sounds had lessened somewhat, but there was definite movement and mutterings coming from their closet.

Duncan advanced quietly and threw the door open.

The shriek almost deafened him.

"Who the bloody 'ell are yer?"

Joly leaned forward on the bed. There was only one person she knew that spoke like that.

"Rhiannon?"

"Joly, is dat yer?"

Joly got out of bed and put on her robe. She walked over to the closet and laughed. Rhiannon was sitting in a tangled mess of clothing with a crystal ball and a half eaten banana held firmly in her hands.

Joly reached out a hand. "Come on out. It's quite safe." She giggled again.

Rhiannon struggled to her feet and stepped out of the closet. She looked at Duncan's white hair.

"Yer must be the missin' 'usband. I'm Rhiannon."

Duncan finally found his voice. "Uhh… hi Rhiannon. Yeah, I'm the missin' husband. Not to sound impolite or anythin', but did you know most people use the door when they come to visit?"

Joly burst into laughter.

Just then a soft knock at the bedroom door interrupted them. Joly opened the door to find Sara standing there, a look a concern on her face.

"Come on in Sara. You might as well meet our unexpected guest."

"By the flamin' way, just where the bleedin' 'ell am I?"

Joly chuckled again. You're in Canada, and without a passport I suppose."

"Canader! Yer puttin' me on!"

Duncan grinned. "Not bleedin' likely." Then he laughed.

"Sara, this is Rhiannon. Rhiannon, our son's nanny, Sara."

"Well chuffed to meet yer, Sara. Canader. *Cor blimey!"*

She looked around the bedroom. "I don't know what 'appened. I was tryin' to get yer in the crystal ball."

"Have you used a crystal before?" Joly asked.

"No. I just got it."

"Ahh, well then, I would think you need some lessons, but not until later."

Sara turned to leave and had a sudden thought. "Should I go and make some tea? Seeing as we're up and all."

"Good idea, Sara. Thanks." Duncan turned to his wife. "Got the spare bedroom ready for an unexpected guest, Darlin'?"

Joly smiled at him. "Always... *darlin'*." She chuckled.

"Come on Rhiannon. Let's go downstairs."

They went down, Rhiannon exclaiming at the size of the old house.

Seated at the table, Rhiannon looked at Joly. "I needed to rabbit to yer. I've been 'avin' dreams; I guess it's more like nightmares. I clock these fings, like it's all mixed together, but its 'orrible." She suddenly looked at the banana in her hand and took a bite.

"Things like what?"

"It's like visions of doom, despair, all manner of evil type stuff. I'm not gettin' much kip."

"Have you seen an old manor house, it has a long covered porch and a small roundish room with a pointy roof that's perched on another piece that sticks out from the main house?"

She nodded. "Ow did yer know dat?"

"It's where we have to go soon. That's where one of the evils was unleashed last October. We will have to go and try to banish it, send it back to where it came from."

Rhiannon shook her head and had another bite of the banana. "I don't fink so. The dreams are naff enough, without goin' anywhere near the kosher fing."

Duncan decided to change the subject. "So with all this, how did you manage to end up in our closet?"

"I'm sorry 'bout dat. I didn't mean to scarper over fer a visit. I just wanted to clock if I could raise Joly in the crystal. I 'ad a devil of a time getting me 'ands on one. 'Ad to 'itch a ride to the Bow bells."

They talked for a while longer and then it was time to get Randy up. He was surprised to see a stranger in their kitchen and acted very shy. This was something new for him and both Joly and Duncan wondered why. Joly finally decided it was because of the way she talked, with her hands waving about as she spoke.

Duncan ran over to Morag's to let her know about the unexpected visitor. She returned with him, and Rhiannon explained once again her reason for trying to reach Joly. She still didn't know why she had ended up in their closet.

Joly and Duncan excused themselves to walk Randy to school.

Morag took Rhiannon's hand in hers, the sense of oneness surprising them both.

"Yer one of them too, the Sisters dat Joly was tellin' me about."

"Yes, I am. Joly knows you're a Sister? She never said anything to me. That's unusual for her."

"She was lookin' fer Duncan. She prolly forgot."

Morag thought back to what had transpired the last time they were in England. She nodded her head in agreement. "You're probably right. It was your friend that talked to Duncan ten years ago?"

"Yes, it was Maddie dat clocked 'im. Where did yer find 'im?"

"East of York, in a small town."

"Yer were jammy. Ten years is a long time. What about the speech thing? Maddie said 'e was autistic."

"He had lost his memory and he did have a bit of a speech impediment, but Joly fixed everything."

"Joly 'as big magic."

"I would imagine you do also. Did Joly explain what it means to be a *Sister of the Triple Moon*?"

"She told me I prolly had super powers of some kind and dat I should be off savin' the bloomin' world wiv yer. I told 'er I didn't 'ave no such thing and dat I wasn't goin' no where."

"I see. And how do you feel about that now, what with suddenly finding yourself in Canada and all?"

"I don't know what I feel. I don't know what to fink. 'Ow did I get 'ere innit? Can yer tell me dat?"

"Certainly dear."

Morag explained about what she often referred to as space travel, but what was in fact was a type of teleportation. True teleportation was instantaneous, with no sense of motion. What witches did was similar, but it wasn't instantaneous and there was a sense of being in the metaphysical plane. Rhiannon was surprised to learn that Morag could travel that way as well.

Joly and Duncan returned and listened as Morag finished her explanation.

"You and I really need to spend some time together. I need to teach you how to properly use a crystal and we will have to work on refining your space traveling, so that you're not ending up in people's closets. Why don't you come over to my place and we'll see what we can accomplish."

Morag turned to Joly and Duncan. "You don't mind if I steal her away, do you? She can stay at my place as well. You have a houseful as it is."

"No, that's fine. Do what you have to do. Keep us posted, though."

"Of course dear. We'll be running along then." She turned to Rhiannon. "Come along dear."

Morag turned to Joly and raised an eyebrow. "By the way Joly, you never told me that Rhiannon was one of the Sisters."

"Oh Gods, I must have forgotten. I'm sorry. I can't believe I didn't tell you."

"You had someone else on your mind." She smiled at her son. "It's alright dear. She's here now, that's all that matters."

Morag and Rhiannon walked across the street, Rhiannon's eyes darting everywhere, taking in the unfamiliar sights.

They went into the living room and Morag picked up her crystal. "Now, you said that all you said was *take me to Joly* and you were there? Is that correct?"

"Yes."

"Well then, I don't think we want to say anything like that, or you'll be gone again. Let's see."

Morag looked into her crystal and thought about Pennsylvania. The crystal immediately responded.

Rhiannon looked on in amazement when she saw the plantation house come into view.

"'Ere now, 'ow did yer do dat?"

"All I did was think about where I wanted the crystal to take me. However, until we figure out the extent of your abilities, I would suggest you don't try that. Perhaps we should check out your space travel and see if we can fine-tune it. What do you think?"

"I fink I'm confused."

"I suppose you are. Come out back with me dear. Do you know how to ground yourself?" Morag led the way to her back yard. She wandered around filling all the feeders, talking continually to Rhiannon, as she did so.

Morag showed her how to properly center and ground herself, how to open her senses and let the pure energy enter her body. They talked about various facets of the craft, Rhiannon seemingly eager to learn. They went back inside and discussed space travel. Morag was somewhat leery about joining Rhiannon, but she had to know how strong the younger woman's powers were.

"Take my hands dear. Now, concentrate on the intended target. In this case, my back yard. Picture it as vividly as you possibly can. Picture the bushes, the flowers, the feeders. Open your senses and smell the flowers, the air. Now, picture the spot where you want to end up. You don't want to land on the fence, or wrapped around a tree. Are you ready?"

Rhiannon, with her eyes squeezed tightly shut, nodded.

Morag closed her eyes and pictured the circle. It was where they had agreed to land. For a few seconds nothing happened. Then Morag could feel it. It was a gentle buzzing sensation that seemed to originate from somewhere in the stomach region. The buzzing grew stronger, and soon her whole body was filled with it. She felt the sensation of movement and knew they were on their way. It should only take a couple of seconds. They had started from the living room.

Suddenly the metaphysical plane they were traveling in went topsy-turvy and she felt herself spinning in every direction, in circles as well as head over heels; she could tell Rhiannon was also spinning. Morag intensified her thoughts of her back yard. She felt a slight tugging against Rhiannon's hand. The traveling took much longer than it should have. The sudden stop caused the breath to be forced from Morag. She opened her eyes and after a quick glance, she shook her head and closed them again. She had no idea where they were, but it certainly wasn't in her back yard.

Once Morag got her breath back, she turned to Rhiannon. "May I ask where we are?"

Rhiannon beamed at her. "We're at me manor."

"*In England?*"

Rhiannon nodded vigorously, still smiling.

"May I ask why you decided we should come here?"

"Well, I 'ad dis thought. Cor blimey guv. I needed to feed me dogs. I 'adn't planned on goin' to Canader yer know."

Morag nodded her head. "Alright. Would you like to feed them and then maybe you'd like to make some arrangements for someone else to feed them in your absence?"

"Me absence? Morag, I don't plan on going back to Canader."

"Perhaps you'd like to put the kettle on for some tea, and then we'll discuss your plans." Morag got to her feet and looked around. They appeared to be at the back of a small cottage. She assumed it belonged to Rhiannon.

Out of nowhere came three very large, very excited dogs, each wanting to be the center of attention. Rhiannon spoke to each one, rubbing behind their ears. Then she led the way around the side of the cottage to the front. The door was unlocked and they walked inside. The room was cool. Rhiannon rekindled the fire and filled the kettle. She bustled about fixing dishes of food for the dogs that were all sniffing Morag and vying for her attention.

"Are yer 'ungry, Morag? I could do wiv a bite to nosh-up."

"Yes, thank you."

While Rhiannon was preparing something to eat, Morag thought about what had just happened. They had been holding hands. They had both been thinking of the same thing to start with, but as soon as Rhiannon had thought about her home, they had been whisked away to it. It was as if she hadn't even been thinking about her backyard. Rhiannon's powers of space travel were obviously far superior to her own, so that would be one of her special powers. She wondered what else Rhiannon was capable of that she didn't know about, or had never given a second thought to.

How was she going to convince Rhiannon to go back to Canada with her? If she refused, she supposed that she would have to stay there a few days and give her some training. She would have to go back and let the others know where she was. Gods, she hated space travel. Oh well, one did what one had to do.

They ate and while Morag helped with the few dishes they had dirtied, she came up with a plan. It might not work, but it was worth a try.

Back home it was early afternoon, but in England it was getting late. Rhiannon had lit some candles and Morag was surprised to see that she appeared to not have electricity.

"How do you survive without power, Rhiannon? Do you have a means to keep your food cool?"

"I shop when I needs somefin'. In the summer, I grows most of me grub. Morag, I'm knackered. It's been a wild day for me. I only 'ave a small Uncle Ned. Did yer want to join me? I don't mind sharin'."

"Thank you for the offer dear, but no. I had best be getting back home. The kids will be wondering where I've disappeared to."

"Will yer come back, ain't it? I'd like to learn more from yer."

"I don't think so dear. Space travel for me is not as easy as it is for you. I guess we'll just have to leave the lessons sit for now."

Morag went and gave Rhiannon a hug, the oneness surprising Rhiannon once again.

"*Cor lummie!* How do yer ever get used to somefin' like dat?"

Morag smiled. "You just do." She pictured her yard and waited. Moments later, she was on her way home.

Pip was prancing through the house, upstairs and down. She looked extremely pleased with herself. She made several trips past Salem and Nefertiti, but neither commented on her odd behavior.

She pranced into Sara's room and turned in a circle. Sara laughed, stroked her back and went back to her drawing.

Every few minutes, she would track down her Mistress and rub up against her legs. Finally, Joly picked her up, cuddled her and set her back down.

"Enough already Pip. Go and lie down or chase a ball or something."

Pip bounded off to prance by Salem again. "I know something you don't."

Salem opened one eye and looked disinterestedly at Pip. He closed the eye again without comment.

"Salem, don't you want to know what it is?"

There was no answer, nor was there any sign he had even heard her.

"Salem? Come on Salem, look at me, talk to me. This is just the greatest news *ever!* And no one knows it except me... not even the Mistress!"

Salem opened one eye again. He licked his lips and sighed. "Just what is it that you would know Pip, that the Mistress doesn't?"

"She's going to have a baby, Salem, *a baby!* The Mistress is pregnant, Salem. Isn't that just the greatest news ever?" She bounced up and down as she talked, excited beyond belief.

Salem leapt to his feet. "*What?* Are you sure, Pip?"

"Oh yes, I'm very sure. I can hear it inside of her. It's very small of course, but I know its there." Pip bounced around the room.

Salem jumped off the chair he had been laying on. "Pip, come here."

Pip sidestepped over to Salem. "What?"

"Listen to me very carefully. You mustn't say anything to anyone, I mean anyone, especially Nefertiti."

"Why, Salem?"

"She's been acting really weird the past few days. Haven't you noticed? She keeps watching both of us, but especially me. It's like she's become some sort of protector. Whenever I go outside, she watches my every move. It's really spooky."

"She's been much nicer since the Mistress came home, Salem, so why can't we tell her?"

"She might get really nasty again, Pip. We don't need that if the Mistress is pregnant. The Mistress needs peace, not fights."

Pip cocked her head. "You're right, Salem, but it's such *great* news. We need to tell *somebody*."

"Pip, you told me. Now leave it at that. I will have to keep a closer eye on her now, and Pip?"

"Yes."

"Be very careful on the stairs, especially if the Mistress is on them."

"Okay, Salem, I will." She turned and pranced out of the kitchen.

"Pip!"

Seconds later, she stuck her head around the corner of the door. "What?"

"For heavens sake, quit prancing all over the place. It's a dead giveaway that something's happened."

She lowered her head. "Yes, Salem." She turned, muttering to herself, "But it's such *great* news."

That night, Randy wrapped his small arms around Joly and laid his head on her tummy. He stayed like that for a minute and then lifted his head. He patted her tummy and looked up at her. "Baby," he stated and laid his head back down.

Duncan laughed. "I wonder just who he's been talkin' to. Not somethin' a kindergarten teacher should be teachin', I don't think."

Joly smiled. She had sensed small changes in her body. It was too soon to tell, but she thought that Randy was right. She thought about Pip and wondered if she had been talking to Randy. She wasn't ready for a baby. She had just gotten her husband back and she was still new to being Randy's Mother. They hadn't used protection, they never had. She thought of Morag and knew she would be ecstatic. Well, if her Gods and Goddesses thought it time for her to have a baby, so be it. She figured nine months would give her the time she needed to get used to the idea.

She thought about her Mother and how upset she had been to be left behind, while the others continued to fight the never-ending battles with the demons. She had kept it a secret as long as she had been able to, but her husband had guessed when she was four months along. She had stayed at home until Joly was nine months old.

Fourteen months. It seemed like a long time, but she thought she would relish the break from all the traveling. She would keep quiet until she was sure... and until the evil from the east had been dealt with.

She ran her hand over Randy's head, still smiling. "Maybe a playmate is expecting a brother or sister."

Duncan looked at her eyes. "Yeah, maybe."

The next day, when Joly was busy with making the beds and vacuuming, Duncan went across the street.

"Maw, I need to talk to you."

"What is it, Son? You sound concerned abut something."

"Yeah, you might say so. I think Joly is pregnant. I don't want her goin' to the states. I don't want her fightin' anything. What do I do, Maw?"

Morag stood with her mouth open. When she finally found her voice, it cracked as she spoke. "Pregnant? Joly?" She shook her head. "What makes you think that?"

"I don't know. I guess it's more a feelin' than anything, but last night Randy patted her stomach and said baby. He wasn't askin', Maw, he was tellin'. He talks to Pip all the time and Pip knows everything that goes on with Joly. Shee-it Maw. What do we do?"

Gods! What a time for this to happen. Damn Pip anyhow. Regardless if Joly was pregnant or not, she was going to have to fight the evil in the southeast. Damn! I'm not a good liar at the best of times. This is fantastic! Oh, how am I going to stay silent? Gods! I can't wait to start shopping for baby things.

"Well dear, about all we can do is wait and see. You've only been back with us for a month, Son. If by chance she is pregnant, it's far too early to tell."

"Wait, Maw? We can't wait! We're goin' to be leavin' any day."

"Duncan. Is she healthy?"

"Yeah."

"Is she a healer?"

"Yeah, but..."

"No! No buts. If by chance she's pregnant, and I doubt she is, we won't know for sure for a while yet. We will go east and do what we have to do."

"Maw..." He was at a loss for words. Couldn't she see how important this was? He slammed his hand down on the table in frustration.

"Duncan, come here, Son." She held her arms out to him.

He hesitated and then went to her. She held him and felt the vibration that was emanating from his very soul. She sent him calming energies and as she did, she wondered how Joly would deal with the news. She remembered their conversation on one of the flights they had taken.

"Morag, my love for Duncan was and is, all encompassing. We just

wanted to be alone with each other."

They had never had the chance to be alone with each other. When Duncan was found, Randy was already part of the picture. She knew Joly had grown in maturity since the conversation, but the possibility of a baby was something else entirely. She remembered all too well the sleepless nights, getting up for feedings, walking a fussy baby across the floor, trying to catch a few winks during the day. She had never regretted a moment of it, but the boys had played hell with her and Brody's time together.

When she felt Duncan was calm, she held him away from her. "Go out back and ground yourself, Son. And ground yourself as often as needed, until you know for sure. There's no point in worrying needlessly over something that might not even be. You were together for three months when you got married. Joly never got pregnant then, why would she get pregnant so fast this time? Randy probably heard something at school."

"That's what Joly said."

"Well, it makes more sense than anything else."

Duncan didn't believe a word of it, but he knew he had nothing concrete to base his suspicions on, so he did as his mother told him, knowing he would be watching his beloved wife very closely.

That afternoon, Morag was down at the mall picking up a few things. Without realizing where she had wandered to, she found herself in the baby department. *Damn!* She shouldn't be there. She started to walk away, but paused when she saw some tiny baby shoes. They were so sweet. There were so many nice things nowadays. Much nicer than when her two had been small. She picked up a pair of the tiny runners. They were white with two red stripes on them. She couldn't resist. She put them in her basket and sent a quick prayer that she wasn't jumping the gun.

Pip was racing through the house, running up and down the stairs just for the sheer enjoyment of it. On her third trip down the stairs, she realized that Joly was heading up them. She remembered what Salem had said and she screeched to a stop, almost falling head over heels down the next step. She sat quietly until Joly had walked past her, and then she resumed her race down the remainder of them. Joly paused and looked at her, shook her head and continued up.

She knew Duncan and Randy were down in the basement and Sara had gone out somewhere. She walked to the fourth bedroom and stood in the doorway. She imagined a crib in the room instead of the bed. She pictured a brightly colored dresser and a change table. She would move her rocking chair in and they would need to get a toy box. She smiled to herself. She shouldn't be thinking about the baby yet. There would be lots of time for that when they returned from the east. She turned and went to Randy's bedroom.

She wondered if it was a boy or a girl. She would know soon enough.

She thought about names as she picked up a few toys and put them away. As much as she loved her parents, she knew she didn't want a little Morgana or Colin in the house. Neither did she want a small Morag or Broderick. She decided that one Duncan was also enough. His middle name was Fraser and she couldn't see herself calling a small child that, either. She certainly didn't want another Joly or an Anne. She thought about Alyce, but she didn't even like the name. She thought about names she had always liked. Her favorite girls name as a child had always been Magi. She knew most people spelled it Maggie, but that was short for Margaret. With only one g and no e, it became a magical name, not short for anything and she quietly tried it aloud. "Magi McEwan." She smiled. *Yes, I like it. What about boys' names?*

In the basement, Duncan was rearranging all of Colin's tools. He didn't have a lot of carpentry experience, but Colin had owned every tool known to mankind. He would have to give it a try and see if he was any good at it.

His thoughts returned to the probability of Joly's pregnancy. He wondered when she would tell him. He knew it definitely wouldn't be until after the fight in Pennsylvania. He wondered what they would name him or her. He didn't care whether it was a boy or a girl. He just hoped that whatever it was, that it had Joly's dark hair and hazel eyes. He thought of Randy and his dark coloring. If the baby had dark hair, at least he wouldn't feel so conspicuous when he got older. Thinking about Randy, he decided they should keep the first letter of his name. He had gone to school with a girl named Doris. Gods, but she had been a goofy one! Her whole family had names that started with the same initial. There had been Doris, Dennis, Debra, David, Deirdre and Donna. He'd always thought it was kind of cool. He started thinking of R names.

Richard, Roy, Raymond, Robert, Reese, Rodney, Rory, Roland, Rudy.

Wait... back up. Rory. Rory and Randy. Rory McEwan. Yeah... that's good.

Roberta, Reba, Robin, Rhonda, Rachael, Rachel, Rae, Rita, Rebecca, Ruth, Regina. Gods, I don't really like any of them. Maybe we should get one of those baby books with all the names and their meanings.

Joly was still thinking about names as she started down the stairs. She never noticed the silent shadow that had been following her from room to room ever since Pip had told him the news.

Salem knew he was in for a long stretch with no sleep. The Mistress did not sit still, so he seemed to be constantly on the move. That was all right. He was there to protect her.

Joly decided she liked the sound of Marty McEwan. Marty was a happy name and she knew it was important to name the child with the kind of name that they wanted the child to grow into. With Duncan as the father, she wanted a happy son, one that would laugh at his goofy antics. Randy already did and that was good. Randy was so easy to please. He was such a great kid. She was sure he would be an awesome big brother to the newcomer.

Veronika lifted the limp body and turned the woman on her side. She began massaging the woman's back, all the while talking softly, the Russian words interspersed with the occasional English word.

When she was finished with the back, she massaged the arms and then the legs.

She gently brushed the now white hair, washed the woman's face and eased another ice chip through the pale lips.

She gathered the top half of the woman to her breast and rocked her, singing a lullaby from her childhood.

This had become a twice daily routine and although Veronika didn't know whether it was of any help to the woman who was lost to another dimension, she felt better doing the little she could.

"*Tsipotchka*, do you know Vorona comes every day to window? He sits on ledge and he looks in at you. I open window, but he don't come in, he just watches you. *Tsipotchka*, how long will you stay away?"

As time passed, Rauna began to see and hear better. The attacks had almost stopped. It was almost like being bullied in the school yard now, the things pushing and shoving her as they passed.

Then she heard it… a silent whisper, more like the touch of a feather, coming from long, long away.

"*Tsipotchka.*"

A leg twitched, which startled Veronika. She felt a tear in her eye. "Yes, *Tsipotchka*, come to me."

Muscles long unused began to spasm, jerking the entire body uncontrollably, but Veronika refused to let go of the woman. As she twitched, Veronika continued talking.

An hour passed and still the muscles continued their foray into limberness.

A sound at the window caused Veronika to look up. The crow was there. She gently laid the woman down and opened the window. "Hello, *Vorona*. Do you sense she is about to wake? Come." She was surprised when the crow entered the room.

She turned to the bed and jumped when she saw the coal black eyes staring at her. Putting her hand to her heart, she smiled.

"*Tsipotchka*, you have returned." She sat on the edge of the bed and ran her hand across the wispy white hair. "I am glad."

She noticed the muscles had finally quit twitching and the woman lay completely still.

"I don't know if you understand me… my English is not good and maybe you don't speak English." She paused, but there was no reaction. The black eyes never left hers. "Sometimes… a voice to listen to is good just to hear, even if you don't understand." She smiled.

"Do you see who is here? *Vorona* waits for you. Come *Vorona*, come and see your *prijate.*"

The crow flew to the side of the bed and walked to the woman's shoulder. He nuzzled her cheek, making small guttural sounds as he did and then buried his head in her hair. Apparently satisfied, he lay down.

The woman's eyes returned to Veronika.

"You are wondering where you are? We are in Jacksonville, Florida." She laid her hand on the other woman's.

"Do you feel it? We are the same… *Sisters of the Triple Moon*. I am Veronika Ivanova. You are safe here, *Tsipotchka.*"

Morag was relaxing after eating her supper. She had the TV on and was watching the news when the phone rang. She usually knew who was calling, but nothing came to her as she picked up the receiver.

"Hello?"

"My Lady, tell me it's really you."

She laughed. "Yes, Jesse, it's really me. How are you?"

"I'm doing alright. And you?"

"I'm fine, thank you. When did you get back to B.C.?"

"How did you… oh, you have call display. I've been here a few days."

"No, I don't have call display. Are you planning on staying?"

"You don't have call display? Then how did…"

"… I know that you were here." She smiled. "I'm a witch, remember."

"Uh, yes, I do remember. How's your partner?"

She smiled again. He wasn't very subtle. "Joly is fine, as is her nanny."

"Uhh… thank you. I guess I should have just asked about Sara."

"Yes, I appreciate when people are up front with me. You didn't answer me, Jesse. I'm not sure if it was intentional or not, but I'll ask again. Are you planning on staying in B.C.?"

"My Lady, you wound me with your accusation."

"Never mind the B.S. and answer me."

She heard his sigh and smiled. He would eventually learn not to be evasive with her.

"It depends."

"On Sara?"

"You don't believe in pulling punches do you, my Lady?"

"No, and again you avoid the question. If you called to dance a tango with me, I don't want to dance and I will say goodbye. If you want answers and help, then quit screwing around."

"Yes, my Lady, and yes to the question."

"Now, how hard was that?"

"My Lady, with you, everything is hard. Have you ever watched an interview with me on TV? Because if you haven't, you should. You would see that I am a master at evading personal questions."

"You sound proud of the fact when you should be ashamed. Why must you be so secretive about everything? You chose a career that puts you in the lime light. Therefore, you should act accordingly."

"Yes, my Lady. Thank you for the sermon. Now if I may, I'd like to see you. I have something to ask of you."

"Ahh, you can be direct when you've a mind to. That's good. I don't drive, so you will either have to come out here and risk seeing Sara, or I will have to take a bus into Surrey. Which one will it be?"

"How did you know I'm in Surrey? Never mind. Don't answer that. I will drive out, that's not a problem. Where do I find you?"

"Three, three, zero..." Morag paused, wondering if she was doing the right thing She gave him her address and directions. She asked him to be there at twelve the next day. She hung up the phone slowly, thinking about what she was doing. She knew Sara usually waited outside, when Joly and Duncan picked up Randy from school.

She also knew Sara wasn't sleeping well. Sara had been over and asked for a tea mixture to help her sleep. Morag had made up a mixture of elderberry, chamomile and peppermint teas and told her to have a cup shortly before she went to bed.

Morag thought life was going to get interesting in the neighborhood. It was a shame she wouldn't be able to stick around to watch.

That night she had a dream. There were several people, but everyone was blurred. It was as if she was looking through a not so sheer curtain. They were in a circle, and in the background she could make out the manor house.

When she awoke, she felt a sense of relief. It was time to leave for Pennsylvania. She had been waiting almost a year for the call. She was glad it had finally come. There were still the other two to deal with, but they were on other continents. They would get to them eventually. They needed to get rid of the nearest one first. She had a feeling it might be the more powerful of the three.

She walked across the street to let Joly and Duncan know. From the look she got from Joly, she was sure that she had also been told it was time. She knew they would spend every moment from now until they left, with Randy. Sara would be free for the next two days.

Morag watched from her living room window as Joly and Duncan walked up the street to pick up Randy from school. Five minutes later, Sara walked out and sat on the steps. Less than a minute later a black car pulled up in front of the house. She watched as Jesse got out and stretched. He glanced around. He and Sara spotted each other at the same time. Jesse stiffened and Sara jumped to her feet, poised to take flight like a frightened bird.

Morag opened her senses and asked the Gods to at least get the two together to talk. She willed the two to walk toward each other. Jesse walked around the front of the car and stopped. Sara hadn't moved. He slowly crossed the street looking directly ahead at Sara. Morag was glad there were no vehicles coming. He would have been flattened.

Jesse reached the sidewalk. He was maybe ten feet away from her. He could see she was terrified. He hadn't wanted to hurt her. He loved her. He needed her. He wondered if he was strong enough to tell her so. He took two more steps and was on the sidewalk that led to the old house.

Sara couldn't believe her eyes. What was Jesse doing there? She wanted to run inside and lock herself away where he would never find her. She couldn't do this hurting thing again. Each time she saw him, it was like the first time he had walked away. She was afraid to breathe. She was so close to crying.

He took two more steps toward her and stopped. "Hello Sara."

She said nothing, so he took two more steps. Another two and he would be beside her. He was afraid she would run and if she did, he would never have the guts to chase her down again. He didn't know what she felt for him, but she had loved him, of that he was sure. He only hoped that somewhere inside of her, some of that love remained.

He ventured a small smile and it was almost Sara's undoing. She felt her heart leap in her chest and she wanted to run to him, to hold him and never let go.

Jesse took the last two steps and looked at the beautiful woman in front of him. He heard her intake of breath and wondered what it meant.

She could smell him, his after-shave, his body odor, his very essence. She needed space to breathe; he was too close.

"Sara, will you go for a walk with me? You don't have to talk, but I'd like you to listen. I have something I want, no, something I need to tell you."

She didn't answer, nor did she move. She felt like she was frozen in time, only able to hear and nothing else.

The quiet was shattered with a shout. "Sara, Sara." Randy came running toward her and she held her arms out as he tumbled into them.

Joly spotted the male figure beside Sara and it took a second to register that it was Jesse Alexander standing on her steps. She walked up to him and put her hand out. "Hello, Jesse, nice to see you again." She turned to Duncan and introduced the two of them. She went on to explain that they had met in Greece. Then she looked over at the window across the street. She turned away from the two on the steps and gave a small 'tsk, tsk' sign with her index finger. She couldn't actually see Morag, but she would have bet every penny in her bank account that she was there watching.

Duncan saw immediately this was the ex-lover in Sara's life. He hoped he wasn't there to cause trouble. Sara was considered a member of the family and he wouldn't take kindly to someone showing up out of the blue to cause her more heartache.

Jesse was surprised to see the young witch had a husband. There had been no mention of one in Greece. Or had there? The crone had said what? Her son was a witch as was her daughter-in-law. Something like that. He wondered why the husband hadn't been in Greece and then he decided it was none of his business. The kid obviously wasn't his, but you couldn't tell by the way that they were interacting.

Jesse turned to Joly. "Would you mind if I stole Sara away from you for a short while?"

"Not at all. Just be sure to return her." She smiled and looked at Sara. She could see Sara would like to have been anywhere but where she was.

Joly laid her hand on Sara's shoulder and sent calming energies to her. Sara was stiff as a board and Joly knew she couldn't breach the shell she had surrounding her in the few seconds she had. She brushed her hand across Sara's cheek and winked at her. She was rewarded with a small smile.

Jesse reached for Sara's hand, but she pulled back, studiously avoiding any contact with him. Wordlessly she walked down the sidewalk and turning right, she walked up the block. She never looked back to see if Jesse was following.

Jesse watched her for a few seconds and wondered at the insanity of it all. She quite obviously didn't want anything to do with him. He looked over at the crone's and wondered if he should just walk over there and say to hell with it.

A voice fluttered through his mind. He shook his head. *What the hell?* The voice came again.

Tell her the truth, all of it.

He was losing his mind. It sounded suspiciously like the crone talking in his head. That wasn't possible, was it?

Anything is possible, Jesse. Just do it.

Shit! It was too weird. He loped to the sidewalk and quickly closed the distance between himself and Sara. When he caught up to her, his hand automatically went to hold hers. When he touched her, she jumped and then she moved away toward the edge of the sidewalk.

"I don't bite, Sara. At least not hard, as you should know."

She still had said nothing. The silent treatment was beginning to get to him. He could handle an outburst or even better, if she would throw herself into his arms, but the silence was unnerving.

She was walking fast and he was aware of her heavy breathing. *Damn it!* How could he get through to her? Suddenly it came to him.

"Sara, please stop walking. Just stand still. We're in the middle of town. I won't touch you."

She walked on as if she hadn't heard him. Several feet farther along, she stopped suddenly. She didn't turn. She just stood there like a statue.

Please Gods, let this work.

He was slightly behind her and he spread out his arms and allowed himself to become one with his surroundings. *I don't care if the whole damn world is watching.* There in the middle of the sidewalk, Jesse Alexander turned invisible.

He took a step toward Sara and leaned over to kiss her neck. She shrieked and turned around in a flash. Her mouth was open to say something, but there was no one there to say anything to.

"Jesse?" He remained silent.

"Jesse? Don't."

"Don't what?"

She jumped. Her eyes went to where his voice had come from and she realized that she could see a slight shimmer in front of her. She reached out and touched a solid form. She withdrew her hand quickly, finding it disconcerting to touch something that she couldn't really see.

She turned away, the tears slowly wending their way to the surface. "What do you want, Jesse?"

"You."

"Don't."

"Will you listen to me; will you let me tell you what happened when I left?"

Sara put her head down. It was too much. She couldn't do this anymore.

"Go away. I don't want to listen to you. Take your invisible self and go back to Greece."

"I will."

Her head shot up.

"But only after you listen to me."

She walked to the curb and sat down. "Talk, Jesse. This is the only chance you will ever get, so you had better make it count." She rested her arms on her knees and laid her head on them.

Jesse allowed himself to become visible once again. He sat beside her, careful not to touch her. He didn't want her to panic; now she had agreed to hear him out. He began his story. He told her about discovering he was a witch, about learning he could make himself invisible, about joining coven after coven and the ridicule he got when they discovered what he could do. He talked more in the following hour than he had probably talked in the past year and a half. He poured his heart out to Sara, holding nothing back. If this was the only chance she would give him, he was going to make it count. He stumbled when he got to the last meeting he had attended. His voice broke as he tried to convey what he had felt. He didn't realize he was crying.

She heard his voice change and turned her head slightly to peek out through her hair at him. She saw the tears and her heart shattered.

He fumbled his way through the part about leaving the meeting, about the humiliation and anger he had felt, the hopelessness and despair. He was a pariah, a misfit, an outcast. He was worthless. He faltered when he told about going to his apartment and grabbing some clothes and the sketch. His voice broke again when he mentioned the realization that he had been wrong to walk out without saying anything to her.

"Sara, I love you. I've always loved you. I've never stopped loving you. Can you ever find it in your heart to forgive me?" He was finally silent, his shoulders heaved as the tears ran down his cheeks. He put his hands in front of his face. He was embarrassed, he was emotionally drained and he was terrified of hearing her answer.

She was silent, too distraught to say anything. The tears trickled down her cheeks, wetting her arms. The breeze running across them caused goosebumps and she shivered, suddenly feeling cold. She wanted his arms around her, but she was afraid. He had walked once, would he walk away again? She knew she couldn't survive another parting from him. She sat up, throwing her head back to get the hair out of her eyes. She sniffled, her nose was running and she had no tissues. She looked at Jesse and saw a broken man. Her Jesse. Her strong Jesse. She knew her first words would set the tone for the rest of their lives, whether they were together or apart.

She reached out her hand and gently laid it on his. His intake of breath was the only reaction she got.

"Jesse, I forgive you."

He looked up at her.

She looked into his eyes and continued. "I'm afraid, Jesse. I love you, but I'm very afraid. I couldn't go through this again. Do you understand what I'm saying?"

He nodded.

"Jesse, I need to know that regardless of whatever ghosts you're fighting, that you won't exclude me from them. I need to know you won't up and disappear on me again. I need to know that…" Her voice broke.

Jesse slid his arm around her and pulled her to him. They sat like that for a long time, not saying anything, each absorbing the essence of the other, the one that had been away for so long.

Joly and Duncan had a day and a half left to spend with their son. They made every second count.

Duncan worried about Joly and the probability that she was pregnant. He knew that demons not only liked to reach in and take the heart from someone, but they also were extremely fond of fetuses. He was thankful she wasn't very far along. The pea sized being inside of her wasn't really worth taking; at least he didn't think it was.

Randy had been playing with his miniature cars and trucks and he'd scattered them everywhere. Joly was walking along the hallway upstairs picking them up and returning them to his toy box. When she was done, she grabbed a hamper of dirty laundry and headed to the stairs with it.

She didn't see the little white car with the oversized tires sitting on the third step. She took the first step and then she took the second.

Salem saw the vehicle and saw disaster happening before his very eyes. He flashed by Joly and screeched to a stop several steps down. He let out a terrible yowl, startling Joly.

"Salem, stop it!" Her foot came down on the car. The car shot ahead as did Joly's foot. She started to fall backwards, but she didn't want the hamper falling on her, so she threw herself forward to let it go. The hamper crashed down the stairs, clothes spilling out with every step it hit. But throwing herself forward had not been the answer. She couldn't regain her balance and now she threw her hands out as her momentum carried her forward to certain disaster.

Salem didn't know if he could do it, but he had to try. He crouched as low as he could and when he sprang to his feet, he launched into the air. He hit his Mistress in the chest so hard that she cried out. She teetered for a second as Salem fell back to the step below. The momentum from his attack finally swung in his favor, and Joly fell backwards onto the steps above.

Duncan had been coming from the kitchen when he heard the hamper thud down the stairs. Not knowing what had fallen he'd raced to the bottom of the stairs in time to see Joly falling forward, Salem springing up and pushing her back and finally he watched as she sat heavily on her backside.

He raced up the stairs and took her in his arms. He was shaking so badly he could hardly hold her. She was a little shaky herself. They sat quietly for a few minutes and then Duncan got mad.

"Don't you *ever*, I mean *ever*, let me catch you doing such a stupid thing, ever again! You could have been hurt real bad. Hell, you could have died. Then where would I be? You just tell me that, Joly McEwan!"

She giggled a nervous little giggle. She knew how close she had come to being badly hurt. She also knew she could easily have lost the tiny life that was growing inside of her. She burst into tears.

"It's okay Darlin', it's okay. You're okay. I didn't mean to yell at you. I love you." He cuddled her close as the tears fell.

Nefertiti watched from the bottom of the stairs. Salem had just saved the Mistress once again. She probably owed him an apology, but she wasn't sure that she was prepared to go quite that far. She did walk up to him and sniffing his nose, she politely said, "Well done, Salem." She walked up the stairs to sniff the Mistress. Yes, she was fine, just shook up.

Pip also went to check out the Mistress, but Pip's concern lie deep inside of her. She listened as she placed her head on the Mistress' tummy. Where was it? There? Yes! There it was. It was still okay. Pip nodded to Salem, as she too thanked him.

When Joly was able to stand, Duncan helped her down the stairs, took her into the kitchen, and made her a cup of calming tea with chamomile, sage, thyme and marjoram.

Joly and Duncan both thanked Salem for his gallant act and then Duncan took Randy to his room and gave him a very serious lecture on leaving his toys laying all over. He emphasized the importance of not having any toys on the stairs at any time.

When Duncan was finished talking to Randy, Pip also went and talked to him.

20. The Gathering

Sara and Jesse slowly walked back to Morag's. Sara was quiet and Jesse still wasn't sure exactly where he stood with her. He was afraid to ask. She had allowed him to hold her hand and he took that to be a positive sign.

"I'm supposed to see Morag. I was going to ask if she would be willing to let me be part of their group. I need to learn about the craft, Sara. I need to learn from someone who is real. Do you understand what I'm trying to say?"

She nodded, but said nothing.

"Sara, I can't stay if I can't see you." He swallowed. "I don't want to push you into anything, but if you won't give me a second chance, there's no point in me going to see her. I'll just get back in the car and leave."

He felt her hand tighten around his. He squeezed back gently.

Sara stopped. She looked at the sidewalk and finally raised her eyes to his. "I need time, Jesse. Go and see Morag. She can teach you a lot. She's a very wise woman. Maybe go with them on their next trip, if she'll have you. I'm not going anywhere. I'll be here. You find out if this is what you've been searching for. When you know the answer to that, then come and see me. You see, I need to know the answer to that also. Until I know this is really what it's all about, I can't give you an answer. I won't take you back only to have you disappear again when you decide this isn't really what you were looking for. I love you, Jesse, but I need to be sure you really know who you are. I also need to know you won't shut me out. Learn to communicate, learn about yourself and learn to share what you know."

"If she allows me in, will I be able to see you?"

"I live with the rest of her group, Jesse. It would be very difficult to avoid one another. Yes, you'll see me, but don't ask me out. I won't go. I told you, I need time. Now, go and talk to Morag."

She reached up and touched her lips to his. She hadn't meant to do that. She had planned to kiss his cheek, but her lips had automatically gone to his. She realized she had needed to taste him, if only for a second.

Jesse was shocked when he felt her lips against his. He wanted to throw his arms around her and never let her go. He savored the momentary touch.

"I do love you, Sara."

She smiled at him then. "I know you do." She turned and walked across the street and into her home.

Jesse watched her go and only after she closed the door did he turn and walk up the steps to Morag's. He raised his hand to knock and the door opened.

"Come in, Jesse." She hugged him and led him into her living room.

"Tea or coffee?"

"Do you have anything cold?"

"Iced tea."

"Yes, please."

While Morag was gone, Jesse looked around the room. He had been surprised to find she lived in an older neighborhood. He'd been under the impression she was fairly well off. He saw that even though everything was spotless, there was nothing even remotely new in the room. The television was small, only nineteen or twenty inches. He hoped she would accept him into the group. She remained an enigma, and he wanted to know her better.

Morag returned with two glasses of iced tea. She sat down across from him and smiled.

"So Jesse, you've had a full afternoon so far. How did you and Sara fare?"

He looked down at the glass in front of him. The crone always pushed. He had a problem with that and knew it was one he was going to have to overcome, if she agreed to his request.

"We talked. I told her everything. She needs, uh, wants me to, uh..." Damn, it was hard expressing himself to this woman with the all-knowing eyes.

"She wants you to discover who you really are, before she'll commit herself again, is that what you're trying to say?"

"Yes."

"And how do you propose to do that?"

"The reason I came out today was to ask you if you would accept me into your group. I need to learn about the craft and as you know, I haven't been too successful. Sara said I could learn a lot from you."

"We leave the day after tomorrow for the states. Be packed and be here tomorrow night. Now, come with me."

He was speechless. He wasn't sure what he had expected her to say, but it certainly hadn't been that.

She led him to the back door and took him out in her yard. He was astounded. None of this was visible from the front of the house. It was like being in a park. He followed her to a circular space hidden in the bushes.

"This is how we center and ground ourselves. This is something we do on a regular basis. The main benefit is to use the earth's energy rather than deplete our own. It also keeps us firmly planted to Mother Earth. It keeps us in touch with the reality of who we are. It allows us to concentrate more fully on the task at hand. It allows us to become one with ourselves and with nature. If every human on earth practiced this, it would be a much better place."

She assumed the Goddess position; her legs slightly spread apart, her arms down and the palms of her hands open and facing front.

"Envision your two bodies, your flesh and blood body and your etheric body or what some would call your aura, as two layers of an onion. To center, you need to line these two layers up so the energy can flow. You will need to line up both sets of chakras as well, and then when they are in line you visualize snapping them together. You must line up each of the seven chakras and snap each one together, starting at the bottom. As you are doing this, you must visualize the seven colors of chakra light, red, orange, yellow, green, blue, indigo and violet joining together, so that when you reach the crown chakra and snap the two of them together, all that will remain is a white light, which will surround you just as your etheric body does."

"Now, visualize a cord of light running from your crown chakra through each of your other chakras, continuing past the root chakra and down your legs deep into Mother Earth. All the way down to the earth's core. This core is full of clean, pure energy and it's there for us to use. Now when your roots have reached the core, draw the clean, pure energy back up your roots all the way through your chakras. See the old stale energy being pushed out and replaced with the fresh, pure energy. When it reaches your crown chakra, allow it to overflow, see the fountain of beautiful energy spilling out and returning to Mother Earth."

He had thought he knew how to ground himself. He discovered he knew nothing. When the crone finally yelled at him the fourth time he did it wrong, he wondered if he would be strong enough to stick it out. He tried it again.

Morag knew she was pushing him, she knew he was beyond being frustrated and she wondered if he would quit, or finally dig deep into his self to discover who he really was.

She knew she needed the okay from the other two to allow him into the group, but she foresaw no problem getting it. She needed to keep Jesse off balance. He was too head strong and far too used to getting his own way. If he was going to become a civilized member of the human race, she was going to have maintain control every inch of the way.

Damn it Jesse, open your chakras; let the energy in!

By his seventh attempt, he was ready to call it quits. He was almost in tears and still the crone kept harping at him. He tried it again.

He felt something. What was that? He could feel something entering his body. It felt... *wonderful.* What was it?

Open wider, Jesse, keep it coming. Yes!

Gods, she had almost been ready to call it a day with him. It had been many years since she had seen anyone who was so tensed up that even when he thought he had opened himself, in reality he was still closed tighter than a drum.

Jesse allowed the energy to flow. He could feel himself calming. It was the most glorious sensation. He couldn't ever remember feeling so peaceful.

"Okay, Jesse. You finally got it, now remember it. You will need to do it several times a day to start with. It will get easier and much quicker. In some instances, it will be needed to help you save your own life or that of a colleague. Never forget *how* to do it and never forget *to* do it."

"Next lesson…"

"My Lady, is this necessary?"

"Yes. If you're going to be part of the group, you need to know at least the basics. We leave in another day and a half to fight one the worst evils out there. What do you know about demons?"

"Nothing."

"How do you fight them?"

"I don't know."

"Is the next lesson necessary?"

He looked at his feet. "Yes, my Lady."

Four hours later, she took him back in the house and fed him supper. When they were finished and Morag was cleaning off the table, she paused.

"Are you ready to quit?"

He cocked his head, unsure of what she was asking. "Quit? Are you asking if I'm ready to quit for good or are you asking if I've had enough for the day?"

"What do you think I'm asking? *Damn it Jesse.* You're a witch. Start using the powers that are inside of you."

Shit! He wished she would quit yelling at him. He wasn't a child, but she sure knew how to make him feel like one.

"You're asking if I'm ready to quit, to walk away. The answer, my Lady, is no."

"Good!" She was silent as she finished putting the dishes in the sink. She ran water, added soap and tossed a tea towel at Jesse. She started washing.

He sat looking at the back of her in amazement. He wondered if he was in over his head. He slowly rose and went to dry the dishes.

She was exhausted, but she wasn't about to let him know it. When the dishes were done and put away, she handed Jesse several candles, a God and Goddess figure and some incense and censor. She took a bell, a chalice, her athame, wand, sea salt and water and her altar cloth and she led him back outside. She showed him how to set up an altar facing the east, with the God items of incense, censor, wand and athame on the right and the Goddess items of the chalice, water and bell on the left. The salt and the pentacle were placed in the center. A white candle was placed on either side.

"There is no hard and fast rule about setting up an altar. You do what feels right to you, but the Goddess items must be on the side that represents her, and the God items must be on the side that represents him."

She lit the altar candles.

"What spells and rituals have you done?"

"Protection mostly, for when I race."

Oh for the love of the Gods! Did this novice know anything?

"Do you call the quarters?"

"Yes."

Amazing.

"The Elements?"

He shook his head.

"I can't hear you, Jesse."

"No my Lady, I've never used the Elements."

"Thank you. We are going to do a very easy ritual tonight, but it's one that uses most of the tools for spell crafting. I would suggest you pay close attention as you will be performing this tomorrow night, without my help."

He couldn't ever remember being so physically tired. Not even when he'd spent night after day on Marathon Plain. But he paid close attention. He was tired of being yelled at; he knew he must look like a complete idiot in the crone's eyes. He watched her every move, where she took things from, where she put them back, what she said and when she said it. He paid attention to which direction she faced as she performed, and when she closed the circle, he was left wondering just how much of it he would remember.

They carried everything back inside and Morag turned to Jesse.

"Do you have robes?"

"I will by tomorrow night."

"Good. We're done for now."

"Thank you, my Lady. I'll see you tomorrow."

He headed out the front door.

"Jesse?"

He turned. "Yes."

"Before you go to bed, center and ground yourself."

"Yes, my Lady. Goodnight."

"Goodnight, Jesse."

He closed the door, wondering where he would find the strength to drive back to Surrey. He looked across the street, but other than a couple of lights that were on, he saw nothing. He got into the rental car and turned around. He drove across the bridge to Matsqui and continued on to Abbotsford.

Morag knew he would never make it to Surrey and was curious to see how far he would get. She went and washed, brushed her teeth, and put her nightie on. She plugged in the kettle and went to her crystal.

She had to smile. He hadn't even made it to the freeway. He was spending the night in Abbotsford. She could have asked him to spend the night, but she was curious to see what time he would show up the next day. Throughout the lessons, she had been carefully planting the seeds of curiosity. He wouldn't wait until night to show up.

She put the crystal down and went to bed.

Veronika propped the woman up with several pillows behind her head. She heated some broth and spoon fed it to her. She talked continuously, sometimes in English, sometimes in Russian.

She had called Sergei. Polina was still at school. Sergei would be over after work.

The crow stayed close to his lady. She left the window open so he could come and go.

She wondered what else she could do.

Rauna's thoughts were interrupted with small electrical impulses that fragmented her senses, and the words of the woman who kept up a steady chatter as she lie there. With only every second or third word making a connection, she wasn't sure what the woman was saying.

She recognized the feeling of oneness that she had felt with Morag and Joly. Crow was with her. She knew she was as safe as she would ever be, but after what she had gone through, she didn't think she would ever truly feel safe again.

She thought she should try to get up, but it seemed too much effort.

She was afraid to close her eyes, afraid she would be taken back to the dark place she had just came from.

She felt movement by her head. Crow peered around the side of her face, looked into her eyes and a soft *krraa* rumbled from his throat. She tried to smile, but her face didn't want to work.

She sensed movement and looked at the door. A smiling young man stood leaning against the opening, his arms folded against his chest.

"Hi there." He advanced to the bed and sat on the edge of it.

"Bad trip, huh?" He reached down and tapped her nose. "You're a lucky lady." He sat and watched her for a while, then squeezed her shoulder and left.

The room grew darker. She didn't want it to be dark. The light continued to fade as evening approached.

Rauna was scared. It was getting too dark. She tried to move and succeeded in grasping the sheet that covered her.

A different voice, loud, came from just out of sight. There was a whirlwind of motion and a small light on the dresser was switched on.

A young girl stood and grinned at her. "Sometimes I wonder about my family. They should never turn this light off. I told *Babushka* that, but she worries about the electric bill." She walked to the bed and eased herself down beside Rauna. She wrapped her arm around her and hugged her. Rauna felt the oneness.

"I'm Polina and I'm going to sleep with you tonight and every night until you are well." She kissed Rauna's cheek.

She jumped to her feet again. "But first, I'm going to feed you. You must be starved. *Babushka* says only broth, so I can't offer you a steak yet." She grinned and swept out of the room.

Rauna wasn't sure why, but she felt calmer. Maybe she was going to be okay.

The next morning, Morag was across the street by eight. She felt invigorated and was ready for anything. Joly was surprised to see her so early.

"I thought I would join you for tea, before you take Randy to school."

"Great. How did you make out with Jesse yesterday? I noticed he was there until quite late."

They walked to the kitchen, where Duncan and Randy were spelling words with alphabet cereal.

"Yes. I have something to ask the two of you."

"Hey, Maw. Look at this. Randy spelled it by himself."

She peered over to see CAT carefully laid out on the table.

"Marvelous! Very good Randy. Why are you buying cereal that's mostly sugar?"

"We don't eat it. We just play with it while we eat the good stuff." He pointed to the counter where a box of oatmeal sat.

"I see."

"What's up, Maw?"

"I wondered how the two of you felt about Jesse joining our little group. He has asked if he could. He is a novice, but willing."

"Cool! Sure thing, Maw. We can always use another body."

"Joly?"

Joly knew Jesse would never have been over at Morag's for as long as he had been, if she wasn't already giving him instruction. She wasn't really sure how she felt about it. A novice would not be able to help them with the Pennsylvania problem. Then again, how did one learn if there was no one to teach him?

"That's fine, Morag. He seemed to be dedicated at Marathon. And Duncan's right. Our circle needs to grow."

"Good. I've asked him to join us on the trip south."

"Fine. At least we have enough room with the van to stretch out now."

Sara joined them and the talk moved to different subjects.

Morag watched Sara, saw the circles under her eyes. She'd not had a good night.

"Your young man is a very willing student."

"Is he? He's not really my young man at present." It hurt her to say that, but she didn't want everyone pushing her to a place that she very strongly wanted to go herself.

Morag drank her tea and they discussed the route they were taking through the states. Duncan said he would pick up some maps later that day and they would go over them that evening after Randy was in bed.

Randy was upset that everyone was leaving again. Duncan said he was going to buy a cell phone so that they could stay in contact more often, rather than just when they were in a hotel or motel.

Morag asked if the cats would be accompanying them. All eyes turned to Joly.

She shrugged her shoulders. "I haven't decided. I know I don't have much time left, but it's going to a long journey. My first thought would be to leave them at home, but I will talk to them later and see what they say about it."

"Yes, all right. You're right though. It is a long time in a vehicle."

When Joly and Duncan took Randy to school Morag went back home to pack a few things and start a load of laundry.

When Duncan and Joly returned home, Joly decided to get the talk over with the cats. She called them and let them know she wanted to talk to them. They lined up in a row close together. Joly lay on the floor and began the meld.

Nefertiti spoke first. "Yes, Mistress?"

"We're going on another trip. This is the big one, the one we've been waiting for. We're driving and I need to know how you feel about a long trip in the van."

"How long of a trip, Mistress?"

"Probably at least a week to get there. Maybe longer. We don't know how long we'll be there, and then another week to drive home again."

"*A week!*" Pip sounded horrified. "Mistress, I don't want to spend a week in your van."

Nefertiti glared at Pip. "Pip, it's not about you and what you want. It's about the Mistress and her needs."

Pip lowered her head. "Yes, Nefertiti. I'm sorry, Mistress."

"No, that's all right Pip. I think I would prefer you to stay home anyhow. You are needed here to translate to Randy when he doesn't understand something."

"Yes, Mistress." Pip was ecstatic. She got to stay at the big house.

"Nefertiti, how do you feel about it?"

"It's as you wish, Mistress. I am here to watch out for you. If you wish for me to go, then I will go."

"Salem, what about you?"

"It's as Neffy… I mean Nefertiti says. We are here to watch out for you. It's hard to do that when you're several days away from us."

"Yes, I understand that. You do need to keep in mind that I will not be climbing any stairs. I will be spending most of my time sitting safely in the van. When we do the banishing, you won't be able to help, whatever happens."

"Mistress, it's your decision to make. We will abide by whatever you say."

"I need to think on it some more. I will talk to you this afternoon."

"Yes, Mistress."

"Go in peace."

Joly got to her feet, wondering what to do. She was afraid to leave both Salem and Nefertiti behind. Nefertiti had been on her best behavior, but how long would it last? What would she do the first time Salem did something that she disapproved of? Nefertiti wasn't young any more. The vet thought she was at least fifteen. A long trip by car would not be easy for her. Salem wasn't a kitten either. The vet said he was between eight and ten. Gods, she didn't know what to do. She went in search of Duncan. He usually had a good answer for any problem she might have.

She discovered he had gone out. Probably to get the maps and the cell phone. She wasn't sure how she felt about traveling with a phone. She was glad that they rarely received any calls. It would be nice to be able to talk to Randy throughout the day though, rather than just in the evening.

She walked upstairs and took the suitcase out of the closet. She wondered if Morag knew what the weather was like in Pennsylvania. She decided it didn't really matter. They would be traveling right across the states and would probably run into all kinds of temperatures. She threw four pairs of jeans in the case, two for her and two for Duncan. She went to the T-shirt drawer and rummaged through it. Undecided, she went and got two sweatshirts and put them on the bed.

Morag was walking up the basement stairs with her clean laundry when she became aware of a shift in the air currents around her home. She had her wards in place and was sensitive to anything that concerned them. She put the laundry down and walked out her back door.

"*Cor blimey*, I fink I got it."

Rhiannon stepped out from the bushes where the circle was hidden, with her crystal in her hand.

Morag shook her head. "Hello, Rhiannon. How are you today?"

Rhiannon smiled at her. "I'm fine, and yer?"

"I'm doing well. Come on in."

Morag poured two glasses of iced tea sat them on the table.

"So what brings you back here?"

"I got to thinkin' about everythin' yer says and everythin' yer showed me. I want to know more, Morag. Will yer show me?

"Is someone looking after your dogs?"

She nodded her head. "Yes, fer a few days."

"Good. Yes, of course I'll show you more, but I would like you to commit to one thing for me."

"I don't want to go to where dis evil place is." She reached into her pocket and pulled out a banana, peeled it and took a bite.

"All right. Then will you agree to give me seven days? One full week, without complaint, without questioning and without hesitation."

Rhiannon thought about it and finally nodded. "I can do dat."

"Well then, the first thing I want you to do is go back home and pack a bag. If you are giving me a week, then I want the full week, all ten thousand and eighty minutes of it. There will be no disappearing to go and do your own thing. You will give me your undivided attention every minute of the day, is that understood?"

"Yes." She finished her tea. "I'll be back soon." She stood and walked to the middle of the room. She looked into the crystal and softly spoke. "Take me 'ome." For a second nothing happened and then she disappeared.

Morag walked across the street to let the other two know that there would be one more joining them on their trip.

Joly was surprised. "How did you convince her to come back?"

"She came back on her own. I thought she would. I had shown her enough to pique her interest. She just needed to think about it and make it her decision."

"Can you teach both Jesse and her at the same time?"

"Of course. It'll actually be easier."

"How's that, Maw?"

"Competition, it's a great thing. They will both be wanting to be the best. I don't expect I'll even have to repeat myself."

She smiled, thinking of the challenges ahead. Could she have Rhiannon whipped into shape before they hit Pennsylvania? She knew from past experience that the more one learned; the more one wanted to know. She was sure that Rhiannon would no more want to leave at the end of the week, than fly to the moon.

She thought about Jesse and his self-absorption. Having to vie for her attention would be the best thing that could happen. He would hate it, but it would make him a much better pupil.

Morag returned home to prepare for her guests. She removed two packages of chicken from the freezer, then she went to Duncan's old room and put clean linens on the bed. She got two sets of towels and facecloths from the linen closet and put one set in each bedroom. She cleaned the bathroom and dusted the living room, finding comfort in doing the common chores.

She sensed Jesse's arrival and looked at the time. It was almost noon. She walked to the front entrance. Wanting to keep him off balance she waited until he was almost to the door, and then she swung it open.

The startled look made it hard for Morag to keep a straight face. She tried for a friendly smile.

"Good morning, Jesse."

"Good morning, My Lady."

He had a medium sized suitcase in one hand and a garment bag in the other.

"Come in, please. Your bedroom is down here." She led him to Stephen's room. "When you're ready, I'll be in the kitchen."

Joly asked Duncan about the cats. He was pleased Pip was staying with Randy. He agreed it would be a long trip for the cats, but especially for Nefertiti. He understood they had traveled everywhere with Joly until she had gone to India, and then again they had been left behind on the Quebec and Australian trips. He thought that given the choice, they would both opt to travel only because they felt it was their duty.

"Well, Darlin', Nefertiti has seniority around here, so perhaps you should allow her the choice. Yeah… she's old, but you know she's healthy and you can't stop the agin' process. It would be nice if we witches had the power of immortality, but we don't. I agree that Salem and her shouldn't both be left behind. She's quite cantankerous. There will be five of us in the van plus all the luggage. Not a lot of room left for a carrier and stretchin' out. If she opts to go, then tell Salem he has to stay home."

"And if she wants to stay here, then what do I do?"

"Tell Salem that for his own safety, he must go with us."

"Yes, that makes sense. Thanks honey."

"No prob. Now, where's that big flashlight I saw the other day?" He wandered off in search of it.

Joly called Nefertiti and melded with her.

"Nefertiti, as you have been with me the longest, I will give you the choice. You may come with us, or if you would prefer, you can stay here and watch out for Randy and Sara."

"Mistress, my place is with you."

"It's a long trip by car. You're sure you want to do this?"

"Mistress, I am healthy. There's not much energy involved with lying down, watching the world rushing by in a blur of motion."

Joly smiled. "Yes, that's true. Fine. I'll let the others know. Salem will remain here."

"Yes, Mistress."

Joly finished the melding and called Salem. She knew she could just tell him he was staying behind, but she wanted to know his thoughts, so she began the melding process one more time.

"Yes, Mistress?"

"Salem, Nefertiti has chosen to make the trip with us. I would like you to stay here and keep an eye on Randy and Sara."

"Yes, Mistress."

"I would take you with me, but there won't be a lot of room, and I am concerned about you and Nefertiti being stuck in such close quarters for such a long time."

"Yes, Mistress. I understand the close quarter's thing. You are right. We would probably lock horns along the way."

"Thank you Salem, for being so understanding."

"It's nothing, Mistress, but may I say one thing?"

"Of course."

"Please, take every precaution on your trip. You need to look after yourself."

"I know I do, Salem." She smiled. "I take it you've been talking to Pip."

"Yes, Mistress. I wasn't aware that you knew."

"Yes, I know. I haven't told anyone. I'll wait until we return."

"Very wise of you. The Mister suspects. He's very concerned."

"Thank you for telling me that. I'll have to be careful. I wouldn't want him sending me back home before the job's done."

"No Mistress. I know you will be successful. Have a safe trip."

"Thank you. Go in peace."

Joly went to find Duncan and let him know what had transpired.

Morag was in the back yard with Jesse when she became conscious of movement along side of the house. She turned in time to see Stephen walk into sight.

"Stephen! What brings you out here today? I was going to call you tonight. We're leaving tomorrow for the States."

"Hello, Mother." He nodded to the stranger sitting at the table. "I don't know. I had a feeling that you were getting ready to leave. I thought I would come out and see how you were doing."

"Wonderful! Stephen, this is Jesse Alexander. Jesse, my oldest son, Stephen."

Jesse jumped to his feet to shake hands. This must be the one that wasn't a witch. He wondered how it felt to be an outsider. He smiled more to himself than anyone else. Gods! He knew very well how it felt to be an outsider.

"Hello, Stephen, my pleasure. You Mother is an amazing woman, but I expect you already know that."

"Jesse. Yes, she is that."

At that moment, there came the sounds of breaking branches and a great lot of cursing.

Morag ran toward the circle with the two men hot on her heels.

Rhiannon lay sprawled amongst the branches of a lilac bush, her bag alone in the circle, and her crystal lying along side of the bush.

"Gods child, are you all right?" She leaned forward to take Rhiannon's hand, but Stephen's hand got there first.

He took one look at the incredibly gorgeous woman lying amongst the branches, and knew he wanted to get to know her. "Here, let me help you up."

Rhiannon was mortified. She had expected Morag to be alone. The image of two very good looking men looking at her in shock would be seared on her brain forever.

"Uhh... thank yer." She reached out to take the stranger's hand. As they gripped one another, she felt a tingling. By the look on his face, she knew he felt it too.

Stephen assisted the young woman to her feet.

Rhiannon tried to straighten herself out as best as she was able, conscious of the scrutinizing she was receiving from everyone.

Morag broke the silence. "What happened dear? Did you think of something else at the last moment?

"Yes. I was tryin' to remember what bushes yer 'ad surroundin' the circle."

"Foolish child. You'll know better the next time."

Rhiannon nodded.

"I'd like you to meet my son, Stephen. Son, this is Rhiannon. I'm sorry dear; I don't know your last name."

"Right. It's Robinson."

"And this is Jesse Alexander. Jesse, Rhiannon Robinson."

Jesse reached out to shake her hand. "My pleasure, Rhiannon. That was some entrance. You may have misjudged, but it was quite an accomplishment just the same."

Rhiannon blushed to her toes.

Morag could sense Stephen's hackles rising, so she took his arm and turned to the other two. "Will you excuse us for a moment, please?" She led Stephen into the house.

"Mother, why did you do that? Now you've left them alone out there."

"Stephen, settle down. Jesse is head over heels in love with Sara. You have no worry there, at all."

"Oh." He seemed nonplussed.

"What's bothering you?"

"Where did she come from, I mean why is she here? Uhh, who is she?"

Morag smiled. Her eldest seemed to be tongue-tied. Two more unfitting people she thought she had never seen, but she thought the Gods must know what they're doing.

"Rhiannon is someone we met in England. She's going with us tomorrow. What else would you like to know?"

He peered out the kitchen window. "Nothing. I was just curious."

Sure you were. "Help me with some refreshments, please."

"Yes, of course."

Outside, Jesse was wondering the same things as Stephen.

"Do you often drop in this way?"

"No. Morag's teachin' me the flamin' ways of the craft. I just discovered I could do dis."

"Morag's teaching you?"

She nodded, a quizzical look on her face.

"You're not going on this trip tomorrow, are you?"

"Yes, I am. Why?"

Jesse was not pleased. He thought the crone would be teaching him exclusively. He wondered if he could come up with an excuse not to go. Then he thought of Sara and knew he would walk on broken glass if the crone demanded it of him.

"No reason. She hadn't said anything. I was just surprised."

"Are yer going wiv us?"

"Yes."

She smiled. "The more the merrier."

"You're Cockney."

"I am."

Morag and Stephen rejoined them. They sat around the table, the conversation sporadic at best. Finally, Morag excused herself and walked over to Joly's.

Duncan answered the door. "Hey Maw, what's up?"

"I have a houseful. I wondered if you, Joly and Randy would like to join us. Sara too, if she doesn't mind seeing Jesse."

"Who else is…?" He spotted the Porsche across the street. "Oh. Stephen's out. Anyone else?"

"Yes, Rhiannon is there. Stephen seems to be all tongue-tied. It's quite strange."

"Stephen and Rhiannon?" He roared. Even picturing it in his mind brought more laughter. "Maw, that's hilarious!"

Joly showed up at the door, smiling at her husband's laughter.

"Hi! You must have said something very funny."

Morag grinned back. "Not really. Stephen seems to be taken with Rhiannon. Duncan finds it humorous. I was wondering if you wanted to join us."

Joly pictured Rhiannon and her colorful language, her cottage without electricity, the fact she was a *Sister of the Triple Moon.* She pictured Stephen with his Jaguar, his fancy office and the monster home that sat on a monstrous property. She shook her head.

"No, I can't see it happening. Did you want to go over, honey?"

"Oh yeah! I wouldn't miss this for the world."

"You go ahead. I'll get Randy."

Morag spoke. "Bring Sara too, if she doesn't mind seeing Jesse."

"Yes, alright."

Duncan left with his Mother and Joly ran upstairs.

She went to Sara's room first. She asked Sara to join them and she agreed. She went to Randy's room and peeked in.

"*Mommy!* Hi you."

"Hi you. Want to go to Gra-Morg's?"

"Yes." He jumped to his feet from the train set Duncan had insisted he needed. He took Joly's hand and they walked slowly down the stairs.

Duncan livened up the gathering. It wasn't long before he had everyone laughing and talking, while Morag was kept busy making iced tea.

Sara joined in the conversation, talking mainly to Rhiannon and Joly, but out of the corner of her eye she kept a close watch on Jesse. She wondered why she had agreed to come, but she knew why. She had needed to see him. She knew he would be gone for the better part of a month. She had wanted to feast her eyes on him one last time. She wanted to feel his arms around her, but she knew she didn't dare. She wanted him so badly she could feel the ache building in her nether regions and she felt it spreading out and consuming her.

Joly wondered if it was her imagination, but she thought Rhiannon seemed to be making an effort to talk the Queen's English, rather than her colorful Cockney.

Stephen was lost in Rhiannon's eyes. He thought he would never get tired of looking at them. They were the most incredible silver color. He wanted to look into them for the rest of his life. He had trouble tearing his gaze away from her when someone addressed him. He watched her lips move as she spoke and wondered what they would taste like. For some reason he imagined them tasting like raspberries. She wore a loose fitting top and he wondered about the size of her breasts. He felt himself harden and could feel the redness stealing up his neck and across his face. He looked at his knees and tried to think about something else. It didn't work. Wherever he looked, he could still sense her; feel her. He couldn't ever remember feeling like this over a woman.

Jesse was conscious of Sara watching him, while trying to appear not to be. He too was watching her, feasting his eyes on her dimpled cheeks, glorying in watching a smile flit across her face, loving her sparkling eyes. Whenever she spoke, he would isolate her words from everyone else's and revel in listening to her musical voice. Gods, but he wanted her. He thought about the next month, of not seeing her, and he felt devastated. He needed to feel her arms around him one more time before they left. He wondered how he could bring it about.

Randy was having a great time. He remembered lots of people gathering in his village, but they never paid any attention to him, other than to feed him. In Gra-Morg's yard, everyone was happy and they all took turns holding and cuddling him. He kept returning to his favorite lap every second or third turn.

"Mommy, your turn." He climbed up and cuddled.

Joly would whisper in his ear. "Mommy's boy." Randy would giggle and nod his head. Then he would get down and go visit someone else's lap. He had gotten over his shyness with Rhiannon and insisted on sitting on her lap.

At first, Rhiannon wasn't sure what to make of it, but she found that she enjoyed the short cuddles. She had never had much to do with children, most people steering their little ones' well clear of her when they saw her.

She was very aware of Stephen sitting across from her. She had never felt so self-conscious in her life. She was having a terrible time remembering to talk properly. Back in her village, everyone was used to her Cockney rhyming slang, but this wasn't her village, it wasn't even her country. When she was with Morag and Joly it didn't seem to matter, but among all these people, she felt terribly out of place. She thought about picking up her crystal and wishing herself back home, but she knew Morag would be disappointed if she did that. She really did want to learn more about the craft, and she didn't want to upset the teacher. She wished Stephen would quit staring at her. It was quite unnerving.

Duncan had his arm around Joly's shoulders and every few minutes he would give her a squeeze. She had her hand resting on his knee and she would squeeze it back, turning her head and grinning up at him. He nuzzled her neck giving her goose bumps. She giggled and smacked his leg.

Emilia heard that Iago Vargas was having a barbecue for a large gathering of friends and neighbors. She had not been invited, but she hadn't expected to be. The day after the fire, White Wind led her to Iago's ranch. Under the cover of darkness the dog had taken her to the steps of the fancy *casa*. The *bastardo* had set fire to her barn and almost killed her two horses. Jacinta still had nightmares and she had to cast a spell nightly to keep them away. She swore he would pay.

Ernesto and Iago had not been close friends but there had been mutual respect. He had always been a fair man and she wondered why her neighbor had changed so much.

Ernesto and she had been to other barbecues he'd had. She knew the routine. Late in the evening when the men were drunk, Iago held a sharp shooting match with prizes. She planned on attending.

She settled Jacinta in bed and waited until she was asleep. She got her rifle and called White Wind. She drove as close to the property line as she dared, then the dog and she walked the rest of the way. She could hear the ruckus long before they reached his *casa*.

White Wind growled and she touched his head to silence him. The rifle shots startled her, until she realized the contest was underway. The bonfire guided them and when she was close enough, she lifted the rifle and peered through the scope. *Where is he?* Half a dozen men were lining up for the next round. She found Iago lounging in an oversized chair, egging the men on. The noise of the men drowned out what was being said, but she watched Iago stand and raise his arm. "*Diosa*, be with me." She sighted in on his back and as his arm lowered, she fired. Her shot was drowned out by the other rifles firing and she watched as Iago crumpled to his chair.

"*Venganza* is mine. *Viento Blanco*, come." She headed back to the jeep.

Morag couldn't quit smiling. She thought of her life a year before and as she looked around, she couldn't believe the changes. Both Duncan and Joly alive and together with one son and possibly another on the way. Stephen, slowly coming down off his high horse, finally rid of that damned twit and most definitely eying up her newest protégé. Sara and Jesse, so much in love, but afraid. They would do well together eventually. They had just needed the nudge to get them talking.

Then there were the changes in herself. She was walking! She was practicing magic. She was living at home. It was all so very wonderful. She still missed her Brody, but she had come to terms with that and moved on. She was very lucky.

She clapped her hands together to get everyone's attention. The talking slowly quieted and all eyes turned to their hostess.

"I hadn't planned on such a large gathering here on the eve of our departure, but I'm so very pleased that it's come about. I have prepared a light buffet supper inside, if you would all like to go and help yourselves. Feel free to eat indoors or out, it matters not to me. After we finish, I would like to have a circle and if Jesse would be so kind, I would like him to lead it. Jesse?"

Jesse could feel his insides shrivel and quiver. In front of all these people? Sara wasn't even a witch. Neither was Stephen. Talk about being centered out. He didn't like it one bit. She was watching him like a hawk. He bet she could tell he was sweating. Well, screw her. If she figured she was going to embarrass him in front of everyone, she had badly misread him.

"No problem, my Lady. My pleasure." He smiled and hoped it didn't look like the grimace that it felt like.

Morag beamed at him. "Wonderful. Feel free to go and eat anytime."

Rhiannon was starving. She got to her feet and headed in the house. As she climbed the steps, she was conscious of someone behind her. She turned as she entered the kitchen to find Stephen watching her.

"H-hello. You're 'ungry too?"

He smiled and she could feel herself melting in the look from his eyes. Gods! What was wrong with her? She'd had boyfriends before, but they sure hadn't made her feel like this.

"You're having trouble with your h's. You keep dropping them."

She was mortified. She didn't have the greatest manners, but she knew one didn't bring up another's shortcomings. She dipped her head with the embarrassment of it.

The soft hand cupped her chin and raised it until she was looking into his eyes. She could feel the tingle clear down to her toes.

"I didn't mean to embarrass you. I wasn't finished. I was going to tell you that every time you dropped one, I would be only too happy to pick it up." He smiled then, a smile that lit up his entire face.

"Corny, wasn't it?"

First she chuckled and then she laughed until the tears streamed from her eyes. Stephen laughed with her and when they were done laughing, he wrapped his arms around her and hugged her. He gave her a gentle kiss on her forehead and then released her.

"Let's go and eat." They loaded their plates and Stephen led her to the dining room where they sat side by side quietly eating, but every so often, glancing at the other and chuckling.

Morag heard the strange laughter coming from the kitchen. Everyone else was talking and didn't notice it. She quickly counted heads and realized she was hearing Stephen. She was dumbfounded. She hadn't heard him laugh like that in years, not since the time he was in the hospital and that was fifteen years ago. Rhiannon was the only other one missing. That she could make Stephen laugh like that was a miracle. She shook her head. She wasn't a matchmaker and they were the oddest couple she could think of. The Gods had a wicked sense of humor. She looked to the skies. "Thank you for bringing her to my son."

When they were done eating, Stephen led Rhiannon out the front door.

"We can't just leave. Your Mother's 'aving a circle. We... I have to be there."

"Just for a few minutes. No one else has even eaten yet. They'll be a while."

He took her hand and they walked down the street.

"You're leaving tomorrow. I want to know all about you before you go."

"I'm... I'm only going for a week. I'll come back."

He smiled. "A week? No, you'll be gone longer than that. I'll dream about you, you know."

"I'll dream about you too. You've bewitched me Stephen. 'Ow did you manage that?"

He stopped and took her in his arms. "Rhiannon, what a gorgeous name. Rhiannon, may I kiss you?"

All thoughts of proper English vanished. "I'd be bleedin' disappointed if yer didn't."

Stephen smiled and leaned his head forward. Rhiannon held her breath. As his lips touched hers they both felt the jolt. It was as if a lightning bolt had shot through the both of them. They quickly drew back, both shocked to their very souls.

"*Cor blimey.*" She spoke so softly he barely heard her.

"My sentiments exactly."

He leaned in to touch her lips again. The jolt was still there, but this time Stephen was prepared for it. He held Rhiannon so she couldn't pull away and he deepened the kiss until she thought he was going to crawl right inside of her, his tongue was everywhere, laving, searching, touching and tickling. She had never been kissed like this and she finally remembered that she was supposed to be responding. Her tongue ran across his, to seek out the secret places in the dark, moist recesses of his mouth. The kiss deepened and time held no meaning for either of them.

Joly went inside to get a plate of food for Randy. She sat at the kitchen table and nibbled on some raw vegetables while he ate.

"Mommy eat."

"Mommy is eating."

"No, Mommy eat."

Duncan came in and overheard the conversation.

"Yes, Mommy should eat. Daddy will fix Mommy some supper, okay?"

Randy grinned. "'Kay."

Duncan filled two plates and set one in front of Joly.

"Gods, there's enough food here for two people."

"Eat, Woman, and shut up." He leaned down and kissed her. He sat down beside her and quickly emptied his plate. Joly picked at her food and finally pushed the plate away.

"Sorry honey. I'm just not hungry."

Duncan silently took her plate and finished it off.

Sara came in, filled a plate and sat down beside Randy.

"Where did Rhiannon go? I haven't seen her for a while."

"I'm not sure. She and Stephen both seem to have disappeared."

"Oh. I didn't realize Stephen wasn't here."

Morag and Jesse were alone outside.

"Are you alright to do the circle? You don't have to, if you don't think you can."

"I can do it, my Lady."

She smiled. "Good. Will you wear your robes?"

"If you wish."

"Will you wear your robes?"

Damn! Quit pushing me!

"Yes, my Lady."

She smiled again and got up to go in the house.

"My Lady?"

She turned. "Yes?"

"You never mentioned another novice."

"No, I didn't, did I?" She turned and walked into the house.

Jesse was angry. The crone was treating him like a two year old. He didn't have to take this shit. He would take Sara for another walk. Tell her that this wasn't working; tell her not to give up on him. There were more real witches out there somewhere. He would keep looking. He got up and headed for the house. Sara hadn't come back outside. He really didn't want to face the crone right now, but he had no choice. He walked into the kitchen to find a lively conversation happening between Duncan, Sara and Morag. The young witch was quiet. She didn't look well. He wondered what was wrong with her.

He tried to get Sara's attention without saying anything, but she was laughing at something Duncan had said and missed his signals. *Shit!* He went and got a plate and filled it. *Screw it! I'll do the damned circle.* He'd show the crone he wasn't stupid. He took his plate and went back outside. He was used to eating alone.

Morag hadn't missed a movement of Jesse's while he was in the kitchen. She saw him signal Sara, saw his look of anger and his look of determination. He was not a happy camper. Good! By the time he went to bed, he'd be a better person. He had a long way to go, but each small step forward was a step in the right direction.

Stephen and Rhiannon slowly walked back to the house, their arms around one another. Every couple of steps they would stop and kiss, a long, deep, down to the bottom of their toes, kind of kiss. Stephen wanted her as he had never wanted anyone ever before. He wondered how the hell he was going to manage to make love to her before the morning.

Rhiannon couldn't believe what was happening to her. She had never felt this way about anyone. She wondered if he made love as wonderfully as he kissed. She couldn't see that happening anytime soon and she was saddened by the thought.

Sara looked at Morag. "Did you want me to take Randy home before you do the circle?"

"No, he's more than welcome to stay for it. We weren't planning on sky clad tonight." She chuckled at the thought. *Now, that surely would have opened Jesse's eyes if I had told him that.*

"You okay, Darlin'?" Duncan had noticed Joly had gotten awfully quiet. That wasn't like her.

She smiled at him. "I'm fine honey, maybe a little tired. I don't know. I seem to have indigestion or something." She patted his hand.

Indigestion? Joly? That didn't sound right. He wondered if he should run home and get Pip. They wouldn't be that much longer. He decided to wait.

The front door opened and Stephen and Rhiannon came in. They were quiet, their arms still around each other. All eyes turned to them. They didn't appear to notice. They walked through the kitchen and out the back door.

Morag shook her head. Duncan grinned and opened his mouth. Morag put her hand against it. "You will say nothing." She lowered her hand. "Be happy for him. He's had many years of misery with that twit."

"Maw, I think it's great! Funnier than hell, but just bloody great!" He chuckled and Morag joined him.

Joly looked over at Sara. "Would you mind running home and getting a jacket for Randy? It's cooling off outside."

"Sure. I think I'll grab a sweater for myself too. How about you two?"

Duncan nodded. "Yes, good plan." He looked at Joly again. She seemed pale.

Joly suddenly shot to her feet. "Excuse me." She headed in the direction of the washroom.

Once there, she barely had time to shut and lock the door, before heaving up the contents of her stomach. She lay over the toilet, retching and coughing. Once she was done, she stood, hanging onto the counter. She leaned over the sink and splashed some cool water across her face. Patting it dry, she went and lowered the toilet lid and sat down. She knew what was wrong. Gods! She didn't need this yet. She had heard of women who had their morning sickness in the evening. She appeared to be one of them. She knew crackers were a remedy to stop the vomiting, but they were also a dead give away to her condition. She wracked her brain thinking about different remedies she might be able to use and not arouse anyone's suspicion.

Peppermint and ginger teas would help. She drank those fairly regularly as it was. She must remember to pack some, for when there was none available. She knew she needed to eat a high protein diet. That she could do. Bananas were good. Cider vinegar was good, but that would draw suspicion. She thought she remembered seeing a recipe for massage oil in her Mother's Book of Shadows. She would have a quick peek before they left. Wild yam root was good too, but again, it would be too noticeable. Lavender oil soaks were also good, but as she was not a bath person, it wouldn't work. Maybe she could use it in the shower. She wondered if it would have the same effect.

A soft knock sounded at the door.

"Coming."

She stood up and looked in the mirror. Yes, there was more color now. Good. She opened the door to find Sara waiting.

"Are you alright? Duncan said you weren't feeling well."

Joly smiled. "I'm fine. I guess I just needed to use the facilities." She reached for the light jacket Sara was holding and put it on.

They headed outside. Everyone seemed to be present with the exception of Jesse. Duncan stood up when he saw Joly. He looked at her closely and was relieved to see the color was back in her face.

"You okay, Darlin'?"

"Never better, *darlin'!*" She laughed and gave him a quick hug.

Stephen and Rhiannon had moved their two chairs slightly away from the others. He sat with his arm around her as if he had been doing it for years.

Morag looked at Stephen and then Duncan. It was amazing. They were sitting exactly the same way, legs crossed at the ankles, one arm around their sweetheart and the other one resting on their leg, with the fingers lightly tapping out some tune known only to themselves.

Randy was cuddling with Sara, and Jesse had gone inside some time ago to put on his robes.

In the bedroom, Jesse sat air-drying on the bed wondering what in Gods teeth he had let himself in for. He knew he wanted Sara and he knew he had to win her trust back, but this way? He also knew he needed to learn about the craft and he knew the crone was probably one of the best. He thought about Marathon Field again. Damn, but he had been scared. He looked at the closet where his new robes were hanging. He did not want to do this tonight. All he wanted to do was look at Sara. He pictured the look on the crone's face as she had addressed him. She had been daring him, he was sure of it. He got to his feet and began dressing.

Rhiannon had never felt so cherished. She'd been on her own for many years and most of them had been spent as an outcast. She had never minded. She was what she was, and she had never been ashamed of it. Living alone made her more aware of who she was. She was looking forward to spending time with others of her kind. She wished Stephen was going with them, but she knew it was better that he wasn't. She would never be able to concentrate fully, if he was there lurking in the background. She turned her head and smiled up at him.

He leaned down and kissed her lips. *She really did taste like raspberries.* They had both gotten used to the jolt of electricity that seemed to surge through them whenever their lips touched. Stephen decided it was some sort of magic, but he found he didn't mind at all.

Morag laid out all the ritual items on the counter. When she was done, she went back outside and joined the others.

There was little talk, everyone preferring the quiet of the evening. The only sounds, the traffic down on the cross street.

Jesse walked into the kitchen with some trepidation. He'd thought the crone would be standing there, with the hint of the 'I dare you' look in her eyes. The kitchen was empty. He saw everything laid out for him. He would have to make two trips. Oh well. Time to get started. He walked over to the counter and put the wand, bell, athame, and two candles in his deep pockets. He picked up the cloth, censor, chalice and carafe of water and walked outside. Ignoring everyone, he strode to the circle and began laying everything out on the altar. He went back to the kitchen and picked up the remaining items, and again silently walked by everyone.

Morag knew he was not centered or grounded. She felt her heart quicken. She hoped she hadn't screwed up. She wondered if she should go to him, but she decided against it. She would hope for the best.

When Jesse had the altar set up and he was sure he had done it right, he stood back and assumed the Goddess position. He knew he should have grounded himself earlier. He probably wouldn't be feeling so annoyed, but the annoyance was a familiar thing and he welcomed it. He knew the crone wouldn't be happy, but if he went on this trip, he would have very little time to be alone with his feelings, so he'd purposefully let himself get riled. He began the centering.

The centering went well, but he had trouble with the grounding. Damn! He had probably let himself go too long. He took a deep breath, trying to calm himself and he started the grounding process one more time.

Joly sensed Jesse was having problems. She had been quite aware of the under currents between him and Morag all afternoon and evening. She patted Duncan on the leg and got to her feet. She disappeared into the bushes.

Jesse heard her coming. He knew it was the crone coming to gloat. *Fine! I'm out of here. I've had enough.* He took a step toward the edge of the circle and Joly walked into view. He stopped abruptly; surprised to see the young witch. She smiled at him and saying nothing, she joined him in the circle. She assumed the Goddess position, taking his hand in hers. He assumed the position again, wondering what it was he was feeling coming through from her hand.

As they stood there, Jesse felt himself grow calmer, more centered. He began the grounding process again and was successful. He felt totally calm and he wondered why on earth he had let himself get so unbalanced earlier. This was surely the greatest feeling. He must remember to try and stay this way. One really didn't need to be mad at the world. This was so much better.

Joly released his hand and headed back to the others. "I think it's time."

Duncan took Randy from Sara, where he had almost been asleep. They all walked to the circle, where they found Jesse quietly facing the east.

Morag asked everyone to spread out inside of the circle's edges. Rhiannon and Stephen still holding hands went to the far side. Joly and Duncan moved over to the right and Sara went to the left. Morag stayed where she was.

They waited. Rhiannon and Stephen were calm and quiet. Duncan was slightly restless, still holding Randy who had his head lying on Daddy's shoulder. He was awake, but just.

Joly stood quietly thinking about Jesse and wondering how he would make out on the trip. She wondered if Morag wasn't pushing him too hard.

Sara stood, feeling out of place. She had no business being there, but she wanted to see Jesse for as long as she could.

Morag thought about the future of all the ones present. She knew Duncan and Joly would be happy the rest of their lives, and she expected that once the babies started, they would just keep coming. She knew that Sara and Jesse would be okay eventually. As much as Sara loved children, she didn't see that happening anytime soon. Rhiannon and Stephen were an enigma. Stephen had sworn he would never have children, but she saw Rhiannon with three. She wondered if Stephen just needed to meet the right person. She could feel the love that was already building inside of him and she smiled. He had told her he didn't know what love was. He was finding out and she was pleased.

Jesse walked to the altar and picked up the athame. Starting at the east point, he walked around the others drawing the circle, encompassing them in it. Back at the east point he raised the athame in both hands.

"*I, Jesse Alexander, conjure you, O Circle of Power.*
As you encircle every tower.
A boundary to protect, shield and contain.
The power raised here shall expel all bane."

He returned to the altar and picked up the bell. He rang it three times and called out,

"*By earth and air, fire and sea,*
Let no harm touch those close to me.
All within this circle round,
Protection sought, protection found."

He rang the bell three more times and placed it back on the altar. He lit the two white altar candles.

He dipped the athame in the chalice of water and called out,

"In the name of the Goddess Isis, I cast out from thee all impurities and unclean spirits."

Jesse dipped the athame into the container of sea salt and called out,

"Blessed be this salt, in the name of the Goddess Isis, that which would malign or hinder shall be cast out and all good shall enter herein."

Jesse retraced the circle with the consecrated tool. He walked to the center again and raised his hands above his head with his fingertips touching.

"Circle of power, circle of protection,
Cone of power, cone of deflection,
We are present of our own free will and accord,
We welcome both the Lady and the Lord."

Jesse went to the altar and lit the incense. The smoke wafted upwards on the night air and the scent of sandalwood reached out to those present. He faced the east holding out the censor in front of him.

"I call upon you Guardian of the East, attend."

He returned the censor to the altar and lit a red candle. He walked to the south.

"I call upon you Guardian of the South, attend."

He walked back to the altar and stood for a moment. He thought he was doing okay so far. He actually felt good. What was next? Oh yes… west. He picked up the chalice of water and walked to the west.

"I call upon you Guardian of the West, attend."

He replaced the chalice, picked up the salt and walked to the north.

Morag was pleased. He had paid attention the previous night. She glanced at Rhiannon who looked to be spellbound. Yes, she was learning too. She smiled. She glanced over at Joly and Duncan. They had unconsciously narrowed the space between them until they now stood side by side. Randy appeared to be asleep on Duncan's shoulder. She looked at her eldest son and grinned. He too, appeared to be completely engrossed in the ritual. She glanced at Sara who never took her eyes off Jesse.

"Winds of the east, blowing through the trees
Fires of the south, glowing in the breeze,
Waters of the west, eddy to the shore,
Terra of the north, steady to the core."

Jesse stood back at the altar, unsure what the next step was. He had two choices. He tried to remember how the crone had done them. It wasn't clear. He reached out his hand and then withdrew it. He felt himself getting flustered and knew he couldn't allow that. He put his head back and opened his hands. He grounded himself.

He felt calmer, but he still wasn't sure what was supposed to happen next.

The crone's words from the previous day sounded in his mind. *Damn it Jesse. You're a witch. Start using the powers that are inside of you.* He looked at the altar again and suddenly he knew what needed to happen next. He knelt at the altar and picked up the goblet of wine.

"In your honor great Goddess Isis, I do drink this toast to you and to the Mother."

He poured some onto the ground and then took a drink. He replaced the goblet and got to his feet. He turned and raised his arms.

"Isis, goddess of protection,
I do honor you and praise you.
Look down upon me with your favor
Hear me and grant me this boon.
The sacred circle protects us here,
I ask that this protection be with us
As we go about our daily lives.
Be with us and keep us safe."

Jesse walked to each of the participants in the circle and drew the sign of the pentacle in the air in front of them. When he reached Duncan and Randy, Duncan gently swung the sleeping child down into his arms, so that Jesse could give him the sign of protection as well.

When he was finished, he returned to the altar.

"As above and so below
The sky, the earth, the universe aglow.
As without and so within
The universe our home, all veils so thin."

"Thank you my Gods and Goddesses for being with us today. Thank you Isis, for answering my call."

He walked to the east.

"Guardian of the East, thank you for attending our Circle. I release you. Return to your home and harm none on your journey."

He walked to each quarter, thanking each Guardian and releasing them. He snuffed out the altar candles He returned to the center and raised his arms.

"The circle is open, yet unbroken."

Jesse turned and started picking up everything from the altar. Morag went to help him. "How do you feel, Jesse?"

He looked at her, wanting to be angry but unable to summon the feeling. He smiled and shook his head. "You know, I can't remember ever feeling this good about something, not even winning a race. The rush is incredible. Thank you, my Lady."

She smiled. "You're very welcome. You did a wonderful job. No errors at all. I would have to give you an A on your report card."

Jesse bowed, "Thank you, my Lady."

Morag knew Sara was waiting, so she took the items from Jesse and headed to the house with them.

Jesse knew Sara was waiting also, and he looked at her as Morag left. He smiled and cocked his head slightly, inviting her to speak first.

She approached him slowly, unsure what to say. He seemed different, not so coiled and tense. She was unsure how to deal with it. She looked into his eyes and was surprised with what she saw there. She wasn't a witch, but she was an artist and she could read faces very well. She could see the contentment, the pride of a job well done, the openness with which he looked at her. She took his hands, needing to feel the contact. He held her hands snugly and she could feel herself melting into a puddle of quivering jelly.

"Jesse…" She truly didn't know what to say.

"Sara honey, come here." He pulled her to his chest and enfolded her in his arms. They stood like that for some time and when she looked up at him, he leaned down and kissed her, a deep soul searching kiss that took them both back in time to when they had been so happy together. A time when they would stop and make love whenever one of them got the urge, a time when their two worlds would disappear with a look, a touch, a heartbeat. When the kiss ended, Jesse murmured in her ear. "I need you, Sara, I need to feel your skin next to mine. I need to feel …"

"Shh… I need it too, Jesse." She reached up and kissed him again.

"That was interesting, Mother. I rather enjoyed it, surprisingly enough." Stephen still held Rhiannon's hand in his, although she had turned and was talking to Joly.

"I thought you might. I guess you'd like to spend the night?"

"Uh… yes. It's late and it's a long drive to the apartment."

"Jesse's in your room. Do you mind sleeping on the roll away?"

"No, that would be fine."

"I'll get you some bedding in a minute, if you want to go down and haul it out of the storage room."

"All right." He turned to Rhiannon. "Come with me?"

She nodded and they headed to the stairs.

Joly and Duncan both hugged Morag, said their good nights and headed across the street with Randy still sleeping in Duncan's arms.

After getting Randy undressed and tucked into his bed, they headed to their room. Duncan started chuckling half way there.

Joly was grinning and she knew what was going through his mind. She smacked him on the shoulder. "You've got a filthy mind, Duncan McEwan. You need to get it out of the gutter, right now."

He laughed. "Gods, Darlin'… musical beds for sure tonight." Wonder where Jesse and Sara will end up?" He grinned.

Joly shook her head. She had been wondering the same thing. "It's none of our business, is it?" She smiled as she climbed into bed.

Duncan joined her and rolled over, half straddling her. "All that lovin' happenin'. Makes a body hot just thinkin' about it." He nuzzled Joly's neck and she felt herself growing warm. She ran her hands down the smooth skin of her husband and searched out his mouth.

"Your bed or mine?" Jesse ran his tongue up the side of her neck, causing goose bumps to rise across her body.

"How big is your bed?" She whispered as she ran her hands down the robe, lifting it in her fingers.

He felt the cool breeze on his legs and thought about taking her right there. "It's a single."

"I have a bigger one. We'll go over there. You going in your robes?" She discovered he wasn't wearing briefs.

He knew he'd never make it that far. He grabbed her hand and led her down one of the paths. They found a spot with grass and Jesse had his robes off in seconds. Sara was still trying to pull her jeans off when he took her arms and pulled her to the ground.

Rhiannon had said goodnight and gone to her room. Stephen was in the basement and Morag, finished with her nightly routine, turned off the lights and headed to her room. She had a thought and walked back to the kitchen. She turned the light on over the stove, nodded to herself and went to bed. She had left the back door unlocked for Jesse, should he return before morning. She was tired, but her mind was awhirl with everything that had happened that day. She found herself tossing and turning, unable to settle down. She decided to get up and make herself a cup of tea. She opened the bedroom door and as she stepped out, she saw the back of Rhiannon disappear around the corner. She smiled and waited a few seconds to give her time to get to the stairs.

Rhiannon's heart was pounding so loud she was sure they could hear it across the street. She had never done this before and she felt like a thief in the night. She made it to the top of the stairs. She didn't want to turn a light on, so she carefully held on to the banister as she descended. Stephen met her half way. He led her unerringly through the dark to the corner where he had placed the cot. He knew where his Mother's room was, and had set it up as far from there as possible.

Rhiannon sat primly on the edge of the small bed, wondering what she was doing. Stephen sat beside her and took her in his arms. Soon, she returned his kisses and caresses as if she had been doing this with him forever.

He fumbled as he removed her nightshirt; his fingers felt like thick sausages that belonged to someone else. He slid out of his boxers and T-shirt and lay beside her. The covers were kicked to the floor, as they discovered the most intimate parts of one another.

Some time later when Stephen went to enter her, she sucked in her breath. "You alright?' He ran his tongue across her breast.

"Stevie, I'm a virgin," was the breathy reply.

He laid his forehead on her breasts and drew in a deep breath.

Stevie? Virgin? Shit! "I'll try not to hurt you."

He guided himself into the moist opening, forcing himself to go slowly. He knew she was ready and he kept up a steady pressure as his manhood went deeper.

She was beside herself. She wanted him so badly. She hadn't planned to tell him, but she hadn't known what to expect. The object that was slowly filling her felt marvelous. She squirmed. He stopped. She lay still and he pushed lightly. She couldn't do this. She wanted more. She bucked up, felt the tearing and cried out. When she connected to him, Stephen's reflex was automatic. He slammed himself home.

They lay still, Rhiannon getting used to the fullness inside her and Stephen coming to grips with what just happened. He'd never been a Casanova in his youth and he and Elise only had sex on the rare occasion that she allowed it. Elise had not been a virgin. Stephen was filled with a wonder he never knew existed. He was in love and he was startled with the revelation. He gently took Rhiannon's mouth in his and began the ritual that was as old as mankind.

Jesse knew Sara was cold, the chill of the night air blowing across their nude bodies made her shiver. He lay beside her, wishing he never had to move again. He rolled over and got to his feet. He pulled Sara up. They dressed and hand in hand, they walked down the side of the house and across the street. They quietly walked upstairs and disappeared into Sara's room.

Sometime in the wee hours of the morning, Stephen awoke and remembered that for the first time in his life, he had forgotten to use protection. Thinking about it, he decided it wasn't all that important. He pulled Rhiannon closer and went back to sleep.

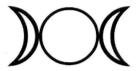

21. The Novices

The sun filled the room and Rauna was glad to see it. Polina had slept with her as promised. She had held Rauna tightly all through the night and Rauna had been able to doze periodically.

The bubbling voice came around the door. "Good morning. I told *Babushka* no broth for breakfast... *eeeww*, so I have hot cereal, cream of wheat." She screwed up her face. "It's what I have to eat when I'm sick, and it hasn't killed me yet." She grinned.

She fed her carefully and then gave her a sponge bath. She put a clean nightie on Rauna and grinned. "Good! Now we're ready for the day. Today we're going to sit you up. Come on now." She leaned forward and pulled Rauna into a sitting position, supported her back while she swung her legs over the edge of the bed.

At that moment Veronika came around the corner. The look of horror caused Polina to laugh.

"*Nyet, nyet*. It's too soon." Veronika rushed to the bed and began to lift Rauna's legs back up.

Rauna reached out a hand to stop her.

They both looked at Rauna. It was her first voluntary movement.

Polina spoke first. *"Awesome!"*

Veronika hugged Rauna. *"Yzumitelno, Tsipotchka!"*

Morag awoke early as usual. She quickly showered and dressed, and then went out to the kitchen. She made coffee knowing Stephen would want some, and a pot of tea for Rhiannon and herself. She idly wondered where Jesse had spent the night. She was going to have to start knocking on doors soon, as they planned to leave fairly early. She began cleaning out her fridge, wanting to take the perishables and milk over to Joly's for Sara to use.

She was surprised when she heard the back door open. She turned to see Stephen and Rhiannon coming in.

"Good morning. You two are up early."

"Good morning, Mother. You know I'm an early riser."

"Yes, you're right. I just thought that you might sleep in a bit later today, that's all."

"Good morning, Morag. It's a beautiful day out there. It'll be nice for driving."

"Yes. Rhiannon, do you have a passport?"

"No. *Oh!* 'Ow am I to get across the border?"

"Yes, that does present a bit of a problem."

"I can help Rhiannon get one. Then perhaps she can meet you somewhere."

"No, I'd prefer it if she came with us. Give me a minute. I think I have an idea."

Joly and Duncan got up early to spend some time with Randy. He had gone bouncing into their room while they were still lying in bed talking. They had their last wrestling match on the bed and then they headed downstairs to prepare breakfast.

Duncan noticed that Sara's door was closed. He elbowed Joly, chuckling under his breath. She smiled and shook her head.

In a stage whisper, he asked if she thought he should go and knock on the door.

"No, leave them be honey."

"Party pooper." He muttered under his breath, grinning as he walked down the stairs.

Behind the door to Sara's room, the two occupants had worked up a sweat and were breathing heavily. Jesse lay astride Sara, his tongue lazily circling her ear.

"I really don't want to go, you know that?"

"But you will, because I want you to."

"Do you really?"

"No."

"Maybe I should stay."

"Jesse…" A warning sounded in Sara's voice.

"I know, I know." He gave her a long kiss and rolled over to get up.

"Come shower with me."

"Sure." She smiled and sat up. They tiptoed down the hall giggling, as they made their way to the washroom.

Downstairs, they heard the creaking of the old floor overhead.

"*Ah-ha!* Something moves above." Duncan broke out into gales of laughter.

"You're so bad." Joly grinned as she set the table.

"Sara up." Randy went to go to the stairs, but Duncan grabbed him before he could escape.

"Oh no you don't little buddy, not today." Duncan started another wrestling match, to take Randy's mind off Sara.

"*Smuggle?* Mother, have you lost your mind?" Stephen was horrified. He's heard many a lame brain idea in his day, but this had to take the cake.

"Oh Stephen, quit being so pompous. It really doesn't become you."

Rhiannon giggled and Stephen turned to her frowning.

"I really don't see what you could possibly find humorous about this."

"Stevie, yer what's 'umorous, uh, humorous. You should see yourself. You look like a cock; all that's missin' is the strut."

Cock? Oh, rooster. "You would go along with this ridiculous idea?"

"Sure Stevie. It'll be a blast."

Stephen picked up his cup of coffee and headed outside. Rhiannon grabbed her tea and followed him.

Stevie? Good Gods! If he was allowing Rhiannon to call him that, then he had fallen hard. Morag chuckled. This was just too funny. She wondered how they were faring across the street. Perhaps she would call and see if they knew where Jesse was. She picked up the phone and punched in their number.

"Good morning."

"Good morning Joly, how's your day going so far?"

"Great! Are you ready, because we're running behind here?"

"No, I'm afraid I'm running behind too. I was wondering if you might know where Jesse is."

"I believe he's upstairs showering."

"Oh, good. I thought he was over there, but I wasn't sure."

"Well, if he isn't, then Sara is making a terrible ruckus for one who is usually very quiet."

Morag smiled. She was happy that the two of them had gotten past their differences. "All right dear, I'll let you get back to that Grandson of mine. We'll be over in a while."

"Okay, see you soon."

Morag peered out the kitchen window, but couldn't see anyone. They must have gone for a walk. She needed to talk to Rhiannon. She would have to do some fast coaching for this to work.

She cleaned up the dishes and finished packing her suitcase. She placed another bag beside it. This one contained different items that they would need to banish the demon.

Jesse and Sara walked down the stairs hand in hand. They walked into the kitchen to find breakfast ready for them.

Jesse was slightly embarrassed and couldn't look anyone in the eye. "Smells good," he mumbled.

"Good morning Sara, Jesse. Sit down and eat. It looks like a gorgeous day out there. It'll be nice for traveling." Joly added some more toast to the already heaping plateful that sat in the middle of the table.

Once Jesse realized that nothing was going to be said about him spending the night, he opened up a bit and joined in the conversation.

Rhiannon reached up and gently ran her finger across the crease in Stephen's forehead. "Don't frown so. Yer face'll freeze that way. Leastwise that's what my Mum always said." She smiled, but the worried look never left her face.

"Rhiannon… would you ever consider relocating to Canada?"

"Relocatin'? You mean move 'ere?"

"Yes." Stephen's frown intensified. He was terrified she would say no.

"Stevie, I'd move anywhere from where I am, if I could afford it."

"I'll cover the costs, whatever they are. How long will it take you to get organized once you're back from this trip?"

"Organized? If you mean packed up, I could be ready in two days."

"Two days? You can't be serious." He smiled then, picturing the insanity he had gone through with trying to move everything he owned out of the mausoleum in two weeks.

"Well, I guess I could do it in one day, if that's what you want."

He shook his head as he smiled into the incredible silvery eyes. "I'm not trying to rush you. Take all the time you need… as long as it's not too long."

She reached up and touched her lips to his. "Stevie, can I bring me dogs?"

Dogs! Dog hair on my clothes, on the furniture; drooling everywhere, muddy paw prints on the carpets and tile, scooping up mountains of crap. Oh no, absolutely not!

"Of course." *No!* That wasn't what he had meant to say. He looked into Rhiannon's eyes again and was lost. *Ahh, what the hell!* They were probably just a couple of small terrier types anyhow.

"When you return, we can fly over together and I'll help you get organized."

"I can't go on a plane, Stevie. No passport, remember?"

"Right. I'll fly over and you can pick me up at the airport."

"Stevie, I don't 'ave a car. I don't even 'ave a license."

He decided he must be dreaming. There couldn't possibly be anyone in this day and age that was a virgin, had no license, no passport, could pack all their worldly possessions in two days and who only asked that she be allowed to bring her two dogs. He shook his head.

"We'll work it out when you return." He took her in his arms and felt the passion rising in his groin as he kissed her.

Rhiannon felt the heat burning in her belly as he rubbed against her and she knew she couldn't be left in this state. She broke away from Stephen and taking his hand she led him deeper into Morag's shrubbery. She pulled him to the ground and threw her arms around him, while taking his mouth in hers.

Stephen felt himself go limp as he thought of his Mother finding them there. He tried to pull away, but Rhiannon deepened the kiss and moved her hand to his ribcage. She began caressing him with light feathery touches and before he knew it, he felt himself responding.

When they finished eating, Sara and Jesse thanked Joly for the breakfast. Jesse said he had to go and pack and Sara decided to walk across the street with him.

Joly and Duncan cleaned up the kitchen.

"Darlin', when we get back, we really need to look into gettin' a dishwasher." Duncan put the last of the clean dishes away.

"Yes, you're right. Where would we put it, though?"

"Have you cleaned out these cupboards yet? Maybe we could free up enough room to remove two of these doors and slide it in there."

"No, I haven't tackled the kitchen yet. You're right though. There's a lot of stuff here I would never use."

Morag peered out the window once again. Where on earth had Stephen and Rhiannon gotten to? They hadn't eaten yet and it was almost time to leave. Jesse and Sara had come in and Jesse's bag sat at the door with hers. She saw that he had dispensed with the garment bag. Another step in the right direction. To some it would seem trivial, but with the traveling they did and some of the remote places they ended up in, one did not need to be packing anything extra. You learned to cram as much as you could, into as small a space as you could. You also learned to pack lightly. It was no picnic dragging a thirty or forty pound bag through the brush or down a remote pathway.

She peered out the window once again and was surprised to see the missing couple walking up the path from the back of the lot. She smiled when she saw Stephen frantically brushing at his knees.

Damn! Grass stains yet. What else could happen? I've never had grass stains in my life. I must remember to tell the dry cleaners what kind of stain it is.

"Stevie, quit fussing so! They're only grass stains. It's nothing to wash them out." She paused and a worried look crossed her face. "They do sell Fels-Naptha soap here, don't they?"

"*Wash!* Rhiannon, I don't *wash* my slacks, I have them dry cleaned."

"Ahh Stevie, what a waste of hard earned money. You wait and see. I'll show you all kinds of ways to save your money. You'll get very rich listening to me." She smiled impishly up at him.

Stephen looked up at the blue sky. He knew he loved her, but he could see there were going to be some major hurdles to cross. He looked down at her beautiful face, looked into her incredible eyes and smiled. There was one thing about it. He knew she wasn't after his money.

"You have to go soon. Mother's lurking behind the curtain. We should go in and have something to eat."

"I'm going to miss you something fierce, Stevie."

He took her in his arms and held her tightly, resting his chin lightly on the top of her head. "I'm going to miss you too. Do you have a cell phone?"

She chuckled. "No Stevie, I don't even have a phone in my house."

He closed his eyes. He could swear she had just arrived from another century.

Pushing her away, he took her hand and led her into the house.

"Your eggs are probably ruined by now." Morag smiled at the two of them. She still couldn't believe that Stephen had finally met his match. Rhiannon would be good for him. She would bring him back to the real world.

"You sit down and eat. I'll be right back." Stephen helped Rhiannon into her chair and leaned over to kiss her forehead. He rushed out the front door and moments later, they heard his car leave.

Rhiannon ate quickly and when she was done, she took her plate and fork to the sink to wash them. She went to the bedroom that she hadn't slept in and quickly repacked her belongings, leaving out clean undergarments. She went and had a quick shower and within twenty minutes, she was ready to leave.

Morag sat with her on the front steps while they waited for Stephen to return and she began coaching her on what had to happen at the border.

They heard the car before it came around the corner. Stephen was speeding, as usual. He stopped in front of Morag's and jumped out. He quickly strode over to Rhiannon and handed her a phone.

"Here. I've already had my number programmed into it. See. Here." He showed her how to operate it. "You call me whenever you want to. I've already programmed your number into mine, so I can call you." He realized that she had been silent since he had returned. He looked at her face. "Is everything all right?"

"Stevie, I love you. Thank you." She smiled up at him.

"I love you too, Beautiful. Come on, try it out."

She touched the buttons and his cell rang. His eyes twinkled as he lifted the phone to his ear and he said, "Hello."

Rhiannon blushed as she raised her phone. "Hi." She spoke so softly he barely heard her.

"Cat got your tongue?" He chuckled and she ducked her head down. He clicked his phone off and sat beside her on the step. "What's wrong?"

"Yer too good to me."

"Rhiannon, you haven't seen anything yet." He put his arm around her and she leaned into him, content to snuggle. He reached across and shut her phone off.

Duncan and Jesse were loading the van, while Joly had one last cuddle with Randy. Nefertiti was sitting at the doorway. Pip and Salem watched their Mistress, both hoping that she would be safe on this trip.

Morag arrived with her milk and perishables. She found Joly curled up on the sectional with Randy.

"How's my favorite Grandson today?"

"Gra-Morg!" Randy jumped down to get a hug.

Joly rose and stretched. "I guess it's that time." She noticed the carrier had been taken out, but Nefertiti was still sitting by the door.

"Come on then, I'll take you out and you can get settled in." She bent down and picked Nefertiti up, carrying her out to the van. She placed her on the rear seat and told her to get comfortable.

Jesse took Sara's hand and put it to his lips. "I'm going to miss you, sweet, sweet Sara."

She smiled. "I'll miss you too, Jess."

Stephen glanced at the Rolex on his wrist. "I think it's time."

Rhiannon sat up leaving the warmth of his side. "Yes. I suppose it is."

Stephen stood and pulled her to her feet. They slowly walked across the street.

Duncan had Randy in his arms. "Daddy... you come home?"

"You know it, Bucko. You be good for Sara."

Randy grinned. "You know it, Daddy. You be good for Mommy." They both laughed.

The next few minutes consisted of many emotional goodbyes. Randy noticed his parents were standing together, Sara and Jesse were standing together and his Uncle Stephen and Rhiannon were standing together. No one was standing with his Gra-Morg, so he let go of Joly and Duncan's hands and went over to be with her. He took Morag's hand in his as he watched everyone saying their goodbyes.

Morag looked down and saw what he was doing. She squeezed his hand lightly and without looking at her, he squeezed back.

Duncan opened the door for Joly. Before she could get in, Randy was clutched onto her leg. She picked him up and gave him another hug and kiss goodbye. Duncan took him and Joly climbed into the van.

Jesse gave Sara one last hug and kiss and slid open the side door for Morag to enter. "My Lady, you have your choice of seats."

"Until we're across the border Rhiannon and I will sit in the back." She climbed in and joined Nefertiti on the back seat.

Duncan handed Randy over to Sara and he walked around to the driver's door.

Stephen gave Rhiannon a kiss on her forehead. "Remember to call me."

"I will." She reached up and softly kissed his lips. She could feel the tears coming, so she quickly turned and climbed in beside Morag.

Morag had picked up Nefertiti and held her on her lap. Once Jesse slid the door closed, she let the cat go. Nefertiti made her way onto the luggage in the back. Joly had tossed in an old blanket and Nefertiti curled up on it and closed her eyes.

Morag could sense that Rhiannon was close to tears, so she took her hand in hers, "You need to concentrate, my dear. If we're going to pull this off, we need to practice."

"Yes, of course. I'm sorry. Dis is all a fair bit weird fer me. I've never been in love before."

"It's the most wonderful feeling in the world. You'll make Stephen very happy, I can tell."

"Really? Do you think so? I want so very much to please 'im. He seems so worldly and sometimes I feel like I'm out of me league."

"Rhiannon, on this journey, I will tell you about Stephen. He's not worldly. It's all a facade to hide a very unhappy soul. Now, come and snug up against me and follow my instructions."

Stephen watched until the van turned the corner and disappeared from sight. He said goodbye to Sara and Randy and got into his car. As it purred to life he thought about the final fight he'd had with Elise. She had been determined to take the Porsche away from him. He had almost given in; he'd gotten so tired of listening to her ranting, but in a moment of crystal clarity, he turned to her and coldly told her to go to hell. She had been shocked speechless. She hadn't said another word to him from that moment on. He shook his head. He should have told her that years ago.

He mentally started a new to-do list as he drove. He needed to check his lease and see if dogs were allowed. If not, how much was it going to cost to break it? He needed to call the airlines and find out the requirements to bring dogs into the country from Britain. If he had to break his lease, what should he start looking for, another house, another apartment, maybe a condo? Maybe he should ask which Rhiannon would prefer.

He wondered if she would want to get her driver's license. He would have to look at some cars. He didn't think she would want anything too big.

He had never been able to figure out what Elise had done with her time when he was at work. Whenever he had asked, she would give some vague answer of being busy. He had paid the bills for two full time housekeepers, so he was never sure what she had been busy with. He didn't think he needed to worry about that happening with Rhiannon. He couldn't picture her wanting even one housekeeper.

Duncan was never too sure what he was going to see in his rear view mirror when he looked in it and he was finding it quite disconcerting. He tried to avoid looking in it, but that seemed to draw his eyes back to it even more frequently. Joly was quiet and he figured she was thinking about Randy. She was having problems with leaving him behind. Jesse was looking out the window but Duncan figured he wasn't really seeing anything. His thoughts were probably on Sara. They made a great looking couple. They seemed to have worked through some of their problems, so maybe things would work out for them after all.

His thoughts turned to his brother. He couldn't help it. He snickered, then he chuckled and finally he laughed. *Gods!* That had to be the craziest thing he'd ever seen. He was glad Elise was finally out of the picture, but Rhiannon? He laughed again.

As they approached the border the traffic slowed to a crawl. Duncan sat tapping his fingers on the steering wheel in time to a Brooks and Dunn tune that was playing on the radio.

Joly turned to see how Morag and Rhiannon were making out. She was shocked to see tears in Jesse's eyes. The man had a heart after all. She was glad to see it. She knew Sara loved him and she hoped that things would work out for the two of them.

The border crossing guard had been on the job for more years than he cared to think about. He was one of the old timers and he knew what to be on the lookout for. He prided himself on doing the best job possible and it had been several years since he'd made an error in judgment. He was able to talk to whoever was at his window, scan their vehicle and at the same time, start scanning the next two vehicles in the line-up. He had two seniors in a Chevy in front of him. Behind them was a Toyota with a young family in it and behind them was a Ford pickup. There was something about the truck that didn't sit right with him. He finished with the seniors and waved them through. The Toyota pulled to a stop.

"Good morning, where you headed today?" He eyed the truck again. A van with several adults was behind the truck. He checked the passports and handed them back to the driver. "You have a good day." He waved them through. The pickup pulled up the window. The driver was in his thirties. He handed his passport over without saying a word.

"Good morning, where are you headed today?"

"Spokane."

"The reason for your visit?"

"My sister's sick. I need to see her."

"Can I get you to pull over there, please?" He pointed to where several other vehicles sat, all being thoroughly searched.

The driver angrily threw the truck into gear and screeched ahead, slamming the brakes on when he reached the designated spot.

The guard shook his head idly wondering what they would find when they searched. He turned his attention to the burgundy van. "Good morning, where are you headed today?"

Duncan grinned as he handed over the three passports and Nefertiti's papers. "Holidays. We've got a whole month to just wander around and sightsee."

The guard looked at the three passports and went to ask for the rest, when he realized there were only three people in the vehicle. He looked hard at the back seat, and mentally reran what he had seen a few minutes before. He was sure there had been at least two, possibly three more people in the van. He knew no one had gotten out. He took another look at the passports. The lone female and the driver both had new ones. The other male was very well traveled. He thought the name sounded familiar. He was sure he'd seen it on TV. He surreptitiously eyed the occupants. No one was fidgeting or sweating. The eye contact was direct. The luggage wasn't excessive for a month's vacation. They were all late twenties, early thirties. He checked the truck behind them. It was a GMC with an older couple in it. Behind it was a SUV with a family. He turned his attention back to the driver in front of him. He handed back the passports and papers. "Enjoy your holiday." He waved them through. He didn't have a bad feeling about the occupants. He had no reason to ask them to pull over, but he didn't remember ever miscounting heads before. He wasn't due to retire for another four years. He wondered if he should start thinking about taking an early retirement. "Good morning, where are you headed today?"

"Say when, Son."

"Not yet. Man, did he give us the once over." Duncan chuckled. He checked the rear view mirror and saw they were far enough away. "Okay, you can come out now." He chuckled again.

Morag dropped her cloak of invisibility, exposing both herself and Rhiannon. Rhiannon wiped viciously at her nose.

"Cor blimey! Me 'ooter was so itchy I thought I was going to 'ave to give us up."

"You can move when you're invisible, but I didn't want to tell you that prior to now. Sometimes staying still is best, especially when one is doing the work for two."

The rest of the day passed uneventfully. Morag talked and coached her two protégés, alternately quizzing them about different things she had previously mentioned. Sometimes she would throw out a question to Joly or Duncan, just to keep them on their toes. She also wanted Rhiannon and Jesse to hear answers from those more experienced.

Joly and Jesse took their turn driving as well. With the three of them alternating, no one had to drive more than three hours which made it easy on all of them. They spent the first night in Ontario, Oregon. They got three rooms, with Morag and Rhiannon sharing.

Morag knew this didn't sit well with Jesse. She sensed his unrest and gently touched his arm. "Ground yourself."

Rhiannon had touched her new phone several times that day, but never picked it up. She told Morag she was going to wait until after supper.

Stephen called first.

Morag could hear him shouting from her bed.

"I've been worried sick about you. I didn't know if you'd been arrested at the border or what. Don't do that to me again, please!"

"I'm sorry, Stevie. I didn't want to bother you at work. I'm sure you would 'ave known if the plan hadn't worked. Someone would have gotten 'old of you."

Morag decided to go for a walk and let Rhiannon have some privacy. As she wandered around she realized she was unconsciously sniffing the air. There was something… what? She turned in a slow circle. It was coming from the south and it wasn't good, whatever it was. She would get her crystal out when she went back inside.

Morag scryed to the south and found something totally unexpected. When she thought about it, she wondered why she was so surprised. This was what they had done for years. There was a demon that appeared to be causing some problems in a park like area outside of a place called St.George in Utah. They would have to go and get rid of it before continuing on.

Morag knocked softly on Jesse's door. He answered immediately. "Do you know how to do a sealing spell?"

He shook his head. Morag went in and showed him how. He asked if it was necessary and she assured him that it was. She told him he should start getting in the habit of always doing one at night.

She walked back to her room and showed Rhiannon how to work a sealing spell. She thought about going to tell Joly and Duncan, but she knew that Nefertiti would be on guard and she had heard how the cat always had sealed the small cabin before Joly was able to resume doing her magic.

She would let everyone know the following morning. There was no point in worrying anyone before it was necessary. She wondered how Duncan would take the news. She hoped he was as ready as he appeared to be.

She washed up and went to bed. She lay there a long time thinking about the two novices and the demon. She'd thought she had two or three weeks to prepare them, but now she had less than twenty-four hours. She hoped it was a weak one. The three experienced practitioners were able to deal with one quite powerful, but they would all have to keep an eye on the other two and that would lessen their concentration and their chance for success. Sometime in the early morning hours Morag finally dozed, but her sleep was a fitful one filled with images of three headed, evil fiendish shapes that kept reaching tentacle like appendages out to her.

Rauna turned on her side. She needed to go to the bathroom, but knew she'd never make it on her own. She didn't even know where it was. She could hear Veronika in another room. Polina had gone out for three hours. She wasn't sure how much time had passed, but she couldn't wait any longer.

She decided to try her voice. "Hello?" It was a whispered croak. That wasn't going to work.

"Crow... get Veronika."

The crow flew off the pillow and disappeared around the doorway.

She heard the scream from the other room, and then a chuckle. She listened to the footsteps coming down the hall.

Veronika appeared.

"*Tsipotchka...* you called." She chuckled again. "*Vorona* startled me."

The raspy voice said, "*Privet. Menia zavut* Rauna."

"Rauna... *vy gavareeteh Rusky. Menia zavut* Veronika."

"Yes... *da.*"

"And I think maybe English, too." She smiled.

"Yes. *Pozhaluista*, I need to use the washroom."

"Of course you do." She bustled over and helped Rauna sit up. With Rauna leaning heavily on Veronika, they made it down the hall and into the washroom.

A short time later, they were back in the hall again.

Rauna croaked, "*Pozhaluista*, can I stay with you? I don't want to be alone."

"Of course you can. I should have thought of that." She led Rauna to the kitchen and sat her in a chair. "Would you like tea?"

"Yes, *pozhaluista.*"

Veronika made the tea and sat with Rauna. As she talked and answered non personal questions, Rauna's voice grew stronger.

The door flew open and Polina charged through. She stopped abruptly when she saw Rauna.

"Hey... you're up! *Sweet!*" She rushed over to hug Rauna.

"*Da*, she's up if you don't knock her to the floor. Polina, this is Rauna. Rauna, this is uncaring Granddaughter, Polina."

"*Babushka*, I'm sorry." She turned and hugged Veronika. "Hello, Grand-mamma. I'm sorry I'm late."

"*Da*, you look sorry." She got up from the table and stirred something on the stove.

"Hello, Polina." Rauna smiled. "Thank you for sleeping with me."

"Hey, no prob. Your soul is empty, dark. You need healing. I'm not really good, but I... "

"*Polina!*"

The shout startled Rauna.

"What?"

"You know what. You leave Rauna alone. She is guest. Treat her as such."

"Yes, *Babushka*. I'm sorry, Rauna. I didn't mean to bring up bad stuff."

"*Polina! Enough.*"

Polina's back was to Veronika, and she rolled her eyes. Rauna smiled. Polina saw and grinned.

Rauna knew her soul was dark. The light had been sucked out of it by the

Abyss. She involuntarily shuddered.

Polina saw, and went to her side. She wrapped her arms around Rauna and held her.

Rauna's nostrils flared. She could smell the Otherworld on the girl and it frightened her. She wondered where Polina had been. She was too young to be making trips through the veils. She blinked away the dark thoughts and concentrated on the warmth of the arms around her.

Veronika watched Rauna's eyes and sensed the darkness had come to the front. "Polina, we take Rauna to room now. You lay with her and keep mouth shut."

"Yes, Grandmamma."

Veronika peered at the eyes as she helped Rauna to stand. They had been so black, but now they looked lighter. Together they led Rauna to the bedroom.

Polina curled up against her and after a while, Rauna felt herself calm. She thought of Joly and wondered where she was. She knew she could use her strong healing powers. She could feel Polina's, but they were much weaker than Joly's.

Over breakfast Morag asked to have a meeting in one of the rooms before they checked out. When they gathered together in Joly and Duncan's room, Morag told them about the demon in Utah. Jesse lost some color when he heard the news, but he said nothing. Joly and Duncan were holding hands and the only sign that they had heard was a tightening of their fingers. Rhiannon was quiet for a few seconds and then she sat heavily on the bed.

She shook her head, her long hair swinging softly with the movement. "*No!* No, no, no. Morag, I want to go 'ome now. I can't do this." She paused, "I need a banana." She jumped to her feet and went and got her cell phone. She rushed outside with it.

Joly took a step forward.

"No dear, leave her be. She'll be back shortly." Morag looked at Jesse. "So, are you ready for this battle?"

"I will be, my Lady, when the time comes. I'm sure you'll see to that." He smiled.

Morag nodded. He was going to be a great asset to their group when his training was finished. "We'll give Rhiannon a few minutes and then we best get the show on the road." Morag took her crystal and had another look at the place they were headed to.

Outside, Rhiannon was frantically trying to reach Stephen. She was upset and crying and she couldn't remember what keys to press on the phone. She knew she had to calm herself down. She took a deep breath and thought about Morag and the grounding lesson. Yes! That was what she had to do. She centered and grounded herself and found she was much calmer. She looked at the phone. She pushed the two buttons and was rewarded with the sound of ringing.

"Stephen McEwan here."

"Stevie..." She burst into tears.

"Rhiannon! What's wrong? What's going on?"

She was unable to speak as she sobbed into the phone.

"Rhiannon, talk to me. I can't help you if I don't know what's going on."

She took a couple of deep breaths as she looked around the motel. A couple of dogs were having a game of tug-o-war with a piece of rope, people were walking down the sidewalk, a housekeeper came around the corner pushing her cart of clean linens. Everything looked so normal. She hesitated and finally spoke into the phone.

"Stevie, I'm sorry. I... your Mum... umm..." She didn't know where to start.

"Rhiannon, tell me one thing. Are you all right?"

"Yes."

"Thank God for that. What's my Mother gone and done this time that has you so rattled?"

She opened her mouth to tell him about the demon. Gods, but she needed a banana! She thought of something and closed it again. She was a witch. This was what witches did. They protected Mother Earth from the evil that would harm her. She didn't want to fight evil or demons. She wanted to grow her herbs and flowers, she wanted to marry Stephen and have his babies. *What?* Where did that come from?

"Rhiannon? You still th...?"

She laughed, which startled Stephen into silence. She laughed again. "I'm sorry, Stevie. I'm being an idiot. I miss you and I'm sorry I called and disturbed you."

"You're not being an idiot. I miss you too and you didn't disturb me. I was just sitting here thinking about you."

"Really?"

"Yes, really. I was wondering what your preference was. A condo, an apartment or a house."

She smiled. "It has to be a house, Stevie. Nothing grand. Something like your Mother's or maybe one even smaller. I don't want anything big like Joly's."

"We'll go shopping together when you get back. Would you like that?"

"Oh yes please, Stevie."

"Where are you headed today? Do you know?"

"A place called St. George in Utah."

"I see. Are you all right now?"

"Yes. I'm okay. They're probably waiting for me, so I should go."

"All right, Beautiful. I love you. Keep safe."

"Love you too, Stevie. Bye."

She pressed the button and headed for the room. She felt invincible after talking to Stephen. She could whip this damn thing with one hand tied behind her back. She opened the door and walked in smiling. "Do we have any bananas?"

Morag started the day coaching Rhiannon and Jesse on the subject of demons. "Demons tend to be a parasitic form of what we know as a spirit." She went on to describe the three types of entities.

Morag watched Rhiannon with interest. Every time there was mention of the demon, she rushed for a banana.

Both Joly and Duncan interrupted on numerous occasions with their point of view on the subject. They reached St. George at six that night. They found a motel and checked in. Once they were organized, they went out to find a restaurant. They were driving down the main street when Rhiannon let out a shriek.

"*Stop. It's Stevie. Look!*"

Duncan thought she was hallucinating, but when he looked to where she was waving, he spotted his brother standing on the sidewalk. He eased over to the first available parking slot and stopped.

Stephen ran across the street and slid open the side door. Rhiannon flew into his arms, almost knocking him to the ground. No words were spoken. They simply held on to one another as if they would never let go.

Duncan finally chuckled. "I hate to interrupt you two, but the rest of us are starvin' to death."

"Sorry." Stephen looked sheepish as he climbed into the van. Jesse moved to sit with Morag and Stephen and Rhiannon took the middle seat. Stephen wrapped both his arms around her and buried his face in her hair.

"How long you been hangin' around waitin' for us, Bro?"

"Uhh, a couple of hours I guess."

Duncan laughed. "Ain't love grand?"

Stephen smiled through Rhiannon's hair. "Yes, yes it is."

Duncan found a restaurant and after they had placed their orders Stephen asked what they were doing in southern Utah.

"I thought you were headed to Pennsylvania."

Morag responded. "We are, but we have a problem here that we need to take care of first."

"What kind of problem?" Stephen looked puzzled. He still didn't know a whole lot about what witches did.

Morag looked around. "There's an entity that's causing problems. We need to get rid of it."

Stephen still looked puzzled. "What kind of entity?"

"The usual kind."

The usual kind. What kind of double talk was his Mother handing him? "I'm sorry, I don't understand."

Rhiannon squeezed his arm and whispered in his ear. "We're here to banish a demon." She reached into her handbag and pulled out a banana.

"*What?*"

Stephen realized he had caused all attention to be focused on their table and he forced himself to speak in a lower tone. "You're not serious?"

Morag sighed. "Very serious. It's what we do, Stephen, it's what we've always done. You would know this, if you had taken your head out of your computers once in a while."

He didn't know what a demon really was. He only knew what television portrayed them as. If those were anything like the real thing, then this could be extremely dangerous. His mind went back to ten years before, when he had gone to England to get his Mother.

"Dad? Colin and Morgana? Is this what happened to them? Fighting an *entity*?"

"Yes, Son."

"My God, are you all crazy?" He looked around the table making eye contact with everyone there. He turned to Rhiannon and looked into her eyes. He wasn't sure what he expected to see, but all he saw was her wide open gaze.

"No, I forbid it! I absolutely forbid it! You're not going." He looked at his Mother. "I don't want any of you to go, but you'll do as you damn well please, anyhow. But Rhiannon is not going to be part of this madness."

Everyone was silent, but all eyes focused on Rhiannon.

"Stevie, come with me." Rhiannon rose and walked toward the door, not once looking back to see if he was following.

Stephen sat there nonplussed. He ran a multi-million dollar business. People listened to him because he knew what he was talking about. Didn't his family understand that what they did wasn't normal? Why did they make him feel like he was the odd one, when he was the only normal one at the table? He shook his head. He needed to talk to Rhiannon. He knew she was being trained, if that was the correct word to use. Well, this was where the training stopped. He wasn't about to have her chasing the very things that had killed his Father. He rose and walked to the door.

As soon as Stephen was outside, Duncan chuckled. "I've got twenty bucks that says Rhiannon will win this round. Any takers?"

"*Duncan!*"

"Sorry Maw, but I figured it was a sure bet." He grinned at her.

She frowned and shook her head at him.

Their meals arrived and the table was silent as they ate, everyone wondering what was happening outside.

Morag wondered why Duncan was so sure that Rhiannon would choose the craft over love. She had never seen Stephen so happy. She hoped this wasn't going to be the end of the romance. She should have sat Stephen down and told him about that night ten years ago. He had a right to know how his Father died. He would never have listened, that's why she had never done it. There was no point in berating herself. There was a time and place for everything, and apparently, this was it.

Jesse was thinking about Sara and he wondered if she would ever try to make him choose. He thought about it and decided no. She was the one that had told him to go and see if it was what he had been looking for. He envied Joly and Duncan. At least they got to stay together.

Duncan thought about his brother and how he almost seemed human since he'd left Elise. He thought about the firewalking and he thought about Rhiannon. If there was to be any hope for Stephen, Rhiannon had to win this round. She was a gutsy gal and he had seen the way Stephen was when she was around. He still would place his money on her.

Joly felt sorry for both Stephen and Rhiannon. They worked so well together, she, by bringing Stephen back to the real world and he, by showing her that there was more to life than what she had experienced. That they operated on two different planes was always going to be a source of disagreement, but this would be their major hurdle. Stephen had slowly been coming around to the idea of the craft, but finding out how his Father had died, must have been a real shock to him. Rhiannon hadn't been with them long enough to hear all the stories, so she was in the dark about so much of what had transpired. How would she argue about that of which she had no knowledge?

Their meal finished, they wondered what to do next. There was no sign of the other two returning.

"I'll go see if I can spot them." Duncan slid his chair back and headed to the door. Outside, he looked up and down the street. Not seeing them, he walked to the corner and looked both ways on the side street. There was no sign of them. He decided it was a good thing and he was whistling as he walked back to the restaurant.

Polina smiled as she walked to school, her thoughts on the previous days trip to see Griffin. She frowned as the memory of her return to her body flicked through her mind. Something had not seemed right and she had searched through her private place, but nothing had been disturbed. The sense of unease had remained with her until she reached *Babushka*'s and found Rauna in the kitchen.

She wanted to talk to Rauna, to find out where in the veils she had been. She and Sergei had travelled to many of them and she wondered if Rauna had been to one that they had been to. No, she decided, that didn't make sense. Rauna had been to a bad place and she and Sergei had never been anywhere bad... well, not too bad anyway.

Her thoughts returned to Griffin. She wanted to spend more time with him, but she was unsure how long it was safe to stay away. She didn't dare ask Sergei and she wondered if she could ask Rauna. Maybe she would wait a few days, until she was stronger. First, she needed to be sure that Rauna would keep the question confidential. There would be hell to pay if either *Babushka* or Sergei found out what she was doing.

"'Ave you even 'eard one word I've said?"

Stephen looked into her eyes and was once again awed by the sparkling, vibrant life he saw there. Without answering, he leaned down and picked something up off the sidewalk. He reached for her hand and carefully placed it in her palm and then he closed her fingers over it. He smiled as she opened her hand. There was nothing there. She raised an eyebrow and looked at him quizzically.

"You were dropping your h's again."

She sighed loudly in exasperation. "Stevie, *have* you *heard* anything I've said?"

He couldn't take his eyes off of hers. He thought of distant stars twinkling in the sky when he looked at the flashing glints of silver lights.

"Do you have any idea how gorgeous you are when you're angry? You have the most incredibly expressive eyes I have ever seen. When you look at me, all I can think of is wanting to make love with you." He reached out and took her hand in his. "Can we compromise?"

"'Ow... uh... How?"

"Let me come with you. Let me see what you and my family are really doing. Let me help if I can. I need to be able to understand what it is you'll be doing whenever you disappear with my Mother."

"And if you don't like what you see, then what, Stevie?"

"I'll have to learn to live with it, won't I?"

"Can you?"

"Can I what?" He needed to take her to bed. He wondered if there would come a time in their lives where they would be able to have long conversations. He couldn't see that happening anytime soon. As soon as he looked at her he needed to undress her, to run his tongue down her smooth belly, to search out the treasure that lay hidden in the thick thatch of auburn hair. He could feel himself hardening and wondered how it was that he had gone through almost forty years of never really thinking about sex, when now all he had to do was look at the woman in front of him and he had an instant erection.

"Can you learn to live with it?"

He tried to bring himself back to the conversation they had been having. He was lost and momentarily disconcerted. *Live with what? I can live with damn near anything if it means waking up to this incredible woman on a daily basis.*

"Yes I can." Damn the consequences. He didn't have a clue what he was agreeing to.

"It'll be up to your Mother, you know?"

"I know." *What the hell does my Mother have to do with the two of us making love? I sure as hell don't need her permission to take Rhiannon to my bed, to any bed, to anywhere I can get her clothes off.*

"Stevie, you're making my insides feel like mush."

He smiled. "Getting warm are you?"

She nodded.

"Come with me." He hoped his erection wasn't too noticeable. He spotted a taxi and waved it over. He gave the name of the hotel where he was staying and hoped they weren't too far away from it. He couldn't wait much longer before he'd be embarrassing himself.

When they reached the hotel, he quickly paid the fare telling the driver to keep the change. Rhiannon started berating him as they walked into the building. "You shouldn't be throwing your money around like that. You'll never be able to save any."

He listened to her as they entered the elevator. She was still talking when he led her to the room. He unlocked the door and guided her in.

She froze in place as she looked around.

The two room suite was elegant in its décor, from the plush gray-blue carpeting, the fine linen wall coverings, and the dark mahogany wood of the furniture. The large fireplace with an off-white brocaded sofa and armchair were directly in front of them, as was a marble topped coffee table, a mini bar was to their right. Farther along was a Chippendale desk and chair. Through the doorway were two queen size beds with large half-oval carved mahogany headboards.

Her voice was so low, he strained to hear her.

"Stevie, you're wasting your money again. You should have gotten a room where we were staying."

"Rhiannon, I can afford this. I don't have to pinch pennies. I'm fairly well off, you know."

He watched as she carefully avoided touching anything. He sensed her fear and discomfort. He felt badly. He had wanted to impress her, to show her that money was no object and to give her a taste of what he wanted her to become accustomed to. He realized he was only thinking of himself again and that he hadn't given any consideration on how she might feel. He thought of the mausoleum and tried to picture Rhiannon in it. All he could visualize was a terrified young woman who was afraid to move. A small house like his Mother's. He thought he understood now. All right. He would have to see what was on the market.

"Rhiannon, we don't have to stay here, if you don't want to. We can go to where you're staying. Would you prefer that?"

"Can you get your money back? For this room?"

He knew he couldn't, but that was unimportant. What was important was that Rhiannon was comfortable. "I'm sure I can. Do you want to wait here while I go and check?"

"No, I'll come with you."

He retrieved his bag and they went to the lobby. He put the bag by a chair and asked Rhiannon to wait while he talked to the desk clerk.

"May I help you, Sir?"

"Yes, we're in room two eleven. We won't be needing the room after all." Stephen placed the key card on the desk.

"I'm sorry to hear that. Was there a problem with the room?"

"No, everything was fine. We have family in town and they're staying elsewhere. My wife wants to be closer to them."

"Of course. Did you use the room?"

"Yes, just the washroom. It's all right. I don't expect a refund."

"Very good, Sir."

He walked over to Rhiannon who was watching everyone that passed by.

"All right, let's get a taxi and go to your place." He was rewarded with a smile that made his heart melt.

"Did you get yer money back?"

"Of course." He felt bad about lying, but he was sure she would never leave the building if she thought he was being charged for a room they weren't using.

They walked outside and found a taxi. Rhiannon didn't know the name of the motel but she gave a detailed description of the two story white building. The driver knew the place she was talking about. They ended up getting a room next to Morag. Stephen would like to have been a little farther away, but Rhiannon was very pleased. She rushed over and knocked on Morag's door.

Morag knew who was there and she wondered if the news was going to be good or bad. She opened the door in time to see Stephen disappear into the room next to hers.

"Hello dear. I take it you're moving next door."

"Morag, you should 'ave seen where Stevie 'ad us. It was 'orrible."

Stephen approached and caught the last of her sentence. "It wasn't horrible. It was elegant and…"

"It was so fancy you didn't dare touch anything in case it broke."

Morag smiled. There was Stephen with his fancy schmancy again. Ahh yes, Rhiannon was going to be so very good for him. They were still together, which she was inordinately pleased to see, but what about the demon?

"We need to talk to you, Morag."

Oh Gods… here it comes. "Well, come in and let's talk." She smiled as she went and sat on the hard chair by the desk. She needed every advantage and sitting on a bed just didn't cut it.

Rhiannon and Stephen sat on the bed.

"Morag, Stevie wants to join us when we banish the demon." She took a bite of her banana. "Is that okay? Can you teach him what you've been teaching Jesse and me?"

Morag knew she had turned white and she could feel the blood rushing through her veins. She had been prepared for several different scenarios, but certainly not the one that had just been presented to her. She willed her heart to return to its normal speed and she drew in a deep breath.

"I see. Can you excuse me for a minute, please?" She rose and walked outside on shaky legs, carefully closing the door behind her.

She centered and grounded herself and when she felt in control once more, she went back inside and sat down.

"Stephen, will you answer three questions for me, please?"

"Yes, Mother."

"What we do as a group is not open to casual observers. If you truly desire to join us in a banishing, you must join our group. Are you prepared to join our group?"

Without hesitation he answered, "Yes."

"If you are accepted into our group, it will not be for a one time event. Are you prepared to make the craft an ongoing part of your life?"

Was he? Being a witch appeared to be a lot more involved than he had thought. He glanced at Rhiannon. She was a witch and apparently would be one for the rest of her life. He wanted to spend the rest of that life with her. He wanted to grow old with her. The craft would be part of his life whether he was personally involved in it or not.

"Yes, I am."

"The decision to allow you into our group is not up to me. There has to be a membership vote. Are you prepared to accept the decision of the membership?"

Hells bells! It would be easier to seek admission into some lowlife biker's club. The membership? The group consisted of his Mother, brother, sister-in-law, Rhiannon and Jesse. Wouldn't that automatically be at least four in favor of? *Shit!* What if they didn't want him?

"Yes, I am."

Morag smiled. "It will be a few minutes while I get the votes." She rose and went out the door.

Morag knocked on Duncan and Joly's door.

Duncan opened it and grinned.

"And the winner is…?" He paused dramatically.

"We have a problem. May I come in?"

"Sure. What happened? Rhiannon going back with big bro'?"

"No." She sat heavily on the bed. "It's not that kind of problem."

Joly smiled. "So what kind of problem do we have?"

"Stephen wants to join our group."

"*What? Maw, come on now, that's not even funny!*"

"Duncan, get a grip. He's entitled to, if he truly desires it."

"He can't. He's not one of us. Shee-it, he'd be the first meal the demon would grab. He's a bit of an idiot, but I really would rather see him stay alive."

"Duncan, please. Be serious for a minute."

"Yeah sure. Sorry. It's just a real dumb idea and I vote no." He turned to Joly. "Darlin'?"

Joly was quiet, a thoughtful look on her face. Morag knew she was thinking about the different things she had seen Stephen do.

"Darlin'?"

"I'd like to reserve my vote."

"*What?* Darlin', have you lost your mind?"

"Honey, I love you, but my vote is mine to make."

"I know, but..." Duncan's voice faded off to nothing. Morag rose and headed for the door. "I'll see what Jesse has to say."

She didn't like it that Joly had chosen to reserve her vote, but that was the way they had always done it. It was her right. She knocked on Jesse's door.

He opened it and waved Morag in.

"My Lady, what's the good word?"

"Jesse, come and sit. I'm not sure if you're aware how our group works. When there's an application for a new member, each one of the group gets a vote. There are three choices. Yes, the applicant is welcome, no the applicant is not welcome and then there is a third choice. One that only one member can make. Once a member has made that choice, all the other members must vote yes or no."

"And that would be...?"

"One person can choose to reserve their vote. In other words, they can withhold their yes or no vote until everyone else has voted."

"So one person can swing the vote either way if it were a tie."

"Exactly."

"So who is applying to get into our group? We don't even know..." His eyes widened and he shook his head. "Stephen?" Jesse said it so softly that Morag saw the movement of his lips more than she heard the word.

She nodded. "Yes, Stephen."

"My Lady, why would..."

Morag cut him off. "Jesse, it not open to discussion. If it was a total stranger, there is a strict procedure we follow. As it is not, I need to hear a yes or a no from you, nothing else. The reserve vote has been taken."

"That's harsh, my Lady."

She smiled. "Maybe so, but it's the way we do it."

She watched the conflicting emotions flit across his face.

"I vote yes, my Lady."

"So be it. Thank you." She went to the door and as she opened it, she turned back to Jesse and smiled as she spoke. "You wouldn't have been thought less of if you had voted no. This is the one time when family truly has no meaning." She walked out and closed the door.

She wondered how Jesse really felt about it. She had watched his eyes and knew he had voted the way he thought was expected of him. She was disappointed. She knew asking Rhiannon was a moot point, but procedure must be followed. She walked back to her room. Rhiannon and Stephen hadn't moved, except to have placed their arms around one another.

"Rhiannon, come with me please." Outside the door Morag spoke softly to her. "I need your vote on whether to let Stephen be part of our group or not. Think carefully on your answer my dear. Be assured, whatever it is, it will go no further."

She saw the look of horror and knew she hadn't expected to have to choose. Rhiannon nodded and walked several feet down the sidewalk. She was motionless for some time. She turned and looked at Morag. She slowly walked back, never breaking eye contact.

"I vote no."

"So be it. Thank you. I'll let you know the result shortly."

"Thank you." Rhiannon went back inside.

Morag was thankful she had the ability to maintain a poker face. She was shocked with Rhiannon's vote. She had been sure the woman would vote with her heart, but she had voted with her mind. She was pleased. This novice was a quick learner.

As shocked as she had been with Stephen's wanting to join them, there was only one way she would vote. She knew he had the power. Her curiosity was aroused. She wanted to know just how strong his abilities were.

She went back to Joly and Duncan's room. She looked at Joly. "The vote's are in. It's tied at two each. What say you?"

Duncan let out a curse.

Morag turned to him with a scowl. "That will be enough from you, young man. Not another word. I mean it!"

He turned and walked to the far side of the room.

Morag regretted her decision to ask the two of them when they were together. She shouldn't have. She knew better, but she'd thought there would be no harm in it. She hadn't realized how strongly Duncan would be against it.

"I vote yes."

"So be it." Without another word Morag turned and left.

Stephen sat with his arm around Rhiannon. His mind was whirling with so many scattered thoughts; he wasn't sure what he was thinking.

The door opened and his Mother walked in. He watched her as she walked to the chair and sat down. He knew why she chose the hard chair. He would have done the same thing had he been in her position. He was impressed. His Mother appeared to be quite intelligent, which wasn't something he had ever given any thought to.

"Stephen McEwan, you have asked for membership into our group. I have three questions for you. Please answer them as directly as possible. Question one. Why have you sought membership with our group?"

Stephen looked his Mother as if he had never seen her before. This wasn't the woman he remembered seeing as he grew up. This wasn't the woman that had always seemed to lean so heavily on his Father. The woman in front of him was a leader, not a follower. How had he so badly misjudged her? He was dumbfounded. He realized that she was waiting for his answer.

"I'm sorry; I don't know how I should address you."

She smiled. "You may continue to call me Mother, as much as I detest it."

His head shot up. "What do you mean?"

"It's a pompous title; one that I feel never suited me. Perhaps someday you might find it in your heart to call me Mom. That would be nice. Your answer, please."

"I have sought membership in your group because... I... uh... need to understand what it is you do... uh... Mom."

"Question two; what do you expect to gain if admitted to our group?"

He hesitated and found the words. "Knowledge. The craft has been part of our family for many years. It's time I knew something about my heritage."

"Question three, what will you contribute if admitted to our group?"

He had failed. Contribute? How could he even pretend to answer that, when he knew nothing about what they did?

He maintained eye contact with his Mother. "I don't know. I don't know enough about the craft to honestly be able to answer that."

"Thank you for being honest. Stephen McEwan, your application to become a member of our group has been accepted. Henceforth, you shall apply yourself to the best of your ability, to become the best witch that you are capable of becoming. The craft will come first and foremost and when you are called, you will not hesitate to answer that call. Henceforth, Mother Earth and all that she represents shall become your creed. Our Gods and Goddesses will become your Gods and Goddesses. You will study under me and I alone will decide when you are ready to bear the title of witch. We would normally have an initiation ceremony, but under the circumstances, we will dispense with it. Do you have any questions?"

"No."

He had not been aware of how nervous he had been. He felt immense relief it was over. He really needed to use the washroom.

Morag rose and opened the door to find the others waiting outside. "Come in. Welcome our newest member." She walked back in and held her arms out to her eldest son.

"Welcome to our group, Son." She hugged him hard, feeling his fear emanating from deep within. She was sure it was an extremely foreign feeling for him.

Rhiannon watched as Joly and Duncan joined Morag in hugging Stephen. She was unsure whether she should be happy or disappointed. She noticed Jesse hanging back. She wondered how he had voted.

Duncan spotted Jesse and waved him over. "Hey Jess, you need to get used to this. We're big on contact and group hugs are common."

He walked over beside Morag and she moved to the side to make room for him. She knew he felt out of place hugging an almost total stranger.

Rhiannon approached Stephen from behind and she wrapped her arms around his waist. Gods, but she loved this man and she prayed fervently to her Gods and Goddesses that she wasn't going to regret asking Morag to allow him to join their group.

Later that evening, Stephen lie on his back in their bed, Rhiannon was draped over his upper torso with her head on his chest. He was thinking about the water thing Rhiannon had done when they had gone into their room. She had stood at the foot of the bed and waved her arms through the air and ordered whatever what there to go into the glass of water she had gotten from the washroom. When she was finished, she had walked outside and taken the glass of water with her. He wasn't sure where she had gone, but when she returned, the glass wasn't with her. He should ask her about it. It was probably something he should know.

"I'm sorry Stevie, I didn't mean for you to have to join the group. I thought you could just come and check it out, you know?"

"Look at me."

She raised herself up and looked into his eyes. He smiled and cupped her jaw in his hands, running his thumbs across her cheeks.

"I could have refused at anytime. You know that. It was my choice to join, so please don't go blaming yourself for something that's not your fault."

"But now you'll have to miss work to travel with us, and you keep throwing money away like it grows on trees."

"Rhiannon dearest, you don't seem to understand. I am not destitute. If I never worked another day in my life, we would never starve."

She thought about that, wondering how many pounds it would take for her to never have to worry about anything ever again. She couldn't even begin to fathom it. Her life had always been a struggle and since she had taken in the three dogs, her situation had worsened. She had been dreading the onslaught of winter, when her garden would no longer sustain her. She turned her attention back to the man who was watching her eyes. She leaned forward and touched her lips to his.

"Stevie, you 'ave to promise me one thing."

"Anything at all my beauty, anything at all."

She thought about what she was going to ask and wondered if she was overstepping her boundaries.

"You said we'd shop for a 'ouse together, right?"

"Yes I did. As I recall we're going looking for a small house, something on the size of my Mother's."

She smiled, amazed at finding such an incredible man. She had been resigned to becoming an old maid.

"When we find one, I'd like to be in charge of the 'ouse'old... oh, sorry... household expenses. I don't know how to convert pounds to Canadian dollars, but I think I can manage on forty pounds a month. If that's too much, I'll make do with thirty-five." She held her breath.

Stephen smiled. She was such an innocent. He hoped she would never change. Forty pounds was roughly equivalent to one hundred dollars. He would happily give her ten times that if she wanted it.

"We'll work it out. Now quit worrying and come here." He pulled her head down to his and ran his tongue along the edge of her lips.

Jesse lay staring at the ceiling. He was undecided about having Stephen as part of their group. He must have some witchcraft abilities to have been accepted, but what they were he had no idea. He wondered if Sara might have some that she didn't know about. Damn, he sure wished she was with him. The thought of Joly and Duncan next door and now Stephen and Rhiannon three doors down had him feeling mighty lonely. *Ah, what the hell!* He got up and headed to the shower, making sure the water was more cold than hot.

Next door, Joly was curled up tightly to Duncan, her head on his shoulder. They hadn't talked about Stephen yet and Joly wondered if Duncan was waiting for her to bring it up. Although Duncan appeared relaxed, she sensed that he was not.

"Honey, you want to talk about it?"

"Not really, Darlin'. You were right when you said it was your vote and I respect that."

"But you don't understand why I did it and I'd like you to."

"Big bro' walked on the coals. He's one of us. I guess I'm just questionin' the timing. Sometime in the next month we'll be fightin' a very dangerous evil. Between him, Jess and Rhiannon, we're going to have our hands full just making sure that nothin' happens to any of them, never mind tryin' to banish the damn thing back to wherever it was summoned from."

"That's why I reserved my vote. I needed to think about the pros and cons. He's smart honey, really smart. I think he'll pick up on your Mom's instruction faster than Jesse will. Tomorrow will be a great initiation for them all. If we made Stephen wait until after Pennsylvania, would we again make him wait until the other two are banished? No, I think I made the right choice. Yes, tomorrow Stephen will get a terrible dose of our reality, but I think it will be all he needs to spur him on. That and the fact that he's so head over heels in love with Rhiannon. He'll be making sure he's the best he can be. He'll be wanting to protect his loved one. You should be able to relate to that." She tipped her chin up to look at Duncan.

He glanced at her and smiled. "You make it sound so reasonable."

"It is reasonable honey. Think about it without thinking of him as your brother. When would be a better time for any novice to train? Tell me that."

Duncan was silent while he ran what she had explained through his mind. He'd had no problem with either Rhiannon or Jess joining them just before the big battle, so maybe he was being prejudiced. The difference was that both Jess and Rhiannon knew they were witches and both were actively pursuing more knowledge. Stephen had been denying anything to do with the craft right up until supper time. Gods, he'd give his eyeteeth to know what Rhiannon had said to him to make him change his mind. Maybe Joly was right though. After the three big ones, the traveling and banishings would lessen greatly. How did a novice learn without experience? He thought of Joly ten years ago. It had been her first banishing. She had been fearsome in her fighting, but he had been so terrified for her. She had been trained all her life in the craft. She knew what to expect. He sighed. He didn't know what to think. It really didn't matter anyway. The votes were in and so was his brother. Only time would tell.

"You're probably right pretty lady. I do tend to think with my heart more than I should." He kissed the top of her head and ran his hand down the curve of her hip. She lifted her face to his and kissed him.

Veronika let Rauna choose the subjects they discussed. She noticed that occasionally Rauna got confused with what was real and what she experienced during her dark time. She remembered things which were an impossibility. Veronika would separate the illusions from reality, and she gently coaxed Rauna forward, back into the land of the living.

When she mentioned the evil of the previous October, Veronika nodded.

"*Da*, it was bad. We will be called soon, I think."

"Yes, I agree. There is something I must do before that happens."

"Can you tell me what?"

"I have to go to Canada, but I'm not sure why."

Veronika nodded. One did what one had to.

"You will stay a few more days. You need more strength before you go."

"Yes, but I must leave soon."

Veronika noticed the eyes were a lighter shade of brown. Good! She was conquering the fear.

22. Initiation

Morag sat nude on the bed, her knees bent and her ankles crossed. She had her hands resting palms up on the insides of her knees. Her body was still damp from her shower. Her head was slightly tipped back as she absorbed the peaceful light that was entering through her crown chakra. She had asked for help and she sat calmly waiting for one of her Gods or Goddesses to answer. Her mind was blank, the only activity being soft, muted colors dancing slowly across her third eye.

She sat without moving for almost two hours. When the answers were given to her, her eyes opened. She stretched her legs to get the circulation back into them, and then she rose and lit a candle. She thanked the powers for answering.

The next morning Stephen gave their room a thorough once-over. He had to admit that the room was quite nice. Everything appeared to be spotlessly clean. It certainly wouldn't have been his first choice, but there was really nothing wrong with it. Watching Rhiannon made it all worthwhile. She was completely at ease. He was amazed at the difference in her and knew he was in for a lot of changes in the way he lived.

"Are you familiar with our Gods and Goddesses, Stevie?"

He smiled and shook his head. "I'm not even familiar with the Christian God, I'm afraid. I never had time. Well, I guess I never made time for any religion."

She picked up a banana and peeled the skin back. "I'll leave the demon talk for Morag, because I don't know much about it myself, but I can tell you about our deities. We have many, some are old, meaning they've been around forever, and some are new, meaning they haven't been around since the beginning of time. Do you know of the Titans?"

"No, I'm afraid not."

"In the beginning, there were the Titans. They ruled the universe until Zeus overthrew them and banished them to Tartarus."

What's Tartarus?"

"It's like a prison for defeated Gods. It's the lowest region in the universe, being as far below earth as the heavens are above. It's said that if an anvil was dropped from the heavens that it would take nine days and nights to reach earth. Then it would take another nine days and nights to reach Tartarus."

He nodded. "I've heard of Zeus, but where did he come from?"

"He was one of the children of the ruling Titan, Cronus and his wife Rhea. He and his siblings were the first Olympians."

"I see. Let's try something." He went to his bag and brought out his laptop. He set it up on the desk and turned it on. When it was ready, he went to a search page and typed in Gods and Goddesses. He scanned quickly through the results and picked one. The page came up. He glanced at it and looked at Rhiannon.

"So we have Greek, Egyptian, Celtic, Norse, Hindi and various other groups. Do we worship them all?"

"They all have their place, yes. You always include all of them in any ceremony. You don't want to anger any of them because you never know when you might have need of one of them." She looked at the computer. "That's sure faster than me trying to teach you. Sorry."

"Hey!" He got up and took her in his arms. "No need to be sorry. This is my life. This is my work. Computers are great. They're a door to worlds that wouldn't normally be open to many. Just think, whenever you want me to learn something new, we can come here to look it up and then whether you're here or not, I can sit and study." He looked at her and saw that she wasn't convinced. "Rhiannon, think of it as a tool. You must use tools in the craft, do you not?"

"Yes, we do."

"Think about how long it would take for you to explain each one these gods to me, what their purpose is and when I might have need of them." He glanced at the computer screen. "That's a pretty long list. How long before I would have the major ones memorized?"

She shrugged. "It would take a long time, Stevie. You never quit learning."

A knock sounded at the door and Rhiannon turned to answer it. Morag stood there smiling.

"Good morning! Are you joining us for breakfast? We're leaving now and as soon as we're done, we'll drive out to the site and look it over. Then we'll return here and see how much you can absorb in one day."

Rhiannon turned to Stephen. "I'm starving. Can we go?"

He walked up to her. "Of course we can. Do I look like the type that would starve my woman?" He picked up the room key and they left.

After breakfast, they drove to the area and once there, Morag and Joly both used their senses to search for the location where the evil being was hiding.

Nefertiti's eyes never strayed from the north and Joly stroked her, as she watched her.

As they approached the north end of the park, the women felt it. Rhiannon, who had been admiring the beauty of the red sandstone, black lava fields and white sandstone, grabbed a banana.

"We need to turn around. There's something not right here. I can feel it."

Morag leaned forward and put her hand on Rhiannon's shoulder, conscious of the ever present banana. As she did, she was aware of Stephen sniffing the air.

"My dear, what you're feeling is the being we are here to banish. Now it would be kind of silly to turn around, wouldn't it?"

Rhiannon turned and faced Morag. "'Ow... I mean how can you be so calm?"

"It's daylight. It won't come out until dark. We're really quite safe for now."

Morag noticed there had been quite a few people at the south end of the park and even in the middle of it, but the area they were in appeared empty of human life, with the exception of the occasional vehicle speeding past them.

"Pull over, Son, when it's safe to do so. We need to go exploring."

Duncan found a spot and parked the van. Everyone got out, including Nefertiti. Joly knew the cat's senses were the strongest, and asked her to guide them to where the demon was hidden. They marveled at the incredibly beautiful scenery, the red sand with the black lava looking like a large lace shawl as it meandered over and around it, the cholla cacti, the red hills, some streaked with black markings and others streaked with white.

They were walking up a small rise when Nefertiti hissed and stopped. They walked to the top and looked across at the large red hill in front of them. Near its base were several small outcroppings of rock, some with large holes in them. The bottom of one outcropping consisted of several cavernous openings divided by rock pillars which Duncan decided looked like the legs of an alien.

Morag's eyes were drawn to one of the holes to the right and slightly above the pillars. She nodded. "Good. Now we know where it is. I think we'll draw our circle right here." She looked around.

"All right everyone, let's check for trouble spots and then we can go."

Stephen looked at Duncan. "What's a trouble spot?"

Duncan grinned. "Gee, Bro', you're askin' your baby brother for help?" He laughed and threw his arm around Stephen. "It'll be dark when we come back. We need to make sure there's nothin' gonna give us any grief, like rocks, sticks, anything that we could trip on and compromise the circle."

They spent the next twenty minutes combing the area for loose debris and when Morag was satisfied, they returned to the van and headed back to town.

When they reached the motel, Morag took the three novices to her room.

She told Joly and Duncan that they could join the group that afternoon if they wished, but the rest of their morning was free.

Duncan waited until the four had disappeared behind Morag's door and then he wiggled his eyebrows at Joly. "Got anythin' in mind to help kill some time?"

She laughed and led him to their room. "I want to call Randy before we do anything. What day in this? *Duncan!* It's your Mom's birthday today."

He slapped his hand across the side of his head in a parody of forgetfulness. "What do you think we should do for her? We're on a long road trip. It's not like we can run out and buy a bunch of stuff."

"I don't know honey. She doesn't really need anything. We could buy her a cake and some candles; leave the big celebration until we're back home. We could have a double celebration, because we're probably going to miss Randy's birthday too."

"Shee-it! Sometimes normal would be good... you know?"

"Do you really think so?"

"No, and you know it. I love being a witch! It's the greatest and it's even better 'cause you're right here with me, bein' a witch along side of me. I love you, Joly McEwan." He grabbed her and gave her a bear hug.

"I love you too, Duncan McEwan, now let me go and phone our son."

He growled in her ear and shook her lightly back and forth. "Never! I've got you just where I want you and there's nothing you can do about it." He lowered his head to the curve of her neck and ran his tongue lightly across her skin.

Joly felt the goosebumps rise along her arms and the heat building in her nether region. She knew Randy wouldn't be getting his call right away as she slid her hands under Duncan's T-shirt.

Morag was pleased with the way the morning was going. The three novices were attentive, inquisitive and open to the ideas she was putting forth.

"We should break for a few minutes. I for one need a drink. Questions, anyone?"

"Mother, this isn't anything to do with what we've been discussing, but I'm curious. Why do you always refer to us as a group? I thought that a group of witches was a coven, yet I've never heard you use the word."

She smiled. "That's actually a very good question, Stephen. If you think back to thirty or forty years ago and picture, say Bettina and me meeting up in a grocery store, what do you think might have happened if one of us had asked the other, 'Have you heard where the coven is meeting next?'"

"There could have been problems, depending on who overheard."

"Exactly. We agreed from the beginning that we would refer to ourselves as a group. That way we wouldn't have to watch what we were saying and where we were when we said it. Also, my feeling is that the word group has a much closer connotation to it. Coven sounds so... I don't know... cold, I guess. It's not personal. Say the words, this is our coven, and then, this is our group."

Stephen did.

"Which one feels better?"

He smiled. "This is our group. Thank you for clearing that up for me."

"No problem. So tell me how do you feel about the morning so far?" Rhiannon joined them, locking her arm through Stephen's.

"I'm finding it really interesting. I'm looking forward to tonight. Will you tell us how we'll get this thing to come to us?"

"We'll cover that this afternoon. I won't be joining you for lunch by the way. I will be staying here to do some meditating."

Jesse had been following the conversation and interrupted. "Does the meditating have something to do with tonight?"

"Yes, it does. I need to try and find out who the entity is."

Stephen raised his eyebrows. "You can do that, through meditation?"

"Yes. Not everyone can, of course, but I do have the ability."

Jesse nodded knowingly. "It's not just a meditation you're going to do, is it?"

Morag looked hard at Jesse. He was ahead of her on this one. Maybe a change in the order of the lessons was called for. "No, it's not. Now, will you excuse me for a minute, please?"

Stephen looked at Jesse. "What's she going to do, do you know?"

He shrugged. "I think she's going on a trip through the veils."

Rhiannon gasped. *"No!"*

Stephen looked at the terror in her eyes and felt his stomach do flip-flops. "What are veils?"

Rhiannon had trouble speaking, she was so upset. "It's...it's... it's the netherworld and such." She shook her head. "No, she can't. It's far too dangerous."

Jesse went and sat beside Rhiannon. "It isn't dangerous, not for those who know how, and besides, she's not necessarily going to the netherworld." He looked at Stephen. "Honest."

Stephen looked perplexed. "What's the netherworld?"

Rhiannon didn't look prepared to answer, so he moved his gaze over to Jesse.

Jesse would have rather had Morag explain it, but she was in the washroom. "The entire universe is made up of different layers, like an onion. One layer is our reality, or universe, whatever you want to call it. There are actually many layers or veils; most of them are inhabited, some by the good guys, some by the baddies. It's possible to access these different layers in order to find out things, just go for a visit, whatever the reason might be. The netherworld is actually just one of the layers."

Stephen looked at Rhiannon. She was pale as a ghost. He hugged her to his side and kissed her temple.

"I know Mother's been doing this kind of stuff all her life. I'm sure she knows what she's doing."

Jesse nodded in agreement. "I'm sure she does." He looked at Rhiannon.

"When you travel back and forth between Britain and Canada, you're traveling through another realm, or veil if you like. You do know that, don't you?"

She nodded. "But it's different. It's a safe veil to travel through."

"You don't think that where Mother is going is safe?"

"I know it's not." She rose and went outside. When Stephen would have followed, Morag spoke from the back of the room.

"Let her go, Son. She needs to center and ground. She'll be fine. When she returns, I'll talk about the veils. I hadn't planned on it, but I see it needs to be touched on."

Rhiannon was bent over, hyperventilating. She knew she had to pull herself together. Her nightmares kept flashing through her mind and she was terrified. She also needed a banana. She had thought Stephen would follow her out and help to calm her fears, but he hadn't. A ragged gasp tore itself from her throat. She stood and assumed the Goddess position. She tried to center herself, but failed. A tear slid down her cheek. She *wasn't* a *Sister of the Triple Moon*. She couldn't be. She couldn't do this. She loved Stephen and had gotten him to join them. He would hate her now, but he would never see her again, so it didn't matter. She needed to get the room key from him. She would get her crystal and her bag and go back home to what she knew.

Joly felt the anguish and rose from the bed, where she had been half watching the news and half thinking about the life inside of her. She reached out and gave Nefertiti a pat as she walked past the foot of the bed. She peered out the window to see Rhiannon attempt to center herself and fail. She quickly opened the door and went to where Rhiannon stood.

She had her arms wrapped around herself and she was twisting from side to side, an intensely pitched hum rose from deep within her. Joly silently put her arms around her and sent the calming energies the other woman so desperately needed. After a few minutes, when Joly felt her heartbeat return to normal, she led Rhiannon to her and Duncan's room.

"Honey, will you get me a bottle of water please?"

"Sure, Darlin'" He went to the little fridge and pulled a bottle out, uncapped it and handed it to Joly. She placed it to Rhiannon's lips. "Take a drink, Sweetie."

Rhiannon took a drink, choked and coughed. "I'm sorry. I should never 'ave come. I'm going 'ome now. I just need to get me crystal ball and me bag. Maybe yer could get them fer me. I don't fink I can face Stevie."

"I want you to center and ground, Rhiannon, please."

"I won't change me mind, yer know."

"Did I ask you to change your mind?"

Rhiannon shook her head. Joly held her hand and helped her to center herself. When she had succeeded, Joly stepped back and let her ground on her own.

"Feel better now?"

"Yes."

"Good. Come and sit down and tell us what happened."

Morag watched as Joly led Rhiannon to her room. She sighed and turned to the two men. She smiled as she went and sat down. "So tell us Jesse, what you know about the veils."

He looked uncomfortable. "I already did, my Lady."

"The veils consist of many layers, some occupied by good guys and some occupied by bad guys. And we can go and visit these layers. Was that what you said?"

"Basically." Gods, she made him sound like he was in kindergarten.

"The veils, also known as layers, realms, worlds, planes, levels are many. There are hundreds, possibly thousands, even hundreds of thousands of them. There is no way to tell how many. We do know that the ones which have been accessed and reported on are numerous. The fact that different people come back and report seeing different entities or different things, means that they are reaching different levels in their travels. The astral plane is actually several planes, so if you were to go astral traveling and you knew that Mike Jones was also astral traveling at the same time, there's a very good chance you wouldn't see him and he wouldn't see you. But the way the veils work, it's also possible that one of you might be able to see the other, but wouldn't be able to communicate because of being on a slightly different plane. An onion is a good representation of the many worlds there are. When you think about peeling an onion, you know there are varying thicknesses, and so it is with the veils. Some are so thin as to be transparent and others so thick, you wonder if you'll ever find your way back out of them."

"And the netherworld?"

"The netherworld is simply one of the many layers."

"You're not going there?"

"No. I need to speak with an entity on a different plane."

"An entity... a demon?"

"No, another type of entity."

"Do these entities ever come to earth?"

"Yes, all the time. Think of anything that's not of our world."

"Are you saying the so called UFOs are from another realm?"

"Think big, Son, very big. The universe, I mean the entire thing is *one* onion. There is *only* one onion. Everything that happens, happens inside that onion, on one layer or another. Yes, the UFOs come from another realm, as do many other beings."

"Beings I would be familiar with?"

Morag smiled. "Does the Ogo Pogo ring a bell, or the Loch Ness monster?"

Stephen's eyes grew large.

"How about dragons, fairies, elves, the abominable snowman, or Bigfoot?"

"You've got to be kidding!"

"Stephen, you know I don't joke about things like this. These are all real, they didn't just spring to life in someone's mind and suddenly the whole world knew about them. They have been seen and as we know, they are not part of our realm. They have come through the veils either accidentally and ended up stuck in our world, or they have travelled here for one reason or another and then gone back to their world."

Jesse grinned. "You didn't mention unicorns."

Morag nodded. "You're right, I didn't. But along with everything else, they too exist."

It was too much for Stephen to digest. He needed to think about something else. "What's dangerous with space travel? I don't want Rhiannon doing it any more, if there's a chance something could happen to her."

"Rhiannon is wrong when she says the veil she travels through is safe." Morag paused when she heard Stephen's intake of breath.

"Its okay, Stephen. The dangers of space travel or teleportation, if you like, are minimal, but there is no such thing as a one hundred percent safe plane to travel in. It is as safe as flying in a plane, traveling by car or crossing the ocean in a ship." Morag felt the heebie-jeebie's creeping over her, just thinking about it. She knew not everyone was as sensitive to the outside forces as she was. Chances were, Rhiannon would never know anything was trying to grab her as she went merrily on her way from one place to another. But Gods, she knew it, she could feel the fingers of a thousand hands reaching, scratching at her skin and clothing, pulling at her hair, trying to get a grip, but never succeeding due to the speed of the travel.

"I've never heard of anything serious happening to anyone teleporting. Not as long as they don't stop, at any rate. It is a safe mode of travel, Stephen."

"I see."

Morag noticed that he didn't sound convinced.

"Rhiannon, two days ago you ran out when Morag said we had to detour to fight a demon. What happened that you changed your mind?"

"I talked to Stevie." She looked around needing a banana. "I ... uhh... somethin' 'appened. I some'ow realized dat it was part of what I was... am. Dat I could run away, but it would just keep followin' me. I don't 'ave a problem with the little things I do, dat most people can't, but it's very over-whelmin', the big stuff. An' I never 'ad to worry about it before. You were raised knowin' about the big magic. I wasn't. I do know about some things. Morag goin' through the veils is dangerous, Joly, very dangerous. What if somethin' 'appened to her? Then what would we do?"

Duncan leaned forward and took her hand in his. "Rhiannon, if somethin' happened to Maw, it would be terrible. We would all miss her somethin' fierce, but life would continue. We would mourn her passing, which we will someday, but hopefully not for a long time to come. But her end would not be ours. You want the worst case scenario? I'll give it to you. If Maw didn't return from the trip today, we would say some prayers for her, wish her a safe trip to Summerland, get in the van, and go and destroy the demon. Then we would leave here and keep headin' to Pennsylvania, because regardless of whether Maw is here or not, that evil has to be banished."

"But Duncan, who would lead us? She 'as the knowledge, we don't."

"Joly would lead us."

Joly cocked an eyebrow at that comment. "Thanks for your vote of confidence honey. It's true, Rhiannon, Morag has been training me in what I believe to be the leadership role. I also know that should something happen to her, while we would all feel her loss greatly, she would expect us to carry on. Duncan is right about that."

"You could do dat?"

"Do what?"

"Lead us, teach us?"

It was not a question to be answered lightly. Joly reached inside her soul and searched out the answer. She was conscious of her life force; her blood pumping through her heart and she could hear the swoosh of it as it was pushed through her veins. Her heartbeat was loud, but steady and comforting. She could hear something else, something foreign that wasn't part of her, and it took her a moment to realize that she was hearing her child. She heard the roaring that always preceded whatever answer she was searching for. She waited a moment and then with a clarity that never failed to astound her, she knew the answer.

"Yes, if it was necessary, I could."

Rhiannon had watched closely and she knew without a doubt that Joly had answered truthfully. "I feel like such an ass. What must Morag be thinkin' of me? What must Stevie be thinkin'? Gods, I am so stupid."

Duncan grinned. "Why don't we go and see? I'm sure you'll find there is no judgin' of the members of this group." He walked to the door. "Comin', Darlin'?"

"Yes, of course. Rhiannon, we all have our fears. You're truly no different than the rest of us."

Rhiannon clasped Joly's hands in hers, the sense of oneness startling her again. She shook her head. "I'll never get used to that. Thank you, Joly.

Sometimes my heart takes over and my head refuses to listen. I appreciate the time you've taken to explain things to me."

Joly hugged her. "That's why we're here. Whether we're related or not, we're all family and we always try to help one another."

Rhiannon walked over to Duncan and gave him a hug. "Thank you."

"You're welcome, Sis!" He laughed and Joly smiled.

"You're so bad."

"I know." He laughed again as he opened the door.

Rhiannon thought about the *sis* comment. She wondered if he had meant it as they were all family in their group, or had he meant something else. Stephen hadn't mentioned marriage, but she knew he was in the middle of getting divorced. It didn't matter to her. She was just thankful to have him in her life and she would take him any way she could get him. He was getting the two of them a house and he was willing to bring her dogs over to Canada, so she knew he was serious about the relationship.

Morag looked up expectantly when she heard them coming. Stephen also heard them and he stood, afraid of what he might see. The door opened and Rhiannon burst through. She smiled when she saw Stephen and she rushed into his arms. Joly and Duncan followed her in.

"Are we welcome, Maw?"

She nodded her head, watching Rhiannon. She seemed to have recovered. Good! She turned and smiled at her two favorite people. Thoughts of Stephen crept into her mind and she felt herself flush. *Gods! I have to quit thinking like that.*

"We were just talking about the veils. Rhiannon, would you like me to go over what we've discussed?"

She pulled herself away from Stephen's chest and turned around. "Yes, please. I would like to understand better, what they're about and what they're capable of."

Morag smiled. "The veils aren't capable of anything. They're just there. It's the inhabitants that one needs to concern themselves with." Morag covered what had been discussed with the two men. She also talked about the dangers of traveling to unknown planes and the ways to ensure that one ended up where they wanted to go, not lost in some dimension no one had ever been to before. By the time she was finished talking, it was lunch time. Morag walked over to Rhiannon and hugged her.

"I appreciate you worrying about me, but I assure you, I have too much to live for, to do anything foolish. I'll see you all back here around two. Have fun."

The five of them left, leaving Morag to do what she needed. She wasn't sure the demon was important enough to even have a name, but it never hurt to check. If it did, it would have to come when summoned. If it didn't, they would have to try to entice it into their circle and that could be time consuming. She used the washroom, had a drink and unplugged the phone. She lit several candles and some sandalwood incense and placed a glass of water at the foot of the bed. She centered and grounded herself and then sat in the middle of her bed.

Sitting cross legged, she lay her hands palms up on the inside of her knees, with her thumbs and forefingers touching. She stared at the glass of water, while concentrating on emptying her mind, visualizing the white light entering through her crown chakra. The chant began as a vibration deep in her throat. The sound slowly rose until she expelled it on her breath, into the air.

"Ooooohhhhhmmmmm."

It was sometime later when she found the entity she was looking for and she asked for the name of the demon that was causing havoc in the vicinity. The spirit, whose only purpose was to answer questions and answer them truthfully, told her what she wanted to know. Morag thanked the spirit and began the journey back to consciousness.

When awareness reached her mind, she opened her eyes and stared vacantly into the space in front of her. It took a long time for the first blink of her eyelids and only then did she finally move. She reached forward and picked up the glass and then went to the washroom. She poured the water into the toilet and flushed. She looked at the time and saw it was almost two. She raised an eyebrow. It had taken longer than normal this time. That didn't sit well with her, as she wasn't conscious of anything out of the ordinary happening. She had hoped to have some time to recover, but unless the others were late returning, that wasn't going to happen. She left the candles burning and snuffed out the incense.

When she was sure that everything was ready for the return of the young people, she went and sat in the hard chair at the desk. She laid her head down on her arms and closed her eyes. Gods, but she was tired. She dozed.

Rauna's recovery advanced steadily, and in a week she felt like a human being again, and not like an empty shell

The sense of urgency overpowered her other thoughts. She must leave now, if she was going to go to Canada before the big meeting. She dressed quickly, called Crow and went in search of Veronika. She found her in the basement doing laundry.

"I must go, Veronika. Thank you for being here, for saving me."

"*Tsipotchka...* you will be missed. Come... I give you lunch to take." She headed up the stairs. A few minutes later, Rauna had enough food to last her several days.

They hugged and Rauna asked, "Will you say goodbye to Polina and Sergei, and tell Polina thank you?"

"*Da.* You take care and we see you soon."

Joly opened her senses and felt the tired woman behind the door. She turned to the others. "She's resting. Why don't we go to our room and talk?" She led the way and waited while Duncan opened the door.

Once they were inside and seated, Joly took the floor. "Some dimensions are easily accessed, others not so easily. Some trips are long, just as others are short. The trip Morag took today was long and hard. I think we'll give her an hour to recuperate. We do need to make good use of the time as it won't be long until we have to go. While Morag has been teaching about the banishing itself, I want to touch on what happens before the actual banishing. Can anyone tell me what size circle we use for a banishing?"

Duncan grinned and waved his hand wildly in the air. "I can teacher, I can."

Everyone laughed.

"Can anyone else?" She looked at Jesse, knowing he had a bit more experience than the other two.

They all shook their heads.

"Okay. The circle for a banishing is usually nine feet in diameter. If there are a lot of participants, it would be twelve feet. Does anyone know why."

Jesse cleared his throat. "We always work in multiples of threes."

"Yes, we do, and nine is the square of three. Nine is a sacred number."

Stephen spoke up, his thirst for knowledge unquenchable. Why do we work in threes?"

Joly smiled. "Three is the number of the universe. All things are comprised of three substances. Terms you might be familiar with are maiden, mother, crone, Father, Son and Holy Spirit, or heaven, earth and hell, past, present, future, animal, vegetable, mineral, there are three primary colors, there's body, mind and spirit and the list goes on."

Stephen laughed. "You made your point. And actually, three is used in the computer industry also."

"Okay, back to the circle. Can anyone tell me what goes in the circle?"

Rhiannon opened her mouth and closed it again. Stephen had only ever seen one circle and he hadn't paid the slightest attention to it. Jesse thought about the circle he'd seen in Greece.

"Symbols?"

"Yes. The sacred circle protects us, but regardless of what kind of ritual you are going to perform, you always want to have that little bit of extra clout. If you're evoking a God or Goddess, you would add symbols that would appeal to that particular God. If you're doing a protection circle, you would add symbols that strengthen the protection. So it is with a banishing, we add symbols that help to keep the entity in its confines, and at the same time help to keep us safe."

Stephen was intrigued. "How does one learn what these symbols are?"

"I'm sure Rhiannon can teach you some of them. Do you have a set of runes?"

"I do. Yes, I can teach them to Stevie. Is that all the symbols there are?"

"Oh no, there are many others, but that would be a good starting place for Stephen. Some of the other common ones are the sun, moon and stars and lightning bolt. There is also the Theban alphabet along with lesser used rune types, but we can cover that later."

"You said to keep it in its confines."

"Yes."

"What would that be?" Stephen was absorbing the information as fast as he could assimilate it.

Joly smiled and glanced at Duncan. She'd been right when she thought Stephen would be a fast learner. Duncan nodded and grinned.

"The only thing that should be used is a pyramidal triangle. You can contain a demon in a pentacle. I've done it, but it's not recommended." She noticed Duncan scowl and knew she'd have to explain what had happened in the Yukon.

"The triangle must be exactly three feet in any given direction. Any more or any less and they can break free of it."

"How do you build the pyramid?"

"That's where the magic comes in. We draw the base, but the actual pyramid is invisible, sort of like a force field if you like. Does that make sense?"

"I think so."

"The triangle must be placed two feet away from the circle, toward the cardinal point that represents the demon. If we can't find out what his point is, we usually use the east."

A knock came at the door and Joly went to answer it. Morag stood there with a sheepish smile.

"You should have woken me. *Gods!* I couldn't believe it when I woke up and saw the time."

"You were tired. You needed the nap. I've been talking about the circle we'll be drawing tonight."

"Oh good. Did you get to the cardinal point?"

"I just mentioned it."

"Tonight the point will be to the south. We have no need of blood; we do have its name."

Morag noticed Stephen lose his color and she laughed softly. "What are you picturing, Son, an animal sacrifice or a human one?"

He realized she was teasing him. Smiling at his Mother he replied, "Mother, as I recall, you put flies outside rather than kill them. I really can't see you slaughtering anything living, but I admit your statement took me by surprise."

Morag laughed. "Okay. Let's get this show on the road. Jesse, what's the first thing we do when we arrive at the location?"

They reviewed everything they had learned and when supper-time arrived they all felt confident that they would be successful that evening.

Duncan drove them to the restaurant that the five of them had gone to for their lunch. Supper would be light due to the upcoming event. Tuna and chicken salads were the most popular. They ate, talking quietly amongst themselves. Occasionally a question was asked with regards to the banishing and Morag was pleased to see that the novices appeared to keeping the evening's event in the back of their minds. She watched Rhiannon, who was still eating bananas. Why?

It seemed that every time the demon was mentioned she needed a banana. There had to be a connection, but what was it? Bananas were an alkalizing fruit that contained lots of potassium, phosphorus, vitamin C and protein.

When they were finished and the dirty dishes had been removed, their server approached the table from behind Morag. In her hands was a cake lit with several candles. The young people began singing happy birthday as the cake came into Morag's view. The server placed it in front of Morag, along with a knife and several small plates. Morag, flushed with embarrassment, put her hands to her cheeks, a smile playing at her lips. She was teased good naturedly when she managed to blow out only half the candles on the first try. She cut the Black Forest cake and served everyone a slice.

Back at the motel, they each handed Morag a card as they left to go to their rooms to start the preparations for the evening.

Morag sat at her desk and opened each card, chuckling at the two her sons had picked. Stephen's said, Have a Wonderful Birthday Mom and Duncan's said, Happy Birthday Mother. The card from Joly stated, Happy Birthday to my Best Friend and the one from Rhiannon said, Birthday Greetings for Someone Special. She smiled at the one from Jesse, which proclaimed For a Special Lady on her Birthday. They all had birds and flowers on them except for Joly's, which also had a cat. She stood them on her desk and headed to the bathroom to have a shower.

The death of Iago Vargas had been ruled accidental. The men were so drunk that by the time it was discovered he was dead, his body was already cool.

Of the three men who had been harassing Emilia, Iago had been the most persistent. With his death, peace once more reigned over her *rancho*.

Jacinta only occasionally had a nightmare and White Wind would let Emilia know if one was in the making.

Emilia knew she was needed in North America. She talked to Marco and he said he would take time off work to stay with Jacinta. The original plan had been to send Jacinta to him, but with the barn burning and the nightmares, Marco agreed she should stay in familiar surroundings. There would have been no horse for her to ride either, as Marco lived in the city.

Jacinta was heartbroken when Emilia told her she was leaving. "No,

Madre, no. Take me with you, please." The tears streamed down her cheeks.

"I can't *niña*. You must stay here with *Tio* Marco and Estrella. *Viento Blanco* will be here also.

You knew this time was coming. We have talked about it."

"I know, but it was never now. It was always sometime later. *Madre*, please take me. I'll be good. I won't get in the way. I promise."

"Oh *niña*... I wish I could." Emilia held the child as she cried, her own tears close to the surface.

Joly quickly called home and spoke to Randy who had been waiting for her to call. She enjoyed talking to him just before he went to bed, knowing that he would sleep better, having said goodnight to her and Duncan. Sara assured them that everything was fine and that the cats appeared to be more relaxed with Nefertiti gone.

While Duncan was talking to Randy, Joly went and talked to Nefertiti. She knew the cat expected to go with them to the banishing and she was hoping to convince her to stay at the motel. With the three novices, her eyes would be busy enough, without having to watch out for the cat too. In the end, she had to compromise. Nefertiti would go with them, but would remain in the van.

Just before the light began to fade, the van headed back to the park. They were all dressed in their street clothes, not wanting to take a chance on possibly being pulled over. Duncan managed to park closer to the site than he had in the morning. They all donned their robes, except for Stephen. He had only packed for an overnight visit, so he'd been forced to go shopping on their lunch break. Duncan had told him to buy loose fitting, comfortable clothing, so he was wearing deep burgundy track pants and a matching jacket. He'd wanted to buy a brown set, but Rhiannon asked him to get the burgundy one.

When they were ready, Duncan grabbed his Mother's case and they began the walk toward the crest of the hill. It was almost dark when they reached the area. Duncan took the length of cord out of the bag and tied one end to a knife which he then pushed into the ground. He tied the other end of the cord to another knife and scribed out the circle. He had done this with his Mother several times in the past, so it was quickly accomplished. While he was doing that, Morag swept the area clean chanting the cleansing spell as she moved around the area. Once the circle was drawn, Joly and Rhiannon set up the altar at the north end, using the suitcase that had carried the supplies and a styrofoam cooler Duncan had picked up earlier in the day. Jesse filled the incense burner and the salt container and Stephen poured the bottled water into the chalice and the wine into the goblet.

Next, Duncan took another piece of cord and measured from the knife in the center toward the southern most point of the circle. With his points for the triangle in place, he drew it in with his athame. Morag was busy drawing in the various symbols and Stephen watched with interest.

Rhiannon sensed the movement first and with a sharp gasp, she froze in place. Stephen went to her side, his nostrils unconsciously flaring. He put his arm around her and looked across at the deepening shadows of the red hill. He shuddered and when Rhiannon felt the tremor, she gave herself a small shake. *Quit being such a ninny, Rhiannon. Wish I had a banana.*

"I'm okay, Stevie." She smiled up at him and gave him a quick hug. She quickly centered and grounded and then went to see if there was anything else she could help with.

Both Joly and Morag knew the demon was ready to exit the hole it had been hiding in. The shadows had reached the rock face and darkness was stealing over the knoll. Morag lit the white God and Goddess candles and assumed her place at the altar. The others went to their places inside the circle and waited.

Morag picked up the bell and rang it three times.

"I call upon you Gods and Goddesses of old,
I call upon you Gods and Goddesses of new.
I call upon the Four Quarters
For that which is right to be done.
I pledged to honor you in all ways,
I vowed to work for the good of all.
The universe maintains a balance.
The balance has been disrupted.
A portal had been opened and evil let loose.
Help me to banish the evil and protect this earth."

Morag picked up a container of holy water and one of sea salt. She started at the east point and walked around the circle sprinkling both as she chanted.

"Sacred circle of power, I consecrate you in the name of the ancient Gods.

Sacred circle of power, I consecrate you in the name of the ancient Goddesses."

She returned to the altar and picked up her athame. Dipping it in the water she called out,

"In the name of the Goddess Hera, I cast out from thee all impurities and unclean spirits."

Dipping the athame in the sea salt, she called out,

"Blessed be this salt, in the name of the Goddess Hera, that which would malign or hinder shall be cast out and all good shall enter herein."

Morag walked to the east point where Duncan stood. She pointed her athame toward the edge of the circle. She stood there for a moment feeling the power building inside her. The white light entered through her crown chakra and flowed through her body. As she felt the energy flowing down her arm, she visualized the light flowing out her fingers, through the athame and down to the ground she pointed at. When she saw the light hitting the ground, she began to slowly walk around the edge of the circle, the light connecting with the salt and water she had sprinkled there earlier. When she reached Duncan again, she raised both her hands with the athame resting in the valley between her thumbs and forefingers.

"With power all around
Our sacred circle is bound."

She placed the athame on the altar, lit a black candle and moved to the side. Jesse approached from the western point and lit the incense. When the smoke rose, he turned and walked to the east point. He carefully walked around the circle, gently waving the smoke toward the outer edge. When he reached Duncan, he returned to the altar and raised the censure in both hands.

"We're not of earth; we're not of air,
We are in between, we are everywhere."

He replaced the incense on the altar and returned to the west. Joly walked to the altar, knelt down and picked up the goblet. Using both hands she raised it high in the air.

"In your honor great Goddess Hera, do I drink this toast to you and to the Mother."

She poured some onto the ground and then she took a drink. She rose, picked up the bell, rang it three times and returned to her place.

Rhiannon could feel the demon watching them. She shivered in the cool night air although she wasn't cold. She wondered if it knew they were about to call it. She looked across at Stephen, who stood on the other side of Morag. She caught his eye and he smiled. She managed a small smile, as she shivered again.

Duncan removed his wand from his pocket and drawing a pentagram in the air, he intoned,

"I call upon Paralda, ruler of air. I do summon you to bear witness and guard this sacred circle."

He walked to the altar and lit a yellow candle, and holding it in both hands, he walked back to his eastern point.

Joly removed her wand and drew the sign of the pentacle in the air.

"I call upon Dijin, ruler of fire. I do summon you to bear witness and guard this sacred circle."

She walked to the altar and lit a red candle and carried it with her to the southern point.

Jesse didn't have a wand yet, so he drew the pentagram with his finger.

"I call upon Niksa, ruler of water. I do summon you to bear witness and guard this sacred circle."

He walked to the altar and lit a blue candle and carried it to his western point.

Morag withdrew her wand and drew the pentagram.

"I call upon Ghob, ruler of earth. I do summon you to bear witness and guard this sacred circle."

Morag walked to the altar and lit a green candle.

They placed their candles on the ground and stepped forward, except for Joly, who was in the two foot space between the triangle and the edge of the circle. With their fingers and wands they pointed at the triangle and chanted in unison.

"We do charge you by the powers of East, South, West, and North;
We do charge you by the powers of Air, Fire and Water and Earth.
Cone of power, you will rise
From the ground to the skies.
Inside this pyramid you will bind
And keep the entity confined.
Cone of power, hear our calls
And reinforce this pyramid's walls."

They all stepped back except for Morag. She held out her cupped hands toward the invisible pyramid and sent her flowing energies toward it.

Stephen's mouth dropped when he saw the pyramid begin to glow.
"Askati, I do command you to attend me."
Duncan stepped forward and the two of them repeated the command.
"Askati, I do command you to attend me."
Joly took a small step forward and the three of them repeated the command, then Jesse stepped forward and it was repeated again. The pyramid shimmered, the soft purples and reds undulating to some unheard beat.

Rhiannon stepped forward and the command was once again issued. Dark smoky mists swirled inside the pyramid.

Stephen stepped forward, hoping his voice wouldn't fail him. The command was issued by all in attendance.
"Askati, I do command you to attend me."
The demon had no choice. They knew it's name. It roared it's displeasure as it fought to escape the magical confines.

Stephen stared. It was real, he could see it. Demons actually existed. It was something like this that killed his Father. He felt the anger rising from the pit of his stomach. He reached in his pocket and withdrew a vial of salt and one of holy water and uncapped them.

The demon saw the movement and sent a spray of reeking mist toward him. Stephen gagged and then he got mad. He was the first to throw the holy water and the demon screamed in agony. It stretched itself to it's fullest size and tried to reach out to grab him. Sea salt hit it from behind.

Rhiannon was frozen in place. She knew she had to move, to help, but she could feel the demon's pain and anger. She felt torn as to whose side she should be on. She felt a hand on her arm. She turned and saw Jesse.

"We need your help." There was deep concern in his eyes and his voice.
Gods, what am I thinking? "Yes, of course." She reached into her pockets

and joined the battle.

The demon was not going to go willingly. It had been released some months before and had been enjoying its new found freedom. How these people had found it, it didn't know, but it did know it wasn't about to go back to where it had been summoned from.

When Joly had thrown the sea salt, she'd had to move fast. She had been at the most dangerous point in the circle. She hadn't been able to leave the southern point until after it appeared and although the pyramid held it, it could reach it's appendages through the pyramid walls. She had stood completely still until it's attention was on Stephen. Then she had thrown the salt to it's right side and she had quickly run to the left.

Duncan had not been happy that his Mother had given the south point to Joly, but it had to be either her or Rhiannon and he had understood Morag's reasoning. South was always represented by a female unless there wasn't one, and Rhiannon was too new to the wiles of a demon. It would have consumed her before she could get around to the other side of the circle.

Rhiannon chanted louder than anyone else. She needed the thing to be gone. She was afraid of it and she was sure it knew that. She knew it was watching her. She threw the salt and cringed as it screamed. An arm-like tentacle whipped out toward her, and she stumbled back. She could smell something burning. She threw the holy water and chanted louder still.

Jesse worked steadily, alternately throwing either the salt or the water, or relieving Morag who was handing the vials out to the rest of the group.

Duncan aimed his wand and almost under his breath, he said the words of banishment. The demon screamed in agony and whipped around searching for someone, something to grab.

The stench of rotten eggs, rancid oils and decomposing filth filled their nostrils. Gagging sounds were heard from several of the group. As more holy water and sea salt were thrown, the demon shrank in size. The fetid odors grew worse and Joly knew some of the group was weakening. She also knew they didn't need much longer. She sent her strength and energies to those who needed them, pointed her wand and threw another vial of salt.

"I command you, Askati, to return to the abyss you spawned from."

The wand glowed and sparked. The demon screamed and slashed out once again, but everyone was standing well back.

It knew it needed sustenance to continue fighting. It had almost been successful once, but the rest of the group was smart enough to keep their distance. Another blast from a wand hit it, punching a fist sized hole in it. The hole instantly filled in, but with a weaker substance than that which had been there before. The demon measured the distance between it and its nearest adversary. They were too far away. It had lost this round, but it knew that someone, somewhere, would release it once again in the future and when that happened, it would be bigger and stronger. It had left a souvenir with the one. Had it been able to laugh, it would have. It let out a final piercing shriek of pain and rage and sent itself back to the abyss that had spawned it.

Sounds of relief were heard and as Jesse eyed the pyramid, he asked, "Is that it? Is it gone now?"

Morag nodded and looked at Stephen. "How are you doing, Son?"

He swallowed hard, the reeking odors having lodged in his throat. "I'm all right, I think."

He in turn went to Rhiannon who had bent over to try and catch her breath, but she saw something that had shocked her into immobility.

"Are you okay?" Stephen put his hand on her shoulder.

She shook her head and slowly stood, lifting the hem of her gown.

Stephen looked and swore.

Morag's head whipped around. "You do *not* use profanity inside our Sacred Circle."

"Mother, come here."

His tone had her moving quickly to him, as well as the others.

The hole in Rhiannon's gown was close to six inches in diameter. The scorch marks that ringed it had left strange hieroglyphic like patterns around the hole. That she'd had a close call with the demon was obvious and Stephen felt himself starting to vibrate. *Shit! Oh... probably not supposed to think that either.* His heart was pounding as he thought of his Mother's legs and of his Father. He grabbed her to him and hugged her tightly.

The others closed in for a group hug with Morag and Joly sending their healing and calming energies to both Rhiannon and Stephen. Minutes later, they separated and Morag eased Stephen aside. She squatted down in front of Rhiannon and checked where the hole lined up. She sucked in her breath. By rights, her legs should have been hit, but she'd obviously had them spread apart at the time of the attack. It was all that had saved her.

Morag stood. "Places everyone."

They slowly moved to their respective points and quarter points. Morag walked to the altar and raised her arms.

"Thank you my Gods and Goddesses for being with us tonight. Thank you Hera, for answering my call."

She walked to the east point where Duncan stood. Together they raised their arms and spoke in unison.

"Guardian of the East, thank you for attending our Circle. We release you. Return to your home and harm none on your journey."

She walked counter clockwise to the north, then to the west where Jesse stood, then to the south where Joly waited. They thanked each Guardian and released them. Morag returned to the east and then continued to the altar. She blew out the white candles, leaving the black one to burn down.

She turned and went to the center of the circle and raised her arms.

"The circle is open, yet unbroken."

Quietly, they began to dismantle the altar and put everything back in the bag. Morag had moved the black candle which was still burning, over to where the pyramid had stood minutes before.

It was the first quarter of the moon and there was little light to see by. They had one flashlight, which they used to ensure that nothing had been missed, and then Duncan guided them to the van. The black candle was left behind, to burn out on its own. It was safe, as there was nothing near it to catch on fire.

When they reached the van, Duncan and Jesse loaded the cooler and suitcase. The three women and Stephen went to climb in, but as soon as the side door was slid back, Nefertiti arched her back and began hissing, spitting and yowling.

Joly had been about to climb in the front seat, but she quickly turned and jumped in the back.

"Nefertiti, what is it?" She opened her senses, but felt nothing. She gently stroked the cat and talked quietly to her, but the growl in the back of her throat remained. Morag got in and also talked quietly to her.

Duncan walked around to the open door and shone the flashlight inside. Nefertiti's eyes were huge and the fear was evident. Rhiannon stepped up to get in and Nefertiti crouched and jumped. She moved so fast Joly didn't have time to stop her. Nefertiti landed on Rhiannon's chest with an unearthly scream, knocking her back to the ground.

Rhiannon, shocked by the unexpected attack was momentarily still, but then the pain of the claws that were sunk into her tender skin mobilized her. She tried in vain to remove the crazed cat, but Nefertiti was having none of it. She hung on, sinking her teeth into the cape, gown and whatever flesh she could find.

Joly grabbed her by the loose skin on the back of her neck and forced her head away from Rhiannon. She shouted at the cat to stop. Stephen went to hit the cat and Duncan grabbed his arm, shaking his head. Morag began prying the claws out of the material and skin. When Nefertiti was finally pried loose, Joly walked away from the van, maintaining a tight grip on the cat. She went and sat on the edge of the road, still talking quietly.

Duncan started the van and turned on the overhead light. Rhiannon had been lucky she was wearing her cape tightly tied at her neck. There were a few scratches on her upper chest, and the cape and gown were shredded in places, but no serious damage had been done.

Stephen was angry. "That damned cat needs to be euthanized. What the hell? Christ, Duncan, say something."

Duncan turned around. "Bro, there's nothin' wrong with Nefertiti. Somethin' set her off, but she's not normally like that, I assure you."

Stephen wasn't placated. "I don't want her on the rest of this trip. You make sure she's…"

Morag cut him off. "Hush now, Stephen. I think I know what the problem is. Rhiannon, your gown is ruined anyway. May I tear the bottom part off?"

She nodded, still upset by the attack. She was huddled in Stephen's arms, with tears perched on her long lashes.

Morag tore off the bottom of the skirt and climbed back outside. In the darkness, she could hear Joly's soft voice. She followed the sound and as she approached, Nefertiti began growling once again.

"Joly, it's Rhiannon's skirt. The demon's scent is on it."

"Oh for…" Her voice trailed off. She would have to meld with the cat when they got back to the motel.

"What do we do? I know you want to study the markings."

"Yes, I do, but I'm not sure how, with Nefertiti being so sensitive."

Duncan had joined them and wondered aloud, "Can we maybe hide the material here somewhere and I'll come back tomorrow and get it?"

Morag nodded. "Yes, that might work. I can transfer the markings to paper before we leave, so the material doesn't have to travel with us."

Duncan turned the flashlight on and wandered around until he found what seemed to be a suitable hiding place. He and Morag covered the material with several rocks and they walked back to the van.

Duncan helped Joly to climb in, as she still had Nefertiti tightly in her arms. The cat had calmed and was quiet.

They drove back to the motel in silence.

Joly and Duncan showered and when they had finished, Joly got down on her stomach to begin the meld.

"Nefertiti, that was unforgivable, what you did tonight. Why would you attack a member of our group?"

"My apologies to Miss Rhiannon, Mistress, but she was bringing evil into our midst. I could not allow that."

"Nefertiti, the demon attacked Rhiannon and burnt a hole in her skirt. Nothing more. You were a little hasty in your attack. I don't understand you sometimes. Either you're too busy making plans on how to do something or you're jumping the gun. I don't…"

"Mistress, it's you that doesn't understand. I know there was a hole, I saw it, but around the hole are symbols. The symbols, when heated, will join and become more evil beings. I couldn't allow Miss Rhiannon in the van, Mistress. The Mister would start it and the warmth would activate the symbols."

Joly frowned. "Are you saying that tomorrow if it's warm, more demons will be on the loose?"

"They aren't demons, Mistress. I don't know what they're called, but they are very small and go undetected by most. Probably even by you and Miss Morag. They crawl inside your nostrils or mouth and suffocate you. Do you know of what I'm talking about?"

Joly shook her head. "No, but maybe Morag knows. I need to go and tell her, and then I guess we need to go back out there and get rid of it."

"Do you know how, Mistress?"

"No, do you?"

"Yes, Mistress. You need to bury it in the bottom of very cold water until all the symbols have been washed away."

"I see. Tie it to a rock and throw it in a lake. Something like that?"

"No, Mistress. It would make sure a fish or something came along and released it. Even a fish hook from someone in a boat. Mistress, you need to keep it with you, to ensure it is done."

"I see, and how do you propose I do that?"

"You have the cooler, Mistress. You could put it on the bottom, cover it with rocks and fill it with cold water and ice."

Joly thought about it. "Yes, I guess we can do that. Thank you, Nefertiti."

"Mistress, I'm sorry about Miss Rhiannon, but you do see that what I did was necessary?"

"Nefertiti, I'm sure there must have been a less violent way to accomplish what you needed to do, but at the moment, I can't for the life of me think of what. I will explain to the others and I'm sure everything will be fine."

"Thank you, Mistress."

"Go in peace, my dear." Joly laid her head on her arms, thinking about the beings in the symbols.

Morag had no idea what Joly was talking about. She'd never heard of such a thing before. She agreed that what Nefertiti had suggested made sense, so the three of them went back to where they had parked earlier. Duncan had placed six inches of water in the bottom of the cooler and then they found a place that sold ice. Duncan bought two bags.

He left the women in the van and walked to where the material was hidden. He uncovered it and walked back to the van. They placed the cooler on the ground and Duncan put the material into the water. As he did, Morag heard a hiss and it frightened her. She felt the goosebumps rising on her arms and she knew that something new was being unleashed in the world. She wondered where it originated.

Duncan piled several heavy stones over the cloth and then he poured in the ice. "Is it okay to cover it, did she say?"

"No, she didn't, but it should be okay, don't you think?"

Morag shrugged. "I have no idea child. I guess, wait and see what Nefertiti says when you get back."

Duncan put the lid on and drove back to town. He left the cooler in the van, knowing it would stay cooler than if it was in their room.

Checkout time was at eleven the next morning. They needed to get some sleep. They said their good nights and went to bed.

In the morning over breakfast, they told the other three about the evil entities in the material. Rhiannon was horrified to think she could have been responsible for all their deaths. Morag explained that whatever it was, it was relatively new to earth and that no one could be held responsible.

Stephen wanted to know how Nefertiti knew about it, if it was so new. Joly thought it was a good question and said she would ask the next time she melded with the cat.

After breakfast, they loaded the van and left St. George. They would check the cooler every three hours when they switched drivers. Nefertiti rode in the front with Joly. She had her ears back and they never quit twitching.

Polina was pissed off. Rauna had left before she could ask her about the veils. *Oh well, I'm a Sister of the Triple Moon. Selene and the Others will watch out for me.*

She set up her altar and prayed. "Goddess, please help me and Griffin to be together forever. I know he seems happy in Summerland, but he died too young. He needs to live and we want to be together."

She heard a noise, paused and turned around. Sergei stood in the doorway. He was smiling, but there was a look of concern on his face.

"Hey Serge… what's up?"

"Be careful what you ask for, Pol, you just might get it."

"Whatever."

"I've just about figured out the formula. Want to help me with it?"

"No, you go ahead. I've got other stuff to do."

"You used to like helping me. I haven't seen much of you the past while. Everything okay?"

"Yeah, everything's cool. I'm just busy, you know?"

"Okay, see you later." He turned to go.

"Serge?"

"Yeah?'

"Uh… never mind. See ya."

She waited until he gone and she went back to praying.

23. Demon-Bitch

They made good time as they headed north to Highway 70 and then east. Three hours later, Duncan pulled over and everyone got out to stretch their legs. Duncan checked the cooler and Jesse took the wheel. They crossed into Colorado around two in the afternoon. Duncan was in the passenger seat talking to Jesse and Joly was sitting with Morag in the back.

Nefertiti refused to go anywhere near the back so she tried to make peace with Rhiannon by going and lying beside her. Rhiannon had forgiven her once she knew what the problem was, but Stephen was still angry at her behavior. Every time Nefertiti moved, he would glare at her.

Duncan was telling Jesse about how he had been a part-time fitness trainer before the accident and that he'd like to get back into it, once they returned home. Jesse said he worked out all the time and had considered opening his own gym, but he'd never gotten around to it.

When it was Joly's turn to drive the two men were so wrapped up in the kind of gym they wanted to build that they sent Morag up front so they could carry on talking. By the time Joly pulled into the hotel in Denver the two men had decided to go into partnership. The gym would be built in Mission. Whenever Stephen heard something that didn't ring quite right from a business point of view he would interrupt and get the two younger men back on track.

Duncan figured that as they were only staying the one night they should share a room with Stephen and Rhiannon. When Stephen vehemently said no, Morag burst into laughter. She couldn't get over how her eldest son had changed since meeting Rhiannon.

"If you don't mind an old woman sharing your room, I'll take that second bed."

"We got no complaint with old women sharin' our room, Maw, but do you have any idea where you're gonna find one?" He chuckled at his own joke and gave Morag a quick hug.

After checking in, Joly called home. The three of them talked to Randy, who had all sorts of things to tell them and he insisted on repeating the whole list to each person.

As soon as Duncan was finished talking to Randy, he went and bought some ice and topped up the cooler. He knew he had to remove the ice and stones and check that the material was still at the bottom. He knew it had to be there, but he also knew he had to see it and for some reason he shivered whenever he thought about lifting the stones. He decided he would wait until after supper. He thought about doing it in the morning which sat better in his mind, but he knew that come morning, he'd still be wanting to put it off.

They went for supper and Duncan and Jesse carried on their conversation about the gym.

Stephen had some questions he wanted answered and he thought it was a good time to ask.

"I was wondering Mother, if you could explain a couple of things to me about last night."

"Of course."

The knife you use to draw in the circle…"

"It's called an athame. I'm sure you noticed that even though it's a double edged blade, it isn't sharp. It is never used for cutting anything. Its purpose is strictly ceremonial."

"I see, and if some fool like me came along and unthinkingly used it to cut something, what then?"

"It would be tossed and a new one would take its place."

He nodded. "What about the broom thing you did at the beginning?"

The three women chuckled. Rhiannon answered. "It's a besom, Stevie."

"A besom? I see. But why do you sweep when the ground is all dirt or sand. What's the purpose?"

Morag responded. "It's the intent, Son. You're casting a Sacred Circle. The area should be clean, so you symbolically sweep and say some magical words to clean it. You need to understand that so much of what's involved with magic is the intent. You will see many things when you are with us, and many of them will be like last night, where we had a full altar setup and candles, the athame and the besom. But you will also find that there will come a time when we will unexpectedly run into a problem and we will have no tools with us. Then you will see magic in its simplest form, because all you ever need is the intent."

"You could have gotten rid of that thing last night without the salt and water?"

"No. We could have confined it without any tools, but we could not have banished it. It was too powerful. We'd still be there, if we hadn't had the salt and holy water. I guess what I should have said is that all you usually need is the intent. Demons are not something that fall under normal everyday magic."

"Why is it I've never seen a demon before? Does one have to acknowledge being a witch to see them?"

Duncan laughed, having overheard the last part of the conversation. "Hell, Stephen, you slept with one for how many years?" He roared with laughter again.

Morag frowned. "Duncan, watch your mouth."

"Sorry, Maw." He snickered again and grinned at Joly, who shook her head and smiled back.

Rhiannon was curious about the woman Stephen had been married to, but she wasn't sure if there was someone she could ask. She looked at Joly and thought maybe she could approach her about it. Joly wasn't related to the woman and might be willing to talk. It was obvious Duncan didn't like her.

"No, one does not have to be a witch to see them, but most people don't go searching for them either. If we never traveled, we probably would never see any."

The table grew quiet as thoughts turned to Broderick, Morgana and Colin and that they would probably still be alive if that had been the case.

Jesse was curious. "How did you get started doing this?"

Morag's smile was bittersweet, as she remembered the beginning. "We were a group of young witches, some just out of our teens. There were nine or ten of us sitting around one night with nothing to do. Someone, I don't even remember who, suggested we should go out and make the world a better place. Everyone thought it was a wonderful idea. There was the usual discussion and arguments of how we should go about doing this. Everyone had a different idea, of course. I think it was Raoul that suggested if we were serious about this, then we should do something that involved using the powers given us. Nothing happened with the idea right away, but the seed had been sown.

We knew of another group that was into the darker side of the craft. We kept our eye on them, not really concerned, but the day came when they got a little carried away. They did manage to conjure themselves a demon, and a nasty bugger it was, too. They weren't prepared for it, of course. It got away on them. One of them approached Brody and told him what had happened. Brody gathered us together and said here was our chance to start doing some good. We all agreed. We did find and defeat that fiend. Of course it gave us all a great feeling to know we had done this. From there, we just kind of carried on. We started watching the news and reading all the papers. Any time we saw something that looked like it might be caused by the supernatural, we would check it out."

"Our group changed, some moved, one died needlessly in a traffic accident. Joly's parents, Colin and Morgana were our best friends. We did everything together. Colin was good with stocks and would tell Brody which ones to buy and which to sell. When we decided to buy a home, it was only natural to buy close together. We lived across the street from each other. Bettina and Raoul married and they stayed active with us. They were good friends too, but Raoul, being Hispanic, had his own way of doing things. They lived about twenty minutes away from us, but we always got together at least once a week. I got pregnant with Stephen and was left at home while the others were out trying to save the world. Once Stephen was old enough to be left with some friends of ours, I rejoined them. Then along came Duncan. Three years later, Morgana became pregnant. She was so upset with having to stay at home but Colin insisted, and rightly so. We left our two boys with her when we were away. Then Joly arrived." Morag looked over to her daughter-in-law and smiled.

The meal finished, they went back to the hotel. Duncan wanted to go to the room with the rest of them, but he knew he needed to empty the cooler.

He drove to a service station and parked by their water hose. He went in and bought two more bags of ice. Opening the back of the van, he lifted the lid off the cooler. He stared at the ice. He really didn't want to do this. He forced himself to pick the cooler up and walked to the curb, where he dumped most of the water and ice out. He walked back to the van and put the cooler down. He stared inside it. He could see a piece of the material poking out from in between a couple of the stones. He knew that was all he needed to do, he'd just wanted to reassure himself, but he found his hand reaching in to remove the rocks.

The material had bunched up in the corner from the cooler being turned on its side. Duncan reached in and picking it up, he smoothed it out. He checked the symbols and saw that they were still very clearly marked. He had the strongest urge to leave the scrap out, to either lay it on the curb and leave it or to take it in the van with him. He knew he couldn't leave it behind, so he put the lid back on the cooler and closed the door. He squeezed the water out of the cloth and laid it on the floor mat in the front. He started the van and turned the heat on high. He wasn't sure why, he didn't really feel cold, but he left the fan blowing hot air onto the floor.

He put the van into reverse and went to back up, but he stopped. He felt light headed or something. He didn't think he should drive until whatever it was, passed. He turned the key off and got out, hoping that some fresh air would help clear his head. He walked around aimlessly, ending up at the pile of melting ice he had dumped. He looked at it wondering what was wrong. He turned to walk back to the van when it hit him.

He ran to the passenger's door and threw it open. He grabbed the material, noting that it was still cold. He ran to the back, opened the door, whipped the lid off the cooler and threw the material inside. He half smoothed it out and quickly covered it with the rocks. He went to the hose and ran two inches of water into the cooler and then he emptied the two bags of ice over it. Slamming the lid back on, he quickly drove back to the hotel.

Back in the room, he related what had happened. "From now on, there must always be two people when that lid comes off. We have to let the others know. We'll have to watch one another, too. I honestly thought I was doing the right thing when I took it up front with me."

In bed, Joly cuddled Duncan, silently sending her calming energies to him. He snuggled against her, his head buried in the curve of her neck. She felt the trickle of a tear rolling down her shoulder and she knew he was terrified of what had almost happened.

The following morning after being told of Duncan's close call the night before, everyone agreed that whenever the back hatch was opened, there must always be at least two people in attendance.

Jesse volunteered to drive the first stretch. Duncan joined him in the front and they continued their talk of opening a gym.

Stephen and Rhiannon talked about their future together. Stephen couldn't wait to get her moved to Canada and Morag smiled as she listened.

Joly sat with Nefertiti on her lap and she thought about the child growing inside of her.

They crossed into Kansas and Joly took the wheel. Morag joined her in the front.

The good weather held and they continued to make good time. Joly had been driving almost three hours when she noticed Morag sit up straighter. Suddenly she sensed it, too. She slowed down and when she saw a pullout, she turned off and stopped.

"My turn, Darlin'?"

"Yes... no. There's something... umm... we need to go, to check out. Nefertiti, wait here please." She got out of the van and sniffed the air. Morag followed her. Soon they were all standing together.

"We need to check it out."

Morag nodded. "Yes, we do."

The wind gusted and the dry autumn leaves rustled across the bare earth. Something wasn't right. The leaves that determinedly clung to the tree branches were still in the cool air. It was only on the ground that the wind blew. Morag looked around, but could see nothing.

"Psst! Everyone."

Joly heard and touched Duncan's arm to stop him. She turned, wondering why Morag was whispering. "What?" She mouthed. Everyone's attention was on Morag.

"Shield yourselves, quickly."

They had placed protective wards around themselves prior to entering the wooded area, but they quickly reinforced them, making doubly sure that they were fully in place.

Rhiannon was the only one who didn't. She shook her head. "It's just the spirits. They mean us no harm."

"What do you mean child?" Morag walked closer to her.

"They're earthbound spirits, unhappy spirits. They need our help."

Morag looked at her in wonder. So that was one of her abilities. She appeared to think it was normal. Morag had thought there would be some things that she wouldn't think to tell about.

They continued on, walking quietly through the dried leaves. The well worn trail said it was used frequently, and they sensed that both animal and man had used it in the past.

The leaves continued to swirl in eddies around their feet. Morag watched them, trying to see whether or not there was a set pattern to their movement.

Joly was in the lead with Duncan on her heels. Rhiannon and Stephen were behind him and Jesse followed them. Morag was a few feet behind all of them. Both Joly and Morag had their senses wide open trying to figure out what it was that had called them to this place. Rhiannon might have been new to this, but even she knew something wasn't right.

Jesse wondered why they were even there. He thought of Sara and wished once again he'd been able to talk her into letting him stay.

Stephen was unaware that his nostrils were flaring as his sense of smell picked up unfamiliar odors.

Morag sniffed the air. There was something... it was very faint. She knew it was something she had smelled before, but she couldn't put her finger on what it was. She whirled around but there was nothing behind her. Odd. She thought she had sensed movement.

Duncan was whistling silently, his lips pursed in some tune only he could hear. His ears were listening to the silence around them. There were no birds singing. He too was aware of the leaves swirling around on the ground. He watched them as they seemed to be trying to get out of the path of their feet.

Joly could smell something. She thought it was fear, but where would it be coming from? Her mouth was slightly open as she walked quietly along, the leaves skittering out of the way of her shoes. She was conscious of the movement of Duncan behind her and she could hear the soft padding of everyone's shoes. Other than those quiet little sounds, there was nothing. She thought about the expression, 'the silence was deafening.' It truly applied to this place.

She thought back to when they had been driving along the highway an hour before. What had called them to this place? Why had she felt the sudden need to stop? Morag had gotten out of the van immediately. She too, had felt it. Not ten words had been spoken since they left the highway.

Rhiannon had been excited when they had gotten out of the van and headed into the woods. She had always had an adventurous streak in her and she loved the woods, but now she was wishing she hadn't come. She didn't like the vibes she was getting. The restless spirits said something was not right up ahead, and she wasn't sure she was ready to face whatever it was.

Stephen didn't have a good feeling about this place. There didn't seem to be anything he could put his finger on, but there was something just not right. Rhiannon's talk of restless spirits didn't sit well with him. He had never believed in the afterlife, ghosts or spirits. He had already learned so much about what was real and what wasn't. He had no reason to doubt what she said was true, but he still had moments of self-doubt with what he was doing.

Jesse could feel the spirits. He hadn't been able to identify what it was until Rhiannon had said, but now that he knew, he realized he should have known all along. He thought of the crone's instruction to him once again. *Use your powers.* He would definitely have to work on expanding his senses.

The bushes and trees were thick through the area and Joly couldn't see very far ahead. As she walked along the gently curving trail she noticed that the bushes, mostly bare of their summer finery, appeared to be thinning out. She felt it before she saw it. She stopped suddenly, the bile rising in her throat. She gagged, swallowed and felt her tummy heave. She looked ahead, seeing nothing.

Duncan almost crashed into Joly; she stopped so fast. He saw she was having trouble keeping from throwing up. He looked around her and wondered what the problem was. The sense of fear slammed into him.
Joly glanced at him and whispered, "Stop Morag, don't let her open her senses."
He whirled around and ran back; he grabbed his Mother, stopping her. He put his hands on either side of her face and looked into her eyes. Quietly, he said, "Maw, don't try to see what's up there. Think about something else."

Rhiannon walked to where Joly stood. The visions slammed into her head and she too, gagged and swallowed. She shook her head. "What is it?" she asked quietly. She watched Joly shrug her shoulders.
Rhiannon felt something touch her arm and she jumped. Stephen stood beside her, peering intently around. He looked pale, but he said nothing.
Jesse was beside him and he had turned a horrific shade of green.

Morag was perplexed. She could see both Joly and Rhiannon were having trouble keeping their lunch down, but she hadn't had a chance to search ahead with her mind before Duncan grabbed her. She could sense the air was no longer clean, but it hadn't been for some time. She could ignore her son, but she knew Joly had given him the instructions and she was curious to see what Joly would do on her own. She went to take a step ahead, but Duncan stopped her, softly saying, "No, Maw."

Joly grounded herself and invited the calming white energy into her soul. They needed to deal with this as quickly as possible, so they could get out of this place.

Jesse, Stephen and Rhiannon saw what Joly was doing, and copied her.

Joly turned and raised her hand to Duncan, signaling him to stay. She nodded to him when she saw he had a hold of Morag. He nodded back, understanding that he was not to let his Mother advance.

Joly followed the path, the fear surrounding her overwhelming in its intensity. Then she spotted the building in the distance. It blended in completely with the gray trunks of the trees.

The four walked quietly toward the building. She sensed there was nobody around, so there was nothing to fear. They reached the door and found it was locked with five padlocks. Joly signaled the other three to stay where they were, while she walked around the building. There were no windows. The building was made of gray concrete blocks and was about twelve feet by sixteen feet.

She felt the anger boiling up inside of her. It started in her heart and burned its way through the rest of her body. While taking several steps back, she pulled her wand out of the back pocket of her jeans and pointed it at the center lock. The fire erupted like a flamethrower and melted the steel. She did this four more times, and when she was finished, the only sign of the locks was a mass of melted metal lying on the ground.

Jesse's eyes almost popped out of his head. S*hit!* These witches would never cease to amaze him. He wondered if he would eventually be able to do half what he had seen them do. He honestly didn't think so. They almost seemed to be some kind of super witches.

Stephen's mouth hung open. He was too old for this. He would never get caught up to them in his learning. *What the hell kind of power was that anyhow?*

Rhiannon had seen Joly in action before, so she wasn't surprised, but she did wonder just what all this witch was capable of.

Joly took a deep breath and stepped forward to open the door. She had thought the visions were graphic when she was outside. They had been nothing compared to what she was hit with, as the door swung open. She turned and emptied her stomach.

Rhiannon also emptied hers. She wanted to go back to where Morag was waiting, but she knew she needed to stay.

Jesse stepped back several feet. The bile rose to his mouth, but he wasn't about to embarrass himself by throwing up. Neither was he going into the building. That was asking too much.

Stephen felt images fighting their way to his consciousness. They were blurred, but the screams that accompanied them were clear and terrifying in their nature.

Morag stood calmly waiting; Duncan's arm was wrapped around her, giving her a sense of security. It was times like this that she missed Brody the most. She missed the feeling of security he had always given her.

She had no idea what was around the corner, but she was glad Joly had taken command. She thought about her daughter-in-law, and how far she had come in the past year. That Duncan had reappeared was a blessing. Joly would have done just as well on her own, but now she had her husband, as well as her son to fight for. She was ready to take on the worse that could be thrown at her. She wondered again if she was in fact pregnant. She had watched Joly closely, but had seen no outward signs of anything different.

Duncan, still upset by the feelings of terror that had assaulted him as he had rounded the corner, held on tightly to his Mother. Not so much to keep her from advancing, but because she was his Mother, and right then, he needed the security she had always given him. He knew it was dumb, he was a grown man, but it didn't matter. He was just thankful she was there.

Joly looked around the large room. The queen size bed dominated the far end. She stood amongst the cameras, the umbrella lighting, and the masses of cords that were laying everywhere. The smell of blood was thick in the air and she could see images of it throughout, even though it had been cleaned not once, but time and time again. It was there on the wall at the head of the bed. It was on the floor on both sides of the bed. The mattress under the sheet was soaked in it. There was even a trail of it running toward the door.

She thought they were called snuff movies. The ones where during the filming, someone was actually murdered. The visions kept slamming at her, visions of women and men, both young and old, the torture, the rapes, the screams, the begging for their very lives. She ran outside and was sick again.

Rhiannon wondered what it was all about. She could tell they made movies there and the large bed suggested pornography, but she didn't understand the rest. She could see the visions and hear the screams, but she couldn't put the two together. In between taking large gulps of air, she asked Joly to explain.

"Do you see the blood?" Joly pointed.

Rhiannon hadn't, but when she knew where to look, it became apparent. It suddenly dawned on her what she was looking at, and she ran back outside and was violently ill.

Stephen looked around the room. He couldn't see the blood, but he could smell it and he still heard the screams. The images sharpened in his mind, although they still weren't clear. He felt his stomach churn and knew he had better leave. He walked outside and took a deep breath. Unconsciously, he put his hands to his ears, trying to block out the sounds of terror that refused to leave him.

Jesse kept retreating. He didn't have to do this. This wasn't normal witch-craft and that was all he had signed on for. When he knew no one could see him, he threw up.

Joly could hear the laughter of one person, a woman. The evil laugh reso-nated through her very soul and she knew she would never forget it. She wondered how she could stop this. Destroying the building would only have the woman moving her business elsewhere.

Joly touched her hand to her stomach. She thought about the precious be-ing growing there and she was sick again. She went back inside and began knocking over the lighting.

Rhiannon saw what she was doing and quickly moved to join her. They smashed the cameras and tore the sheets on the bed. They ripped holes in the umbrellas and bent the stands.

Suddenly Joly had a thought. "Rhiannon, where's the power?"

"What do yer mean?"

"We're in the middle of no where. Where's the source of power? There's got to be a generator."

They searched but couldn't find it.

"Do you think they pack it with them?"

"Maybe."

Joly decided she would notify the authorities and hoped they would catch the killer, but in the meantime, this would slow her down. When they were done, they walked out and headed back toward the others.

She sensed movement out of the corner of her eye and turned. There was nothing. She walked toward the trees and again saw something out of the corner of her eye. She whirled around. Nothing. She stood and opened her senses. The visions of the horrors that had taken place inside the building slammed into her again and again. She pushed herself past them and looked for something else. She closed her eyes and willed the air around her to speak.

"It's the spirits of the dead, Joly. They can't rest; they're lost and confused. They don't know they're dead."

Joly opened her eyes and walked farther into the trees. She allowed herself to be led by whatever unseen force was guiding her. Rhiannon followed.

They could smell it before they reached it. It wasn't far, maybe thirty or forty feet from the back of the building. There had been no attempt to hide it or disguise it. The pit itself was about fifteen feet in diameter and appeared to have been dug down two or three feet. The bodies had simply been thrown in. A rough attempt to cover them with loose earth had failed to stop the hungry animals. The stench of the decomposing bodies was overwhelming. They both bent forward retching and gagging. When their stomachs were empty, Rhiannon grabbed Joly and together they clung to one another. Joly turned and leading Rhiannon by the hand, they walked back to the others.

Duncan, Stephen and Morag saw the sickness on Joly and Rhiannon's faces and they moved toward them. They wrapped their arms around the two women and sent them the love they both so badly needed at that moment.

Joly cried then, for all the poor innocent souls that had met their end in that horrid building. She thought of the child growing inside of her and she thought about Randy. The visions of the horrors that had been done to other people's children, grown or not, slammed into her again. She broke away from the others and threw up again, this time it was mostly dry heaves as she had already emptied her stomach of everything that was in it. When she was done, Duncan took her in his arms again.

Rhiannon was shaking uncontrollably in Stephen's arms and Morag wrapped her arms around the two of them sending her calming energies.

Rhiannon slid to the ground and she wrapped her arms around herself. She began rocking back and forth, emitting a humming noise from deep in her throat. Morag understood that it was her usual way to deal with something terrible. She squatted down beside her and held on to her once again. Stephen knelt on the other side of her and softly rubbed her back, not knowing what else to do.

When Joly had calmed, she turned to the others. "We need a circle."

Morag looked around. There wasn't room where they were.

"Where do you want to cast it?"

Joly thought of the clearing near the building, but she didn't want to subject Morag to the horrors that were there. She shook her head.

"I don't know."

Jesse waved his arm. "Follow me." He'd seen a small clearing when he'd been looking for some privacy.

They left the trail and walked through the bushes. The clearing was small, but large enough for the six of them.

Morag wasn't sure what the circle was for, so she stood back and left Joly in command.

They had no tools with them, so Joly cast the circle with her wand. She called the Gods and Goddesses and the four quarters. She stood in the center and raised her arms.

"May the Gods and Goddesses hear me. Help us to bring peace to those who have died violently and needlessly."

Morag frowned. *What had they found?*

"Earth bound the spirits lie,
They know not why they had to die.
Give them peace and let them rest,
Let them know they did their best.
Take their fear and take their pain,
For all who die are born again.
Remove the darkness and give them light,
The time has come to give them flight."

Joly looked up at the sky, unsure of which direction she was facing. It was late afternoon and the sun was low in the sky. She couldn't see it with all the trees, but she could see where the light was strongest. She turned to the north.

"Your bodies mingle with the earth
Wait now, for in time comes rebirth."

She turned to the west...

"Your blood has joined with the water
Rest now, every son, every daughter."

And then the south.

"Your breath still floats in the air
Sleep now, knowing you're everywhere."

She turned to the east.

"Your spirit's are ablaze like a fiery flame
Rise now, and know you'll live again."

Raising her arms again, Joly thanked the Gods and Goddesses and bade the elementals to depart. She closed the circle knowing she could do no more there.

Rhiannon went to her and hugged her. "That was beautiful, Joly. Thank you."

She smiled a small, sad smile. "I hope it was enough."

Rhiannon turned to Stephen. "Stevie, will you come with me to check?"

He didn't want to go anywhere, except back to the van, but he gamely took her hand and let her lead him back toward the building. He watched as Rhiannon turned this way and that. His nostrils were flaring, but he sensed nothing.

"They're gone, Stevie. Joly did it." She smiled up at him. After a brief kiss, they walked down the trail to where the others waited.

"They're gone, Joly. It's okay now."

She smiled. "I'm glad. Now, let's get out of here, before it gets dark."

As they walked, they noticed the leaves were no longer swirling on the ground.

Morag wondered about the memorial. Who had died? Sons and daughters meant both sexes. Violently and needlessly? Murder obviously. She wondered how many. She was pleased with the way Joly had taken command and she had done an admirable job of the service. She thought maybe it was time to let Joly take command of the group. She thought about Pennsylvania. Perhaps she would wait and see.

Duncan stopped at the next town, and Joly called the police from a pay phone. She gave them a description of the place and directions on how to find it. She also told them that they were looking for a woman. She walked back to the van and looked around.

"You okay, Darlin'?"

"Uhh… yeah. I think I need a cup of tea."

"Sure thing, Darlin'. Come on Maw, let's go find a restaurant." He jumped out of the van, walked around and opened the door for Morag. The other three followed her out.

They walked down the street, Duncan with his arm around Joly, and Morag and Stephen walking beside Rhiannon with Jesse behind them. They found a coffee shop and ordered tea. No one said anything as they sat in silent contemplation. They drank their tea and started walking back to the van.

"I think maybe we should just call it a day and go find a hotel."

"*No!*" Joly raised voice startled the others, and caused several people passing by to look in their direction.

"No… I need to get away from here. Sorry. I didn't mean to yell."

"No prob, Darlin', we can keep on goin'. I just thought you might not feel up to travelin'."

"I'll be fine, once we're away from here."

The laughter from across the street stopped her in her tracks. Her entire body stiffened as she turned around to face the direction it had come from. Half a dozen women stood chatting outside a real estate office.

"What is it, Darlin'?"

She shook her head, unable to speak as the visions ran rampant through her head once again. *The laughter… I'll never forget the laughter.* She knew she could walk over to the women and quite calmly kill the one that caused all the suffering. She also knew that she wouldn't. The woman needed to suffer as much as the innocent had suffered.

She choked down the bile that had again risen in her throat. "The demon-bitch that caused the suffering back there. She's in that group of women."

Morag looked across the street, as did the others.

"Which one is it?"

"I don't know. I only recognized the laugh."

"Are you sure child?"

"Yes."

Morag laid her hand on Joly's arm. "What do you want to do?"

"I don't know. Yes, I do know. I'd like to kill her. You didn't see. I'm glad you didn't see. It was horrible. Murder is seldom right, but this was far worse." The tears welled up in her eyes again. She looked across at the women who were innocently chatting, unaware a monster was in their midst.

She unconsciously put her hand to her stomach. Both Morag and Duncan watched. They looked at each other and Duncan nodded. It was an *I told you so* nod and Morag nodded back. She no longer had to wonder if her daughter-in-law was pregnant.

"Call the authorities dear. Let them handle it."

"Yes, I suppose you're right."

One of the women in the group noticed the six people across the street. She brought it to the attention of the others. They wondered if the people were prospective clients. One broke away from the group and walked across the street.

"Hello. My name is Sharon Littleton. I couldn't help but notice you looking over at the office. Do you have need of a realtor?" She was smiling broadly, as she sized up each of them. She noticed the younger woman seemed upset. Husbands and wives almost always quarreled over buying a house. She was used to it.

The calculating look that she gave Jesse caused goosebumps to break out on his arms and legs. He shivered and wanted nothing more than to get out of there.

Joly couldn't help herself. She tried to talk herself out of it, but it was no use. She moved so fast, the others didn't see what she was about to do until it was already over. She drew her arm back and punched the woman as hard as she could in the face. The woman lifted off her feet, flying backwards into the street, directly in front of a oncoming bus. The thunk of the vehicle hitting her echoed through everyone's heads.

"*Damn!* Let's get out of here." Morag grabbed Joly's arm and started walking quickly to the van. Duncan grabbed her other arm, propelling her along. Rhiannon, Stephen and Jesse hurried along behind them. They reached the van and Duncan opened the passenger door, pushing Joly in. He slammed the door shut and ran around to the other side. Stephen slid open the back door and the four of them quickly climbed in. Duncan started the van and backed out of the spot they were parked in.

He eased out into the traffic and headed out of town.

Morag turned around to see what was happening behind them. All attention appeared to be on the woman on the pavement. She saw no one looking in their direction.

Duncan stopped at a mall on the outskirts of the town. He went to a pay phone and called the police. He said what needed to be said. "The building in the woods. The woman in charge was just hit by a bus." He hung up and got back in the van. He drove until they reached a place called Junction City.

He stopped at the first decent looking motel he came to and took four rooms. He topped up the cooler with Stephen looking on and then the two of them went and found a grocery store. They bought cheese, fruit, cold cuts and buns. They drove back to the motel where the others were waiting in Morag's room.

The television was on, tuned to a news channel and Morag updated them. "The woman is alive. No one seems too sure what happened. They did mention that three couples had been talking to her just prior to the accident."

Duncan smiled. "Three couples? Maw, you and Jess holdin' out on the rest of us?"

She smiled back at him. "Well, Son, it does work in our favor if that's what they think."

"And they're calling it an accident?"

"Yes."

Duncan breathed a sigh of relief. He knew it was imperative they get to Pennsylvania and he really didn't want to be running from the law for the rest of the trip. He noticed Joly was very quiet and wondered how he was going to get her mind off everything that had happened.

They ate quietly, and when they were finished, Duncan, Joly, Stephen and Rhiannon left to go to their rooms.

Jesse stayed behind, not wanting to be alone.

"So my Lady, tell me what your take is on the day's events."

"I'd rather hear yours."

He should have known that was coming. When was he going to wise up?

"Well, I think we should have steered clear of that business out in the bush."

"Why?"

We're witches. That wasn't anything to do with the craft. That was strictly police business."

"I see. And what about the spirits that Joly laid to rest?"

"Anyone could have done that."

"Jesse, tell me what our purpose in life is."

"We're here to protect Mother Earth."

"And what else?"

"To destroy evil and help others."

"That is correct. Now tell me again please, about the spirits that Joly laid to rest."

He thought about where the crone was going with her questions. Once again, he apparently had screwed up.

"It was an ugly business. Perhaps I was hasty in saying we should have left it alone, but I still don't feel we should be interfering where the law is concerned. Isn't that why we have laws and police?"

"As I didn't see what everyone else saw, it's difficult for me to make a sound judgment call on what did or didn't happen. However, I do know Joly. She did in fact call the authorities, as did Duncan. Now, tell me please, where was the interference?"

"Joly and Rhiannon destroyed everything in the place. That was after Joly melted all the locks on the door."

"Do you know why they destroyed everything?"

Jesse shrugged. "Probably to stop more horror movies from being made."

"Ahh. So they were in fact trying to stop evil from happening?"

"I suppose." He wished she would quit twisting his words. Whenever he said anything that made perfect sense, the crone would turn it around and make it look like he didn't know what he was talking about.

"As this also took place before we got to the town, then Joly didn't know at the time who was responsible, correct?"

"No, I guess not."

Morag nodded. "Let's do a summation. Evil things are happening in a locked building. Joly senses this and melts the locks and discovers the tools that are used for an evil purpose. She somehow knows the perpetrator is a woman, but she doesn't know who. She wants to call the authorities, but she also wants to make sure the woman is at least temporarily out of business. She destroys the tools of the trade. Do I have it right so far?"

"I think so."

"Now we have the spirits of the victims wandering about, earthbound from their violent deaths. The woman has caused much grief. Even if she were arrested and put in jail, the spirits would still be there, confused and unhappy, because they don't know what happened to them. Should we just leave the spirits to suffer, and hope that somewhere along the line someone with the power will happen along and put an end to their suffering? Or should we take a few minutes of our time and put the spirits to rest?"

Jesse looked down at his shoes. The crone had a way of making him feel small and he really hated it.

"My Lady, once again, you have successfully made me look like an uncaring, unthinking person. I'm not sure how you keep doing this, but for one, I really am a caring person, just ask Sara. And two, I'm really getting tired of being made to look like a fool."

He stood and headed for the door.

"Jesse, come here and sit down. I'm not finished with you yet."

He turned and looked at Morag. ""But I, my Lady, am finished with you." He reached for the doorknob.

"You were the one who chose to stay and spar with me. You don't like losing do you, Mr. Alexander? Well, that being the case, perhaps you should turn around and stay. You never know, you just might learn how to put forth a winning argument."

With his one hand on the doorknob, he leaned his head against the door. *Why don't I have the guts to walk out? I'm tired of the crap the crone keeps dishing out. I want to go back and see Sara.*

Sara wanted him to learn from the crone, to discover who he really was. She wouldn't be happy to see him back on her doorstep. No, he needed to stick it out. He turned around and faced Morag.

"Do you think it'll be anytime soon?"

"What?"

"This winning argument I'm going to put forth."

Morag laughed. She stood and hugged him. "You are a character, Jesse. Now ground yourself and then I'll tell you my take on the day's events."

Joly called home, but there had been no answer. She was still sitting at the desk looking pensively into the mirror.

Duncan watched her and decided it was time to bring her back from wherever her mind had wandered. He went and stood behind her, massaging her shoulders as he looked at her reflection.

"Darlin', is there something you want to tell me?"

"What do you mean?"

He lifted her to her feet and turned her around. He took her head in his hands and leaned forward to kiss her on her forehead. "You know what I mean pretty lady." He smiled at her and placed his hand on her stomach.

"Honey…" She felt so bad. She had never kept a secret from him before.

"Shh, it's okay. I know you wanted to wait until we got home."

"I wasn't even really sure honey. Not at first."

"I know." He ran his hand across her abdomen and grinned.

"So tell me, Darlin', are we having a son or daughter?"

"I don't know yet. Which do you want it to be?"

"Darlin', as long as it looks like you, I don't care."

"Why me?"

"Because you're beautiful and I love you."

"Oh honey." She put her arms around him and laid her head on his chest.

"Got any names picked out?"

He felt her shaking and knew she was laughing. Good, she was out of the blue funk she'd been in. "Well?"

"Yes." She wondered if he would like her choices. She looked up at his face.

"What do you think of Magi, m-a-g-i?"

"Magi McEwan." He thought about and decided it sure beat anything he'd come up with.

"I like it, Darlin', sounds just about perfect, and if it's a boy?"

"Marty."

"Marty McEwan? Sounds like you expect him to be born wearin' a Stetson hat and cowboy boots."

"*Honey!* It's a happy name. I wanted something that sounded like sunshine and rainbows."

"Marty? Well, unless you've got a horse tucked up..."

She punched him on the shoulder. He laughed. "Sorry, Darlin."

Grinning, she looked at him. "So... what would you call him?"

There was no hesitation. "Rory."

She was surprised. He'd obviously been thinking about names for sometime. She wondered how long he'd known.

"Rory McEwan. I like it."

"Well, I was thinkin' about Randy you know, and Randy and Rory just kind of went together."

"You're right, they do."

"So we're decided then? Rory or Magi. Work for you?"

"Yes." Gods, but she loved this man of hers.

He was still massaging her stomach and she felt the heat building. She ran her tongue across his lips and he sucked it into his mouth and then ran his tongue across the tip of hers.

She moaned and rubbed herself against him. He was already hard.

Rhiannon and Stephen were snuggled together on the bed. Rhiannon was exhausted. The spirits talking to her had always tired her out, but she never had so many talking at once. She had been overwhelmed by all the voices.

Stephen sighed and she turned to the man beside her. "You okay, Stevie?"

"I think so. I find it really strange having these things happening to me, though. I always said there was no... what's the word, witchyness or magic in me, and now I find I'm feeling things that aren't there, I hear things which have happened in the past. Do you understand what I'm trying to say?"

"Sure, Stevie. Wait until you do somethin' innocent like look in a crystal and find yourself across the ocean in a strange closet."

He chuckled. She'd told him the story and he wondered who had been the most shocked, Rhiannon or Duncan and Joly?

He thought about Joly and how he'd decided he was going to make her his next wife. She was a good person, but now he'd spent some time with her, he was extremely glad that she was Duncan's wife and not his. He glanced down at Rhiannon and felt his heart race. *Gods, but I love her!*

Gods? Where the hell had that come from? He smiled to himself. He was spending far too much time with his family. He pictured himself saying that at his next board meeting and inwardly cringed.

The next morning Duncan asked Joly when she wanted to let the others know about the pregnancy.

She shook her head. "I don't know. I think after the trip."

"Maw, too?"

"What do you think?"

"I think Maw's just waiting for confirmation."

Joly giggled. "I'm not much of a secret keeper am I, if everyone already suspects. What gave it away?"

"I knew as soon as Randy patted your tummy and said baby. To be honest, I went and told Maw. I didn't want you coming on this trip at first."

"And now?"

"I think I'm okay with it now."

"Okay, let's go tell your Mom, but I would just as soon not say anything to anyone else yet."

"Sure."

They went and knocked on Morag's door.

When she opened it and waved them in, she commented, "You two are up early this morning."

"Yeah well... we... uh... got somethin' to tell you." Duncan's eyes were bright and he was grinning from ear to ear.

She went and sat down. "Well, what are you about to surprise me with at this early hour?"

Duncan had his arm around Joly and he looked down at her. "Go ahead, Darlin', it's your news to tell."

Joly smiled and walked over to Morag. "I understand you already suspect, but I thought you'd like confirmation. You're going to be a Grandma again."

Morag's face lit up. "Oh, that is wonderful news! Congratulations to both of you. When can we expect to know if it's a boy or a girl and when are you due? Do you know?"

"Probably late May or early June and I'm hoping to know the sex by the thirtieth so I can tell Randy as part of his birthday gift."

"Well, now we can have fun picking out a name." She hugged Joly.

"Too late, Maw."

"What do you mean?"

"Baby already has a name."

Joly smiled and Morag noticed her eyes were misty.

"Oh. Well, that was fast. What have you decided on?" She was disappointed. She'd hoped to help with the decision.

They told her and she decided she was pleased with their choices. She thought of the tiny shoes sitting in her dresser at home and knew she was going to have trouble not buying every baby thing she came across.

They swore her to secrecy and went back to their room.

After breakfast, more ice was added to the cooler, and the three men proceeded to load the van. Morag was still in her room when something on the television caught her ear. She quickly turned up the volume. The police had found the building in the woods and also discovered a mass grave site near it. The aerial shots taken from a helicopter didn't show a lot of detail, but the news was chilling just the same. They were still unearthing bodies, but had so far found sixteen. Most were too badly decomposed for immediate identification, but three had been identified. One was a twenty-two year old girl that had gone missing from college the month before, one was a male in his late teens and the third was a male in his early thirties. The investigation was ongoing and the police had received an anonymous tip with regards to a possible suspect that they were checking out.

Immediately after that, the news mentioned the bus accident and that the woman, a well known realtor, was in stable condition. Due to injuries to her spine, she was not expected to walk again.

Morag thought to herself; what goes around, comes around, and she clicked the television off.

Stephen decided it was his turn to drive. Morag, Joly and Duncan looked at him in trepidation.

Morag finally spoke. "Son, if Duncan says you can drive, fine, but I don't want to see you driving this van like you drive your car. Is that clear?"

Stephen took offense. "I'm a damn good driver and you know it. Why would you even say that?"

"Why? Because whenever you come home, you usually take the corner on two wheels, that's why."

He had the sense to look guilty. "Uh, well, I'm usually in a hurry, for one reason or another." He looked at Duncan. "I promise to keep all four wheels on the pavement."

Duncan laughed. "Sure, Bro, why not?" He handed Stephen the keys.

Rhiannon headed for the front seat and the others climbed in the back. Nefertiti still refused to go near the cooler, so when Morag and Jesse took the middle seat, she joined them. In the back seat, Duncan pulled Joly close and started nuzzling her neck.

She squirmed and playfully slapped his leg. "Stop it."

Duncan chuckled. "Darlin', all we need is a curtain in front of us, what do you think?"

Morag turned around and gave him a glaring look. "You might also consider having it soundproofed." She laughed as she shook her head and turned to the front.

24. A Snake and a Thunderbird

Two hours later, they crossed into Missouri. Stephen was telling Rhiannon about his business. He couldn't wait to show her how to use a computer.

Stephen noticed his three hours were up. He glanced in the rearview mirror. Jesse appeared to be sleeping, as did Duncan and Joly. He wasn't tired, so he decided to continue on.

He tried to get Rhiannon to talk about herself, but she didn't have too much to say. From the bits he did get out of her, it appeared she'd had a fairly hard life. He was looking forward to spoiling her, but he knew he was going to have to ease into it. She was tight with a dollar. He smiled to himself when he thought about opening a bank account for her. He'd have to start it small, with maybe five thousand dollars. *Damn!* That didn't seem like very much. Maybe he'd start it with ten thousand. Yes, that was better.

Stephen looked across at Rhiannon. "Talk to me, my beauty. You're being awfully quiet."

Rhiannon didn't know what to talk about. Her life had been quiet and uninteresting for the most part. She had never hidden the fact that she was different from most people, so had consequently been ostracized from what many would call a normal life. She had been on her own since she was fourteen when her Mother died. She had never known her father or who he was. A chance encounter with a handsome stranger, her Mother had slept with him. She had been a virgin and decided she wanted to know what joining with a man was all about. As far as she knew, her Mother had never lain with another man. She was the end result of the one night's experiment.

She thought about Maddie and smiled. Maddie had been her Guardian Angel throughout so much of her young life. Maddie had been her first teacher in primary school. She had seen something in Rhiannon that no one else did, and although she hadn't exactly taken her under her wing, she had always seemed to sense when Rhiannon needed encouragement or help with something. Maddie would search her out, take her aside and inquire how she was doing.

After Maddie had fallen down some stairs and broken her hip and leg, Rhiannon tried to repay her by doing her shopping and generally looking out for her. Maddie was a proud woman and refused to accept what she referred to as charity. She allowed Rhiannon to do the occasional shopping for her, but would never allow her to do anything else. As Maddie's home had grown more slovenly with her inability to care for it herself, Rhiannon had tried to get her to agree to let her do some cleaning, but she refused. Rhiannon finally decided that if Maddie was content to live in her own mess, then who was she to try and change her. As Maddie had grown more reclusive and Rhiannon's time was taken up with trying to survive, they had grown apart, but whenever she did stop by to visit, Maddie was always pleased to see her.

Rhiannon looked at Stephen. She wanted Maddie to meet him, but she thought back to when Joly had first entered the house. Rhiannon never gave any thought to the smells inside. They were a part of Maddie and therefore immaterial. She knew Stephen would have trouble with them also. If they could arrange to be in the village on a Monday morning, Maddie would be out doing her weekly shopping. It was usually the only day she left her home.

Rhiannon watched the scenery flashing by. Stephen was a very good driver. She wondered why everyone seemed to think he wasn't. She'd only known him six days and it felt like forever. She wondered how she had managed for so many years without him. She knew the universe had a master plan for everyone. There was a reason she had been alone for so long, she just didn't know what it was. Perhaps it was to teach her to be thrifty. The Gods knew she was going to have a difficult time with Stephen and his money. He'd said he could go the rest of his life and never have to work another day. She shook her head thinking about it. If he actually planned on staying home with her, then she would have to shop very carefully. She hoped she could stretch her grocery money to include the occasional bones for the dogs. They so loved a treat.

Duncan had settled down, and was dozing with Joly in his arms. She had her eyes closed, but she was wide-awake, thinking about her unborn child.

Joly knew the three hours was up, but Duncan was snoring softly in her ear and she didn't want to disturb him. She noticed Jesse's head swaying back and forth and knew he was also asleep. Her thoughts returned to the baby. She should know within the next two weeks whether it was a girl or a boy. She laid her hand on her stomach. *Grow strong little one, Momma loves you.*

She thought about being a *Sister of the Triple Moon* and was happy that her child wasn't going to be one. While it was an honor, she wouldn't wish her life on a child. She tried to remember what her Father had said about it. Only in times of dire trouble to Mother Earth, did the Sisters appear. Would the banishing of the three demons be the completion of their duties?

She wondered about Morag and her heritage. She idly wondered how the knowledge of such people remained constant. She decided it had to be passed down by word of mouth.

Morag was deep in thought about her forthcoming grandchild. Rory was a Gaelic name and she liked it. She hoped if it was a boy he would have red hair, as Rory meant ruddy or red. Magi was an old name with a new spelling, but she had to admit she liked it. It wasn't Gaelic or Scots and she was pretty sure it wasn't Welsh. She didn't think the kids had given any thought to their heritage when they chose the names, something she herself was very big on and one of the reasons she had been hoping to have a say in naming the newest McEwan. She wondered if a future child would be given a Welsh name to honor Joly's heritage on Morgana's side. She couldn't see the future clearly when it came to the McEwan babies, but she knew without a doubt that Joly and Duncan would have at least six. It was times like this she wished she could see more clearly. She would dearly love to know how many boys and how many girls. *Ah well, one couldn't be blessed with everything and she did have more than her share of blessings.*

Jesse jerked awake and looked around. A glance at his watch told him it was somebody else's turn at the wheel. He gave himself a few minutes to wake up and then he reached forward to tap Stephen's shoulder.

"Whenever you're ready, I'll take over."

"Sure. I'll stop in the next town. It's just about time for lunch, anyhow."

They stopped for lunch, checked the cooler and Jesse drove them through St. Louis, where they began a gradual northeasterly ascent toward Pennsylvania. Duncan took the wheel and night found them in Terre Haute, Indiana.

They were on the road early the next morning with Joly driving. Morag had joined her in the front, as the three men were back to discussing the gym. Stephen appeared to have appointed himself business manager, and Morag smiled as she listened to her two sons argue amicably back and forth. Jesse almost seemed to be part of the family when it came to talking about the gym. He argued comfortably with both Duncan and Stephen. She knew she was going to have to get back to talking about the craft with the novices, but she would give them a break for a couple of days.

Two and half hours later they crossed into Ohio.

They stopped for lunch and Jesse and Stephen checked the cooler. It had been four days since Duncan had looked at the material. They decided they would check it again that night. All three men planned on being in attendance.

Duncan took the wheel shortly before they entered West Virginia. When they reached Breezewood, Pennsylvania, Morag asked Duncan to stop. "We might as well find a place to stay for tonight. We're close. We'll fine tune the location in the morning."

Neither the first nor the second hotels he stopped at, took pets. The third hotel accepted cats, and they were soon registered and in their rooms. Morag decided to stay with Duncan and Joly again.

They went to the hotel's restaurant for supper, and then the three men went out to check the marks on the material.

Rhiannon asked Joly to join her in her room. Once there, Rhiannon sat on the bed looking terribly distressed, so Joly went and sat beside her.

"Something's wrong. What is it? I can't help you, if you don't tell me."

"Joly, I'm so very embarrassed. I don't know who to talk to or to ask."

"We're all family here. There can't possibly be anything so terrible, as you're making it out to be."

Rhiannon's hands fidgeted in her lap as she stared at them. "It's a personal question that I need the answer to."

Joly smiled. "Okay."

"It's about money."

"Okay."

Rhiannon chanced a glance in Joly's direction. She found a kind and caring face looking at her in concern.

"Joly, the meals, the hotels, the petrol, everything. Who's paying for it?"

Joly chuckled and Rhiannon was horrified.

"I'm sorry, I shouldn't have laughed. Of course you're wondering about the money and someone should have taken the time to explain it to you." She hugged Rhiannon and explained about the investments made by her Father and Broderick, the bank accounts that had sat unused for the most part for nine years. Joly told her about never having to work as long as she lived and that Duncan didn't have to either, but by choice, he wanted something to do with his time. She told her about Stephen's company and that he was a millionaire several times over.

Rhiannon was quiet as she digested the information. "You're saying you have more money than you will ever spend?"

"Yes, as long as I don't start buying planes and ships and small countries." She grinned.

Rhiannon smiled back, understanding a joke had been made.

Stephen was a millionaire. She couldn't even begin to fathom how much money that was, or what it meant when it came to the kind of lifestyle he was accustomed to.

"Do yer fink Stephen and me will do okay together?"

"You're worrying too much. It shows in your speech. Everything will be fine, I'm sure. You just need to keep loving him like you do. I don't think he had much love from his ex."

"That will be easy to do. I'm sorry about the way I talk. I feel comfortable when I'm with you, and I forget."

"I don't mind. I like the way you talk, and I know it must be hard for you not to slip back into it. I also know you're trying very hard to talk properly and I'm sure Stephen appreciates it."

"He teases me about dropping my h's."

Joly laughed.

They talked until the men returned and then Joly left to go back to her room. She told Duncan and Morag about Rhiannon's concerns regarding money.

Duncan grinned. Joly had told him about the tiny cottage with no power.

"She must be finding this trip pretty wild. Talk about culture shock." He laughed. When he thought about it, he was amazed she had taken as long as she had to say anything.

Morag felt badly. She had meant to talk to Rhiannon about their finances, but with Jesse and Stephen and everything else that had been happening, it had completely slipped her mind.

She had scryed the area while Joly was with Rhiannon. They were very close. The old manor house was deserted and there was nothing lurking around the immediate area.

Duncan told them that the marks in the material were still dark, but he didn't think they were as dark as before.

Polina didn't understand what was happening. Three times she had come back from seeing Griffin, and something wasn't right when she returned to her body. She knew her private place hadn't been discovered, but something was happening, and she had no one she could ask.

She wanted to ask Sergei, but she didn't know how to without him asking all kinds of questions that she didn't dare answer. And lately, he either wasn't around or he was talking to *Babushka* about the demon fighting. *Damn demon anyhow. There's more important stuff to do.*

She kicked a rock and her toe caught it wrong. "*Owww!* Damn it anyhow!"

She wished she was old enough to get drunk. That's what she felt like doing. *Stupid!* She didn't even know anyone who drank. Not in her crowd anyhow. She saw another rock, went to kick it, thought twice about it and walked past it.

The following morning after breakfast was finished, the cooler checked and the van loaded, Morag told Stephen to keep heading east. He found interstate 76 and did fine until they approached Harrisburg. He asked if he should stay on the same highway.

Morag said nothing, wanting to see if Stephen would be able to figure it out himself. She knew his senses were opening and she wondered how much more he would discover he could do.

Stephen was getting frustrated. He had asked twice and no one was answering him. He decided if no one was going to direct him, he'd go where the van took him. He took an exit that soon had them heading north.

Jesse watched with interest. So it wasn't just him that was being tested. The crone was testing her own son, as well. He smiled to himself and felt a great weight fall from his shoulders. She wasn't picking on him; it was her way of instructing. As he smiled to himself, he became aware of something strange happening. He felt like his head had cracked open and all sorts of information was streaming through it. None of it made any sense. He leaned forward and put his hands to his head.

Morag touched him on the arm. "Let it be, Jesse. It's what you've been waiting for. It'll sort itself out, if you give it time."

Her voice came from far away, but he understood every word. "What is it, my Lady?" The light show in his mind was incredible. The pinks, the blues, the reds, the purples were streaming through like water blown from a hose.

"You've just opened your mind. It's a bit of a shocker to start with, but you'll get used to it."

She watched his facial expressions with interest. Whatever he had been using as the block had just released in one big bang. She wondered what the catalyst had been.

Stephen slowed as he approached another exit. He tried letting his mind decide. He wasn't sure, so he kept going. Fifteen minutes later he pulled off to the side of the road.

"Hey, Bro'… what's happenin'?" Duncan sat up from where he'd been curled up with Joly.

"Uh… I think I screwed up. Well, actually I did screw up. We're heading the wrong way." He stared ahead through the windshield, not wanting to see the faces of his passengers.

Morag tipped her head back and closed her eyes. Her nostrils flared. "No, I don't think so."

"Mother, we're headed northwest."

She opened her eyes and sat up, looking around. "Maybe so, but wherever we are, it's where we're supposed to be." She reached down and picked up her crystal, which had been resting in a small bag tucked under her feet. She slid open the door and climbed down. She leaned against the side of the van and asked the crystal to take her where it needed to go.

As the mists receded, she was taken to a small town directly ahead. She was smiling as she got back into the van.

"You're doing just fine, Stephen. I wonder… were you following your senses?"

He looked at his mother with a startled expression. "You can do that? I mean… we can do that?"

"Absolutely." She smiled again as she relaxed in her seat. How ironic. They were headed to a town called East Salem.

Duncan chuckled. "Just follow your beak, Bro'." He kissed Joly on her forehead and rubbed his hand across her belly.

Rhiannon chuckled. "Beak. That's funny. I call it a 'ooter, umm, hooter."

Duncan laughed. "Same difference."

Stephen pulled back on the highway, a thoughtful expression on his face.

His mother had not told him where they were going. He wondered if he would pass the test. Just thinking about it made him break out in a cold sweat.

"Relax, Son. You're doing fine. Don't try to push the feelings, let them lead you. You will make a mistake if you force what's happening inside. Ground yourself, relax and go with what feels right."

He nodded and grounded himself. He reached over and squeezed Rhiannon's hand, smiling as he did.

"Talk to me my beauty. Help me take my mind off this… thing."

Morag leaned forward and rested her hand on Stephen's shoulder. "It's not a thing, it's an ability and it's one that all witches have. Have you ever thought about why you've been so successful?"

"Hard work, Mother, and determination."

"Yes, but did you ever veer from the path you set for yourself? Did you ever make a major error in judgment?"

"No, never."

"That's because you were listening to your inner self and when you do that, you won't go wrong."

Jesse listened to the conversation with interest. He thought about the times he'd made an error in judgment and he'd made many of them. As he thought about it, he realized that he usually knew he was making a wrong choice, but he'd gone ahead and followed through with them anyhow.

Stephen passed several side roads and tried to not think about what he should be doing, but to allow whatever senses he had to guide him. Another road appeared heading to the north and almost without realizing it, he reached down and clicked his turn signal on. He slowed and smiled to himself. *Maybe there was something to this after all.*

Fifteen minutes later, they passed a figure sitting beside the road. Stephen was about fifty feet past the person, when he slammed on the brakes. He pulled over to the side of the road and leapt out of the van. As the rest of them watched, he jogged toward the person who had gotten up and was walking toward them. They stood talking for a minute and then Stephen and the person continued walking back to the van.

Morag knew this was the reason for the detour. She hoped it was another Sister. Stephen slid the side door open and poked his head in. "We have another passenger. This is Rauna."

Morag was shocked at the white hair, but she smiled and held her arms out. "Welcome back, my dear. We've missed you. Hello Crow, it's nice to see you, too."

"Morag? I'm so happy to see you." She leaned forward to receive her hug. She spotted Joly in the back seat curled up with a white haired man and wondered where he had come from. "Hello, Joly."

"Rauna, you're a sight for sore eyes. You have no idea how many times I've wondered how you were doing." Her eyes traveled up to the white hair. "You've been having some adventures I see, and not necessarily good ones."

"I'm happy to see you, too." She ran her hand across her hair and smiled. "Looks pretty weird, huh?"

She stopped smiling and sighed. "It was horrible. I'm still scared of shadows… and shadows seem to have so much more life now, than before."

Joly hugged her and felt the traces of fear emanating from her soul.

She noticed Rauna glancing at Duncan. "This is my husband, Duncan. Honey, you've heard about Rauna."

"Hi Rauna, nice to see you. Heard a lot about you."

"Hello." She looked confused.

Joly explained about finding him in England.

"How nice for you."

Morag introduced the others and Rauna slid in the back seat beside Joly. From the center seat, Nefertiti glared at Crow as they moved passed. Crow ignored her.

Stephen turned around and headed back to Harrisburg. Forty-five minutes later, he was back on the highway and heading east.

"Did you want to stop for lunch or keep going?"

They decided to keep going. An hour and a half later, they arrived in Allentown.

"We're very close, but let's stop for lunch." They drove down the main street looking for a restaurant. Morag looked in her crystal. She chuckled. "The sorcerer chose his location well. I wonder if it was intentional."

"How's that, Maw?"

"We're heading to a town called Bethlehem."

After eating, they drove the short distance to Bethlehem. It was mid afternoon. They decided to find a place to stay and they would check out the location the next day.

Rauna and Morag took a room together. Morag wanted to hear about Rauna's travels, but especially what happened to her that caused the white hair.

Rauna told her about some of her adventures. She had trouble speaking about the Abyss and Morag hugged her, telling her it was alright. She understood. She knew about the Abyss; that Rauna had been able to return at all was a miracle.

Rauna told her about Veronika and Polina both being Sisters. Morag nodded. So that was how she had been called back. Now it made sense. She was pleased to hear there were more Sisters, but when she heard Polina's age, she knew they'd only found one Sister for this battle.

When she heard about Sergei also being a witch, she was pleased. If he were to come with Veronika they would welcome the extra help. The more there were to fight the monster, the better their chances were in defeating it.

The next morning, Duncan stopped Stephen as he was about to get in the back seat. "You wanna drive, Bro'?"

"Why? I drove yesterday."

"You got the power, Bro'. You guided us to Rauna. I thought maybe you might want to take us the rest of the way."

Stephen looked at their mother. Her face was unreadable. He glanced around at the others. Jesse had a slight smile and looked pleased that it wasn't him under the gun. Both Joly's and Rauna's faces were as expressionless as his mother's. Rhiannon looked concerned, although she was smiling at him.

"Sure, why not?" He took the keys from Duncan and climbed in the driver's seat.

Thirty minutes later they were traveling down a dirt road and when he came to a seldom used lane where the weeds were taking over, he stopped. A yellow pipe gate was closed across the entry and he got out to look at it. When he saw it wasn't locked, he pushed it open. He drove through, stopped to close it and slowly drove forward. The pine trees were tall and thick along the roadside and the canopy above them blocked out much of the daylight. The growth on the roadway was abundant with vines and weeds and the van lurched over unseen obstacles.

"Stop here, Stephen." Joly commanded. She sensed evil and fear although it wasn't strong. She knew what she was feeling was from some time ago, and that there was nothing there at the moment to be afraid of. She felt the need to approach on foot, to better sense the feelings left behind.

Stephen stopped in the middle of the narrow road. Everyone got out, including Nefertiti, who had had her fur raised and her ears laid back for several miles.

Joly looked at Rhiannon and Rauna. They both appeared curious. The three men looked to be okay. She glanced at Morag, who was looking in her crystal. She appeared to be fine. She began walking down the lane. Toward what, she wasn't sure. The weeds were thick in places and she was carefully picking her way through them. There were kudzu vines everywhere and she didn't want to catch her shoe under a tendril and trip. Nefertiti was walking beside her. Duncan was two steps behind her and the others were following them.

As Joly moved to the side to avoid a particularly thick spot of growth, Nefertiti growled and spit. Joly was concentrating on the path she was taking and the evil she sensed ahead, and didn't notice.

Duncan heard Nefertiti's growl, but as he wasn't too familiar with the cat's ways, he ignored it, thinking she must have spotted a mouse or something. He heard a rattling sound, and paused. He knew that sound, but couldn't place it. He knew it was what Nefertiti was growling at, and he stepped forward to stop Joly.

Two steps farther and Nefertiti was springing through the air. Duncan was conscious of a flash of movement in front of Joly and heard Nefertiti scream in pain.

Joly stopped in her tracks as she saw the snake leap toward her. She saw Nefertiti airborne in front of her and heard her scream as the snake's fangs struck her side. She fell to the ground, her muscles spasming several times and then she was still. Duncan was beside Joly in an instant and pulling her backwards.

"*Snake!* There's snakes here. Get back to the van. Watch where you're walkin'." He was yelling as he pulled Joly along. She was fighting him and he knew she wanted to go back to the cat, but he didn't know where the snake was, or if there were more of them.

Joly pulled herself free and ran back to where Nefertiti lay. Duncan ran after her with his heart in his throat. Joly picked the cat up, and only then did she allow Duncan lead her back to the van where everyone was waiting inside. Duncan opened the door and they both got in.

Joly looked at Nefertiti and saw the light fading from her eyes. Her thoughts were fragmented with the horror of what just happened. She willed herself to concentrate, to open her senses and allow the healing power to enter her and flow into Nefertiti. The cat's eyes cleared for a moment and Joly heard her thoughts.

"It's alright, Mistress. I had to save you. Thank you for..." Her eyes dimmed again and the light slowly faded away. Joly couldn't feel a heartbeat and her tears fell as she opened her mind.

The healing light entered and filled her. She became one with the universe, she could hear her blood pumping through her veins, could hear the staccato beat of her heart as it raced with the fear of losing a loved one. She went deeper into herself and became aware of another sound. She concentrated on it. It was the baby's life force and the outer edges of her lips turned up.

Of the others, only Morag and Rauna were calm. Jesse, Rhiannon and Stephen were awestruck with the power they were seeing. The white light continued to surround Joly and she slowly disappeared in the ethereal mist.

Joly thought about all she and Nefertiti had been through together. She saw the cat sitting regally looking out the window of the small cabin; saw her looking like a fur ball as she hissed at the demon that had showed up there. She saw Nefertiti checking out the wards she had placed, Nefertiti horrified by Salem's calling her Neffy, Nefertiti trying to get her to her feet in the alley in London. She saw Nefertiti sitting proudly in the bay window of their home, Nefertiti laying in the yard soaking up the sun, Nefertiti's head as it continuously swung from side to side searching for evil. And in amongst all these pictures was the one she had seen only a short time ago, of seeing Nefertiti and the snake collide, hearing her scream and watching as she fell to the ground.

Her mind drifted as the power surged through her. She listened to her blood swooshing through her veins, her heartbeat, strong and steady; she heard the baby's heartbeat and something else. She went further into herself. There was another heartbeat, very faint. *Nefertiti? Come on sweetie, hang in there. We can do this.* She allowed herself to join with Nefertiti.

Duncan held her, and the white light glowed as it surrounded the two of them and Nefertiti. He spoke quietly to his Mother. "How long do we let her try?"

"I would suggest you don't move, Son. She's no longer there."

Stephen asked what she meant.

"She's left her body. You're looking at her shell."

"Are you serious?"

"Very.'

"So where is she?"

"I'm not sure, but possibly she's gone searching for Nefertiti's soul. She can't bring her back, so I really don't know what's happening there."

Rauna asked, "Would you like me to go and find her, fetch her back here?"

"No dear, she needs to do this her way."

Duncan spoke quietly. "We'll need a circle. Any ideas?"

Morag picked up her crystal. "I'll check."

She scryed the area. There was a beautiful and peaceful property nearby. It appeared deserted and there was a road of sorts going into the trees. She found an area that would suit their purposes.

"There's a place nearby. I'll guide you there when she returns."

"What about the snakes, Mother?"

"They won't be a problem. Joly had not shielded herself when she left the van. An almost fatal mistake on her part. It's a lesson I hope all of you have learned. Never ever set foot on strange land without protecting yourself."

Duncan laid his head on Joly's, careful not to move her and thought back to a time many years before, when she had lost a feline friend. She had been fourteen and Hebe had been with her since she was a toddler. The black shorthair had always been part of their lives and he too had cried when she developed an incurable cancer. Hebe had fought valiantly, refusing to give in to the disease for over two years. He knew now that it was Joly's healing powers that had kept her alive for so long. If Joly had known how powerful her powers were, she probably could have healed Hebe. When the time had come and Hebe asked Joly for release from the pain, she had screamed to the Gods about the unfairness of it. Their group had gathered, and in a circle they asked for understanding to be given to Joly. He was never too sure what message she had received, but she appeared to finally accept the reality of Hebe's death and although she had been quieter for several weeks, he had never seen her cry for the cat again.

She had shaved her eyebrows in accordance with the ancient Egyptian custom, which showed that a valued feline from the household had passed away. It had caused a bit of a stir at school, but within a week, half the girls had followed suit, thinking Joly was starting a new fad.

Joly concentrated on the faint, erratic heartbeat and visualized the healing energy going into the cat's blood stream, separating the light yellow toxins from the blood, and the flow of the poison reversing direction. She watched as it oozed back out of the two small puncture holes. She saw the wounds slowly close; the tissue inside whole again. She removed herself from Nefertiti's body and joined with her own. She listened to the heartbeat grow stronger and when she felt a small movement, she sent prayers of thanks to Diana, Goddess of all animals.

The white light slowly dissipated and the others watched as Joly lifted her head and stretched her neck. She looked down at the furry bundle in her arms. "Talk to me, Nefertiti."

The cat's eyes opened and Joly was rewarded with a small purr of thanks. Joly looked at Duncan. "She's going to be okay honey." She smiled and her entire face lit up.

Morag smiled. *Thank the Gods!* She had been concerned how Joly would handle the cat's death when she needed her total concentration for the evil at hand.

"Take us back to the hotel, Son. There has been enough excitement for today. Joly, may I ask where you went?"

"Nefertiti was hanging on by a thread. I went in to get the poison out."

Stephen backed the van out and they returned to the hotel. Morag knew Joly and Duncan would want to stay with Nefertiti so she gathered the others in her room. She decided to take advantage of the time to resume coaching the novices.

Stephen asked about the circle that had been mentioned, so Morag explained what they did when a beloved pet or familiar died.

"There are actually two different services. One is for a pet; one is for a familiar. Never make the mistake of mixing the two up. Every animal can be a pet, only a few are actually familiars."

"How do you know the difference?" Stephen was having a problem with the idea of plans to give Nefertiti a special send off. He thought she had gotten what she deserved after attacking Rhiannon.

Morag knew how he felt about Nefertiti, and hoped she could explain it so he would have kinder feelings toward the cat.

"Had we been walking down that road with a pet, Joly would quite likely be dead right now, for the simple reason a pet would not have jumped in front of her to save her. Animals do not purposely put themselves in danger, as their will to live is as strong in them, as it is in us. Granted, you do hear about the occasional dog or cat that saved their master from a burning home, but think about it. If you were an intelligent animal and you knew that you were going to die from smoke or flames, and you knew your master could open the door to let you out, what would you do? You go and wake the master to let you out. The master thinks you've saved his life, which you have, but only because you were trying to save your own." She paused and took a drink of water.

"A familiar is not a pet and should never be treated as one. A familiar is a witch with a fur coat. No, that's a fallacy. There are also feathered familiars like Crow, and reptilian skinned familiars. A familiar is a partner in the relationship and is treated as such. Familiars can have different powers and some have very strong powers. They're not really much different from us. Joly has some pretty strong powers. You two boys do not. Neither does Duncan."

"Why are her powers so strong?" Jesse had wanted to know the answer to that question since he'd watched her melting the steel locks.

"Jesse, you've been patient to this point with regards to things that you've seen and that you are probably aware you will never in a million years be able to do. Please bear with me and be patient for a while longer. It will all be explained to you soon."

Stephen's interest was aroused. "Did Nefertiti have special powers?"

"Yes, she did. She was capable of casting protection spells and for nine years she kept guard over Joly who was trying to recover from the loss of her parents and Duncan. She saved Joly's life in England and she continued to watch out for her ever since. Two months ago in Greece, Nefertiti and Joly's other two cats all helped to protect her. Pip ended up with an injured paw and Salem had his side slashed open by a sword that was being thrust straight at Joly."

Rhiannon gasped, "That's awful!"

"We were lucky. Joly still ended up with a broken arm and I had three broken ribs, but it goes with the territory. When you fight evil forces, you have to expect injuries occasionally. Isn't that right, Rauna?"

Rauna nodded.

Stephen looked thoughtful. "What you're saying, Mother, is that all of Joly's cats are familiars."

"Yes, they are."

"Why would she need three and others, like you, don't have any?"

"Joly was alone for nine years. I expect because of that, they found their way to her. You have to remember she was in pretty bad shape mentally for most of that time. I spent nine years in those prisons you put me in and they frowned on anyone talking to the birds, never mind having a pet or a familiar."

"Mother, they weren't prisons; they were very expensive..."

"They were *prisons*. It might have been different if I'd been able to go home once in a while, but I wasn't."

Stephen's face turned red and he said nothing.

Jesse asked, "She left her body and said she went to remove the poison. What am I missing here? Where did she go?"

"I would assume she went inside of Nefertiti. That's where the poison was."

Stephen looked up at the ceiling and shook his head.

"Having a problem believing that, are you?"

"Mother, I'm having problems believing a lot of things, but I'm also seeing things I've never seen before, so just give me some time."

Rhiannon asked, "The snake. Was it really a rattler?"

Morag nodded thoughtfully. She'd wondered if the thought had crossed anyone else's mind. "It's difficult to say. There are rattlers in this part of the world but ..." She left the rest unsaid. They would probably never know whether the evil had earmarked Joly as soon as she set foot on the property, or whether a fluke in nature caused the reptile to be where it was.

Polina struggled to move, at least she thought she was struggling, but she wasn't sure. She knew she was back in her body because she could see the trees, but she couldn't seem to move. She tried to turn over. She was still face up. *What the heck?* She closed her eyes and attempted to ground herself, but something was interfering. She could hear crackling in her head.

She heard something and opened her mouth to yell, but no sound came out, and she didn't think her facial muscles had moved.

Maybe I'm too weak; maybe I stayed too long with Griffin. She was getting scared. She decided to rest a bit and then try again.

She awoke with a start. It was dark. *Gods, I'm busted.* She turned over and... no, she hadn't turned over at all. She began crying. She thought she was crying, but she felt no tears on her cheeks.

She heard something. *What's that?*

Griffin? Is that you? She listened for a minute and giggled. Her spell was working. Griffin was coming; he was crossing over, being reborn.

Griffin, talk louder. I can't make out what you're saying. She listened again. It was definitely Griffin talking, but his words weren't clear.

Hurry up Grif. I've got to get home. Mom will be going crazy. She tried moving again, but had no more luck than before.

The crackling in her head popped and spit. It sounded like electrical wires when they short-circuited.

She listened through the noises. *Grif... are you coming?* Silence. *Griffin, are you still here? Griffin?*

This wasn't how she envisioned it. She'd thought he would just appear, solid and whole. She hadn't counted on a lengthy struggle.

What? Come to you? No, Griffin. You have to come to me.

She thought she felt cold, but she wasn't sure. Everything seemed so... Otherworldly. It was quite strange.

Otherworldly? Oh Gods, what have I done?

What had Sergei said? "Be careful what you wish for, Pol..."

She knew what had happened. She was caught in between the two worlds. Griffin wasn't coming to her. She was going to him... *forever!*

Nooo... I don't want to die. I'm only seventeen. Oh Gods, help me please. I've been so stupid. I screwed up. Please let me go home and I totally promise never to mess around with this stuff ever again.

The following morning they returned to the property. Morag ensured that everyone had shielded themselves before she allowed a door to be opened. Once again, they approached on foot, with Joly leading the way. Duncan walked beside her, her hand gripped tightly in his own. They had left Nefertiti at the hotel, something the cat had not been pleased about, but Joly was insistent.

The old manor house came into view and Joly stopped, her nostrils flaring with all the ancient fear and evil she was being bombarded with. She resumed walking slowly forward, and with every step she took, her mind screamed at her to turn around and get out of there. She didn't understand the feelings.

Rhiannon was squeezing Stephen's hand so tightly that it hurt, but he said nothing. He could feel the fear, and wondered again how he'd managed to get through so many years without knowing he had this ability. He suddenly remembered the previous All Hallow's Eve and how he'd sensed something wasn't quite right. *He had known!*

Joly reached the steps and Duncan tried them first, ensuring that they would hold their weight. Joly approached the door and stopped. *Gods, but she didn't want to do this!*

Morag had moved forward and now stood on the other side of Joly. She reached back for Rauna's hand, took Joly's hand and together they centered and grounded. Behind them, the other three also joined hands and did the same.

Joly reached forward, turned the knob and pushed. Complaining softly, the door swung open. Joly hesitated and then entered. As the fear assaulted her, she unconsciously ducked her head down, bringing her shoulders up.

Morag walked past her and circled the large entryway which had several doorways leading off it and a wide staircase ascending to the second floor.

She advanced through the high ceiling room, looking everywhere, missing nothing. She walked into the next room and the next. Joly followed her closely, her nostrils flaring. Duncan was one step behind Joly, with Rauna on his heels. Stephen and Rhiannon were behind them and Jesse brought up the rear.

"Do you hear it?" Morag asked.

All three women answered. "Yes." The haunting crying had started almost as soon as they entered the house.

Rhiannon gripped Stephen's hand. "It's children... they're so afraid."

Morag nodded as she approached the room with all the windows. She paused without entering.

Joly took the lead and slowly walked through the doorway. The evil overpowered her and she stopped to ground herself.

The others clustered around the door watching.

Joly circled the room one hesitant step at a time, the others watching her, unsure whether they should enter or not.

Morag entered the room and Joly held her hand up. "Stay away from the center." She continued her slow circle of the room, pausing every so often, a frown marring the smooth contours of her face.

"This is where it will return to. It hasn't been here recently, so it must come soon." She quickly subtracted the days left. "It has twenty-three days." She continued walking slowly; stopping at the corners, peering through the dirty glass, looking at the ceiling where the remnants of a light fixture hung. She examined the lace curtains which were smoke covered, and walked toward the back of what appeared to be an altar with the remains of two candles. She stood looking at it, scowling the whole time. She advanced closer to the center of the room and stopped again. She slowly allowed her senses to open and she staggered.

Duncan was beside her in an instant, holding onto her arm. Because she had not expected anyone to touch her, she had not encircled herself with protection. Duncan was assaulted with every vision she was seeing and feeling. He pulled his hand away and the visions disappeared. "*Shee-it!*" He shook his head. He did not envy his wife.

Jesse had gone to check out the second floor. He'd felt useless standing around doing nothing. He had managed to conquer the queasiness he'd been feeling from the overpowering fear that pervaded the whole building. He was slowly making his way up the stairs and had reached the landing. He paused and peered up into the gloom, trying to make out what was at the top of the stairs. He thought he saw movement and quickly blinked to clear his vision. That was when the bottom fell out of his world.

One second there was a solid wood beneath him, the next, there was nothing. Both feet went through at the same time. There was no warning, no ominous sounds of cracking wood, nothing. He dropped hard and automatically threw out his arms. As they connected with the surrounding floor, his descent was abruptly halted. The wind was knocked out of him and both arms were stinging from the force of the connection with the floorboards. He drew in a couple of deep breaths and moved one arm trying to get better leverage to push himself up. He heard the creak of the floor above him and looked up. *Damn!* He still couldn't make out anything. He squinted and quickly blinked. *What the hell?* He could have sworn that two red eyes were looking back at him. His heart was hammering and he quickly began lifting himself up out of the hole with the strength of his arms. He had inches to go to free his backside, when something reefed on his legs and pulled him back down.

Jesse screamed and the sound died as it left his mouth. He screamed again when there was another tug on his legs. He began kicking for all he was worth as he levered himself back up through the hole. His butt was clear. He threw himself to the side of the hole and rolled. He hit the top step and kept on rolling. As he thumped and crashed down the stairs, he was sure he heard laughter above him. When he hit the bottom, he lay still for a moment and then he was up on his feet and running out the front door. He finally stopped, gasping for breath some thirty feet from the house. When his breathing became more controlled, he turned and looked back at the house. His stomach was roiling again and he fought to maintain control. He glanced up to the second floor and saw a curtain dropping back into place. He retched.

Joly and the others checked out the entire ground floor. They came across a room in the back that different from the rest. As they filed through the doorway, everyone felt completely at peace.

Rauna attempted to enter, but was repelled by the wards that had somehow remained strong through the years. She understood that once one had been to the Abyss, innocence was lost, never to be regained. She knew she would always carry the echo of her time in that dark place. She stood outside the door and watched.

Joly turned from the window and the others were startled to see an ethereal glow surrounding her face.

"What do you see child?"

"It's incredible... the love in this room. I feel as though I could stay here forever. The love and the laughter... it's... it's so very beautiful."

"And the evil?"

"Bad word. Please don't say it here. Don't spoil perfection." Joly slowly circled the room, the rapture never leaving her face.

"We need to go, dear."

"In a while." Joly continued her slow walk around the room.

Morag reached over to Duncan and signaled him to bring Joly from the room.

He walked over to her and put his arm around her. "Come on, Darlin'."

"Do you feel it honey?"

He felt it. It *was* incredible. He understood why she didn't want to leave. He didn't either.

Morag saw the glow on her son's face and knew they were in trouble. She saw that Rhiannon was smiling, and her eyes glistened with happiness. She had built many shields throughout the years, but all had been to keep evil away from her. Could she build one to keep love out?

Stephen walked across the room, took his brother's arm and guided Duncan and Joly through the door. As soon as all three were through, he dropped his hand and bent over leaning his hands on his knees. He took several deep breaths and stood, shaking his head. "That was close. That room is really something!"

Morag put her arm around Rhiannon and led her out. They saw Joly and Duncan clinging to each other with tears streaming down their cheeks.

Duncan wiped his arm across his face and gave his Mother a lop-sided grin. "Man… that was some experience. Did you feel it, Maw?"

She nodded. "Yes, I did." She left it unsaid that she hadn't felt it as strongly as he and Joly had.

Rauna could feel the house being hugged, overwhelmed, and covered with black storm clouds of evil. She knew that whatever was outside was very, very bad, and she was not going to lose these women she had come to think of as family.

The air around Rauna began to shimmer. Iridescent waves of light undulated up and down her body. Rauna threw her arms out, stamped her feet and her body became opaque, it grew fainter until it was translucent. The crow on her shoulder spread his wings and wrapped them around Rauna's head like a black halo. The two appeared to melt into each other, becoming one.

Stephen's mouth dropped open and his eyes grew large. *Now what the hell's happening?* He felt Rhiannon's hand squeezing his and he gently released it to put his arm around her.

The light was playing tricks on the occupants of the room. Feathers appeared to emerge on Rauna's arms and fingers, and then she began to grow.

A shadow manifested itself and Rauna became two. The large feathered creature had the beak of an eagle and was darker than the night. It rose up toward the high ceiling of the room, still growing in size. The other part of the shadow separated from the winged beast and Rauna crumpled to the floor.

A wing tip brushed Joly's face, and she cringed as she watched the almost transparent creature disappearing through the high ceiling. She shook her head. "Rauna," she cried, as she headed toward the still body.

Morag was faster. She threw herself in between Joly and the figure lying on the floor. "No! Leave her; she's alright."

Morag rolled her eyes and looked at the ceiling. "Damn fool child!"

"What the hell was that?" Joly wrapped her arms around Duncan, as disbelief covered her face.

"Use your head, child. You know of astral travel."

"That... that... *thing* was no astral traveler!"

Morag shook her head. "Rauna is a Shaman. They have different powers than you or me. That *thing* was nothing more than a Thunderbird. Now, we need to get that girl back here, before she's hurt."

Stephen found his voice. "How do we do that?" He still had his arm tightly around Rhiannon and she eased herself out of his death grip to walk closer to Rauna.

"We need to call her back. She doesn't know what she's up against. She could quite possibly get lost in whatever dimension she's in. Let's gather around her, just be careful not to move her." Morag looked around. "Where's Jesse?"

No one had seen him leave.

"We'll go look for him." Joly and Duncan headed to the next room. "*Jesse?* Where the heck did he go? *Jesse?*" They called Jesse from each of the rooms as they passed through. When they got to the front door and looked outside there was still no sign of him.

"Honey, run to the van and see if he's there. I'll walk around back."

"Sure, Darlin'." Duncan jogged down the steps and loped across what once had been a lawn.

Joly walked around to the back of the huge house, she noted the out buildings, an over grown area that she could tell had at one time been a garden; there was a maze and what looked to have been a arbor. She was looking at something that wasn't there, but should have been. Something was out of kilter. What was wrong with what she was seeing? She heard a faint shout and turned back, retracing her path to the front.

Duncan spotted her. "Jesse's hurt. Come on!"

She ran. Duncan's legs were longer and he stayed ahead of her as he ran down the driveway.

Jesse sat on the ground, leaning against the van. His one eye was swollen shut and a dark red streak ran from the outer corner of his eye down through his cheek, ending just below his lips. His jeans were shredded down one leg and his T-shirt was marked with blood and grime.

"Gods, Jesse, what happened?" Joly tenderly touched the red mark on his face. It was a bruise. The skin wasn't broken. She held her hand to the mark and called forth her powers to heal.

Jesse's one good eye looked at her. He ran his tongue over his lips and tried to speak. Nothing happened.

"I need a bottle of water, please."

Duncan reached in the van and returned with one. She uncapped it and held it to Jesse's lips. He drank thirstily.

Joly moved her hand up to the swollen eye.

Jesse licked his lips and tried again. "The demon's there."

Joly quit concentrating. *"What?"*

"Yeah, I saw it. It tried to grab me."

Joly stared hard at him. His good eye stared back at her, unwavering in its directness. *It wasn't possible. One of them would have known if it had been there.* She pictured Rauna as she had last seen her. Had she also somehow sensed something the rest of them had missed? She resumed her healing and when she felt the skin under her fingers move, she lifted her hand.

Jesse blinked and both eyes opened. The swelling was almost gone.

"Where else are you hurt?"

"My leg. It feels like its broken, but it can't be."

"Why not?"

"I ran out of that place and both legs were working."

She ran her hand down his denim clad leg. She sensed the break in the fibula and held her hand against it.

"It is broken, Jesse. You'll have to take it easy for a couple of days, to make sure it's strong enough to take whatever punishment you give it next."

"How can it be broken? I was running on it."

"Adrenalin is an amazing thing. People do the impossible all the time when their adrenalin is running high. Do you feel up to telling us what happened?"

Jesse told them what he had seen and felt. He didn't know how his jeans had ripped, but he'd hit his face on the newel post at the bottom of the stairs. He told them about screaming and the sound dying as it left his mouth.

"We didn't hear anything." Joly looked at the front of his shirt. "Where did the blood come from?"

"My nose. It was bleeding and I used my shirt to wipe it."

She ran her finger over his nose. It wasn't broken. She sent the power to his leg for a few more minutes and asked him to stand.

He pushed himself to his feet and tried a token step. There was no pain. He grinned. "Wow! You do all kinds of things, don't you?"

Joly smiled gently at him. "Yes, I do. Do you hurt anywhere else?'

"No, not really. I'm a little stiff, but I'll work out the kinks."

She shook her head. "It's not necessary to have pain. Here, let me do a quick general on you."

"A quick general?"

"Sorry, I'm doing a quick general healing, meaning an all over healing, rather than concentrated in one place."

"Oh."

The three sat on the floor and softly chanted Rauna's name continually, doing it in a round robin, so that her name was always being said by one of them. There had been no sign of any change and the two novices wondered as they chanted, what would happen next.

The monstrous bird hit the floor with a loud thud, its legs straddling the still form of Rauna.

Rhiannon gasped and pushed herself backwards. The ten foot tall bird towered over the three sitting on the floor.

Stephen was dumbfounded. It was just too much to comprehend. Where had it just come from? He moved back, stood, and looked at the ceiling, but it was intact.

Morag pushed herself to her feet and walked around to face the bird's head. She could feel its confusion and when it finally focused on her, it was with a look of cold-blooded rage.

The light from the window played on the shiny feathers creating tiny rainbow fireworks. Morag saw her reflection in the birds jet black eye. The bird lay on top of Rauna and began to lose density.

Its tail brushed Rhiannon's face and she quickly jumped to her feet, moving back to stand beside Stephen.

Morag was reminded of someone removing one slide after another from a stack... the bird became diffuse and Rauna started to emerge. Finally, Rauna stood there in her own shape, still looking at Morag with the same ruthless fury in her golden eyes.

"So that was a demon," she said. "Hate them..."

Morag stepped forward and wrapped her arms around Rauna, sending calming energies to the angry young woman. Stephen and Rhiannon joined them for a group hug.

Then they made their way to the front door.

A few minutes later Joly was done. Jesse stretched and smiled at Duncan." It must be nice to have your own built-in healer around."

"Yeah, its okay, but I'd take Joly any way I could, even with no powers." He looked back at the mansion in the distance.

"I guess we better go and help Maw."

Joly nodded in agreement, but looked at Jesse. "Rauna's in trouble. We need to help her return from wherever she's gone to."

Jesse shook his head. "I'd just as soon wait here."

"Sure. We shouldn't be too long." Joly put her hand into Duncan's and they walked toward the house.

Jesse watched them walk away and knew he didn't want to be alone. He lit out after them, calling for them to wait. When he caught up to them, Joly surprised him by taking his hand in hers. She smiled at him and explained the little she knew about thunderbirds.

The calming energies she was sending to him had the needed effect. He felt his heartbeat slow, but he was still glad when he saw the others coming toward them.

The two groups met half way and they headed for the van and drove away from the place of evil. Instead of leaving with some of their questions answered, it seemed there were now even more questions.

Morag was deep in thought as to how the demon could have been there without their knowledge. She knew only the very powerful ones had the ability to cloak themselves in invisibility, but that wasn't normally their way. And if it had been the demon, it also meant that it was far more powerful than any she had dealt with before.

After lunch, they gathered in Morag's room to discuss the morning's events.

Rhiannon was subdued and Morag asked if she had anything she wanted to share. Rhiannon looked undecided; she opened her mouth and then closed it again. Stephen put his arm around her.

"What's wrong, Beautiful?"

Rhiannon chewed on the side of her mouth, frowning, as she studied the floor. Finally, she raised her head and looked at Morag. "Somethin' isn't right there. The big room was filled with evil, the back room was filled with love, but it was the other rooms that felt wrong."

"Wrong, how?"

"I'm not sure. There was just somethin' that wasn't right about them."

Joly told about having the same sense of wrongness as she stood at the back of the house. "It was like something was missing that should have been there."

Rhiannon nodded her head vigorously. "Yes! That's it. The other rooms... somethin' was missing."

Morag delved into her memory banks and retraced her steps through each of the rooms. She found nothing unusual. "Joly, what did you see as you circled the front room?"

"Images of different things, people, furniture, I sensed fragmented thoughts and voices that weren't really clear. The room is filled with memories of fear, harsh words and hatred."

"And in the center?"

"There was a circle, a rooster was sacrificed, there were thirteen people, and the leader sicced the demon on his followers. It was horrible. The demon got them all except for one and the leader killed him."

"Hmm… it sounds like he didn't want to leave any witnesses. He too, will have to be dealt with. I'm wondering if he should be our next priority. As long as he's on the loose, he can command the two remaining demons to do his bidding.

Tell me about the happy room."

Joly smiled, the feeling of well being surging through her as she thought about it. "Gods, it was just so incredible. There was a woman and several children, all girls of varying ages. There were images of sewing, doing crafts, drawing and painting, playing games. It was… I can't express it… the love… the love was so intense, like there was nothing else, just them and the room.

I know there are happy homes with good feelings, but this wasn't like that. I don't know what else to say about it… other than it was like a magical space where unhappiness wasn't allowed in."

"So there were no unhappy thoughts at all?"

"None."

Morag nodded. That answered that question. It was definitely a magical room. The woman would have been a sorceress, a powerful one at that, if she could block out all negativity. She wondered about the rest of the house. What had happened that this woman felt the need to shield one room from the rest? "The children, were they the woman's?"

"I believe so."

"Rauna dear, what did you see in the veil you traveled to?"

"A demon. I tried to kill it, but it disappeared after I hurt it. I had my talons dug deep into it and it screamed a hideous scream. Then it just vanished. I don't know where it went. I could go back and search for it."

"Rauna, Rauna, Rauna. *No*, you will *not* go and search for it. You will *not* face it down in another veil. What you did was very foolish and you are damned lucky to have returned unharmed."

"But I am a Shaman. I can do this."

"You forget child, I studied under your Father. You cannot defeat a demon in its own territory. I do know what I'm talking about. It would be nice if we could, then someone could go and get rid of them all and we would never have to worry about them ever again.

I would like to go back tomorrow. There are a couple of things I'd like to try and I'd like to check the property itself."

Joly listened as Duncan sang in the shower. A smile creased the outer edges of her eyes. She laid her hand on her belly. She was homesick. She wanted to see Randy. They had been gone ten days and it felt like a month. She absentmindedly stroked Nefertiti. Her thoughts turned to the problem at hand. An invisible demon, children crying, people in danger, the list went on.

Duncan came out of the bathroom naked as usual. He sat on the edge of the bed. "A dollar for your thoughts pretty lady."

She smiled. "I don't think they're worth a dollar, but I was just thinking about the demon and all the crap that seems to be surrounding it. I can't figure out why Rhiannon and I are both seeing something missing."

"Well, Darlin', you'll figure it out. I tell you though; I'm not lookin' forward to goin' back there, 'specially after what happened to Jess. I'm thinkin' we should all stick together from here on in, but it'll take three times as long to check everythin' out."

"I think as long as we're outside, it'll be okay. I wouldn't want to split up inside though. I wonder if it really was the demon. I should have been able to sense the essence of it, even if I couldn't sense it."

"A poltergeist maybe?"

"No… I don't think so. Maybe a wrath poltergeist. Gods knows, the house probably has several of them, by the feel of it."

"Hmm. I suppose, but what about the red eyes?"

"Maybe Jesse imagined the red eyes. He was terrified. The mind plays tricks when you're not thinking straight."

"True, but Jess is a pretty level headed guy. I don't see him as the type to freak out over imagined thoughts."

"I don't know honey. I think we figured we would come away from there with some answers, but all we seem to have is more questions."

"Ain't that the truth." He pulled the covers off Joly, covering Nefertiti. She bobbed her head as she tunneled her way out. Duncan grinned.

"Go have your shower, Darlin'. Time's a wastin'."

Rhiannon was pacing and it was driving Stephen crazy. "Come and sit down. I can't think when you're walking back and forth."

"Stevie, I can't. There's somethin' I should know, but I can't figure it out. Gods, what's wrong with me?"

"There's nothing wrong with you. You're beautiful, and I love you." He stood and took her in his arms. He tilted her head up and kissed her. She was still for a moment and then she reached forward and returned it.

25. Kiss of Death

Jesse sat on the bed across from Morag. "Thank you, my Lady, for letting me spend the night here."

She smiled. "No problem, Jesse. I'm glad you were able to get some sleep. How do you feel about going back there today?"

"I think I'm all right with it, as long as I keep someone else in my sight."

"Good." She picked up the phone as Rauna came out of the washroom. She called the other two rooms to see if they were ready to go.

Jesse hadn't been able to stay alone in his room and he felt dumb about it, but he'd needed human companionship, and the crone hadn't appeared unduly surprised. He sensed Rauna also had fears that needed human contact.

He had lain for what seemed like hours listening to the gentle breathing, soft snoring and other sounds from the other bed. He didn't know what time he'd fallen asleep, but he'd slept like a rock, and he felt good this morning.

Back at the property, they fanned out at the end of the driveway. No one was too sure what they were looking for, but Morag told them they would know it if they happened upon it. She had decided there was safety in numbers. Joly and Duncan had gone to the right. Rhiannon and Stephen had gone to the left. Morag, Rauna and Jesse walked to the house and went along side of it and around to the back. She wanted to see if she would pick up on what Joly had sensed. At the rear of the house, they began exploring. They wandered through the overgrown garden; they walked around the half dead maze. Jesse wanted to walk through it, but Morag said no.

"With half of it dead, it looks like it would be easy to find your way back out, but I have a feeling that's not the case." She also sensed that there were untold horrors to be found in its center.

They checked the arbor, all signs of any rose bushes long gone with the passage of time. They walked to the out buildings. The barn roof had caved in, along with one side of the barn. Jesse stuck his head through a window opening on the side that still stood, but could see nothing. There was an evil feel to the place and in his minds eye, he saw a whip being used on some-one's back. He shuddered and returned to Morag's side.

They toured what appeared to be the milk house, the outside kitchen and laundry room, the carriage barn, smoke house and another building that Morag wasn't sure about. She noticed Rauna had returned to the maze. She stood and watched, but Rauna made no move to enter it.

Farther along were two smaller buildings, both half burnt. As they approached, Morag reached out and took Jesse's arm. He stopped.

"What is it, my Lady?"

"Let's turn around. We will learn nothing there."

"What were they?"

"Slave cabins." She began walking back toward the main house.

"Rauna, come on dear, I think we're done here."

"Did you see what Joly saw?"

"No, I didn't."

They walked back to the front where the others were waiting. Duncan and Stephen were sitting on the steps talking; while Joly and Rhiannon stood back, looking up at the second floor.

Morag spoke sharper than she intended. "Don't even *think* about going up to the second floor!"

"We weren't. Jesse said he saw a curtain moving. We were trying to see if any of the windows were broken, but they all seem to be intact."

Placated, Morag said, "I'm getting hungry, but it's up to you. Do you want to have another look inside or not?" She noticed Rauna was looking back to the side of the house.

Jesse shook his head as he took several steps toward the road and van.

Duncan looked at Joly and grinned. "What say you, Darlin'?"

"I don't know. What will have changed since yesterday?"

"You won't find that out unless you go in."

"Yes, alright. If everything is the same, we won't need to check back, except for when the time comes to…" Her voice faded, but everyone knew what had been left unsaid.

They grounded and shielded themselves and entered. Joly and Morag circled each room as they came to them.

Morag came to a stop in the third room. "I know what's missing here."

Joly and Rhiannon responded in unison. "What?"

"There's no recent past. Every sense, every memory is from months past."

"Maybe no one's been in here for that long."

"The thirteen from last Samhain. They had to have come through here, but this room has no memory of them." She walked back through the previous two rooms.

"These rooms don't either." She walked toward the room off to the left, confirming that each room had no memory of the ones' who had released the evil. "In fact, these rooms have no memory of us being here yesterday and now I think about it, there was nothing at the back that said Joly was there."

"What? That's impossible!" Jesse didn't understand Morag's powers, but he knew she told the truth.

Back in the sunroom, Joly allowed her senses to open, and she saw all that had taken place on the thirty-first of October, the year before. She smelled the same smells the participants had, she felt the fear of the twelve, felt the gloating victory of the leader and saw the demon come to life in the circle.

Her stomach rebelled and she threw up where she stood. Duncan went to her side, but he made sure she was back to normal, before he touched her.

"Come on, Darlin', enough is enough. Let's go." He led her out the door and Rauna followed.

Morag had one more thing she wanted to check and that was the stairs where Jesse had fallen through. She stood at bottom of the staircase, looking up. It was strange. The staircase was open; there should have been enough light to see all the way up, but the upper half of the stairs was in deep shadow. She wanted to see the landing, but she wasn't about to take any unnecessary chances. She shielded herself in a protective bubble, and cautiously began the ascent.

The others could see that her feet were barely touching the steps; she almost appeared to be floating up the stairs. As her eyes reached the landing, she suddenly somersaulted in mid air, and hung upside down, her eyes now facing those below. There was no movement from her except for her eyes, which were flashing in every direction.

"*What the hell?*" Stephen took several steps before Rhiannon grabbed his arm and stopped him.

"*No, Stevie!* Go get Joly. Somethin's wrong."

It wasn't until Stephen left that Rhiannon realized her mistake. She and Jesse were now alone in the building. She took a step backwards and screamed as something touched her arm.

Jesse let out a nervous laugh. "Sorry, I didn't mean to scare you."

Movement from above caught their eyes. Morag was spinning slowly, head over heels, each completed cycle a little faster than the one before.

Jesse headed for the stairs and quickly ran up them, waiting for the unknown. *What the ...?* He was running, but Morag was no closer to him than when he started. He looked at his feet. They appeared to be climbing. He looked up at Morag. She was still no closer.

From the floor, Rhiannon couldn't believe her eyes. Jesse was running full out and not going anywhere. He looked like he was pedaling an invisible bicycle. She went to the bottom of the stairs and held on to the newel post.

"Jesse, talk to me, please."

He didn't appear to hear her.

She went to reach up to touch him and discovered her hand refused to part with the wood. She tried to move the other one, but it too, was stuck fast. *"Jesse!"* She was terrified. He still looked up the stairs.

"Stevie! Oh Gods, where is everyone?" She started to cry.

Joly and Duncan wandered to the back of the house. Rauna felt drawn to the maze, so she followed them. She wasn't sure why, but she found herself at the entrance peering in. She saw no harm in going in a little way. She took two steps inside and discovered a different world. The wind vanished and the light was different, harsher somehow. The dead shrubs of a second before appeared whole and healthy. *Weird!*

She stepped back out and found the worn garden, dead bushes and the light breeze. She looked around, but Joly and Duncan had disappeared. She stepped back inside.

"All turns right and I cannot go wrong." She thought of Ariadne, Theseus and Minotaur and laughed. "I can always send Crow up if I lose my way."

As she moved forward through the walls of yews, she heard something. She stopped and listened. There were murmurings, whining and soft sobbing. She continued on and the sounds grew louder.

She stopped and closed her eyes. "Oh... that one..." She remembered some of the demons in the Abyss. They had made her feel things that had never happened; remember things that had not happened to her. And when she walked in the Abyss and heard the sounds of abuse, she remembered someone else's memories.

She remembered and felt what had happened in the maze. "Oh, wickedness..." She stood there until she got the feelings and memories manageable, and then continued deeper into the maze. The voices grew stronger as she approached the center, and the whispers were continuous in her ears. At the center, the feelings surrounded her, the voices, the crying, the fear overwhelmed her, and she felt like she was back in the Abyss. She threw her hands over her ears and screamed, *"Stop that! Stop that now!"* But it didn't stop.

Outside, Stephen hadn't seen anyone, so he had ran back to the van. They weren't there. He yelled their names, but heard no response. He ran back to the house and around the side to the back. He saw no one. He shouted their names again. He thought he heard a muffled reply, and ran toward the out-buildings, calling them every few seconds.

He heard a faint shout and veered off to a smaller building. He ran through the door and almost fell over Joly who was on her knees hanging on to one of Duncan's arms. He had fallen through the floorboards. All that was visible was his head, shoulders and arms.

Joly's breath came in ragged gasps. "It's the water cistern. We don't know how deep it is."

Stephen leaned over and grabbed Duncan's other arm. He looked at Joly. "On three... one, two, three."

They pulled, and slowly Duncan came up through the jagged, rotten wood. They backed up and kept pulling until he was clear of the hole, and they dragged him out of the building.

Duncan lay on the ground and wiped the perspiration from his face. "Thanks, Bro'. I was getting' a little worried there."

"Why the hell would you walk on rotten boards to start with? *Shit!*"

"Hey, bro', I didn't. I was standin' in the door lookin' in and all of a sudden someone pushed me."

Stephen's head whipped around to look at Joly.

"Don't even go there, Bro'! She was over at one of the other buildings." He pushed himself to his feet.

Stephen stared at Duncan, wondering what was going on. He remembered why he had gone looking for them. "*Mother!* She's in trouble." He turned and ran back to the house, the other two following close behind. They ran into the foyer. No one was there. Stephen panicked.

"Mother! *Mom!*" He looked wildly about. "Rhiannon? *Rhiannon!*"

Joly put her hands on his arms. "Stephen, you need to relax." She sent her energies into him and felt him calming.

"Center and ground, Stephen."

"There isn't time. Everyone's missing. You didn't see what happened to Mom." His voice broke and his shoulders shook.

"Listen to me. You can't help anyone if you don't have it together. Now, center and ground. I'll help you." She held on to Stephen's hands. She was conscious of Duncan heading into another room.

"No Duncan! Don't separate. Stay here." He appeared not to hear her. She hung on to Stephen and dragged him behind her as she rushed after Duncan, who had disappeared around the corner.

"*No honey-y-y!*" She ran around the corner and crashed into him. Her abrupt stop caused Stephen to slam into her.

Duncan turned and looked blankly at her, and as she watched, his beautiful blue eyes turned red.

Joly was too angry to be afraid. "Get out of there *now*, you bastard!" She could feel the heat rising inside of her and she knew she had to gain control.

"Stephen, no matter what happens, do *not* let go of me!" She slapped his hands around her waist.

Duncan's face grimaced and laughed. It was his laugh, but it wasn't. It was a malevolent laugh that went on and on.

Joly pictured roots growing from her feet and she sent them to the center of the earth, where she spread them out. Then she absorbed the pure energy and brought it up through her body until it overflowed from the top of her head and spilled back on the ground below the floor, returning to Mother Earth. She envisioned Father Sun high in the sky and asked for the healing light. She pictured it like a laser, descending from the sun and shooting into her crown chakra. She felt it filling her body and she knew Stephen would be feeling the power. She had to go slowly.

Duncan's mouth finally quit laughing. It opened again in a parody of a smile. "Well, *Darlin'*, feel up to some wild sex? How about you, *Bro'?*" The face inched closer to Stephen and its fetid breath exhaled in Joly's face. She gagged and swallowed.

"*Bro'!* I'm talkin' to you. Let's have a wild orgy with this wife of mine. Me first, and you can watch and learn a thing or two, then you. And then we can both have a go at her, what do you think?" The obscene laughter echoed through the room and Duncan's arm raised up to slap Stephen's shoulder. The smell of scorched cotton wafted on the air, as the vulgar mouth continued on with what it was going to do to Joly's body.

Joly grabbed Duncan's hands and as she did, she slowly opened her mind and allowed the healing energies to flow into both Stephen and Duncan.

As soon as the energy touched Duncan's hands, steam rose from them. His face twisted into grotesque rubbery mask-like shapes, his mouth opened in a silent scream. Giant pustules erupted on his face.

Joly continued opening her mind and the steam grew thicker. It emanated from all of Duncan's body and clothes. Duncan's face began to melt, the pustules oozing black slime, his skin and the slime dripping onto the front of his shirt. Joly could feel the skin on his hands oozing and she knew what the demon was trying to do. If the connection were broken by her holding on to skin that was no longer attached, then it would win. She released one hand and grabbed Duncan around the waist and then she released the other hand. She held onto Duncan tightly, as she continued to open her mind.

The demon tried to remove Joly's hands, but she was having none of it. It pushed against her shoulders, but she didn't budge.

The white light filled her and the excess began flowing outwards. It surrounded them and still she hung on. Her pure, healing powers were flowing into Duncan's shell. She could hear his skin sizzling like bacon in a hot frying pan, she felt the humidity from the steam, and she could feel pieces of skin and flesh dropping on her. The air grew fetid, smelling like a backed up sewer, and mixed in with those smells was the scent of barbecued flesh. He grew thinner as his flesh melted away and she felt the bones of his ribcage.

With all the love she had for him concentrated in her eyes and her voice, she whispered, "I love you honey." With her heart and her soul exuding unending love, she reached up to kiss the melted skin and slime draped teeth. The sizzle sounded like cold water drops hitting a hot burner and the steam billowed out around his face. His hands waved aimlessly through the air.

The scream was unearthly. It reverberated through the room, echoing and bouncing back. The room shook with the menacing, unleashed power of evil.

Joly felt Stephen's grip lessening. "No, Stephen, don't let go."

She held on to Duncan and sent him her love with every breath she took.

The scream ended abruptly; the silence overwhelming. Joly was left in a void where there was only the calming, white light.

Veronika lit the white candle and prayed. "Goddess, hear me, hear my prayer. Please help to heal my Polina and make her whole again. We must go soon to help Gaia and rid her of the evil that has been summoned. We are the *Sisters of the Triple Moon* and she is one of us."

"*Babushka?*"

She turned from the altar and smiled at Sergei. "Yes?"

"I'm sorry; I didn't mean to interrupt you."

"It's alright. What is it?"

"I talked to Lyn. She said Pol had a boyfriend, Griffin, but nobody's ever seen him. She thought maybe the internet. I hacked her computer. There's nothing there except a couple of poems." He handed Veronika two pieces of paper. She read them, her eyes returning to one line.

"*I come to you on the wings of a dream.* Sergei, you smell the Otherworld on her, as do I. Would she go and meet somebody there?"

"No *Babushka*, she's not that stupid." He took the paper and reread it. Shaking his head, he looked at his Grandmother. "I'll check, okay?"

"Da... I think you better." She looked in the room. Polina lay curled up in a fetal position, her eyes open, but unseeing. *Now it makes sense.*

"If that is what she did, then she is caught. You go and make sure. I will prepare. If I have to break the thread that is holding her... it is dangerous. We could lose her. I must make sure everything is just so."

Gradually, Joly's hearing returned as she continued hugging the shell that had been her husband. For the longest time nothing happened, and then ever so slowly she could feel Duncan's body filling out and solidifying. The steam quit billowing, the putrid odors lessened and vanished, and soon two arms wrapped themselves around Joly.

"Gods, but I love you, Darlin'." He kissed the top of her head.

She reached up and kissed him. "I love you, too."

She let go of him and pointed her hands to the floor. She released the excess energy and realized Stephen was still clutched on to her. She removed his hands from her waist. "It's all right now. It's gone, Stephen. You need to release the energy." He said nothing as she showed him how.

They walked outside. Joly stopped Stephen and laid her hand on his shoulder over the brown imprint left from the demon's hand. She sent her healing energies to the second degree burns that lay under the pale blue shirt, and then they headed to the van where Morag, Rhiannon and Jesse waited.

When Rhiannon saw Stephen, she flew out of the door and into his arms. He held her tightly, tears streaming down his cheeks. He looked at his mother and finally spoke.

"You all right, Mom?"

She smiled. "Yes, Son, I'm all right." She looked back at the house.

"We need to get Rauna. I'm pretty sure she went into the maze. Let me have a look." She reached for her crystal.

The crystal took her to the center of the maze where Rauna was circling and twirling around, her fists punching thin air. Her mouth was open in a silent unending scream and suddenly she wrapped her arms around a shrub and appeared to be trying to pull it out of the ground.

"We need to get her fast. She's in trouble."

They ran to the back of the house. At the entrance to the labyrinth, they listened, but there was no sound.

"Let's pray it's not an island maze. Keep one hand on the right wall at all times. Let's try staying about ten feet apart and see where it puts us."

Joly led the way. Ten minutes later, there was still silence. They took turns calling Rauna, but got no response. Another ten minutes and there was still nothing and no sign of the center. They had hit several dead ends and had to retrace their steps.

Morag suggested they go back to the entrance. It wasn't until they were standing by the opening that they noticed Rhiannon was crying. Stephen held her tightly, murmuring to her as he tried to calm her.

"Rhiannon dear, what did you hear?"

She sobbed and sniffled. "The children… oh Gods, Morag… the poor little girls." She burst into tears again.

Morag knew there was no time to lose. "Rhiannon, pull it together please. You need to go in and get Rauna. It's the only way."

"Me?"

"Space travel dear. You can do it. The center is clear. You might slam into Rauna on arrival, but better that than leaving her there."

"I need me crystal. I don't 'ave it wiv me."

Stephen hugged her and kissed her temple. He knew she was rattled.

"I think we both know you don't really need your crystal to travel. Time is of the essence. You must go *now*."

"Yes… alright." She grounded and when she felt calm, she visualized the maze with a clear center. Nothing happened. She could feel the panic starting and she willed it away. She held her hands in front of her, cupped as though her crystal was in between them. She visualized the crystal and softly said, "Take me to the center of the maze." She pictured the maze and felt the soft buzzing. She was conscious of a split-second of movement and she slammed into something solid.

The scream was deafening. She turned and saw Rauna reefing on a yew, trying to bodily rip it out of the earth. The crow was clutched on to her shoulder, barely able to maintain a grip.

Rhiannon threw herself on the older woman, wrapped her arms around her, and pictured Stephen waiting for her. "Take me to my man." The screams drowned out her voice, but the universe heard her plea. The buzzing sounded in her head and Rauna suddenly stilled.

Seconds later, they stood with the others. Joly went to Rauna.

Morag signaled for a circle to be made around them and they held hands, as they sent their love to the desperate woman in Joly's arms.

Joly wrapped her arms around the terrified woman and sent her calming, healing energies to Rauna. The fear was overwhelming, and Joly allowed the white light to spill over and encircle the two of them.

She felt the quivering cease, the fear lessened and Rauna grew calm. She wriggled in Joly's arms and she released her friend. She smiled at Rauna, as she shook the excess energy to the ground. "You okay now?"

"Yes… thank you."

They walked back to the van.

On the way to the hotel, the two groups updated each other with what had happened. Morag told the tale of what had transpired on the stairs.

"It seems Jesse used to play with psi balls…"

"I hate to interrupt, but what's a psi ball?" Stephen asked.

"It's a ball of energy. You concentrate and focus on gathering the energy, usually between your hands and you form it into a ball. Anyhow, Jesse got very good with doing it. He could throw them; he could build them with his mind and he got so he was able to have several built at the same time; a very unusual ability. While he was climbing and going nowhere, he knew he had to do something, so he built psi balls and threw them around the room. Some of them were so concentrated I could see them. I'm not sure how many there were, but I could hear them whizzing by me. It must have gotten to be too much for the entity to keep avoiding them, and keep us under its power too. We were all quite suddenly released. I dropped to the steps, Jesse ran up them and Rhiannon was right behind him."

When the entity released them, she suggested they head back to the van to wait for the other three. She knew Jesse and Rhiannon would feel more secure in familiar surroundings, even though the truth of the matter was that there was nowhere on that Gods forsaken property that was safe. She watched the other three in the crystal while they waited. Morag knew she had never prayed so hard in her life. When she saw Duncan become possessed, she had almost cried out, but she hadn't wanted to frighten Rhiannon and Jesse any more than they already were. She had bit her tongue so hard it still hurt. She watched as *it* taunted Joly and Stephen, and she had wondered if she was destined to lose both her sons, as well as Joly.

She knew Joly's powers were mighty, but she had not thought they were so strong as to defeat a demon with healing and love. She shook her head again thinking about it. She'd never heard of such a thing being possible. *Gods, but theirs was a powerful love!* She pictured the melted, oozing flesh and wondered if it had been Brody standing there; could she have done what

Joly did, and kissed it? Not only kissed it, but kissed it with passion. She truly didn't think so.

She thought about the snake. Had it been the entity? They had seen no sign of snakes on the property since. Assuming it was, that meant one attempt on Joly's life; one on Duncan's plus the possession; one on Jesse's plus the stair pedaling, and it had simply played with Rhiannon and herself. It had trapped Rauna in the maze and Stephen had been left alone. Was there a reason behind the specific attacks? She didn't need to keep rehashing the events, but again, there were more questions than answers.

Her thoughts turned to Rhiannon. She was a Sister, but other than the space travel and sensitivity to voices from veils other than theirs, she had shown no signs of any other powers. She knew she was going to have to spend more time with her. They needed to know what her power was. She decided she would devote two hours a day to Jesse, Stephen and Rauna; the rest of the time would be Rhiannon's. She thought about the bananas she consumed, and knew that somehow they had something to do with the unknown power. She had been unable to figure out what.

The time had also come to tell Jesse and Stephen about the *Sisters of the Triple Moon*. She'd been putting it off, but too much had happened. Too many questions were going to be asked.

Jesse called Sara. He needed to hear her voice. Only when she answered the phone, did he quit quivering inside. He hadn't thought the psi balls would do anything. He'd just needed something to keep his mind occupied while his legs had kept pumping and going nowhere. Two episodes on stairs in two days. He knew it would be awhile before he'd go near any stairs again.

He wished he'd been there to see the possession. It couldn't have been as bad as they made it out to be. They went overboard when they made movies and he'd seen them all. Melting flesh, steam rising, sizzling... maybe they had been hypnotized or something.

Morag lie down with Rauna and cuddled her close. *Gods, this poor child.* She had always had a problem with Shamanism, and she now saw why. To be ruled solely by the element of air was so restricting, so overpowering. To always have one foot in the Otherworld and the other foot on earth's plane had to be a terrible way to live. To define what was happening in the real world must take continual concentration. Rauna appeared well adjusted to the life she lived, and Morag knew that it was in part thanks to her Father that this was so.

When one was ruled by air, situations that arose required rationality. No wonder Rauna had so much trouble understanding demons. There was nothing rational about the entities from Tartarus.

She idly wondered why a Shaman would be picked as a Sister. There appeared to be no logical reason that she could see. She looked toward the ceiling of the room and smiled. *Sorry my Goddess, I don't mean to question you.*

Rauna enjoyed being held by Morag. It gave her a measure of comfort against the dark shadows that seemed to be everywhere.

She thought about the *Sisters of the Triple Moon* and wondered again how she could be one of them.

She had made several trips to the Otherworld hoping for enlightenment, but all she had found was the typical indifferent attitude of the Otherworld when it came to *High Magick*. It just wasn't the shamanic way, so the Otherworld wasn't interested.

Her spirit guide had come with cryptic messages that made it all even more incomprehensible and basically told her only what she already knew, that it was her decision whether she joined the Sisters or not. It would not go against her work as a witch, just push it to another level, and she knew if the Sisters wanted her to be with them, she was "good enough."

She thought about Morag and Joly and knew they welcomed her as one of them. That she had no special powers didn't appear to bother them. Veronika had also accepted her without question. These women were so incredibly amazing and she felt blessed to know them.

The paths of Goddess were mysterious indeed, and often it was impossible to see what was behind the next corner. There was a reason why she was led into these events and to meet these people, and it was not her place to question it. When it was time, she'd know. But all this was so strange to her, that she felt lost... and she never felt lost.

Rhiannon held Stephen, her fingers combing through his short red hair. His head lay on her chest, his ear against her heart. Its steady rhythmic beating giving him some semblance of peace. He thought about his orderly, normal life of ten days prior and wondered just how he had come to be where he was. The question was a moot one. The red eyes once again forced themselves into his mind and he shuddered. He felt the calming circles being rubbed on his back. He'd heard of possession, had seen the movie The Exorcist, but hadn't believed any of it. *Well, I'm certainly a believer now.* He decided Joly was made of steel, not flesh and blood. No mortal human could possibly have done what she did. Maybe she was an alien. That made as much sense as anything else he'd seen the past few days.

Rhiannon knew that as long as this man depended on her, she would be there for him. She had not wanted to fight demons, but it seemed that she was destined to, whether she wanted it or not. She had seen the possessed dogs and she never wanted to see anything like that ever again. She was thankful she hadn't been there, when Duncan was taken over. She still didn't understand what had happened on the stairs. Morag had said they'd discuss it later. She was looking forward to it. She felt so backwards compared to the others and she welcomed understanding, even when it was about something she'd just as soon not know.

Duncan was asleep in Joly's arms. She had seen to it, so he would have a brief respite from the horrors of the day. As she lay there thinking about what had happened, a sudden vision replaced everything in her mind.

She and Duncan were at home and it was summer time. Randy was rolling a ball to a giggling, dark haired little girl. Her chubby fingers grabbed at the ball, missed, tried again and were successful. Laughing, she rolled the ball back to Randy and then she clapped her tiny hands together.

The vision rolled away and Joly smiled. They were going to have a girl. Duncan was getting his wish. She looked exactly like Joly had at the age of two. She touched her hand to her tummy. *I love you, wee Magi McEwan.* She thought about the date. The moon was full. *Thank you Goddess.* She mentally computed the days and discovered Magi would be born in June, the month of the Strawberry Moon.

That afternoon they gathered to go over what had taken place in the morning. Morag ran through the time line. The demon or whatever it was; she was still puzzled about the invisibility thing, had first played with the three of them on the stairs, then when it was chased away with the psi balls, it had coaxed Rauna into the maze, then pushed Duncan onto the rotten boards of the cistern. When that failed also, apparently it got angry, and that's when it took over Duncan's body. She frowned.

"Just so you know. This is not normal demonic behavior. First off, demons like to be visible. They also are not known for their sense of humor."

"*Humor!* There was nothing humorous about what took place today." Jesse sounded angry.

"Maybe not to you and me, but think about it. Had you been watching it on television, you probably would have laughed to see a woman whipping around in mid air, a man pumping his legs like crazy on the stairs but going nowhere and another woman trying to get to them, but glued fast to a post. No, it wasn't funny at the time, but trust me when I say it was playing with us, because that's exactly what it was doing."

Stephen asked, "It's gone now, right? It won't be back?"

"Yes, it's gone, thanks to Joly. That particular entity won't be back, but that's not to say there's nothing else hanging around. We've had some pretty weird things happening, so we need to stay vigilant."

"You're saying that entity wasn't the one we came to banish?"

"No, it wasn't. I will know that fiend when I see it. Where this one came from, I have no idea. Perhaps it just wandered in and liked the feeling of evil that surrounds the place. Maybe it didn't like being disturbed. We'll never know."

26. Sisters of the Triple Moon

The following morning, Morag and Rhiannon had an intense session. Morag needed to know what Rhiannon's main power was. She grilled her about her entire life, her dreams, her accidents, her toys, birthdays, pets, school, and her parents. Morag asked about the unknown father. Rhiannon knew nothing about him other than she thought his name was Willie. By mid afternoon, Morag was exhausted and had accomplished nothing. She had grilled Rhiannon on what happened when she was angry, sad, happy, distraught, and content. Rhiannon swore there was nothing she hadn't thought of and that there *was* no unknown power.

Morag asked her about her craving for bananas.

"I… don't know. Every time I 'ear the word demon or fink about it, I 'ave to 'ave a banana. It's so dumb."

"No, it's not dumb. Your body is preparing for something. You feel no changes within you?"

Rhiannon shook her head. "No, nothin'."

At three, Stephen and Jesse arrived at Morag's room. They were surprised to find Joly and Duncan there as well. Morag was chewing on her lower lip as she stared at her feet, while she waited for everyone to get settled.

She looked up, her gaze going first to Jesse and then Stephen. "I'm going to explain to you two boys about something which I am sure you're curious about. You've both seen Joly in action and at different times you've questioned how she can do the things she does. First of all, Joly is not the only one with what you might call extra-ordinary powers. Rhiannon is also a part of this rather exclusive membership, as are Rauna and myself. Unfortunately, we're still trying to figure out what Rhiannon's powers are. So… where do these powers come from and why are they limited to a chosen few?"

Morag glanced at her feet again. There was nothing wrong with telling the other members of their group about the Sisters. Her problem lay in the timing. New information tended to stay at the forefront of a person's mind and she was concerned that one or both of the boys would be more inclined to watch what the women were doing, instead of paying attention to what they were supposed to be doing. A dangerous concept when one put it in the same sentence as fighting the ultimate evil.

"In the days of the Titans, there was an oracle... a prophecy that the Gods themselves would not be able to destroy the Titans, but that with the help of a mortal, the Titans would indeed be destroyed.

Gaia, concerned that this might happen did two things. First, she decided to ensure that the memories and some of the Titans powers would always be available to ensure the continuity of Mother Earth. As Gaia and Mother Earth are one and the same, she was ensuring her own survival, but it does work to the benefit of us mortals." She smiled. "She entrusted these memories and powers to her Granddaughter Selene, our moon. When something happens that will cause a shift in the balance of Mother Earth, Selene brings forth the *Sisters of the Triple Moon* to keep the balance in check. Selene picks the carriers of the future *Sisters of the Triple Moon*, ensures the child will be female, sends a vision to someone close to the child letting them know the importance of the upcoming birth and generally oversees the raising of and the indoctrinating of the new Sister."

Rhiannon asked, "If this is so, how come I never knew and I don't have this power you keep looking for?"

"Well my dear, there is no way I can answer that with one hundred percent accuracy, but my guess would be that your Mother knew and hadn't got around to telling you when she passed away. The reason I say this, is because I witnessed that very thing with Joly. Her parents, specifically her Mother, didn't want Joly to feel pressured, and as there was no sign of any big evil throughout her childhood, Morgana stayed silent, content with Joly having only the basic working knowledge of any normal witch. I did not and do not agree with her. Joly's Dad told her on her eighteenth birthday. Thank the Gods he did, or I would be training another novice today."

"You call them *Sisters of the Triple Moon*, any particular reason?" Jesse asked.

"That is how they... we... are known, and we are made known to each other when we touch, by a feeling of... oneness, completeness. It's hard to describe. We also are named according to our sir name. Whatever the first initial is, our name must also begin with that initial."

"Why?"

"I think it has something to do with the fact that in the beginning, everyone only had one name. Possibly when mankind began using two names, Selene decided to keep confusion to a minimum."

Jesse asked, "How did you find out you're one of these sisters?"

She nodded. "It was my Grannie who was told, and she began teaching me the ways of the craft before I could talk. We moved to Canada when I was five and she continued teaching me via my mind, until she was satisfied I had the knowledge I needed."

Stephen asked, "Why the age difference? If there's a group of you, shouldn't you all be born in the same generation?"

"A built in safety factor, I suppose. If the evil we were born to defeat managed to wipe out some of us, being born a couple of generations apart ensures continuity and eventual success."

"That makes sense. Now I have a really dumb question."

"Stephen, what did I tell you when you were a child?"

He thought for a moment and shook his head. "I'm not sure."

"There is no such thing as a dumb question."

"Right. I'd forgotten that."

"What's the question?"

"I have only ever seen one moon. Where does the triple enter into it?"

"Actually you see the triple moon every month. The first quarter, the curved sickle that opens to the left, the full moon, and the third quarter or the curved sickle that opens to the right. Also, the three phases of the moon represent the life cycle of every woman, the new moon being the maiden, the full moon represents the mother and the third quarter is the crone, or old woman."

Stephen looked at Rhiannon. "Did you know that?"

"Sure Stevie, I thought everybody knew that."

Stephen waved his hand in the air. "Question?"

"Shoot."

"You said Gaia did two things. What was the second one?"

Morag chuckled. "I see you're paying attention. The second thing she did was to look for a drug that would prevent the destruction of the Titans by even mortal hands. However, she hadn't bargained on Zeus catching wind of what she was up to, and he prevented Selene, Eos and Helios from appearing long enough for him to destroy the drug before Gaia could find it." She smiled sadly. "And as everyone knows, the Titans were indeed destroyed."

"You said Selene is the moon. Who were the other two you just mentioned?"

"Eos is the dawn and Helios is the sun. What Zeus did was to keep Mother Earth in absolute darkness and while she unable to see anything, he destroyed the drug."

"So it was a good thing she did the Sister of the Triple Moon thing."

Duncan laughed.

Morag frowned at him. "Your brother is trying to learn something here."

"Sorry Maw." He snorted again. ""I've known this stuff forever. It just seems weird listening to my *big* brother trying to get it right."

They talked about Joly's powers and discussed what other powers there could be.

"There are many available powers, not all strong, not all obvious. Rauna is a shaman. She travels to other veils, sky walks, and has incredible knowledge of the old ways. I can do just about anything that is called for. I have no single strong power like Joly, but like Rauna, I have knowledge. And I have not come across anything yet, that I can't figure out the answer to. There are powers that involve electricity, light, shadows, minerals, water, air, and electromagnetism. The list is endless.

I was told many years ago that all Sisters have knowledge of two elements. I don't know if this is true, but I have no reason to doubt it. Joly has water and fire. She's also a healer. Both Rauna and Rhiannon have air. And with all the bananas being consumed, I would think Rhiannon's other power is something to do with geokinetics... rocks, minerals or possibly the earth itself."

As soon as the meeting broke up, and everyone went to their rooms, Stephen asked Rhiannon about the power they were trying to find. She shook her head. "I don't know, Stevie. Your Mum has been over my whole life with me and there isn't anything there."

He hadn't been far off when he thought Joly might be an alien, but the love of his life was also one. He considered what it meant and how it might affect their relationship. Future generations... that meant children. He and Rhiannon weren't using protection. As he thought about it, he decided that maybe being a father wouldn't be a bad thing after all. He knew Rhiannon would be an excellent mother. Maybe that was why he'd never wanted children. He knew Elise was too much of a narcissist to ever be any good with anyone other than herself.

It had been ten days since they'd picked up the material. After supper that night the men emptied the cooler to have another look at it. The marks were definitely lighter. The desire to keep the scrap close was not as strong either, and Duncan breathed a huge sigh of relief.

The following days were spent quietly, with Morag and Rhiannon going for long walks and talking about Rhiannon's childhood in England. While they were away, Joly and Duncan would talk to Stephen, Jesse and Rauna, teaching them about demons, magic and whatever they picked for the topic of the day. They spent several days in deserted areas, with Joly and Duncan teaching the others how to use a wand. They had to quit doing that when Duncan accidentally set fire to a farmers hay field.

At three in the afternoon, Morag would take over with Rauna, Stephen and Jesse, grilling them on what they had learned that day, and what they remembered from previous days. Rhiannon would join Joly and Duncan and learn about the day's topic.

Each day after breakfast and again after supper, they would drive out to the manor and check for signs of anything different, but day after day everything appeared to be the same.

It was almost two weeks later when a couple of things of things happened.

They had driven out to the estate after supper as they always did. As the front of the van touched the property, they were assaulted with visions of untold terror and overwhelmed with feelings of total and utter despair.

Duncan was at the wheel and he slammed on the brakes, almost ripping the gearshift off the steering column as he threw it into reverse and backed onto the cross road. They were all gasping for breath.

"Now we know." Morag swallowed.

"Know what?"

"What we're here to fight."

"Gods! That is one powerful mother." Jesse felt the sweat trickling down the middle of his back.

Rhiannon was silent, her fingers clenched to Stephen's arm. She alone had understood the message it had sent them. The warning was very explicit. They were *not* to return. She knew the others understood the feelings it sent, but she had heard the words in her mind.

Morag thought about the demon of ten years prior. This one was far stronger. There had been eight in their group with two Sisters, one of whom had not discovered her powers. This time they had seven in their group with four Sisters, and again, one who had not yet discovered her powers. Yes, the odds were better even though their numbers were less. She still didn't like it. *Gods, where are the others? Where's this Veronika? What's the date and where is the moon? Oh. Yes, the timing is perfect.* The dark of the moon was the following night. She would have to check and see what time it actually fell. It didn't give them much time to prepare, but they had been preparing for three weeks. They were as ready as they were going to be.

Her thoughts turned to Rhiannon again. Gods! She didn't understand why they had found no power. Oh well, it was too late to worry about it now.

There hadn't been time to teach the novices to speak Greek with any fluency. Both Jesse and Rauna knew the language and learned the chants easily. Morag assured Rhiannon and Stephen that the words said in English would be fine, just as long as they were said. They went over the chants time and again. There was no room for error. The rules for banishment were precise. The sentences must be exact, or else expect failure.

Joly had wondered what she would feel when the time came. She touched her hand to her tummy and felt the determination well up through her. This *thing* had no business in their world and she was glad she was part of those who would banish it back to where it belonged. She wanted, no, she *needed* a safe world for her children to grow up in. She was ready.

Stephen was silent beside Rhiannon. He hadn't been prepared for the strength of the feelings. He hoped he was ready to face such an evil. He was worried about Rhiannon. She was supposed to have some super power, and it hadn't surfaced. She wasn't sleeping well because of it. He would have to ask his mother for an herb tea. She needed more rest. He had found her in the washroom that morning, looking like the wrath of God. She had been sick and although she recovered quickly, he knew something wasn't right.

Rhiannon's thoughts had also turned to the morning's episode. She had been violently ill, but it wasn't anything serious. She had felt the small changes within her body and thought she might be pregnant. The sickness of the morning had only served to confirm it. She wondered how Stephen would feel about it. She thought of her Mother and her struggle to keep a roof over their heads and food on the table. She bowed her head and looked at her flat stomach. Gods, she didn't want to have to go through what her Mother had. She prayed to the Goddess that Stephen would at least understand, even if he couldn't be happy about it.

Duncan drove back to the hotel, his one hand resting on Joly's knee. His mind had been back in Mission when he'd turned onto the property. The blast of evil had startled him badly. He knew better than to grow lax. He shook his head. *Stupid!*

The following day, Morag checked the moon's time and found they would need to be at the house in the wee hours of the morning. She suggested everyone be in bed early that night.

Stephen was able to get Morag alone at lunch time. He asked about a tea for Rhiannon. She knew Joly had several kinds and said she would give him one at supper.

They spent the day going over the entire plan.

They broke for supper at four. At the restaurant, the three men all settled for chicken, while the women opted for salads. Rhiannon had her supply of bananas with her, but as the talk was light, she left them alone.

Rauna was very playful and told jokes and made everyone smile and laugh. She sang and told short stories, which in turn got Duncan started.

Morag, returning from the ladies room, couldn't believe the noise coming from their table. It did not sound like there were any major worries. She hoped they were right.

Stephen saw her and went to meet her. She handed him several packages of chamomile and peppermint tea. "It's good for upset tummies and also will help to relax her."

"Thanks."

Back at the hotel, they were all in bed by eight.

They were at the property by three in the morning. They left the van parked on the road. The walk in to the house was at least a half mile. Jesse and Duncan carried the bags. Joly and Duncan went first. The glow from the flashlight was swallowed by the darkness. They took their first steps on the land. Nothing happened. They took another and then another. Joly signaled Rhiannon. She and Stephen stepped onto the land. Nothing. They took two more steps and turned to signal Morag. She, Rauna and Jesse stepped forward. Nothing. They all advanced slowly, one step, stop, next step, stop. They were halfway there when the hurricane force gust of fetid air whooshed over them, knocking them to the ground. No one was able to stand, the wind was too vicious. They put the flashlights away and advanced on their hands and knees, dragging the cases behind them. For every knee that was brought forward, the gale force wind would try to blow them back. They hung onto the kudzu vines and inched forward.

It was a long and arduous trip in the dark to the steps of the house, but they finally reached it. They crawled up the steps hanging on to the balusters, as the wind tried to blow them back down. The tears caused by the vicious winds, blew across their cheeks and back into their eyes, the salt causing more tears. Half blind, they inched along the veranda to the door. Duncan reached up and turned the knob. Nothing happened. He wrapped Joly's hand around the bag and stood. He put his shoulder into the door and pushed. The door pushed back. Jesse crawled forward and stood beside Duncan. Together they pushed. It opened a crack and slammed shut. Stephen joined them. The three pushed together and they managed to open the door several inches.

Duncan wedged his foot in the opening and Stephen did the same. The door pushed against their feet, crushing them, but they didn't give in to the forces of evil. They heaved again and forced the door open once more. Stephen stepped forward and managed to get his body in between the jamb and the door. He twisted sideways, and felt the skin peel back on his shoulder. He shoved one shoulder against the jamb, the other against the door. He slowly spread his feet apart, until Duncan was able to squeeze through. Once he was inside, he stood and grabbed the door and pulled as Stephen pushed. Jesse squeezed in and the three of them held it open enough that the four women could get through. As soon as they were all in and the door was released, it slammed shut, the sound reverberating through the room.

There was sudden silence in the old house, the only sounds were the heavy breathing of the three men. Morag pulled the flashlight out of her pocket and pushed the switch. Nothing happened. She shook it and tried it again. Still no light. She reached around and felt someone. She wasn't sure who it was, but she took a hold of the hand and squeezed. She sensed it was Rauna and gave her another quick squeeze.

Duncan and Stephen were both trying to get their flashlights to work but they had no better luck than Morag. It appeared the demon had drained the batteries. The sound of a match being dragged across the sandpaper surface of the striker brought a small flame that was quickly blown out from another gust of wind. The momentary light had been enough for everyone there to see that they were all accounted for and to orient themselves. Joly took Duncan's hand and began crawling toward what she hoped was the doorway to the next room. Duncan stopped her long enough to find someone else's hand and placed it on his leg. They crawled across the floor, the silence overwhelming them. A small whisper and everyone stopped. The sound of another match being struck and again a moment of dim light. Joly had led them true. She was only a foot away from the door. She crawled forward another few inches. Duncan stopped her. He pushed the bag forward. As he pushed it into the doorway, the bag was sucked out of his hands. A heartbeat later, the door slammed shut.

Duncan dropped his head down. That had been too close. He squeezed Joly's hand. *Now what?*

The door whipped open, slamming against the wall on the other side.

Duncan eased forward reaching out for the wall. He found it and slid his hand to the door frame. He tucked Joly's hand in his waistband and reached for the wall on the other side. Finding it, he searched for the frame on that side. He slid forward and got to his knees. He removed one of his shoes and wedged the toe into the crack between the door and the frame. Holding it there, he slid forward. Nothing happened. He inched into the room, dragging Joly behind him. He sat with his back against the door and squeezed Joly's hand. She reached back and tugged on whoever was holding on to her leg. One by one they entered the room. The only sounds were their breathing and the sliding of their jeans and shoes across the floor.

Another match was struck. The light flared up and stayed lit. They quickly stood and crossed the room. Duncan again blocked the door open. They filed through one at a time. Another match was lit. The scent of evil was swirling around them.

They had decided not to enter the sunroom. Too much evil was ingrained into the very fabric of the room. They were in the room next to it. Although the sense of evil was in the room, the room itself appeared benign. It was a large room; possibly a music room or a second sitting room. Jesse lit another match. Morag reached in the bag, handed Jesse a candle and grabbed her besom. She quickly swept the floor while Duncan and Stephen measured out the double circle. Joly and Rauna took the sea salt and holy water and walked around the perimeter sealing it. No one spoke, but the same thought was in everyone's mind. Where had the dark beast gone? It had done a good job of slowing them down and then suddenly nothing.

The idea of a second decoy bag had worked to their advantage. They still had everything they needed. They drew in the triangle, set up the small altar and lit the candles. They hadn't bothered with their robes, as they had expected to be repelled every inch of the way.

"What was that?"

"What?"

"That."

They all felt it then. A deep rumble that seemed to come from the very bowels of the earth. The house shook slightly and then there was silence.

Duncan shrugged. "Don't know." He went back to what he'd been doing.

They heard it again, but this time it was louder. The house shook once more, but this time it vibrated enough that it creaked and groaned with the movement.

"Earthquake?"

No one moved. Morag opened her senses to see what was happening. The others figured it out at the same time. Rauna yelled first.

"*Get out! Get out now!*" She ran toward the door.

The house shook harder. Jesse grabbed Morag and ran. Stephen and Rhiannon were right behind them. Duncan reached for Joly's hand, but it had vanished. He whirled around to see her at the altar.

He went to take a step and the floor tilted. He slid away from Joly. He heard the shouts of the others in the next room. "*Darlin'?*"

Joly slid down the tilted floor and crashed into the wall.

Flames licked at the dry wood where the candles had fallen. The wood and wall coverings were a natural accelerant and the fire whooshed up the walls.

"Come on." Duncan grabbed her hand and headed to the door. The flames were bright and they could see their way into the next room. Another rumble and the house shook again. Somewhere, glass was heard breaking. The flames licked at their heels as they scampered across the uneven flooring. They were through the next door and were halfway to the outside door when the floor tilted on its side. Duncan and Joly were thrown onto the wall. The creaking of timbers and joists along with the snapping and crackling of the flames deafened them to any other sounds.

They crawled toward the door, the heat and smoke causing disorientation. Joly could feel the draft and she headed that way. Duncan stopped her.

"*Wrong way!*" he shouted, pulling her back.

She shook her head. "*No! It's right!*" She turned and screamed.

The demon stood in the flames. The three heads were watching them and each mouth was open in a parody of laughter.

Duncan grabbed her around her waist and half ran, half crawled in the other direction. The smoke was thick and he was choking on it. Hands grabbed him and he was separated from Joly. He fought like a wild man, he kicked and punched, and screamed her name.

"*Duncan!* Stop it, she's okay. *Christ!* Quit fighting me!" Stephen wrestled his brother toward the door. They were finally through and the cool air hit Duncan's face.

"*Joly?*" He choked out her name in between coughs. He was blinded from the smoke.

"Here." She wrapped him in her arms and he cried, partly from the smoke and partly from relief.

A groaning sound grabbed their attention and as they watched, the roof of the building slowly sank into the flames.

"We have to go." Stephen wrapped Joly and Duncan in his arms and half dragged, half led them away.

The flames lit up the sky and the roadway. As they walked and stumbled through the thick grass and vines, they heard chilling laughter coming from the burning building.

Elaine Tenborg

While the younger ones slept most of the day, Morag was busy. She meditated, she took a trip through the veils, she made a list of things they would have to buy to replace everything they had lost, and she prayed. She knew who they were up against and the demon was far stronger than she had first thought. *We need help. Where are the others?* She remembered Joly's chilling words from Alyce. *"You will not all survive these fights."* Surely the others hadn't already perished. *Where is this Veronika?*

When Stephen and Rhiannon appeared, she got them to take her to town, where she purchased all the necessary items.

She had not been happy with having the circle inside the old house. She knew things tended to go very wrong in a confined space. She had given in to the others against her better judgment. When they had agreed to have the circle, not over the original one but nearby, she should have insisted that they have it outside the windows of the room where the demon had been summoned. She shook her head. It wouldn't have mattered. It was too strong for what they had planned, but at least now they knew. They would be better prepared for it the next time. The only thing they did have right was the time. The banishment had to take place after three in the morning.

Jesse showed up shortly after they returned, and Joly and Duncan arrived an hour later. Duncan's eyes were burning from the smoke, and Joly had done a healing on them and cleared the residual smoke from his lungs.

Morag took command immediately. She was not about to let anyone override her again and she made it clear her word was law. Joly hung her head, knowing it was she who had placed them in so much danger that morning. She had been sure she had it right and with her belief evident for all to see, the others had sided with her.

"Joly, there is no need for guilt. We all make mistakes. We're human and nothing can change that, not even the fact that we're *Sisters of the Triple Moon*. Had I been sure I was right, I would have overridden you, but I erred also, so the fault is not yours alone. Will you share the failure with me?"

Morag needed Joly's undivided attention. She would not get it as long as she was feeling sorry for herself.

Duncan squeezed her around the waist. They had discussed the morning's events while she healed him. He knew it wasn't all her fault and told her so. She wasn't much more than a novice herself, with only a year of hardcore spell craft and rituals behind her. He told her she was bound to make mistakes and it didn't sit well with her. He also knew she was somewhat diversified with being pregnant, but he was careful not to mention that.

Joly looked at Morag and gave her a small smile. "Yes, I'll share the failure with you." There. She no longer had to carry the burden alone. She sat up straighter and leaned into Duncan.

They spent the next two hours practicing what they would need to do to have a successful ending. Then they went out to the manor in the daylight to begin their preparations. Once the circle was drawn and blessed, the demon couldn't touch it. It could make it difficult for them to get to it, but they hoped to take it by surprise.

Even though the sun was shining when they got to the estate, it was dark and eerie under the canopy of the trees. The smell of the burned house was strong. Tendrils of smoke still rose from the burnt out rubble. The one back corner appeared to still be intact. They walked around to check it out. The door to the enchanted room was closed and the room had not been touched.

"Did anyone close the door when we left the room?"

No one had. Joly stepped across the rubble, and headed toward the door.

"Joly! *No!* Come back here... *now!*"

She stopped and looked around, shook her head, and turned to walk back to the others.

They walked around to the side where the sunroom windows had been. There were broken branches and tree limbs everywhere.

"Think we'll get this cleaned up before dark?" Duncan looked doubtful.

"We will if you start working instead of standing there with your hands in your pockets." Morag already had her arm half loaded with smaller branches.

It didn't take long once they got started. The three men hauled away the large stuff and the women gathered up all the smaller items. They checked to make sure nothing else hazardous was nearby and when they were done, Morag picked up her new besom and swept the area clean. Duncan and Jesse measured out the circle and then carefully measured the triangle at the northern side. There would be no room for error. This demon was very powerful. He was one of the kings in the abyss he had been summoned from. Rhiannon and Joly set up the altar. Rauna drew in the circle.

They called the Gods and Goddesses; they called the Four Quarters and the Elements. The circle was blessed. They dismissed the Elements, the Quarters and the Deities. Morag cut in a door with her athame so they could enter and leave without compromising the sacred space. They walked out of the circle as the sun was setting. Morag pointed the athame and closed the invisible gate behind her.

They could feel the evil building as they hurried back to the van.

They had a light supper and went back to the hotel to get some sleep.

Three in the morning found them gathered in Morag's room. They were all freshly showered and wearing their robes.

Stephen felt extremely uncomfortable in his. It was his first time wearing it and the idea of a dress by any name, didn't sit well with him. Rhiannon had run her fingers up underneath it and tickled him. She'd grinned wickedly, and said, "I like it."

"Are we clear on how we're doing this?" Morag still didn't like the plan, but she knew it was the only way.

Everyone nodded or murmured, "Yes."

Jesse picked up the bag and they got into the van. The drive to the estate was completed in silence.

Duncan parked on the dark road. There were no street lamps this far out of the city. They got out of the van and gathered by the driver's door. Everyone centered, grounded and shielded.

Morag took Rhiannon's hand in hers. "Be safe."

Rhiannon squeezed her hand and replied, "You too."

Morag stepped in between Duncan and Joly. Rhiannon stepped in between Stephen and Jesse. Rauna stepped in between the two men and they formed a tight circle.

Morag checked that her athame was in her belt. "Remember… eight seconds." She hung on tightly to Duncan and Joly and visualized herself at the gate of the circle. Slowly the gentle buzzing started in her stomach and then moved to fill her body. It reminded her of a bee hive. She was conscious of the feeling of movement and the grabbing at her from the invisible hands. Suddenly they were there. She quickly let go of the other two and grabbed her athame. She murmured the words to open the gate. They quickly filed in. Duncan was no sooner through, when Rhiannon and the other three stood where he had just moved from. The four quickly entered and Morag pointed the athame and closed the door.

The wind howled around them. The trees dipped and swayed. The noxious odors of the beast swirled around the circle.

Morag lit the candles. The wind couldn't violate the sacred space. The flames hardly stirred. The beast grew angrier, the winds screamed around them, but they paid it no attention.

They began the ritual. They called the Gods and Goddesses, the Quarters and the elements. They raised the Cone of Power. They lit the quarter candles and poured the wine. Then they called the demon. First, they called it individually and then they called it as a group.

"Εντολη ι εσεις, βασιλιας Μυβαχηυτασ, για να παρευρεθει σε μἐ."

"*I command you, King Mubachutas, to attend me.*"

They repeated the chant and felt the power rising in the circle. They knew it could take a long time to get the demon inside. Demons on earth's plane didn't like obeying any human, but they were forced to obey the one who summoned it from the abyss it called home. They also were forced to attend anyone who called it by its name. It could fight the calling, but it would eventually have to appear.

"Εντολη ι εσεις, βασιλιας Μυβαχηυτασ, για να παρευρεθει σε μἐ."

"*I command you, King Mubachutas, to attend me.*"

The winds howled outside the circle. Branches cracked and broke off trees, falling and bouncing off the invisible cone. The sickening odors of things long dead wafted over and around them. They continued chanting. All eyes concentrated on the glowing triangle in front of them.

Rhiannon had volunteered to stand at the dangerous point behind the triangle. Stephen had vehemently disagreed, but Rhiannon insisted. She had practiced space travel enough that she knew she would be able to get away faster than Joly or Rauna could. Stephen knew he would be the first one to throw the sea salt and holy water. He remained calm due to the grounding, but his heart was in his throat.

"Εντολη ι εσεις, βασιλιας Μυβαχηυτασ, για να παρευρεθει σε μἔ."
"I command you, King Mubachutas, to attend me."
The colors in the pyramid began changing. Rhiannon got ready to move.
"Εντολη ι εσεις, βασιλιας Μυβαχηυτασ, για να παρευρεθει σε μἔ."
"I command you, King Mubachutas, to attend me."
Dark smoky mists appeared.
"Εντολη ι εσεις, βασιλιας Μυβαχηυτασ, για να παρευρεθει σε μἔ."
"I command you, King Mubachutas, to attend me."
They were overwhelmed with the smell of excrement. A dark appendage snaked out of the pyramid. Stephen threw the sea salt and holy water.

Rhiannon vanished.
Stephen quit breathing.
She reappeared beside him.
His heart resumed beating.
And the fight began in earnest.
"Εμεις εξοριζω εσεις πισω απο οπου κληθηκατἔ."
The demon screamed as it was hit with the sea salt, holy water, herbs and the charges from the wands.
"We banish you back to wherefrom you were summoned."
Morag handed out the vials as she kept chanting.
"Σας διαταζω Μυβαχηυτασ,για να επιστρεψω στη θεση που προηλ θατε απὄ."
Rhiannon and Stephen chanted in English. "I command you Mubachutas, to return to the place you came from."

Rauna pointed her wand and let the feeling flow from her soul, as Joly had taught her. When she felt the power trickle down her arm, she said the Greek words and watched as the charge spit from the end of the wand. She had a direct hit and when the demon screamed, she wanted to dance.

The fight continued. At the altar Morag replaced Jesse, Jesse replaced Rauna, Rauna replaced Rhiannon, and Rhiannon replaced Stephen who re-placed Duncan.

They didn't seem to be making any headway. It appeared to be a standoff. Morag didn't show it, but she was slowly becoming concerned.

The demon slashed out at the humans and released another blast of fetid, noxious odors.

"Αδεια τωρα εσυ που ανηκετε στο χαος."

The demon was getting angry. It had had enough of the pain. The humans didn't seem ready to give up. They didn't seem to be getting tired. They had not come close enough for it to grab any of them. They were smarter than it had first thought. It dispersed another salvo of reeking, putrid air, so thick it formed as a mist in the circle.

When the demon saw that the nauseous scents had little effect, it changed tactics and sent them an overpowering scent of perfumes.

The cloying sweetness was worse than the fetid odors of the moment before. Rhiannon gagged and retched, Jesse gagged, then Rauna and finally Duncan. Morag wasn't faring much better.

Joly knew the time had come to use extreme measures. She began to feel the ice building inside of her. The sight of her friends getting sick angered her, but when her beloved also fell victim to the overwhelming smells, she knew no reasoning. The cold started in her heart and the ice flowed through her veins. When she felt it reach her fingers, she raised her hands and with a voice of tempered steel, she spoke the words and released the power,

"Σας διαταζω Μυβαχηυτασ, για να επιστρεψω στη θεση που προη λθατε απο."

She was conscious of Stephen repeating the words. "I command you Mubachutas, to return to the place you came from."

The icy blast of minus one hundred and ten degree cold hit the demon. It was as if it had been submerged into a vat of dry ice. The tentacles froze where they were, looking like dead branches sticking out of the pyramid.

Moments later Morag shook her head. "Very nice, Joly, but can you tell me how we banish it when it's frozen solid on our plane?"

The others were quickly breathing in the fresh air that had returned with the freezing of the monster.

Stephen approached the pyramid. "Can she unfreeze it bit by bit and banish the pieces?"

"I wish it were that easy. Unfortunately, it must go as a complete unit."

Slowly, their eyes left the pyramid, as they discussed what to do next. Even with grounding, they were slowly tiring.

No one noticed a faint glow coming from inside the pyramid. No one saw the branch like appendages flutter and move. No one was aware of the red eyes that opened, blinked and focused on them.

"Anyone willing to take a walk to another veil with a friendly, frozen monster?" Duncan chuckled, knowing that it couldn't be done. They had no way of knowing which veil it belonged in, and it had to return to the one it had come from.

"He's joking." Stephen's arm was around Rhiannon's waist, and he felt the tightening of her stomach muscles. He knew how she felt about the veils.

The tentacle slowly snaked out toward the two who were closest. It undulated in the cool air as the last of the freezing was worked out of it. When it sensed it was as limber as it should be, the tentacle whipped out and grabbed the cape, snapping it backwards.

Stephen was jerked off his feet. He hit hard, grunting as his tailbone connected with the ground. Rhiannon screamed. With their arms interlocked around one another, she was pulled down with him.

It sensed victory and another tentacle snaked out to help the first as it reached toward Stephen's head.

Duncan threw himself on top of Stephen causing another groan as the air was forced from his lungs.

The head was still not within reach. Angrily, the second tentacle went to help the first, grabbing another piece of the cape and slowly dragging it toward the pyramid.

Stephen was choking. He couldn't breath. He tried to move an arm. Duncan was laying on the one and the other was still under Rhiannon.

Seeing Stephen and Duncan sliding toward the beast, Jesse threw himself on top of Duncan and screamed at Rhiannon. *"Untie the fucking cape!"*

Her one arm was caught under Stephen, so she wriggled around and reached up to his neck. Everything had twisted and she had to search to find where it was tied. When she felt the bow, she grabbed an end and prayed it wouldn't turn into one of those knots that were impossible to undo. She pulled.

The beast let out a blast of noxious odors that left a tangible mist hovering in the cool night air.

Morag choked and gagged as Joly pointed her wand and threw the sea salt.

It screamed in pain from the salt and again as the charge from the wand connected to one of the appendages. The tentacle involuntarily released the cape and was withdrawn back into the pyramid.

"It's off," Rhiannon gasped.

Jesse slid off Duncan and when they were side by side they each grabbed one of Stephen's legs and pulled.

As his cape was reefed into the pyramid, Stephen was pulled out its reach.

It screamed in rage and sent another burst of gut-wrenching stench to those who would send it back to its prison.

Joly sent the gift of heat. She knew it was impossible to incinerate it, but the fire might slow it down. She allowed the heat to build and when she was filled with it, she pointed her wand and again spoke the words of banishment. The flame shot out the end of it.

"Εμεις εξοριζω εσεις πισω απο οπου κληθηκατε."

The flame hit true and as the demon screamed, it returned her fire with the overwhelming scent of perfumes. She gagged and swallowed.

She sent the fire again.

A female voice cut through the darkness of the night.

"Open the gate. We're here to help."

Duncan paused and then moved over to where Morag was standing handing out the sea salt and holy water. "Go, Maw." He grabbed several vials and began passing them out.

Morag stumbled as she walked to the back side of the circle. She stopped and quickly grounded herself. Revived, she picked up her athame and murmuring the magical words, she opened the gate. She was surprised to see three women enter the sacred ground. All three were in their robes and Morag wondered if one was Veronika. The first woman whipped her wand out of her pocket and aimed it at the evil being. She screamed the words with such feeling; one would have thought she had a personal stake in the fight.

"Αδεια τωρα εσυ που ανηκετε στο χαος."

The charge left the end of her wand and hit the demon so hard they could see the vibration inside the pyramid. It screamed in agony and rage. The air filled with the scents of every person's worse nightmare. The reeking, fetid odors of rotting flesh, sewage, and rancid cooking oils slammed into them. The stench of scorched meat and urine added to the foul scents assailing them.

Morag held her breath, quit watching the woman and rejoined the fight.

The newcomers were fresh and fought with a vengeance, giving the others a reprieve. Duncan kept passing the salt and holy water. Each of their group took a turn at grounding and centering, and then rejoined the fray.

"Σας διαταζω Μυβαχηυτασ,για να επιστρεψω στηυ αβυσσο που ω οτοκησατε απο."

"I command you Mubachutas, to return to the abyss you spawned from."

The demon howled, it screamed and it overwhelmed them with feelings of despair.

The first time Rhiannon felt the despair, she quit fighting and stood, looking alone and lost in the circle. Joly spotted her and knew what had happened. She quickly snapped her out of the trance she had gone into.

The three women fought with the surety of experience. Some of the Sisters powers were evident. Fire balls and forked electrical charges joined the sea salt and holy water. They all had wands.

The battle raged on and those who grew tired were able to take a break while others fought in their place.

The bright light overhead was almost Jesse's undoing. They all glanced up as the sky over the circle glowed with an unearthly golden orange light.

Jesse had stepped in to throw the holy water and with the distraction of the light, forgot to step back. One of the strangers grabbed him as the demon's appendage touched the edge of his cloak. The scorched scent of burnt material rose up and tickled his nose.

Overhead, all eyes were fastened on the article that hovered there.

"*Ho!* Can a weary traveler join the party? I assure you, I come well prepared." The male voice had the sound of laughter in it.

Morag took one last look at the sword that dangled high in the air, and she went to open the gate. Whoever was on the other side had excellent levitation abilities.

The sight that greeted her had her shaking her head. He looked like he'd arrived from fighting with the three musketeers. The pirate type boots came up over his knees; mostly covering the shiny black satin pants. The velvet tabard had a pentagram sewn in trapunto design across the front of it and the flared sleeves of the pirate shirt all but hid his hands. He removed the large feathered hat and bowed low before her.

"My Lady. Thank you for admitting me. My sincerest apologies for arriving so late. I will explain everything after we are done with this spawn from hell."

He stood up, replaced the outlandish velvet hat back on his head and looked up at the sword that hung above. He raised his hand and the sword slowly descended into it. He sheathed it and from a pocket he withdrew a small vial.

"May I use some of your salt, please?" The smile was boyish in extreme.

Morag wondered if this was Sergei. She nodded and remembered she had yet to close the gate. She replaced the besom across where she had drawn the door in and again, pointing her athame, she murmured the words that would protect those inside.

The circle wasn't overly large and with eleven people inside it, along with the three foot triangle that contained the demon, there was not a lot of room for movement. One of the women joined Duncan with handing out the vials. He was surprised when he saw her close up. He'd thought the women were in their thirty's or forties, but this one beside him was much older than that. He thought she was older than his mother.

The male walked around until he was near the side of the pyramid. He grinned at the beast within.

"Mubachutas, your time on this plane is short. Any last requests?" He laughed and the monster covered him with the stench of excrement. He choked. "Now that wasn't even nice." He uncapped the vial, carefully tucking the lid back in his pocket and then he stood with both hands out toward the demon.

The tentacle whipped out and missed the hand by less than an inch.

"Naughty, naughty!" The young man laughed again, as he waved his pointed finger back and forth.

Everyone's eyes were glued to the outlandish costumed gentleman.

One of the women turned to Duncan for another vial and as she quickly turned back so as not to miss anything, her foot caught on her gown. She threw out her arm to try and regain her balance. Her hand slammed into the back of the woman next to her. The woman stumbled ahead two steps.

It all happened so fast, no one was even sure of what had happened. One second the woman was there, the next, she was a blur of movement as she was pulled into the pyramid. She never even had time to cry out.

The young man soberly stepped back a half a pace. He bowed his head and as he raised it, his arms were on the move. The salt flew from his left hand and as the demon screamed, the right hand was throwing the contents of the other vial.

"Δεν ανηκετε σε αυτο το πεπλο. Σας διαταζω Μυβαχηυτασ, για να επιστρεψω στην αβυσσο που ωοτοκησατε απο."

The liquid hit the demon and everything in the pyramid turned blue. The sound that escaped from the demon deafened them all. The blue flame in the pyramid burned transparently. They watched as the beast writhed in agony.

Joly regained her senses first and sent another burst of heat to the beast. An electrical charge followed and then a fireball. Jesse had managed to gain control of his thoughts and he whipped up a couple of psi balls and tossed them into the triangular prison.

"Σας διαταζω Μυβαχηυτασ,για να επιστρεψω στηυ αβυσσο που ω οτοκησατε απο."

A tentacle shot out of the small prison and threw a blue flame at Jesse. Joly deflected it with a flame of her own.

The monster screamed and sent dozens of blue flames toward Morag. Joly had trouble deflecting them all. One escaped her return fire and hit Morag's cape. The blue flames shot up it and she quickly untied and removed it. There was no heat from the small fire and in moments only a pile of ash remained where the cape had lay seconds before.

Morag knew why she was being targeted. It had sensed her when it was summoned, and knew she was responsible for the predicament it was in.

The man in the feathered hat stood quietly chanting. He had thrown nothing since the liquid ingredient that had erupted into flames. The smile had returned to his face and it looked out of place amid the demon's screams and the desperate moves of the witches. They continued their chanting, reaching for another vial, throwing, chanting. Joly continued deflecting the blue flames.

It appeared to be a standoff.

The young man glanced over at the others. "Where are the spurs? Let's finish this exercise and be done." He looked at the demon and resumed chanting.

Spurs? Morag wondered if she had heard him right, because if she had, she had no idea what he was referring to. She replaced Duncan at the altar, while he went and grounded himself, drawing much needed energy from the earth. Feeling somewhat revitalized, he rejoined the group.

From the group, Rhiannon stepped forward. Stephen reached out to stop her, but Morag's hand was there to stop him. Rhiannon took another step forward. Her eyes were focused solely on the apparition in the pyramid. She appeared unaware of anything else.

Jesse could see she was in a trance. He wondered if he should tell some-one. Before he had a chance, Rhiannon raised her arms and pointed her index fingers at the demon.

Carefully enunciating each word, concerned that her English accent would fail her, she said the words, "Leave now, you who belongs to Tartarus. You do not belong to this veil. I command you Mubachutas, to return to the abyss you spawned from."

From her fingertips millions of tiny gold slivers shot toward the pyramid.

The demon saw them coming and knew what they were. The unearthly scream deafened all within the circle. The tiny barbs disappeared into the pyramid and for seconds it glowed brightly, then quicker than a blink it went black.

The scream was unending. Appendages reached, withdrew and reached again. It knew its time was limited on this plane and it needed to feed, it needed more strength. It whipped around stretching out as far as it was able.

The young man was no longer smiling. He looked confused as he stood there quietly. He finally shook his head and looked at Morag.

"That shouldn't be."

As she had no idea what he was referring to, she said nothing, continuing with the chanting and throwing.

"I have no more acid, but perhaps another shot of spurs..." His voice trailed off and he took a step closer. That he was puzzled was obvious.

Rhiannon closed her eyes and drew on her inner power. She felt the prickle of a million tiny barbs rushing through her. She held out her hands and pointed her fingers.

"Return to whence you were summoned. I command you Mubachutas, to return to the abyss you spawned from."

The golden spurs flew from her fingertips. The demon screamed in rage and pain. The air grew heavy with the reeking, fetid odors of a world not of their plane. The tentacles cut another swath through the group, finding noth-ing to pull into its web of hate.

It screamed again, the nauseous smells visible in the air. The more it tried to repel the magical barbs the deeper they dug in. Its strength was going fast. It needed more blood. The red eyes squinted as it judged the distance of every participant in the circle. It gathered up all of its remaining strength and compacted it into one condensed last desperate try for freedom. It literally threw itself through the confines of the pyramid, with only a small portion remaining inside. The young man hadn't expected it, hadn't moved back and suddenly he was no more.

The youngest of the women cried out. *"Noooo..."* The others sensed her grief, but there was no time for consoling.

The demon screamed a victory scream and grew stronger. The vile odors also grew stronger and the witches renewed their efforts. The psi balls, the flames, the mini lightning, the herbs, the sea salt and holy water, none of it seemed to have any lasting effect on the monster.

Rhiannon threw more barbs and wondered what she was throwing. She could feel them inside, almost like tiny bugs, multiplying by the dozens.

The demon grew weaker, but it wasn't about to let them know that. It roared, it raged, it sent wave after wave of noxious gases to those that would condemn it to another eternity in Tartarus. The spurs did their work, with every undulation, every movement from the demon; they cut the phantom, weakening it until finally, it was visibly losing its strength.

The witches had the upper hand and sensed victory was near. The appendages had quit reaching; the demon was too busy trying to retain its hold on the plane it was in.

They chanted and continued throwing the sea salt, herbs and holy water. The heavy duty artillery was no longer needed. Jesse threw one last psi ball, grinning as he did. He was feeling euphoric about being part of something so right, so good, and he felt ready to walk on air. The loss of the two strangers wasn't enough to subdue him.

Rauna smiled. It was a new way of fighting, but it felt good. She twirled her wand in a circle, felt the power emerge from her soul and rush down her arm. The tip of the wand sparked and the charge spiraled to the pyramid. It looked awesome in the darkness. She laughed and did a little dance.

The demon had quit fighting. It wondered if it could trick one of the others into moving closer. *It needed blood!* The spurs were ripping it apart. The spurs alone would not have bothered it, but the acid had been the catalyst. The special blend ate the protective energy field that held its essence together, leaving the remaining energy to be diffused by the damaging spurs. More blood would help to stop the diffusing process and rebuild the protective outer energy field.

No one moved closer, but the sea salt and holy water kept raining down upon it. The energy kept separating and finally it knew it had no choice. It had to return to its prison. With a final scream of rage and hatred, it gathered itself up and took itself from the earth's plane.

In Argentina, Marco was taking a sip of hot coffee when he heard the blood curdling scream. The coffee slopped down the front of his shirt, burning his chest. At the same instant the dog howled and shivers of doom raced down his back. He understood the cries of pain, and knew he had said the final goodbye to his beloved sister. He allowed himself a minute of mourning and then went to console his niece.

It was over. Everyone grounded and breathed a sigh of relief.

Morag went to the older woman and hugged her. She felt the oneness. "Thank you for coming. Are you Veronika?"

The old woman smiled softly with tears glistening in her eyes. "You're welcome. Yes, I'm Veronika." She looked at the triangle and shook her head. "How do I tell his Mother?"

"These things are never easy, my Sister. He was Sergei?"

"Yes."

"I'm so sorry."

"This is Polina, Sergei's sister."

Morag wrapped her arms around the young girl. The feeling of oneness enveloped her, along with something else. Rauna had said she was seventeen. She had no business being at the banishing, but she had fought an experienced fight. "You are very brave. Thank you for coming and helping us."

The girl nodded her head, but said nothing.

Veronika hugged Rauna. "I am happy to see you again, *Tsipotchka*."

"It's nice to see you too. I'm sorry about Sergei." Rauna returned the hug.

Morag watched as Rhiannon pointed her fingers to the earth and released thousands more of the tiny golden objects. She went over and peered at the ground, wanting to take one home to study. There was nothing there.

They gathered up the tools and closed the circle. It was a tired group that made their way back to the van that morning. It had taken them five hours to banish the demon.

Veronika didn't drive, so they gave her and Polina a ride to their hotel.

"We need to speak, Veronika. Can we pick you up for supper?" Morag asked, not wanting the woman to disappear on them.

She thought about it, before answering. "I need to go home. To tell my daughter. What do you need to speak about?"

"Your Grandson... Sergei. The liquid he used, he called it an acid. I would like to know more about it."

"His lab is in my basement. You are welcome to come, to see. I will give you address."

Polina looked uncomfortable. She lowered her head and said something so quietly no one caught it.

"I'm sorry. What did you say dear?"

"I can show you, if you come."

Morag placed her hand on Polina's arm. There was something not quite right with the girl, but she decided it was probably the shock of losing her brother. "Thank you, Polina."

Joly quietly asked, "Did you know the other woman?"

Veronika shook her head. "She was called Emilia. She come from South America, from Argentina. She said her daughter was a Sister, but was too young to fight this evil."

They said goodbye and drove to their hotel.

That night the men checked the cloth in the cooler. There were no signs of any marks left on it. They drove out to the river and wrapped it around a rock. Then they wound wire around the rock and tied it off, careful to remove the sharp ends. Stephen threw it as hard as he could and they watched as the rock hit the water near the middle. They threw the cooler in the first trash container they came to.

Morag could still feel the darkness coming from Rauna and suggested she make the trip to Vancouver with them. The time spent close to Joly would continue to heal her soul. Rauna agreed as she liked being with the women, and she understood that she needed to remain near Joly.

Nefertiti was pleased they were going home. She had felt useless having to stay in the hotel room all the time. She could feel the Mistress' power and knew she no longer needed protection.

She'd had time to think and decided that perhaps she was being too hard on the other two felines. She found she actually missed the company of Salem and Pip. The Mistress was right. Not everyone was born to royalty. She would try to be more tolerant when they got home.

She was glad to see the cooler was gone along with the evil beings in it. She wished she knew where she remembered them from, but there appeared to be a blank spot in her memory. This really bothered her, but try as she might; she could only narrow it down to a time when she was quite young, probably about two or three in human years.

Joly asked to stop in the town where the bus accident had occurred. She made some inquiries and found where Sharon Littleton was hospitalized. Joly needed to see her. The others waited in the van while she went in on her own.

She entered the room and saw the woman on the bed. She walked up beside it and looked down at the woman. Sharon opened her eyes and when she saw who was standing there, the fear in her eyes made Joly smile.

"You remember me. Good. I'm glad you get to live with your memories. I was afraid you wouldn't remember. Goodbye." She smiled and left.

They made it home the night before Randy's fifth birthday.

Coming soon.

Sisters of the Triple Moon

Book two: *Witches Brew, Demon Stew*

About the Author

Elaine Tenborg lives in Hinton, Alberta, a small town nestled in the foothills of the Canadian Rockies. She works as a night auditor and desk clerk for a major hotel chain.
She is married and has three cats, none of which are familiars.